FIC
Verne, Jules, 1828-1905.
The mysterious island

JAN   2002

W9-DDC-648

Discarded

FLESH PUBLIC LIBRARY
124 W. GREENE ST.
PIQUA, OH 45356-2399

THE MYSTERIOUS ISLAND

L'ILE MYSTÉRIEUSE

par Jules VERNE

154 Dessins

par J. FÉRAT

JULES VERNE

THE MYSTERIOUS ISLAND

Translated by Jordan Stump

Introduction by Caleb Carr

*With illustrations from the original 1875 edition
by Jules-Descartes Ferat*

FLESH PUBLIC LIBRARY
124 W. GREENE ST.
PIQUA. OH 45356-2399

THE MODERN LIBRARY

NEW YORK

2001 Modern Library Edition
Translation, translator's preface, and biographical note
copyright © 2001 by Random House, Inc.
Introduction copyright © 2001 by Caleb Carr

All rights reserved under International and Pan-American
Copyright Conventions. Published in the United States by
Random House, Inc., New York, and simultaneously in Canada
by Random House of Canada Limited, Toronto.

MODERN LIBRARY and the TORCHBEARER Design are registered trademarks
of Random House, Inc.

LIBRARY OF CONGRESS CATALOGING-IN-PUBLICATION DATA
Verne, Jules, 1828-1905.
[Ile mystérieuse. English]
The mysterious island / Jules Verne; translated by Jordan Stump; and with an
introduction by Caleb Carr.
p. cm.
ISBN 0-679-64236-6
I. Stump, Jordan, 1959- II. Title.
PQ2469.I43 E5 2002
843'.8—dc21   2001037414

Modern Library website address:
www.modernlibrary.com

Printed in the United States of America

2 4 6 8 9 7 5 3 1

JULES VERNE

In Nantes, France, where Jules Verne was born on February 8, 1828, a memorial plaque describes him as a "novelist and precursor." Indeed, a celebrated playwright, novelist, and short story writer, Verne was also something of an inventor; in his works, technology and science are central and realistic elements, which led to Verne's reputation as the father of science fiction. His childhood in a seaport town engendered a love of the sea and adventure and even prompted him to run away at age eleven to become a ship's cabin boy (his father quickly rescued him). Though his parents, Pierre and Sophie Verne, prepared young Verne to follow his father's lead into the law, his school years in Paris inspired Verne to pursue a career as a writer instead.

Verne lived on Paris's Left Bank, where he met several famous literary men such as Victor Hugo and the elder Alexandre Dumas, and where he also witnessed the revolution of 1848. He began writing stories and plays, and was encouraged when Dumas produced his play *Broken Straws* at the Théâtre Historique in June of 1850. This was followed by numerous ephemeral dramas and an historical novella, *Martin Paz* (1852). Verne took a job as secretary to the Théâtre Lyrique in 1852, and his stories ran in the magazine *Musée des Familles*.

Verne abandoned his bohemian lifestyle in 1857 when he married Honorine Morel, a widow with two young daughters, and became a stockbroker. He continued to write plays, with some success, in his spare time. In 1861, his only son, Michel, was born, and Verne met Félix Tournachon, an artist-inventor with an interest in balloon flight. Soon thereafter, Verne completed his first famous work, *Five Weeks in a Balloon* (1863). An immediate hit that combined geography and adventure, the novel marked the beginning of Verne's series of *voyages extraordinaires* and a life long association with publisher Pierre-Jules Hetzel. Verne quit the stock exchange when Hetzel contracted him to write two major stories per year, to be published in magazine and book form.

A plethora of didactic tales followed, and Verne was hailed for his ability to weave narrative and mechanical detail. The subterranean world revealed in *A Journey to the Center of the Earth* (1864) both entertained readers and served as a geology lesson. *From the Earth to the Moon: Passage Direct in 97 Hours and 20 Minutes* (1865), set in postbellum America, centered on space exploration. The two-volume *The Adventures of Captain Hatteras* (1865) combined two stories of escapades at the North Pole. At the same time, Verne's publisher asked him to work on an illustrated geography of France, a tedious job that forced Verne into convalescence in the fishing village of Le Crotoy, where he bought a boat. He took his first trip to America with his younger brother before publication of *Captain Grant's Children* (1868), a mystery about young castaways.

While at Le Crotoy, Verne worked on the novel that some call his masterpiece, *Twenty Thousand Leagues Under the Sea* (1870), a chronicle of the enigmatic Captain Nemo's journey on the *Nautilus*. Also in 1870, when Verne was at the height of his fame and skill, he published *Round the Moon*, a sequel to *From Earth to the Moon*. In July of that year, the Franco-Prussian War erupted, and Verne organized a coast guard at Le Crotoy. He continued to write, producing *A Floating City, and the Blockade Runners*, a one-volume novel and short story, in 1871, and *The Fur Country*, a novel, in 1873.

Around the World in Eighty Days also appeared in 1873, garnering world wide publicity for Verne and his unlikely hero, Phileas Fogg. In 1874, Verne and his family moved to Amiens, and he published *Dr. Ox's Experiment, and Other Stories*. Utilizing a variation of his desert island theme, Verne brings Capt. Nemo into contact with shipwrecked Americans in the three-volume *The Mysterious Island* (1874–1875). After this novel, Verne's prose became darker, although his output remained substantial. The well-received *Michael Strogoff, the Courier of the Czar* (1876) was followed by *Hector Servadac: Travels and Adventures Through the Solar System* (1877) and other works set in foreign lands, most notably, *The Begum's Fortune* (1879).

Verne's love of the sea never waned, and he often took his family on cruises. While traveling in 1884, Verne met Pope Leo XIII, who praised the moral value of his fiction. *Mathias Sandorf* (1885) is a colorful novel from that period. In 1886, he made a momentous return to science fiction with *The Clipper of the Clouds* (also titled *Robur the Conqueror*), in which a rudimentary helicopter appears. That same year, Verne suffered two setbacks: a mysterious attack by his nephew, in which Verne was shot in the leg, and the death of his friend and publisher, Hetzel.

Embarking on yet another career, Verne took up local politics in 1888 by becoming a city councilor at Amiens. He also produced many novels over the next few years, including *Topsy Turvy* (also titled *The Purchase of the North Pole*) in 1889, *The Carpathian Castle* in 1892, *Propeller Island* in 1895, and *For the Flag* in 1896. For much of Verne's career, Edgar Allan Poe had been a major influence, especially in *An Antarctic Mystery* (also titled *The Sphinx of the Ice-Fields*), published in 1897 as a sequel to Poe's *Narrative of Arthur Gordon Pym*. Some minor detective novels followed, such as *The Master of the World* (1904).

With his eyesight failing, due to diabetes, Verne completed more than one hundred books before his death on March 24, 1905. He was among the most translated authors in the world, though many poor translations marred his work. Verne, whom science fiction novelist Arthur C. Clarke has called, "one of the best storytellers who ... ever lived," also left many manuscripts to be published posthumously, including *The Lighthouse at the End of the World* (1905), *The Survivors of the Jonathan* (1909), *Yesterday and Tomorrow* (1910), *The Barsac Mission* (1919), and *Paris in the Twentieth Century* (1994).

CONTENTS

List of Illustrations

INTRODUCTION: "FOR IT HOLDS A SECRET"

Caleb Carr

During the modern era, it has become commonplace to affectionately dismiss *The Mysterious Island* as little more than Jules Verne's diverting, microcosmic testament to man's triumph over the earth's other creatures, as well as its elements. By placing five (and later in the story six) castaways on a deserted island and minutely detailing how they use their scientific knowledge and native ingenuity to harness the resources of the place and transform it into a bustling hive of agriculture and manufacture, Verne hoped, in the opinion of such commentators as Isaac Asimov, to reassure Industrial Age citizens that they could survive when stripped of their technological conveniences. "That small inner uncertainty," Asimov wrote of the book during the 1980s, "of 'How can I ever get along if civilization fails me?' is allayed." The "point of the story," he continued, is "that human beings using their hands and brains can supply all their wants if only nature is kind."

This rather trite view of what is arguably Verne's most important and self-revelatory book resonates today with those who see in such contemporary phenomena as the television series *Survivor* a similar desire on the part of a new generation dominated by technological innovation to assert their basic physical and mental skills. But just as *Survivor* is an artifice that tells us as much about its creators and how they perceive the world as it does about its audience and their views, so *The Mysterious Island* offers important insight into its extraordinary author, insight contained in a series of character-related messages that Verne fought hard to defend against editorial elimination. On the simplest level, these messages are hinted at in the very *title* of the book: Verne did not call it "An Island Tamed," or "Man Against the Island"—he called it *The* Mysterious *Island,* with a purpose that was evident to at least some early reviewers. Writing in the French paper *Le Temps,* for example, one such critic correctly identified the book as very different from Verne's other works: "For," he explained simply, "it holds a secret." That secret was far more than merely the solution to the mystery of the island: it was an explanation, perhaps unconscious but nonetheless apparent, of the paradox that lay at the very center of Jules Verne's complex soul and intellect, an explanation embodied in the long-awaited revelation of the motivations of the greatest character that ever sprang to life from the novelist's pen.

———

In October 1875 Jules Hetzel, the enterprising, innovative Frenchman who had built an empire publishing the likes of Victor Hugo and Georges Sand in both serialized and bound formats, brought out the final volume of the latest novel by another of his most popular authors. Titled "The Secret of the Island," this collection of chapters—which also ran in serialized form in one of Hetzel's magazines—had been awaited by Jules Verne's fans with anticipation that was even more than the usually feverish. For while in its early chapters *The Mysterious Island* had seemed little more than another of Verne's captivating but numerous shipwreck (or, in this case, balloon-wreck) tales, the book had, during its considerable magazine run, gradually proved to be something very different. In fact, it was exactly what its title promised: a mystery.

Such was indeed an intriguing surprise, for Jules Verne was certainly not known as a mystery writer. The master (if not, purely speaking, the originator) of what would come to be called "science" or "speculative" fiction, Verne had originally set out to become what he himself described as a "geographical author": his object was "the teaching of geography, the description of the earth. For each new country I have to invent a new story." By "country" he by no means meant mere nations: the center of the earth and outer space had proved two of the most popular "countries" through which Verne, by anchoring his work in highly dramatized but no less extensive research complemented by uncanny extrapolation, had taken his readers. And while there had certainly been *questions* involved in both *Journey to the Center of the Earth* and *From the Earth to the Moon*—What would Professor Lindenbrock's party find at the earth's core? Would the Barbicane team return from their moonshot safely?—they were the sorts of immediate situational questions characteristic of adventure stories. Deep probing of character and motivation had always been absent: Verne himself had stated flatly that, in his books, "The characters are secondary, whatever you may say." (A declaration that would become an unfortunate tradition for much of science fiction.)

Certainly the rules of adventure rather than mystery had dominated in Verne's other two masterworks from the period prior to 1875, *Around the World in Eighty Days* and *Twenty Thousand Leagues Under the Sea*. Nowhere in either of these books did Verne employ what was becoming, in the post–Edgar Allan Poe era, the increasingly formalized basis of the mystery genre: a series of inexplicable activities, usually violent, on the part of an unknown agent whose obscure personal and psychological motivations were revealed during the climax of the tale. Verne had, on one occasion, *tried* to pursue such a course: in his original conception of *Twenty Thousand Leagues*, he had intended to explain the misanthropic attitude and actions of Captain Nemo by casting him as a Polish nobleman whose struggles against Russian aggression had resulted in his family's murder by the vicious invaders. These events were to have been the cause of Nemo's separating himself from what he deemed savage mankind by descending beneath the waves in his submarine *Nautilus*, from which domain he would occasionally lash out in vengeance at the ships of the surface world.

But Jules Hetzel, ever attuned to the public mood in France and abroad, had decided that Verne's intended motivation for Nemo was too controversial: not only did Hetzel's publications do a healthy business in Russia, but the publication of *Twenty Thousand Leagues* coincided with the signing of a treaty between France and the tsarist empire. This was not the first time Verne had felt the force of Hetzel's editorial censure: earlier in Verne's career, Hetzel had exercised even more drastic caution regarding the young author's political and social views when Verne submitted a novel titled *Paris in the Twentieth Century*. Set in the 1960s, the book described a city consumed by runaway materialism and shrouded in pollution caused by automobile fumes, a city where people commonly possessed such luxuries as photo-telephonic facsimile machines but forsook even basic cultural knowledge. Hetzel had pronounced all this not only depressing but implausible, and refused to publish it. (The book did not resurface until the 1990s, when it became a best-seller.)

Verne had not forgotten the experience: faced with Hetzel's demand that Nemo's motivation for sinking ships and living under the sea be tempered, the author angrily conceded, declaring in protest that if he was barred from a controversial political explanation he would give the brooding captain *no* stated motive. Hetzel readily agreed to this idea, for to his way of thinking it was Verne's enthusiasm for science and adventure that were most valuable and popular, not his troublesome worries about the fate of mankind. Thus Nemo never explains, in *Twenty Thousand Leagues*, the specific origins of his consuming hatred of the world above the waves—a fact that places the book squarely in the genre of action-oriented science fiction, and removes it from the realm of mystery.

But by 1873 Verne, now enormously successful and something of a French national institution, was ready once more to lock horns with Hetzel on the subjects of mystery and motivation. His cagey old publisher and friend had remained a formidable and cautious taskmaster: Verne, the author of many tales of trouble at sea, had long desired to write his own contribution to yet another genre of popular fiction called *robinson-ades,* that is, stories that followed the precedent of Daniel Defoe's *Robinson Crusoe* by telling of a person or group of people who, marooned on a deserted and uncharted island, usually in the South Pacific, use their human ingenuity to triumph over the forces of nature. But Verne's first foray into this genre—titled *Uncle Robinson,* in obvious tribute to the originator of such tales—had been rejected by Hetzel: the first time the publisher had exercised his veto since *Paris in the Twentieth Century.* Hetzel's reasoning then had been that the characters in *Uncle Robinson* had been "too inert!" "Drop all these people and begin with new ones," the publisher went on. "It's important that everything be extraordinary."

In the years that followed, Verne had followed this direction (though in a way that he had reason to think might tweak Hetzel); and by 1873, after carefully reading and absorbing at least one more popular robinsonade—James Fenimore Cooper's *The Crater*—Verne was hard at work on a fresh attempt, one that he cleverly ensured would be both accepted and successful by placing at its heart the hand (unseen, for most of the book) of none other than Captain Nemo, who had already become a fixture in international popular culture.

Indeed, the success of *Twenty Thousand Leagues,* along with that of his other books, emboldened Verne to rebuff nearly all of Hetzel's editorial concerns about *The Mysterious Island* from the first, and in no uncertain terms: "The sum of things imagined in this work is greater than in the others," he declared, and when Hetzel expressed some reservation or other Verne would explode with, "you're succeeding in disgusting me with the book," or "I ask you whether I need to be in possession of all my composure." Hetzel backed off almost every time, for he knew that the novel's plot and details were indeed complicated, both scientifically and dramatically: what Verne had begun by describing as "a chemical novel" in fact did contain long passages detailing basic and not-so-basic chemical—as well as agricultural, mechanical, and physical—descriptions of how the castaways conquer the rather impossibly varied environment of their island. (Never much of a traveler, Verne incorporated carefully researched ecological aspects of every continent into what his characters called Lincoln Island, apparently oblivious, empirically, to the impossibility of such coexistence.) Yet even more important than these encyclopaedic scientific details was the careful weaving throughout of an actual *mystery:* an unexplained presence on the island that repeatedly acts in the castaways' favor, saving them from harm and providing them with needed supplies.

Verne builds the questions and tension surrounding this presence masterfully: at first the castaways, and even we readers, can almost believe that the events for which the unseen agent is responsible are unrelated, or perhaps simply coincidental or unusual natural occurrences. When we can no longer deny that it must be a human being at work, we are nonetheless unsure that said person's intentions are purely benevolent. For if they are, why would he hide himself and disguise his actions so carefully? We share the frustration of Cyrus Smith, the American engineer who leads the colonists: when it is put to him by the journalist Gideon Spilett that the seemingly related yet inexplicable events may all be the result of chance, he declares: "Chance! Spilett! I don't believe in chance, any more than I believe in earthly mysteries."

This protest carries weight: for under Cyrus Smith's leadership, and thanks to his seemingly inexhaustible knowledge and ingenuity, the castaways have created everything from a thriving farm to an iron refinery to electric batteries for a telegraph (assisted, admittedly, by the fact that their island contains deposits of nearly every metal ore and chemical known to man). Yes, we as readers and surrogate members of the team have enjoyed the creation of a comfortable, safe, and idyllic environment, and we bridle somewhat at the idea that it has ultimately been secured by some hidden benefactor who refuses to reveal himself. Yet simultaneously we are, of course, secretly happy and relieved that the man exists. As Verne himself puts it, again discussing Smith: "The engineer was both moved and irritated by his invisible protective force, for next to this their own [the castaways'] actions paled into insignificance." By the commencement of the third section of the book we can understand the anticipation that Verne's fans felt on its publication: Who is the hidden agent? What are his intentions? How does he appear and disappear with such skill, without ever being seen, and why does he possess such an array of advanced implements and instruments, if he lives on a deserted island?

And above all, why has Jules Verne, supposed champion of ingenuity, science, and self-sufficiency, included such an uncharacterisitic, such an unquantifiable and inexplicable, such a *mysterious* element in this story?

———

It was Jules Hetzel who played the crucial role in establishing the myth of Jules Verne as a rational priest of scientific benevolence—for in truth, Verne himself was deeply ambivalent about the social and moral implications of the scientific advances that were going on around him. That technological progress was an unstoppable force he did not doubt: toward the end of *The Mysterious Island* Cyrus Smith—one of the characters through which Verne expresses his hopeful side most clearly—tells Captain Nemo (who has by then been revealed as the castaways' unseen benefactor) that his mistake in fighting against the surface world "was to believe that you could bring back the past. You struggled against progress, which is a good and necessary thing. This is an error that some admire and some condemn." And yet when the final volcanic destruction of the island occurs, Verne sums up all that Smith's party have been through with words that echo the engineer's tone, but incline toward a very different conclusion: "The colonists had tried to fight off this invasion; they had tried, but all their efforts were for naught. Man is no match for such cataclysms, and mad indeed is he who struggles against the forces of nature!" (So much for the body of the book's action, which concerns little *but* the castaways' struggle against the forces of nature.)

From the beginning of his career, Verne had expressed similarly contradictory thoughts, sometimes, as in the case of *The Mysterious Island*, within one volume, and sometimes in different books. There had been and was to be no greater expression of his ambivalence about science and progress than *Paris in the Twentieth Century,* the book that Hetzel—rightly convinced that the public desired stories that would morally rationalize the Industrial Revolution—had refused to publish; yet even in various early works that did see the light of publication there were hints of Verne's discomfort. As early as 1872, for example, Verne amused his public with *Dr. Ox's Experiment,* a tale in which a scientific man creates great mischief by pumping oxygen through the gas lines of a town stricken by lethargy and apathy; the townspeople eventually become so "lively," however, that they declare war on a neighboring community.

But later in life Verne's dark doubts about science and scientists grew distinctly less amusing (and as a result less popular). In 1889 he produced *The Purchase of the North Pole,* in which some of his earlier heroes—the Barbicane team of *From the Earth to the Moon*—make a return appearance; but this time they are engaged in a sinister endeavor. Having bought up large amounts of unclaimed territories around the pole, they plan to construct a giant gun similar to the one that sent them to the moon; but the gun's only purpose is to produce a recoil so severe that it will knock the earth off its axis, melting the polar ice and making it possible for the now-incorporated Barbicane & Co. to exploit the natural resources that lie beneath. Jules Verne, the man who had become popular largely because of his rapturous writings about the promise of science, had evolved into an observer who was openly alarmed about the uses that might be made of those same scientific advances.

It is this side of Verne's character that is hinted at in the revelation of Captain Nemo's true name and past at the climax of *The Mysterious Island.* Finally Verne was able to tell the tale of a lesser country subjugated by a greater, and of a brave aristocrat whose attempts to save that smaller country result in the destruction of all he holds dear. Verne decided to switch the culprit in the tale from one toward which he felt no special antipathy—Russia—to one he actively detested: Great Britain. And to fill the role of victim he turned his eyes toward India, making Nemo, in his earlier life, "Prince Dakkar," a handsome and wealthy young man who had been one of the leaders of the Sepoy Uprising. In Verne's version (a version very close to fact) Britain had used all of its technological military might to crush the rebellion, an act that Verne clearly deplored; this, despite the fact that India at the time was a violent, backward nation dominated by tribal and religious wars—hardly the sort of place that a prophet of the redemptive power of rational science would hold up as a model.

There is much in the tale of Verne's own life to explain this inner ambiguity and philosophical dichotomy. As a man he often spoke of his supposed boyhood desire to go to sea, like one of the youths in his books; but in truth he tried but once, for when he was caught in the harbor by his father he earnestly pledged never to make another attempt. And while his characters might be starry-eyed adventurers, Verne himself was, from early adulthood to old age, eminently bourgeois: preoccupied with money, not-so-secretly anti-Semitic (he remained convinced of the guilt of Captain Dreyfus throughout his life, even when the facts of the case came out), and a believer in conservative, indeed fairly oppressive, family values. Though he abandoned his father's profession, the law, he did so only to take up an unsuccessful career as a stockbroker, writing on the side but never really living so much as visiting *la vie bohème.* He married a woman who was every bit as bourgeois as himself, and who had no use for his writing until it became the source of a substantial income; even then, her lack of either imagination or understanding was a constant irritant that often drove her husband from the house. This situation was aggravated by the birth of a son, whose infant cries distracted and annoyed Verne when he was trying to work: and in the years that followed the relationship only deteriorated from there. Though he professed to be unconcerned with awards and rank, Verne prized his membership in the Legion of Honor and remained bitter about his exclusion from the French Academy to the day of his death.

In short, Jules Verne's personal life was as characterized by contradiction as was his writing; and in *The Mysterious Island* we get a palpable sense of that inner tension more than in any of his other books. The desire to portray the castaways as masters of their own fate, contrasted with the constant undercutting of their self-sufficiency through the introduction of the "unseen hand"; the inability to decide which is the mightier or more magnificent force, man's ingenuity or nature's raw power; and above all the self-revelatory philosophical dichotomies inherent in both Nemo himself and in the mythological captain's contrast to and discussions with the engineer Cyrus Smith; from all these things we can divine that the true secret the book holds is the considerably—indeed, sometimes terribly—contradictory and troubled nature of Verne's beliefs and spirit. Yet despite the opinion of Jules Hetzel (and others since) that it was Verne's talent for scientific research that made him stand out as an author, it was in fact precisely this inner conflict that made him great, and keeps his books alive. For such an air of uncertainty and self-doubt is, ultimately, essential to all great novelists—no matter how unhappy it may make both them and those who choose to share in their lives.

———

Jordan Stump's new translation of *The Mysterious Island* makes the book new, even—or perhaps I should say especially—to anyone who spent his or her childhood reading and re-reading the English text that was standard for so many generations. It is not simply that details such as character names have been restored to the original ("Cyrus Smith," for example, has until now always been "Cyrus Harding" in American editions—as if the character himself were not vigorous and remarkable enough!); but Stump's understanding and faithful rendering of Verne's French idiosyncracies, as well as the otherwise knowledgable author's ignorance of American habits of speech and behavior (despite his deep admiration for America, Verne spent a total of one week in the United States), make us understand how very much of a universal fantasy and parable the tale is—while simultaneously allowing us to comprehend much more of the book's humor than did the old standard. It is to be hoped that Mr. Stump's considerable efforts will be enough to call *The Mysterious Island* to the attention of the *Survivor* generation; for when the "unseen hand" on the island is that of Captain Nemo rather than a television network, a world of truly ageless adventure, amusement, and, yes, *mystery* await.

———

CALEB CARR is the author of the bestselling novels *The Alienist, The Angel of Darkness,* and *Killing Time,* and the nonfiction books *America Invulnerable: The Quest for Absolute Security from 1812 to Star Wars* (with James Chace) and *The Devil Soldier: The Story of Frederick Townsend Ward.* Carr is a contributing editor of *MHQ: The Quarterly Journal of Military History* and has written for *The World Policy Journal, Time,* and *The New York Times,* among other publications. He is also the editor of the Modern Library War series and has worked for the Council on Foreign Relations. Carr was born in Manhattan and grew up on the Lower East Side, where he still lives.

TRANSLATOR'S PREFACE

Jordan Stump

The Mysterious Island ranks among the best-known works of one of France's best-loved writers, and among the few nineteenth-century French novels with which an American schoolchild might possibly be expected to have some acquaintance. For well over a hundred years it has been continuously offered up to the English-speaking world in various guises, including comic books, CD-ROMs, and a memorably unfaithful film adaptation; but until this year, only once has it been translated into English in its entirety. First published in Great Britain in 1876 and many times reprinted since, W.H.G. Kingston's version has no doubt fired countless imaginations in the past century-and-a-quarter, judging by the well-thumbed copy in my public library and, no doubt, in yours. It is a perfectly creditable rendering—it could hardly have enjoyed such tangible success if it were not—and the fact that I am now prefacing a new translation of Verne's novel should not be construed as a dismissal of Kingston's work. His is not so much a deficient translation as a dated one—for it is a sad (or from a translator's point of view, a happy) fact that translations date. Language changes, readings evolve, new stylistic conventions emerge (is this not what Verne means by *progress?*), and the result is that a translation such as Kingston's might seem somewhat lifeless to a modern reader, something less than engrossing, which is precisely what *The Mysterious Island* should not be. Verne can be didactic, he can be prolix, he can even be laborious, but he should never seem drab. Hence, to a publisher's mind, the need for a new translation. For my part, of course, such justifications are entirely superfluous: the sheer pleasure of dealing with Verne's writing, and with a book I have loved since childhood, was reason enough to leap unhesitatingly into the task.

But I most emphatically do not mean to say that this new translation attempts to "update" the first. The lifelessness of Kingston's version is not entirely his fault, nor entirely the work of passing time: there *is* a certain formality in Verne's writing, and a certain stilted quality to his dialogue. That, to me at least, is a potent part of his charm, and to attempt to punch up Verne's prose would be to do him and his readers a great disservice. The present translation sets out not to modernize Verne for contemporary tastes, then, but to offer the contemporary reader a truer taste of the particular nature of his writing: at once formal and playful, passionate and controlled. For, despite his reputation as a visionary, Verne is a very nineteenth-century sort of writer; there is, in his style of course, but also in his unique blend of realism and melodrama, in his unrelenting faith in progress, and even in his unconsciously insensitive treatment of race relations, something distinctly archaic, something perfectly familiar to us today but at the same time just a little distant. This seems to me a quality of capital importance, and I endeavored to keep it utmost in my mind as I translated *The Mysterious Island*, attempting to communicate the quality of his writing without modernizing it, but also without descending into pastiche.

To put it more concisely, I have done here what any translator does: I have tried to offer the American reader an experience as similar as possible to my own experience of the original work. But this is no simple thing. Indeed, it is a very complicated thing, and a reader who compares my translation to Kingston's will find not that mine simply hews more closely to Verne's text than his, nor that it departs from Verne's text more boldly, but that it sometimes hews, and sometimes departs, for fidelity is a strange and labyrinthine undertaking. Nowhere is this truth illustrated more clearly nor encapsulated more neatly than in the question of the proper name, and if the reader would indulge me I would like to consider that problem for a few moments here.

One fundamental difference will immediately leap out at any reader of this translation familiar with Kingston's version: the name of the engineer who acts as the castaways' leader is no longer Cyrus Harding, but

Cyrus Smith. It is indeed the latter name that he goes by in Verne's book; no doubt Kingston had good reasons for making this change, but whatever they were they have surely outlived their usefulness, and I have thus reverted to Veren's nomenclature here, as I have for the sailor Pencroff, whom Kingston renames Pencroft. The case of young Harbert poses a more difficult problem. Kingston calls him Herbert; should I follow his lead and assume that "Harbert" represents Verne's attempt to transmute "Herbert" into French? There are good arguments to be made on both sides, but in the end I think not. For one thing, "Herbert" is a perfectly acceptable (if uncommon) name in French, and Verne could certainly have used it as is, if such had been his wish; for another—given that "Harbert" is unattested as a Christian name in both French and English—we cannot even say with any certainty that this is meant to be the child's first name rather than his last. And of course "Harbert" is a wonderful name in any case, calling to mind both "Harvard" (as Verne tells us, he was educated by the best teachers in Boston) and "harvest" (he is a budding expert in the field of botany); for a variety of reasons, then, it seems more right to me than "Herbert," and so once again I have chosen to remain closer to Verne than Kingston.

But sometimes, not paradoxically, fidelity requires a change to the original. Another castaway bears the name Gédéon Spilett in Verne's text; here, as distinct from Harbert's case, it seems unambiguously clear that Verne has chosen the French version of an English name, and—finding it unlikely that an American might be named Gédéon—I naturally opted for Gideon. The name of the sixth castaway requires a similar change, but for a different reason. Verne calls him Nab, short for Nabuchodonosor, who is none other than the biblical king we know as Nebuchadnezzar; hence my choice to rebaptize him Neb. Another abbreviated name seemed to call for another change, for yet another reason: the character Verne calls Jup derives his name from Jupiter, but while a French reader would instinctively pronounce "Jup" with a long *u*, as in "Jupiter," an American would, I think, naturally pronounce it with a short *u*, rhyming it with "cup." This seemed too great a loss to me, and so I did not hesitate to rename him Joop.

Verne adds yet another layer of complication to the problem of the proper name—which, I remind the reader, I dwell on here as an emblem or illustration of the complexities of fidelity generally—when he has his castaways name the various parts of the island onto which fate has dropped them. Verne does not merely give us the French versions of the names they invent; ever the stickler for authenticity, he further records the names they "actually" choose in the fictional world of the novel, which is to say the *English* names. Unfortunately, these do not always seem particularly likely as products of an anglophone mind. Thus Verne translates the wetland dubbed the *Marais des Tadornes* as "Tadorn's-fens," which—leaving aside the hyphen and the uncapitalized *f,* which are only a matter of typographical convention—I found simply too unnatural to leave as is. There is no reason why "tadorn" should not be a word in English, but the fact remains that it isn't one, and while the French *des* might well signify a possessive, here it clearly does not (and certainly not a singular possessive). I thus renamed this area Shelduck Fens (admiring that rather erudite "fens," and so choosing to keep it despite its slightly implausible sound), and it was in a similar way, and for similar reasons, that Verne's "Mandible-cape" became Cape Mandible, "Claw-cape" became Cape Claw, "Flotson-point" became Flotsam Point, and so on.

It should be clear from the above that Verne's English is not always perfect; but—to further compound the problem of fidelity—these minor solecisms are not the only lapses to be found in *The Mysterious Island*. Verne wrote quickly, and while for the most part his text betrays a remarkably precise and careful mind, it is nevertheless not entirely free of errors and inconsistencies. What is a translator to do when the author errs? Does the rule of fidelity require me to reproduce the mistake just as it is, or to correct it so as not to hamper the reader's pleasure? Again, there are arguments to be made on both sides. My own solution—almost, but not quite, invariably—has been to stick with Verne's version, even at the risk of confusing the novel's audience. These lapses are few, and generally slight enough to pass unnoticed by most readers; but for the sake of the psychic equilibrium of those blessed with a particularly acute eye for detail, it might be best to catalogue a few of Verne's small missteps here.

One such error deserves special mention at the outset, for Verne openly acknowledges it in his text: twice linking the events of *The Mysterious Island* to two prior novels published under his name, he concedes the uncomfortable chronological incompatibility of the three tales—but ingeniously explains the problem away even as he calls it to our attention (see his footnotes in Chapter 17 of Part II and Chapter 16 of Part III). More commonly, however, Verne's lapses appear simply to have eluded the eye of the author and his proofreaders. Chapter 15 of Part II, for instance, is prefaced by an erroneous heading; the events it describes take place not in that chapter but in the following one (whose heading bears almost—but not quite—the same words as its predecessor). I have chosen not to correct that error; nor have I deleted the narrator's use of the toponym "Flotsam Point" before the castaways have so named it, nor his one-time use of the name "Grant Islet" for the small patch of land otherwise known as Safety Island. Occasionally, though, where the error seemed too jarring to be worth keeping, I have corrected Verne's slips. The final lines of Part I, for instance, recount an incident with a peccary, which Verne once refers to as "an inoffensive rodent." Given that rabbits figure prominently in the few pages leading up to this passage, it seems very possible that he briefly forgot the nature of the animal in question (or perhaps he originally intended this incident to involve a rabbit and later changed his mind, neglecting to remove the allusion to the rodent order). In any case, given that this is a moment of some dramatic tension, I thought it best not to distract the reader with such a trifling inconsistency, and simply changed "rodent" to "peccary," just as I have corrected a small problem of chronology (a matter of one hour) that might mar the reader's enjoyment of a great climactic sequence in Part III, Chapter 15. I hope that the reader will forgive me these small interventions, and will not think me capricious for having reproduced some of Verne's errors and not others. Such are the decisions translators are sometimes called upon to make: we all want to be faithful, but faithful to what? To each word? To the text as a whole? To the reader? To all of them at once, preferably—no simple thing, again.

Only very rarely have I imposed my editorial authority over Verne's text, however; indeed, I believe I have just named the only two overt instances. In those, as throughout this translation, my goal was to respect the nature of Verne's work while at the same time producing a living book rather than a slavish reproduction: a book which would retain the foreign quality of the original (its Frenchness, its nineteenth-century-ness) while remaining as gripping a read for the twenty-first-century reader as for Verne's original audience. How well I succeeded in this effort is of course for the reader to decide; for my part, I can only say that I found this an unfailingly engrossing and happy task, and that the nine months I spent on *The Mysterious Island* were among the most agreeable of my life as a translator. Luckily, like Cyrus Smith, I had a number of able hands helping me with my project, and I would like to take this opportunity to offer thanks. I owe a tremendous debt of gratitude to MJ Devaney of Random House, for her untiring help and encouragement; to John McGhee, for his superb copyediting; to Professor Nancy Lindsley-Griffin, for help with the rudiments of metallurgy and vulcanology; to Robert Stump, who cleared up certain mysteries in the realms of meteorology, astronomy, and geometry; to Josh Graml of the Mariners' Museum Research Library, whose assistance with shipbuilding arcana proved invaluable; and most of all, by far, to Eleanor Hardin, whose sympathetic reading and unerring advice shaped this translation more than I can say.

One final word. I said at the beginning that Kingston's translation is the only complete *Mysterious Island* to have appeared in print *until this year,* but as fate would have it another new translation of Verne's novel, by Sidney Kravitz, is set to be published by New England University Press at roughly the same time as this one. I have not seen Mr. Kravitz's text, and he has not seen mine; but, given the nature of translation, I have no doubt that there will exist both fascinating similarities and fascinating differences between our respective versions. The conscientious reader is thus encouraged to buy a copy of both.

———

JORDAN STUMP is an associate professor of French at the University of Nebraska–Lincoln. He has published articles on the Marquis de Sade, Georges Perec, and Raymond Queneau, among others; he is also the author of *Naming and Unnaming: On Raymond Queneau,* and has translated novels by Marie Redonnet, Eric Chevillard, Patrick Modiano, and Christian Oster. His translation of Claude Simon's *The Jardin des Plantes* won the 2001 French-American Foundation Translation Prize.

PART ONE

THE CASTAWAYS FROM THE SKY

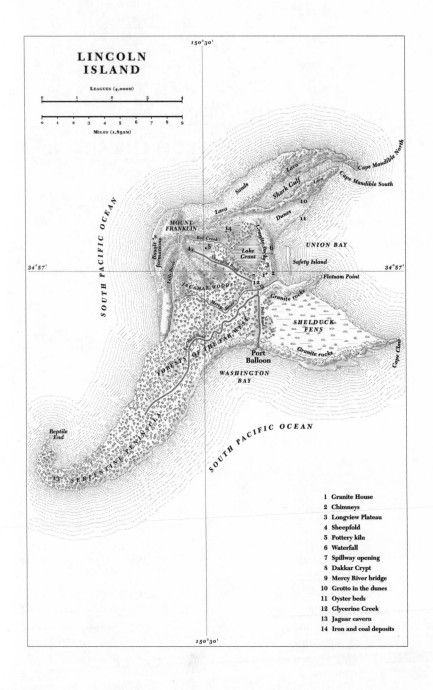

LINCOLN ISLAND

Leagues (4,000M)

0   1   2   3   4

0   1   2   3   4   5   6   7   8   9

MILES (1,852M)

SOUTH PACIFIC OCEAN

150°30'

Cape Mandible North

Cape Mandible South

Lava

Lava

Sands

Lava

Shark Gulf

10

Lava

11

Dunes

MOUNT FRANKLIN

14

Creek

Red Creek

5

Lake Grant

6

UNION BAY

Basalt's formation

4

Falls River

Serpentine River

Mandible River

7

8   3

1   2

Safety Island

34°57'   34°57'

12   9

Flotsam Point

JACAMAR WOODS

Mercy River

Fork River

Granite rocks

SHELDUCK FENS

Granite rocks

Cape Claw

Port Balloon

WASHINGTON BAY

Road

FORESTS OF THE FAR WEST

SOUTH PACIFIC OCEAN

Reptile End

13

SERPENTINE PENINSULA

150°30'

1 Granite House
2 Chimneys
3 Longview Plateau
4 Sheepfold
5 Pottery kiln
6 Waterfall
7 Spillway opening
8 Dakkar Crypt
9 Mercy River bridge
10 Grotto in the dunes
11 Oyster beds
12 Glycerine Creek
13 Jaguar cavern
14 Iron and coal deposits

I

The Great Storm of 1865.—Shouts in the Air.—A Balloon in a Whirlwind.—The Torn Fabric.—Nothing but Water.—Five Passengers.—The Events in the Gondola.—A Shoreline on the Horizon.—The Outcome of the Drama.

"Are we rising?"

"No! Quite the reverse! We're sinking!"

"Worse than that, Mr. Cyrus! We're falling!"

"For the love of God! Drop some ballast!"

"That's the last sack emptied!"

"Is the balloon climbing now?"

"No!"

"I think I hear waves crashing!"

"We're over the ocean!"

"We can't be more than five hundred feet above it!"

Just then a powerful voice rent the air, and the following words rang out: "Everything heavy overboard!... everything! And God save us!"

Such were the cries echoing over the vast emptiness of the Pacific Ocean on March 23rd, 1865, at about four o'clock in the afternoon.

Surely no one will have forgotten the terrible northeasterly gale that was unleashed at the vernal equinox of that year. The barometer fell to 710 millimeters, and the storm went on unabated from the eighteenth to the twenty-sixth of March. Great was the devastation it wrought, in America, Europe, and Asia alike—a vast diagonal swath of destruction eighteen hundred miles wide, from the thirty-fifth parallel north to the fortieth south! Shattered cities, uprooted forests, shorelines ravaged by crashing mountains of water, ships slammed against the shore—by the hundreds, according to the dossiers of the Bureau Veritas—whole regions leveled by cyclones that smashed everything in their path, a human toll that numbered in the thousands, both on land and at sea: such was the scene in the wake of the cyclone, and such were the tokens of its fury. In the ranks of natural disasters, it outstripped even the horrific devastation witnessed at Havana and on the island of Guadeloupe, on October 25th, 1810, and July 26th, 1825, respectively.

Now, even as these many catastrophes were unfolding at sea and on land, another drama, no less prodigious, was being played out in the turbulent skies.

For a balloon, wafted along atop a whirlwind like a toy ball, and caught up in the rotational movement of the column of air, was traveling through the heavens at a speed of ninety miles an hour,* spinning in circles as if seized by some aerial maelstrom.

Beneath the appendix on the underside of the balloon swayed a gondola holding five passengers, scarcely visible in the dense mists and sea spray that suffused the air.

Whence came this aerostat, this plaything of the terrible storm? From what point on the globe had it taken flight? It could not have set off in the middle of the cyclone, of course, and the cyclone's first symptoms had appeared on the eighteenth—five days before. The reasonable conclusion would thus be that the balloon had come from far, far away; indeed, given the speed of the wind, it could not have traveled less than two thousand miles in every twenty-four-hour period!

But, caught up in the storm as they were, the passengers had no point of reference, and hence no means of gauging the distance they had traveled. Indeed, a very curious phenomenon must then have been at work: the violent winds propelled them at a terrific speed, and yet they themselves had no sense of their own motion. Forward they sped, ever turning circles, as perfectly unaware of their rotation as of their horizontal movement. Their gaze could not penetrate the thick mass of fog below them; and around them all was gray mist, forming a veil so opaque that they could not say whether it was day or night. No glimmer of light, no sound from land, no ocean roar could have reached them through that vast dark-

---

*That is, 46 meters per second or 155 kilometers per hour (nearly 42 four-kilometer leagues).

ness so long as they remained at high altitude. Their rapid descent alone had alerted them to the peril they faced above the waves.

But now, relieved of all heavy objects such as ammunition, weapons, and provisions, the balloon had once again risen into the upper levels of the atmosphere, to an altitude of 4,500 feet. Realizing that the sea alone lay beneath the gondola, and believing the dangers awaiting them above to be less formidable than those below, the passengers did not hesitate to jettison even the most vital elements of their equipment; their only thought was to prevent any further loss of the precious gas, the soul of their conveyance, that held them aloft over the abyss.

The night passed, full of fears that might have proven fatal for less vigorous souls. Then daylight returned, and with the sunrise the storm began to abate. A newfound calm settled over the atmosphere in the first hours of that twenty-fourth of March. By dawn the clouds had grown more billowy, and had lifted higher into the sky. Over the next several hours, the whirlwind gradually expanded and weakened. The winds, once hurricane-force, were now at the "near-gale" level, meaning that the speed of the atmospheric levels' translatory motion had fallen by half. The balloon was still caught up in a wind that would have caused a prudent sailor to take three reefs in his sail; nevertheless, the perturbation of the atmosphere had greatly decreased.

By eleven o'clock, the air had cleared noticeably at the lower altitudes. The atmosphere was bathed in the sort of damp limpidity that is often seen, and even felt, in the wake of a major meteorological phenomenon. It seemed not so much that the cyclone had moved on to the west as that it had simply exhausted itself. Perhaps, once the center had collapsed, its energy had dispersed in sheets of electricity, as sometimes happens with typhoons in the Indian Ocean.

At about this same hour, it became evident that the balloon was once again sinking through the lower levels of the atmosphere, slowly and continuously. Worse yet, it seemed to be deflating little by little, the envelope growing longer, distended, no longer spherical but ovoid.

By noon, the aerostat hovered no more than two thousand feet above the sea. Its volume was fifty thousand cubic feet,* and it was thanks to this that it had stayed so long afloat; for a balloon with such a capacity can travel both high and far.

---

* Approximately 1,700 cubic meters.

Now the passengers jettisoned the last few objects weighing down the gondola, the small remaining store of foodstuffs, even the utensils crammed into their pockets, and one of them, hoisting himself onto the ring that encircled the ropes of the net, tried to tie off the aerostat's appendix with a sturdy knot.

It was clear that the passengers could not hope to maintain the balloon in the upper reaches of the atmosphere. A great quantity of gas must have escaped from the envelope into the open air!

They were finished!

For no continent lay beneath them, not even so much as an island. Not a single landing place as far as the eye could see, not a single solid surface in which to cast anchor.

Only the vast ocean, whose waves continued to crash with an inconceivable violence! The sea, with no visible end, not even from an altitude that offered a view of forty miles in every direction! Only a liquid plain, relentlessly tossed and whipped by the winds, which appeared from this height as an endless cavalcade of frenzied waves topped by a vast expanse of foaming whitecaps! No land in sight, not a ship to be seen!

The descent would have to be halted, no matter what the cost, for if left to fall unchecked the balloon would soon vanish into the billows. It was thus to this urgent task that the passengers of the gondola now turned their efforts; but no matter how they struggled, the balloon only continued to sink, all the while moving at great speed with the direction of the wind, from northeast to southwest.

A truly terrible situation now faced the aerostat's wretched passengers! They were clearly no longer in control of their craft. Their exertions had no effect. The envelope of the balloon was deflating before their eyes; the gas was escaping, and they had not the slightest hope of preserving it. The descent was accelerating perceptibly, and, at one hour past noon, the gondola hung only six hundred feet above the ocean.

For the leak had proved impossible to stem, and the gas flowed unhindered through a tear in the fabric of the balloon.

By ridding the gondola of its contents, the passengers had prolonged their aerial suspension by a few hours. The catastrophe could be delayed, but it could not be prevented; and unless some land appeared before nightfall, the passengers, the gondola, and the balloon would disappear forever beneath the waves.

One final maneuver was left to them, and it was to this that they now turned in desperation. It should be plain to see that the aerostat's passengers were men of great mettle, able to look unflinching into the face of death, without a single murmur of complaint. They were determined to fight to the very last, to do whatever they must to slow their fall. The gondola was nothing more than a sort of wicker basket, incapable of flotation; once it had dropped to the surface of the water, it would inevitably sink like a stone.

At two o'clock, the aerostat was scarcely four hundred feet above the waves.

Just then, a manly voice—the voice of one whose heart was impervious to fear—made itself heard. To this voice responded other voices, no less forceful than the first.

"Has everything been thrown out?"

"No! There are still ten thousand francs in gold!"

And at once a heavy sack fell into the water.

"Is the balloon climbing now?"

"A little, but it will soon be sinking again!"

"What's left to throw overboard?"

"Nothing!"

"One thing!... The gondola!"

"Hang on to the net! and off with the gondola!"

For this was their one last means of lightening the aerostat. The ropes attaching the gondola to the ring were cut, and when it had fallen away the aerostat climbed two thousand feet higher.

The five passengers had clambered into the netting above the ring, and clung to the network of interlaced ropes, staring down at the abyss.

The static sensitivity of balloons is well known. To jettison even the lightest object is to provoke an immediate vertical displacement, for the apparatus acts like a balance of mathematical precision as it floats in the air. Thus, when it is unburdened of a relatively large weight, its upward movement will naturally be sudden and considerable. Such was the result in this case.

But after stabilizing in the upper altitudes for a brief moment, the aerostat once again began to sink. The gas still leaked from the rip, and the rip was beyond repair.

The passengers had done everything within their power. No human intervention could save them now. There was nothing left to do but hope for assistance from God.

At four o'clock, the balloon was only five hundred feet above the surface of the water.

A resounding bark was heard. There was a dog with the passengers, clinging to the interlaced ropes alongside its master.

"Top's seen something!" one of the passengers cried.

Then, at once, a loud voice rang out:

"Land! Land!"

Still carried southwest on the wind, the balloon had traveled some hundreds of miles since dawn, and a slightly elevated coastline now appeared in that direction.

But that shore was still thirty miles leeward. It would take no less than an hour to reach it, and only on condition that the balloon not be blown off course. They could not say if it was an island or a continent, for they scarcely knew toward what part of the world the cyclone had carried them! In any case, inhabited or not, hospitable or not, that land was their only hope!

But by four o'clock it was all too evident that the balloon could no longer stay aloft. Even now it was skimming the surface of the sea. Several times already the peaks of the enormous waves had lapped at the bottom of the net, further adding to its weight, and the aerostat only half floated in the air, like a bird with lead shot in its wing.

A half-hour later, the land lay only a mile distant; but the balloon, exhausted, limp, distended, creased with great folds, had lost all but a small pocket of gas at the top. It could no longer bear the weight of the passengers who clung to its net; soon they were half submerged in the water, and buffeted by the furious waves. The slack sheath of the balloon now acted as a sort of sail, catching the great gusts and speeding over the water like a ship with a tailwind. Perhaps it would be blown to shore!

It was only two cables from land when four terrible cries burst from four breasts at once. Just when it had begun to seem certain that the balloon would never rise again, a huge wave had washed over it, and it had taken an unexpected leap upward. As if suddenly freed of a part of its burden, it climbed to an altitude of fifteen hundred feet; there it encountered a sort of eddying wind, which, rather than carrying it directly toward the coastline, drove it along almost parallel to the shore. Finally, two minutes later, it obliquely approached the land, and at last came to rest on the sands of the shoreline beyond the reach of the waves.

Each helping the next, the passengers extricated themselves from the

The balloon at last came to rest on the sands...

ropes of the net. Freed of their weight, the balloon was caught up by the wind, and, just as an injured bird sometimes briefly comes back to life, it disappeared into the heavens.

Five men and a dog had once occupied the balloon's gondola, but only four were thrown onto this beach.

The one missing had evidently been carried off by the great wave that had struck the net. Relieved of his weight, the aerostat had made one final climb, only to fall to earth a few moments later.

And as these castaways—for such indeed they were—set foot on land, their thoughts turned at once to the missing member of their party. As one man, they cried:

"He might be trying to swim ashore! We've got to rescue him! rescue him!"

II

An Episode in the War between the States.—The Engineer Cyrus Smith.—Gideon Spilett.—Neb, the Negro.—The Sailor Pencroff.—Young Harbert.—An Unexpected Question.— Rendezvous at Ten O'Clock.—A Tempestuous Departure.

Those whom the storm had tossed onto this shore were not professional aeronauts, nor amateur devotees of airborne travel. They were prisoners of war, driven by their own daring to flee in the most extraordinary of circumstances. A hundred times over, they should have perished! A hundred times over, their ripped balloon should have cast them into the abyss! But Providence had a stranger fate in store for them; and so, on this twenty-fourth of March, having fled the city of Richmond, then besieged by the troops of General Ulysses Grant, they found themselves seven thousand miles from the capital of Virginia, the principal Secessionist stronghold in the terrible civil war. Their journey through the airs had lasted five days.

Here, then, are the curious circumstances of the prisoners' escape—an escape that was to lead to the catastrophe we have just seen.

Cyrus Smith, born and raised in Massachusetts, was an engineer possessed of a first-rate mind. The Union government had entrusted to him the task of overseeing the railways, an asset of immense strategic value in the conduct of the war. A true Yankee, thin, bony, lanky, about forty-five years of age, his close-cropped hair had already begun to gray, as had his thick mustache. He had one of those fine "numismatic" heads, seemingly made for the express purpose of being stamped into medallions; his gaze was intense, his mouth resolute, his physiognomy that of a wise scholar from the École Militaire. He was the sort of engineer who insists on beginning his career wielding the hammer and the pick, just as some generals are eager to start out as simple soldiers. Thus, along with an ingenious mind, he displayed supreme physical dexterity. His muscles gave proof of remarkable fitness. A true man of action as well as a man of mind, he moved through the world effortlessly, impelled by a great vital expansiveness, with the sort of sturdy persistence that defies every threat of failure. Very learned, very practical, very *débrouillard,* as French soldiers say in speaking of an unusually resourceful person, he was also a man of superb temperament; whatever the circumstances, he never failed to retain his mastery over himself, nor to meet the three necessary conditions for human achievement: an active mind and body, an impetuous desire, and a powerful will. His personal motto could well have been that chosen by William of Orange in the seventeenth century: "I have no need of hope in order to undertake, nor of success in order to persevere."

Cyrus Smith was bravery personified, an eager participant in every battle of this civil war. Beginning in the Illinois volunteers under Ulysses S. Grant, he had fought at Paducah, Belmont, Pittsburg Landing, the siege of Corinth, Port Gibson, Black River, Chattanooga, Wilderness, on the Potomac, everywhere—and had proved himself a valiant soldier, one worthy of a general who liked to say, "I never count my dead!" A hundred times over, Cyrus Smith should have ended up in the ranks of those formidable Grant refused to count, for he threw himself into combat with unstinting and selfless abandon. But his luck had never failed him until the day he was injured and captured on the battlefield at Richmond.

And another important figure had fallen into the Southerners' hands that day: none other than the honorable Gideon Spilett, the reporter for the *New York Herald,* assigned to follow the changing fortunes of the Northern forces for the duration of the war.

Gideon Spilett belonged to that remarkable breed of chroniclers, a race of men peculiar to England and America—men such as Stanley, men who stop at nothing in their quest to obtain the most precise information and transmit it to their newspaper with the greatest possible speed. A Union newspaper such as the *New York Herald* is a veritable power in its own right, and its delegates are truly envoys to be reckoned with. Gideon Spilett occupied a place of honor in their very first ranks.

A man of great merit, energetic, quick, full of ideas, ever ready for a challenge, a world traveler, at once soldier and artist, fearless in his counsel, resolute in his actions, insensitive to pain, fatigue, and danger in his quest to learn the facts—for himself first of all, and only then for his newspaper—a true champion of curiosity, a towering figure in the domain of information, of the unprecedented, the unknown, the impossible, he was one of those intrepid observers who write their stories amid a hail of bullets, who "chronicle" events as cannonballs rain down around them, and for whom every sort of peril means good fortune.

He, too, had witnessed every battle, direct from the front lines—revolver in one hand, notebook in the other—and never did his pencil quiver as the grapeshot flew all around him. He took care not to overburden the wires with incessant and unnecessary telegraphs; rather, his dispatches were short, concise, and clear, each of them shedding light on a single significant matter. But his serious character was enlivened by a certain touch of humor; thus, after the Black River affair, firmly resolved that his newspaper would have the results of the battle before the rest, he maintained his place at the window of the telegraph agency for more than two hours by transmitting the first few chapters of the Bible. It cost the *New York Herald* two thousand dollars, but the *New York Herald* was the first to know.

Gideon Spilett was a tall man of at most forty years. His face was framed by reddish-blond side whiskers. His eye was calm, alert, fast-moving—the eye of a man who has learned to note every detail of a scene in a single moment. Endowed by nature with a sturdy constitution and a solid frame, his exposure to every climate under the sun had tempered him like a bar of steel dipped into cold water.

For ten years Gideon Spilett had been the *New York Herald*'s star reporter, and its pages were graced with both chronicles and drawings from his able hand, as skillful with a pencil as with a pen. He had been captured in the middle of a description and sketch of the battle. The last words written in his notebook were as follows: "A Southerner has trained his sights on me, and..." And missed, for, as he inevitably did, Gideon Spilett emerged from that predicament without a scratch.

Cyrus Smith and Gideon Spilett, who knew each other only by reputation, were transported to Richmond. The engineer soon recovered from his wounds, and it was during his convalescence that he made the reporter's acquaintance. The two men took an immediate liking to each other, and each greatly enjoyed the other's company. Soon these fast friends shared a single goal: to escape, to rejoin Grant's army, and to fight once more in its ranks for the sake of federal unity.

The two Americans had resolved to take advantage of any possible opportunity; but although they had been granted the right to move freely throughout the city, Richmond was too closely guarded to allow any hope of escape.

It was then that Cyrus Smith was joined by a servant, one whose devotion to his master knew no bounds in this world or the next. This intrepid soul had been born to a slave couple on the engineer's lands. An abolitionist in both heart and mind, Cyrus Smith had given the Negro his liberty many years before, but the liberated slave refused to leave his master's side. He loved Cyrus Smith above all else on earth; indeed, he would gladly have died in his place. He was a young man of thirty, vigorous, agile, graceful, intelligent, gentle, calm; sometimes naive, but always cheerful, kindly, and eager to be of use. His name was Nebuchadnezzar, but he answered only to the familiar abbreviation Neb.

Learning of his master's imprisonment, Neb had immediately left Massachusetts for Richmond. By dint of strength and cunning, risking his life twenty times over, he found his way into the besieged city, and soon the two were reunited. Truly, words cannot express Cyrus Smith's delight at seeing his servant again, nor Neb's joy at rejoining his master.

Neb had succeeded in entering Richmond, but finding a way out was a very different matter, for the federal prisoners were closely watched. Only by some highly unusual circumstance might their dreams of escape be realized, and such a circumstance seemed unlikely to arise, and difficult to bring about.

In the meantime, Grant relentlessly pursued his operations. His victory at Petersburg had been hard-won. He had united his forces with Butler's, but their combined efforts had little effect at Richmond, and there was no reason to believe that liberation was close at hand. The reporter found this ordeal particularly excruciating, for his ever-curious eye could find nothing new to observe within the city's walls. He had only one thought: to leave Richmond, no matter what the cost. Several times already he had tried his luck, only to be turned back by one insurmountable obstacle or another.

And so the siege continued. The prisoners were impatient to escape in order to rejoin Grant's army; but a similar impatience tormented a certain part of the besieged citizenry, who longed to flee and rejoin the separatist forces. Among these was one Jonathan Forster, a rabid Secessionist. As we know, the prisoners of the Confederacy could not leave the city; but we must also recall that the same constraint faced the Confederates, surrounded as they were by the troops of the Northern army. The governor of Richmond had long since lost all possible means of communication with General Lee, and it was vitally important that the city's plight be made known, so as to speed the arrival of reinforcements. It was then that this Jonathan Forster had the idea of using a balloon to pass beyond the lines of the besiegers and make his way to the separatists' headquarters.

The governor approved his plan. An aerostat was fashioned and placed at the disposal of Jonathan Forster and the five Confederates who would accompany him into the heavens. They were issued weapons on the chance that they might need to defend themselves upon landing, and a supply of provisions on the chance that their aerial voyage might be a long one.

The balloon's departure was set for March 18th. The launch would take place by night, and with a moderate northwest wind the aeronauts could hope to arrive at Lee's camp only a few hours later.

But that northwest wind proved to be no gentle breeze. On the morning of the eighteenth, it was clear that a terrible storm was on its way. Soon the tempest had grown so fierce that Forster's departure had to be called off, for in such conditions an attempted launch would have placed the balloon and its passengers in mortal danger.

Thus the balloon sat fully inflated in Richmond's central square, ready to cast off as soon as the wind began to calm. With mounting impatience, the townspeople watched for some change in the weather.

So passed the eighteenth of March, and then the nineteenth, and still the storm gave no sign of easing. The balloon remained tied to the ground, bent double by the lashing wind, and no effort was spared to keep it safe from harm.

The night of the nineteenth went by; but the next morning they found that the storm had grown still wilder than before, and continued to intensify. Departure was out of the question.

That day, Cyrus Smith was accosted in a Richmond street by a man he had never set eyes on before. The stranger was a sailor who went by the name of Pencroff, somewhere between thirty-five and forty years of age.

His body was powerfully built, his skin deeply tanned by the sun, his eyes bright and fast-blinking, but his face was fine and strong. This Pencroff was a Northerner who had sailed every sea of the globe and lived through every sort of adventure that might conceivably befall a featherless two-legged creature. Needless to say, his was an enterprising spirit, always ready for a challenge and dismayed by nothing. Early that year Pencroff had gone to Richmond on business, accompanied by a young boy of fifteen, Harbert Brown of New Jersey—his captain's son, an orphan whom he loved like his own child. Unable to leave the city before the first stages of the siege, he had, to his great displeasure, found himself imprisoned, and now he, too, had only one idea: to flee by any means possible. He knew the engineer Cyrus Smith by reputation, and he knew how impatiently a man of such determination must yearn for his freedom. Thus he did not hesitate to approach him that day, and without preamble he asked him:

"Mr. Smith, have you had enough of Richmond?"

The engineer only stared at the stranger, who now added in a low voice:

"Mr. Smith, would you like to escape?"

"When?..." he answered at once—an almost involuntary response, bursting from his lips before he had even examined the stranger who had addressed him thus.

But once he turned his penetrating gaze toward the sailor's trustworthy face, he could not doubt that he had before him an honest man.

"Who are you?" he asked curtly.

Pencroff introduced himself.

"Very well," answered Cyrus Smith. "And by what means do you suggest we escape?"

"In that do-nothing balloon tied down in the square. You'd almost think they left it there expressly for us!"

There was no need for the sailor to finish his sentence. The engineer had understood after a single word. He gripped Pencroff by the arm and led him to his lodgings.

There the sailor laid out the details of his plan, which was in fact exceedingly simple. They would be risking nothing but their lives. The cyclone was at the height of its violence, but surely an engineer as clever and daring as Cyrus Smith would know how to pilot an aerostat. If Pencroff had known the technique himself, he would have set off already—

"Mr. Smith, would you like to escape?"

with Harbert, of course. He had seen far worse than this, and he was not about to be put off by a mere windstorm!

Cyrus Smith listened to the sailor in silence, but his eyes shone all the while. Here was his opportunity. He was not the sort of man to let it slip away. It was a very dangerous plan, and thus a feasible one. Under cover of darkness, they could elude the guards and approach the balloon, then slip into the gondola and cut the ropes that held it down! To be sure, their lives would be at risk; but success was not out of the question, and were it not for this tempest... But were it not for this tempest, the balloon would already be gone, and the opportunity he had so long sought after would never have arisen!

"I'm not alone!..." said Cyrus Smith, by way of conclusion.

"How many would you like to take with you?" asked the sailor.

"Two: my friend Spilett and my servant, Neb."

"That's three," answered Pencroff, "and, with Harbert and myself, five. And the balloon was made to hold six..."

"That's enough. We will go!" said Cyrus Smith.

That "we" implicated the reporter, but the reporter was not the shrinking kind, and when told of this plan he wholeheartedly agreed to take part. He was surprised that such a simple idea had not occurred to him. As for Neb, he would follow his master anywhere he might wish to go.

"Until this evening, then," said Pencroff. "We'll take a stroll around the balloon, all five of us, just seeing the sights!"

"Until this evening, at ten o'clock," answered Cyrus Smith, "and God grant the storm not abate before then!"

Pencroff took his leave of the engineer and returned home, where young Harbert Brown was expecting him. The brave child was aware of the sailor's plan, and it was not without a certain anxiety that he awaited news of his interview with the engineer. Resolute indeed were these five men, as we can plainly see—for resolute they must be to launch themselves into the heavens in the midst of a howling gale!

No! The storm did not abate, and neither Jonathan Forster nor his companions would have thought of facing its wrath in that frail gondola! It was a terrible day. The engineer had only one fear: that the aerostat might be ripped into a thousand pieces by the wind while it was still held fast to the ground. For several hours he lingered in the almost deserted square, keeping a close eye on the apparatus. Pencroff did the same, his hands in his pockets, now and then yawning like a man trying vainly to kill time, but all the while dreading that the balloon might tear open before his eyes, or even break its moorings and disappear into the heavens.

Evening came, and soon a deep darkness settled over the city. Billows of mist scudded along the ground, dense as clouds. A mix of snow and rain was falling. The air was cold. A sort of veil hung over Richmond. The violent tempest seemed to have imposed a truce on besiegers and besieged alike, and the cannons fell silent in the face of the cyclone's blast. The streets of the city were deserted. On a night such as this, it scarcely seemed necessary to guard the lurching aerostat tied down in the square. Clearly, events were conspiring to favor the prisoners' departure; but the voyage itself, through the wild, howling winds!...

"Foul seas!" Pencroff said to himself, clapping his hat to his head as the wind sought to carry it off. "But we'll get through it, all the same!"

At nine-thirty, Cyrus Smith and his companions slipped into the square from different directions. They found themselves in profound darkness, for the wind had extinguished the gas lamps. The enormous aerostat itself was nearly invisible, still bent to the ground by the roaring winds. Bags of sand had been tied to the net to weigh down the balloon, and a thick cable was attached to the gondola, threaded through a ring encased in the pavement.

The five prisoners met near the gondola. They had not been seen; indeed, so dark was the night that they could scarcely see one another.

Without a word, Cyrus Smith, Gideon Spilett, Neb, and Harbert took their place in the gondola while Pencroff, on the engineer's order, untied the packets of ballast one after another. A few moments later his work was done, and the sailor rejoined his companions.

The cable alone now held the aerostat to earth. There remained only for Cyrus Smith to give the order to cast off.

Just then, a dog leaped into the gondola. It was Top, the engineer's dog, who had broken his chain and come running after his master. Fearing the excess weight, Cyrus Smith wanted to send the poor animal away.

"Ah well! One more!" said Pencroff, throwing two bags of sand from the gondola.

And with this he threw off the cable. At once the balloon rose obliquely into the air and passed over the roofs of the surrounding buildings. The gondola struck two chimneys on the way, and they toppled as the balloon vanished into the distance.

The storm was still raging with horrific violence. The engineer could not hope to land by night, and when daylight returned the fog refused him even the briefest glimpse of what lay below. Only five days later did the clouds finally part to reveal the boundless sea beneath them, and still the winds propelled the aerostat at a terrific speed!

The five men had begun their voyage on March 20th; as we have already seen, four of them were thrown onto a deserted shoreline on March 24th, more than six thousand miles from their native land!*

And the one missing, the one to whose aid the four survivors immediately raced, was their natural leader, the engineer Cyrus Smith!

---

* On the 5th of April, Richmond was finally captured by Grant; the separatist revolt was crushed, Lee retreated to the west, and the cause of American unity triumphed.

III

Five O'Clock in the Afternoon.—The One Missing.—Neb's Despair.—Searching Northward.—The Islet.—A Difficult Night.—Morning Fog.—Neb in the Water.—A View over the Land.—Fording the Channel.

A powerful wave had swept the engineer through the torn lattice of the net. His dog disappeared along with him. The loyal beast had voluntarily thrown itself into the water in an attempt to rescue its master.

"Come along!" cried the reporter.

And, oblivious to their own exhaustion, the four men, Gideon Spilett, Harbert, Pencroff, and Neb, set out to begin their search.

Poor Neb was weeping in rage and despair. Cyrus Smith meant more to him than anything in this world, and he could not bear the thought of losing him.

Not two minutes had passed from the moment of his disappearance to his companions' landfall, and they had reason to hope that they might yet be able to save him.

"We've got to look for him! Look everywhere!" cried Neb.

"Yes, Neb," answered Gideon Spilett, "we'll look for him, and we'll find him!"

"Alive?"

"Alive!"

"Does he know how to swim?" asked Pencroff.

"Yes!" answered Neb. "And besides, Top's with him!..."

Hearing the roar of the sea, the sailor only shook his head!

The engineer had vanished some half-mile north of where the castaways now stood. If he had succeeded in swimming directly to shore, they might find him no more than a half-mile away.

It was nearly six o'clock. The night was dark, and a fog had come up to make it still darker. The castaways walked northward along the eastern shore of the land where fortune had tossed them—an unknown land, whose position on the globe they could not have begun to guess. The ground was sandy and sprinkled with stones, apparently devoid of vegetation. Their progress was slowed by a number of small holes scattered over the uneven surface. As they advanced, large birds emerged from these holes and took off with a great beating of their heavy wings, fleeing in all directions and vanishing into the night. Others, more agile, rose up in flocks and passed overhead like low clouds. The sailor recognized them as two sorts of common seagulls, and their piercing shrieks clashed with the roar of the crashing waves.

From time to time the castaways stood still, calling out as loudly as they could and listening for some response from up the coastline. If they were indeed near the spot where the engineer might have come ashore, the dog, Top, would surely answer their cries, even if Cyrus Smith could not. But no bark could be heard through the roar of the waves and the clattering hiss of the surf. And so the little band resumed its forward march, searching the shoreline's every fold and inlet.

After twenty minutes' walk, the four castaways found they could go no farther; the land had come to an end, and only the foaming waves lay before them. They found themselves at the end of a narrow spit, lashed by the furious sea.

"We're on a promontory," said the sailor. "We'll have to turn around and keep to the right to reach the mainland again."

"But what if he's here?" answered Neb, pointing offshore, where the enormous waves shone white in the darkness.

"Well, let's call out for him!"

And together the four voices rose up in a powerful shout, but still no answer came. They waited for a lull in the wind. They tried again. Nothing.

And so the castaways turned around and followed the opposite side of the promontory. The ground was just as sandy and stony as before; nevertheless, Pencroff observed that the shoreline was steeper, and that they were now walking uphill. From this he deduced that a long slope lay before them, leading to an elevated shoreline whose form could dimly be seen through the darkness. The birds seemed less numerous here, and the sea calmer and quieter. The agitation of the waves was visibly abating, and the sound of the surf could scarcely be heard at all. This side of the promontory evidently formed a semicircular cove, protected by the narrow spit from the turbulence of the open sea.

But to continue in this direction was to travel southward, which is to say away from the spot where Cyrus Smith might have found his way to shore. They continued another mile and a half, and still the shoreline showed no sign of curving northward again. Nevertheless, the promontory whose point they had just rounded had to be connected to the larger mass of land. The castaways' strength was fading fast, but still they bravely struggled on, ever hoping to come upon some sudden turn that would send them back in their original direction.

Imagine their disappointment, then, when after a two-mile walk they found themselves standing on an elevated point formed of smooth boulders, their progress once again blocked by the sea.

"We're on an islet!" said Pencroff. "We've just crossed it from one end to the other!"

The sailor's observation was correct. The castaways had been tossed not onto a continent, nor even an island, but onto an islet no more than two miles in length, and clearly little wider.

Could this arid, stony islet, this desolate refuge for a handful of seabirds, be part of a more sizable archipelago? There was no way to know. The balloon's passengers had had only the briefest glimpse of land through the fog—a glimpse far too fleeting and vague to allow them to gauge its size. Just then, however, Pencroff's well-trained eye, long accustomed to penetrating the darkness, caught sight of an indistinct shape toward the west, indicating a raised seacoast.

But for the moment, in the deep darkness of the night, they could not determine to what sort of system, simple or complex, this islet might belong. Nor could they hope to reach that other shore, for their way was blocked by the sea. They thus had no choice but to put off until the next day their search for the engineer, who, alas! had as yet given no sign of his presence.

"Cyrus's silence proves nothing," said the reporter. "He might well be unconscious or injured, and so simply unable to respond for the moment. We must not give up hope."

The reporter then proposed that they light a fire on one end of the islet to serve as a signal for the engineer. But their search for wood or dry twigs proved fruitless. Sand and stone, and nothing else.

We might easily imagine the depth of the castaways' pain, greatly attached as they were to the intrepid Cyrus Smith. It seemed all too clear that they could do nothing to save him for now. They would have to wait for daylight. To be sure, the engineer might have succeeded in saving himself, and might even now have found refuge somewhere along the shore—or he might have sunk lifeless into the sea, and vanished forevermore!

The next few hours were long and difficult. The biting cold tormented the castaways, but they paid little heed to their suffering, and never thought of taking a moment's rest. Unconcerned for themselves, thinking only of their leader, hoping and wanting to keep on hoping, they walked back and forth over the arid islet, continually returning to its northernmost point, nearest the site of the catastrophe. They listened, they shouted, they tried to make out some desperate appeal. Their voices must have carried far out to sea, for a kind of calm had descended over the atmosphere, and the ocean's roar had begun to fade as the waves grew less violent.

At one point, a shout from Neb seemed to echo back to the islet. Harbert remarked on this to Pencroff, adding:

"That would prove there's land close by, somewhere to our west."

The sailor nodded his assent. Besides, he knew what he had seen, and if his sailor's eye had glimpsed a coastline, however indistinctly, then the coastline had to be there.

But that distant echo was the only answer that came to Neb's cries, and only silence could be heard from the great empty space off the islet's eastern shore.

Meanwhile, the sky was gradually clearing. Toward midnight a few stars appeared, and if the engineer had been with his companions he would have pointed to those stars as proof that they had left the northern hemisphere. For the North Star was nowhere to be seen; the constellations were not those that looked down on the northern half of the New World, and the Southern Cross glimmered over the earth's South Pole.

The night went by. At five o'clock on the morning of March 25th, the upper reaches of the sky began to change color. The horizon remained dark, but with the first gleams of daylight an opaque mist rose up from the sea, reducing visibility to no more than twenty paces in any direction. The fog unfurled in thick wreaths, slowly drifting over land and sea.

This was a setback. The castaways' gaze could not penetrate the veil of fog. Neb and the reporter looked out over the ocean while the sailor and Harbert tried to distinguish the shoreline to the west. But still not the slightest patch of land could be seen.

"No matter," said Pencroff. "I may not be able to see the shore, but I can feel it...it's there...it's there...as sure as we're no longer in Richmond!"

But the fog was not slow to lift, for it proved to be only a fair-weather haze. Bright sunshine was warming its upper layers, and its warmth filtered through to the islet's surface.

By six-thirty, three quarters of an hour after sunrise, the fog had already become more translucent. It grew thicker above them, but at ground level it steadily dissipated. Soon the entire islet was revealed, as if it had come down from a cloud; then the sea appeared, a circular flat surface unbounded toward the east, but delimited in the west by a high, steep shoreline.

Yes! there was land there, and so their survival was assured, for the moment at least. The islet was separated from shore by a channel some half-mile wide, and a swift and powerful current could be detected in its waters.

One of the castaways, obeying his heart alone, now launched himself straight into that flowing current, without consulting his companions, without speaking a single word. It was Neb, burning with impatience to reach that shoreline and follow it northward. No one could have held him back. Pencroff called out to him, but in vain. The reporter was about to set out after his companion.

Pencroff quickly strode toward him.

"You want to cross the channel?" he said.

"Yes," answered Gideon Spilett.

"Well, believe me, you'd do better to wait," said the sailor. "Let Neb rescue his master on his own. If we set foot into that channel the current could sweep us straight out to sea. Just look at the way it's rushing along. Now, if I'm not mistaken, this is an ebb current. You can see from the sand that the tide's running out. So I'd advise you to be patient; when low tide comes, we'll look for a spot where we can ford the channel."

"You're right," said the reporter. "We must try to stay together..."

Meanwhile, Neb was struggling vigorously against the current, crossing the channel obliquely. They could see his black shoulders emerging from the water at every stroke. The current was relentlessly pulling him seaward, but little by little he was nearing the shore. It took him more than half an hour to cross that half-mile channel, and he came ashore several thousand feet downstream from his point of departure.

Neb emerged from the water at the foot of a towering granite wall and shook himself off; then he set off at a run, and soon disappeared behind a rocky point that jutted out into the sea across from the northernmost end of the islet.

Neb's companions had looked on in terror as he performed this daring feat; then, once he had disappeared from sight, they once more turned their gaze toward that expanse of land where they hoped to find some sort of refuge. Waiting for the tide to recede, they ate a few shellfish they had found scattered over the sand—a meager repast, but a repast all the same.

The coastline that faced them formed a vast bay, ending in a very sharp spit to the south, devoid of vegetation and very wild in appearance. That spit jutted fantastically from the shore, buttressed by huge granite boulders. Toward the north the bay grew broader, and the gently curved shoreline ran southwest to northeast, ending in a tapering cape. A distance of perhaps eight miles separated the ends of the two arms that embraced the bay. The islet lay some half-mile from shore, like the greatly enlarged carcass of an enormous whale. At its widest point, it measured no more than a quarter-mile across.

The shoreline across from the islet took the form of a sandy beach, studded with black rocks now gradually uncovered by the receding tide. Beyond the beach rose a sort of sheer granite wall, crowned by a capriciously scalloped crest at an altitude of at least three hundred feet. This wall continued some three miles down the beach. To their right it came to a sudden stop where a section seemed almost to have been cut away by a human hand; but to the left, beyond the promontory, the wall became an irregular cliff of conglomerate stones and rubble, a long chain of prismatic shards gradually sloping away into the distance and eventually merging with the boulders of the bay's southern point.

No trees could be seen on the plateau atop the cliffs—only open tableland of the sort that overlooks Cape Town, on the Cape of Good Hope, but on a smaller scale. So, at least, it appeared from the islet. To the right, on the other hand, the cutaway in the granite wall revealed a rich mass of greenery. Here the castaways discovered a tangled mass of tall trees stretching far into the distance—a welcome sight for eyes grown weary of the harsh lines of the granite facade.

Finally, some seven miles northeast of the plateau, a towering white peak glistened in the solar rays, the snowcap of a distant mountain.

They still could not say whether the shore before their eyes belonged to an island or a continent. Let us nonetheless note that a geologist would have instantly recognized the chaos of boulders to their left as volcanic in origin, and as the product of some ancient plutonian process.

Gideon Spilett, Pencroff, and Harbert scrutinized the shore with the greatest attention, for it was here that they might be forced to live for many years to come; and it was here that they might die, if the shipping routes lay too far away!

"Well," asked Harbert, "what do you think, Pencroff?"

"Well," answered the sailor, "there's some good and some bad, as in all things. We shall see. But now there's no doubt, the tide's running out fast. In three hours we'll see if we can't make our way across, and once we're there we'll try to find some way out of this, and we'll look for Mr. Smith!"

Pencroff's prediction was accurate. Three hours later, at low tide, the greater part of the channel's bed lay uncovered. Only a narrow strip of water now separated the islet from the shore, and this they could easily ford.

And so, around ten o'clock, Gideon Spilett and his two companions doffed their clothes and rolled them into bundles. Carrying these bundles on their heads, they waded into the water, whose depth was no more than five feet. The water proved too deep for Harbert, but he swam like a fish, and so made his way in fine fashion. They reached the opposite shore without difficulty. There, soon dried by the sun, they dressed again, having successfully protected their clothes from contact with the water, and discussed their next move.

IV

*The Lithodomes.—The Mouth of the River.—The "Chimneys."—
The Search Continues.—The Green Forest.—A Supply of Fuel.—
Awaiting the Ebb Tide.—From Atop the Crest.—The Timber
Raft.—Back to the Shore.*

Telling the sailor he would rejoin them later at this precise spot, the reporter now set off up the shoreline in the direction the Negro Neb had taken a few hours before. He soon disappeared around a bend in the coastline, desperate for news of the engineer.

Harbert had asked permission to accompany him.

"Stay here, my boy," the sailor had told him. "We have to set up some sort of camp, and look for something a little more filling than shellfish to eat. Our friends will need sustenance when they return. To each his own task."

"I'm ready, Pencroff," answered Harbert.

"Good!" replied the sailor. "We'll do fine. Let's go about this methodically. We're tired, we're cold, we're hungry. What we have to do, then, is find shelter, fire, and food. There's wood in the forest, and eggs in the nests: all that's left is to find the house."

"Well," Harbert answered, "I'll look for a cave in those rocks. I know I'll find some sort of hole we can all squeeze into!"

"That's right," said Pencroff. "Off we go, my boy."

And so they set out along the towering wall of stone, down a beach broadly exposed by the receding tide. Unlike their companions, however, they set off toward the south. A few hundred paces from where they had come ashore, Pencroff had espied a narrow rift that he thought must serve as an outlet for a river or stream. And it was important, on the one hand, to locate a source of drinking water in the immediate area; on the other, the possibility that the current had drawn Cyrus Smith in that direction was not to be ruled out.

As we know, the wall of rock stood some three hundred feet high, but its surface was completely solid. Even at its base, scarcely lapped by the water, it offered not the slightest crack which might serve as a temporary dwelling. It rose up sheer and vertical, its hard granite uneroded by the waves. At its summit a host of seabirds wheeled through the air, most particularly various species of the palmiped order, with long, compact, pointed beaks—extraordinarily noisy birds, little intimidated by what must have been the first human intrusion into their solitude. Among those palmipeds, Pencroff spotted a number of skuas, which are a sort of gull sometimes referred to as stercorarii, as well as a few smaller gulls nesting in the crevices of the granite. A rifle shot fired into that teeming flock would have brought down a great many birds; but to fire a rifle shot one needs a rifle, and neither Pencroff nor Harbert were so equipped. Besides, gulls and skuas are scarcely edible; even their eggs have a foul taste.

But Harbert, wandering off some distance to his left, soon spotted a cluster of seaweed-covered rocks, which the incoming tide would submerge a few hours later. Amid the slippery wrack that covered those rocks he found an abundance of bivalve mollusks, which hungry men could ill afford to scorn. Harbert called out to Pencroff, who hurried to join him.

"Why! Mussels!" cried the sailor. "That'll make up for the eggs we don't have!"

"These are no mussels," answered young Harbert, closely examining the mollusks that clung to the rocks. "They're lithodomes."

"And can we eat them?" asked Pencroff.

"Certainly."

"Well then, lithodomes it shall be."

Pencroff did well to place his trust in Harbert. The boy had a real gift for natural history, and had always felt a veritable passion for that science. His father had encouraged him, enrolling him in the courses of Boston's finest teachers, who looked on this intelligent, hardworking child with great affection. His naturalist's instincts would more than once be put to use in the days to come, and in this, his first attempt, he did not go astray.

The rocks were covered with clusters of these creatures, whose oblong shells clung tenaciously to the stone. The lithodome is a variety of burrowing mollusk, which bores holes into even the toughest rock, and its shell is rounded at both ends, unlike that of a common mussel.

Pencroff and Harbert made a good meal of these lithodomes, which they had found lying half-open in the sunshine. They ate them like oysters, and found their taste quite peppery—no small consolation for ones without pepper or any other sort of condiment.

Their hunger was thus quelled for the moment, but not their thirst, which the consumption of these naturally spiced mollusks only intensified. Now was the time, then, to look for fresh water, which they supposed would not be hard to find in a region as capriciously craggy as this one. Filling their pockets and handkerchiefs with an ample supply of lithodomes, Pencroff and Harbert returned to the foot of the plateau.

Two hundred paces farther on, they came to the rift where Pencroff believed a small river must lie. Here the wall of rock seemed to have been split open by some violent plutonian force. The base of the wall framed a small cove, sharply angled at the far end. The river measured a hundred feet across here, and its banks were scarcely twenty feet wide. The water flowed almost straight inland between the granite walls, which gradually receded upstream from the mouth; then it made an abrupt turn and disappeared into a thicket some half-mile farther on.

"Here's our water! There's our wood!" said Pencroff. "Well, Harbert, all we need now is a house!"

The river was wonderfully clear. The sailor determined that the water was potable at the low point of the tidal cycle, when the incoming tide did not flow into the river. Once this crucial point had been established, Harbert looked again for some cavity where they might find shelter, but his efforts were not repaid. Everywhere the wall was smooth, flat, and vertical.

Nevertheless, at the very mouth of the river, beyond the reach of the sea even at high tide, a series of rockslides had formed, if not a cave, at least a pile of enormous boulders of the sort commonly found in granitic areas, and which are often referred to as "chimneys."

Pencroff and Harbert found a passage that took them deep into this mass of boulders. The sandy corridors were lit by the sunlight filtering through the gaps between the stones, some of which remained in place only by the most miraculous prodigies of equilibrium. But along with the

A series of rockslides had formed a pile of enormous boulders.

light came the wind—like a draft in a hallway—and with the wind the biting cold of the outside air. Nevertheless, the sailor was convinced that by blocking off certain segments of the corridors and plugging some of the gaps with stones and sand, they might make the "chimneys" inhabitable. The corridors were formed like the typographical figure &, which is used as an abbreviation for *etcetera*. After closing off the upper loop, which lay open to the southerly and westerly winds, they could no doubt turn the lower section to their own purposes.

"This is just the thing," said Pencroff, "and if we were ever to see Mr. Smith again, he'd know how to put this labyrinth to good use."

"We will see him again, Pencroff," cried Harbert, "and when he comes back he must find more or less livable accommodations waiting for him. And that's just what this will be, if we can build a hearth in the left-hand corridor, with an opening to let the smoke escape."

"That we will, my boy," answered the sailor, "and these Chimneys"—for such was the name Pencroff had chosen for this temporary abode—"will do very nicely. But the first thing we must do is lay in a supply of fuel. I imagine the wood will come in handy for plugging up the holes. Just listen to that wind blowing through them—it's like the devil's own trumpet!"

Harbert and Pencroff left the Chimneys, and, turning the corner of the rift in the rock, they followed the left bank of the river upstream. The rapid current carried a number of dead branches toward the sea. The incoming tide—which was even now becoming perceptible—must have been forceful enough to reverse the flow of the current for some distance upstream, and it now occurred to the sailor that this ebb and flow might be put to use for the transportation of heavy objects.

After a fifteen-minute walk, the sailor and the boy came to the sudden bend where the river turned off to the left. From that point onward, it ran through a forest of magnificent trees. Although it was late in the season, these trees had not lost their leaves; for they were of the conifer family, which can be found the world over from the far north to the tropics. The young naturalist took particular note of the deodar cedars, a species that grows abundantly in the Himalayan zone, which filled the air with a delightful scent! Among these lovely trees grew clumps of pines, their opaque crowns spreading wide. Dry branches snapped in the deep grass underfoot, with a series of sharp, explosive cracks.

"Right, my boy," Pencroff said to Harbert, "I may not know the names of all these trees, but at least I know enough to classify them as 'firewood,' and, for the moment, that's the only classification we require!"

"Then let's gather our fuel!" answered Harbert, immediately setting to work.

It was an easy harvest. There was no need to pull branches from the trees, for enormous quantities of dead wood lay at their feet. But while the firewood was plentiful, the problem of transporting it was not so easily solved. The wood was very dry, and would burn rapidly. Hence the necessity of bringing a considerable quantity back to the Chimneys, more than the two men could carry themselves. So Harbert observed.

"Well! my boy," the sailor answered, "there must be some way to transport this wood. There's always a way to do anything! If we had a cart or a boat, nothing could be easier."

"But we have the river!" said Harbert.

"Right you are," answered Pencroff. "We'll let the river do the work for us, like a road that carries you along on its own. Timber rafts weren't invented for nothing!"

"Except," Harbert observed, "that our road is moving in the wrong direction, since the tide's coming in!"

"We'll just have to wait for it to go out again," answered the sailor, "and then we'll let it bring our fuel back to the Chimneys for us. In the meantime, we must build a timber raft."

Followed by Harbert, the sailor returned to the bend where the river first entered the forest. They each carried a bundle of wood proportional to their respective strengths. They found yet more dead branches in the tall grass of the riverbank, where in all likelihood no human foot had ever trod before. Pencroff immediately set about constructing his raft.

Into a sort of eddy created by a stone outcropping that broke the river's current, the sailor and the boy placed large pieces of wood tied together with dry vines. These formed a sort of raft atop which their branches were successively stacked, finally forming a load larger than twenty men could have carried on their backs. Within an hour the work was done, and the raft, moored to the bank, awaited the reversal of the tide.

This left several hours to fill, and, by mutual accord, Pencroff and Harbert resolved to find a route to the upper plateau for a more extensive view of their surroundings.

Two hundred paces beyond the bend in the river, the wall of rock, now a mere pile of rubble, declined at a gentle slope and finally disappeared at the edge of the forest. It was like a natural staircase, which Harbert and the sailor thus began to climb. Their vigorous legs soon brought them to the crest, and they found their way to a point overlooking the mouth of the river.

On reaching this spot, they first turned their gaze toward the ocean they had crossed in such fearsome conditions! They looked with deep emotion over the northern part of the coast, the scene of their catastrophe. It was here that Cyrus Smith had disappeared. They searched the water's surface for some remnant of their balloon, to which a man might be clinging for his life. Nothing! Only a vast desert of water, and an equally deserted shore. No sign of the reporter or Neb, but perhaps they were simply too far away to be seen.

"It seems to me," cried Harbert, "that a man like Mr. Cyrus would never let himself be drowned like any ordinary person. He must have found his way ashore somewhere. Don't you think, Pencroff?"

The sailor sadly shook his head. He had lost all hope of seeing Cyrus Smith again; still, not wanting to dash Harbert's hopes entirely:

"No doubt, no doubt," he said. "I daresay our friend the engineer could find his way out of a situation that would be the death of anyone else!..."

As he spoke, he scrutinized the coastline with great attention. His gaze wandered over the sandy beach, rimmed with a line of shoals to the right of the river's mouth. The tide had not yet submerged these rocks, and from shore they looked like small groups of amphibians lying still in the surf. Beyond the shoals, the sea sparkled in the rays of the sun. To the south a narrow point blocked his view, and he could not determine whether the coastline extended farther in that direction or turned to run southeast and southwest, which would have meant that they were then on the coast of an elongated peninsula. At the northern edge of the bay a low, flat shoreline could be seen curving gently into the distance; here there were no cliffs, but only a broad expanse of sand, exposed by the low tide.

Pencroff and Harbert now turned to face west. Their gaze was immediately drawn to the snowcapped mountain six or seven miles distant. A vast wooded area ran from its lower slopes to a point some two miles from shore, and the broad swaths of color that enlivened those woods betrayed the presence of numerous evergreens. From the edge of that forest to the shoreline itself lay a broad plateau strewn with isolated stands of trees. To their left they could sometimes see the glint of the river through the clearings. Its sinuous course seemed to wander toward the mountain's foothills, where its source must lie. Two walls of granite towered over the bend in the river where the sailor had left his raft; but while the walls on the left bank remained smooth and abrupt, those on the right slowly sank lower and lower, the solid wall of rock becoming separate boulders, the boulders stones, and the stones pebbles, until it finally reached the end of the point.

"Are we on an island?" murmured the sailor.

"If we are, it must be a big one!" answered the boy.

"Big or small, an island is still only an island!" said Pencroff.

But this important question could not yet be answered; they would have to settle it another time. In any case, whether island or continent, this land appeared to be fertile, pleasing to the eye, and varied in its resources.

"That's a good thing, at least," Pencroff observed, "and, in our misfortune, we must not forget to give thanks to Providence."

"God be praised, then!" Harbert answered, his devout heart full of gratitude to the Author of all things.

For a long while Pencroff and Harbert examined the shores to which destiny had brought them; but such an inspection could not begin to tell them what the future might have in store.

They now started back along the southern crest of the granite plateau, formed by a long string of anarchic boulders of the most fantastic shapes. Here they found hundreds of birds nesting in the holes in the rocks. Harbert leaped onto a boulder, and a great flock took flight.

"Ah!" he cried. "These are no seagulls!"

"What kind of birds are they, then?" asked Pencroff. "By gad, they look like pigeons!"

"They are indeed, but these are wild pigeons, or rock doves," Harbert answered. "You can recognize them by the double band of black on their wings, their white tails, and their ash blue plumage. And rock doves are entirely edible, so their eggs must be delicious; and seeing as they've left some behind in their nests!..."

"We won't give them a chance to hatch, except as omelettes!" Pencroff merrily replied.

"But what will you make your omelette in?" asked Harbert. "Your hat?"

"Well now!" answered the sailor. "I don't know that I'm up to that. We'll just have to make do with hard-cooked eggs, my boy, and I'll gladly deal with the hardest ones myself!"

Pencroff and the boy carefully examined the clefts in the granite, and they did indeed find eggs in some of the cavities! Several dozen were collected and stored in the sailor's handkerchief; then, since the time of high tide was approaching, Harbert and Pencroff began to climb down to the river again.

It was one hour past noon when they arrived at the bend. The current was already changing direction. They would now let the ebb tide carry the timber raft to the mouth of the river. Pencroff had no intention of allowing the raft to drift unchecked; nor did he intend to climb onto the branches in order to steer. But a sailor is never at a loss for solutions where ropes and cables are concerned, and soon Pencroff had twisted together a number of dry vines to form a rope several fathoms long. This vegetal cable was tied to the rear of the raft, and the sailor held the rope while Harbert kept the floating wood in the current by means of a long pole.

The procedure worked like a charm. The enormous load of wood followed the river's course downstream, restrained by the sailor as he walked along the bank. The river was deep, and there was no danger of the raft's running aground; thus, by two o'clock, it had arrived safely at the river's mouth, only a few steps away from the Chimneys.

V

The Chimneys Made Livable.—The All-Important Question of Fire.—The Matchbox.—A Search of the Beach.—Return of Neb and the Reporter.—One Single Match!—The Crackling Hearth.—The First Dinner.—Their First Night on Land.

Once the timber raft had been unloaded, Pencroff's first concern was to block off the drafty corridors to make the Chimneys suitable for habitation. Soon the galleries of the & that lay open to the southerly winds had been sealed with walls of sand, stones, interlaced branches, and wet earth. The upper loop was now completely closed off, with one narrow, sinuous conduit left open in the lateral section as a vent for the smoke from their fireplace. The Chimneys were thus divided into three or four separate chambers, if we may so call these dark dens, scarcely suitable for a wild beast. Only the main chamber, at the center of the labyrinth, was large enough to stand up in; but at least the occupants were protected from the weather. A fine sand covered the ground, and, all things considered, they could well make do with this until they found something better.

Harbert and Pencroff pursued their conversation as they worked.

"Do you think our companions might have found some shelter better than this?" asked Harbert.

"Could be," answered the sailor. "But when in doubt, a man must take action! Better too many strings to your bow than no string at all!"

"Oh," Harbert said more than once, "let them bring Mr. Smith back to us, let them find him, and then we will have nothing more to do but give thanks to Heaven!"

"Yes!" murmured Pencroff. "That one was a man, a real man!"

"Was..." said Harbert. "Do you despair of ever seeing him again?"

"God save me from such a thought!" the sailor answered.

Soon the Chimneys were fit for human habitation, and Pencroff declared himself pleased with their work.

"Now," he said, "our friends can return. At least they'll find livable accommodations."

There was nothing more to do but build a hearth and prepare the evening meal—an uncomplicated and simple task. Large, flat stones were laid out beneath the narrow conduit at the far end of the leftmost corridor. Some of the fire's heat would escape with the smoke, of course, but enough would be trapped inside to maintain a suitable temperature. They stowed their supply of wood in one of the chambers, and the sailor arranged a small pile of logs and kindling on the stones of the hearth.

As he was seeing to this, Harbert asked if he had any matches.

"Certainly," answered Pencroff, "and a good thing too, I must say, for without matches or tinder we'd be in a most uncomfortable position!"

"We could always make fire the way the savages do," answered Harbert, "by rubbing two sticks of dry wood together."

"Well, just you give it a try, my boy, and we'll see if you get anything more than cramped arms for your pains!"

"But it's a perfectly simple procedure, and a very common practice in the Pacific islands."

"I wouldn't want to contradict you," Pencroff answered. "Maybe the savages know just how to go about it, or maybe they use a particular sort of wood, but more than once I've tried to start a fire that way, and it got me nowhere at all! So, I must confess, I have a certain preference for matches! Where are my matches?"

Pencroff reached into his jacket for the matchbox that never left his person, as he was an inveterate smoker. He found nothing. Next he searched through his trouser pockets, but—to his profound astonishment—met with no greater success than before.

"Now there's a silly thing—something more than silly, as a matter of fact!" he said, looking at Harbert. "The box must have fallen out of my pocket, and now I've lost it! What about you, Harbert, do you have anything, a flint, say, or anything we could use to start a fire?"

"No, Pencroff!"

Vigorously scratching his forehead, the sailor stepped outside, with Harbert not far behind.

They scoured the beach, the rocks, and the riverbank, but in vain. The box was made of copper, and they could not have failed to see it.

"Pencroff," asked Harbert, "are you sure you didn't throw the box overboard when we were in the balloon?"

"That's just what I took care not to do," answered the sailor. "But with all that shaking and tossing about, a small object could easily disappear. My pipe is gone as well! That cursed box! Where could it be?"

"Well, the tide is running out," said Harbert. "Hurry, let's go and look where we came ashore."

Their chances of finding the box here were slim indeed, since at high tide the waves must have tossed it in all directions, like the pebbles that littered the beach. Nevertheless, they were right not to dismiss the possibility. Harbert and Pencroff sped off to the place of their landfall the day before, some two hundred paces from the Chimneys.

There they undertook another exhaustive search, among the pebbles and in the hollows of the rocks. No success. The box would surely have been carried off by the waves if it had fallen from his pocket here. The sailor hunted through the shoals uncovered by the receding tide, but still he found nothing. This was a serious loss, in the circumstances, and for the moment an irreparable one.

Pencroff could not conceal his keen disappointment. His brow was deeply furrowed. He did not speak a single word. Harbert tried to console him by observing that the matches had probably been dampened by the seawater, and would thus be useless to them in any case.

"No, no, my boy," answered the sailor. "It was a solid copper box with a watertight seal! What are we to do now?"

"Don't worry, we'll find some way to start a fire," said Harbert. "Mr. Smith or Mr. Spilett will know what to do, even if we don't!"

"Yes," answered Pencroff, "but in the meantime we have no fire, and it's a sad meal our companions will find waiting for them when they come back!"

"But," Harbert said with some agitation, "surely they must have matches or tinder!"

"I don't think so," the sailor answered, shaking his head. "Neither Neb nor Mr. Smith is a smoker, and I fear that Mr. Spilett cares more for his notebook than for his matches!"

Harbert made no reply. The loss of Pencroff's box was a great setback, that much was clear; but the boy remained confident that they would find some way to start a fire. As for Pencroff, he was not the sort to give up without a struggle, nor even with a struggle; nevertheless, he could not share Harbert's optimism, having a far greater experience of the world. In any case, there was nothing to be done but await the return of Neb and the reporter. But they would have to forgo the meal of hard-cooked eggs he had intended to prepare, and the prospect of a diet of raw flesh seemed an unpleasant one, both for the others and for himself.

The sailor and Harbert renewed their supply of lithodomes before returning to the Chimneys, in case their dreams of a fire might turn out to be impossible. Then they made their way homeward in silence.

Pencroff kept his gaze fixed on the ground, still searching for the elusive box. He even walked from the mouth of the river to the bend where the timber raft had been moored. He returned to the plateau, looking this way and that, and searched through the tall grass at the edge of the forest—all in vain.

It was five o'clock in the evening when he and Harbert returned to the Chimneys. It need hardly be said that they hunted for the box in every corridor, down to the darkest corners; but eventually they were forced to accept that it was truly lost.

At about six o'clock, as the sun was disappearing behind the highlands to the west, Harbert, who was out walking on the beach, called to Pencroff that Neb and Gideon Spilett had returned.

They were alone!... The boy's heartache was beyond words. The sailor's forebodings had been borne out. The engineer Cyrus Smith was nowhere to be found!

The reporter came to the beach and silently sat down on a rock. Exhausted, famished, he had not the strength to utter a single word!

As for Neb, his reddened eyes showed how long he had wept, and a fresh flood of uncontrollable tears said all too clearly that he had given up hope!

The reporter told his companions of their search for Cyrus Smith. He and Neb had walked more than eight miles up the coastline, well beyond the point where the balloon had plunged for the next-to-last time, just before the disappearance of the engineer and the dog, Top. The shoreline was deserted. Not a trace of life, not a footprint. Not a single pebble freshly overturned, no sign scratched into the sand, no indication that any human being had ever set foot on that vast beach. If the island was inhab-

The reporter silently sat down on a rock.

ited, it was plain to see that no native ever approached this section of the coastline. The sea was as empty as the shore, and it was there, clearly, a few hundred feet from the beach, that the engineer had gone to his grave.

Just then Neb stood up, his hopeful nature rebelling at such a conclusion.

"No!" he cried. "No! He is not dead! No! That cannot be! Not him! Me, yes! Anyone else, maybe! but him, never! He's the kind of man who can find his way out of anything!..."

Then, his strength abandoning him:

"Oh! I can't go on!" he murmured.

Harbert ran to him.

"Neb," said the boy, "we'll find him! God will bring him back to us! But in the meantime, you must be dying of hunger! Eat, eat just a little, I beg you!"

And with these words he offered the poor Negro a few handfuls of shellfish, a meager and unsatisfying meal!

Neb had gone many hours without food, but nevertheless he refused. Without his master, Neb could not or would not go on living!

As for Gideon Spilett, he devoured his share of shellfish; then he lay on the sand at the foot of a boulder, dead tired but composed.

Harbert came to him, and taking his hand:

"Sir," he said, "we have found shelter, where you'll be more comfortable than here. Night is falling. Come and rest! Tomorrow, we'll see..."

The reporter stood up and allowed the child to lead him to the Chimneys.

On the way, Pencroff approached the reporter, and, as casually as he could, asked him if by any chance he might have a match on him.

The reporter stopped, looked through his pockets, found nothing, and said:

"I did, but I must have thrown them away..."

The sailor called to Neb, asked the same question, and received the same answer.

"Damnation!" cried the sailor, unable to restrain himself.

The reporter heard this, and, turning to Pencroff:

"No matches?" he said.

"Not one, and consequently no fire!"

"Oh!" cried Neb. "If my master were here, he'd know how to make you a fire!"

The four castaways stood motionless, staring at one another in consternation. Harbert was the first to break the silence, saying:

"You're a smoker, Mr. Spilett, you always have matches on you! Maybe you haven't looked closely enough? Look again! We only need one!"

Once again, the reporter searched the pockets of his trousers, his vest, his cardigan, and finally, to Pencroff's great joy and astonishment, he felt a small stick of wood trapped in the lining of his vest. He grasped the piece of wood through the fabric, but he could not pull it out. It had to be a match, and the only match they had; it was thus vitally important that they not abrade the phosphorus coating the tip.

"Would you like me to try?" the boy asked.

And very adroitly, taking care not to break it, he managed to extract the little piece of wood—that miserable, precious splinter, so desperately important to these poor wretches! It was in perfect condition.

"A match!" cried Pencroff. "Oh, it's as good as a boatload of them!"

He took the match and returned to the Chimneys, with his companions close behind.

That tiny piece of wood, that worthless little stick, so freely and carelessly used in inhabited lands, would here have to be treated with the utmost care. The sailor assured himself that it was quite dry. Then, his examination complete:

"We'll need paper," he said.

"Here, take this," answered Gideon Spilett, tearing a sheet from his notebook after a moment's hesitation.

Pencroff took the reporter's piece of paper and knelt down before the hearth. He slipped a few handfuls of dried grass, leaves, and moss beneath the sticks, arranging them with great care so that the air would circulate unhindered and speed the ignition of the dead wood.

Then Pencroff twisted the piece of paper into a cone, as pipe smokers do when a strong wind is blowing, and placed it among the dried moss. He picked up a slightly rough stone and carefully wiped it off; then, his heart beating fast, he held his breath and lightly scraped the match over its surface.

His attempt met with no success. Pencroff had not applied enough pressure to the match, for fear of flaking away the phosphorus.

"No, I can't do it," he said, "my hand is shaking...I wouldn't be able to strike it properly...I can't...I don't want to!..." and, standing up again, he delegated the task to Harbert.

The child had never known a moment as tense as this. His heart was pounding. Surely Prometheus himself could not have felt a greater awe as he stole the secret of fire from the heavens! Nevertheless, he did not hesitate, but quickly put match to stone. A faint crackle was heard, and a wispy bluish flame appeared, producing an acrid smoke. Harbert gently turned the match on end to feed the flame, then slipped it into the paper cone. Within a few seconds the paper had caught fire, and at once the dry moss began to burn.

A few moments later the dry wood was snapping, and a merry flame, encouraged by the sailor's vigorous breath, gleamed in the darkness.

"Finally!" said Pencroff, standing up again. "I've never had such a fright in all my life!"

No sight could have been more welcome than the fire that now burned on the hearthstones. The smoke flowed easily through the conduit, the chimney drew just as it should, and soon a pleasant warmth was spreading through the chamber.

They would have to take care never to let the fire go out again, and to keep a few hot embers beneath the ash at all times. But this was only a matter of persistence and attention, for there was no lack of wood, and they could replenish their supply whenever they needed to.

Pencroff's first thought was to put the fire to use and cook up a dinner more nourishing than a handful of lithodomes. Harbert brought him two dozen eggs. Sitting in a corner against the wall, the reporter watched these preparations in silence. His mind was occupied by three thoughts at once. Is Cyrus still alive? If so, where could he be? If he survived the fall, why has he not found some way to alert us to his whereabouts? As for Neb, he was on the beach, pacing endlessly back and forth. He had become nothing more than a body without a soul.

Pencroff knew fifty-two recipes for preparing eggs, but for the moment he had no choice. His only option was to bury them beneath the hot ashes and let them be hardened by the slow heat.

After a few minutes the eggs were done, and the sailor offered the reporter his share. Such was the castaways' first meal on this unknown shore. The hard-cooked eggs proved to be quite delicious, and since the egg contains all the elements necessary for the nourishment of man, the wretched little group took great pleasure in their meal, and soon found themselves in better cheer.

Oh! if only one of their number were not missing! If all five of the prisoners who had escaped their confinement in Richmond had been together, nestled within that pile of rocks before that bright, crackling fire, on that dry sand, perhaps their only thought would have been to give thanks to Heaven! But the most ingenious, the wisest as well, he who was their uncontested leader, Cyrus Smith, was, alas! not among them, and his body had been denied even a proper burial!

Thus passed the twenty-fifth of March. Night had come. Outside, they could hear the whistling of the wind and the monotonous crashing of the waves against the shore. The pebbles clattered loudly as the surf dragged them back and forth.

The reporter had retired to the end of a dark corridor after hastily noting down the events of the day: the first sight of the new land, the engineer's disappearance, the exploration of the shoreline, the incident of the matches, etc. Finally, spurred on by his profound fatigue, he found solace in slumber.

Harbert fell asleep at once. As for the sailor, he spent the night near the hearth, keeping one eye on the fire, and he did not spare the fuel.

Only one of the castaways spent the night outside the Chimneys: the inconsolable, desperate Neb, who, all night long, despite his companions' urgings to rest and regain his strength, wandered the beach, calling for his master!

VI

The Castaways' Inventory.—Nothing.—Charred Linen.—An Excursion into the Forest.—The Flora of the Forest.—A Jacamar in Flight.—Signs of Wild Animals.—The Trogons.—The Capercaillies.—An Unusual Sort of Fishing.

Dropped from the skies onto an unknown shore, the castaways now took inventory of their possessions, and few words indeed would be needed to draw up that list.

For they had nothing, nothing but the clothes on their backs at the moment of the disaster. To be sure, Gideon Spilett had kept hold of his notebook and watch—out of pure carelessness, no doubt—but they had not a single weapon, not a single tool, not even a pocketknife. The gondola's passengers had thrown everything overboard in their attempt to lighten the aerostat's burden.

No hero invented by Defoe or Wyss, no Selkirk or Raynal shipwrecked at Juan Fernández or in the Auckland archipelago ever found himself as utterly bereft as this. Either they enjoyed an abundant supply of resources from the wreck of their ship—seeds, animals, tools, ammunition—or else some new wreckage was driven to their shore, offering all they required for their survival. Never were they forced to face nature unarmed. No such luck for our castaways: no utensils, no instruments of any sort. Starting from nothing, they would have to create everything!

Now, if Cyrus Smith had been among them, if the engineer could have contributed his practical expertise and inventive mind, perhaps not all hope would have been lost! But alas! they could not be sure they would ever see Cyrus Smith again. The castaways would have to place their trust in themselves alone—and in Providence, which never abandons those whose faith is sincere.

But the first question to be settled was this: should they settle permanently on this shore without attempting to discover to what continent it belonged? Should they not first determine whether the area was inhabited, or whether they found themselves on some deserted island?

These questions would have to be resolved as quickly as possible, for their answers would determine the castaways' next steps. Nevertheless, on Pencroff's advice, they agreed to wait a few days before setting out to explore. The necessary provisions would have to be gathered, and some nourishment more fortifying than eggs and mollusks found. And above all, the explorers would have to regain their strength before exposing themselves to long periods of fatigue with no shelter in which to lay down their heads.

The Chimneys would do for the moment. A fire had been lit, and it would not be difficult to keep the embers burning. They had a plentiful supply of shellfish and eggs on the beach and among the boulders. The hundreds of pigeons that flocked on the plateau could be killed with blows of a club or hurled rocks, if need be. Perhaps there was edible fruit to be found in the trees of the nearby forest? And of course, there was fresh water nearby. Thus it was agreed that they would remain at the Chimneys for a few days before setting out on an exploratory expedition, either along the coastline or inland.

This plan was particularly pleasing to Neb. As stubborn in his convictions as in his premonitions, he was in no hurry to abandon the scene of their disaster. He did not believe—he refused to believe—in the loss of Cyrus Smith. No, he found it inconceivable that such a man could meet his end in such an ordinary way, carried off by a sea swell and drowned among the waves a few hundred paces from land! Until the tides had washed the engineer's body ashore, until he, Neb, had seen his master's corpse with his own eyes, and touched it with his own hands, he would never believe he was dead! This idea had taken root in his obstinate heart. An illusion perhaps, but an illusion to be respected, which the sailor had no desire to demolish! In his own mind, all hope was lost: the engineer had simply perished in the sea. But there was no arguing with Neb. He was like a dog who refuses to leave the spot where his master fell; indeed, so profound was his grief that he seemed unlikely to survive him.

At dawn on that morning of March 26th, Neb once again set out northward down the shore, back to the place where the sea had no doubt swallowed poor Cyrus Smith.

That day's breakfast was composed solely of pigeon eggs and lithodomes. Harbert had found some salt in the hollows of the boulders, left behind by the evaporating seawater, and this mineral made a most welcome addition to their diet.

As the meal was ending, Pencroff asked the reporter if he would like to accompany Harbert and himself into the forest, for they were planning a hunting expedition! On reflection, however, someone had to stay behind to tend the fire, and to lend assistance in the very improbable event that Neb might require it. And so the reporter stayed at the Chimneys.

"To the hunt, Harbert," said the sailor. "We'll find our ammunition along the way, and we'll cut down our rifles in the forest."

They were about to set out when Harbert observed that, given their lack of tinder, they would do well to provide themselves with a substitute.

"Such as what?" asked Pencroff.

"Charred linen," answered the boy. "That can be used as tinder when there's nothing else at hand."

The sailor thought this an eminently sensible idea. The only drawback was that it would require the sacrifice of a bit of handkerchief. Nevertheless, the benefits outweighed this small disadvantage, and soon one corner of Pencroff's checked handkerchief was reduced to a half-burned rag. This inflammable material was carefully stored away in the central room, stuffed inside a small cavity in the rock, well protected against wind and moisture.

It was then nine o'clock in the morning. The sky was dark and threatening, and a stiff wind blew from the southeast. Harbert and Pencroff turned away from the Chimneys, casting one final glance back at the smoke curling up from the heap of rocks; then they headed upstream along the left bank of the river.

Once they had entered the forest, Pencroff broke two thick branches from the first tree he came to, transforming them into bludgeons, whose sharp points Harbert blunted against a rock. Oh! what wouldn't he have given for a knife! The two hunters now pressed onward through the tall grass of the riverbank. The watercourse gradually narrowed as it proceeded southwest after the bend, and its banks formed a deep trough covered over by the double arch of the trees. So as not to lose their way, Pencroff resolved to stay close by the river, which would always lead them back whence they had come. But the bank was not without obstacles: here, trees with flexible branches that drooped down to the water, there, vines or brambles that they had to beat down with their sticks. Harbert, lithe as a young cat, sometimes slipped between the broken stumps and disappeared into the undergrowth; but Pencroff called him back at once, admonishing him never to venture off alone.

Meanwhile, the sailor carefully observed the form and nature of their surroundings. On that left bank the ground was even, sloping imperceptibly uphill away from the river. Sometimes the terrain was damp and marshy, suggesting the existence of a vast network of subterranean waters trickling slowly through the bedrock and into the river. Sometimes, too, they found small streams running through the brush, which they crossed without difficulty. The opposite bank appeared more uneven, and in that direction the river valley was more broadly exposed. Trees covered the hillside, growing from a series of natural terraces and obstructing the view beyond. Walking would have been difficult on that right bank, for it was full of sudden declivities, and the trees overhanging the water held fast thanks only to the strength of their roots.

It need hardly be added that this forest, like the shoreline they had already explored, was devoid of any sign of human life. Pencroff found only the fresh spoor and footprints of various quadrupeds, though of what species he could not say. Harbert agreed that some of these had clearly been left by dangerous animals, which they would surely have to face some day; but nowhere did they see the mark of an ax on a tree trunk, nor the remains of any extinguished fire, nor any footprint, and perhaps this was for the best. Here in the middle of the Pacific Ocean, the presence of man was very likely more to be feared than desired.

Harbert and Pencroff advanced quite slowly, scarcely speaking, for simply walking was an arduous task on this bank. An hour went by, and they had covered little more than a mile. Thus far, their hunt had proved less than fruitful. Nevertheless, they saw many birds singing and fluttering among the boughs, eyeing them warily as if justifiably apprehensive at the sight of men. Coming to a swampy area in the forest, Harbert pointed out a bird with a long, pointed beak, anatomically similar to a kingfisher, but distinguishable from the latter by its rather coarse plumage, overlaid with a metallic sheen.

"It must be a 'jacamar,' " said Harbert, trying to move within striking distance of the creature.

Pencroff found the fresh spoor of various quadrupeds.

"Now's our chance to see what a jacamar tastes like," the sailor answered. "I do hope the bird's in a mood to be roasted!"

At that moment, a stone, thrown with skill and strength by the child, struck the bird where the wing joined the body; but the blow was not strong enough, for the jacamar fled as fast as its legs could carry it, and disappeared in the blink of an eye.

"Oh! I'm so clumsy!" cried Harbert.

"Not at all, my boy!" answered the sailor. "That was a direct hit, and many a hunter would have missed the bird altogether. Come now! Don't be discouraged! We'll get him next time!"

The exploration continued. As the hunters penetrated deeper into the forest, the trees became more widely spaced and majestic, but none bore any edible fruit. Pencroff looked in vain for one of those precious palm trees, so useful for so many domestic needs, whose presence has been attested as far north as the fortieth parallel of the boreal hemisphere, although only up to the thirty-fifth of the austral. But they found nothing but conifers: more deodars, such as Harbert had already spotted, a number of Douglas pines, much like those of the northwestern coast of North America, and even some fine fir trees standing fifty feet high.

Just then, a flock of small birds with beautiful plumage and long, iridescent tails burst from the undergrowth and flew off in all directions. Their loosely attached feathers fluttered to the ground in their wake, leaving a fine down over the forest floor. Harbert picked up a few of these feathers, and, after examining them:

"Those were 'trogons,' " he said.

"I'd be happier with guinea fowl or black grouse," answered Pencroff; "but tell me now, are they good to eat?"

"They are, and in fact their flesh is very tender," Harbert answered. "Furthermore, unless I'm mistaken, it's quite easy to approach them and kill them with a club."

The sailor and the boy slithered through the tall grass to the foot of a tree whose lower branches were lined with rows of such birds. The trogons were waiting for insects to fly past, for this was their principal food. Their feathered talons could be seen tightly clenching the new branches that served as their foothold.

Now the hunters stood upright, and, wielding their sticks like scythes, cut down whole rows of trogons. The birds made no attempt to fly away, but blindly allowed themselves to be slaughtered. A hundred bodies lay lifeless on the ground before the others decided to flee.

"Well now," said Pencroff, "that's just the game for hunters like us! You could catch them with your bare hands if you wanted to!"

The sailor strung the trogons onto a flexible stick, as hunters do with larks, and the exploration continued. They soon found that the river was curving slightly in a southward loop, but the detour would surely not be a long one, since the river had to have its source in the mountains, fed by the melting snow.

As we know, the primary goal of this excursion was to procure the greatest possible quantity of game for the inhabitants of the Chimneys, and this goal had so far gone unmet. Thus, the sailor returned to the hunt with redoubled vigor, and cursed whenever some animal fled through the tall grass before he had even caught sight of it. If only the dog, Top, were here! But Top had disappeared along with his master, and had no doubt perished beside him!

At around three o'clock in the afternoon yet more birds were discovered in a stand of junipers, busily pecking at the aromatic berries. Suddenly a veritable trumpet blast resounded through the forest. This strange, sonorous fanfare was produced by a kind of gallinacean known in the United States as a "capercaillie." Soon they spotted several pairs of these birds, with brown tails and variegated fawn and brown plumage. Harbert recognized the males by the two pointed pinions formed of the upswept plumes on their necks. Pencroff immediately resolved to bring down one of these gallinaceans, no matter what the cost; for they were fat as hens, with flesh as fine as that of the hazel grouse. But this proved no easy thing, as they fled at once when the sailor approached. After several fruitless attempts, whose only result was to frighten the capercaillies, he said to the boy:

"We clearly can't kill them when they're flying off, so we'll have to try to catch them with a line."

"Like a carp?" cried Harbert, astonished at this idea.

"Like a carp," answered the sailor, in all seriousness.

Pencroff had found a half-dozen capercaillie nests among the grass, and in each of them two or three eggs. He took great care not to touch the nests, whose owners would surely not be slow to return. His idea was to lay a series of fishing lines among them—lines fitted not with nooses, but with hooks. He led Harbert away from the nests, then sat down to prepare his strange contrivances with all the care of a fervent disciple of Izaac Walton.* Harbert watched him work, understandably intrigued if somewhat dubious. The lines were made of thin vines tied together, fifteen or twenty feet long. Large, sturdy thorns with curved points, gathered from a thicket of dwarf acacias, were tied to the ends of the lines to serve as hooks. As for the bait, it took the form of large red worms they had found crawling in the dirt.

When he was done Pencroff slithered off through the grass, skillfully concealing himself from view, and placed the hooked ends of his lines near the capercaillies' nests; then he returned, took up the other ends, and hid with Harbert behind a thick tree. They waited patiently. It must be said that Harbert did not share the optimism of the inventive Pencroff.

A good half-hour went by, but eventually, as the sailor had predicted, several pairs of capercaillies returned to their nests. They hopped here and there, pecking at the ground, oblivious to the hunters, who had taken care to remain downwind of the gallinaceans.

The boy took a most lively interest in the scene now unfolding before him. He held his breath, like Pencroff, who stared at the birds wide-eyed, his mouth open, his lips puckering as if he were about to savor a morsel of capercaillie meat.

Meanwhile, the birds were strolling among the hooks, paying them little mind. Pencroff began to jerk gently on the lines, causing the bait to move just as if the worms were still alive.

The sailor's emotion at this moment was considerably more intense than that of an ordinary fisherman, who never sees his prey gliding through the water toward the hook.

The quivering worms soon attracted the gallinaceans' attention, and they attacked the hooks with their beaks. Three capercaillies, no doubt particularly famished, swallowed the bait and the hook all at once. Suddenly Pencroff gave a strong tug on the line, "reeling them in," and a loud flutter of wings showed that the birds had been caught.

"Hurrah!" he cried, running toward his prize, gathering the birds up in his arms.

Harbert applauded. He had never before seen birds caught with a line; but the sailor, in all modesty, admitted that he had done this more than once, and that he could not take credit for the invention.

* The author of a well-known treatise on angling.

"And in any case," he added, "in our present circumstances, I'm sure we'll see stranger things than this!"

The capercaillies were bound by the feet, and Pencroff, happy not to be returning home empty-handed, and observing that the light was beginning to wane, thought it best to start back.

They set out downstream with the river showing them the way, and at about six o'clock, rather weary from their excursion, Harbert and Pencroff found themselves once again inside the Chimneys.

VII

*Neb Has Not Returned.—The Reporter's Thoughts.—Dinner.—
A Bad Night Coming.—The Terrible Storm.—A Departure by
Night.—Fighting the Rain and Wind.—Eight Miles from Home.*

Gideon Spilett was standing motionless on the beach, arms folded over his breast, looking eastward over the sea. The horizon was obscured by a large, black cloud swelling ever higher into the sky. The wind was already strong, and freshening as the light faded. The sky had taken on a particularly menacing look. In short, the first signs of a severe windstorm were beginning to manifest themselves.

Harbert entered the Chimneys, while Pencroff headed toward the reporter. Absorbed in his thoughts, he did not see the sailor approaching him.

"We're going to have a bad night, Mr. Spilett!" said the sailor. "Rain and wind, just the way the petrels* like it!"

Turning around, the reporter caught sight of Pencroff, and his first words were these:

"How far from the coast do you suppose the balloon might have been when it was struck by the wave that carried off our companion?"

The sailor was not expecting such a question. He thought for a moment, then answered:

"Two cables at most."

"And what is a cable?" asked Gideon Spilett.

---

* Seabirds that take particular pleasure in tempests.

"A hundred and twenty fathoms, more or less, or six hundred feet."

"So," said the reporter, "Cyrus Smith would have disappeared twelve hundred feet from shore, at most?"

"More or less," answered Pencroff.

"And his dog, too?"

"His dog, too."

"What surprises me," the reporter went on, "assuming that our friend did indeed perish, is that Top must have died as well, and neither the dog nor his master have washed ashore!"

"Nothing surprising in that, in these heavy seas," said the sailor. "Besides, the current could have carried them farther down the coastline."

"And is it indeed your opinion that our companion died among the waves?" asked the reporter, once again.

"That is my opinion."

"My own opinion," said Gideon Spilett, "with all due respect for your greater experience, Pencroff, is that the double fact of Cyrus's and Top's complete disappearance, living or dead, strikes me as both inexplicable and unlikely."

"I wish I could think as you do, Mr. Spilett," answered Pencroff. "Unfortunately, there's no doubt in my mind."

With this the sailor returned to the Chimneys. A lively fire crackled in the hearth. Harbert had thrown in an armload of dry wood, and the flames cast powerful rays of light into the dark corners of the corridor.

Pencroff immediately set about preparing dinner. He thought it a good idea to supplement the usual menu with some sort of pièce de résistance, for they were all in need of a good restorative. The strings of trogons were set aside for the next day, but they plucked two capercaillies, and soon, skewered on a stick, the birds were roasting over a roaring fire.

It was now seven o'clock in the evening, and Neb had still not returned. This prolonged absence filled Pencroff's mind with anxiety. He must have been thinking that some accident had befallen the Negro in that unknown terrain, or that in his grief he had committed some desperate act. But Harbert drew an entirely different set of conclusions from Neb's absence. To him, if Neb had not come back, it could only be because some new discovery had come to light, obliging him to prolong his search. And such a development could only mean good news concerning Cyrus Smith. Why would Neb not have come home, if not because some new ray of hope had detained him? Perhaps he had found a trail, or a footprint, or a bit of wreckage, which had set him on a new path? Perhaps he was at this very moment following some tangible lead? Perhaps he was even at his master's side? ...

Such was the boy's reasoning, and such were his words to the others. His companions let him talk on. Only the reporter nodded in agreement. To Pencroff, the most likely explanation was that Neb's search had brought him farther up the shoreline than the day before, too far for him to have returned yet.

Nevertheless, urged on by certain vague premonitions, Harbert several times expressed his intention to go and look for Neb. But Pencroff replied that this would serve no purpose, that in this darkness, and in such terrible weather, he had no chance of discovering any trace of their companion, and would do better to wait where he was. If Neb did not appear the next day, Pencroff would not hesitate to join in Harbert's search.

Gideon Spilett seconded the sailor's opinion concerning the importance of staying together. Harbert had no choice but to abandon his plans, but two heavy tears fell from his eyes.

The reporter could scarcely hold back from embracing the good child.

The bad weather had now descended on them in full force. A windstorm of incomparable violence was passing over the coastline from the southeast. They could hear the sea, then at ebb tide, crashing against the line of shoals. Atomized by the tempest, the rain took the form of a liquid fog, a stream of ragged vapors scudding low over the coastline. The smooth pebbles on the beach hissed as they were blown along by the gusts, with a sound like a load of gravel being dumped from a wheelbarrow. Kicked up by the wind, the sand intermingled with the driving rain, doubling the unbearable force of its assault. Particles both mineral and aqueous filled the air. Great whirlwinds swirled between the mouth of the river and the granite wall. The gusts thrown out by that maelstrom had no other route to follow but the narrow valley leading to the river's source, and they howled through it with irresistible violence. The smoke from the fireplace was often blown back through the conduit and into the Chimneys' corridors, poisoning the atmosphere.

This is why, as soon as the capercaillies were cooked, Pencroff let the fire die down, maintaining only a few hot embers buried under the ash.

At eight o'clock Neb still had not reappeared; but they could now suppose that the fierce weather alone had delayed him, and that he must have taken shelter in some cavity to await the end of the storm or at least the return of daylight. As for setting off to meet him, or to search for him, in these conditions it was clearly out of the question.

The fresh fowl was the only dish at supper. They were delighted to have meat set before them, and superb meat it was. Pencroff and Harbert, their appetite overstimulated by a long excursion, devoured their share with great enthusiasm.

Then each retired to the corner where he had slept the night before, and Harbert was not slow to fall asleep beside the sailor, who had stretched out full length before the hearth.

Outside, as the night wore on, the force of the storm became truly terrifying. It was a gale not unlike the one that had carried the prisoners from Richmond to this spot of land in the Pacific. Tempests are a frequent occurrence at the equinox, and many are the catastrophes they bring about. And most awesome of all are those that develop over the open sea, where no obstacle blocks their fury! It is easy to understand, then, that a coastline such as this one, exposed to the east, which is to say directly facing the onslaught of the storm and struck by its full fury, was lashed with a violence that no description can adequately convey.

By the greatest of good fortune, the pile of boulders they called the Chimneys was sound and solid. It was formed of enormous granite blocks, some of which, however, more precariously balanced than the others, seemed to tremble ominously in the raking winds. Pencroff sensed this, and as he pressed his hand to the walls he felt a series of rapid shudders running through the rock. But he rightly repeated to himself that there was nothing to fear, that their improvised retreat would not collapse. Nevertheless, he could hear stones falling onto the beach as they were wrenched from the summit of the plateau by the force of the eddying wind. Some of them even rolled onto the upper section of the Chimneys, or shattered against its boulders as they fell. Twice the sailor stood up and crawled to the opening of the corridor to look outside. But these minor rockslides posed no real threat, and he returned to his place by the hearth, whose embers crackled beneath the ash.

Harbert slept soundly despite the fury of the whirlwinds, the tumult of the storm, the thunder of the tempest. Even Pencroff was finally overcome by sleep, accustomed as he was to all weathers after his many years at sea. Only Gideon Spilett remained awake, uneasy. He cursed himself for not having accompanied Neb. As we know, he had not given up hope.

The sailor crawled to the opening of the corridor.

He shared Harbert's premonitions, and he could not shake them from his mind. Neb was foremost in his thoughts. Why had he not returned? He tossed and turned on his sandy bed, paying little mind to the battling elements. Sometimes his eyes closed for a moment, grown heavy with fatigue; but some sudden thought threw them open again almost at once.

The night wore on, and it might have been two o'clock in the morning when Pencroff, then deep in slumber, felt someone shaking him roughly.

"What is it?" he cried, immediately awake, recomposing his thoughts with the alacrity peculiar to men who ply the sea.

The reporter was bending over him, and saying:

"Listen, Pencroff, listen!"

The sailor cocked his ear, but heard only the howling wind.

"It's the wind," he said.

"No," answered Gideon Spilett, listening again, "I thought I heard..."

"What?"

"A dog barking!"

"A dog!" cried Pencroff, leaping to his feet.

"Yes...barking..."

"That can't be!" answered the sailor. "And besides, how, with the roar of the tempest..."

"There...Listen..." said the reporter.

Pencroff listened more closely, and indeed, during a brief lull in the wind, he thought he could make out a distant bark.

"Well?" said the reporter, gripping the sailor's hand.

"Yes...yes!" answered Pencroff.

"It's Top! It's Top!..." cried Harbert, who had just awoken, and the three of them raced toward the entrance to the Chimneys.

They had to struggle to make their way outside. The wind continually pushed them back. But at last they succeeded, bracing themselves against the boulders to keep their footing. They looked around them; they could not speak.

They found themselves in complete darkness. Sea, sky, and land melded into one unrelieved mass of black. There seemed not a single atom of light to be found in the atmosphere.

For several minutes the reporter and his two companions remained as they were, crushed by the winds, soaked by the rain, blinded by the sand. Then the wind fell once again, and they heard what sounded like a distant bark.

It could only be Top! But was he alone or accompanied by another? No doubt alone, for if Neb were with him he would have made directly for the Chimneys.

Unable to make himself heard, the sailor squeezed the reporter's hand in such a way as to signify: "Wait!" Then he disappeared into the Chimneys again.

He reemerged a moment later, carrying a bundle of burning twigs. These he threw heavenward with all his might, giving a sharp whistle at the same time.

Like a prearranged signal, long-awaited, this whistle was answered by a less distant bark, and soon a dog rushed headlong into the corridor. Pencroff, Harbert, and Gideon Spilett followed him inside.

An armload of wood was thrown onto the coals. A bright flame illuminated the corridor.

"It's Top!" cried Harbert.

It was indeed Top, a magnificent Anglo-Norman cross, blessed with the finest qualities of those two breeds: great speed in the legs and a very keen sense of smell, the two signal qualities of the hound.

It was the engineer Cyrus Smith's dog.

But he was alone! Neither his master nor Neb accompanied him!

But how could his instincts have led him to the Chimneys, having never before set eyes on this place? It seemed inexplicable, especially in the inky darkness of the night, and in such a storm! And more inexplicably still, Top was neither tired nor breathless, nor even splashed with mud or peppered with sand!

Harbert drew Top toward him, cradling the dog's head in his arms. Top permitted this embrace, and rubbed his neck against the boy's hands.

"If we've found the dog, we'll find the master as well!" said the reporter.

"God willing!" answered Harbert. "Let's go! Top will guide us!"

Pencroff made no objection, sensing that Top's arrival might prove all his conjectures wrong.

"Off we go!" he said.

Pencroff carefully covered the embers in the hearth. He placed a few pieces of wood under the ashes so they would find a fire burning on their return. Then, on the heels of the dog, whose sharp, repeated barks seemed to urge him to make haste, he hurriedly led the reporter and the boy outside, taking what remained of their dinner with him.

The tempest, nearing its peak, howled with terrific force. The moon was then new, and not the faintest glimmer of light shone through the clouds. They could only trust in Top's instincts, and so they did. The reporter and the boy followed behind the dog, with the sailor bringing up the rear. Conversation was impossible. The rain was not heavy, since it was atomized by the force of the gale, but the wind was terrible.

One very fortunate circumstance worked to the favor of the sailor and his two companions: the wind was blowing from the southeast, and consequently it pushed them along from behind. The wind-borne sand, which would have been unbearable otherwise, struck only their backs; so long as they never turned around it did nothing to interfere with their progress. In short, they often advanced more quickly than they intended, and were forced to quicken their pace so as not to be knocked off their feet. Nevertheless, their newfound sense of hope redoubled their strength. Now, at least, they knew they were not searching at random. They did not doubt that Neb had found his master, and that he had sent the faithful dog to alert them. But was the engineer alive, or had Neb sent for his companions so that they might pay their last respects to poor Smith's corpse?

They were careful to keep their distance from the wall of rock, but soon an angled outcropping allowed them to stop and catch their breath. A wedge of stone sheltered them from the wind, and they paused for a brief rest after their fifteen-minute trek, which had been more a run than a walk.

For the moment they could hear one another, answer one another, and when the boy mentioned Cyrus Smith's name, Top let out a series of short barks as if to say that his master had been saved.

"Saved, is that it?" Harbert repeated. "Saved, Top?"

And the dog barked again in response.

They started off again. It was about two-thirty in the morning. The tide was coming in—higher than usual, for it was a syzygy tide, swollen still further by the driving winds. Great waves roared over the line of shoals, with a force that suggested they would soon wash over the islet, even now submerged by the incoming tide. No longer would the shoreline be protected by that long, natural breakwater; it would soon be exposed to all the fury of the open sea.

The sailor and his companions emerged from their shelter and headed back into the storm. Hunched over, backs to the wind, they hurried ever onward behind Top, who seemed to know precisely where he was going. He led them northward; to their right an endless line of waves crashed deafeningly against the shore, while on their left lay a dark landscape, invisible in the darkness. But their senses told them it was fairly flat, since the gale-force winds now passed directly over their heads, without the backlash they had felt when the gusts were blocked by the granite wall.

At four o'clock in the morning, they calculated that they had traveled a distance of five miles. The clouds had lifted somewhat, and no longer scudded over the surface of the ground. The air was less damp, and the wind came in sudden gusts, drier and colder than before. Pencroff, Harbert, and Gideon Spilett must have suffered cruelly in their thin clothes, but not a single complaint escaped their lips. They were resolved to follow Top wherever the intelligent beast might lead them.

Daylight began to appear toward five o'clock. At the zenith, where the mists were not as thick, the contours of the clouds emerged against a gray background, and soon a more luminous line appeared along the ocean horizon beneath a band of darkness. The approaching waves glimmered here and there, and the spume was white again. At the same time, the irregular terrain to their left was slowly unveiled, dim gray against the black.

By six o'clock in the morning, the day had dawned. High above them, the clouds sped swiftly past. The sailor and his companions were now six miles from the Chimneys, on a very flat beach rimmed by a line of offshore boulders scarcely visible above the water, for the tide was now at its highest. To the left they found a wild, sand-covered landscape of scattered dunes, some of them strewn with bristling cardoon plants. The shoreline was smooth and straight, protected from the ocean winds only by an irregular chain of hillocks. Here and there stood a twisted tree or two, leaning westward, branches permanently blown away from the sea. Well inland, toward the southwest, the edge of the forest could be seen curving away.

Just then, Top's agitation increased tenfold. He ran ahead, returned to the sailor, and seemed to urge him to pick up the pace. The dog then left the beach and sped off through the dunes, guided by his remarkable instincts.

They followed close behind. The area seemed absolutely deserted. There was not a single living creature in sight.

This great expanse of sand was peppered with hillocks, and sometimes even hills, unevenly and capriciously scattered through the landscape. It was like a little Switzerland of dunes, and only the most prodigious feat of canine instinct kept them from losing their way.

Five minutes after they had left the beach, the reporter and his companions arrived at a sort of deep hollow in the side of a particularly lofty dune. Here Top stopped, and gave a sharp bark. Spilett, Harbert, and Pencroff entered the small cavity.

They found Neb kneeling over a body outstretched on a bed of grass...

It was the body of the engineer Cyrus Smith.

It was the body of the engineer.

VIII

Is Cyrus Smith Alive?—Neb's Story.—The Footprints.—An Unanswerable Question.—Cyrus Smith Speaks.—The Revelation of the Footprints.—Return to the Chimneys.—Pencroff Aghast!

Neb did not move. The sailor spoke only one single word.

"Alive?" he cried.

No answer came from Neb. Gideon Spilett and Pencroff went pale. Harbert clasped his hands and stood motionless. But it was clear that the poor Negro, absorbed in his own pain, had neither seen his companions nor heard the sailor's words.

The reporter knelt down over the motionless body, unbuttoned the engineer's shirt, and applied his ear to his breast. A minute—a century!— passed as he listened for a heartbeat.

Neb sat up a bit and looked on, unseeing. No man's face could have been more altered by despair. Neb was unrecognizable, haggard with fatigue, broken by pain. He was sure his master was dead.

After a long and careful observation, Gideon Spilett arose.

"He's alive!" he said.

Now Pencroff knelt over Cyrus Smith; his ear, too, caught the sound of a beating heart, and he felt the engineer's faint breath on his lips.

On the reporter's instructions, Harbert hurried outside to look for water. Some hundred paces away he found a limpid stream meandering through the sands, obviously swollen with the previous night's rainfall. But nothing to carry that water in, not a single seashell to be found among the dunes! The only solution was to soak his handkerchief in the stream and run back to the cave as quickly as he could.

Fortunately, the wet handkerchief was enough for Gideon Spilett, who wanted only to moisten the engineer's lips. Those few drops of cool water produced an almost immediate effect. A sigh escaped Cyrus Smith's breast; it even seemed that he was trying to speak.

"We'll save him!" said the reporter.

With these words, Neb's hope was restored. He undressed his master to examine the body for wounds. They found no contusions, nor even abrasions, on his head, torso, or limbs—much to their surprise, for Cyrus Smith's body must have been tossed and dragged over any number of rugged stones. Not even his hands had been damaged. How could it be that the engineer's body displayed no trace of the violent struggle he must have put up as he attempted to cross the shoals?

But this question could be resolved later. Cyrus Smith would tell them what had happened as soon as he had strength enough to speak. For the moment, their task was to bring him back to life, and they thought that a friction rub might offer the best chance of success. This plan was put into action, using Pencroff's peacoat. Warmed by the rough massage, the engineer began to move his arms slightly, and his breathing became more regular. He was dying of exhaustion; were it not for the reporter and his companions, Cyrus Smith would clearly never have survived.

"You thought your master was dead?" the sailor asked Neb.

"Yes! dead!" answered Neb. "And if Top hadn't found you, if you hadn't come, I would have buried my master and gone to my death beside him!"

It was by a slender thread indeed that Cyrus Smith's life had hung!

Neb then told them everything that had happened. The day before, he had left the Chimneys at dawn and followed the shoreline northwest until he came to the region he had visited before.

There—with no real hope, by his own admission—Neb had scoured the beach, among the boulders, in the sand, for any minuscule clue that might guide him. He examined with particular attention the area left uncovered at high tide, for beyond that line the ebb and flow of the surf would have washed away any potential clues. Neb was not hoping to find his master alive. He was now searching only for a corpse, a corpse that he would bury with his own hands!

Neb searched for some time, to no avail. No human being seemed ever to have set foot on this deserted shore. Beyond the reach of the waves lay millions of seashells, all unbroken and undisturbed. Over the entire beach, a distance of some two to three hundred yards,* he could find no trace of a landing, neither ancient nor recent.

And so Neb decided to continue a few miles farther up the coastline, for the currents might have carried the body to some still more distant point. A body floating in the waters off a flat shoreline is nearly always washed ashore sooner or later. Neb knew this, and he refused to give up the search until he was reunited with his master one last time.

"I walked another two miles along the shore. I searched the shoals when the tide was low, the beach when it was high, and I had nearly given up hope when yesterday, about five o'clock in the evening, I found footprints in the sand."

"Footprints?" cried Pencroff.

"Yes!" answered Neb.

"And could you follow these footprints back to the shoals?" asked the reporter.

"No," answered Neb, "only up to the high tide mark. From there to the shoals they must have been washed away by the waves."

"Go on, Neb," said Gideon Spilett.

"When I saw those footprints, I was mad with joy. They were clear and sharp, and heading toward the dunes. I followed them for a quarter-mile, running, taking care not to rub them out. Five minutes later, as night was falling, I heard a dog barking. It was Top, and Top led me here, to my master's side!"

Neb finished his tale with an evocation of the great wave of grief that washed over him on discovering the engineer's body. How he tried to make out some last glimmer of life in his master's inanimate form! He had found the dead body he sought, but now he wanted him alive! But all his efforts proved vain! There was nothing more to do but pay his last respects to the one he loved so well!

Neb's thoughts had then turned to his companions. Surely they would want to see their unfortunate friend one last time! Top was there. Could he not rely on the faithful beast's keen intelligence to summon others? Neb spoke the reporter's name several times, as Top knew him better

---

* A yard is an American unit of length, equivalent to 0.9144 meters.

than the rest. Then he showed him the way southward, and the dog sped off down the coastline.

We know already how, guided by an instinct that could almost be called supernatural—for the animal had never set foot in the Chimneys before—Top arrived at his destination.

Neb's companions listened to this story in rapt attention. They could not understand why, after what must have been a terrible struggle against the waves and rocks, Cyrus Smith bore not the merest trace of a scratch. Equally inexplicable was the fact that the engineer had somehow found his way to this hollow, hidden away among the dunes over a mile from shore.

"So, Neb," said the reporter, "it wasn't you who brought your master to this place?"

"No, not me," answered Neb.

"It's obvious Mr. Smith came here on his own," said Pencroff.

"Obvious, yes," observed Gideon Spilett, "but not believable!"

Only from the mouth of the engineer would they ever learn the story behind all this, and that would have to wait until he had recovered the capacity for speech. Happily, life was beginning to return to his body. The friction rub had restored his circulation. Cyrus Smith moved his arms again, then his head, and once more a few incomprehensible words issued from his lips.

Kneeling down, Neb spoke his master's name, but the engineer seemed not to have heard, and his eyes remained closed. Only his movements showed that he was alive. His senses remained as deadened as ever.

They had no fire in that grotto, nor any way of producing fire, to Pencroff's deep regret; for he had neglected to bring along their charred linen, which he could easily have set alight by striking two stones together. The engineer's pockets were empty, save the watch in his vest pocket. They would have to transport Cyrus Smith back to the Chimneys at once. To this the castaways unanimously agreed.

Meanwhile, their ministrations seemed to be bringing the engineer back to consciousness more rapidly than they had dared hope. The water applied to his lips was slowly reviving him, and now Pencroff thought of supplementing that water with the congealed juices of the capercaillie meat he had brought with him. Harbert ran to the beach and brought back two large bivalve seashells. The sailor made up a sort of elixir, and introduced it between the engineer's lips. Cyrus Smith absorbed the mixture with what appeared to be great eagerness.

He opened his eyes to find Neb and the reporter kneeling over him.

"Master! Master!" cried Neb.

The engineer heard these words. He recognized Neb and Spilett, then his two other companions, Harbert and the sailor, and weakly he pressed their hands with his own.

A few words escaped his lips—the words he had spoken before, no doubt, expressing the thoughts even then tormenting his mind. This time his words were understood.

"Island or continent?" he murmured.

"What!" cried Pencroff, unable to hold back this exclamation. "By all the devils, what do we care if it's an island or a continent, so long as you're alive, Mr. Cyrus? We'll see to that later."

The engineer nodded slightly and seemed to fall asleep again.

They respected his need for rest, and the reporter immediately began making preparations for his transport, hoping to make it as comfortable as it could be. Neb, Harbert, and Pencroff left the grotto and headed toward a tall dune crowned with a clutch of stunted trees. As they walked, the sailor could not prevent himself from repeating:

"Island or continent! Imagine thinking of that when you're down to your final breath! What a man!"

On reaching the top of the dune, with no tools but their own two arms, Pencroff and his companions stripped the largest branches from a rather stunted tree, a sort of maritime pine wizened by the endless wind; these were then used to make a litter, lined with leaves and grass, for the engineer's return to the Chimneys.

This took them some forty minutes, and it was ten o'clock when the sailor, Neb, and Harbert returned to Cyrus Smith's side, where Gideon Spilett had remained.

The engineer then awoke from his sleep, or rather from the stupor in which they had first found him. His cheeks, once deathly pale, had begun to regain their color. He sat up a little and looked around him, seemingly wondering where he was.

"Are you strong enough to listen to me, Cyrus?" said the reporter.

"Yes," answered the engineer.

"If you want my opinion," the sailor said, "Mr. Smith will be able to listen to you all the better if he takes a little more of this capercaillie gelatin—for this is capercaillie meat, Mr. Cyrus," he added, offering him another helping of gelatin, this time mingled with a few shreds of meat.

Cyrus Smith chewed these morsels while the rest of the meat was shared among his three equally hungry companions, who found the meal rather frugal.

"Right!" said the sailor. "We've got more food awaiting us at the Chimneys, for you should know, Mr. Cyrus, that not too far south of here we have a house with rooms, beds, a hearth, and a kitchen, nicely stocked with several dozen birds that our Harbert calls trogons. Your litter is ready, and as soon as you feel up to it, we'll take you home."

"Thank you, my friend," the engineer answered, "just another hour or two and we can leave...And now, talk to me, Spilett."

The reporter then gave him an account of all that had happened. He told Cyrus Smith of everything he could not have witnessed: the balloon's final plunge, the landing on that unknown and apparently deserted shore—perhaps an island, perhaps a continent—the discovery of the Chimneys, their search for the engineer, Neb's devotion, all that they owed to the intelligence of faithful Top, etc.

"But," asked Cyrus Smith, his voice still weak, "you didn't pick me up off the beach?"

"No," answered the reporter.

"And it wasn't you who brought me to this hollow?"

"No."

"How far are we now from the shoals?"

"About a half-mile," answered Pencroff, "and if you're surprised, Mr. Cyrus, we're every bit as surprised to find you here!"

"Indeed," answered the engineer, gradually coming back to life, deeply intrigued by these details, "that's a very odd thing indeed!"

"But," the sailor replied, "can you tell us what happened after you were carried off by the wave?"

Cyrus Smith tried to recall the events. He remembered little. Ripped from the aerostat's net by the powerful swell, he had sunk several fathoms below the waves. Coming to the surface again, he vaguely sensed a living presence not far away, struggling to stay afloat, invisible in the darkness. It was Top, who had thrown himself from the net to come to his rescue. Looking up, he could no longer see the balloon, which had shot back up into the heavens once rid of his and the dog's weight. He found himself no less than a half-mile from shore, amid the raging waves. He swam with all his might, attempting to fight the current. Top kept him afloat, his jaws clamped over the engineer's clothes; but he was caught up in a storm current that pushed him ever northward, and after a half-hour's struggle he sank into the deep, pulling Top along with him. From that moment until his reawakening in the arms of his friends, he remembered nothing.

"Nevertheless," said Pencroff, "you must have washed ashore somehow, and found the strength to come to this place, since Neb found your footprints!"

"Yes...I must have..." answered the engineer, deep in thought. "And you've seen no trace of any other human being on this shore?"

"Not a trace," answered the reporter. "Besides, if by chance some good Samaritan had happened along just when he was needed most, why would he have abandoned you after pulling you from the waves?"

"You're right, my dear Spilett. —Tell me, Neb," added the engineer, turning to his servant, "you're quite sure it wasn't you...you mightn't have gone blank for a moment...and during that time...No, that's absurd...Are any of the footprints still intact?" asked Cyrus Smith.

"Yes, master," Neb answered, "there are some on this very dune, out of the wind and rain. The rest were all worn away by the storm."

"Pencroff," said Cyrus Smith, "do me a favor and take one of my shoes, and see if it fits the print!"

The sailor did as the engineer asked. Guided by Neb, he and Harbert went to examine the prints. Meanwhile, Cyrus Smith said to the reporter:

"This all seems quite inexplicable!"

"It does indeed!" answered Gideon Spilett.

"But let us not belabor these questions just now, my dear Spilett. We shall discuss all this later."

After a moment, the sailor, Neb, and Harbert returned.

There was no doubt. The engineer's shoes conformed perfectly to the surviving footprints. It was thus indeed Cyrus Smith who had left them behind him as he walked.

"Well then," he said, "I must not have known what I was doing! I must have somehow gone blank at one point, just as I thought Neb might have done! I must have walked like a man asleep, unaware of my own footsteps, and it must have been Top who led me here, acting by instinct alone after pulling me from the waves...Come, Top! Come here, my dear dog!"

The magnificent beast leaped forward to join his master, barking, and Cyrus Smith did not spare his caresses.

This was clearly the only possible explanation for the events surrounding Smith's rescue, and Top was given full credit for saving his master's life.

As noon approached, Pencroff asked Cyrus Smith if he felt in a condition to be transported, and by way of response the engineer arose, bearing witness to the extraordinary force of his will. Nevertheless, he had to lean on the sailor to keep from falling to the ground again.

"Right! Good!" said Pencroff. "Bring the gentleman's litter!"

The litter was brought. The crosspieces had been blanketed with moss and long blades of grass. Cyrus Smith was laid out atop the branches, and they set off toward the shore with Pencroff at one end of the stretcher and Neb at the other.

They had an eight-mile walk ahead of them, and they knew their progress would be slow, with frequent stops for rest; they were thus expecting a journey of six hours at least before they finally reached the Chimneys.

The winds were still strong, but fortunately the rain had stopped. Lying on his stretcher, the engineer propped himself up on one arm and observed his surroundings, gazing with particular attention in the direction of the sea. He said nothing, but only stared around him, and there can be no doubt that the layout of this landscape, its varied terrain, its forests, its diverse flora, were soon engraved in his mind. Nevertheless, after two hours' travel, fatigue overtook him, and he fell asleep on his litter.

At five-thirty, the little band arrived at the bend in the granite wall, and soon after at the Chimneys.

They stopped and gently set the litter on the sand. Cyrus Smith was sound asleep, and did not awaken.

To his great surprise, Pencroff then discovered that the violent tempest of the day before had considerably altered the look of the place. Some rather serious rockslides had occurred. Large boulders lay on the beach, and the shore was covered with a thick carpet of vegetation, kelp, and seaweed. The sea had overrun the islet, and flooded the beach up to the very foot of the great wall of granite.

At the entrance to the Chimneys the ground had been deeply rutted by the relentless assault of the waves.

A grim foreboding ran through Pencroff's mind. He rushed into the corridor.

He fell asleep on his litter.

A moment later he reappeared at the entrance, standing motionless, staring at his companions...

The fire had been extinguished; the ashes were nothing more than mud. The charred linen was nowhere to be found. The sea had flooded the corridors, leaving only devastation behind it, leaving only ruin and destruction inside the Chimneys!

IX

Cyrus Is Here.—Pencroff's Efforts.—Two Sticks Rubbed Together.—Island or Continent?—The Engineer's Plans.—Where in the Pacific?—Deep in the Forest.—The Maritime Pine.—A Hunt for Capybaras.—Promising Smoke.

With a few words, Gideon Spilett, Harbert, and Neb were informed of the situation. This incident, whose consequences might well prove grave—or so at least Pencroff thought—elicited a range of emotions from the worthy sailor's companions. Lost in his joy at being reunited with his master, Neb did not even listen, or rather refused to let himself be troubled by Pencroff's words of warning.

As for Harbert, he seemed to share the sailor's apprehension to some extent.

And the reporter, hearing Pencroff's words, answered simply:

"Ye gods, Pencroff, that's of precious little concern to me now!"

"But I'm telling you we have no fire!"

"Pshaw!"

"Or any way to light one."

"Enough!"

"But, Mr. Spilett..."

"Isn't Cyrus Smith here with us?" answered the reporter. "Is our friend the engineer not alive? He'll find a way to start a fire, you can be sure of that!"

"And with what?"

"With nothing at all."

How was Pencroff to answer this? He could not answer at all, for deep down he fully shared his companions' faith in Cyrus Smith. In their minds, the engineer was nothing less than a microcosm, a composite of all human science and intelligence! One could be no worse off with Cyrus on a desert island than without Cyrus in the most bustling city of the Union. With him, they would never lack for anything. With him, they need never despair. If someone were to come along and tell this intrepid little band that a volcanic eruption was about to rip this patch of land apart and cast it into the depths of the Pacific, they would answer, unperturbed: "Cyrus is here! Go and talk to Cyrus!"

In the meantime, though, the engineer had sunk back into an exhausted stupor after the rigors of his trip to the Chimneys, and for the moment they could not avail themselves of his ingenuity. Their dinner would have to be a light one, for all the capercaillie meat had been consumed, and they had no means to cook any of their other game. Besides, their reserve supply of trogons had vanished. Some other solution would have to be found.

Their first concern was to bring Cyrus Smith into the central chamber. There they succeeded in gathering together a few shreds of relatively dry seaweed and kelp to make his bed. A long, profound slumber would no doubt restore his strength more effectively than any abundant repast.

Night had come, and with it a sizable drop in the temperature under the effect of a northwesterly wind. And since the sea had demolished the barriers Pencroff had installed in the corridors, the cold winds swept through their quarters and rendered the Chimneys virtually uninhabitable. These conditions would have been dangerous to the engineer's health had his friends not stripped off their jackets and peacoats and carefully covered him up against the cold.

Dinner would have to be limited to the inevitable lithodomes, of which Harbert and Neb made an ample harvest on the beach. Nevertheless, the boy supplemented these mollusks with a large heap of edible seaweed, which he had collected from tall rocks washed by the waves only when the seasonal tides were at their peak. This seaweed was of the Fucaceae family, a variety of sargasso that, when dried, exudes a gelatinous substance rich in nutritive elements. After taking their fill of lithodomes, the reporter and his companions sucked on this seaweed, finding its taste to be quite tolerable. Indeed, it should be noted that these aquatic plants occupy a place of some considerable importance in the diets of the indigenous peoples of the Asiatic coasts.

"This is all very well!" said the sailor. "But now's the time for Mr. Cyrus to come to our aid."

The cold had grown quite bitter, and to their great regret they had no way to shield themselves against it.

Profoundly vexed, the sailor struggled to light a fire, with Neb's assistance. He had found some dry moss, and, striking one pebble against another, he managed to produce a few sparks; but the moss was not sufficiently flammable, and refused to catch. In any case, the sparks thrown off by the stones were nothing more than tiny shards of incandescent flint, far fainter and more fleeting than those produced by the piece of steel in an ordinary lighter, and the sailor's efforts were doomed to failure from the start.

In spite of a profound lack of confidence in the procedure, Pencroff then tried rubbing together two pieces of dry wood, as the savages do. To be sure, could his and Neb's exertions have been transformed into heat, as the new theories suggest, they might easily have powered the boiler of a steamship! But their efforts could not bring about a fire. The pieces of wood grew warm, nothing more, and far less so than the experimenters themselves.

After an hour's work, Pencroff was bathed in sweat, and he threw down the pieces of wood in rage.

"The day someone convinces me that the savages light their fires that way," he said, "will be a very warm day indeed, even in the middle of winter! I'd have an easier time lighting my arms on fire by rubbing them together!"

The sailor was wrong to doubt the technique. It is perfectly true that the savages start fires by means of this rapid friction. But not every sort of wood is suitable for the procedure, and it requires a certain "know-how," as people sometimes say, and it seems that this "know-how" was the one thing that Pencroff lacked.

The sailor's bad humor was not long-lived. The two pieces of wood he had dashed to the ground were soon picked up by Harbert, who rubbed them with renewed vigor. The doughty sailor could not hold back a burst of laughter as he watched the adolescent struggle to succeed where he had failed.

"Rub, my boy, rub!" he said.

"I'm rubbing," answered Harbert, laughing, "but I'm only trying to

Pencroff tried rubbing together two pieces of dry wood...

warm myself the way you did, instead of sitting here shivering. Before long I'll be as warm as you, Pencroff!"

And so he was. Nonetheless, for tonight at least, they would have to abandon all hope of a fire. Gideon Spilett repeated for the twentieth time that Cyrus Smith would not be so easily deterred, and with these words he stretched out on the sand in one of the corridors. Harbert, Neb, and Pencroff followed suit, while Top slept at his master's feet.

The next day, March 28th, the engineer awoke at about eight o'clock to find his companions gathered around him, eagerly awaiting this moment. Just as the day before, his first words were:

"Island or continent?"

This, clearly, was his idée fixe.

"Well!" answered Pencroff, "we don't have the faintest idea, Mr. Smith!"

"You still don't know? ..."

"But we will soon," Pencroff added, "with you to guide us."

"I think I might be well enough to try," answered the engineer, rising to his feet without too much difficulty.

"Now there's a fine sight!" cried the sailor.

"I was more exhausted than anything else," answered Cyrus Smith. "A bit of food, my friends, and I'll be good as new. —You do have a fire, I suppose?"

This question did not meet with an immediate response. But after a few moments:

"Alas! we have no fire," said Pencroff, "or rather we no longer do, Mr. Cyrus."

And the sailor told him of the previous day's events. He brought a smile to the engineer's lips with the story of the lone match, as well as his abortive attempt to start a fire in the manner of the savages.

"We'll see to that," answered the engineer, "and if we can't find some sort of substitute for tinder..."

"Yes?" asked the sailor.

"Well then, we'll make matches."

"Chemical matches?"

"Chemical matches."

"You see? Simple as that," cried the reporter, slapping the sailor on the shoulder.

Pencroff remained unconvinced, but he did not protest. The castaways stepped outside. The weather was fine again. A brilliant sun was rising over the sea, and the prismatic granules embedded in the vast granite wall gleamed with a dazzling golden light.

After a quick survey of his surroundings, the engineer sat down on a large boulder. Harbert offered him a few handfuls of mussels and sargasso, saying:

"This is all we have, Mr. Cyrus."

"Thank you, my boy," answered Cyrus Smith, "this will do nicely—for this morning, at least."

And he ate his unsubstantial meal with relish, washing it down with a little cool water drawn from the river in a large shell.

His companions looked on in silence. Then, his appetite more or less sated, Cyrus Smith crossed his arms and said:

"So, my friends, you still don't know whether fate has left us on an island or a continent?"

"No, Mr. Cyrus," answered the boy.

"We'll know tomorrow," the engineer went on. "Until then, there's nothing to be done."

"Yes, there is," answered Pencroff.

"What would that be?"

"Fire," said the sailor, who had an idée fixe of his own.

"We'll see to that soon enough, Pencroff," answered Cyrus Smith. "Tell me, did I indeed see a mountain off to our west as you were bringing me here yesterday?"

"That's right," answered Gideon Spilett, "and no small mountain, by the look of it…"

"Good," answered the engineer. "Tomorrow we'll climb to the top, and we'll see whether this is an island or a continent. Until then, I repeat, there's nothing to be done."

"Fire!" repeated the obstinate sailor.

"Yes, yes, we'll make a fire!" Gideon Spilett replied. "Patience, Pencroff!"

The sailor looked at Gideon Spilett with a look that seemed to say, "If we had to depend on you, our first meal would be a mighty long time coming!" Nevertheless, he kept his peace.

Cyrus Smith had made no response to the sailor's plea. The problem of fire did not seem to trouble him in the least. He remained lost in his thoughts for a few moments; then, turning his attention to his companions again:

"My friends," he said, "our situation may well be deplorable, but it is extremely simple. Either we are on a continent, in which case, by dint of exertions great or small, we will reach some inhabited area; or else we are on an island, in which case there are two possibilities. If the island is inhabited, we will do what we can to remedy our situation with the help of its people; if it is deserted, we will do what we can to remedy our situation ourselves."

"That seems clear enough," answered Pencroff.

"But, whether island or continent," asked Gideon Spilett, "where do you think the cyclone has brought us, Cyrus?"

"I have no way of knowing precisely," the engineer answered, "but in all probability we are somewhere in the Pacific. The wind was blowing from the northeast as we left Richmond, with such force that it could not have changed direction for some time. Assuming that our course was a southwesterly one, then, we must have passed over North Carolina, South Carolina, Georgia, the Gulf of Mexico, the narrowest part of Mexico itself, and then some portion of the Pacific Ocean. I would estimate the distance traveled by our balloon at no less than six to seven thousand miles; and assuming that the wind shifted by no more than half a quarter, we must have come to either the Mendana archipelago or the Pomotou islands—or even, if our speed was greater than I have supposed, as far as New Zealand. If the latter hypothesis proves to be true, our return home will be an easy thing. We'll have no difficulty finding someone to assist us, whether Englishman or Maori. If, on the contrary, we find ourselves on the shore of a deserted island in some Micronesian archipelago, we may at least be able to establish that fact from atop the great cone I glimpsed yesterday, and then we will do what we must to make a life for ourselves here, as if we were never to leave again!"

"Never!" cried the reporter. "Did you say 'never,' my dear Cyrus?"

"It seems wisest to assume the worst from the beginning," answered the engineer, "and let anything better come as a surprise."

"Well said!" answered Pencroff. "And we must also hope that this island, if that's what it is, doesn't lie too far from the shipping routes! Now that would be a stroke of bad luck!"

"We won't know what we're facing until we climb the mountain. That must be our first priority," said the engineer.

"But Mr. Cyrus," asked Harbert, "will you be strong enough to make the climb tomorrow?"

"I hope so," answered the engineer, "assuming that you and the good Pencroff will prove intelligent and skillful hunters."

"Mr. Cyrus," answered the sailor, "while we're on the subject of hunting, if I could feel as certain that we'll be able to roast our catch as I am of bagging some game..."

"Just bag it, Pencroff," answered Cyrus Smith.

And so it was agreed that the engineer and the reporter would spend the day at the Chimneys, studying the shoreline and plateau. Meanwhile, Neb, Harbert, and the sailor would return to the forest to replenish their supply of firewood, and help themselves to any furred or feathered beast that might come their way.

They set off at about ten o'clock in the morning, Harbert full of confidence, Neb full of joy, and Pencroff muttering to himself:

"If I find a fire burning when I come home again, it'll only be because the god of thunder himself came by and lit it!"

The trio followed the usual path up the riverbank; on reaching the bend, the sailor stopped short and asked his two companions:

"Shall we begin as hunters or loggers?"

"Hunters," answered Harbert. "Look, Top's already picked up a scent."

"To the hunt, then," said the sailor, "and then we'll come back and gather some wood."

With this, Harbert, Neb, and Pencroff broke three large branches from the trunk of a young pine tree and ran off after Top as he bounded through the tall grass.

This time the hunters did not follow the course of the river, but penetrated directly into the heart of the forest. The trees were much as they had seen earlier, primarily pines. Where the forest grew less dense, the isolated pines were often quite tall and well developed, which suggested that the island lay at a latitude higher than the engineer supposed. They found a number of clearings studded with weathered stumps and strewn with dead wood, offering an inexhaustible supply of fuel. Then, on the other side of the clearings, the undergrowth became dense again, forming an almost impenetrable mass of green.

Finding their way through this vast woodland, without path or trail, was no easy task. Every now and then the sailor marked their route by breaking small branches in a way they could easily recognize on the return trip. But perhaps they were wrong not to have stayed close by the riverbank as he and Harbert had done in their first expedition, for after an hour's walk no game had yet been spotted. Top ran along beneath the low branches; a number of birds were flushed out, but never came within striking distance. Even the trogons eluded their search, and it began to seem that they would be forced to return to the marshy area where the sailor had so successfully shown his skill at capercaillie fishing.

"Well! Pencroff," said Neb in a sarcastic tone, "if this is the catch you promised to bring back to my master, we won't need much of a fire to roast it!"

"Patience, Neb," answered the sailor, "if anything's lacking on our return, it won't be fresh game!"

"You have no faith in Mr. Smith?"

"Of course I do."

"But you don't believe he's going to make us a fire?"

"I'll believe it when I see the wood burning in the hearth."

"You will, since my master said you would!"

"We'll see!"

But the sun had not yet reached the highest point of its journey through the heavens, and so their explorations continued, marked by Harbert's fortuitous discovery of a tree bearing edible fruit. It was a maritime pine, which produces a superb nut, highly esteemed in the temperate zones of America and Europe. The pine nuts were perfectly ripe, and on Harbert's suggestion his two companions sampled them with great pleasure.

"Well, now," said Pencroff, "seaweed for bread, raw mussels for meat, and pine nuts for dessert, that's what I call a meal fit for people without a single match in their pockets!"

"We mustn't complain," answered Harbert.

"I'm not complaining, my boy," Pencroff replied. "I'm simply restating my opinion that there has been a certain lack of meat in our meals of late!"

"Top's seen something!..." shouted Neb, hurrying toward a thicket into which the dog had disappeared, barking. Top's barks were intermingled with a strange sort of growling.

The hunters found Top locked in combat . . .

The sailor and Harbert ran after Neb. If there was game to be found, this was no time to be discussing how they might cook it; the only question now was how they might best get their hands on it.

The hunters entered the undergrowth to find Top locked in combat with some sort of animal, his jaws clamped over the beast's ear. It was a quadruped some two and a half feet long, piglike in appearance, blackish brown in color but lighter on its belly, its body covered with coarse, sparse bristles, and toes that appeared to be united by a membrane.

Harbert believed it to be a capybara, one of the largest members of the Rodentia order.

The capybara made no attempt to fend off the dog's attack. It stupidly rolled its great eyes, set deep within a thick layer of fat. This could well have been its first sight of men.

Testing the weight of his club in his hand, Neb was about to dispatch the rodent when the latter ripped itself from the dog's jaws, leaving a shred of ear between his teeth. It let out a loud growl and threw itself against Harbert, half knocking him over, then disappeared into the woods.

"Oh! that miserable!..." cried Pencroff.

Immediately the trio hurtled forward on Top's heels, but just as they were about to catch up, the animal disappeared into the waters of a large pond shaded by venerable pine trees.

Neb, Harbert, and Pencroff stopped and stood motionless. Top had thrown himself into the water, but the capybara, concealed at the bottom of the pond, remained out of sight.

"Let's wait here," said the boy. "He'll soon have to surface to take a breath."

"Won't he drown?" asked Neb.

"No," answered Harbert, "his webbed feet show that he's virtually an amphibian. Now let's keep an eye out for him."

Top swam circles in the water. Pencroff and his two companions took up position on two points of the bank, ready to cut off the capybara's retreat, while the dog swam over the surface of the pond, continuing his search.

Harbert was not mistaken. After a few minutes the animal returned to the water's surface. With one bound Top was upon it, preventing it from diving again. A moment later the capybara was dragged to the water's edge and dispatched with one blow of Neb's club.

"Hurrah!" cried Pencroff, who had a certain fondness for that cry of triumph. "All we need now is some hot coals, and we'll gnaw this beast down to the bones!"

Pencroff slung the capybara over his shoulder, and, judging by the height of the sun that it must be about two o'clock, called for an immediate return to the Chimneys.

Once more the hunters availed themselves of Top's excellent instincts: with the intelligent animal's help, they soon found their way back to the path that had brought them into the forest. A half-hour later, they arrived at the bend in the river.

As before, Pencroff quickly built a timber raft, although with no fire this seemed a sadly pointless endeavor. And so they returned toward the Chimneys, following their raft downstream.

But the sailor was not fifty paces from home when he stopped, once again let out a great hurrah, and, one hand outstretched toward the break in the cliffs:

"Harbert! Neb! Look!" he cried.

A long stream of smoke was swirling over the boulders!

X

The Engineer's Invention.—Cyrus Smith Preoccupied.—Setting Out for the Mountain.—The Forest.—Volcanic Soil.—The Tragopans.—The Mouflons.—The First Plateau.—The Bivouac.—The Summit of the Cone.

A few moments later, the three hunters found themselves before a crackling fire. Cyrus Smith and the reporter were awaiting their return. Pencroff looked first at one, then at the other, never speaking, the capybara still in his hand.

"That's right, my dear fellow!" cried the reporter. "Fire, a real fire, just the thing to roast that magnificent animal for a feast this evening!"

"But who lit it? ..." asked Pencroff.

"The sun!"

Gideon Spilett had answered truthfully. It was indeed the sun that had provided the heat that so astounded Pencroff. The sailor could not believe his eyes, so utterly dumbstruck that he never thought of asking the engineer how he had done it.

"Does this mean you have a lens, sir?" Harbert asked Cyrus Smith.

"No, child," he answered, "but I made one."

And he displayed the device with which he had simulated the action of a magnifying glass. It was nothing more than the two crystals he had removed from his and the reporter's watches. By filling them with water and sealing the rims together with sticky clay, he had constructed a veritable lens, with which he had concentrated the solar rays onto a clump of very dry moss and so induced the process of combustion.

The sailor examined the device, then looked at the engineer, still silent. But the look in his eyes spoke volumes! If Cyrus Smith was not a god, he was at least, and most certainly, more than a man in Pencroff's eyes. Finally he recovered his voice, crying:

"Write that down, Mr. Spilett, write that down on your piece of paper!"

"I already have," the reporter answered.

Then, with Neb's help, the sailor set up a spit, and soon the capybara, carefully gutted and cleaned, was roasting over a bright, crackling fire like a suckling pig.

The Chimneys were once again inhabitable, not only because of the fire spreading its warmth through the corridors, but also because the protective walls of stone and sand had been rebuilt.

As we see, the engineer and his companion had put their day to good use. Cyrus Smith's strength was almost fully restored now; he had even climbed up to the high plateau to test his endurance. There his eye, well practiced in the art of judging elevations and distances, had long remained fixed on the peak he intended to scale the next day. The mountain lay some six miles to the northwest, and he estimated its elevation at 3,500 feet above sea level. Consequently, an observer standing on its summit would have a view of at least fifty miles in all directions. Cyrus Smith thus believed they would have no difficulty resolving the "continent or island" question, to which he rightly gave primacy over all others.

Their dinner was a pleasant one. The capybara meat was declared superb. Sargasso and pine nuts rounded out the meal, during which the engineer spoke only rarely, preoccupied as he was with thoughts of the day to come.

Once or twice, Pencroff ventured some idea concerning the tasks that lay before them, but Cyrus Smith, whose mind clearly worked in the most methodical way, merely shook his head.

"Tomorrow," he repeated, "we will know what sort of land we are dealing with, and we will take action accordingly."

After the meal was over, still more armloads of wood were thrown onto the fire, and the denizens of the Chimneys, including faithful Top, fell into a profound slumber. No incident troubled the tranquillity of the night, and the next day—March 29th—they awoke rested and refreshed, eager to set out on an excursion that promised them a more definite understanding of their fate.

All the necessary preparations had been made. The leftover capybara would sustain Cyrus Smith and his companions for the next twenty-four hours. Furthermore, they hoped to supplement their store of provisions as they walked. Since the crystals had been reaffixed to the engineer's and the reporter's watches, Pencroff charred a bit more linen to use as tinder. As for flint, they were sure to find great quantities of it along the way, given the island's plutonian origins.

It was seven-thirty in the morning when the explorers left the Chimneys, armed with their clubs. At Pencroff's suggestion, it was agreed that they would follow the usual path through the forest—the most direct approach to the mountain—and perhaps find a different route for their return. They rounded the southern extremity of the granite wall and followed the left bank of the river, veering off at the southwesterly bend. They found the trail that had been blazed through the green trees the previous day, and by nine o'clock Cyrus Smith and his companions were nearing the western edge of the forest.

The ground, previously flat and regular, first marshy, then dry and sandy, had begun to slope upward slightly as they progressed from the shoreline to the interior. A few animals had been spotted amid the thick trees, immediately taking cover on catching sight of the castaways. Top ran to flush them out, but his master immediately called him to heel. This was not a time for hunting; that they would try again later. The engineer let nothing distract him from his idée fixe. Indeed, he paid precious little mind to the landscape around him—its configuration, the resources it might offer. His only goal was the mountain they were about to climb, and he headed straight toward it, never wavering.

At ten o'clock they took a few minutes' break. Now that they were out of the forest, the region's orographic system lay fully exposed to their gaze. The mountain was formed of two cones. The first, truncated at an elevation of about 2,500 feet, was bolstered by a number of irregularly shaped foothills, branching out like the talons of some immense claw sunk into the ground. Between the foothills lay narrow forested valleys. The trees grew sparser at higher elevations, and a few small stands could be seen growing here and there up to the truncation of the first cone. The vegetation seemed less dense on the northeast side of the mountain, which was marked by deep gouges, no doubt carved out by flowing lava.

A second cone grew from the first, slightly rounded at the peak and tilted a little to one side, like a huge round hat pulled down over one ear. It seemed to be made of bare earth, studded with a great number of reddish boulders.

Their goal was the summit of the second cone, and the crest of the foothills no doubt offered the surest route.

"We are on volcanic terrain here," Cyrus Smith said, and with his companions in tow he began a gradual ascent along the ridge of a foothill, which would lead them to the first plateau by way of a sinuous and therefore relatively untiring route.

The ground was peppered with outcroppings, clearly created by the convulsive force of the plutonian process. Erratic blocks of stone lay here and there, as well as piles of basalt, pumice, and obsidian rubble. Conifers grew in isolated stands, while a few hundred feet below, deep in the narrow gorges, these same trees formed thick forests, virtually unpenetrated by the rays of the sun.

As they continued to ascend the lower slopes in this first stage of the climb, Harbert called the others' attention to pawprints indicating that large animals had recently come this way—perhaps wildcats, perhaps some other species.

"Those beasts might not be happy to find trespassers on their territory!" said Pencroff.

"Well," answered the reporter, who had hunted tigers in India and lions in Africa, "we'll just have to find some way to get rid of them. But in the meantime, stay on your guard!"

The slow ascent continued. Their route was a long one, made still longer by meanders and obstacles that forced them into prolonged detours. Sometimes the ground suddenly fell away, and they found themselves on the edge of a deep crevasse that they had to find some way around. Many times they were obligated to retrace their steps in search of some practicable route, compounding their fatigue and slowing their progress still further. At noon, when the little band stopped for lunch by a small cascade beneath a large stand of pine trees, they were only halfway to the first plateau, which, they now realized, they would in all likelihood not reach until nightfall.

Their view over the ocean was considerably broader from where they now stood. Nevertheless, to their right, the narrow southeastern promontory obstructed the horizon, and they could not yet determine whether this coastline might take a sudden turn and rejoin the mass of land beyond their line of sight. To the left, they could see a few miles farther northward than before; nevertheless, as soon as they turned northwest, their view was completely blocked by the oddly shaped crest of a foothill, nestling against the central cone like some titanic buttress. For the moment, then, they could form no preliminary idea of the answer to the question that Cyrus Smith was hoping to resolve.

They resumed their ascent at one o'clock. They now turned obliquely toward the southwest and into another dense forest. There, in the shelter of the trees, several pairs of gallinaceans from the pheasant family were spotted. These were "tragopans," with fleshy wattles hanging from their necks and two thin cylindrical horns sprouting from behind their eyes. They were roughly the size of roosters, and while the females were uniformly brown, the males were resplendent in their red plumage strewn with small, white, teardrop-shaped spots. With a single stone, vigorously and skillfully thrown, Gideon Spilett killed one of these tragopans, and Pencroff stared longingly at the cadaver, his appetite sharpened by the fresh mountain air.

With the forest now behind them, the alpinists clambered a hundred feet up a very steep, rubble-strewn slope, giving one another a boost when required, and so reached another, higher patch of level ground. Here the soil took on a volcanic look, and the trees were few and widely scattered. Now they would turn east again, making switchbacks as they advanced, for the flanks of the mountain were extremely steep, and nearly impossible to climb in a straight line. Every colonist's mind was focused on the task of choosing the spot where he would next place his foot. Neb and Harbert walked at the head of the group, Pencroff at the tail, with Cyrus and the reporter in the middle. The animals that frequented these slopes—and there was no lack of prints—could only have been such sure-footed, supple-spined beasts as chamois or izards. They spotted a few such beasts, but Pencroff had a different name for them, crying out at one moment:

"Sheep!"

The alpinists drew to a halt. Some fifty paces away, they saw a half-dozen large animals with massive horns curved backward and flattened at the tip, and a woolly fleece concealed beneath long, silky strands of light brown hair.

These were no ordinary sheep, but a species widespread throughout the mountainous regions of the temperate zones, to which Harbert gave the name of mouflons.

"Do they have legs and chops like any other mutton?" asked Pencroff.

"Yes," answered Harbert.

The alpinists clambered up a very steep, rubble-strewn slope . . .

"Well then, they're sheep!" said Pencroff.

Standing motionless amid the basalt rubble, the beasts looked on in astonishment, as if seeing human bipeds for the very first time. Then, their fear suddenly aroused, they bounded away over the rocks and disappeared.

"Until we meet again!" Pencroff cried out to them, in a tone so comical that Cyrus Smith, Gideon Spilett, Harbert, and Neb could not help but laugh.

The climb continued. Some of the slopes were capriciously striated by old lava flows. Small solfataras sometimes blocked their path, and they had no choice but to find some way around them. Here and there they found crystalline sulfur deposits, as well as various other materials such as are commonly thrown from a volcano before a great eruption of lava: pozzolanas with irregular, deeply charred grains, whitish ashes composed of countless small crystals of feldspar.

As they neared the first plateau, formed by the truncation of the lower cone, the climb became markedly more rigorous. By four o'clock they had passed the timberline. Only a few tortured, stunted pines stood here and there, and their life must have been a hard one, battered as they were by the strong sea winds, which blew even more fiercely at this altitude. Fortunately for the engineer and his companions, the weather was fine and the atmosphere serene, for at an altitude of three thousand feet a strong wind would have greatly hampered their mobility. The sky was cloudless, the air wonderfully transparent. A perfect calm lay over the landscape. They could no longer see the sun, now concealed, along with half the western horizon, behind the vast screen of the upper cone. Stretching off to the shoreline, its enormous shadow grew ever longer as the earth's radiant star sank slowly toward the sea, its diurnal course drawing to a close. Vapors began to rise in the east, more mist than cloud, taking on all the colors of the spectrum under the effect of the solar rays.

Only five hundred vertical feet now separated them from the plateau where they hoped to set up camp for the night, but those five hundred feet grew to more than two miles thanks to the zigzag path the explorers were forced to follow. They had, so to speak, no earth beneath their feet. Eroded by the wind, the striae offered only an occasional foothold, and the angle of the slope was so obtuse that they more than once found themselves sliding down an old lava flow. Night was slowly falling, moreover, and the darkness was almost complete by the time Cyrus Smith and his companions arrived at the plateau of the lower cone, greatly fatigued after their seven-hour ascent.

Their next task was to arrange a campsite and restore their weary bodies, first with a good dinner and then with a sound sleep. The upper tier of the mountain rose up from a base of boulders among which they had no difficulty finding shelter. There was little wood to be had in the area; nevertheless, they thought they could build a fire with the mosses and dried brambles that dotted the plateau here and there. The sailor laid out a number of flat stones on the ground to serve as a hearth while Neb and Harbert set off to gather fuel. They soon returned with a load of brambles. Two pieces of flint were struck together, the sparks fell onto the charred linen, and a few moments later, encouraged by Neb's careful breath, a good fire crackled atop the hearth in the shelter of the boulders.

The purpose of this fire was to counteract the chilly nighttime temperatures, and not to cook the pheasant, which Neb reserved for the next day. The leftover capybara and a few dozen pine nuts formed the menu for this meal, which was over before six-thirty in the evening.

Cyrus Smith then conceived the idea of using the last glimmers of daylight to explore the broad circular platform supporting the mountain's upper cone. Before taking his rest, he wanted to know if there might be a path around the base of the cone, as its flanks might well prove too steep to allow access to the summit. He could not chase this insistent preoccupation from his mind, for it was possible that, on the side from which the tilted hat emerged, which is to say the north side, the plateau would offer no practicable path. And if, on the one hand, they could not reach the summit of the mountain directly, nor, on the other, find some way around the base of the cone, they would have no means of observing the western regions of this land, and the purpose of their ascent would be in part defeated.

Thus, despite his great fatigue, the engineer left the task of preparing the campsite to Pencroff and Neb, and to Spilett that of noting down the day's events, and set off northward around the circular rim of the plateau with Harbert at his side.

The night was fine and peaceful, the darkness not yet complete. Cyrus Smith and the boy walked close together, in silence. In some places the plateau lay open before them, and they made their way without difficulty. In others they could find only the narrowest passages through the rubble, so narrow that they were forced to walk single file. Finally, after a twenty-minute walk, Cyrus Smith and Harbert found they could go no farther. From here on, the escarpment between the two peaks became a vast pile of rubble, its slopes inclined at nearly seventy degrees, and hence quite impossible to cross.

The child and the engineer had no choice but to abandon their hopes of a route around the cone; but now they saw that a direct ascent to the summit was not out of the question.

For before them they found a great fissure in the mountainside. The rim of the upper crater had crumbled here, forming a sort of spout through which the liquid eruptive materials had flowed in the days when the volcano was active. Inside, the hardened lava and encrusted scoria formed a sort of broad natural staircase, offering easy access to the top.

One glance was all Cyrus Smith needed to realize the use they could make of this geological phenomenon, and unhesitatingly, with the boy close behind, he entered the enormous chasm amid the gathering gloom.

They still had a thousand vertical feet to climb. Would the interior slopes of the crater be practicable? The engineer intended to press on until something forced him to stop. Fortunately, the long, sinuous incline formed a sort of huge spiral ramp within the volcano, greatly facilitating their ascent to the summit.

As for the volcano itself, they did not doubt that it was entirely inactive. Not a single wisp of smoke escaped its flanks. Not a single flame could be seen in the deep cavities. Not a rumble, not a murmur, not a shudder emerged from the dark shaft, which seemed to plunge straight down to the bowels of the earth. No sulfurous vapors permeated the atmosphere inside the crater. The volcano was not merely asleep; it was utterly extinct.

Cyrus Smith's plan met with complete success. Little by little, he and Harbert saw the upper crater broadening above their heads as they climbed the interior walls. The diameter of the circle of sky framed by the rim grew perceptibly larger as they advanced. With each step that Cyrus Smith and Harbert took, more stars entered their field of vision. The magnificent constellations of the southern sky glimmered above them. At the zenith, pristine, shone the splendid Antares of Scorpio, and not far away, the well-known Beta Centauri, which is thought to be the star nearest our terrestrial globe. As the crater flared ever broader, they saw the star Fomalhaut in the constellation of Pisces; then the Southern

Triangle, and finally, almost at the Antarctic pole, the sparkling Southern Cross, the counterpart of the North Star in the boreal hemisphere.

It was nearly eight o'clock when Cyrus Smith and Harbert set foot on the upper crest of the mountain, at the very summit of the cone.

The darkness was now complete, limiting visibility to no more than two miles. Did the sea surround this unknown land, or was it joined in the west to some continent of the Pacific? They still could not say. A band of clouds lay over the western horizon, heightening the darkness of the night, and the eye could not determine whether the meeting of heaven and water was as straight and unbroken there as on all other sides of the island.

But on that horizon there now appeared a vague gleam, slowly descending as the cloud climbed toward the zenith.

It was the slender crescent of the moon, soon to disappear from view. But the meager light it cast afforded a clear glimpse of the horizon beneath the rising cloud, and the engineer could see its quivering form briefly reflected on the surface of the water.

Cyrus Smith grasped the boy's hand, and, in a somber voice:

"An island!" he said, just as the lunar crescent sank beneath the waves.

XI

Atop the Cone.—Inside the Crater.—The Sea All Around Them.—No Land in Sight.—Bird's-Eye View of the Coastline.— Hydrography and Orography.—Is the Island Inhabited?— Naming the Bays, Gulfs, Capes, Rivers, Etc.—Lincoln Island.

A half-hour later, Cyrus Smith and Harbert were back at the campsite. In a few words, the engineer told his companions that the land onto which chance had tossed them was indeed an island, and that the next day they would consider their situation. Then each settled down to sleep as best he could, and, nestled among the basalt boulders in the tranquil night air some 2,500 feet above the sea, the "islanders" enjoyed a deep sleep.

The next day, March 30th, after a hasty breakfast of roast tragopan, the engineer expressed his intention to climb back to the volcano's summit for a more careful examination of the island on which they had been imprisoned—perhaps for life. A second ascent might show them whether their island lay close by some other land, or at least on the route followed by ships visiting the archipelagoes of the Pacific Ocean. This time his companions accompanied him, eager to see the island on which they would have to rely for their every need.

It must have been about seven o'clock in the morning when Cyrus Smith, Harbert, Pencroff, Gideon Spilett, and Neb left their campsite. None of them expressed the slightest anxiety concerning their situation. They had faith in themselves, to be sure, but it must be noted that the foundation of Cyrus Smith's faith was not identical to that of his companions. The engineer was confident that they would wrest from the grasp of untamed nature everything required for their survival, while the others feared nothing simply because Cyrus Smith was with them—a slight difference that we should have no difficulty understanding. Pencroff, especially, had lost the capacity for despair ever since the relighting of the fire; no matter what sort of barren, desolate rock he might find himself on, he would never lose hope with the engineer at his side.

"Ah well!" he said. "We managed to get out of Richmond, and without the authorities' permission! Devil if we won't find some way to leave this place as well, since no one's trying to hold us back!"

Cyrus Smith led them along the route he had taken the previous evening. They rounded the cone along the escarpment, and soon they reached the great rift in the mountainside. The weather was magnificent. The sun slowly rose through a serene sky, covering the entire eastern flank of the mountain with its rays.

They now began their climb up to the rim of the crater. It was just as the engineer had glimpsed it in the darkness, a vast funnel flaring ever broader as it rose to a height of one thousand feet above the plateau. Beneath the rift, broad lava flows had snaked over the slopes of the mountain, strewing the path with eruptive debris all the way down to the lower valleys that rutted the island's northern regions.

The crater's interior slopes were no steeper than thirty-five to forty degrees, and so presented no obstacle to their ascent. Traces of the ancient lava flows were all around them, no doubt dating back to a time when the magma spewed from the very summit of the cone, before the formation of the lateral rift offered a more direct route to the exterior.

As for the volcanic chimney linking the crater with the subterranean realm, they could not gauge its depth by sight, for the bottom was swallowed up by the darkness. But there was no doubt that the volcano was completely extinct.

By eight o'clock, Cyrus Smith and his companions were standing at the summit of the crater, on a conical outcropping that bulged from the northern rim.

"The sea! The sea, everywhere you look!" they cried, as if unable to hold back the word that had made islanders of them.

The sea, indeed, an immense circular surface of water all around them! Perhaps Cyrus Smith had secretly hoped that on returning to the summit he might catch sight of some coastline, some nearby island that he could not discern in the darkness of the previous night. But no: there was nothing to be seen from there to the horizon, a distance of more than fifty miles in every direction. No land. No sail. The entire area was devoid of any sign of life, and the island occupied the center of a circumference that truly appeared to be infinite.

For several minutes the engineer and his companions stared out over the ocean, motionless and mute. With their gaze they searched every last inch of the water's surface, and in every direction. But even Pencroff, with his extraordinary visual acuity, saw nothing. If there were land to be seen on the horizon, even a single dim, shimmering form, the sailor could not have failed to spot it, for nature had furnished the sockets in his skull with nothing less than two telescopes!

Their gaze now shifted from the ocean to the island laid out at their feet, and the first question was put by Gideon Spilett, as follows:

"How big do you think the island might be?"

The fact is that it did not appear very large amid the unending sea.

Cyrus Smith thought for a few moments; he carefully gauged the perimeter of the island, accounting for their present elevation; then:

"My friends," he said, "I think I might safely estimate the length of our island's coastline at more than one hundred miles."*

"And its surface area? ..."

"That would be difficult to judge," the engineer answered. "The coast-line is far too irregular to say."

If Cyrus Smith's estimation was accurate, the island was more or less the same size as Malta or Zante, in the Mediterranean; but at the same time it was much more capriciously shaped than those islands, and less marked by capes, promontories, spits, bays, coves, and inlets. Its truly curious form was a wonder to behold, and when at the engineer's sugges-tion Gideon Spilett made a sketch of its outline, they found that it resem-bled some fantastic beast, a sort of monstrous pteropod asleep on the surface of the Pacific.

Here, then, is the exact configuration of the island, which it will be important to understand, and which the reporter immediately mapped out as accurately as he could.

A broad concavity on the eastern shoreline, where the castaways had landed, created a vast bay delimited to the southeast by a narrow cape, which a point had concealed from Pencroff during his first exploration. To the northeast the bay was closed off by two further capes, between

---

* Approximately forty-five leagues of four kilometers.

which lay a narrow gulf that resembled the half-open jaws of some formidable shark.

From the northeast to the northwest, the coastline was rounded, like the flattened skull of a wild feline, then bulged outward in a vague and amorphous way. It was in the center of this bulge that the volcanic mountain lay.

From there, the coastline ran from north to south in a relatively straight line, indented by a narrow cove some two thirds of the way down, then ending in a long tail, like the caudal appendage of a gigantic alligator.

That tail formed a veritable peninsula extending more than thirty miles into the sea, starting from the aforementioned southeastern cape; it curved in such a way as to create a broad, open roadstead, which extended the full length of this strangely shaped island's southern coast.

At its narrowest point, which is to say between the Chimneys and the cove that lay at the same latitude on the western shore, the island measured no more than ten miles; but at its longest, from the jaw on the northeast to the end of the tail on the southwest, the distance was fully thirty miles.

As for the interior of the island, its general appearance was as follows: heavily forested over the southern half, from the mountain to the shore, but arid and sandy in the north. Between the volcano and the eastern shore, Cyrus Smith and his companions were surprised to discover a lake, framed by green trees, whose existence they had not previously suspected. Seen from this elevation, the lake seemed to be at the same level as the sea, but, after some reflection, the engineer explained to his companions that its elevation was probably closer to three hundred feet, for the broad expanse into which it was set was simply the continuation of the plateau that ended near the shore.

"So this is a freshwater lake?" asked Pencroff.

"Unquestionably," answered the engineer. "It must be fed by the waters flowing from the mountain."

"I can see a little stream running into it," said Harbert, pointing out a narrow band of water whose source no doubt lay in the western foothills.

"Indeed," answered Cyrus Smith, "and since that stream feeds the lake there must undoubtedly be a spillway on the seaward side, to carry off the overflow. We'll have a look at that on our way home."

That sinuous little rivulet, along with the river they had already found,

"I can see a little stream," said Harbert.

constituted the whole of the island's hydrographic system, or so at least it appeared to the eyes of the explorers. Nevertheless, beneath the dense greenery that forested two thirds of the island, there might well have been other small watercourses flowing toward the sea. Indeed, this seemed almost beyond question, given the fertility of the region, its many magnificent specimens of flora and fauna characteristic of the temperate zones. In the island's northern reaches they could find no trace of flowing water. A few stagnant pools in the marshes to the northeast, perhaps, but that was all; the rest was dunes, sand, a pronounced aridity that stood in stark contrast to the opulent vegetation blanketing the greater part of the island.

The volcano did not lie at the island's center, but rose up from the northwestern quadrant, and seemed to mark a boundary between the two zones. To the southwest, south, and southeast, the first foothills disappeared beneath masses of verdure. To the north, on the other hand, the network of foothills was clearly visible, slowly dying away as they neared the sandy plains. The lava must have flowed to this side in the age of the volcano's eruptions, and a broad causeway of hardened lava ran from its flanks to the narrow jaw that formed the northeastern gulf.

Cyrus Smith and his friends spent an hour in this way, atop the summit of the mountain. The island was spread out before their eyes like a vast relief map tinted green for the forest, yellow for the sand, blue for the water. They considered their new home in its entirety, and nothing escaped their gaze save the ground beneath the leafy canopy of the forest, the farthest recesses of the shadowy valleys, and the interior of the narrow gorges furrowing the terrain at the foot of the volcano.

There remained one vital question, whose response would determine the castaways' future.

Was the island inhabited?

It was the reporter who posed this question, and after their close examination of the island's every region they sensed that it could only be answered in the negative.

Nowhere could they discern any sign that human hands had been at work. No cluster of huts, no isolated cabin, no fishery on the coastline. No smoke drifted through the air, betraying the presence of man. It is true that a distance of thirty miles separated the observers from the farthest point of the island—the end of the tail to their southwest—and even with Pencroff's eyes it would have been difficult to discover any sign of human habitation there. Nor could they lift the curtain of greenery that covered three fourths of the island, to see if some village might lie concealed beneath it. But in any case the inhabitants of these cramped patches of land amid the Pacific waves generally preferred to live by the shore, and here the shore appeared to be utterly deserted.

Until they had made a more complete exploration, then, they could assume that the island was not inhabited.

But was it ever visited, however briefly, by the natives of other islands? This was a question not easily answered. No land could be seen within the circle of their vision, whose radius measured fifty miles. But a distance of fifty miles is no obstacle for a Malay prau or a great Polynesian pirogue. It all depended on the position of the island, whether it lay isolated in mid-Pacific or near that ocean's archipelagoes. Could Cyrus Smith determine its latitude and longitude, without instruments? A difficult task. Given this uncertainty, then, they thought it best to take precautions against the possibility of a landing by natives from the surrounding areas.

The exploration of the island was now finished, its configuration determined, its relief cataloged, its hydrography and orography appraised. The layout of the forests and plains had been broadly sketched out on the reporter's map. There was nothing left but to make their way back down the mountain's flanks and explore the lowlands in order to form some idea of the island's animal, vegetable, and mineral resources.

But before calling on his companions to set off again, Cyrus Smith addressed them in a calm, serious voice:

"Here, my friends, is the modest patch of land onto which the hand of the Almighty has cast us. This is where we shall live, perhaps for some time. Perhaps, too, we will be rescued someday, if by chance some ship should happen by . . . I say 'by chance' because our island is none too large; it lacks even a port in which a ship might take shelter, and I fear that it may well lie off the usual shipping routes, too far south for ships frequenting the archipelagoes of the Pacific, and too far north for those traveling to Australia by way of Cape Horn. I don't wish to conceal any aspect of our situation from you . . ."

"And you're quite right, my dear Cyrus," the reporter quickly rejoined. "You are dealing with men here. They have faith in you, and you can count on them. —Do you not agree, my friends?"

"I will obey you in all things, Mr. Cyrus," said Harbert, clasping the engineer's hand.

"My master, always and everywhere!" cried Neb.

"As for me," said the sailor, "may I lose my good name if ever I shrink before a task, and with your help, Mr. Smith, we'll make our island a little America! We'll build cities, we'll construct a railway, we'll lay telegraph lines, and one fine day, when the island has been completely transformed, completely developed, completely civilized, we'll go and offer it to the Union! I only ask one thing."

"And what is that?" asked the reporter.

"That we no longer think of ourselves as castaways, but as colonists, whose mission is to colonize this land!"

Cyrus Smith could not hold back a smile, and the sailor's motion was adopted. Then the engineer thanked his companions, adding that he was relying on their energy and on help from above.

"Well, let's be off to the Chimneys!" cried Pencroff.

"One moment, my friends," answered Cyrus Smith. "I think it would be a good idea to give a name to our island, and also to the capes, promontories, and streams we have before us."

"Capital," said the reporter. "That will greatly simplify things in the future, when we have to give or receive instructions."

"Right you are," said the sailor. "It's no small thing to be able to say where you're going or where you've come from. At least we'll feel like we're somewhere!"

"The Chimneys, for instance," said Harbert.

"Right!" answered Pencroff. "That was a handy name to have, and it came to me just like that. Shall we keep that name for our first dwelling, Mr. Cyrus?"

"Yes, Pencroff, since that was the name you gave it."

"Good! and the rest will be easy," the sailor cheerfully replied. "Let's give everything names, like the Robinsons, whose story Harbert used to read to me: 'Deliverance Bay,' 'Whale Island,' 'False Hope Point'!..."

"Or else we could name them after Mr. Smith," answered Harbert, "Mr. Spilett, Neb!..."

"My name!" cried Neb, his smile revealing his gleaming white teeth.

"Why not?" Pencroff replied. " 'Port Neb,' that's grand! And 'Cape Gideon'..."

"I'd rather we gave them names borrowed from our own land," the reporter answered, "so as to remind us of America."

"Yes, for the principal locations," Cyrus Smith then said, "for the bays or seas, I most certainly concur. Let us, for example, give to that vast eastern bay the name Union Bay, to the broad indentation to the south the name Washington Bay, to the mountain on which we now stand, Mount Franklin, to the lake spread before us, Lake Grant. These are fine and noble names, my friends, which will serve to remind us of our homeland and the great citizens who have honored her; but for the rivers, gulfs, capes, and promontories before us, let us rather find designations that recall their particular form. Those will be far easier to remember, and more practical as well. The island's curious forms will only make our task the easier. And, in the coming days, each time we happen upon some new geological feature—streams and rivers in the forests, coves or inlets along the shore—we will find names for them by the same method. What do you say, my friends?"

The engineer's suggestion was unanimously approved. The island lay before their eyes like an unfolded map on a table, and they had only to give a name to every bulge and concavity along the coastline, to every element of the island's relief. Gideon Spilett would note them down as they proceeded, and the geographical nomenclature of the island would be settled.

First of all, for the two bays and the mountain, they adopted the engineer's suggestions: Union Bay, Washington Bay, and Mount Franklin.

"Now," said the reporter, "for that peninsula jutting from the southwestern corner of the island I suggest the name Serpentine Peninsula, and for the hook at its farthest point the name Reptile End, for to me it looks very like the tail of a great reptile."

"Adopted," said the engineer.

"Next," said Harbert, "on the other side of the island, that gulf that looks so like an open jaw might be called Shark Gulf."

"A fine idea!" cried Pencroff. "And we'll round it out by naming the two halves of the jaw Cape Mandible."

"But there are two capes," the reporter observed.

"Well then," answered Pencroff, "we'll have Cape Mandible North and Cape Mandible South."

"I've got that written down," Gideon Spilett replied.

"We have yet to name the point on the southeast coast," said Pencroff.

"In Union Bay?" answered Harbert.

"Cape Claw," Neb immediately answered, as eager as the others to become the godfather of some part of his domain.

And, in truth, Neb had found an excellent name, for the cape did indeed resemble the powerful claw of the fantastic animal evoked by the island's singular outline.

Pencroff was delighted with this game, and his pleasure was contagious. Soon the colonists' slightly overexcited imaginations had devised the following names:

for the river that provided their drinking water, not far from where the balloon had dropped them, the Mercy—in sincere thanks to Providence;

for the islet on which the castaways had first set foot, Safety Island;

for the plateau atop the towering wall of granite, above the Chimneys, overlooking the whole of the vast bay, Longview Plateau;

finally, for the great swath of impenetrable forest blanketing Serpentine Peninsula, the Forests of the Far West.

The naming of the visible, known parts of the island was thus complete; new names would be found for each new discovery in times to come.

As for the orientation of the island, the engineer had determined from the height and position of the sun that Union Bay and Longview Plateau lay roughly to their east. But the next day, by noting the exact times of the rising and setting of the sun, and observing its position midway between those two times, he would discover the precise location of the north, for in the austral hemisphere the high point of the sun's apparent arc over the earth will always lie to the north of an observer on the ground, and not to the south as in the boreal hemisphere.

Now their work was done, and the colonists were about to descend Mount Franklin and return to the Chimneys when Pencroff cried out:

"Well, what a lot of scatterbrains we are!"

"Why is that?" asked Gideon Spilett, who had closed his notebook and risen to his feet, ready to set off for home.

"What about the island? How can we have forgotten to find a name for the island?"

Harbert was about to suggest that they give it the name of the engineer, an idea his companions would have warmly applauded; but before he could speak Cyrus Smith said simply:

"Let us give it the name of a great citizen, my friends, a man now engaged in a fight for the unity of the American republic! Let us call it Lincoln Island!"

The engineer's suggestion was answered by three loud hurrahs.

And that evening, before they slept, the new colonists spoke together of their distant land; they discussed the terrible war, and the blood spilled over her fertile fields; they did not doubt that the South would soon be vanquished, and that, thanks to the noble labors of Grant, of Lincoln, the cause of the North—the cause of justice—would soon triumph!

The date was March 30th, 1865. They could not have known that sixteen days later a terrible crime would be committed in Washington, and that Abraham Lincoln would be felled on Good Friday by a fanatic's bullet.

XII

The colonists of Lincoln Island took one last look around them, then circled the crater along its narrow rim; a half-hour later, they were back on the plateau where they had camped the night before.

It then occurred to Pencroff that this would be a good time for breakfast, and this led to the question of setting their two watches, one belonging to Cyrus Smith and the other to the reporter.

As we know, Gideon Spilett's watch had never been touched by the seawater, since he had been thrown directly onto the sand, beyond the reach of the waves. This instrument was a veritable pocket chronometer, manufactured to the most exacting standards, and the reporter was careful to rewind it each and every day.

As for the engineer's watch, it had inevitably run down as he lay half lifeless among the dunes.

The engineer thus now rewound his timepiece; estimating by the height of the sun that it must be approximately nine o'clock in the morning, he set it to that time.

Gideon Spilett was about to do the same when the engineer stopped him with a gesture, saying:

"No, my dear Spilett, wait. You've left your watch on Richmond time, have you not?"

"Yes, Cyrus."

"Consequently, your watch is set to the longitude of that city, which is roughly the same as that of Washington?"

"Surely."

"Leave it just as it is. Take great care to rewind it faithfully, but do not adjust the hands. It might be of use to us."

"How so?" the sailor thought to himself.

Their appetite was such that the store of game and pine nuts was soon exhausted. But this did not trouble Pencroff, for he was intending to replenish their supply on the way home. Top, whose share was quite mean, would surely find some new game among the undergrowth. The sailor then thought of asking the engineer if he could create gunpowder, as well as one or two hunting rifles, believing that neither of these would prove particularly difficult for his companion.

As they left the plateau, Cyrus Smith suggested that they take a different route to return to the Chimneys. He wanted a closer view of Lake Grant and the glorious forest that surrounded it. And so they set out along a ridge through the foothills, where the creek that fed the lake probably had its source. The colonists had already begun to make free use of the proper names they had just chosen, and this greatly eased their exchange of ideas. Harbert and Pencroff—one young and the other slightly childlike—were enchanted, and as they walked, the sailor said:

"This is the stuff, Harbert! Don't you think? We can't possibly lose our way, my boy. Whether we pass by Lake Grant or return to the Mercy through the Forests of the Far West, either way, we can't help but reach Longview Plateau, and consequently Union Bay!"

It had been agreed that they would take care not to stray too far from one another as they walked. The thick forests were undoubtedly home to many dangerous animals, and they would have to remain on their guard. Pencroff, Harbert, and Neb generally walked ahead of the others, preceded by Top, who searched every nook and cranny around him. The reporter and the engineer stayed together, Gideon Spilett taking note of every incident, the engineer generally silent, occasionally straying from his path to pick up some object, some mineral or vegetable substance, which he then pocketed without comment.

"What the devil is he picking up?" murmured Pencroff. "I can't see anything worth bending over for, no matter how hard I look!"

By ten o'clock the little troop was descending the lower slopes of Mount Franklin. Nothing grew here but bushes and an occasional tree.

Pencroff walked ahead of the others, preceded by Top.

Before them lay a plain, about a mile long, leading up to the edge of the woods; the arid, sunbaked soil beneath their feet was of a yellowish tint. Large blocks of basalt—which, if Bischof's findings are accurate, must have taken some 350 million years to cool and solidify—lay scattered over the deeply rutted plain. They saw no sign of hardened lava, however, whose flow was confined to the volcano's northern slopes.

Cyrus Smith's hope was that this route would soon bring them to the creek, assuming that its course ran beneath the trees on the edge of the plain. But suddenly he saw Harbert sprinting toward him from up ahead, while Neb and the sailor hid behind the rocks.

"What is it, my boy?" asked Gideon Spilett.

"Smoke," answered Harbert. "There's smoke coming from between the rocks, not a hundred paces away."

"Men, here?" cried the reporter.

"Let's not show ourselves until we know who we're dealing with," answered Cyrus Smith. "If there are any natives to be found on the island, I'm more reluctant than eager to meet them. Where's Top?"

"Top's gone on ahead."

"And he isn't barking?"

"No."

"That's odd. All the same, let's try to call him back."

A few moments later, the engineer, Gideon Spilett, and Harbert had joined their two companions, and, like them, they took cover behind a basalt boulder.

From there they clearly saw billows of smoke rising through the air. The smoke was of a very distinctive yellow color.

Called to heel by his master's discreet whistle, Top immediately returned. The engineer signaled to his companions to stay where they were, then slipped between the rocks.

The colonists remained crouching behind the boulder, perfectly still, awaiting the results of this exploration with some apprehension. Then a shout from Cyrus Smith brought them running. Soon they were by his side, and at once they were struck by the disagreeable odor that impregnated the atmosphere.

The smoke had caused the engineer no small alarm at first, and with good reason; but the very characteristic odor soon allowed to him guess its source.

"This fire," he said, "or rather this smoke, is the work of nature itself.

This is nothing more than a sulfurous spring, thanks to which we'll have an effective treatment for any cases of laryngitis that may arise."

"Well now!" said Pencroff. "Pity I don't have a cold!"

The colonists proceeded toward the source of the smoke. There they saw a sodic sulfurous spring flowing abundantly between the rocks. Reacting with the oxygen in the air, the water gave off a sharp odor of hydrosulfuric acid.

Cyrus Smith dipped his hand into the stream and found the water viscous to the touch. He took a sip and discovered its taste to be faintly sweet. As for the temperature, he estimated it at ninety-five degrees Fahrenheit (thirty-five degrees centigrade above zero). And when Harbert asked him how he had reached this conclusion:

"Quite simply, my boy," he said, "because as I immersed my hand in that water, I felt no sensation of heat or cold. Therefore, its temperature must be that of the human body, which is approximately ninety-five degrees."

The sulfurous spring was of no particular use to them for the moment, and so the colonists continued toward the edge of the dense forest, a few hundred paces distant.

There, as they had supposed, they found the swift and limpid waters of the stream, flowing between high banks of red earth, whose color indicated the presence of iron oxide. Taking note of this color, they immediately dubbed it Red Creek.

It was nothing more than a large stream, deep and clear, fed by snowmelt from the mountain, half rill, half torrent, here flowing peacefully over the sand, there roaring over submerged rocks or tumbling in a lively cascade. Its course toward the lake covered a distance of a mile and a half; its width ranged from thirty to forty feet. The water was fresh, which suggested that the same must be true of the lake. And this might prove most advantageous, if they could find lodgings on the lakeshore more comfortable than the Chimneys.

As for the trees overhanging the creek banks a few hundred feet downstream, the majority belonged to the various species that flourish in the moderate zones of Australia or Tasmania, rather than the conifers that predominated in the areas around Longview Plateau. The trees had not yet lost their leaves, for this was early April, the equivalent of our October, which is to say the beginning of fall. The explorers discovered casuarina and eucalyptus trees, some of which, when spring returned, would produce a sweet manna in every way comparable to the manna of the East. There were stands of Australian cedars as well, in clearings carpeted with the tall grass known as "tussac" in New Holland; but the coconut tree, so abundant throughout the archipelagoes of the Pacific, appeared to be entirely absent from this island, which no doubt lay at too low a latitude.

"Pity!" said Harbert. "It's such a useful tree, with such wonderful fruit!"

A host of birds flocked among the sparse branches of the eucalyptus and casuarinas, where they had plenty of room to spread their wings. Black, white, or gray cockatoos; parrots and budgerigars, their plumage striped with all the colors of the rainbow; "king parrots," bright green with a red crown; blue lories; "blue-mountains"—they fluttered here and there, keeping up a deafening chatter, and with their brilliant and varied colors, it almost seemed the colonists were looking at them through a prism.

Suddenly, a strange concert of discordant voices burst from the middle of a thicket. In rapid succession the colonists heard birdcalls, the cries of quadrupeds, and a sort of clicking that they might well have thought to be emanating from the lips of a native islander. Forgetting the most elementary principles of prudence, Neb and Harbert leaped into the brush. Very fortunately, they found no fearsome beast or dangerous native, but simply a half-dozen birds whose varied songs emulated the sounds around them, and which they recognized as "blackcocks." A few well-placed blows from their clubs put a stop to the birds' mimicry, and promised the colonists an excellent dish for the evening's dinner.

Harbert also pointed out some magnificent pigeons with bronze-colored wings, some topped with a superb crest, others shrouded in green, like their fellows in Port Macquarie; but there was no way to reach them, no more than the ravens or magpies that fled before them in great flocks. A rifle loaded with grapeshot would have brought about a hecatomb of feathered creatures, but their only projectile weapons were stones, their only handheld weapons clubs, and these primitive implements were useless to them in the present circumstances.

Their insufficience was all the more clearly demonstrated a little later, when a band of quadrupeds fled past them—veritable flying mammals, hopping, bounding, making thirty-foot jumps, springing over the thickets at such great speeds and altitudes that they almost seemed to be leaping from tree to tree like squirrels.

"Kangaroos!" cried Harbert.

"Are they edible?" answered Pencroff.

"Braised kangaroo can rival the finest venison!" replied the reporter.

Before Gideon Spilett could finish this enticing sentence, the sailor was already after the kangaroos, followed by Neb and Harbert. Cyrus Smith called them back, to no avail. But the hunters' pursuit of their elastic prey proved no less vain, for the creatures bounced over the land like rubber balls. After a five-minute sprint, the hunters were quite out of breath, and the herd disappeared into the undergrowth. Top met with no more success than his masters.

"Mr. Cyrus," said Pencroff, when the engineer and the reporter had caught up with them, "Mr. Cyrus, we are in desperate need of rifles, as you see. Would it be possible to make some?"

"Perhaps," the engineer answered, "but let us begin by making bows and arrows, and I have no doubt that you'll soon become an archer every bit as accomplished as any Australian hunter."

"Bows and arrows!" said Pencroff, disdainfully. "Those are children's toys!"

"Now, don't be proud, friend Pencroff," answered the reporter. "Blood has been spilled by bows and arrows for many centuries, and all over the world. Gunpowder was only invented yesterday, and war is as ancient as the human race—alas!"

"Why, you've got a point there, Mr. Spilett," answered the sailor. "I should learn to think before I open my mouth. Beg pardon!"

Meanwhile, Harbert returned to the subject of kangaroos, in his unbounded enthusiasm for the study of natural science:

"Besides," he said, "what we just saw were the most difficult to catch of all the kangaroos. They were giant kangaroos, as we can tell from their long gray fur; but, if I'm not mistaken, there also exist black and red kangaroos, rock kangaroos, kangaroo rats, and we'll have a much easier time with those. There are no fewer than a dozen species..."

"Harbert," the sailor sententiously replied, "to my mind there's only one species of kangaroo, the 'kangaroo on a spit,' and that's the one we'll be missing tonight!"

They could not help but laugh on hearing Professor Pencroff's new classification. The good sailor could not conceal his regret at finding himself reduced to eating blackcock for dinner; but fortune was soon to smile on him again.

For Top, sensing that his own dinner was at stake, went nosing about hither and yon with an instinct sharpened by a ferocious appetite. Indeed, there would be precious little left over for the hunters if any game happened to find its way between his jaws, for Top seemed to be hunting purely on his own account; but Neb kept a close eye on him, and he was right to do so.

At about three o'clock the dog disappeared into the brush, and muted growls soon signaled that he was battling some sort of animal.

Neb ran forward, and, to be sure, he soon found Top greedily devouring a quadruped; ten seconds later it lay unrecognizable in the dog's stomach. Fortunately, however, he had come across a full nest, and had clearly felled three beasts at once, as two other rodents—for such was the order to which these animals belonged—lay on the ground, their necks neatly snapped.

Neb reappeared triumphant with a rodent in either hand. The beasts were somewhat larger than hares, with rudimentary tails and yellow coats sprinkled with greenish spots.

They had seen such animals before, and they remembered the name given to them by the people of their native land. They were maras, a variety of agouti, a little larger than their tropical counterparts—veritable rabbits of the Americas, with long ears, and jaws armed with five molars on each side, by which they can be distinguished from the agouti.

"Hurrah!" cried Pencroff. "The roast is here! Now we can go home."

After this brief interruption, their journey was resumed. The limpid waters of Red Creek still flowed beneath the vaulted branches of the casuarinas, banksias, and giant gum trees. Superb Liliaceae stood twenty feet tall. Other arborescent species unknown to the young naturalist overhung the stream, which could be heard murmuring in its cradle of verdure.

The stream was growing ever broader, and Cyrus Smith deduced that they were nearing its mouth—which, in fact, suddenly appeared before them as they emerged from a dense grove of beautiful trees.

The explorers had arrived at the western shore of Lake Grant. The spot was worthy of a closer look. That expanse of water, approximately seven miles in circumference and with a surface area of two hundred fifty acres,* was surrounded by a heterogenous forest. Looking east, through a

---

* Approximately two hundred hectares.

curtain of greenery picturesquely lifted at certain places, they saw the glinting horizon of the sea. To the north, the curve of the lakeshore was slightly concave, contrasting with the acute angle of its lower point. Numerous aquatic birds frequented the shores of this miniature Ontario, the "thousand islands" of its American homonym represented by a cluster of rocks emerging from the surface a few hundred feet from the southern shore. On these rocks lived a small community of kingfishers; serious and still, they perched overlooking the water, watching for fish to swim past, then abruptly dived with a piercing cry and reappeared holding their prey in their beaks. Elsewhere, both on the lakeshore and on that small islet, wild ducks strutted about in the company of pelicans, moorhens, redbeaks, philedons with their brush-shaped tongues, and one or two splendid menuras, whose tails imitate the graceful curve of a lyre.

The water of the lake was fresh, limpid, slightly dark, and—judging by the number of bubbles rising to the surface and forming concentric circles atop the water—unquestionably full of fish.

"What a magnificent lake!" said Gideon Spilett. "I can easily imagine living here!"

"And that's just what we'll do!" answered Cyrus Smith.

Hoping to return to the Chimneys by the shortest route, the colonists made for the angle formed by the junction of the two shores at the southern end of the lake. Not without difficulty, they struggled through thickets and brush never before thrust aside by human hand, and so proceeded toward the coastline and the north end of Longview Plateau. They traveled two miles in this direction; then, after the last curtain of trees, the grass-covered plateau appeared, and beyond it the unending sea.

To return to the Chimneys, they had only to continue obliquely across the plateau for a distance of one mile, then follow the slope down to the first bend of the Mercy. But the engineer was curious to know how and by what route the excess water flowed out of the lake, and so they continued northward for another mile and a half, beneath the trees. The spillway very likely lay somewhere in this vicinity, no doubt created by a rift in the granite. In other words, this lake was nothing other than a natural basin that had been gradually filled by the waters of the creek, and somewhere, no doubt, its overflow cascaded down the cliffs and continued onward to the sea. If such was the case, the engineer thought they might be able to make use of the waterfall's power, currently lost to the sea and profiting no one. And so they followed the shoreline of Lake Grant over the

Neb and Pencroff prepared a dish of grilled agouti …

plateau; but after another mile in that direction, Cyrus Smith had still not succeeded in discovering the spillway. Nevertheless, he knew that it had to exist, somewhere not too far away.

It was then four-thirty. The task of preparing their dinner called the colonists back to their home. The little band retraced its steps, and Cyrus Smith and his companions returned to the Chimneys by way of the left bank of the Mercy.

A fire was lit. The kitchen duties had naturally fallen to the Negro and the sailor, and soon Neb and Pencroff had skillfully prepared a dish of grilled agouti, greedily devoured by all.

Once the meal was over, just as they were about to surrender to their exhaustion, Cyrus Smith pulled from his pockets a number of small mineral samples, and spoke these few words:

"My friends, this is iron ore, this is a pyrite, this is clay, this is lime, this is coal. This is what nature has offered us. She has done her part in our common task! —And tomorrow we'll set about doing ours!"

XIII

*Top's Contribution.—Making Bows and Arrows.—A
Brickyard.—The Pottery Kiln.—Various Kitchen Utensils.—The
First Stew.—The Artemisia Plant.—The Southern Cross.—An
Important Astronomical Observation.*

"Well, Mr. Cyrus, where shall we begin?" Pencroff asked the engineer the
next morning.

"At the beginning," answered Cyrus Smith.

And the colonists would indeed have to start at the "beginning." They
lacked even the tools needed to make tools. The work that lay ahead of
them was far more daunting than that of nature herself, who, "having
plenty of time, spares every effort." Time was precisely what they lacked,
as the requirements for their subsistence would have to be met at once.
To be sure, they had nothing to invent, thanks to the long history of
human ingenuity; but they would be forced to create with their own
hands every object they might need. Their iron and steel were as yet
merely ore, their pottery clay, their clothes and linen only vegetal fibers.

It should also be said that these colonists were "men" in the fullest and
most admirable sense of the word. The engineer Smith could not have
been backed up by a more intelligent set of companions, nor ones more
devoted and zealous. He had questioned them at length. He knew all
their aptitudes.

Gideon Spilett was a reporter of great talent, with some knowledge of
all things because in his profession he had to know how to speak of all
things; both intellectually and physically, he had much to contribute to
the colonization of the island. He never balked at any task, and, passion-

ate hunter that he was, he would gladly make a duty of what had once been only a pleasure.

Harbert, that fine boy, already remarkably learned in the field of natural sciences, would be of no less considerable use to their common cause.

Neb was devotion personified. Nimble, intelligent, tireless, sturdy, bursting with good health, he knew a bit about working a forge and could not fail to be of great help to the colony.

As for Pencroff, not only had he sailed every ocean on the globe, he had also been a carpenter in the construction sites of Brooklyn, a tailor's assistant in his government's fleet, a gardener and farmer during his holidays, etc., and like all seagoing folk he was ever ready for anything, and competent in everything.

It would truly have been difficult to bring together five men better suited to this struggle against fate, or more likely to triumph in the end.

"At the beginning," Cyrus Smith had said, and by this he meant the construction of an apparatus which could be used to transform natural substances. As we know, heat plays a central role in all such transformations. And they had plenty of fuel, wood and coal both, close at hand and ready to use. Their first task, then, was to build a kiln.

"What will we use the kiln for?" asked Pencroff.

"To make pottery," answered Cyrus Smith.

"And what will we make the kiln with?"

"Bricks."

"And the bricks?"

"Clay. Come with me, my friends. I propose that we build our kiln where all the necessary raw materials can be found, as that will spare us the effort of transporting them. Neb will bring along some provisions, and we'll have all the fire we need to cook our meals."

"Very well," answered the reporter, "but how do we know we'll have all the food we need, since we have no weapons to hunt with?"

"Oh! if we only had a knife!" cried the sailor.

"Yes?" asked Cyrus Smith.

"If we only had a knife, I'd make a bow and arrow quick as you please, and our larders would be full of game!"

"Yes, a knife, some sort of sharp blade..." said the engineer, half to himself.

Just then his gaze settled on Top, who was running back and forth along the beach.

Suddenly a light appeared in Cyrus Smith's eyes.

"Here, Top!" he said.

The dog ran to his master. He took Top's head between his hands, and, removing the animal's collar, he broke it into two pieces, saying:

"Here are two knives, Pencroff!"

The sailor let out two great hurrahs in reply. Top's collar was made of a narrow band of tempered steel. They had only to sharpen the edges against a piece of sandstone, then file away any remaining imperfections with still finer sandstone. A plentiful supply of that arenaceous stone could be found on the beach, and so, two hours later, the colony's tool collection had acquired its first two elements: two sharp blades, fitted into sturdy wooden handles.

Thus they made their first tool. This achievement was celebrated as a veritable triumph, and not without reason. A crucial achievement it was, and a timely one.

The hour had now come to set off. Cyrus Smith's intention was to return to the lake's western shore, where he had found the lump of clay he brought back to the Chimneys the day before. And so they walked alongside the Mercy, then across Longview Plateau, and after a journey of five miles at most they arrived at a clearing some two hundred paces from Lake Grant.

Along the way, Harbert had discovered a tree whose branches the Indians of South America use to make their bows. It was a "crejimba" tree, a member of the palm family, but with inedible fruit. Long, straight branches were cut from the tree and stripped of their leaves. These they now shaped, tapering them at the ends but leaving them thicker in the middle. Next they would need to find a plant that could provide them with a bowstring, and so they did: a species of the Malvaceae family, a *hibiscus heterophyllous*, whose fibers are remarkably tough, almost comparable to animal tendons. With this Pencroff constructed several bows of no small range and power. All they needed now were arrows. These were easily made from straight, rigid, unknotted branches; but if they were to be effective as weapons they would need a sharp point made of some material similar to iron, and this would not be so easy to find. But, as Pencroff told himself, he had done his part; the rest he would leave up to chance.

The colonists arrived at the area they had visited the day before. Here the soil was composed of the very kind of figuline clay used to manufacture bricks and tiles, ideally suited to their present purpose. The procedure was not an arduous one. They had only to thicken the figuline with sand, form this material into bricks, and bake them over a wood fire.

Ordinarily, bricks are formed in wooden molds, but the colonists would have to make do with their hands. That day and the next were devoted to this task. The clay, first diluted with water and then kneaded by the workmen's hands and feet, was divided into identical blocks. Without a machine, an experienced worker can produce up to ten thousand bricks in a twelve-hour period; but in their two days of work, the five brickmakers of Lincoln Island produced no more than three thousand. These were then laid out in rows on the ground, there to remain until they were dry enough to proceed to the baking process, three or four days later.

On April 2nd, Cyrus Smith turned to the question of the island's orientation.

The day before, he had noted the precise hour at which the sun disappeared beneath the horizon, correcting for refraction. Just as precisely, he observed the time of its reappearance the following morning. A total of eleven hours and thirty-six minutes had elapsed between sunset and sunrise. Thus, six hours and twelve minutes after rising that day, the sun would reach the exact midpoint of its journey, and the point that it then occupied in the heavens would be due north.*

At the appointed hour, Cyrus Smith carefully observed the position of the sun. He then located two trees that lay in perfect alignment with the celestial sphere at that moment, giving him an invariable indicator of the meridian's direction, which he would need for his subsequent endeavors.

Two days remained before the bricks would be ready for baking, and these were devoted to the renewal of their fuel supply. Branches were cut from around the clearing, and every branch and twig lying beneath the trees was collected. This pause also offered an excellent opportunity for hunting, of which the colonists took full advantage, for Pencroff now possessed several dozen arrows armed with very sharp points. These points were provided by Top, who had brought down a porcupine, an animal of no great value as a foodstuff, but incontestably useful for its abundant spines. These were fixed firmly to the ends of the arrows, which had been

---

* The sun did indeed rise at 5:48 in the morning and set at 6:12 in the evening on that date and at that latitude.

feathered with cockatoo plumes to ensure that they would fly straight and true. Harbert and the reporter soon became expert bowmen.

The inhabitants of the Chimneys would thus never lack for game: capybara, pigeon, agouti, capercaillie, etc. Most of these animals were killed in the forests on the left bank of the Mercy, to which they gave the name Jacamar Woods in memory of the feathered beast that Pencroff and Harbert had pursued in the course of their first exploration.

They ate this game fresh, but they preserved a number of capybara hams as well, spicing them with aromatic leaves and smoking them over a fire of green wood. Very nourishing their meals were, but after many meals of roast meat, night after night, they would have been delighted to hear a humble stew bubbling merrily on the stove. But the stew would have to wait until they had a pot, and the pot would have to wait until they had built a kiln.

Their wanderings in the woods surrounding the brickyard had more than once confronted them with evidence of large animals. The species could not be determined, but the prints showed them to be armed with fearsome claws. Cyrus Smith urged his companions to remain on guard at all times, for the forest might very well be filled with such dangerous beasts.

And he was right to do so, for one day Gideon Spilett and Harbert spotted an animal that looked very much like a jaguar. The feline did not attack, and in this they were fortunate, as they could have been badly wounded. But as soon as they had procured real weapons—which is to say the rifles that Pencroff was pleading for—Gideon Spilett vowed to wage a merciless war against these beasts, and rid the island of them forever.

No work was done to improve their living conditions in the Chimneys over the next few days, for the engineer was hoping to find more suitable accommodations in the near future, even if it meant building a house with their own hands. They merely laid fresh litters of moss and dried leaves atop the sand in the Chimneys' corridors, and on these rather primitive mats the workers, thoroughly exhausted after their busy day, fell into the deepest, most untroubled sleep.

They also counted up the number of days they had spent on Lincoln Island since their landing, and they kept careful track of this from then on. On April 5th, which was a Wednesday, it had been twelve days since the wind had tossed the castaways onto this shore.

On April 6th, the engineer and his companions gathered in the clearing for the baking of the bricks. Naturally, this procedure would take place in the open air, and not in a kiln; or rather, the stack of bricks would be nothing other than an enormous kiln which would bake itself. Bundles of twigs were laid out on the ground to serve as fuel, and these were surrounded with row after row of dried bricks, which soon formed a large cube with gaps in the walls to act as vents. The building of this cube took up the entire day, and it was only that evening that they set the bundled twigs alight.

No one slept that night. They all stayed up to keep a careful watch over the fire, ensuring that it did not die down.

The procedure took forty-eight hours, and succeeded flawlessly. While they waited for the smoking pile of bricks to cool, Neb and Pencroff, under the direction of Cyrus Smith, used a sledge made of interlaced branches to haul in several loads of limestone—a very common stone, abundant in the area north of the lake. Once the heat had broken down the stones, they would produce great quantities of rich dry lime, as pure as if it had been produced by the calcination of chalk or marble. Mixed with sand, whose effect is to attenuate the shrinkage of the cement as it dries, this lime would furnish an excellent mortar.

The result of these various labors was that on April 9th the engineer had at his disposal several thousand bricks and a good quantity of lime, ready for use.

Without a moment wasted, they now began to construct the kiln in which they would fire the various pieces of clay pottery required for their domestic needs. The undertaking posed no great difficulty. Five days later, the kiln was loaded with coal—an exposed vein of which the engineer had discovered near the mouth of Red Creek—and soon the first wreaths of smoke were billowing from a chimney some twenty feet tall. The clearing had been transformed into a factory, and Pencroff was not far from believing that this kiln would provide them with all the many products modern industry has devised.

For the moment, however, the colonists confined themselves to simple pottery, unextraordinary in appearance but most useful for cooking food. The raw material was nothing other than the clay found in the soil, to which Cyrus Smith added a little lime and some quartz. The substance thus produced was in fact precisely what is known as "pipe clay," and with this they made pots, cups molded over small round stones, plates, large

The colonists confined themselves to simple pottery.

jugs and basins to hold water, etc. The form of these objects was graceless and imperfect; but after they had been fired at high temperature, the kitchen in the Chimneys was equipped with an array of utensils as precious to them as the finest porcelain.

Curious as to whether the clay Cyrus Smith had compounded truly deserved its name, Pencroff now undertook to make a number of rather crude pipes, which he found charming; but alas! there was no tobacco to fill them with. And, it must be said, for poor Pencroff this was a terrible privation.

"But the tobacco will come along in time, like everything else!" he sometimes repeated, in his moments of absolute and enthusiastic confidence.

These tasks occupied the colonists until April 15th. They never failed to put their time to the best possible use. When they were potters, pottery was their sole concern. When the time came for Cyrus Smith to change them into blacksmiths, they would be blacksmiths. But—since the next day was a Sunday, and not just any Sunday, but Easter—they unanimously agreed to sanctify it with a day of rest. These Americans were religious men, conscientiously observant of the Bible's teachings, and their present circumstances could only heighten their faith in the Author of all things.

The evening of April 15th, then, they returned to the Chimneys to stay. They brought the rest of the pottery with them, and the kiln was extinguished until such time as it was needed again. This return was marked by a fortunate incident: the engineer's discovery of a substance they could use as a replacement for tinder. As we know, that spongy, velvet-textured matter is derived from a certain kind of mushroom, of the polyporus variety. When properly treated, it becomes extremely inflammable, especially when it has been saturated with cannon powder or boiled in a solution of nitrate or potassium chlorate. But so far they had never come across such polypores, nor even morels, which can be put to the same use. That day, catching sight of a plant belonging to the artemisia family, which includes among its principal species absinthe, citronella, tarragon, Alpine genepi, etc., the engineer pulled several handfuls of shoots from the ground. Then, offering them to the sailor:

"Here, Pencroff," he said, "this will make you happy."

Pencroff carefully scrutinized the plants, which were covered with long, silky bristles, and a cottony down on the leaves.

"Why, what is it, Mr. Cyrus?" asked Pencroff. "Merciful heavens! Is it tobacco?"

"No," answered Cyrus Smith, "it's artemisia, Chinese artemisia to be specific, and for us it will be tinder."

For that artemisia, when carefully dried, furnishes a highly inflammable substance, later made considerably more so when the engineer impregnated it with potassium nitrate, deposits of which could be found here and there on the island, and which is nothing other than saltpeter.

That evening the colonists gathered in the central chamber to enjoy a most agreeable dinner. Neb had prepared a stew of agouti and spiced capybara ham, to which they added the boiled tubers of *Caladium macrorhizum,* a sort of herbaceous plant of the Araceae family, which grows to the size of a small tree in the tropical zones. These rhizomes were delicious to eat, and very nutritious, rather similar to the substance sold in England under the name "Portland sago." They served as a kind of substitute for bread, which the colonists of Lincoln Island still lacked.

Once dinner was over, before retiring for the night, Cyrus Smith and his companions stepped out onto the beach for some fresh air. It was eight o'clock in the evening. The night promised to be a magnificent one. The moon, which had been full five days earlier, had not yet risen; but the horizon was already silvered by the gentle, pale nuances of what could be called the lunar dawn. At the zenith of this southern sky the circumpolar constellations shone brilliantly, and the brightest of all was the Southern Cross, which the engineer had hailed a few days earlier from atop Mount Franklin.

For many minutes Cyrus Smith silently observed that splendid constellation, which bears two stars of the first magnitude at its summit and base, a star of the second magnitude in the left crosspiece, and a star of the third magnitude in the right.

Then, after several moments' thought:

"Harbert," he asked the boy, "today is the fifteenth of April, is it not?"

"Yes, Mr. Cyrus," Harbert answered.

"Well then, if I'm not mistaken, tomorrow will be one of the four days of the year on which real solar time coincides with mean time—which is to say, my boy, that tomorrow, give or take a few seconds, the sun will reach its highest point in the sky precisely when the clock shows noon. And so, if the weather is fine, I believe I can calculate the island's longitude to within a few degrees."

"Without instruments, without a sextant?" asked Gideon Spilett.

"Yes," replied the engineer. "And since the sky is so pristine tonight, I will try to determine our latitude this very evening by calculating the height of the Southern Cross, which is to say the southern celestial pole, above the horizon. For you understand, my friends, that it is not enough to have discovered we are on an island; before we embark on the project of making a life for ourselves here, we must, insofar as possible, determine our island's distance from the American continent, or the Australian continent, or the principal archipelagoes of the Pacific."

"Indeed," said the reporter, "rather than building a house, we might well do better to build a boat, if it turns out we're no more than a hundred miles from inhabited land."

"And that is why," replied Cyrus Smith, "I shall try to determine Lincoln Island's latitude this evening, and at noon tomorrow I will attempt to calculate its longitude."

If the engineer had owned a sextant, a device that uses reflection to make extremely precise measurements of the angular distance between objects, this undertaking would have been a simple one. That evening, by the height of the celestial pole, and the next day by the arrival of the sun at its highest point, he would have obtained the island's coordinates. Lacking such a device, he would have to find another solution.

Cyrus Smith thus returned to the Chimneys. By firelight, he carved two flat rulers and joined their ends together to form a sort of compass whose arms could be separated at any width. The pivot point was fixed by a thick acacia thorn, plucked from among the firewood.

Having constructed this instrument, the engineer returned to the beach; but since he had to determine the height of the celestial pole above a precisely determined horizon—the horizon of the sea, that is—and since the southern horizon lay concealed behind Cape Claw, he had to find a more suitable standpoint. The ideal place would of course have been the island's south-facing shoreline, but that would have required him to cross the deep Mercy, which seemed too great a nuisance.

Consequently, Cyrus Smith resolved to make his observation from atop Longview Plateau, remembering that he would have to take into account his elevation above sea level—a height that he intended to calculate the next day by a simple procedure of elementary geometry.

The colonists thus climbed to the plateau by way of the left bank of the Mercy, and positioned themselves on the ridge that ran from northwest to southeast, formed by the line of capriciously shaped rocks over-looking the river.

This part of the plateau stood some fifty feet higher than the bluffs of the right bank, which sloped in two directions, to the far end of Cape Claw and to the southern coast of the island. No obstacle blocked their view from this point; the horizon was unobstructed over half of its circumference, from the cape up to Reptile End. To the south, the first glimmers of the rising moon shone over the horizon, clearly distinguishing sky from ocean, and allowing a precise observation of the level of the sea.

At that time of the year, the Southern Cross lay in an upturned position, with the alpha star, the closest to the austral celestial pole, at the bottom.

This constellation is not situated as directly over the Antarctic pole as the North Star is over the Arctic pole. The alpha star lies at approximately twenty-seven degrees, but Cyrus Smith was fully aware of this, and planned to correct for the discrepancy in his calculations. He was also careful to observe the star at the precise moment of its passage over the meridian, which would greatly ease his task.

Thus, Cyrus Smith pointed one arm of his compass at the ocean horizon and the other at the alpha star, just as he would have done with the telescopic lens of a repeating circle, and the angle of the two arms gave him the angular distance between the alpha star and the horizon. In order to fix this angle permanently, he used thorns to attach a third strip of wood between the other two, running transversely from one arm of the compass to the other, and so maintaining the angle of their separation.

There was nothing more to do but calculate the size of this angle and make the necessary adjustment to compensate for his elevation above the sea, which meant that he would have to measure the height of the plateau. The width of the angle would give him the height of the alpha star, and consequently that of the celestial pole above the horizon, which is to say the latitude of the island, since the latitude of any point on the globe is invariably equal to the height of the celestial pole above the horizon at that point.

These calculations were set aside until the following day, and at ten o'clock, the colonists were sound asleep.

XIV

Measuring the Granite Wall.—An Application of the Theorem of Similar Triangles.—The Island's Latitude.—An Excursion Northward.—A Bed of Oysters.—Plans for the Future.—The Sun at its Zenith.—The Coordinates of Lincoln Island.

The next day, April 16th—Easter Sunday—the colonists emerged from the Chimneys at daybreak and undertook to wash their clothes and linen. The engineer planned to make soap as soon as he could find the necessary raw materials: soda or potash, fat or oil. The all-important question of new clothing would also be dealt with in due time. In any case, their present clothes were more than sturdy enough to withstand the rigors of manual labor, and could be counted on to last another six months at least. But all of this would depend on the location of the island with respect to inhabited lands, and that they would determine this very day, weather permitting.

As it happened, the morning sun was rising over an unsullied horizon, promising a magnificent day, one of those fine autumn days that are like summer's final farewell.

Their task, then, was to complete the measurements taken the day before by gauging Longview Plateau's elevation above sea level.

"Won't you need an instrument like the one you used yesterday?" Harbert asked the engineer.

"No, my child," the latter answered, "we'll proceed in a different way this time, but the measurement will be no less precise."

Ever desirous of new knowledge, Harbert followed the engineer as he strode away from the granite wall. Pencroff, Neb, and the reporter busied themselves with other tasks in the meantime.

Cyrus Smith had chosen as his tool a sort of straight rod, about twelve feet long. He measured its length as precisely as possible by comparing it to his own height, which he knew to within a sixteenth of an inch. Harbert carried a plumb line—a simple stone tied to the end of a flexible fiber—that Cyrus Smith had handed him.

Having come to within some twenty feet of the water's edge, and about five hundred feet from the perpendicular granite wall, Cyrus Smith sank his rod two feet into the sand. He used the plumb line to ensure that it stood perfectly perpendicular to the line of the horizon, then carefully braced it so that it would maintain this position.

With this, he backed away until he reached a point where, as he lay on the ground, the visual ray leaving his eye touched both the tip of the rod and the peak of the granite wall. He carefully marked this point with a small stick.

Next, speaking to Harbert:

"Do you know the basic principles of geometry?" he asked.

"A little, Mr. Cyrus," Harbert answered, somewhat reluctant to commit himself.

"Do you remember the properties of two similar triangles?"

"Yes," answered Harbert. "Their corresponding sides are proportional."

"Well, my child, I've just constructed two similar triangles, both of them right triangles: the first, the smaller one, has as its sides the perpendicular rod, the distance from the small stick to the bottom of the rod, and, as its hypotenuse, my line of sight; the second has as its sides the perpendicular wall, whose height we are here to measure, the distance from the stake to the base of the wall, and once again, as its hypotenuse, my line of sight—which, as it happens, is the continuation of the hypotenuse of the first triangle."

"Oh! Mr. Cyrus, I understand!" cried Harbert. "Just as the distance from the stick to the rod is proportional to the distance from the stake to the base of the wall, the height of the rod is proportional to the height of the wall."

"Precisely, Harbert," the engineer answered, "and once we have measured the first two distances, knowing as we do the height of the rod, a

He lay on the ground...

simple proportional calculation will give us the height of the wall, which will be much easier than trying to measure it directly."

The two horizontal distances were now determined; as their measuring stick they used the rod itself, knowing its length above the sand to be exactly ten feet long.

The first distance, between the stick and the point where the rod had been thrust into the ground, measured fifteen feet.

The second distance, between the stick and the base of the wall, was five hundred feet.

Having completed their measurements, Cyrus Smith and the boy returned to the Chimneys.

There the engineer took a flat stone that he had brought back from one of his excursions, a sort of slaty schist on which figures could be scratched with a pointed seashell. He now drew up the following ratio:

$$15 : 500 :: 10 : x$$

$$500 \times 10 = 5,000$$

$$5,000 \ / \ 15 = 333.33$$

From which it was established that the granite wall measured 333 feet in height.*

Cyrus Smith then picked up the instrument he had constructed the day before. The angle of separation between the two strips of wood gave him the angular distance from the alpha star to the horizon. He very carefully measured the degree of that angle, using a circle which he had divided into three hundred sixty equal parts. The angle measured ten degrees. Hence, the total angular distance between the celestial pole and the horizon, adding the twenty-seven degrees separating the alpha from the antarctic celestial pole, and reducing to sea level the elevation of the plateau where he had made his observations, proved to be thirty-seven degrees. Cyrus Smith thereby concluded that Lincoln Island was situated at thirty-seven degrees south latitude, or rather, allowing a deviation of five degrees to compensate for the approximative nature of the measurements, that it must lie somewhere between the thirty-fifth and fortieth parallels.

In order to complete his calculation of the island's coordinates, the

---

* In English feet, which are equivalent to thirty centimeters.

engineer would now have to determine its longitude. This he intended to do that very day, at noon, when the sun would reach its highest point in the sky.

It was decided that they would use their day of rest for a long walk—or, more precisely, an excursion—to the area between the north end of the lake and Shark Gulf; if time permitted, they would pursue their explorations as far as the southern shore of Cape Mandible South. They would stop for lunch amid the dunes, and return home at nightfall.

At eight-thirty in the morning, the little band was walking along the channel that separated their shore from Safety Island. Great flocks of birds could be seen striding gravely over the sand across the channel. These were diving birds of the penguin species, easily recognized by their disagreeable cries, reminiscent of the braying of an ass. Pencroff considered them purely from an alimentary point of view, and he was not entirely displeased to learn that their flesh is quite edible, although almost black in color.

They also discovered a number of large amphibians crawling over the islet, probably seals, which seemed to have chosen this place as a refuge. This time the question of comestibility did not come up, for it is well known that their oily flesh has a detestable taste; nevertheless, Cyrus Smith observed them with great interest, and, without further explanation, announced to his companions that they would soon be paying a visit to the islet.

The colonists walked along a shoreline strewn with innumerable shells, some of which would have been the pride of any amateur malacologist's collection: *Phasianellae, Terebratulae, Trigoniae,* and many more. Of far greater interest to them, however, was a vast oyster bed, exposed at low tide, which Neb pointed out between the rocks some four miles from the Chimneys.

"Neb knows how to put his time to good use," cried Pencroff, observing this expanse of *Ostraceae* lying just offshore.

"A happy discovery indeed," said the reporter. "I've heard it said that every oyster produces fifty to sixty thousand eggs a year; if that's true, we have an inexhaustible supply."

"Yes, but oysters are not particularly nourishing," said Harbert.

"That's true," answered Cyrus Smith. "The oyster contains very little nitrogenous material, and a man attempting to live on oysters alone would need to eat no fewer than fifteen to sixteen dozen per day."

"Well!" answered Pencroff. "We can each have dozens of dozens, and there'll still be plenty more! What do you say we bring some along with us for lunch?"

And, without awaiting a response, knowing full well that his suggestion was approved in advance, the sailor and Neb plucked a generous helping of mollusks from the rocks. Neb had woven a sort of net out of hibiscus fibers, which he was now using to carry their lunch; they placed the oysters inside, then continued down the shoreline between the dunes and the sea.

From time to time, Cyrus Smith consulted his watch. His observation of the sun had to be made at exactly noon, and he would need some time beforehand to make the necessary preparations.

The terrain in this region was extremely arid, and it continued unchanged up to the point that closed off Union Bay, which they had dubbed Cape Mandible South. The colonists had before them only a vast expanse of sand and seashells, mixed with volcanic debris. A few seabirds frequented this desolate coastline: gulls, large albatrosses, and wild ducks, which understandably aroused Pencroff's desire. He fired off a few arrows, but without success, for the birds rarely landed, and it was next to impossible to shoot them down in mid-flight.

This led the sailor to repeat once more to the engineer:

"You see, Mr. Cyrus, we're in desperate need of hunting rifles. You must admit, these bows and arrows leave much to be desired!"

"I quite agree, Pencroff," answered the reporter, "but it's up to you! Find us some iron for the barrels, steel for the hammers, saltpeter, coal, and sulfur for the powder, mercury and nitric acid for the fulminate, and lead for the bullets, and Cyrus will make us some first-class rifles."

"Oh!" answered the engineer. "I'm sure we can find all that somewhere on the island; the greater problem is that a firearm is an extremely delicate instrument, impossible to build without very specialized and precise tools. But we shall see about that later."

"Why," cried Pencroff, "oh, why did we have to jettison all our weapons, and all our tools, and even our pocketknives?"

"But if we hadn't thrown them overboard, Pencroff, we're the ones who would have ended up being dumped into the sea!" said Harbert.

"Why yes, that's very true, my boy!" answered the sailor.

Then, moving on to another idea:

"But I've just thought of something: what must Jonathan Forster and his cohorts have thought the next morning when they found the square empty and the balloon vanished!"

"Now, that is truly the least of my concerns!" said the reporter.

"And to think this was all my own idea!" said Pencroff with a self-satisfied air.

"And a wonderful idea it was, Pencroff," answered Gideon Spilett, laughing. "Just look where it's got us!"

"I'd rather be here than in the hands of the Southerners!" cried the sailor. "Especially since Mr. Cyrus was so kind as to join us!"

"I couldn't agree more!" answered the reporter. "Besides, what do we lack here? Nothing!"

"Except for…everything!" answered Pencroff, who then let out a great laugh, his broad shoulders quaking. "But we'll find a way out of here one fine day!"

"And perhaps sooner than you imagine, my friends," the engineer then said, "if it turns out that Lincoln Island is not too distant from some inhabited archipelago or continent. We'll know within the hour. I have no map of the Pacific Ocean, but I have a very clear picture of its southern reaches in my memory. The latitude that I determined yesterday puts Lincoln Island somewhere between New Zealand to the west and the Chilean coast to the east. But the distance between those two lands is at least six thousand miles. We have now to determine where the island lies within that expanse of ocean, and that is precisely what we will learn from our longitude, which we will soon know, hopefully with sufficient accuracy."

"The Pomotou archipelago would be the closest to us in latitude, wouldn't it?" asked Harbert.

"Yes," answered the engineer, "but it's more than twelve hundred miles from here to there."

"What about that way?" asked Neb, following this conversation with great interest, and now pointing southward.

"That way there's nothing," answered Pencroff.

"It's true, nothing," added the engineer.

"Well, Cyrus," asked the reporter, "what if it turns out that Lincoln Island is only two or three hundred miles from New Zealand or Chile?…"

"Well then," answered the engineer, "instead of building a house, we'll build a ship, and our friend Pencroff will be her captain…"

"Right you are, Mr. Cyrus," cried the sailor, "I'd gladly accept a promotion . . . as soon as you find a way to build a seaworthy vessel!"

"We'll do just that, if the need arises!" answered Cyrus Smith.

But as they spoke the hour of the observation was quietly drawing near. How would Cyrus Smith go about determining the exact moment when the sun reached its meridian? Harbert could not begin to guess.

The observers were then at a distance of six miles from the Chimneys, not far from the expanse of dunes where the engineer was discovered following his mysterious rescue. Here they stopped and laid out their lunch, for the time was now eleven-thirty. Harbert went to fetch some fresh water from the nearby stream, bringing it back in a jug that Neb had included among the provisions.

While the others were seeing to these preliminaries, Cyrus Smith prepared for his astronomical observation. He chose a standpoint on the beach at a spot made perfectly level by the receding waves. The bed of fine sand was as smooth as a mirror, without a single grain protruding above the rest. But in the end it mattered little whether the area was horizontal or not, nor whether the six-foot rod stood perfectly perpendicular in the sand. Indeed, Cyrus Smith had given it a southward tilt, pointing it away from the sun, for we must not forget that because their island lay in the austral hemisphere, the colonists of Lincoln Island saw the radiant star describe its diurnal arc above the northern horizon rather than the southern.

Harbert then understood how the engineer would determine the high point of the sun, which is to say its intersection with the island's meridian—or, to put it another way, the precise moment of noon in this location. In the absence of any other sort of instrument, he would use the shadow cast onto the sand by the rod; the measurement would be approximate, but sufficiently exact for his purposes.

For the shadow would attain its minimum length at noon precisely, and he would have only to follow the end of that shadow as it moved over the sand, watching for it to begin growing longer again after a period of continuous diminution. By leaning his stick away from the sun, Cyrus Smith was making the shadow longer, and consequently the changes in its length would be more easily observed. For the longer the hand of a timepiece, the more easily the motion of its point can be detected, and the rod's shadow was nothing other than the hand of an enormous timepiece.

When he believed the moment had come, Cyrus Smith knelt down; then, using a series of small sticks thrust successively into the sand, he began to mark the gradual shrinking of the rod's shadow. Looking over his shoulder, his companions followed this operation with bated breath.

The reporter held his chronometer at the ready, waiting to announce the time shown when the shadow reached its shortest length. Furthermore, since Cyrus Smith was performing this operation on April 16th, the date on which real solar time and mean time coincide, the hour indicated by Gideon Spilett would be the current real time in Washington, which would make their calculations all the easier.

Meanwhile, the sun continued its slow advance; the shadow of the rod gradually shrank, and, when it appeared to Cyrus Smith that it was beginning to grow longer again:

"What's the time?" he said.

"One minute past five o'clock," Gideon Spilett answered at once.

There remained only the elementary task of adding up the figures. As we have just seen, there was a difference of approximately five hours between the meridians of Washington and Lincoln Island, which is to say that when it was noon on Lincoln Island it was already five o'clock in the evening in Washington. Now the sun, in its apparent motion around the earth, travels one degree every four minutes, or fifteen degrees per hour. Fifteen degrees multiplied by five hours made seventy-five degrees.

Therefore, since Washington lies at 77°3′11″, or, for all intents and purposes, simply 77 degrees from the Greenwich meridian—which the Americans, in accord with the English, use as the starting point for the measurement of longitude—it followed that the island was situated at 77 degrees plus 75 degrees west of Greenwich, which is to say at 152 degrees west longitude.

Cyrus Smith announced this result to his companions, and, reckoning in a margin of error as he had done for the latitude, he believed he could affirm that Lincoln Island was located somewhere between the 35th and 37th parallels, and between the 150th and 155th meridians west of the Greenwich meridian.

As we see, he estimated the potential deviation that might arise from observational errors at five degrees total for both directions, which, since one degree equals sixty miles, gave a margin of error of three hundred latitudinal or longitudinal miles.

But this possibility of error was of no real significance as they considered their present situation, as it now seemed quite clear that the distance from Lincoln Island to any other land or archipelago was far too great to attempt in some fragile, handmade boat.

For by Cyrus Smith's calculations, the island lay at least 1,200 miles from Tahiti and the islands of the Pomotou archipelago, more than 1,800 miles from New Zealand, and more than 4,500 miles from the American coastline!

Cyrus Smith searched through his memories, but he could not recall a single island at the coordinates he had just determined.

XV

The Prospect of a Winter on Lincoln Island.—Metallurgical Considerations.—Exploration of Safety Island.—The Seal Hunt.—Capture of an Echidna.—The Kola.—What Is Known as the Catalan Method.—Fabrication of Iron.—How to Produce Steel.

The next day, April 17th, the sailor's first words were addressed to Gideon Spilett.

"Well, sir," he asked him, "what shall we be today?"

"Whatever Cyrus pleases," the reporter answered.

As it turned out, after having been brickmakers and potters, the engineer's companions were now to become metallurgists.

The day before, the exploratory excursion had continued after lunch to the point of Cape Mandible, nearly seven miles distant from the Chimneys. They came to the end of a long line of dunes, and the ground took on a volcanic appearance. Gone were the towering granite walls of Longview Plateau, replaced by a bizarre, capricious line of rocks framing the narrow gulf between the two capes, formed of mineral matter thrown out by the volcano. On reaching this point the colonists retraced their steps, and by nightfall they were back at the Chimneys. They did not sleep, however, until they had definitively settled the question of an attempted departure from Lincoln Island.

The twelve hundred miles separating the island from the Pomotou archipelago was a considerable distance. Such a stretch of sea could not be crossed in an open boat, especially with winter coming on. Pencroff stated this in no uncertain terms. Furthermore, even with the proper tools, the task of building a boat, no matter how crude, was in itself a difficult undertaking; and since the colonists had no tools whatsoever, they would first have to make hammers, axes, adzes, saws, augers, planes, etc., all of which would take some time. Thus it was decided that they would spend the winter on Lincoln Island, and that they would now search for some lodgings more comfortable than the Chimneys in preparation for the cold weather to come.

Their most pressing task was to use the iron ore found by the engineer in the northwestern part of the island to make either iron or steel.

As a general rule, the earth contains no metal in its pure form, but only in combination with oxygen or sulfur. To give them their exact names, the two samples brought back by Cyrus Smith were magnetic, noncarbonate iron on the one hand, and pyrite—which is to say iron sulfide—on the other. It was the former, the iron oxide, that they would now refine with coal, removing the oxygen in order to obtain iron in its pure form. This they would accomplish by exposing the ore to high temperatures in the presence of carbon, either by the rapid and simple "Catalan method," which has the advantage of transforming the ore directly into iron, or else by the blast-furnace method, which first changes the ore into pig iron, then the pig iron into iron by removing the remaining 3 to 4 percent of carbon.

Now what did Cyrus Smith need? Iron, not pig iron, and his goal was to find the fastest smelting process he could. Besides, the ore he had gathered was already very pure and very rich. It was a sort of oxidulated ore that, in its natural state, takes the form of amorphous dark gray lumps; when processed, it produces a black dust, crystallizes into regular octahedrons, provides natural magnets, and is used in Europe to make iron of the finest quality, particularly in Sweden and Norway. Not far from the deposits of iron ore lay deposits of vegetal coal that the colonists had already exploited. All the necessary elements for the treatment of the ore thus lay close at hand, which would greatly simplify their task. Indeed, it is to just such a circumstance that the British steel industry owes its extraordinary productivity; for there, as here, the ore and the coal used to refine it are excavated from the same soil and at the same time.

"So, Mr. Cyrus," Pencroff said to him, "we're going to smelt the iron ore?"

"Yes, my friend," answered the engineer, "and to that end—you'll like this—we will begin with a seal hunt on the islet."

"A seal hunt!" cried the sailor, turning to Gideon Spilett. "We need seals to make iron?"

"If Cyrus says so!" answered the reporter.

But the engineer had already left the Chimneys, and, with no further explanation forthcoming, Pencroff made ready for the hunt.

Soon Cyrus Smith, Harbert, Gideon Spilett, Neb, and the sailor had gathered on the beach, at a point where the channel could be forded at low tide. The water was no more than knee-high, and the hunters had no difficulty wading across to the islet.

This was the first time Cyrus Smith had set foot upon the islet, and the second for his companions, since it was here that the balloon had first dropped them.

They came ashore to find several hundred razorbills staring at them unsuspectingly. The colonists could easily have killed them with their clubs, but they had other prey on their minds, and a mass slaughter of razorbills would only frighten the amphibians lying on the sand several cable lengths away. Also spared were a number of innocent penguins, with stumpy, flat, finlike wings and plumes of a scaly appearance.

The colonists continued cautiously toward the northern point, picking their way over a surface pockmarked with small holes that were nothing other than seabird nests. Just offshore they saw large black spots skimming along the surface of the water, looking for all the world like exposed shoals that had somehow been endowed with the gift of mobility.

These were the amphibians they had come to hunt. The colonists would have to wait until the beasts came ashore, for thanks to a narrow pelvis, short, dense fur, and a smooth, tapering shape, these seals were excellent swimmers, nearly impossible to catch in the water. Once on land, however, their short, webbed feet limit their movement to a slow, inefficient crawl.

Pencroff knew the habits of these amphibians, and he advised his companions to wait until they had stretched out on the sand to bask in the rays of the sun, for the solar warmth would soon lull them to sleep. The hunters would move to block any attempted retreat, and then club them over the muzzle.

The little band hid among the rocks that littered the shoreline, and waited in silence.

An hour passed; then the seals came ashore and lay luxuriating on the

The colonists continued cautiously.

sands. There were a half-dozen of them. Pencroff and Harbert split away from the group and skirted the point of the island so that they could attack from the rear and cut off their retreat. In the meantime, Cyrus Smith, Gideon Spilett, and Neb crawled along the line of rocks toward the theater of the coming struggle.

Suddenly the sailor raised himself to his full height, letting out a loud battle cry. The engineer and his two companions leaped forward with great vigor and blocked the seals' access to the sea. Two of these animals, struck with great force, soon lay dead on the sand, but the others succeeded in reaching the water, and so made their escape.

"Seals, as requested, Mr. Cyrus!" said the sailor, striding toward the engineer.

"Very good," answered Cyrus Smith. "We'll use them to make bellows for our forge!"

"Bellows!" cried Pencroff. "You lucky seals!"

The engineer needed wind to treat the ore, and this was indeed his intended use for the amphibians' skin. They were of average size, no more than six feet long, with heads roughly the size of a dog's. There was no point in attempting to transport a weight as immense as that of these two beasts. Neb and Pencroff set about skinning them on the spot while Cyrus Smith and the reporter continued their exploration of the islet.

The sailor and the Negro adroitly carried out their work, and three hours later Cyrus Smith found himself with two fine sealskins, which he planned to use just as they were, untanned and untreated.

The colonists waited for the tide to recede, then crossed the channel and returned to the Chimneys.

Next came the frustrating task of stretching the skins taut over wooden frames and stitching them together with fibers, trying not to leave holes through which air might escape. They were forced to start over several times. Cyrus Smith's only tools were the two steel blades from Top's collar; nevertheless, he was so dextrous, and his companions assisted him with such intelligence, that three days later the little colony had acquired a set of mechanical bellows by which air would be injected into the ore as it was being heated—a necessary condition for the procedure's success.

The morning of April 20th marked the inauguration of the "metallurgical period," as the reporter called it in his notes. It will be remembered that the engineer planned to build his forge on the site of the coal and iron ore deposits, which lay at the base of the northeastern foothills of Mount Franklin, some six miles distant. To return to the Chimneys at the end of each day was out of the question; thus, it was agreed that the little colony would build themselves a small hut so that they could pursue this all-important task day and night.

With their plans now settled, they started off at first light. Neb and Pencroff dragged the bellows on a sledge, along with a supply of vegetal and animal foodstuffs, which they would supplement with any game they might find along the way.

Their route took them in a diagonal northwesterly direction, through the densest area of Jacamar Woods. They hacked out a path as they went, which would thereafter serve as the most direct way from Longview Plateau to Mount Franklin. The trees were enormous, most of them belonging to species they had already encountered. Harbert pointed out some new ones, though, most notably dragon trees, which Pencroff termed "pretentious leeks"—for, despite their size, they belonged to the Liliaceae family, like onions, chives, shallots, and asparagus. The woody roots of these dragon trees are delicious when cooked, and can furthermore be fermented to produce a very pleasant liqueur. They stopped to gather a supply of these roots, then started off again.

The journey through the woods was a long one, lasting an entire day, but offering an excellent opportunity to study the island's flora and fauna. The fauna was Top's responsibility, and he ran through the tall grass and undergrowth, indiscriminately flushing out all manner of game. Harbert and Gideon Spilett killed two kangaroos with their bows and arrows, as well as an animal with a strong resemblance to both a hedgehog and an anteater—to the former because it rolled into a ball bristling with sharp spines, to the latter because it had claws for burrowing, a long, slender snout ending in a birdlike beak, and an extendable tongue covered with small barbs to capture the insects that formed its principal food.

"And when we put him in a stew," Pencroff naturally inquired, "what will he look like then?"

"Like an excellent cut of beef," answered Harbert.

"We ask for nothing more," the sailor replied.

In the course of this excursion, they spotted a number of wild boars, who made no attempt to attack them. They were beginning to think they would meet up with nothing more formidable than this, when in the middle of a dense thicket the reporter saw an animal he took to be a bear nestled in the lower branches of a tree a few paces away. He calmly began a sketch of this beast. Fortunately for Gideon Spilett, the animal in question did not belong to the fearsome Plantigrade family. It was nothing more than a "kola," more commonly known as a "sloth," the size of a large dog, with coarse, dirty-looking fur and sharp, curved claws that allowed it to climb into trees and feed on the leaves. Learning the name of this beast, whose occupations they did not disturb, Gideon Spilett erased *bear* from the caption of his sketch, wrote in *kola* instead, and they resumed their walk.

At five o'clock in the evening, Cyrus Smith gave the signal to stop for the night. They were now out of the forest, at the edge of the first looming foothills that shored up the eastern flank of Mount Franklin. Red Creek flowed along a few hundred paces away, providing an unlimited supply of fresh drinking water.

They quickly set up their campsite. Less than an hour later, a hut made of branches interlaced with lianas and insulated with sticky clay stood among the trees at the edge of the forest, offering reasonably comfortable accommodations. They put off their geological researches until the next day. Dinner was prepared, a good fire blazed before the hut, the spit turned, and at eight o'clock they fell into a restful slumber. Nevertheless, one of the colonists stayed up to tend the fire, lest some dangerous animal might be on the prowl in the vicinity.

The next day, April 21st, Cyrus Smith and Harbert went off to locate the terrain, formed in the mists of prehistory, where the sample of ore had been discovered. An exposed deposit was found near the source of the creek, beneath one of the northeastern foothills. Inside its gangue of fusible material, the ore was very rich in iron, and was thus perfectly suited to the refining process the engineer intended to use: a simplified form of the Catalan method, commonly practiced in Corsica.

For, strictly speaking, the Catalan method requires kilns and crucibles, in which the ore and coal are arranged in alternating layers before they are exposed to the heat of the fire. But Cyrus Smith wanted to avoid any unnecessary steps, and so planned simply to make a cube-shaped pile of ore and coal, into the center of which he would direct the flow of air from his bellows. This must have been the technique used by Tubalcain and the first metallurgists of the inhabited world. And if it had worked for Adam's grandchildren, if it was still successfully practiced in lands rich in ore and fuel, it could not fail to work for the colonists of Lincoln Island.

After the ore, the coal was gathered from exposed deposits they had found a small distance away. They broke the bits of ore into small pieces and scraped away any visible impurities from the surface. Next the coal and ore were arranged in successive layers to form a large pile, just as a charcoal maker does with the wood he wishes to carbonize. In that way, under the influence of the air injected by the bellows, the coal would be transformed into carbonic acid, then into carbon monoxide, whose role is to reduce the iron oxide—to rob it of its oxygen, in other words.

The engineer now proceeded to the next step of the process. The seal-skin bellows were set up near the pile of ore, fitted with a tube made of heat-resistant clay, previously fired in the pottery kiln. Powered by a mechanism of fiber ropes and counterweights held fast by a frame, they expelled a continuous stream of air which not only raised the temperature at the pile's center, but also contributed to the chemical transformation that would produce pure iron.

This was no simple procedure. It took all the colonists' patience and ingenuity to see it through; but in the end they succeeded, and the final result was a bloom of iron, not unlike a sponge in appearance. This they now had to hammer and weld—to forge, in other words—so as to drive out the liquefied gangue. Ill-equipped but ever resourceful, our black-smiths obviously lacked the hammer required for this procedure; but, after all, their situation was no different from that of the first metallurgist, and they simply did as he must have done.

The first bloom was fitted with a handle and used as a hammer to forge the second on an anvil of granite, and in this way they produced a crude but usable metal.

Finally, on April 25th, after much effort and weariness, several bars of iron were forged and transformed into tools—pliers, tongs, picks, pick-axes, etc.—which Pencroff and Neb deemed genuine beauties.

But pure iron was not enough for their needs; what they truly required was steel. Now, steel is a combination of iron and carbon that is derived from either a removal of excess carbon from pig iron, or an addition of carbon to pure iron. In the former case, the decarbonization of pig iron produces natural steel or puddle; in the latter, the carbonization of iron results in cementation steel.

Cyrus Smith chose the latter course, since he already had pure iron at his disposal. The carbonization process could not have been simpler: he

This was no simple procedure.

merely had to heat the metal with powdered coal in a crucible of heat-resistant clay.

The operation succeeded flawlessly, and the resulting steel, which is malleable both cold and warm, was thoroughly hammered. Under his skillful guidance, Neb and Pencroff produced a number of ax heads; these were heated until they glowed bright red, then tempered by a sudden immersion in cold water.

Other instruments—crudely formed, needless to say—were fabricated in the same way: plane blades, axes, hatchets, strips of steel that would later be shaped into saws, carpenter's chisels, then blades for pick-axes, shovels, picks, hammers, nails, etc.

Finally, on May 5th, the first metallurgical period came to a close, and the blacksmiths returned home to the Chimneys, soon to take up yet another trade in their project to civilize Lincoln Island.

XVI

The Housing Question Reconsidered.—Pencroff's Fancies.—An Exploration of the North End of the Lake.—The Southern Edge of the Plateau.—The Serpents.—The End of the Lake.—Top's Agitation.—Top Swims.—An Underwater Struggle.—The Dugong.

The date was May 6th, which corresponds to November 6th in the northern hemisphere. The sky had grown ever cloudier over the past few days, and the time had come to think of the necessary preparations for winter. Nevertheless, the temperature had not yet dropped to any appreciable extent, and a centigrade thermometer transported to Lincoln Island would still have registered an average of ten to twelve degrees above zero. Such temperatures need hardly surprise us, for Lincoln Island, situated in all probability between the thirty-fifth and fortieth parallels of the southern hemisphere, must have enjoyed the same climatic conditions as Sicily or Greece in the north. But just as Greece and Sicily are sometimes subjected to extreme cold, and even snow and ice, so would Lincoln Island have its share of harsh wintertime temperatures. It was thus necessary to take certain precautions before the cold weather came.

In any case, even if the cold of winter was not yet a threat, the rainy season was not far off, and on that isolated mid-Pacific island, exposed to all the meteorological extremes of the open sea, storms would no doubt be frequent, and potentially violent.

The question of finding lodgings more comfortable than the Chimneys had thus to be seriously considered and promptly resolved.

Pencroff naturally felt a certain fondness for the refuge he had discovered; nevertheless, he fully understood the importance of finding another. Once already the sea had come to pay a call on the Chimneys, in the circumstances we remember, and laying themselves open to a second such accident was out of the question.

"Besides," said Cyrus Smith as they discussed this matter, "we must consider the question of security."

"Why? The island is uninhabited," said the reporter.

"That's very likely true," answered the engineer, "although we have not yet explored it fully; but even if there is not another human being to be found on these shores, I fear there may be dangerous animals living hereabouts in great numbers. We would do well to shield ourselves from every possible aggression, so that one of us will not always have to stay awake and tend the fire. My friends, we must be ready for anything. This area of the Pacific is often frequented by Malay pirates..."

"What?" said Harbert. "This far from land?"

"Yes, my boy," answered the engineer. "Those pirates are intrepid sailors as well as fearsome brigands, and we must take measures accordingly."

"Well then," answered Pencroff, "we shall fortify ourselves against savages of both the two-legged and four-legged variety. But, Mr. Cyrus, would it not be a good idea to start by exploring the island from one end to the other?"

"That would be best," added Gideon Spilett. "Who knows? Perhaps on the opposite shore we'll come across the very sort of cavern we tried without success to find on this side?"

"Very true," answered the engineer, "but you're forgetting, my friends, that we must have a source of fresh water near our new home, and that we saw neither stream or river as we looked west from the summit of Mount Franklin. Here, on the other hand, we have both the Mercy and Lake Grant, and this is no small advantage. Furthermore, since our shoreline faces east, it is not exposed to the trade winds as the other is, for in this hemisphere they inevitably blow from the northwest."

"Well then, Mr. Cyrus," answered the sailor, "let's build a house at the edge of the lake. We have plenty of bricks and tools. We've been brickmakers, potters, ironworkers, blacksmiths, so devil if we can't become masons!"

"Yes, my friend, but before we make that decision we have some exploring to do. If we could find a home constructed by nature herself we would be spared a great deal of work, and we would undoubtedly have an even surer refuge, defended against enemies from within and without alike."

"Quite right, Cyrus," answered the reporter, "but we've searched the length of the granite cliffs, and there's not a hole to be found, not even a crack!"

"No, not one!" added Pencroff. "Oh! if only we could dig out a cavern high in that wall, high above the ground, completely out of reach, that would be a fine thing indeed! I can see it now, in the cliff face overlooking the sea, five or six rooms..."

"With windows for light!" said Harbert, laughing.

"And a staircase to get up!" added Neb.

"You can laugh," cried the sailor, "but why? What makes you think it's so impossible? Don't we have picks and pickaxes? Don't you think Mr. Cyrus knows how to make gunpowder so we can blast? Isn't it true, Mr. Cyrus, that you'll make us some powder whenever we need it?"

Cyrus Smith listened as the enthusiastic Pencroff laid out his rather fanciful plans. To tunnel through that mass of granite would be a Herculean task, even with dynamite. It was really most unfortunate that nature had not already undertaken the greater part of the labor. But the engineer's only answer to the sailor was a promise to give the wall of granite a closer inspection, from the mouth of the river to the bend that marked the northern end of the cliffs.

They examined the cliff face with great care, over a distance of about two miles. Nowhere in the vertical wall did they find a single cavity of any description. Even the nests of the rock doves wheeling over the cliffs were nothing more than small pits in the irregular edge of the crest.

These were very discouraging results, and clearly it would be madness to dream of carving out a dwelling in the solid rock with powder or picks. Pencroff had in fact discovered the only temporarily inhabitable dwelling along the entire coastline—the Chimneys—which they now had no choice but to abandon.

The colonists' explorations brought them to the northern bend in the wall, at which point it began to slope gently down to the beach. From there westward, the wall was little more than a sort of embankment, a dense agglomeration of stones, earth, and sand filled in by plants, shrubs, and grasses, no longer vertical but sloped at an incline of less than forty-five degrees. Here and there an occasional granite outcropping could still be seen jutting abruptly from the formation. Stands of trees grew in terraces over its flank, which was carpeted with a dense growth of grass. At the base of the embankment this vegetation died away, and a long sandy plain ran from there to the water's edge.

Cyrus Smith had good reason to believe that this was where he would find the cascade that carried the excess lakewater to the sea. For the continuous flow of Red Creek clearly brought in more water than the lake could contain, and somehow, by some invisible route, the excess ran down to the shore; and yet none of the engineer's previous explorations, from the mouth of the stream to Longview Plateau, had shown him that mysterious route.

Thus, the engineer suggested that they climb the embankment and return to the Chimneys by way of the highlands, which would allow them to explore the lake's northern and eastern shores.

The proposition was accepted, and a few minutes later Harbert and Neb had arrived atop the plateau. Cyrus Smith, Gideon Spilett, and Pencroff followed behind at a statelier clip.

Two hundred paces from where they now stood, the lovely waters of the lake shimmered in the solar rays. An enchanting landscape stretched out before them. The eye delighted in the many majestic stands of trees, now turning various shades of yellow. The black bark of a few enormous fallen trunks, cut down by old age, stood out against the lush, green carpet covering the ground. A population of cockatoos, veritable mobile prisms, hopped from one branch to the next, chattering noisily all the while. It was as if the sunlight were broken down into its constituent parts as it passed through that singular network of branches.

Rather than proceeding directly to the lake's northern shore, the colonists followed the edge of the plateau in hopes of returning to the right bank of the creek's mouth. This involved a detour of a mile and a half at most—an easy walk, with nothing to bar their way between the scattered trees. The edge of the plateau clearly marked the limit of the island's fertile zone; even here, the vegetation was far less luxuriant than anywhere between the creek and the Mercy.

Cyrus Smith and his companions walked cautiously over this unknown terrain. Their only weapons were bows, arrows, and sticks armed with sharp steel blades. To their relief, however, no wild animals confronted them. Such beasts very likely preferred the thick forests of the south; but the colonists soon had the unpleasant surprise of seeing Top encounter a large serpent, fourteen to fifteen feet in length, which Neb promptly vanquished with a single blow of his club. Cyrus Smith examined the reptile and assured his companions that it was not venomous; it was a member of the family of diamond pythons, which are an important food source for the natives of New South Wales. But they could easily come upon others whose bite might prove fatal, such as deaf adders, with forked tails, which suddenly spring up from underfoot, or hooded cobras, endowed with two earflaps that allow them to strike with great speed. Once his initial surprise had passed, Top gave chase to those reptiles with a relentlessness that could well have proven fatal. His master was thus frequently forced to call him to heel.

Soon they reached the mouth of Red Creek, where the mountain's waters flowed into the lake. On the opposite bank, the explorers recognized the point they had visited after their descent from Mount Franklin. Cyrus Smith noted the speed and volume of the creek's flow; clearly, nature had somewhere provided an outlet for the excess from the lake, and he thought it important to discover that spillway, for if it took the form of a waterfall, as he believed it must, its mechanical force could be harnessed to very good use.

And so the colonists began to make their way around the steeply inclined lakeshore, each choosing his own path but never straying too far from the others. The water appeared to be full of fish, and Pencroff immediately conceived a project to construct a number of fishing rods with which to exploit the lake's abundance.

They followed a zigzag route around the point at the lake's northeastern end. It could well have been here that the overflow drained off toward the sea, for this far end of the lake extended almost to the edge of the plateau. But such was not the case, and the colonists pursued their exploration of the lakeshore as it began to curve southward, parallel to the seacoast.

On this side the lakeshore was less wooded, but a few scattered groups of trees added to the picturesque beauty of the place. The view encompassed the whole of Lake Grant. No breath of wind ruffled the water's surface. Beating the undergrowth, Top flushed out flocks of various sorts of birds, which Gideon Spilett and Harbert greeted with flights of arrows. One of these avians was hit by an arrow adroitly fired by Harbert, and fell into a marshy area filled with tall grasses. Top scurried off after it, and returned with a beautiful swimming bird, slate-colored, with a short beak, a very elaborate frontal plate, toes broadened by scalloped edges, and wings bordered in white. It was a "coot," the size of a large partridge—one of the macrodactyls, midway between wading birds and palmipeds. Not a particularly sumptuous sort of game fowl; its taste leaves much to be desired. But Top would surely prove less demanding than his masters, and it was agreed that the coot would serve as his dinner.

The colonists continued along the lake's eastern shore toward the area previously explored. To the engineer's profound astonishment, he still saw no sign of the spillway, and he made no attempt to conceal his surprise as he spoke with the reporter and the sailor.

Just then, Top, heretofore quite sedate, began to show signs of extreme agitation. The intelligent beast ran back and forth along the shore, abruptly stopping to stare into the waters, one paw raised as if to point at some invisible game. Then he began to bark furiously, as if he wanted something from his masters, and suddenly fell silent again.

At first, Cyrus Smith and his companions paid no mind to Top's odd behavior; soon, however, his barking became so insistent that the engineer grew concerned.

"What is it, Top?" he asked.

The dog came bounding toward his master, his demeanor suggesting genuine terror, then hurtled off toward the lakeshore again and suddenly leaped into the lake.

"Here, Top!" shouted Cyrus Smith, loath to let his dog venture into unknown and uncertain waters.

"What could be down there?" asked Pencroff, staring at the water's surface.

"Top must have smelled some sort of amphibian," answered Harbert.

"An alligator, no doubt?" said the reporter.

"I don't think so," answered Cyrus Smith. "It's not likely we would find an alligator at this high a latitude."

Top had returned to the shoreline in response to his master's call, but still he could not contain his excitement; he plunged into the tall grass, and, guided by instinct, seemed to be following some hidden creature slithering along the shore just beneath the surface. Nevertheless, the water remained perfectly calm, without a single ripple or eddy. Several times the colonists stopped on the shore and stared searchingly into the lake. They saw nothing. Something mysterious was afoot.

The engineer was deeply intrigued.

"Let's see our explorations through to the end," he said.

A half-hour later, they had arrived at the southeastern corner of the lake, and so found themselves once more on Longview Plateau. Their inspection of the lakeshore now had to be considered complete, and yet the engineer had learned neither where nor how the excess water spilled from the lake.

"Nonetheless, I know there's a spillway somewhere, and if it isn't outside, then it must be buried deep inside the granite cliffs along the shore!"

"Is it really so important that we resolve this question, my dear Cyrus?" asked Gideon Spilett.

"It is indeed," answered the engineer, "for if the excess flows through the interior of the cliffs, we may be able to find a cavity inside the rock that we could make livable by altering the water's course."

"But is it not possible, Mr. Cyrus, that the water drains from the very bottom of the lake," said Harbert, "and flows to the sea through some sort of conduit deep underground?"

"That may well be," answered the engineer, "and if so—if nature has done none of the labor for us—then we shall have no choice but to build our house ourselves."

The colonists were preparing to set out across the plateau and return to the Chimneys, for it was now five o'clock; but just then Top once more manifested a tremendous agitation. He barked furiously, and before his master could hold him back, he threw himself into the lake again.

As one man, they ran to the water's edge. The dog was already more than twenty feet from shore, and Cyrus Smith was urgently calling him back when a huge head emerged from the surface of the shallow water.

Harbert immediately recognized the animal's species by its conical head, its large eyes, and the long, silky whiskers that graced its snout.

"A manatee!" he cried.

It was in fact not a manatee, but what is known as a "dugong"—a member of the Cetacean order, distinguishable from the manatee by the open nostrils at the top of its muzzle.

The enormous animal launched itself toward the dog, who tried in vain to escape and return to shore. His master could do nothing to save him, and before Gideon Spilett or Harbert could think of arming their bows, the powerful dugong had dragged Top into the water's depths.

His iron pike at the ready, Neb was about to dive into the lake and attack the formidable beast in its own element, in hopes of rescuing the dog.

Top was launched into the air . . .

"No, Neb," said the engineer, restraining his courageous servant.

Meanwhile, a struggle was going on beneath the water; an inexplicable struggle, for in these conditions Top clearly could not last long; a fierce and furious struggle, it seemed, judging by the churning of the water's surface; a struggle, finally, that could not fail to end in the dog's death! But now Top abruptly reappeared in a nimbus of foam. Launched into the air by some unknown force, he shot up to a height of ten feet above the surface of the lake, then fell into the water again with a great splash, and soon returned to shore none the worse for wear, miraculously spared what had seemed an inevitable death.

Cyrus Smith and his companions looked on, uncomprehending. And—more inexplicably yet!—it seemed that the underwater struggle continued still. Under attack from some powerful animal, the dugong must have released the dog in order to fight for its own life.

But the battle did not last long. The waters grew red with blood, and the body of the dugong, emerging from a spreading pool of scarlet, soon washed onto a small beach at the southern corner of the lake.

The colonists came running. The dugong was dead. It was an enormous animal, fifteen feet long, weighing easily three to four thousand pounds. On its neck they found a large gaping wound, clean and straight, rather like a sharp blade might make.

What sort of amphibian could have slain the dugong with this one terrible blow? They could not say. Somewhat shaken by these events, Cyrus Smith and his companions returned to the Chimneys.

XVII

A Visit to the Lake.—The Revealing Current.—Cyrus Smith's Plans.—Dugong Blubber.—Use of the Pyritic Schist.—Iron Sulfate.—How Glycerine Is Made.—Soap.—Saltpeter.—Sulfuric Acid.—Nitric Acid.—The New Waterfall.

The next day, May 7th, Cyrus Smith and Gideon Spilett left Neb to prepare breakfast and climbed to Longview Plateau while Harbert and Pencroff walked up the river in search of yet more firewood.

The engineer and the reporter soon came to the small beach at the southern end of the lake, where they had left the body of the amphibian. Flocks of birds had descended on the fleshy mass and had to be chased off with stones, as Cyrus Smith wanted to harvest the dugong's blubber for the colony's domestic needs. Furthermore, the animal's flesh was fully edible; indeed, so prized is its meat in certain regions of Malaya that it is reserved for the tables of the native princes. But that was Neb's affair.

For at the moment Cyrus Smith's mind was on other things. The previous day's incident had not faded from his memory, but continued to occupy his thoughts. He yearned to know the secret of that underwater combat, to learn what sort of beast, what relative of the mastodon or other aquatic monster, could have dealt the dugong such a curious wound.

He lingered at the edge of the lake, watching, observing, but the tranquil waters only glimmered merrily in the rays of the newly risen sun. Clearly there was nothing to be seen here today.

This lake resembled nothing so much as a great basin, filled by the continual flow of Red Creek. Near the shore the water was quite shallow;

but the bottom steadily fell away, and the middle of the lake was probably very deep indeed.

"Well, Cyrus," said the reporter, "there doesn't appear to be anything out of the ordinary in these waters!"

"No, my dear Spilett," answered the engineer. "I simply don't know how to explain yesterday's incident!"

"I must admit," Gideon Spilett replied, "that the amphibian's wound is curious, to say the least, and I find it equally difficult to explain how Top could have been thrown from the water with such force. It was exactly as if some mighty arm had launched him into the air and then dispatched the dugong with a dagger!"

"Yes," answered the engineer, lost in thought. "There's something here that I can't understand. But for that matter, my dear Spilett, do you understand how I was snatched from the waves and carried into the dunes? I presume not. My sense is that there is a mystery in all these things, which we will no doubt discover one day. Let us keep a careful watch, then, but we mustn't speak too much of these singular incidents before our companions. Let us keep our remarks to ourselves, and continue our work."

As we know, the engineer had not yet discovered the route followed by the overflow from the lake; nevertheless, having seen no sign of flooding at its edges, he knew that the spillway existed. But now, to his surprise, Cyrus Smith observed a rather pronounced current in the waters of the lake. He threw in some small pieces of wood, and at once they began to drift toward the southern corner. He followed along the shore until he arrived at the lake's southernmost point.

Here he found a sort of depression in the water, as if it were draining through some fissure in the lake bottom.

Cyrus Smith knelt down and cocked his ear over the surface of the lake. It was then that he clearly heard the sound of an underground waterfall.

"This," he said, rising to his feet, "is where the water drains from the lake. There must be a conduit running through the granite directly to the sea, and we may well be able to turn that cavity to our own use! Now, let's see if I'm right!"

The engineer cut a long branch from a tree, stripped it of its leaves, and probed beneath the water. Soon he discovered a large, open hole no more than one foot below the surface. This was the opening by which the overflow drained from the lake—the goal of his long and heretofore fruitless quest. The force of the current was such that the branch was ripped from the engineer's hands and vanished immediately.

"There's no doubting it now," Cyrus Smith repeated. "This is the entrance to the spillway, and our next task will be to uncover it."

"How?" asked Gideon Spilett.

"I shall lower the level of the lakewater by three feet."

"And how are you going to do that?"

"By creating another outlet with a greater capacity than this one."

"Where, Cyrus?"

"Where the lakeshore lies closest to the sea."

"But the shore is solid granite there!" objected the reporter.

"Well then," answered Cyrus Smith, "I'll have to blast through it. The water will pour through the new spillway, and the level will drop sufficiently to uncover this hole..."

"And the water will tumble over the rocks onto the beach, like a waterfall," added the reporter.

"And that waterfall will be a very useful thing for us to have!" answered Cyrus. "Come along, come along!"

The engineer led his companion away. The reporter's faith in Cyrus Smith was absolute, and he little doubted that this new undertaking would succeed. But how would he break through the solid granite of the lakeshore? How could he hope to demolish that stone without blasting powder, and with only the simplest of tools? Was the engineer not embarking on a project that would prove simply beyond his capacities?

When Cyrus Smith and the reporter returned to the Chimneys, they found Harbert and Pencroff busily unloading their timber raft.

"Soon the lumberjacks will have finished their work, Mr. Cyrus," said the sailor, laughing, "and whenever you're ready for the masons..."

"No, not masons, but chemists," answered the engineer.

"That's right," added the reporter, "we're going to blow up the island..."

"Blow up the island!" cried Pencroff.

"Well, part of it, at least!" replied Gideon Spilett.

"Listen, my friends," said the engineer.

And he presented his findings. He felt sure that a more or less sizable cavity existed within the mass of granite beneath Longview Plateau, and his intention was to find a way inside. The first step would be to uncover the opening, now accessible only to the rushing waters; to this end, they would lower the water level by providing the lake with a more sizable outlet. Hence the need to create an explosive substance, for in no other way could they hope to produce a sufficient gash in the solid stone of the shoreline. It was to this project that Cyrus Smith would now turn, using the minerals nature had placed at his disposal.

Needless to say, this plan was hailed with great enthusiasm by all, especially Pencroff. A spectacular explosion, shattering granite, a waterfall where none was before, the sailor could think of nothing finer! And he could just as well be a chemist as a mason or bootmaker, if it was chemists the engineer needed. He was prepared to become whatever was required, whenever the need arose—"even a dancing-and-deportment master," as he told Neb.

Neb and Pencroff were charged with the task of rendering the dugong's fat and preserving its flesh for use as food. Off they went at once, never thinking to question their orders, for their confidence in the engineer was entire.

Dragging the sledge behind them, Cyrus Smith, Harbert, and Gideon Spilett set off upstream toward the coal deposits in search of pyritic schist, which is often found in recent transitional terrains. Indeed, Cyrus Smith had already collected a sample of that stone in his previous explorations.

They spent the entire day transporting the pyrites to the Chimneys, and by evening they had several tons.

The next day, May 8th, the engineer began his operations. This pyritic schist was composed primarily of coal, silica, alumina, and iron sulfide, the latter in excess. Cyrus Smith's task was to isolate the iron sulfide and to transform it into sulfate as rapidly as possible; from this iron sulfate, he could then extract sulfuric acid.

For this was his real goal. Sulfuric acid is one of the most widely used of all chemical products, and the industrial vigor of a nation can be measured by the quantity of sulfuric acid it consumes. This substance would later be of great use to the colonists for making candles, tanning animal hides, etc., but for the moment, the engineer had another purpose in mind.

Cyrus Smith chose a work site behind the Chimneys, carefully leveling the surface of the ground. He lay down a pile of branches and split logs and set the pieces of pyritic schist atop them, leaning against one another like in a house of cards; this was then covered with a thin layer of pyrites, crumbled to the size of walnuts.

The wood was set alight, and its heat caused the coal and sulfur within the schists to catch fire. More layers of crushed pyrites were piled on, soon forming a sizable heap. This was then covered over with earth and grass, with holes here and there to serve as vents, just as if the colonists were carbonizing a pile of wood to make charcoal.

Now they waited for the transformation to take place. It took no less than ten or twelve days for the iron sulfide to be changed into iron sulfate and the alumina into aluminum sulfate—two equally soluble substances, unlike the remaining silica, burned coal, and ashes.

As this transformation was taking place, Cyrus Smith turned his attention to other projects. These colonists were more than zealous. They were tireless.

Neb and Pencroff had rendered the dugong's fat and stored it away in great earthenware pots. The goal was to isolate one element of that fat, glycerine, by a process of saponification. This could be done in two ways: the fat could be treated with soda or with lime. Either of these substances would react with the fat to produce a soap, while at the same time isolating the glycerine—and it was this glycerine that the engineer was hoping to obtain. There was no lack of lime, as we know; but treatment with lime would produce only calcareous soaps, insoluble and consequently worthless, whereas treatment with soda would provide them with soluble soap, invaluable for many varied domestic purposes. Thus, ever the practical soul, Cyrus Smith resolved to attempt to produce soda. Would this be a difficult undertaking? No, for the shoreline was rich in aquatic plants, salicornes, ficoides, and all the variety of Fucacea that we know as kelp and wrack. They collected a large quantity of these plants, dried them, then burned them in open pits. The combustion of the plants was carefully maintained over several days, so that the heat would remain intense enough to melt the ashes; and the end result of this incineration was a compact, grayish mass, known to mankind for centuries as "natural soda."

Having successfully made soda, the engineer now used it to treat the rendered fat, producing, on the one hand, a soluble soap, and on the other, the neutral substance we know as glycerine.

But his work was not yet done. Cyrus Smith needed one more substance for his preparation: potassium nitrate, which is better known by the name niter or saltpeter.

Cyrus Smith could have produced this substance by treating potassium carbonate, which is easily extracted from plant ashes, with nitric acid. But he had no nitric acid; indeed, this was precisely what he was trying to obtain. That way lay only an inescapable vicious circle. Fortunately, nature herself could provide him with the necessary saltpeter; he had only to collect it. For Harbert had discovered a deposit of that salt in the north end of the island, at the foot of Mount Franklin, ready to be purified and used.

These various tasks were accomplished after eight days, before the transformation of sulfide into iron sulfate was complete. The colonists used the remaining time to make heat-resistant pottery from moldable clay, and to build a specially designed brick furnace with which they would distill the iron sulfate once they had derived it. They finished this work around May 18th, just as the chemical transformation was nearing its end. Under the engineer's skillful leadership, Gideon Spilett, Harbert, Neb, and Pencroff had become the most able workers in the world. Necessity is the finest master, moreover—the most effective of all teachers, and the most closely attended to.

Once the fire had completely reduced the pile of pyrites, the resulting matter, consisting of iron sulfate, aluminum sulfate, silica, charcoal residue, and ashes, was shoveled into a water-filled basin. They stirred this mixture, let it rest, then poured it off into another vessel, obtaining a light-colored liquid that held the iron sulfate and aluminum sulfate in suspension; the other substances had been left behind as solids, since they were not soluble. Finally, once the liquid had partially evaporated, the crystals of iron sulfate precipitated out, and the mother liquor, that is, the unevaporated liquid containing the aluminum sulfate, was discarded.

Cyrus Smith thus had at his disposal a rather large quantity of iron sulfate crystals, and from these he would now extract sulfuric acid.

In industrial practice, the apparatus used to produce sulfuric acid is a costly one. Indeed, the process requires sizable factories, specially designed tools, platinum machine parts, acid-proof leaden containers for the transformation itself, etc. The engineer had nothing of the sort, but he knew of a considerably simpler technique for producing sulfuric acid, commonly practiced in Bohemia, which in fact has the advantage of producing a more concentrated product. It is by this technique that the substance known as Nordhausen acid is made.

One last step remained before Cyrus Smith would attain his goal: the incineration of the iron sulfate crystals in a covered vessel, from which the sulfuric acid would be distilled as a vapor, then condensed as a liquid.

This was the purpose of the heat-resistant pottery, into which the crystals were now placed, and of the oven, whose heat would distill the sulfuric acid. Everything proceeded according to plan, and on May 20th, twelve days after he had begun, the engineer held in his hands the agent for which he would later find a great number of varied uses.

But what did he now intend to do with this agent? Quite simply, to make nitric acid—a simple procedure, since saltpeter, when treated with sulfuric acid, produces that very acid by a process of distillation.

But what, in the end, was he intending to do with the nitric acid? That his companions did not yet know, for he had never explained the precise nature of his work.

Meanwhile, the engineer was nearing his goal, and, with all the extensive preliminaries now behind him, one final step gave him the substance he required.

He collected the nitric acid and introduced it into the glycerine, which he had concentrated by evaporation in a double boiler; and the result, even without the concurrence of a refrigerant, was several pints of an oily, yellowish liquid.

Cyrus Smith had performed this final step alone, away from the others, far from the Chimneys, as it carried a certain risk of explosion. But soon he returned to his friends with a small vial of liquid, saying simply:

"Nitroglycerine!"

For such was the awesome compound he now held in his hands—a substance whose explosive force can be ten times that of ordinary blasting powder. Little wonder that it has been the cause of so many terrible accidents! To be sure, once men learned to transform it into dynamite by mixing it with some porous substance such as clay or sugar, this dangerous liquid became less of a threat to its user. But dynamite was not yet known at the time of the colonists' stranding on this island.

"That juice is going to blow up our rocks?" said Pencroff, slightly dubious.

"Yes, my friend," answered the engineer, "and this nitroglycerine will prove all the more powerful because the granite is extremely hard, and will therefore put up a greater resistance to its explosive force."

"And when will we see this, Mr. Cyrus?"

"Tomorrow, as soon as we have dug a blasting hole," answered the engineer.

The next day—May 21st—at dawn, the miners gathered on the eastern shore of Lake Grant, at a point where the lakeshore lay only five hundred paces from the sea. The plateau sloped away from the water, which was held back only by its granite embankment. Thus, if they could create a fissure in the embankment, the water would pour out, flow over the inclined plateau, and fall onto the beach. This would lower the level of the waters in the lake and uncover the entrance to the spillway, which was their ultimate goal.

They would thus have to break through the rock. Under the engineer's direction, Pencroff skillfully began to bore a hole in the outer face of the granite. They chose a spot in the horizontal ridge at the water's edge, and began to carve out a small tunnel, running diagonally through the rock to a point well below the water level. In this way, the force of the explosion would shatter the granite and allow the water to flow through in large quantities, thus lowering its level to the desired extent.

This was slow work. Knowing that he would need a powerful blast, the engineer planned to devote no less than ten liters of nitroglycerine to the operation. But Pencroff and Neb, working by turns, finished their blasting hole before four o'clock in the afternoon.

There remained the problem of the detonation itself. Ordinarily, nitroglycerine is detonated by means of fulminating caps, whose small explosions set off the larger one; for some kind of shock is required to provoke the detonation. If the nitroglycerine were simply set alight, it would burn, but it would not explode.

To be sure, Cyrus Smith could have made a detonating cap. Lacking any other form of fulminate, he could easily concoct something similar to cotton powder, since he had nitric acid at hand. Packed into a cartridge and inserted within the nitroglycerine, this substance could be detonated with a fuse, so engendering the explosion.

But Cyrus Smith knew that nitroglycerine has the peculiar property of detonating when subjected to some kind of blow. He resolved to exploit this attribute, and fall back on the blasting cap only if this technique should fail.

Indeed, a blow from a hammer is enough to set off the explosion of a few drops of nitroglycerine dribbled onto a hard stone; but in the present

Pencroff began to bore a hole…

circumstances the one who swung the hammer would unavoidably become a victim of his own operation. Therefore, Cyrus Smith conceived the idea of suspending a heavy mass of iron over the blasting hole, by means of a simple frame and a length of vegetable-fiber rope. To the middle of this rope was tied one end of another long fiber, coated with sulfur, which was then left trailing along the ground over a distance of several feet. Once this second strand of rope was lit, it would burn until it reached the first, which, catching fire in turn, would break, and several pounds of iron would be dropped onto the nitroglycerine.

This device was erected; then the engineer, urging his companions to keep their distance, filled the blasting hole with nitroglycerine, dribbling a further few drops onto the surface of the rock beneath the mass of iron hanging from its rope.

With this, Cyrus Smith took the end of the sulfur-coated fiber, lit it, and with all possible speed returned to join his companions at the Chimneys.

He estimated that the flame would take twenty-five minutes to reach the second fiber, and indeed, twenty-five minutes later, the air was rocked by an explosion of inexpressible violence. The entire island seemed to tremble on its foundation. A great spray of stones was launched into the heavens with the force of a volcano. The Chimneys' very boulders shuddered as the shock wave hit them. More than two miles from the site of the blast, the colonists were thrown to the ground.

They stood up, returned to the plateau, and ran toward the embankment, hoping to find it ripped open by the explosion...

A triple hurrah burst from their breasts! The wall of granite had cracked wide open! A rushing stream of water surged through the fissure, poured across the plateau, white with foam, came to the ridge, and plunged three hundred feet down to the beach!

XVIII

Pencroff Has No Further Doubts.—The Former Spillway.—A Descent Below Ground.—The Route Through the Granite.—Top Vanishes.—The Central Cavern.—The Shaft.—A Mystery.— Blows from a Pick.—The Return.

Cyrus Smith's plan had succeeded. Nevertheless, as was his wont, he simply looked on, expressing no satisfaction, his lips sealed, his gaze fixed. Harbert could not contain his enthusiasm; Neb leaped for joy; Pencroff shook his great head and murmured these words:

"Quite a piece of work, is our engineer!"

The nitroglycerine had done its job most effectively. The new outlet was quite broad, allowing the escape of at least three times as much water as the old one. As a result, not long after the operation, the level of the lake had dropped by at least two feet.

The colonists returned to the Chimneys to collect their picks, pikes, and fiber ropes, as well as a flint and some tinder; then they returned to the plateau, with Top at their side.

Along the way, the sailor could not prevent himself from saying to the engineer:

"You do know, Mr. Cyrus, that with that charming cordial you've concocted we could easily blow up the entire island?"

"Without a doubt—the island, the continents, the earth itself," answered Cyrus Smith. "It's simply a question of quantity."

"Could we not use this nitroglycerine as ammunition for firearms?" the sailor asked.

"No, Pencroff, it's far too sensitive for that. But we can easily make cotton powder, or even ordinary gunpowder, now that we have nitric acid, saltpeter, sulfur, and coal. Unfortunately, what we do not have are weapons."

"Oh! Mr. Cyrus," answered the sailor, "where there's a will..."

Pencroff had clearly deleted the word *impossible* from Lincoln Island's dictionary.

Arriving at Longview Plateau, the colonists headed immediately toward the end of the lake, where they hoped to find the entrance to the former spillway now fully exposed. If so, the spillway would be dry and passable, and they could attempt to survey its interior configuration.

A few moments later, the colonists reached the southern end of the lake, and one glance was enough to tell them that their hopes had been realized.

For there, within the lake's granite cradle, and well above the waterline, they saw the long-sought-after hole. They approached it by a narrow ledge, also revealed by the receding waters. The fissure measured approximately twenty feet in width, but no more than two feet in height. Its shape was that of a sewer in a street gutter. There was no easy way inside; but Neb and Pencroff took up their picks, and in less than an hour they had expanded the opening to a practicable size.

The engineer than knelt down and discovered that the channel of the spillway sloped at an angle of no more than thirty to thirty-five degrees. It could thus be explored on foot, and so long as the inclination did not increase, they could easily follow it down to the level of the sea itself. And if, as seemed very likely, some great cavity existed inside the granite wall, it might very well prove to be usable.

"Well, Mr. Cyrus, what's keeping us?" asked the sailor, eager to set off into the narrow corridor. "Top's gone on without us, as you see!"

"Very well," answered the engineer. "But we'll need light. —Neb, go and cut us some pine branches."

Neb and Harbert ran toward the lakeshore, shaded by conifers and other green trees, and returned with a load of branches that were bundled together to form torches. The torches were lit with the flint, and Cyrus Smith led the colonists into the dark tube once filled by the waters of the lake.

Contrary to what they might have supposed, the diameter of the passage grew larger as they progressed, meaning that the explorers soon found themselves able to stand upright as they made their way down the slope. Worn smooth by eons of flowing water, the granite surface was treacherously slick, and they had to take great care not to fall. The colonists thus tied themselves together with a rope, as alpinists do in the mountains. Fortunately, occasional irregularities in the surface offered footholds, making their descent less perilous. Drops of water still clung to the rocks, gleaming like prisms in the torchlight and creating the illusion of innumerable stalactites. The engineer examined the black granite walls. He found no strata, no faults. The stone was quite solid, its grain extremely dense, suggesting that the tunnel dated back to the very origins of the island. It was not flowing water that had created this passage. Pluto, not Neptune, had drilled it with his own hand, and the walls showed traces of an eruptive process that the lakewater had not entirely effaced.

The colonists descended at a very cautious pace. An intense emotion took hold of them as they ventured farther into the mass of rock, realizing that they were very obviously the first humans ever to have set foot here. They did not speak, but their minds were full of thoughts, and more than one of them must have been thinking that some octopus or other giant cephalopod might well still be lurking in these inner cavities, which led directly to the sea. Great vigilance would thus be required.

But at the same time, Top was at the head of the little group, and they knew they could rely on the dog's sagacity. He would not fail to sound the alarm should the need arise.

After a sinuous descent of one hundred feet or so, Cyrus Smith suddenly stopped and waited for his companions to catch up with him. Here the tunnel broadened somewhat to form a cavern of some size. Drops of water fell from the vaulted ceiling, but not as a result of percolation through the stone; they were simply the last traces left by the torrent that had for so long roared through this cavity. The air was slightly damp, but seemed entirely free of mephitic fumes.

"Why are we stopping, my dear Cyrus?" said Gideon Spilett. "This is a nicely secluded retreat, well hidden in the depths of the rock, but surely there's no way we could live here."

"Why not?" asked the sailor.

"Because it's too small and too dark."

"Couldn't we enlarge it, hollow it out, cut openings to let in air and light?" answered Pencroff, who now doubted the feasibility of no project.

"Let us go on," answered Cyrus Smith, "and continue our explo-

The colonists descended at a very cautious pace.

rations. Somewhere farther down, we may find that nature has already seen to that."

"We're only one third of the way down," Harbert observed.

"Approximately one third," answered Cyrus Smith, "for we have come about a hundred feet from the entrance, and it may be that a hundred feet farther on..."

"Where's Top?" asked Neb, interrupting his master.

They glanced around the cavern. He was nowhere to be seen.

"He must have gone on ahead," said Pencroff.

"Let's try to catch up with him," answered Cyrus Smith.

They resumed their descent. The engineer carefully noted every deviation in the tunnel's path, and despite its many meanders he had little difficulty keeping track of his general direction, which was ever toward the sea.

The colonists had descended a further fifty vertical feet when their attention was alerted by a series of distant sounds from the cavity's depths. They stopped and listened. The sounds reached their ears clear and undistorted, carrying through the corridor like a voice through an acoustic tube.

"That's Top barking!" cried Harbert.

"Yes," answered Pencroff, "that's our fine dog all right, and barking furiously!"

"We have our pikes," said Cyrus Smith. "Stay on your guard, and forward march!"

"This is getting more interesting by the moment," Gideon Spilett murmured into the ear of the sailor, who nodded in agreement.

Cyrus Smith and his companions hurried to the dog's assistance. Top's bark grew ever louder. They sensed an unusual rage in his sharp yelps. Was he struggling with some animal he had surprised in its lair? As we might well suppose, the colonists were now consumed by an irresistible curiosity, without a thought for the danger they faced. No longer did they creep down the corridor; now they let themselves slide over the rock, as it were, and a few minutes later, sixty feet farther down, they finally met up with Top.

Here the corridor opened into a vast, majestic cavern. They found Top running to and fro, barking with rage. Pencroff and Neb waved their torches in the air, sending great washes of light skimming over the asperities in the granite, while Cyrus Smith, Gideon Spilett, and Harbert stood with their pikes at the ready, waiting to face whatever may come.

But the great cavern was empty. The colonists searched it from one end to the other. There was nothing, not an animal, not a living being! And yet Top continued to bark. Neither caresses nor threats could silence him.

"Somewhere in this cavern there has to be another outlet, to let the lakewater drain into the sea," said the engineer.

"Right you are," said Pencroff. "Let's take care not to fall into any holes."

"Go, Top, go!" cried Cyrus Smith.

Aroused by his master's words, the dog ran toward one end of the cavern, and there his barking doubled in intensity.

They followed him, and, by the light of their torches, they saw a deep shaft opening up in the granite. This was the way seaward for the water that once flowed through these rocks, and this time the tunnel was not a sloping, practicable corridor, but a vertical hole, impossible to enter.

They shone their torches into the shaft. They could see nothing. Cyrus Smith pulled a burning branch from a torch and dropped it into the abyss. The crackling resin lit the interior walls, growing brighter as its fall accelerated, but still nothing could be made out. Then the flame disappeared, indicating by a faint hiss that it had struck water, which is to say that it had dropped to the level of the sea.

Calculating the duration of its fall, the engineer was able to estimate the chasm's depth at some ninety feet.

This meant that the floor of the cavern was situated ninety feet above sea level.

"Here is our new home," said Cyrus Smith.

"But there was something here," answered Gideon Spilett, his curiosity still unsatisfied.

"Well, whatever that something may have been, amphibian or other, it made its escape through that hole," answered the engineer, "and it has left this place to us."

"All the same," added the sailor, "I wish I could have been Top, fifteen minutes ago. He surely wasn't barking at nothing!"

Cyrus Smith looked at his dog, and if one of his companions had been standing near enough, he would have heard him murmur these words:

"Yes, I do believe Top knows more about a great many things than we do!"

Nevertheless, the colonists' wishes had to a great extent come true. Aided by their leader's marvelous wisdom, fortune had served them well. They now enjoyed possession of a vast cavern, whose capacity they could not estimate by the dim light of their torches, but which it would certainly be easy to divide into rooms with brick walls, and so to make their own, if not as their house, at least as a spacious apartment. The waters had abandoned it, never to return. It was theirs for the taking.

Two difficulties remained: first, the problem of lighting this cavity sunk deep within the solid rock; second, the need for an easier access to it. They could not dream of illuminating their home through the ceiling, of course, given the great thickness of the granite slab above their heads; but perhaps they could pierce a hole in the far wall, which faced the sea. During the descent, Cyrus Smith had attempted to judge the slope of their path, and consequently the length of the tunnel, and from this he deduced that the exterior granite wall could not be particularly thick. If a hole could be cut to provide light, the problem of access could be solved at the same time; for if they could cut windows they could surely cut a doorway as well, and then construct a ladder running up the cliff face.

Cyrus Smith laid out his ideas for his companions.

"Well then, Mr. Cyrus, let's get to work!" answered Pencroff. "I have my pick, and I know I can get through that wall! Where should I start?"

"Here," answered the engineer, pointing the energetic sailor toward a concavity where he thought the wall might be thinner.

Pencroff attacked the granite, and for the next half hour he sent shards of rock flying in all directions through the torchlight. Sparks leaped from the stone beneath his pick. Neb relieved him, then Gideon Spilett after Neb.

The work went on for two hours, and they were beginning to fear that the wall might be thicker than the pick was long; but just then, as Gideon Spilett struck one final blow, the tool crashed through the wall and fell outside.

"Hurrah! and again hurrah!" cried Pencroff.

The wall was only three feet thick.

Cyrus Smith admired the view from the opening, which overlooked the shore from an elevation of some eighty feet. Before him lay the beach, the islet, and, beyond that, the endless sea.

And at the same time, through that opening—which was quite large, for a considerable stretch of rock had crumbled—the exterior light poured in, producing a magical effect as it illuminated this splendid cavern! The leftmost area of the cave measured no more than thirty feet high by thirty feet wide by one hundred feet deep, but to the right they now discovered an enormous cavern whose vaulted ceiling soared to more than eighty feet. Here and there, granite pillars supported the vaulting like the columns of a cathedral's nave. Atop those columns, as atop the lateral piers of a great church, here dipping to form arches, there bulging over ogival ribs, obscured in the dark aisles whose capricious forms were only dimly visible in the gloom, ornamented with a profusion of outcroppings like so many pendentives, this vaulted ceiling was a miraculous blend of all the wonders of Byzantine, Romanesque, and Gothic architecture at once. And yet here the only craftsman was nature! Nature alone had carved this enchanted Alhambra from a block of granite!

The colonists were mute with wonder. They were expecting a cramped little cavity, and they had discovered a marvelous palace! Neb took off his hat, as if he had found himself transported to a veritable temple!

Cries of astonishment burst from every breast. The hurrahs resounded, echoing down the dark naves and slowly fading as they reached the end.

"Oh, my friends!" cried Cyrus Smith. "Once we have sufficient light, we can use the left-hand area for bedrooms, storerooms, a kitchen, and we'll still have this marvelous cavern for our study room and museum!"

"And what will we call this place?..." asked Harbert.

"Granite House,"* answered Cyrus Smith, and his companions greeted this name with another round of hurrahs.

The torches were now almost completely consumed, and since they would have to find their way uphill through the passage to return to the plateau, they decided to put off until the next day the task of settling into their new home.

Before they left, Cyrus Smith knelt once again over the dark vertical shaft connecting the cavern with the sea. He listened carefully. There was

---

* We should understand the word *house* to mean "palace" here, for in English this word can be used to refer to dwellings both grand and humble. See, for instance, Buckingham House or Mansion House, in London.

not a sound to be heard, not so much as a splash from the water, which even under this mass of rock must sometimes be tossed by the undulations of the ocean swells. Another bundle of burning sticks was dropped. The walls of the shaft were lit for a moment, but—no more than the first time—nothing suspect was revealed. If some sea monster had been lurking there when the water suddenly drained away, it would now have returned to the open sea through the underground conduit where the lakewater once flowed.

For many long minutes the engineer remained motionless, his ear cocked, his gaze lost in the depths of the abyss, speaking not a single word.

The sailor then approached him, and, touching his arm:

"Mr. Smith?" he said.

"What is it, my friend?" the engineer answered, as if just returned from the land of dreams.

"The torches will be burning out soon."

"Let's be off!" answered Cyrus Smith.

The little band left the cavern and began to ascend through the dark tunnel again. Top brought up the rear, still growling now and then in a very curious way. It was a difficult climb. The colonists paused for a few moments when they reached the upper grotto, which formed a sort of landing halfway down that long granite staircase. Then they resumed their ascent.

Soon the air became fresher. The water droplets had evaporated, and the walls no longer glimmered as they passed by. Their light was fast dimming. Neb's torch soon went out; they would have to hurry if they did not want to be forced to find their way out through total darkness.

This they did, and not long before four o'clock, just as the sailor's torch was going out in turn, Cyrus Smith and his companions emerged from the spillway entrance.

XIX

Cyrus Smith's Plans.—The Facade of Granite House.—The Rope Ladder.—Pencroff's Dreams.—Aromatic Herbs.—A Natural Rabbit Warren.—Water for the New Home.—A View from the Windows of Granite House.

The next day, May 22nd, they began the process of adapting the new abode to their needs. The colonists were eager to abandon the meager shelter of the Chimneys for this vast, solid retreat deep within the living rock, protected from waters both oceanic and atmospheric. The Chimneys would not be abandoned, however, for the engineer intended to use their former home as a workshop for some of his more ambitious projects.

Cyrus Smith's first concern was to determine the precise location of Granite House's facade on the cliff face. He went to the foot of the enormous wall, and since the pick must have fallen vertically as it slipped from the reporter's hands, he would have only to find that pick in order to discover the spot where the hole had been made in the granite.

The pick was easy to find, and, to be sure, a hole could be seen some eighty feet up the wall, directly above the point where the pick had sunk into the sand. A number of rock doves came and went through the narrow opening, just as if they assumed Granite House had been discovered specially for them!

The engineer intended to divide the leftmost portion of the cave into several rooms preceded by an entryway, and to illuminate it with five windows cut from the facade, along with a door. Pencroff agreed with the five windows, but he could not see the usefulness of the door, since the spillway offered them a natural staircase into Granite House.

"My friend," Cyrus Smith answered, "if we can easily enter our home through the spillway, others will be able to as well. My idea, in fact, is to barricade the spillway at its entrance, to seal it off permanently—and even, if need be, to conceal the entrance altogether by building a dam and raising the water level in the lake."

"And how shall we get in?" asked the sailor.

"By an exterior ladder," answered Cyrus Smith. "With a solid rope ladder that we can pull inside when required, our home will be completely impregnable."

"But why all these precautions?" said Pencroff. "So far the animals haven't seemed particularly fierce. And as for hostile natives, there's not a living soul on the island!"

"Are you quite sure of that, Pencroff?" asked the engineer, looking at the sailor.

"We can't be sure, of course, until we've given it a complete going over," answered Pencroff.

"Indeed," said Cyrus Smith. "There is much yet to be explored. But in any case, even if we have no domestic enemies, they might well come from outside, for the Pacific can be a very rough neighborhood. We must defend ourselves against any eventuality."

There was wisdom in Cyrus Smith's words, and Pencroff prepared to carry out his orders without further objection.

The "apartment" of Granite House would thus be lit by five windows and a door in the facade. They would also cut a large picture window and a series of bull's-eyes, allowing light to flood into the marvelous nave that would serve as their great room. Eighty feet above the ground, the facade of their new house faced east, and the rising sun greeted it with its first rays. The facade ran from the angled precipice at the mouth of the Mercy to a point directly above the pile of rocks that formed the Chimneys. Thus, the strongest winds, blowing from the northeast, would strike it only obliquely, for it was sheltered by the very orientation of the cliff face. For the moment, until they could build window frames, the engineer intended to keep out the wind and rain with thick shutters, which could be concealed if the need arose.

The first task was to cut the openings in the facade. With picks alone this would have been a long and arduous process; and, as we know, Cyrus Smith was not a man for half measures. He still had a certain quantity of nitroglycerine at his disposal, and he made good use of it. He took great care to localize the effect of his explosive, and under its force the granite shattered precisely where the engineer wished. Then the pick and pickax were brought in to shape and refine the forms of the bedroom windows, the vast main window, the bull's-eyes, and the door. They carefully smoothed away all the irregular edges, and a few days after the work had begun, Granite House was amply lit by the rising sun, even in its most secret depths.

Cyrus Smith planned to divide the living quarters into five sections, each of them overlooking the sea: first, an entryway with a door to which the ladder would allow access, then a kitchen, thirty feet wide, a dining room measuring forty feet, a dormitory of the same size, and finally, at Pencroff's insistence, a "guest room" adjoining the great nave.

These rooms, or rather this series of rooms forming the living quarters of Granite House, would not occupy the full depth of the cavity. A corridor would run along the back wall of the chambers, separating them from a long storeroom with ample space for utensils, provisions, and reserves. Perfectly watertight, their storeroom would offer ideal conditions for the preservation of all the many products they had gathered from the island, flora and fauna alike; furthermore, its vast size would allow their reserves to be warehoused in the most practical and efficient manner. And as if this were not enough, there was also the small grotto above the great cavern to serve as the colonists' attic.

The plans were drawn up; there was nothing more to do but carry them out. The miners now became brickmakers again; then, once the bricks had been formed and fired, they were brought to the foot of Granite House and left on the sand.

So far, Cyrus Smith and his friends had always used the spillway to enter the cavern. For this they had to climb up to Longview Plateau after a detour along the riverbank, then descend two hundred feet through the corridor, then climb the same distance again when they wanted to return to the plateau, all of which involved a certain expense of both time and energy. Cyrus Smith thus resolved to proceed immediately to the fabrication of a solid rope ladder, which, once drawn inside the cave, would make the entrance to Granite House perfectly inaccessible.

The ladder was constructed with great care, and its uprights, made of stout bulrush fibers braided with the aid of a small winch, were as sturdy as a thick cable. The rungs were furnished by a variety of red cedar tree with light, solid branches. Through the hard work of Pencroff's able hands, the ladder was soon finished and ready for use.

More ropes were made from plant fibers, and a sort of crude pulley block was installed at the door, by which the bricks could be hoisted into Granite House with great ease and speed. The transformation of the cave's interior could now begin in earnest. They had plenty of lime at hand, and several thousand bricks; with these they quickly erected rudimentary interior walls, and in a very short time the leftmost portion of the cavern was divided into five chambers and a storeroom, in accordance with the plan they had devised.

All this was done under the direction of the engineer, who also wielded the hammer and trowel. No sort of manual labor was alien to Cyrus Smith, and in all things he served as an example to his intelligent and devoted companions. They worked confidently, merrily even, with many a lighthearted quip from Pencroff—Pencroff the ropemaker, the carpenter, the mason—communicating his good humor to the entire group. The sailor's faith in the engineer was complete and unshakable. He thought him capable of any enterprise, and incapable only of failure. The question of clothes and shoes—a serious question indeed—as well as such other problems as illumination for the long winter nights, the cultivation of the fertile areas of the island, the transformation of wild flora into civilized flora, everything seemed simple to him with Cyrus Smith's help, and anything was possible, given time. He dreamed of canalized rivers to ease the transportation of the earth's bounty; he dreamed of quarries and mines, of machines for every industrial purpose, of railways—yes, railways!—whose network of tracks would certainly cover Lincoln Island one day.

The engineer never once interrupted Pencroff's wild flights of fancy; he would not have dreamed of crushing even one of his worthy friend's exaggerated dreams. He knew how contagious enthusiasm can be. He even smiled to hear him speak, and said nothing of the anxieties that the future sometimes aroused in him. For in this part of the Pacific, so far from the shipping routes, he might justifiably fear that they would never be rescued. The colonists would have to rely on themselves, and themselves alone, for the distance between Lincoln Island and any other land was such that to attempt the voyage in a handmade boat—inevitably small and frail—would be a most serious and perilous undertaking.

But, as the sailor often said, they were a hundred arm-lengths ahead of the Robinson Crusoes of yesteryear, for whom any success seemed a miracle.

And it is true: they "knew," and the man who "knows" succeeds where others unavoidably falter and perish.

Harbert distinguished himself in these labors. He was intelligent and active, quick to understand, careful in his execution. Cyrus Smith found himself growing increasingly attached to the boy, and Harbert felt a strong and respectful friendship for the engineer. Pencroff could see the close bond of sympathy forming between those two souls, but he felt no jealousy.

Neb was Neb. He was as he would always be, the very embodiment of courage, zeal, devotion, and self-abnegation. He shared Pencroff's absolute faith in his master, but he displayed it less ebulliently. To every eruption of the sailor's enthusiasm, Neb always seemed to respond, "Nothing could be more natural." He and Pencroff were great friends, and had quickly come to speak together in the most familiar and amicable terms.

As for Gideon Spilett, he always did his share of the common labors, and, to the sailor's great astonishment, he did not prove to be the least handy of the bunch. A journalist of great talent, quick and agile of mind, to be sure—but no less skillful with his hands!

The ladder was installed on May 28th. It comprised no fewer than one hundred rungs over a length of eighty feet. A ledge that jutted felicitously from the wall some forty feet up allowed Cyrus Smith to divide the ladder into two halves, greatly reducing the weight of the ladder and the difficulty of scaling it. The outcropping was carefully leveled with their picks, and the upper end of the first ladder was anchored to this landing while the lower end trailed loose on the beach; a rope tied to the lowest rung would allow the colonists to pull the ladder up to the landing, making Granite House utterly inaccessible from below. As for the second ladder, they attached it at both its lower end, which rested against the ledge, and its upper end, tied to the doorjamb itself. This greatly eased their ascent. Furthermore, Cyrus Smith had plans for a hydraulic elevator, which would spare the inhabitants of Granite House both time and energy.

The colonists soon grew accustomed to using the ladder. They were spry and nimble, and the sailor Pencroff, quite used to clambering over the ratlines of ships' shrouds, was happy to give lessons in this art. He had to give lessons to Top as well, of course, and with his four legs, the poor dog was scarcely built for such an exercise. But Pencroff was a conscientious teacher, and in the end Top climbed the ladder with all the casual ease of a veteran circus dog. The sailor's pride in his pupil would be difficult to express. But sometimes, and on more than one occasion, Pencroff carried him on his back, and this was entirely to Top's liking.

Despite the haste with which these projects were carried out—for the bad weather was not far off—the question of alimentation was never neglected. The reporter and Harbert had become the provisioners for the colony, and every day they spent a few hours hunting for fresh game. Their excursions never took them beyond Jacamar Woods on the left bank of the river, for, with neither bridge nor boat, the Mercy was an insurmountable barrier. The immense woodland they had dubbed the Forests of the Far West thus remained unexplored for the moment. They were saving that important excursion for the return of the fine weather the following spring. But there was no lack of game in Jacamar Woods; kangaroos and wild boars abounded, and the hunters' pikes, like their bows and arrows, served them well. Furthermore, in the southwestern corner of the lagoon, Harbert discovered a natural rabbit warren, a slightly marshy, willow-strewn plain, its air scented by aromatic herbs such as thyme, mother-of-thyme, basil, savory, and all the fragrant Labiae species of which rabbits are so inordinately fond.

With such a fine dinner awaiting them, as the reporter observed, it would have been surprising if there were no rabbits to be found there; thus, the two hunters searched the warren with great care. If nothing else, they had here an abundance of useful plants. Any naturalist would have been delighted at this opportunity to study the varied specimens of the vegetal kingdom. Harbert collected several handfuls of basil, rosemary, balm, betony, etc., all endowed with various therapeutic properties, some of them expectorants, astringents, or febrifuges, others antispasmodics or antirheumatics. And when Pencroff later inquired into the purpose of this harvest of herbs:

"To keep us well," answered the boy, "and to treat ourselves when we're ill."

"Why should we ever be ill, since there are no doctors on the island?" Pencroff replied, in all seriousness.

There was no answering Pencroff's question, but the boy continued gathering the herbs all the same, and his project was warmly received at Granite House, particularly because in addition to the rest he had brought back a notable quantity of *Monarda didyma*, which in northern America goes by the name of Oswego tea, and produces an excellent beverage.

Finally, the two hunters' painstaking search brought them to the heart of the warren. The ground was perforated like a sieve.

"Burrows!" cried Harbert.

"Yes," answered the reporter, "so they are, quite clearly."

"But are they occupied?"

"That's the question."

The question was soon answered, for a moment later, hundreds of small, rabbitlike animals erupted from the ground and went fleeing in all directions, with such speed that Top himself could not have outrun them. The dog and hunters gave chase, but the rodents easily eluded them. Nevertheless, the reporter was determined not to leave this place until he had bagged at least a half-dozen of the quadrupeds. He had immediate plans for them in the kitchen, of course; but he was also thinking of catching a number of rabbits for domestication, which they could easily do by laying snares at the mouths of the burrows. But for the moment they had no snares, nor anything to make snares with. What they could not accomplish by cunning they would thus have to accomplish by sheer persistence; and so they resolved to search from den to den, thrusting a stick into the holes to flush out any rodents taking shelter within.

Fourteen such animals were pulled from their dens over the next hour. A closer inspection showed them to be very similar to the rodent known in Europe as the "American rabbit."

Their catch was brought back to Granite House for their evening meal, and warmly praised by all the colonists. The warren was clearly no small discovery; it would be a precious resource for the colony, and an apparently inexhaustible one.

The interior walls were finished on May 31st. There was nothing left but to furnish the chambers, which would be their project for the long winter days. A fireplace was constructed in the room they had designated as the kitchen. Now they would have to find a way to channel the smoke outside, and for this purpose Cyrus Smith made a fat pipe from the same clay they had used for their bricks. The pipe could not, of course, be routed through the stone to the upper plateau, and so a hole was made in

A small hole was bored in the rock . . .

the granite just above the kitchen window; the pipe would run from the hearth to that opening, precisely like an ordinary tin stovepipe. Perhaps—probably, in fact—the fireplace would smoke when the east winds blew hard against the facade, but this was a rare occurrence, and in any case such details were of little concern to master Neb, the cook.

Once they had laid out the interior of the cavern, the engineer turned to the project of blocking off the opening of the spillway to prevent any access to their home by that route. Large boulders were rolled over the orifice and solidly cemented into place. Cyrus Smith did not yet carry out his plan to return the water to its original level and so submerge the opening. Nevertheless, he took care to conceal his barricade by planting an abundance of grasses, bushes, and shrubs among the rocks, knowing that they would grow exuberantly in the course of the coming spring.

But the channel through the granite would not go entirely unused. It was Cyrus Smith's plan to bring a small stream of fresh water from the lake into their new lodgings, and it was through this channel that the water would flow. A small hole was bored in the rock beneath the surface of the lake, and from this pure and inexhaustible source Granite House would draw some twenty-five to thirty gallons* of water each day—more than enough for their needs.

Their new home was now fully livable, and it was high time, for the cold weather was near. They had yet to make window glass to protect them from the cold winter winds; nevertheless, thick shutters allowed them to seal off the openings in the facade, and this proved reasonably effective.

On the outcroppings around the windows, Gideon Spilett had very artistically arranged a variety of plants and feathery grasses, giving the simple openings in the rock a picturesque frame of greenery, to delightful effect.

The inhabitants of this solid, salubrious, and safe refuge could not help but marvel at their own handiwork. The windows afforded an extensive view over an unbounded horizon, broken only by the two Cape Mandibles to the north and Cape Claw to the south. Union Bay spread out magnificently before their eyes. Yes, these gallant colonists had good reason to be pleased, and Pencroff was not sparing in his praise of what he quaintly called "his apartment five floors above the mezzanine!"

---

* One gallon equals approximately four and one-half liters.

XX

The Rainy Season.—The Question of Clothing.—A Seal Hunt.—Candle Making.—Indoor Projects.—The Two Bridges.—Return from the Oyster Beds.—What Harbert Found in His Pocket.

This month of June, which corresponds to the month of December in the northern hemisphere, marked the true onset of winter. It began with showers and gusts of wind, one upon the other without surcease. The guests of Granite House now learned the full value of a dwelling protected from inclemencies. The Chimneys would have offered them a very mean shelter against the rigors of winter, not to mention the continual fear that the fierce waves, propelled by the winds of the open sea, would once again pour into their home. Indeed, Cyrus Smith thought it necessary to take certain precautions against this threat, for they would do well to protect the Chimneys' forge and kilns as best they could.

The various labors that occupied the colonists over the month of June left plenty of time for hunting and fishing, and their store of foodstuffs never dwindled. As soon as he could find the time, Pencroff planned to set a number of animal traps from which he expected great things. He had already made a number of snares from tough plant fibers, and not a day went by without a fresh catch of rodents from the rabbit warren. Neb spent hours salting or smoking animal carcasses, and their larders were bursting with delicious preserved meats.

They now turned their full attention to the question of clothing. The colonists had no other garments than those they were wearing when the balloon cast them onto this island. Their clothes and linens were sturdy and warm, and they treated them with great care, keeping them in a state of impeccable cleanliness; nevertheless, it would soon all have to be replaced, and if the coming winter turned out to be a harsh one, their wardrobe would likely prove woefully deficient.

Here Cyrus Smith's ingenuity was confounded. They had rightly dealt with the most serious issues first—the fundamental questions of food and shelter—and now the cold weather might come upon them at any time, before the problem of clothing had been resolved. They had no choice but to endure this first winter as best they could. When spring returned, they would undertake a serious hunting expedition to the slopes of Mount Franklin, in search of the mouflons they had sighted before. Once they had harvested their fleece, the engineer would find a way to weave it into warm, sturdy cloth... How? That he would have to consider at greater length.

"Well, we'll just have to warm our feet by the fire here in Granite House!" said Pencroff. "There's plenty of firewood, and no reason to spare it."

"Besides," answered Gideon Spilett, "Lincoln Island lies at a comparatively low latitude, so the winter may well not prove all that rigorous. Did you not say, Cyrus, that the thirty-fifth parallel is equivalent to the latitude of Spain, in the other hemisphere?"

"I did," the engineer responded, "but winters can be very harsh in Spain! They have no lack of snow and wind, and it might well be the same on Lincoln Island. Nevertheless, it is an island; and, as such, its temperatures will hopefully prove more moderate."

"And why is that, Mr. Cyrus?" asked Harbert.

"Because, my boy, the sea can be thought of as an immense reservoir for the summer's warmth. Once winter comes, the sea returns that heat to the atmosphere; thus, any land lying near the sea enjoys temperatures somewhat less warm in the summer, but not as cold in the winter."

"We'll see," answered Pencroff. "I prefer not to spend my time worrying about how cold it will or will not be. One thing is certain: the days are already shorter now, and the evenings longer. Perhaps we should consider the question of lighting?"

"Nothing could be simpler," answered Cyrus Smith.

"To consider?" asked the sailor.

"To resolve."

"And when shall we begin?"

"Tomorrow, with another seal hunt."

"So we can make tallow?"

"Fie, Pencroff! So we can make candle wax."

Such was indeed the engineer's plan, and a perfectly realistic plan it was; for already they had lime and sulfuric acid, and the islet's amphibians could be counted on to provide all the fat they required.

It was June 4th, Pentecost Sunday, and they unanimously agreed to observe the occasion. All work was suspended, and prayers were offered up to Heaven. But their prayers were now prayers of thanksgiving. The colonists of Lincoln Island were no longer the wretched castaways that had been tossed onto the islet. They no longer entreated Providence; they simply expressed their gratitude.

The next day, June 5th, they set out for the islet in rather unsettled weather. Once more they had to wait for low tide to ford the channel, and in light of this they resolved to try their hands at building a small boat. This would ease their crossings to the islet, and would also afford a faster route up the Mercy for the exploration of the island's southwestern quadrant, which was planned for the first fine days of spring.

On the islet they found a great herd of seals, of which a half-dozen were handily killed with the pikes. Neb and Pencroff quickly flayed them, and they returned to Granite House with the blubber and skin, the latter to be used in making sturdy new shoes.

The hunt had yielded some three hundred pounds of fat, all of which would be used for the fabrication of candles.

This was an extremely simple procedure, and if the results were not absolutely perfect, they were at least usable. If Cyrus Smith had had only sulfuric acid to work with, he could have heated it with an inert fatty compound—in this case, seal blubber—to extract the glycerine; then, from this new substance, he could easily have separated the olein, margarine, and stearin with boiling water. But in order to simplify his task, he chose to saponify the fat with lime. This produced a chalky soap which could be treated with sulfuric acid, causing the lime to precipitate out as a sulfate and leaving the fatty acids free.

He now had a compound of three acids: oleic, margaric, and stearic. The first, being a liquid, was driven off by pressure; the two left behind were precisely what he needed for his candles.

All this took no more than twenty-four hours. After several failed attempts, they succeeded in making wicks from vegetal fibers, and once these were inserted into the liquefied substance they had genuine hand-molded stearic candles. To be sure, they were neither bleached nor polished, nor were the wicks impregnated with boric acid to make them vitrify and disappear as they burned; but once Cyrus Smith had constructed a fine pair of snuffers, these candles were greatly appreciated during the long nights in Granite House.

The next month was spent in continual indoor labor. In light of the carpentry projects to come, they had to make improvements to their rudimentary tools, and build new tools to add to their collection.

Among these was a pair of scissors, thanks to which the colonists were finally able to cut their hair and, if not shave their beards, at least trim them to their liking. Harbert had none, Neb scarcely at all, but their companions' luxuriant whiskers easily justified the work involved in fashioning this new implement.

They expended much time and labor in the fabrication of a small handsaw; in the end, their efforts were repaid with an instrument capable of separating ligneous fibers most effectively, if rather laboriously. With this it became possible to make furniture, and soon Granite House was graced with tables, chairs, cupboards, and bed frames—although their bedding remained limited to eelgrass mattresses. The kitchen was a pleasure to behold, with its clay cookware lined up on the shelves, its brick oven, its stone sink, and Neb attended to his tasks there as gravely as any chemist in his laboratory.

But the furniture makers soon had to make way for the builders. The new stream created by the nitroglycerine blast necessitated the construction of two rudimentary bridges, one on Longview Plateau, the other on the beach itself. For the plateau and the beach were now transected by a rushing torrent, and the colonists needed a way across in order to reach the north of the island, now accessible only by way of a long detour to the west, beyond the source of Red Creek. Clearly, the best solution was to build bridges on the plateau and the beach. Over the next few days, then, great trees were felled, and their trunks, some twenty-five to thirty feet long, were squared off with an ax and laid across the flowing waters. No sooner were the bridges in place than Neb and Pencroff found an occasion to use them, visiting the oyster beds they had discovered offshore from the dunes. They took with them a sort of crude chariot, a replacement for the cumbersome sledge, and returned with several thousand oysters. A new bed was made for the mollusks among the rocks at the mouth of the Mercy, and soon they were perfectly acclimated to these surroundings. The oysters were of the very finest quality, and the colonists quickly made them an almost daily part of their diet.

Thus, although they had as yet explored only a small portion of their domain, Lincoln Island already provided the colonists with virtually everything they required, and an exploration of the secret recesses of the vast forest that stretched from the Mercy to Reptile End seemed sure to offer up still more and greater treasures.

One privation, however, continued to weigh on the colonists of Lincoln Island. There was no lack of nitrogenous meats, nor of vegetal products with which to vary their diet; the fermented roots of the dragon trees gave them a slightly acidic beverage, a sort of beer that they found vastly preferable to plain water; they had even made sugar, without canes or beets, by collecting the liquor distilled by the *Acer saccharinum,* a sort of maple of the Acerineae family that flourishes in moderate zones all over the world, and which the island possessed in great number; they concocted a very pleasant tea with the monarda they had found in the rabbit warren; finally, they had plenty of salt, the only mineral product that enters into the human diet... but there was no bread.

Perhaps, in times to come, the colonists would develop some sort of substitute, using sago flour or starch from a breadfruit tree—for the southern forests were likely home to such flora—but for the moment they had nothing.

Providence, however, was about to intervene in the colonists' favor. To be sure, its gift was of an infinitesimal size. Nevertheless, despite all his intelligence, all his ingenuity, Cyrus Smith would never have been able to produce what Harbert found one day, by the greatest of chances, as he was stitching up the lining of his jacket.

The rain was pouring down, and the colonists were sitting together in the great room of Granite House. Suddenly the boy cried out:

"Look, Mr. Cyrus! A grain of wheat!"

And he showed his companions a grain, one single grain, which had slipped through a hole in his pocket and landed in the lining of his jacket.

The presence of this grain was explained by a favorite occupation of Harbert's during his stay in Richmond: the feeding of a small number of ringdoves offered to him as a gift by Pencroff.

"A grain of wheat?" the engineer asked excitedly.

"Yes, Mr. Cyrus, but only one, no more than one!"

"Well, my boy," cried Pencroff with a smile, "that'll do us no end of good, I daresay! What on earth are we to do with one grain of wheat?"

"Make bread," answered Cyrus Smith.

"Bread, cakes, pies!" replied the sailor. "Come now! I'll say this at least, there'll be no danger of choking on the loaf of bread we make from that grain of wheat!"

Harbert attached no real importance to his discovery, and was about to throw the grain away, but Cyrus Smith took it, examined it, and found it to be in good condition. Then, looking the sailor square in the face:

"Pencroff," he asked him calmly, "do you know how many ears of wheat one grain can produce?"

"One, I suppose!" answered the sailor, surprised at this question.

"Ten, Pencroff. And do you know how many grains one ear of wheat holds?"

"Why, no."

"Eighty, on average," said Cyrus Smith. "Therefore, if we plant this grain, our first harvest will bring in eight hundred grains, which will produce, at second harvest, six hundred forty thousand, at third harvest five hundred twelve million, at fourth more than four hundred billion grains. That's how it adds up."

Cyrus Smith's companions listened in silence. The numbers were staggering, but perfectly accurate.

"Yes, my friends," the engineer continued. "Such is the mathematical progression of nature's fecundity. And yet what is the multiplication of the grain of wheat, whose ear bears only eight hundred grains, compared to a poppy plant, which produces thirty-two thousand seeds, or a tobacco plant, which produces three hundred sixty thousand? Within a few years, were it not for the many destructive forces that hinder their fecundity, such plants would cover the entire surface of earth."

But the engineer's brief discourse was not over yet.

"And now, Pencroff," he continued, "do you know how many bushels four hundred billion grains would make?"

"No," answered the sailor, "but what I do know is that I am an ass!"

"Well, more than three million, Pencroff, assuming thirty thousand grains per bushel."

"Three million!" cried Pencroff.

"Three million."

"In four years?"

"In four years," answered Cyrus Smith, "and even in two, if, as I hope, we can expect to make two harvests per year at this latitude."

Pencroff could think of no other reply than his customary hurrah.

"So, Harbert," the engineer added, "you have made a discovery of the greatest significance. Everything, my friends, everything can be of use to us in our present circumstances. I beg of you, never forget that."

"No, Mr. Cyrus, no, we won't forget," answered Pencroff, "and if ever I find one of those tobacco seeds that can be multiplied by three hundred sixty thousand, you can be sure I won't throw it to the winds! And now, do you know what we must do next?"

"We must plant that grain," answered Harbert.

"Yes," added Gideon Spilett, "and with all the care it deserves, for it bears within it all our future harvests."

"Oh, let it grow!" cried the sailor.

"It will grow," answered Cyrus Smith.

The date was June 20th, an ideal time to sow that one precious grain of wheat. They first thought of starting it in a pot; but, on reflection, they resolved to place their faith in nature, and to entrust it to the earth. And so they did, that very day, and it need hardly be added that every possible precaution was taken to ensure the success of this new venture.

The sky had cleared, and the colonists climbed to the plateau above Granite House. There they chose a spot well sheltered from the wind, and warmed by the noonday sun. The area was cleared, thoroughly hoed, even searched for insects and worms; they added a layer of good soil rectified with a bit of lime, and surrounded the plot with a wooden palisade. Finally the grain was pressed into the damp earth.

Was this not rather like the laying of the first stone of some great edifice? Pencroff was reminded of the day he had lit his single match, and of all the care that went into that operation. But this was a far more serious matter. For the castaways would surely have managed to produce fire somehow, by one method or another, but no human power could ever bring back that grain of wheat, if, by some great misfortune, it should die!

XXI

Below Zero.—Exploration of the Southeastern Marshes.—The
Culpeo Foxes.—View of the Sea.—A Discussion of the Future of
the Pacific Ocean.—The Endless Labor of the Infusoria.—What
the World Will Become.—The Hunt.—Shelduck Fens.

From that moment on, not a day went by without Pencroff paying a visit
to what, in all seriousness, he called his "wheatfield." And unhappy was
the lot of any insect venturing onto that terrain! It was shown not the
slightest mercy.

Toward the end of June, after a period of interminable rains, the cold
weather settled in. By the twenty-ninth, a Fahrenheit thermometer
would have indicated only 20 degrees above zero (6.67 degrees centigrade below freezing).

The next day, June 30th, corresponding to December 31st in the
northern calendar, was a Friday. Neb observed that the year was ending
on a very gloomy day; but Pencroff answered that the next year would no
doubt begin with a fair one—which was far more significant.

In any case, it began with bitter cold. Ice began to accumulate at the
mouth of the Mercy, and the surface of the lake was soon entirely frozen.

They had to replenish their fuel supply more than once. It occurred to
Pencroff that they should bring a number of large timber rafts down the
Mercy before it froze. The current was a tireless engine, and they used it
to convey the floating wood until the cold brought it to a standstill. They
supplemented their supply of firewood with several cartloads of coal,
which required a journey to the foothills of Mount Franklin. The powerful heat it provided was greatly appreciated on the bitterest days of win-

ter, such as July 4th, when the temperature dropped to eight degrees Fahrenheit (thirteen degrees centigrade below zero). A second fireplace was installed in the dining room, and this became their common workroom.

At times such as this, Cyrus Smith might have been understandably pleased with himself for having directed a small rivulet from Lake Grant through Granite House. Drawn from below the frozen surface, the liquid water flowed through the spillway and trickled into an interior reservoir dug out from one corner of the storeroom; as this reservoir overflowed, the excess cascaded down the shaft and so out to sea.

The weather was cold but perfectly dry, and so the colonists resolved to spend a day exploring the southeastern corner of the island from the Mercy to Cape Claw. This was a vast marshy area, sure to be full of great flocks of aquatic birds, and they believed it might offer good hunting.

They estimated the distance at eight to nine miles each way, which meant that the day would be a long one. The entire colony would take part in the exploration, since it involved a completely unknown region. Thus, at six o'clock on the morning of July 5th, Cyrus Smith, Gideon Spilett, Harbert, Neb, and Pencroff—dressed as warmly as possible, armed with pikes, snares, bows and arrows, and carrying an ample supply of provisions—left Granite House, preceded by Top, who gamboled as he ran on before them.

They wanted to take the shortest route, and the shortest route was to cross the Mercy by way of the vast sheet of ice that now covered it.

"But," the reporter correctly remarked, "this is no replacement for a real bridge!"

And so the construction of a "real" bridge was inscribed in the list of future tasks.

This was the first time they had set foot on the right bank of the Mercy, and their first trek through the tall, majestic pines that grew there, now covered with snow.

But before they had traveled a half-mile, an entire family of quadrupeds bolted from the dense thicket that was their home and scurried away, alarmed by Top's barking.

"Oh! they look like foxes!" cried Harbert, as he watched them race off into the distance.

And indeed, they were foxes, but foxes of great size, and as they ran they let out a series of piercing barks, much to Top's astonishment. At

The shortest route was to cross the Mercy.

once he broke off his pursuit and allowed the swift animals to make their escape.

The dog had every right to be surprised, given his ignorance of the natural sciences. The foxes' coats were reddish gray, their tails black with a white tassel at the end, but it was their bark that revealed their nature. Thus, Harbert unhesitatingly identified them by their true name: culpeos. These culpeos are commonly found in Chile, the Malvinas, and in all regions of the Americas lying between the thirtieth and fortieth parallels. Harbert was deeply disappointed that Top had not managed to get hold of one of the carnivores.

"Can they be eaten?" asked Pencroff, who unfailingly considered the island's fauna from a very specific point of view.

"No," answered Harbert, "but zoologists have not yet determined whether their pupils are diurnal or nocturnal, meaning that they might be more properly classified as dogs."

Cyrus Smith could not help but smile on hearing the boy's observation, seeing it as further evidence of a fine and serious mind. As for the sailor, once he had learned that the foxes could not be classified as foodstuffs he lost interest entirely. He nevertheless observed that it might be a good idea to defend their property against such four-legged marauders once they began raising animals at Granite House, and this no one contested.

Once they had passed Flotsam Point, the colonists found a long beach, washed by the waters of the sea. It was then eight o'clock in the morning. The sky was clear, as is often the case during prolonged periods of cold weather; but, warmed by the exertion of their walk, Cyrus Smith and his companions did not suffer too cruelly from the cold. Besides, there was no wind, and in such conditions low temperatures are considerably easier to tolerate. A bright but unwarming sun was then rising from the ocean, like an enormous disk hanging low on the horizon. The sea was an untroubled sheet of blue, reminiscent of a Mediterranean gulf in fine weather. Cape Claw, curved like a yataghan, could be seen tapering away some four miles to the southeast. To the left, the marsh abruptly ended in a rocky spit, newly lit by the golden beam of the solar rays. Nothing, not even a sandbar, stood between this part of Union Bay and the open sea; clearly, no ship would be safe from the howling easterly winds here. By the perfect tranquillity of the water, by its uniform blue color, unsullied by the yellow tint of a shallow spot, and finally by the absence of reefs, they sensed that the bottom must be very steeply inclined, and that a profound abyss lay beneath that serene and even surface. The first trees of the Far West forests lay four miles behind them, to the west. They might have been forgiven for thinking that they were standing on the desolate shore of some ice-strewn antarctic island. The colonists stopped here for breakfast. A fire of brush and wrack was lit, and Neb prepared a collation of cold meat, to which he added a few cups of Oswego tea.

They observed their surroundings as they ate. The region was truly sterile, in stark contrast to the western half of the island. This led the reporter to reflect that if chance had first dropped the castaways onto this beach, they would have imagined their future domain in the most deplorable terms.

"Indeed, I don't believe we would ever have reached land," answered the engineer, "for the water is uncommonly deep, without a single rock to cling to. In front of Granite House there were sandbanks at least, and an islet, which greatly increased our chances of survival. Here, nothing but the abyss!"

"It seems odd to me," observed Gideon Spilett, "that an island as small as this should have such a varied landscape. One would expect to find such a great variety of features on a major continent, but never on an island. You might almost think that the rich, fertile western half of Lincoln Island were bathed by the warmth of the Gulf of Mexico, while its northern and southeastern shores looked out onto Arctic waters."

"You're right, my dear Spilett," answered Cyrus Smith. "The same idea has occurred to me. In both form and nature, this island strikes me as a very strange place. It seems to possess all the geographical richness of a continent, and I would not be surprised to learn that that is precisely what it was at some time in the past."

"What's that? A continent in the middle of the Pacific?" cried Pencroff.

"Why not?" answered Cyrus Smith. "Why should Australia, New Ireland, everything that the English geographers call Australasia, together with the Pacific archipelagoes, why should all that not once have constituted a sixth region of the world, as important as Europe or Asia, as Africa or the two Americas? I find it in no way inconceivable that every island emerging from this vast ocean might be a mountaintop from a continent now undersea, but high above the waters in prehistoric times."

"Like Atlantis," answered Harbert.

"Yes, my child...if Atlantis existed, that is."

"And you believe Lincoln Island was a part of that continent?" asked Pencroff.

"It's entirely probable," answered Cyrus Smith. "Furthermore, that would do much to explain the diversity of its landscape."

"And the considerable number of animals still living on it," added Harbert.

"Yes, my boy," answered the engineer, "and you've given me another argument to support my hypothesis. We have already noted the large numbers of animals that live on our island; more curiously yet, these fauna belong to the most varied species. There must be a reason for this, and to my mind it must be that Lincoln Island was once part of a vast continent, which gradually sank below the Pacific."

"So one fine day," replied Pencroff, still not entirely convinced, "the remains of that ancient continent could disappear as well, and there will be nothing left between America and Asia?"

"No," Cyrus Smith answered, "for there will be new continents, which billions and billions of tiny living creatures are building at this very moment."

"Building! And what do you call those masons?" Pencroff asked.

"Coral infusoria," answered Cyrus Smith. "It was their never-ending labors that created the island of Reao, the atolls, and all the other coral islands in the Pacific Ocean. It takes forty-seven million infusoria to attain a weight of one grain,* and yet, from the sea salt they ingest and the solids in the water they assimilate, these tiny creatures produce calcareous deposits, and those deposits form gigantic undersea substructures, as hard and durable as granite. In the distant past, during the earliest epochs of the earth's creation, nature produced land through upheavals of molten rock; but now nature has given these microscopic animals the task of replacing that agent, whose dynamic power has obviously diminished with the cooling of the earth—as is proved by the number of extinct volcanoes to be found all over the globe. And I do believe that, as century follows on century and one generation of infusoria follows on another, the Pacific will one day become a vast continent, which the men of the future will inhabit and civilize just as their predecessors have done."

"That will take some time!" said Pencroff.

"Nature has all the time she needs," the engineer answered.

* One grain weighs fifty-nine milligrams.

"But what's the use of new continents?" asked Harbert. "Surely the surface area of the earth's inhabited lands is enough for all humanity, and nature never creates unnecessarily."

"No, never, you're quite right," the engineer replied, "but here is how in times to come there might be a need for new continents, in this very region where the coralligenous islands now lie. This seems to me, at least, a plausible explanation."

"We're listening, Mr. Cyrus," answered Harbert.

"This is my idea: scholars generally agree that one day our world will meet its end, or rather that animal and vegetal life will no longer be possible, owing to the intense cold that will eventually fall over the earth. What they do not agree on is the cause of that cooling. Some say that it will come as the result of the cooling of the sun after millions of years; others, the gradual extinction of our world's internal fires, which have a greater influence on the earth than is generally supposed. I myself hold with the latter hypothesis, basing my assumption on the fact that the moon is nothing other than a world gone cold, utterly uninhabitable even though the sun continues to spread its heat over the surface. If the moon has gone cold, then, it must be because its internal fires—to which, like any other body in the stellar realm, it owes its origin—have burned out. In any case, no matter what the cause, our globe will eventually grow cold, but only little by little. And what will happen then? Sometime in the future, the temperate zones will become as uninhabitable as the polar regions are now. Therefore, the human and animal population will set out for latitudes more directly exposed to the influence of the sun. An immense migration will begin. Europe, central Asia, North America will gradually be deserted, as will Australasia and the southern reaches of South America. This human migration will have an equivalent in the vegetable realm. Plant life will recede toward the Equator, along with the animals. The central parts of the southern Americas and of Africa will become the most densely populated continents. The Laplanders and Samoyeds will find the climatic conditions of the polar seas on the shores of the Mediterranean. And how can we assume that the equatorial regions will not prove too small to contain and feed all the people of the earth? Thus, why should nature, foreseeing this great migration, not even now be laying the foundation for a new continent in the area of the Equator, and why should she not have charged the infusoria with the task of constructing it? I've given these matters a great deal of thought, my friends, and I seriously believe that the look of our world will someday be completely transformed: with the appearance of these new continents, the old ones will be covered by the sea; and, in centuries to come, some new Columbus will go and discover the islands of Chimborazo, of the Himalayas, or of Mont Blanc, the last traces of an America, an Asia, and a Europe now far below the waves. And finally these new continents will themselves become uninhabitable; the heat will fade, as from a body abandoned by its soul, and life will disappear from this earth, if not definitively then at least momentarily. After this, perhaps, our spheroid will rest, and remake itself in death so as to come alive again in more favorable conditions! But that, my friends, is known only to the Author of all things, and with my delving into the secrets of the future I've let myself wander far from our discussion of the infusoria and their labor."

"My dear Cyrus," answered Gideon Spilett, "to my mind these theories are nothing short of prophecies, and I have no doubt they will indeed come true one day."

"God alone can say," said the engineer.

"This is all well and good," Pencroff then said, having listened in rapt attention, "but can you tell me, Mr. Cyrus, was Lincoln Island built by your infusoria?"

"No," answered Cyrus Smith, "it is of purely volcanic origin."

"So it will disappear some day?"

"Very likely."

"I hope we won't be here."

"No, don't worry, Pencroff, we won't be here. We have no intention of dying here, and every intention of escaping someday."

"In the meantime," answered Gideon Spilett, "let us occupy this land as if it were to be our home for all eternity. There is no room for half-measures."

So ended their conversation. Breakfast was over. The explorations resumed, and the colonists entered the wetlands.

This was a real marsh, extending as far as the rounded shoreline at the island's southeastern end, over an area of twenty square miles. The soil consisted of a siliceous clay silt mingled with abundant vegetal debris. It was covered with conferva, reeds, sedge, bulrushes, and an occasional bed of grass, thick as a plush carpet. Here and there ice-covered ponds glimmered in the solar rays. Neither flood nor rainfall could have formed this watery landscape. The explorers immediately concluded that the marsh was fed by infiltration through the soil, and so indeed it was. And they had good reason to fear that in warm weather the atmosphere might be charged with dangerous miasma, of the kind that engenders paludal fevers.

Above the aquatic plants covering the surface of the stagnant waters, the air was full of birds. An experienced swamp hunter or decoy man would not have wasted a single shot here. Wild ducks, pintails, teals, and snipes could be seen in great numbers, apparently untroubled by the colonists' presence, for such birds are not overly fearful by nature.

A rifle loaded with lead shot would certainly have brought them down by the dozens, but the colonists had to make do with their bows and arrows. The catch was not as generous, but the silent arrow has the advantage of not frightening the prey, which the detonation of a firearm would have sent flying to all the corners of the marsh. For the moment, then, the hunters contented themselves with a dozen birds whose white bodies were encircled by a cinnamon-colored band, with green heads, flat beaks, and wings of black, white, and red. Harbert recognized these creatures as "shelducks." Top contributed his agility to the capture of the fowl, whose name was given to this marshy region of the island. The colonists had found an abundant reserve of aquatic game, which they could exploit at their leisure. Furthermore, several of the species they found in these marshes could no doubt be, if not domesticated, at least acclimated to the environs of the lake, where they would be all the closer at hand.

At around five o'clock in the evening, Cyrus Smith and his companions started home again through the newly named Shelduck Fens, then crossed the Mercy on the ice bridge.

By eight o'clock they were back in Granite House.

XXII

The Animal Traps.—The Foxes.—The Peccaries.—A Sudden Wind from the Northwest.—Snowstorm.—The Basketmakers.— The Worst Cold of the Winter.—The Crystallization of Maple Sugar.—The Mysterious Shaft.—Plans for an Exploration.— The Lead Pellet.

The cold remained intense until August 15th, although the temperature never dropped below the minimum previously observed. When the atmosphere was calm, the cold could be borne without difficulty; but when the wind blew, life was hard indeed for men with no winter clothes. Pencroff found himself wishing that Lincoln Island were populated by bears, rather than foxes or seals, whose fur leaves much to be desired.

"Bears," he said, "are generally well dressed, and I'd like nothing so much as to borrow a nice warm greatcoat, just until the winter's over."

"But," Neb answered with a laugh, "those bears might not want to lend you their greatcoats, Pencroff. They're not known for their kindness toward strangers!"

"We'd force them, Neb, we'd force them," answered Pencroff in an impressively authoritarian voice.

But there were no such formidable carnivores on the island, or at least none had shown themselves as yet.

Nevertheless, Harbert, Pencroff, and the reporter set about laying animal traps on Longview Plateau and at the edges of the forest. To the sailor's mind, any animal at all, of whatsoever sort, would be a good catch, and any rodents or carnivores who might grace the traps with their presence would find a warm welcome at Granite House.

The nature of these traps could not have been simpler: a hole was dug in the ground and covered with branches and grass to conceal the orifice, with some sort of odorous bait at the bottom, and that was all. Their placement was not left up to chance; rather, the traps were dug only where an accumulation of pawprints indicated the frequent passage of quadrupeds. The traps were checked daily, but over the first few days the only game they bagged were culpeos, such as they had already sighted on the right bank of the Mercy.

"Really now! isn't there anything but foxes around here?" cried Pencroff, discovering a third such creature sitting sheepishly in the hole. "Good-for-nothing brutes!"

"Oh, that's where you're wrong," said Gideon Spilett. "They're good for something!"

"And what would that be?"

"For bait, to attract other animals!"

The reporter was not mistaken, and from then on the traps were baited with fox carcasses.

The sailor had also made snares from bulrush fibers, and these proved considerably more profitable than the traps. Rarely did a day go by without a rabbit caught in the noose. Night after night, an unending stream of rabbits appeared on their dinner table, but Neb was a master at sauces, and the dinner guests never thought of complaining.

Once or twice, however, in the second week of August, the pit traps offered the hunters something other than culpeos, and far more useful: wild boar, of the sort they had spotted north of the lake. This time Pencroff did not have to ask if the animals were edible. Their resemblance to the pigs of America or Europe plainly showed that they were.

"But I have to tell you, Pencroff," Harbert said to him, "they're not pigs."

"My boy," answered the sailor, leaning over the hole and pulling out a representative of the family Suidae by the tiny appendix that served as his tail, "please let me believe these are pigs!"

"But why?"

"Because I want to!"

"You're fond of pigs, Pencroff?"

"I'm very fond of pigs," the sailor answered, "especially their feet, and if they had eight instead of four, I'd be twice as fond of them!"

The animals in question were in fact peccaries, and their dark coats showed them to be of the tayassu species, one of the four that comprise

"Please let me believe . . ." said Pencroff.

that family. As with all other peccaries, their snouts were armed with long, curving canine teeth. These creatures ordinarily live in herds, and they were no doubt abundant throughout the island's forests. In any case, to Pencroff's great delight, they were edible from head to foot.

The island's weather changed abruptly on August 15th, as the wind shifted to the northwest. The temperature rose a few degrees, and soon the atmospheric vapors began to produce snow. The entire island was covered by a white blanket, transforming its appearance before the colonists' eyes. This snow fell continuously for several days, and by the end it had accumulated to a depth of two feet.

Now the wind suddenly freshened, and from Granite House they could hear the sea crashing over the shoals far below. Sometimes the fiercely eddying wind blew the snow into tall, rotating columns, like the waterspouts that are sometimes seen pirouetting over the water in mid-sea, and which can be subdued by cannon fire from a nearby ship. Nevertheless, the winds were blowing from the northwest, and not from Union Bay, so that the orientation of Granite House protected it from a direct assault. But with the blizzard howling as wildly as any polar tempest, neither Cyrus Smith nor his companions could venture outside; thus, to their deep regret, they remained imprisoned for five days, from August 20th to the 25th. They could hear the tempest roaring through Jacamar Woods, and they helplessly imagined the damage it must be wreaking. Many trees would be uprooted, no doubt, but Pencroff consoled himself with the thought that this would spare them the trouble of chopping them down.

"If the wind wants to be our lumberjack, so be it," he sometimes said.

And in any case, there was nothing they could do to stop it.

How thankful they were to Heaven for having offered them such a solid and indestructible home! A part of their gratitude went legitimately to Cyrus Smith, but after all it was nature that had created this vast cavern; he had merely discovered it. Here they were safe, and beyond the reach of the tempest's fury. A house of brick and wood on Longview Plateau would never have withstood the force of the gale. As for the Chimneys, the sound of crashing waves told them all too clearly that their former home had been flooded again; the sea must have washed once more over the islet, and now furiously battered the boulders. Here in Granite House, however, surrounded by rock as impervious to wind as to water, they had nothing to fear.

The colonists did not sit idle during these few days of sequestration. The storeroom was full of wood, already cut into planks, and with these they completed their collection of furniture. A number of tables and chairs were built, and very sturdy tables and chairs they were, for the colonists did not spare the lumber. They were rather heavy and inconveniently difficult to move, but Neb and Pencroff were quite proud of their work, and would not have traded their crude furnishings for the finest pieces from the studio of André Boule.

Next the furniture makers became basket weavers, and in this new industry they met with no less success than before. They had discovered a dense grove of willows near the northern corner of the lake, where purple osiers grew in great number. Pencroff and Harbert had made a harvest of these useful shrubs before the rains began, and now the dried fronds were ready for use. Their first attempts were rather shapeless, but the basket weavers summoned up all their skill and intelligence, consulting one another, searching through their memories, each attempting to outdo the others; thus, they soon owned a small collection of urns and baskets of varying sizes. These they stowed away in the storeroom, and Neb had a fine supply of specially designed receptacles to hold his rhizomes, pine nuts, and dragon-tree roots.

The weather changed once again in the last week of August. The temperature dropped slightly, and the winds grew calm. The colonists hurried outside. The beach was buried beneath two feet of snow, but they could easily walk on its frozen surface, and Cyrus Smith and his companions took advantage of the moment for a visit to Longview Plateau.

What a change! They had last seen these woods as a variegated mass of green, particularly here, where conifers predominated; but what they now had before their eyes was a uniform expanse of white. From the summit of Mount Franklin to the shoreline, the forests, the meadows, the lake, the river, the beaches, everything was white. The waters of the Mercy flowed beneath an arch of ice, which shuddered and cracked with every ebb and flow. Flocks of birds—ducks and snipes, pintails and guillemots—skimmed in their thousands over the solid surface of the lake. The rocks around the cascade at the edge of the plateau were bristling with ice. The water seemed to spurt from a monstrous gargoyle, carved with all the fanciful imagination of a Renaissance artist. For the moment, they could not gauge the extent of the gale's damage to the forest; that would have to wait until the vast layer of white had melted away.

This was also an opportunity for Gideon Spilett, Harbert, and Pencroff to check their traps. They hunted for the holes beneath the blanket of snow, taking great care not to fall in, which would have been both dangerous and humiliating: caught in their own traps! But they succeeded in avoiding this misfortune, and found the traps perfectly intact. No animals had been caught, despite the profusion of pawprints surrounding the pits, some of them armed with formidable claws. Harbert immediately informed his companions that some carnivore of the feline genus had passed by this place, justifying the engineer's fear that dangerous animals lurked on Lincoln Island. Ordinarily, no doubt, these beasts remained in the dense Forests of the Far West; only at the urging of their empty bellies had they ventured onto Longview Plateau. Perhaps they could smell the inhabitants of Granite House?

"Tell me, what sort of felines are these?" asked Pencroff.

"Tigers," Harbert answered.

"I thought tigers could only be found in warm climates?"

"In the New World," answered the boy, "they have been seen from Mexico to the pampas of Buenos Aires. And since Lincoln Island lies at more or less the same latitude as the provinces of La Plata, it would hardly be surprising to find tigers here."

"Well then, we'll keep an eye out," answered Pencroff.

But the snow eventually dissipated as the temperature rose. Rain began to fall, speeding the dissolution of the blanket of white. The colonists ventured outside to replenish their supply of essentials: from the vegetal domain, pine nuts, dragon-tree roots, rhizomes, maple sap; from the animal, rabbits, agoutis, and kangaroos. This brought them into the forest, where they found many trees toppled by the recent storms. The sailor and Neb took the cart to the coal deposits, and brought back several tons of fuel. On the way, they found that the chimney of the pottery kiln had lost a good six feet of its length to the violent winds.

The colonists replenished their store of firewood as well, and the newly liberated current of the Mercy was once more put to use to transport their timber rafts. They could not be sure that the worst of winter was indeed behind them.

The colonists also paid a visit to the Chimneys, and congratulated themselves on having moved before the onset of the storms. The destructive force of the sea was all too plain to see. Propelled over the islet by the strong ocean winds, the waves had laid waste to their former home, covering the stones with a thick layer of wrack and filling the corridors with sand. While Neb, Harbert, and Pencroff were out hunting or gathering firewood, Cyrus Smith and Gideon Spilett turned to the task of clearing out the Chimneys, and they found the forge and furnaces more or less undamaged, fortuitously protected by an accumulation of sand piled atop them by the winds before the onslaught of the sea.

Their new supply of fuel was soon put to good use, for the rigors of winter were not yet past. The month of February is marked by great temperature swings in the boreal hemisphere, as we know. The same was evidently true in this austral hemisphere, and the end of the month of August, corresponding to February in North America, did not defy that climatic law.

Around the twenty-fifth, after yet more alternating rain and snow, the wind shifted to the southeast, and suddenly the cold grew extremely sharp. By the engineer's estimations, a Fahrenheit thermometer's column of mercury would have registered no less than eight degrees below zero (22.22 degrees centigrade below freezing), and this intense cold lingered for several days, made all the more painful by a cutting wind. Once again the colonists were forced to take refuge inside Granite House, and, with the openings in the facade sealed off as tightly as possible, leaving only a tiny gap to provide ventilation, their consumption of candles was considerable. In an attempt to economize, the colonists often relied on the fireplace alone for light, and here they did not spare the fuel. Occasionally two or three of them made their way down to the beach, finding it littered with sea ice washed ashore at high tide; but they soon returned to Granite House, clinging to their ladder only with difficulty, for in this intense cold the rungs left their fingers painfully raw.

The hours passed slowly as they sat imprisoned inside Granite House, and they searched desperately for some occupation to fill their days. But now Cyrus Smith thought of a task they could easily perform within their four walls.

As we know, the colonists had no sugar other than the liquid substance they had extracted through deep incisions in the bark of maple trees. This liquor was collected in jars for various culinary purposes, growing more delicious as it aged, slowly whitening and taking on a syrupy consistency.

But there was a better way, and one day Cyrus Smith announced to his companions that they would now become refiners.

"Refiners!" answered Pencroff. "Sounds like warm work!"

"Very warm indeed!" answered the engineer.

"In that case, there's no time like the present!" the sailor answered.

Do not let the word *refining* summon up images of complicated factories teeming with workers and machines. No! The process by which the sugar would be crystallized could not have been simpler. They set the liquor to boil in large earthenware jars, and as it evaporated a foam covered its surface. Once it began to thicken, Neb dutifully stirred it with a wooden paddle so as to speed the evaporation and prevent it from taking on an empyreumatic taste.

After a few hours' boiling over an excellent fire, which did the workers as much good as the substance under treatment, a thick syrup had formed. This was then poured into clay molds of various shapes they had fired in the kitchen's own oven, and the next day the syrup had cooled into hard loaves and tablets. It was sugar, somewhat reddish in color, but almost transparent, and of an impeccable flavor.

The cold persisted until mid-September, and the prisoners of Granite House began to chafe against their imposed captivity. Yearning for the open air, they went out nearly every day; but these sorties never lasted long, and they soon returned to the task of improving the interior of their dwelling, chatting as they worked. Cyrus Smith spoke to his companions of many things, most particularly the practical applications of science. The colonists had no library at their disposal, but the engineer was a book in himself, a book ever to hand, ever open to the requisite page, a book that answered all their questions, freely and frequently consulted. And so the time passed, and the worthy colonists never feared the future.

Nevertheless, it was time for this captivity to come to an end. They were all eager for, if not the return of fine weather, at least an end to this unbearable cold. If only they had clothes that could withstand the frigid blasts of winter, how many excursions they would have made to the dunes or to Shelduck Fens! The hunting would surely have been fine, and the animals unwary. But Cyrus Smith insisted that no one risk his health, for he needed both arms of every man present, and his advice was respected.

But it must be said that, apart from Pencroff, none rebelled against this imprisonment more impatiently than Top. The faithful dog had developed a severe case of cabin fever. He came and went from one room to the next, and expressed his displeasure at this detention in his own way.

Cyrus Smith often noticed that Top growled in a curious manner whenever he went near the dark shaft that plunged from the floor of the storeroom toward the sea. He endlessly circled the shaft, which had been covered with a wooden panel. Sometimes he even tried to slip his paws beneath this covering, as if to lift it up. Then he gave a distinctive yelp, expressing both anger and anxiety.

This ritual was repeated several times under the engineer's watchful eyes. What could be down that hole to trouble the intelligent animal so? The shaft led to the sea, that was certain. Did it lead to other tunnels running through the island's foundation? Did it communicate with other caverns deep in the rock? Might some sea monster occasionally come to the bottom to breathe? The engineer did not know what to conclude, and in spite of himself his mind devised the most bizarre and convoluted explanations. Throughly trained in the study of scientific realities, he could not forgive himself for wandering into the realm of the strange, and even the supernatural; but why should an unfailingly levelheaded dog such as Top, who never so much as howled at the moon, so obstinately persist in exploring that abyss with his nose and his ears, if not because something about it aroused his apprehension? Top's behavior intrigued Cyrus Smith more than he himself found it reasonable to admit.

In any case, the engineer expressed his puzzlement only to Gideon Spilett, for nothing would be gained by exposing the others to involuntary reflections inspired by what might be nothing more than a mad whim of his dog.

Finally the cold eased. There was rain, there were blustery showers mingled with snow, there were cloudbursts and sudden gusts of wind, but these did not last. The ice had dissolved, the snow melted; the beach, the plateau, the banks of the Mercy, the forest were once again practicable. The return of spring delighted the inhabitants of Granite House, and soon they spent their days in the open air, returning only to sleep or dine.

They did a great deal of hunting in the second half of September, which led Pencroff to renew, with redoubled insistence, his request for the firearms that he claimed Cyrus Smith had promised to make. Knowing full well that specialized equipment was required to make even a rudimentary rifle, the engineer continually demurred and delayed. And furthermore, he remarked, Harbert and Gideon Spilett had become skillful archers, and all sorts of excellent animals—agoutis, kangaroos, capybaras, pigeons, bustards, wild ducks, snipes, all manner of game both feathered and furred—regularly yielded to the assaults of their arrows;

consequently, there was no need for haste. But the stubborn sailor did not see things quite that way, and he would allow the engineer no peace until he had fulfilled his longing. Gideon Spilett seconded Pencroff.

"If, as we might well suppose," he said, "the island is home to dangerous animals, we will have to find a way to fight them off and exterminate them. There may come a time when this will be our most pressing task."

But for the moment it was clothing, not firearms, that concerned Cyrus Smith. The colonists' clothes had survived the winter, but they could not count on them to last until the next. They were in urgent need of skins of carnivorous animals or wool from ruminants, and, remembering the great numbers of mouflons they had seen on Mount Franklin, he began to think of raising a herd of these beasts for the colony's needs. A pen for their domestic animals, a yard for fowl; in a word, a sort of farm: these were the two most pressing projects for the coming spring.

Consequently, and with a view to these future constructions, it became urgent to survey the unexplored portions of Lincoln Island, that is, the towering forests that stretched from the right bank of the Mercy to the end of Serpentine Peninsula, as well as the entire western coast. But for this they would need more predictable weather, and a further month went by before this exploration could be undertaken in confidence.

They were awaiting this moment with some impatience when an incident occurred that further excited the colonists' desire to better acquaint themselves with the entirety of their domain.

It was October 24th. Pencroff had gone to check the traps, still baited each day in hopes of fresh game. Peering into one of the holes, he found three animals—a female peccary and its two young—which would be welcomed with pleasure into their kitchen.

Pencroff returned to Granite House, enchanted at his catch, and as always the sailor made a great display of his prey.

"Well now! We have a fine meal in store for us, Mr. Cyrus!" he cried. "And you're invited too, Mr. Spilett!"

"I accept with pleasure," the reporter answered, "but what are we to be served?"

"Suckling pig."

"Oh, really? suckling pig is it, Pencroff? From the way you were talking, I thought perhaps you'd brought us a baby partridge in truffle sauce!"

"How's that?" cried Pencroff. "You're not going to turn your nose up at suckling pig, by any chance, are you now?"

"No," answered Gideon Spilett, with no great enthusiasm, "although it would be nice to vary the menu from time to time..."

"Now, now, Mr. Journalist," shot back the sailor, who never liked to hear his capture disparaged, "let's not be particular! Just think how happy you would have been to sit down to a meal like this seven months ago, when we first landed on this island!..."

"Yes, yes, you're right," the reporter answered. "Man is never perfect, and never content."

"In any case," Pencroff replied, "I'm counting on Neb to prove his worth. Look! These two little peccaries can't be more than three months old! They'll be as tender as young quails! Here, Neb, come along! I'll oversee the preparation personally."

And with Neb in tow the sailor disappeared into the kitchen and lost himself in his culinary endeavors.

They let him do as he pleased. He and Neb prepared a magnificent feast: the two little peccaries, kangaroo soup, a smoked ham, pine nuts, dragon-tree drink, Oswego tea—the best sort of meal imaginable. But among all these dishes, the succulent peccaries, braised to perfection, would be the pièce de résistance.

At five o'clock, dinner was served in the dining room of Granite House. The kangaroo soup was steaming on the table. It was pronounced excellent.

The soup was followed by the peccaries, which Pencroff insisted on carving himself, serving each of the dinner guests a colossal portion.

The suckling pigs were truly delicious, and Pencroff was devouring his share with great enthusiasm when suddenly a cry and an oath escaped his lips.

"What is it?" asked Cyrus Smith.

"I...I...I've just broken a tooth!" the sailor answered.

"No! Pebbles in your peccary?" said Gideon Spilett.

"It would seem so," answered Pencroff, raising his hand to his lips and extracting the object that had cost him a molar!...

It was not a stone...It was a pellet of lead.

PART TWO

THE OUTCAST

I

*Concerning the Lead Pellet.—The Construction of a Canoe.—
Hunting.—From Atop a Kauri Tree.—No Sign of Human
Presence.—Neb and Harbert Fishing.—An Overturned
Tortoise.—The Tortoise Disappears.—Cyrus Smith's
Explanation.*

It was now seven months to the day since the passengers of the balloon
had been cast onto the shores of Lincoln Island. In all this time, no matter how they searched, no human being had ever shown his face. Never
had a plume of smoke betrayed the existence of other men on their
island. Never had any sign of human handiwork borne witness to even a
fleeting presence, neither recent nor ancient. The island did not appear to
be inhabited; indeed, by all indications, it never had been. And now these
deductions were rocked to their very foundations by a simple metal pellet, found in the body of an inoffensive peccary!

For that piece of lead had come from a firearm, and how could the shot
have been fired if not by a human hand?

Pencroff set the pellet on the table as his companions stared in deepest astonishment. A million thoughts ran through their minds as they
pondered this incident, so banal on its surface and yet so profoundly significant in its consequences. The sudden eruption of some supernatural
being into their midst would not have left them so thoroughly dumbfounded.

Cyrus Smith was the first to formulate the implications of this baffling
and unexpected finding. He picked up the pellet, turned it over in his
hand, turned it again, palpated it between thumb and index finger. Then:

"You feel certain," he asked Pencroff, "that the peccary wounded by this lead pellet was no more than three months old?"

"If that, Mr. Cyrus," answered Pencroff. "It was still suckling at its mother's teat when I found it in the hole."

"Well," said the engineer, "this proves that a rifle has been fired on Lincoln Island, sometime within the past three months at most."

"And that a lead pellet," added Gideon Spilett, "hit, but did not kill, this little animal."

"This is beyond doubt," Cyrus Smith continued, "and here are the consequences to be drawn: either the island was inhabited before our arrival or men have landed here sometime in the past three months. Did those men come to this place voluntarily or involuntarily? Did they land here deliberately, or were they shipwrecked? That we cannot know for the moment. As for their origins, European or Malay, enemies or friends of our race, that we cannot begin to guess; nor can we say whether they are still living on the island or have already sailed away. My friends, these are crucial questions, and we cannot allow them to go unanswered."

"No! a hundred times no! a thousand times no!" cried the sailor, rising from his seat. "There is no one on Lincoln Island but us! Damn! it's not a large island, and if it was inhabited we would have seen someone, I'm sure of that!"

"It would be very surprising if we hadn't, it's true," said Harbert.

"But not nearly as surprising, I daresay," the reporter observed, "as a peccary born with a lead pellet in its body!"

"Unless," Neb said in all seriousness, "the pellet was in Pencroff's..."

"Oh, come now, Neb," the sailor shot back. "You're not suggesting I could have had a lead pellet in my jaw for five or six months without knowing it? Where would it have been hiding?" the sailor added, opening his mouth to reveal thirty-two magnificent teeth. "Look closely, Neb, and if you find a single hollow tooth in that set of choppers, I'll gladly authorize you to pull a half-dozen!"

"Neb's hypothesis does seem most unlikely," Cyrus Smith replied, unable to repress a smile despite the gravity of his thoughts. "There can be no doubt that a rifle has been fired on the island sometime in the past three months at most. But I would suppose that whoever has landed on these shores must have been here only a very short while, or has long since left. If the island were inhabited the day we surveyed it from atop Mount Franklin we would have surely seen some sign of life, or we would

"Look closely, Neb."

have been seen ourselves. Thus, sometime in the past few weeks, and not before, a storm must have thrown a small group of castaways onto our shores. In any case, whatever the solution to this mystery may be, it is vitally important that we discover it at once."

"We must proceed with great caution," said the reporter.

"I am of the same opinion," Cyrus Smith answered, "for unfortunately we cannot rule out the possibility of a landing by Malay pirates!"

"Mr. Cyrus," asked the sailor, "before we set off in search of answers, would it not be a good idea to build a boat? That way we can easily travel up the river or along the shoreline, if need be. We have to be ready for anything."

"It's a fine idea, Pencroff," the engineer answered, "but we have no time to lose. And it would take at least a month to build a boat..."

"A real boat, yes," the sailor answered, "but we're not intending to put out to sea. I promise you that in five days at most I can build a canoe sturdy enough to ply the Mercy."

"Five days to build a boat?" cried Neb.

"Yes, Neb, an Indian-style boat."

"Made of wood?" the Negro asked, apparently unconvinced.

"Made of wood," answered Pencroff, "or rather bark. I repeat, Mr. Cyrus, five days is all I need!"

"Five days, then!" the engineer replied.

"But in the meantime, let's keep a watchful eye!" said Harbert.

"Harbert is right, my friends," Cyrus Smith answered, "and I must ask that you limit your hunting excursions to the immediate area of Granite House."

The dinner ended less merrily than Pencroff had hoped.

Thus, the island was or had been inhabited by someone other than the colonists. This could no longer be disputed after the incident of the lead pellet, and such a revelation could not fail to arouse the deepest anxieties in the colonists' minds.

Cyrus Smith and Gideon Spilett discussed all this at great length before they slept. They wondered if the incident might bear some relation to the inexplicable circumstances of the engineer's rescue, or to other curious events upon which they had already remarked. Nevertheless, after considering every aspect of the question, Cyrus Smith finally said:

"In the end, would you like to know my opinion, my dear Spilett?"

"Yes, Cyrus."

"Well, here it is: we can explore the island as meticulously as we please, but we will find nothing!"

Pencroff set to work the next morning. His intention was to build not a boat with ribs and planks, but a simple flat-bottomed craft, ideally suited for the Mercy, especially near the source where the water's depth was minimal. Strips of bark would be carefully joined together to form a lightweight hull, easily carried overland should natural obstacles require a portage. Riveted nails would hold the strips of bark in place, and clamp them securely enough to keep the craft perfectly watertight.

For this he would need trees with exceptionally strong and supple bark. As it happened, the recent gales had blown down a number of Douglas pines, which met these conditions perfectly. Many such trees now lay flat on the ground; the colonists had only to strip them of their bark, but the crudeness of their tools made this an exceedingly difficult task. Nevertheless, they found a way in the end.

Gideon Spilett and Harbert did not stand idly by as the sailor and the engineer labored, for they had taken on the responsibility of providing food for the colony. The reporter could not help but admire the boy's remarkable dexterity with the bow and the pike. He was no less struck by Harbert's fearlessness, tempered by that particular sangfroid that we might rightly call the "daring man's reason." Keeping Cyrus Smith's admonition in mind, the two hunting companions never ventured farther than two miles from Granite House, but the forest furnished a sufficient tribute of agoutis, capybaras, kangaroos, peccaries, etc., and while the traps were more often empty now that the cold weather was past, the warren continued to offer up the usual contingent of rabbits—more than enough for the entire colony of Lincoln Island.

As they hunted, Harbert and Gideon Spilett often spoke of the incident of the lead pellet and of the engineer's conclusions, and one day—it was October 26th—Harbert said to him:

"But Mr. Spilett, do you not find it extraordinary that none of the castaways who might have ended up on this island have ever appeared in the area of Granite House?"

"Quite astonishing, if they're still here," answered the reporter, "but not at all astonishing, if they aren't!"

"So you believe they've already left the island?" Harbert replied.

"It seems more than likely, my boy. If they had been here for any length of time—and especially if they were still here—some incident would have betrayed their presence in the end."

"But if they had some way to leave," the boy observed, "then they weren't castaways, were they?"

"No, Harbert, or at least they were what I would call temporary castaways. It may well be that some gale drove them onto the island without demolishing their craft, and that they put to sea again once the storm had passed."

"One thing is certain," said Harbert. "Mr. Smith has never seemed particularly eager to find other men living on our island."

"Indeed," the reporter answered, "he is convinced that the only souls who sail these waters are Malays, and those gentlemen are a bad lot, best avoided."

"It isn't out of the question, is it, Mr. Spilett," Harbert replied, "that we might eventually find some sort of evidence that they'd been here, and settle the question once and for all?"

"I wouldn't say no, my boy. An abandoned campsite or a burned-out fire might give us a lead, and that's just what we'll be looking for in our upcoming explorations."

The day of this conversation, the two hunters were strolling through an area of the forest near the Mercy remarkable for its beautiful trees. Among these were a number of those superb conifers that the natives of New Zealand call "kauris," which can grow to prodigious heights; here they towered more than two hundred feet above the ground.

"I have an idea, Mr. Spilett," said Harbert. "What if I climbed to the top of one of those kauris? I imagine I could see for miles."

"A fine idea, my boy," the reporter answered, "but are you sure you can climb a giant like this?"

"I can always try," answered Harbert.

The boy nimbly hoisted himself up into the lowest branches. The form of the kauri made the climbing relatively easy, and a few minutes later he had arrived at the summit, far above the vast carpet of greenery created by the forest's rounded treetops.

From this height, the view encompassed the entire southern area of the island, from Cape Claw in the southeast to Reptile End in the southwest. To the northwest stood Mount Franklin, obstructing the view over a good quarter of the horizon.

From his observatory, Harbert had a commanding view of the island's unexplored areas, where the suspected strangers might once have found shelter, where perhaps they sheltered still.

The boy looked around him with great attention. First at the sea, where he saw nothing—not so much as a sail, neither on the horizon nor in the island's waters. Nevertheless, since the mass of trees hid the coastline, a ship, especially one whose masts had been sheared off, could have been moored very close to land and remained invisible to Harbert's eye.

Nor was there anything of note to be seen in the Forests of the Far West. The trees formed an impenetrable dome over several square miles, uniformly dense, without a single clearing. So opaque was the veil of trees that Harbert's gaze could not follow the course of the Mercy back to its source amid the foothills. Perhaps there were other creeks flowing westward, but even from this height he could not be sure.

Nevertheless, even if Harbert could make out no sign of a campsite, perhaps he might spot some plume of smoke revealing the presence of men? There was not a cloud in the sky, and the slightest vapor would have stood out distinctly against the blue background of the heavens.

For a moment Harbert thought he could descry a slender thread of smoke rising to his west, but on closer inspection he realized he was mistaken. He looked as closely as he could, and his eyesight was excellent...No, there really was nothing.

Harbert climbed down to the foot of the kauri, and the two hunters returned to Granite House. There Cyrus Smith listened to the boy's account, shook his head, and said nothing. It was quite clear that this question would not be decided until they had made a thorough exploration of the island.

Two days later—October 28th—another incident occurred, whose explanation once again remained elusive.

As they were strolling along the beach some two miles from Granite House, Harbert and Neb happened upon a magnificent specimen of the Cheloniidae family. It was a tortoise of the genus *Mydas*, whose shell was streaked with wonderful green gleams.

Harbert saw the tortoise wending its way seaward through the rocks.

"Help me, Neb, help me!" he cried.

Neb came running.

"What a beautiful animal!" said Neb. "But how will we capture it?"

"Nothing could be simpler, Neb," Harbert answered. "If we turn the tortoise on its back it won't be able to get away. Take your pike and do as I do."

Sensing danger, the reptile had withdrawn into its shell. Its head and feet vanished from sight, and it sat motionless as a stone.

Harbert and Neb then inserted their pikes beneath the animal's sternum, and, working as one, they eventually succeeded in turning it onto its back. The tortoise measured three feet in length, and must have weighed at least four hundred pounds.

"Well!" cried Neb. "Our friend Pencroff is going to be a very happy man!"

Indeed, friend Pencroff could hardly fail to be overjoyed, for the flesh of these tortoises, which feed exclusively on eelgrass, is wonderfully flavorful. For the moment, all that could be seen of the tortoise was its small, flattened head, flaring broadly toward the back, with two large temporal indentations sunk beneath an arch of bone.

"Now what will we do with it?" said Neb. "We can't drag it all the way to Granite House!"

"Let's leave it here, since it won't be able to turn over again," answered Harbert. "Then we can come back with the cart."

"All right."

Nevertheless, just to be sure, and although Neb thought it quite needless, Harbert took the added precaution of wedging two large stones beneath the animal to prevent it from rolling over. With this the two hunters returned toward Granite House along the shoreline, now made broad by the receding tide. Hoping to give Pencroff a pleasant surprise, Harbert made no mention of the "superb specimen of the Cheloniidae family" he had overturned on the sand; but two hours later, he and Neb took the cart and returned to where they had left it. The "superb specimen of the Cheloniidae family" was gone.

Neb and Harbert looked at each other, and then looked around them. There was no mistake; this was indeed where they had last seen the tortoise. The boy even found the stones he had used to keep it on its back, proof that they had not simply come to the wrong spot.

"Well now, look at that!" said Neb. "Do those things know how to turn over?"

"Apparently," answered Harbert, utterly confounded, gazing at the pebbles that littered the beach.

"Pencroff isn't going to be happy about this!"

"And Mr. Smith is going to be very hard put to explain the animal's disappearance!" thought Harbert.

"Well then," said Neb, eager to cover up this misadventure, "we won't tell anyone."

"On the contrary, Neb, we must tell them," Harbert answered.

And so they set out once again toward Granite House, pulling the empty cart behind them.

Finding the engineer and the sailor hard at work on their boat, Harbert told them what had happened.

"Oh! you bunglers!" cried the sailor. "That's fifty soups at least you let get away from you!"

"But Pencroff," Neb replied, "it wasn't our fault the beast got away! I'm telling you, we turned it over!"

"Well then, you didn't turn it over far enough!" came the intractable sailor's quaint response.

"Not far enough!" cried Harbert.

And he told them of the care he had taken to brace the tortoise with stones.

"Then it must have been a miracle!" Pencroff answered.

"I thought, Mr. Cyrus," Harbert said, "that once a large tortoise was set on its back it could never roll onto its feet again?"

"That's perfectly true, my child," Cyrus Smith answered.

"Then how could it have?..."

"How far from the water did you leave the tortoise?" asked the engineer, pausing in his work to ponder this incident.

"Fifteen feet at most," Harbert answered.

"And was the tide out at the time?"

"Yes, Mr. Cyrus."

"Well," the engineer answered, "what the tortoise could not do on the sand it must have done in the water. The rising tide must have lifted it off the beach, and then it must have rolled over and calmly paddled out to sea."

"Oh! what a bungle we made of it!" cried Neb.

"That's exactly what I had the honor of telling you just now!" answered Pencroff.

Such was Cyrus Smith's explanation, and a perfectly plausible explanation it was. But was he truly convinced that this was the explanation? That we cannot say.

II

The Canoe's Maiden Voyage.—Wreckage on the Shore.—The Towline.—Flotsam Point.—Inventory of the Crate: Tools, Weapons, Instruments, Clothing, Books, Utensils.—Pencroff's Disappointment.—The Gospel.—A Bible Verse.

The little bark boat was indeed finished on October 29th. Pencroff had kept his promise, and a sort of canoe, its body reinforced by flexible cre-jimba branches, had been constructed in five days. A bench in the back, a second bench in the middle for stability, a third bench in front, a gunwale to support the oarlocks, a scull to steer with, such were the craft's features. It measured twelve feet long and weighed no more than two hundred pounds. The launching procedure was extremely simple. The light canoe was carried onto the beach below Granite House, and slowly the rising tide lifted it off the sand. Pencroff jumped in, steering with the scull, and soon pronounced the boat ready for use.

"Hurrah!" cried the sailor, who was not above celebrating his own triumph. "With this we can go around..."

"The world?" asked Gideon Spilett.

"No, the island. With a few stones for ballast, a mast in front, and a little sail, which Mr. Smith will make for us one day, we can go wherever we please! Well, Mr. Cyrus, and you, Mr. Spilett, and you, Harbert, and you, Neb, don't you want to try out our new craft? Come along! We have to be sure it will hold the five of us!"

This was indeed an essential experiment. With a stroke of the scull, Pencroff pulled closer to the beach through a passage between the shoals, and it was agreed that they would make a trial run this very day, following the shoreline up to the end of the rocks on the island's southern shore.

As they were climbing aboard, Neb shouted:

"Pencroff, your boat's taking on water!"

"It's nothing, Neb," the sailor answered. "We have to let the wood swell to seal the joints! That might take two days or so, but then our canoe will have no more water in its belly than the most inveterate tosspot. In with you!"

They climbed into the boat, and Pencroff pushed away from shore. The weather was magnificent, the sea as calm as a small lake, and as unthreatening as the stately current of the Mercy.

Neb took one oar, Harbert the other, and Pencroff remained astern to guide the little craft with the scull.

They crossed the small channel and skimmed past the islet's southernmost point. A light southerly breeze was blowing. No swell could be felt in the channel or beyond; only a series of slow undulations rippled the surface and gently rocked the canoe. They continued a further half-mile from shore for a fuller view of Mount Franklin.

Next Pencroff turned back toward the mouth of the river. They followed the curve of the shoreline, gliding past the marshes of Shelduck Fens toward a sharp spit that jutted far into the sea.

This spit lay some three miles from the Mercy along the curving shore. The colonists resolved to make for the end, and to continue past it only as far as necessary for a view of the coastline up to Cape Claw.

And so the little boat paddled on, never more than two cables from land, avoiding the numerous shoals now disappearing beneath the rising tide. The granite cliffs grew ever less lofty from the mouth of the river to the spit. Here they took the form of piled granite rocks, capricious, irregular, and utterly wild in appearance, quite unlike the sheer curtain of stone beneath Longview Plateau. It was as if some monstrous wheelbarrow full of boulders had been emptied here. Jutting two miles from the forest into the sea, the spit was entirely devoid of vegetation, like a giant arm emerging from a sleeve of greenery.

Propelled by the two oars, the boat glided smoothly through the water. Pencil in one hand, notebook in the other, Gideon Spilett made a rough sketch of the shoreline. Neb, Pencroff, and Harbert chatted as they observed this new area of their domain, and as the canoe continued southward the two Capes Mandible appeared to move with them, closing off Union Bay ever more tightly.

As for Cyrus Smith, he did not speak, but simply looked, and the intense watchfulness of his gaze gave him the look of one observing some alien and unknown land.

After three quarters of an hour the canoe had nearly arrived at the end of the spit. Pencroff was preparing to make his way around it when Harbert stood up and pointed to a dark spot on the shore, saying:

"What's that I see on the beach?"

All eyes turned toward the spot in question.

"You're right," said the reporter, "there's something there. It almost looks like a wrecked ship, half sunk into the sand."

"Oh!" cried Pencroff. "I see what it is!"

"What is it?" asked Neb.

"Barrels, barrels! And maybe they're full!" the sailor answered.

"To shore, Pencroff!" said Cyrus Smith.

A few brisk oar strokes brought the canoe into a small cove, and the passengers leaped onto the beach.

Pencroff was not mistaken. There were indeed two barrels half buried in the sand, firmly tied to a voluminous crate. Kept afloat by the buoyancy of the barrels, the crate must have drifted over the sea for some time before finally washing ashore on this beach.

"Does this mean there's been a shipwreck in the vicinity of the island?" asked Harbert.

"Clearly," answered Gideon Spilett.

"But what could be in that crate?" cried Pencroff with understandable impatience. "What could be in that crate? It's sealed shut, and we have no way of opening it! Well, a good hard rock will fix that!"

Raising a heavy stone above his head, the sailor was about to bash in one of the crate's walls; but the engineer stopped him, saying:

"Pencroff, can you control your impatience for just one hour?"

"But, Mr. Cyrus, think of it! Everything we need might be inside this box!"

"We'll see to that, Pencroff," the engineer answered, "but we mustn't destroy the crate. It might well prove useful at some point. Let's bring it back to Granite House, where we can open it without violence. It has floated this far already, so we can certainly guide it to the mouth of the river."

"But what could be in that crate?"

"You're right, Mr. Cyrus, and I was wrong," the sailor answered. "Sometimes my curiosity gets the better of me!"

The engineer's suggestion was a wise one. The canoe could never have held all the objects the crate might contain, for if two empty barrels were required to keep it afloat, its contents must have been quite heavy. It would thus be best to leave it as it was and tow it back to the beach below Granite House before attempting to open it.

But where had this piece of flotsam come from? This was a very important question. Cyrus Smith and his companions carefully combed the area for several hundred paces in all directions. They found no other debris of any sort. Harbert and Neb clambered up an elevated boulder for a better view of the sea, but the horizon was as empty as ever. No crippled ship, no sail, nothing.

And yet there clearly had been a shipwreck. Might this discovery be connected to the incident of the lead pellet? Perhaps the strangers had landed on some other shore of the island? Perhaps they were still there? In any case, the colonists realized with relief that the strangers could not be Malay pirates, for the crate was clearly of American or European origin.

They returned to the crate, which measured five feet long by three feet wide. Its walls were of oak, covered with a thick skin held down by copper nails. Great care had been taken to keep it watertight. The two fat barrels were hermetically sealed, but a knock showed them to be empty. They were held to the side of the crate by strong ropes, tied with what Pencroff easily recognized as a "sailor's knot." The crate appeared to be in perfect condition, having washed onto a sandy beach rather than a shore of jagged rocks. A careful examination suggested that it had not been in the ocean long, and had only recently reached this shore. No sign of seepage could be found; whatever it contained must therefore have survived undamaged.

It seemed obvious that the crate had been thrown from a crippled ship in the vicinity of the island, and that the passengers had taken the precaution of lightening it with this flotation device in hopes that it would reach the shore, to be recovered later.

"We will tow the crate to Granite House," said the engineer, "and inventory its contents; then, if we discover any survivors of the presumed shipwreck, we will return the crate to its rightful owners. If we find no one…"

"We'll keep it for ourselves!" cried Pencroff. "But for the love of God, what could be in there?"

Even now the incoming tide was lapping at the crate; soon it would be floating free atop the water. A rope was partially unwound from one of the barrels to serve as a tug line. Pencroff and Neb used their oars to dig a trench in the sand to ease the crate's movement, and soon, with the crate in tow, the little craft began its trip around the spit, now christened Flotsam Point. The crate was quite heavy, and the barrels could scarcely keep it afloat. The sailor trembled lest it come untied from the barrels and sink straight to the bottom; fortunately, however, his fears were not borne out, and an hour and a half later—for it took them that long to make the three-mile return trip—the canoe landed on the beach before Granite House.

The boat and the crate were hauled onto the sand, and as the tide was already receding, they were soon beyond the water's reach. Neb went to find some tools with which to gently force open the crate, and they proceeded to the inventory. Pencroff made no attempt to hide his profound emotion.

The sailor first detached the two barrels and set them aside for later use, for they were in excellent condition. Next the locks were broken with a pair of pliers, and the box was immediately thrown open.

A second envelope of zinc lined the inside of the crate. Great pains had clearly been taken to protect the contents from contact with water, no matter how heavy the seas.

"Oh!" cried Neb. "Do you suppose there could be canned food in there?"

"I sincerely hope not," answered the reporter.

"What I'd like more than anything..." said the sailor in a quiet voice.

"What's that?" asked Neb, who had overheard him.

"Nothing!"

They slashed the sheet of zinc and folded it back. Little by little, various objects of the most diverse sorts were extracted and laid on the sand. Pencroff greeted each new object with renewed hurrahs, Harbert clapped his hands, and Neb danced...like a Negro. There were books to make Harbert leap for joy, and kitchen utensils that Neb could have smothered with kisses!

The colonists had good reason to celebrate, for in the crate they found a profusion of tools, weapons, instruments, clothing, and books. Here is the precise account of their windfall, as recorded in Gideon Spilett's notebook:

Tools:	3 knives with multiple blades
	2 woodsman's hatchets
	2 carpenter's hatchets
	3 planes
	2 adzes
	1 double-bladed ax
	6 cold chisels
	2 rasps
	3 hammers
	3 drills
	2 augers
	10 sacks of nails and screws
	3 saws of various sizes
	2 boxes of needles
Weapons:	2 flint rifles
	2 percussion-cap rifles
	5 cutlasses
	4 sabers
	2 kegs of gunpowder, each containing some twenty-five pounds
	12 boxes of percussion caps
Instruments:	1 sextant
	1 pair of binoculars
	1 telescope
	1 box compass
	1 pocket compass
	1 Fahrenheit thermometer
	1 aneroid barometer
	1 complete photographic kit, with lens, plates, chemicals, etc.
Clothing:	2 dozen shirts of unknown cloth, similar to wool but clearly of vegetal origin
	3 dozen stockings of the same fabric
Utensils:	1 iron cauldron
	6 casseroles of tin-plated copper

3 iron platters
10 aluminum dishes
2 kettles
1 small portable oven
6 table knives

Books: 1 Bible, including the Old and New Testaments
1 atlas
1 dictionary of diverse Polynesian dialects
1 dictionary of the natural sciences, in six volumes
3 reams of white paper
2 bound registers with blank pages

"Whoever owned this crate," said the reporter after the inventory had been drawn up, "he surely knew how to think ahead! Tools, weapons, instruments, clothes, utensils, books, everything we need is here! You'd almost think he was expecting to be shipwrecked, and had prepared for it in advance!"

"Indeed, everything we need is here," murmured Cyrus Smith in a pensive tone.

"One thing is certain," added Harbert, "the ship that carried this crate and its owner was no Malay pirate ship!"

"Unless," said Pencroff, "the crate's owner had been captured by pirates..."

"That seems awfully far-fetched," the reporter answered. "I find it far more likely that some crippled American or European vessel drifted into this area, and the passengers attempted to salvage what they needed most by packing this crate and launching it into the sea."

"Is that your opinion as well, Mr. Cyrus?" asked Harbert.

"Yes, my child," the engineer answered, "that might be how it happened. Perhaps, as or before the ship began to sink, the passengers collected their most vital possessions and put them in the crate, in hopes of finding them somewhere on shore..."

"Even the photographic kit?" the sailor retorted, unconvinced.

"I do not entirely understand why that was included," answered Cyrus Smith. "It would have been better for us, and for any other castaways, if they had packed a more complete assortment of clothing or a more ample supply of ammunition!"

"But on all these instruments, these tools, these books, is there no sort of mark, no address that might show us their origin?" asked Gideon Spilett.

This was indeed worthy of investigation. Each object was closely examined, especially the books, instruments, and weapons. In contradiction to common practice, neither the weapons nor the instruments bore the mark of their manufacturer; furthermore, they were in perfect condition, and apparently unused. The same proved true of the tools and utensils: everything was new. This seemed to prove that the objects had not been collected and thrown into the crate; on the contrary, the choice of objects must have been carefully considered, and clearly great pains were taken to arrange them in an orderly way. This was further confirmed by the second envelope of metal protecting them from contact with water, which could hardly have been welded together in the ship's last desperate moments.

The dictionaries of the natural sciences and of the Polynesian dialects were both written in English, but bore no publisher's imprint, and no date of publication.

The same was true of the Bible, a beautifully printed quarto, again in English, which showed signs of frequent readings.

As for the atlas, it was a magnificent work, with maps of every region of the globe and several planispheres depicted in accordance with the Mercator projection. This time the nomenclature was in French—but still no date of publication or publisher's mark.

No matter how closely they inspected these various objects, then, no sign of their provenance could be found, nor any indication of the nationality of the ship that must have passed so near their island. But wherever this crate had come from, it had made rich men of the colonists of Lincoln Island. So far, they had attempted to meet their needs by transforming the products offered by nature herself; and thanks to their intelligence they had succeeded admirably. But did it not seem that Providence had now set out to reward them with these various products of human industry? For this they unanimously offered thanks to Heaven.

Nevertheless, there was one among them whose desires remained unsatisfied. This was Pencroff. Evidently the crate lacked something for which he felt an overpowering longing. As the objects were pulled from the crate, his hurrahs grew progressively quieter; and once the inventory was complete, he could be heard to mumble these words:

"Mr. Smith, I am a superstitious man."

"This is all fine and dandy, but it would seem there's nothing in that box for me!"

Which led Neb to ask him:

"Well, my word, friend Pencroff, what were you hoping for?"

"A half-pound of tobacco!" Pencroff answered in all seriousness. "With that my happiness would be complete!"

The others could not help but laugh on hearing the sailor's remark.

In light of this unexpected discovery, a serious exploration of the island seemed more vital than ever. And so it was agreed that they would set out the next day at dawn, following the Mercy toward the western coastline. If some little band of castaways had landed somewhere along that shore, they very likely lacked the resources necessary to their survival, and the colonists were duty-bound to come to their aid at once.

They spent the rest of the day bringing the various objects inside Granite House and carefully laying them out in the great room.

As it happened, that day—October 29th—was a Sunday, and before the colonists went to bed, Harbert asked the engineer if he might like to read some passage from the Gospel.

"Gladly," Cyrus Smith answered.

He picked up the holy book, and was about to open it when Pencroff stopped him, saying:

"Mr. Smith, I am a superstitious man. Open it at random, and read us the first verse your eye lights on. We might find that it applies to our situation."

Cyrus Smith smiled at the sailor's idea. Ceding to his wishes, he let the book fall open, and found a small bookmark between two pages.

Suddenly his gaze was drawn to a red cross penciled in the margin next to verse 8 of chapter 7 of the Gospel according to Saint Matthew.

And he read this verse, which runs as follows:

For every one that asketh receiveth; and he that seeketh findeth...

III

Departure.—The Rising Tide.—Elms and Hackberry Trees.—
Various Plants.—The Jacamar.—Appearance of the Forest.—
The Giant Eucalyptus.—Why These Are Called Fever
Trees.—Bands of Monkeys.—The Waterfall.—A Camp for
the Night.

The next day, October 30th, everything was ready for their long-planned exploration, now grown so urgent in light of recent events. For things had taken such a turn that the colonists' first concern might well be not to ask for help, but to offer it.

It was agreed that they would follow the Mercy as far as the course of the river would take them. A large part of their journey would thus be accomplished without exertion, and the explorers could transport their provisions and weapons well into the island's western regions.

In preparation for this journey, they had to consider not only what to take with them, but also what they might be bringing back to Granite House. If, as all signs indicated, there had been a shipwreck on the coastline, then they would no doubt find an abundance of salvageable wreckage. The cart would of course have performed this task far more efficiently than their fragile canoe; but they would have had to drag that crude, heavy cart behind them as they went, and this seemed too great a burden. Pencroff expressed his regret that the crate did not contain, along with his "half-pound of tobacco," a pair of sturdy New Jersey horses, which would indeed have made a most welcome addition to the colony!

Neb stowed the provisions in the boat: smoked meats and a few gallons of beer and fermented liqueur, enough to sustain them for three days, the maximum Cyrus Smith allowed for this exploration. They further intended to resupply themselves with provisions en route, should the need arise, and Neb was careful not to forget the small portable oven.

By way of tools, the colonists took the two woodsman's hatchets, which would be used to hack out a path through the dense forest; by way of instruments, they brought the spyglass and the pocket compass.

For their weapons they chose the two flint rifles, preferable to the cartridge rifles in that the latter required percussion caps, whereas the former used only flints, which they could easily replace. Nevertheless, they took one of the carbines as well, along with a few cartridges. They had no choice but to bring some of the fifty pounds of powder they had found in the kegs, but the engineer was planning to formulate an explosive substance that would allow them to use that supply more sparingly in the future. In addition to these firearms, they brought the five cutlasses in their leather sheaths; thus equipped, the colonists could venture into the vast forest with some hope of emerging from it again.

It need hardly be added that Pencroff, Harbert, and Neb were thoroughly delighted to find themselves so armed, although Cyrus Smith made them promise not to fire a single shot unless strictly necessary.

The canoe was pushed into the sea at six o'clock in the morning. The colonists embarked, Top included, and paddled toward the mouth of the Mercy.

The tide had begun to rise a half-hour before. They would thus enjoy a favorable current over the next few hours, and it was important to take full advantage of this, for eventually the outflowing tide would begin to impede their progress upriver. The current was quite strong, for the moon would be full three days later, and the propulsive force of the oars was not needed to keep the canoe gliding swiftly between the high riverbanks; the colonists had only to keep their craft within the river's current.

After a few minutes, the explorers arrived at the bend in the Mercy, where Pencroff had constructed his first timber raft seven months earlier.

Here the river made a sharp turn and began to run obliquely toward the southwest, in the shadow of the tall evergreens.

The banks of the Mercy were wonderful to behold. Cyrus Smith and his companions could not help but gaze in rapt admiration at the beautiful effects nature so effortlessly achieved with a simple palette of water and trees. The forest changed as they advanced. The slopes to the right of the river were covered with magnificent specimens of the Ulmaceae family, the precious smooth-leafed elm, so highly prized by builders for its ability to withstand long periods of submersion. And there were other species from that same family as well, among them hackberry trees, whose nuts produce a very useful oil. Farther on, Harbert sighted a number of lardizabalas, whose flexible boughs can be macerated in water to produce excellent ropes, and two or three Ebenaceae with beautiful, curiously striated black trunks.

They stopped from time to time, whenever they found a suitable landing place. Then Gideon Spilett, Harbert, and Pencroff took up their rifles and explored the surrounding area, with Top leading the way. In part these were hunting expeditions; but more than that they were a search for useful flora. Soon the young naturalist's fondest wishes were granted, for he discovered a sort of wild spinach of the Chenopod family, as well as many cruciferous plants belonging to the cabbage genus, which they could easily "civilize" by transplantation; there was cress, horseradish, turnips, and finally some small bushy stalks, slightly downy, about a meter high, which produced seeds of an almost brown color.

"Do you know what this plant is?" Harbert asked the sailor.

"Tobacco!" cried Pencroff, who had clearly never seen his most beloved plant anywhere but in the bowl of his pipe.

"No, Pencroff!" Harbert answered. "It's not tobacco, it's mustard."

"Mustard is fine with me!" answered the sailor. "But if by chance you might spy a tobacco plant somewhere around here, my boy, please do me the favor of not overlooking it."

"We'll find one someday!" said Gideon Spilett.

"Will we indeed!" cried Pencroff. "Well, when that day comes, I don't believe there will be anything more to wish for!"

These various plants were uprooted with great care and transported to the canoe, where Cyrus Smith still sat, lost in meditation.

The reporter, Harbert, and Pencroff made several such forays, sometimes on the right bank of the Mercy, sometimes on the left. The latter was not as steep, but the former was more densely wooded. Consulting his pocket compass, the engineer determined that the river flowed virtually straight southwest to northeast after the first bend, over a distance of some three miles. But its direction would very likely change a little farther on, for at some point the Mercy would turn northwest, toward the foothills of Mount Franklin where it found its source.

One of their brief hunting excursions allowed Gideon Spilett to capture two pairs of gallinaceous birds with long, slender beaks, elongated necks, and no apparent tail. Harbert rightly identified them as "tinamous," and it was resolved that they would be the first guests of the future poultry yard.

But so far the rifles had kept their silence. The first detonation to be heard in the Forests of the Far West was provoked by the appearance of a beautiful bird not unlike a kingfisher in appearance.

"I recognize him!" Pencroff shouted, and we might well say that his rifle fired of its own accord.

"What do you recognize?" asked the reporter.

"The bird that got away from us in our first excursion, whose name we gave to this part of the forest."

"A jacamar!" cried Harbert.

It was indeed a jacamar, a magnificent bird with coarse iridescent plumage. A few lead pellets sent it plummeting to earth, and Top brought it back to the canoe along with a dozen "touraco lories," scansorial birds approximately the size of a pigeon, gaily daubed with green, but with a crimson swath on their wings and upright crests festooned with a white border. It was the boy who had brought down this prize catch, and he made no attempt to conceal his pride. As game, the lories were superior to the jacamar, whose flesh is somewhat tough; but it would have been difficult to disabuse Pencroff of the notion that he had killed the king of all edible fowl.

At ten o'clock in the morning, the canoe came to a second bend in the Mercy, roughly five miles from its mouth. Here they stopped for breakfast, lingering a good half-hour in the shelter of the tall, graceful trees.

The river still measured sixty to seventy feet wide, and five to ten feet deep. The engineer had noted the numerous tributaries that fed it, but these were no more than rills, entirely unnavigable. As for the forests, first Jacamar Woods and now the Forests of the Far West, they extended as far as the eye could see. Nowhere could the explorers detect any sign of human presence, neither among the towering trees nor along the shady banks of the Mercy. It was evident that no woodsman's ax had ever struck these trees, that no pioneer's cutlass had ever slashed the lianas slung between the tree trunks amid the dense brush and tall grass. If there were castaways on the island, they had clearly not yet left the shoreline, and there was nothing to be gained from prolonging the search in this thick mantle of greenery.

For this reason, the engineer felt a certain impatience to reach the western shore of Lincoln Island, still at least five miles distant in his estimation. They resumed their navigation, and although the Mercy now appeared to flow not toward the coast but rather toward Mount Franklin, they resolved to continue using the canoe so long as there was water beneath its keel to keep it afloat. This would spare them both effort and time, for if they set out on foot they would have to cut their way through the dense undergrowth with their hatchets.

Soon their favorable current began to wane, either because the tide was receding—and in fact it must have been receding at this hour—or because they were now too far from the mouth of the Mercy to feel its effect. They had no choice but to deploy the oars. Neb and Harbert took up their positions on the bench, Pencroff at the scull, and they pursued their course upstream.

As they penetrated farther into the Far West region, they found the woods growing less dense. The trees were more widely spaced, and often stood in isolated clusters. But precisely because they were more widely scattered, they profited all the more from the circulation of the pure, open air, and they were truly magnificent to behold.

What splendid specimens of the characteristic flora of this latitude! With one single glimpse of these forests, a skilled botanist could have immediately named the parallel that ran through Lincoln Island!

"Eucalyptus!" Harbert cried.

For such were the superb trees now before their eyes, the last giants of the subtropical zone, like the eucalyptus of Australia and New Zealand, which lie at the same latitude as Lincoln Island. Some of them soared to a height of two hundred feet. Their trunks measured twenty feet around at the base, and their bark, striated by the interlacing trails of a perfumed resin, might have been as much as five inches thick. Nothing could be more wonderful, nor more singular, than these enormous specimens of the family Myrtaceae, with the sun shining through their foliage and dappling the forest floor!

The ground beneath these eucalyptus trees was carpeted with cool grass, and a flight of birds arose from among the tussocks, gleaming in the luminous rays like winged carbuncles.

"Now, those are what I call trees!" cried Neb. "But are they good for anything?"

"Pshaw!" Pencroff answered. "There must be giant plants, just as there are giant humans. They're only good for sideshows!"

"I believe you're mistaken, Pencroff," answered Gideon Spilett. "I've heard that eucalyptus wood has proven extremely valuable in cabinet-making."

"And I would add," said the boy, "that the eucalyptus belongs to a family with many invaluable members: the guava tree, which produces guava fruit; the clove tree, from which we have cloves; the pomegranate tree, which gives us pomegranates; the *Eugenia cauliflora,* whose fruit can be used to make a very tolerable wine; the ugni myrtle, which contains an excellent alcoholic liquor; the caryophyllus myrtle, whose bark produces fine cinnamon; the *Eugenia pimenta,* the source of the Jamaican pepper; the common myrtle, whose berries make an excellent substitute for pepper; the *Eucalyptus robusti,* which produces a delicious sort of nectar; the *Eucalyptus gunnii,* whose sap can be fermented to make beer; and indeed all the trees known as 'trees of life' or 'ironwood,' for the family Myrtaceae comprises no fewer than forty-six genera and thirteen hundred species!"

They listened indulgently as the boy delivered this spirited little botany lesson, Cyrus Smith with a smile, Pencroff with a pride that no words can convey.

"That's all very well, Harbert," Pencroff answered, "but I'll wager none of the useful specimens you've just mentioned are giants like these!"

"You're right, Pencroff."

"Which only proves my point," the sailor answered. "Giants are good for nothing!"

"That's where you're wrong, Pencroff," the engineer then said. "These very eucalyptus in whose shade we stand serve an invaluable purpose."

"And what would that be?"

"They purify the region in which they grow. Do you know what these are called in Australia and New Zealand?"

"No, Mr. Cyrus."

"They call them 'fever trees.' "

"Because they cause fevers?"

"No, because they prevent them!"

"Good. I'll note that down," said the reporter.

"Note it down, indeed, my dear Spilett, for it has been demonstrated that the simple presence of eucalyptus trees is sufficient to neutralize paludal miasma. They are a natural prophylactic. As a test of their powers, they have been planted in certain unwholesome swamplands of southern Europe and northern Africa, and the state of the inhabitants' health has gradually improved. Intermittent fevers are unknown in any region forested with these Myrtaceae. This fact is now beyond dispute, and a happy fact it is for the colonists of Lincoln Island."

"Oh, what an island! What a blessed island!" cried Pencroff. "I tell you, there's not a single thing it lacks...except..."

"That will come, Pencroff, that will come," the engineer answered. "But now it's time we were off again. We must push on as far as the river will bear our canoe!"

They pursued their explorations among the eucalyptus trees for another two miles at least. Still the forest continued as far as their eyes could see, covering both sides of the Mercy, whose course now wound sinuously between tall green banks. Often their progress was blocked by tall grass and even jagged rocks, which made navigation an arduous task. The action of the oars was hampered, and Pencroff had to push the boat along with a pole. They could sense the water gradually becoming shallower, and they knew that the moment was not far off when the canoe's journey would have to come to an end. The sun was sinking low over the horizon, and the shadows of the trees grew ever longer. Realizing that they would not reach the western shore before nightfall, Cyrus Smith resolved to set up camp wherever the water became too shallow for the canoe. He estimated the distance to the coast at five to six miles, too far to attempt in the dark through unknown forests.

And so they pushed on tirelessly through the forest, which now grew thicker again, and more densely populated as well; for, unless the sailor's eyes had deceived him, he had spotted several bands of monkeys running through the undergrowth. Indeed, every now and then two or three such creatures could be seen standing at some distance from the canoe and watching the colonists pass by, unafraid, as if, seeing men for the first time, they had not yet learned to fear them. The explorers could easily have shot down one of these quadrupeds with their rifles, but Cyrus Smith forbade this needless massacre, much to the chagrin of Pencroff, ever the avid hunter. Smith's decision was a prudent one, for these monkeys are quick and remarkably agile, and can thus prove redoubtable adversaries, and it was best not to provoke them with an inopportune act of aggression.

The sailor, of course, considered the monkeys purely from the alimentary point of view, and it is true that such herbivores make excellent game; but there was no lack of provisions to hand, and it would have been a mistake to expend their ammunition for no reason.

By four o'clock, the Mercy was becoming increasingly choked with water plants and rocks, and so extremely difficult to navigate. The banks soared ever higher, and already the river was entering the first foothills of Mount Franklin. Its source could thus not be far away, since it was fed by the waters running off the mountain's southern slopes.

"Within a quarter of an hour we'll have to stop, Mr. Cyrus," the sailor said.

"Well then, we shall stop, Pencroff, and set up camp for the night."

"How far do you suppose we might be from Granite House?" asked Harbert.

"Approximately seven miles," the engineer answered, "but the bends in the river have brought us far to the northwest."

"Are we to continue paddling up the river?" the reporter asked.

"Yes, as long as we possibly can," Cyrus Smith answered. "Tomorrow, at daybreak, we will abandon the boat and continue on foot to the coast. This will take two hours or so, I hope, and then we will have nearly a full day to explore the coastline."

"Onward!" Pencroff replied.

But soon the bottom of the canoe was scraping the stony riverbed, whose width had shrunk to no more than twenty feet. A dense arch of greenery hung over the water, shrouding it in near-total darkness. They could clearly hear the sound of falling water, indicating the presence of a natural dam several hundred paces upstream.

And indeed, at one last bend in the river a cascade appeared through the trees. The boat ran aground against the riverbed, and a few moments later it was moored to a trunk on the right bank.

It was about five o'clock. The last rays of the setting sun slipped beneath the dense branches and obliquely struck the little waterfall, causing its pulverized spray to glimmer with all the colors of a prism. Beyond that the Mercy disappeared into the brush, where it was fed by some hidden spring. Downstream it became a true river thanks to the various rills feeding into it here and there, but now it was only a limpid, shallow rivulet.

Here they would camp for the night, and a charming spot it was. The colonists disembarked, and a fire was lit beneath a stand of spreading hackberry trees, among whose branches Cyrus Smith and his companions could take refuge should the need arise.

Their supper was soon devoured, for their hunger was great, and now there was nothing more to do but sleep. Nevertheless, a number of suspicious growls had been heard before the daylight faded, and so a further supply of fuel was added to the fire, so as to protect the sleepers with the crackling flames. Neb and Pencroff kept watch by turns, and they did not spare the firewood. Perhaps they were not mistaken when they thought they saw shadowy animals prowling around the campsite, among the undergrowth and through the branches; but the night passed without incident, and the next day, October 31st, at five o'clock in the morning, they were all on their feet, ready to set out again.

IV

Toward the Coastline.—Bands of Quadrumanes.—A New Waterway.—Why the Tide Does Not Affect It.—A Forest Shoreline.—Reptile End.—Gideon Spilett Inspires Harbert's Envy.—The Crackling Bamboo.

It was six o'clock in the morning when the colonists resumed their journey after a cursory breakfast, hoping to find the shortest possible route to the island's western shore. How long would it take them to reach it? Cyrus Smith had said two hours, but this would of course depend on the nature of the obstacles they encountered. The forest was extremely dense in this region of the Far West, like a single immense thicket composed of many varied species. They would no doubt be forced to hack out a path through the grasses, brush, and lianas, and to keep their hatchets ever in hand—along with their rifles, judging by the wild cries they had heard in the night.

They now determined the precise location of their campsite in relation to Mount Franklin. The volcano stood no more than three miles to their north, meaning that a straight southwesterly route would unfailingly bring them to the western shore.

They conscientiously checked the mooring of the canoe and set off. Pencroff and Neb carried sufficient provisions to nourish the little troop for at least two days. There was no need for hunting now, and indeed the engineer urged his companions not to call attention to their presence with unnecessary gunfire.

They began to chop their way through a thicket of mastic shrubs a short distance above the cascade. Compass in hand, Cyrus Smith led the way.

The forest was now composed of trees familiar to the colonists from Longview Plateau and the environs of the lake: deodars, Douglas pines, casuarinas, gum trees, eucalyptus, dragon trees, hibiscus, cedars, and other species. They were generally of middling size, for their great density hampered their growth. Forced to create their path as they went, the colonists' progress was slow; but as they proceeded, the engineer formulated a plan to link this new path with the route to Red Creek.

Slowly the colonists descended the low slopes that formed this region's orographic system. The terrain was very dry, but a luxuriant growth of vegetation suggested either that some hydrographic network lay beneath the soil or that they were approaching another stream. Nevertheless, Cyrus Smith could not recall having seen any watercourse other than Red Creek and the Mercy during his expedition to the crater.

Yet more bands of monkeys appeared over the first few hours of this trek, apparently startled and astonished at what must have been their first sight of men. In jest, Gideon Spilett wondered whether such strong, agile quadrumanes might look on them, his companions and himself, as their own degenerate brothers! And it must be admitted that, entangled in lianas at every step, their progress continually halted by tree trunks and brush, the colonists did not compare particularly well with the lithe creatures who raced effortlessly through the woods, leaping from branch to branch. The monkeys were numerous, but fortunately showed no sign of hostility.

A few wild boars were spotted as well, along with agoutis, kangaroos, and other rodents. There were even two or three kolas, and Pencroff longed to send two or three gunloads of lead flying their way.

"But," he said, "hunting season is over. So frolic away, my friends, leap and fly in peace! We'll have more to say to you on the way back!"

At nine-thirty in the morning, their southwesterly path was abruptly blocked by an unsuspected waterway, thirty to forty feet wide, crashing noisily over the rocks that littered the steep slope of the streambed. The creek was deep and clear, but quite impossible to navigate.

"We're cut off!" cried Neb.

"No," Harbert answered, "it's only a stream. We can easily swim across."

"There's no need for that," Cyrus Smith answered. "The creek clearly runs toward the sea. Let's stay on this side and follow the bank. I'd be very surprised if it doesn't lead us directly to the shore. Off we go!"

"Just one moment," said the reporter. "The name of this creek, my friends? We mustn't neglect our geography."

"Right you are!" said Pencroff.

"Name it, my boy," said the engineer, speaking to the child.

"Wouldn't it be better to wait until we've observed it all the way to its mouth?" Harbert asked.

"So be it," answered Cyrus Smith. "Let's keep close to it, and let's not stop again."

"Just one more moment!" said Pencroff.

"What is it?" asked the reporter.

"Hunting is forbidden, I know, but I suppose fishing is allowed?" said the sailor.

"We have no time to lose," the engineer answered.

"Oh! five minutes!" Pencroff replied. "I'm only asking for five minutes, for the sake of our lunch!"

Pencroff lay down on the bank and thrust his arms into the running water. Soon he had brought out several dozen beautiful crawfish, which had been swarming among the rocks.

"Now, there's a good thing!" cried Neb, coming to the sailor's assistance.

"I'm telling you, this island has everything, everything except tobacco!" Pencroff murmured with a sigh.

In less than five minutes they had taken in a miraculous haul, for the creek was alive with crawfish. After remarking on their cobalt blue tests and the small barb that armed their rostra, they stored the crustaceans in a bag and resumed their journey.

Their progress was considerably faster and easier on the bank of this new creek. Still they found no trace of any human footprint. From time to time, they discovered prints left by large animals coming to this stream to quench their thirst, but nothing more than that. The lead pellet that wounded the peccary and cost Pencroff a molar had apparently not been fired anywhere in this region.

Cyrus Smith observed the rapidity of the current flowing toward the sea, and concluded that he and his companions were farther than they thought from the western shores. For the ocean tide must now be rising, and it would have reversed the creek's current if the mouth were only a few miles distant. But no: the water was simply coursing over the natural slope of the streambed. This greatly surprised the engineer, and he carefully consulted his compass to assure himself that some imperceptible bend in the stream had not brought them back toward the middle of the Far West.

As they advanced, the creek gradually widened, and its waters grew less tumultuous. The forest was equally dense on both banks, and equally opaque; but the woods were undoubtedly deserted, for Top was not barking, and the intelligent animal would not have failed to sound the alert if he had detected the presence of strangers nearby.

At ten-thirty, to Cyrus Smith's great surprise, Harbert suddenly stopped and shouted back to the others:

"The sea!"

A few moments later, the colonists joined Harbert at the edge of the forest and saw the island's western shore stretching out before them.

How different it all was from the eastern coastline, where fate had dropped them so many months before! No wall of granite, no shoals, not even a sandy beach. The forest was the shoreline. The last row of trees leaned over the water, continually lashed by the waves. It was not a shoreline at all in the usual sense—carpeted with sand or paved with rocks— but simply the edge of a remarkable forest populated by the world's most beautiful trees. The riverbank, slightly elevated, overlooked the waters of the open sea. Overlying its granite bedrock, the rich soil of the forest floor was densely planted with magnificent trees of many species, just as in the thickest forests of the island's center.

The colonists found themselves in a cove of no great size, too small even for two or three simple fishing boats, which served as an outlet for the creek. The cove had one very unusual feature: rather than flowing gently seaward over a regular slope, the creek's waters rushed down from a height of more than forty feet—which explained why the rising tide could not be felt upstream. For even at their strongest, the ocean tides would never reach the streambed, as high above the sea as the upper reach of a canal, and it would no doubt take millions of years for the rushing water to erode that massive granite apron and flow smoothly into the sea. Thus, by common accord, they gave this new waterway the name "Falls River."

Across the river, the forest continued northward for another two miles;

The riverbank was slightly elevated.

then the trees became sparser, and farther on a number of picturesque bluffs could be seen receding into the distance, nearly straight north. To the south, on the other hand, from Falls River to Reptile End, the shoreline was one long row of magnificent trees, some of them straight, some leaning, all washed by the slow undulations of the sea. And this was the direction they would now travel, as far as the end of Serpentine Peninsula, for here, unlike the arid wastelands to the north, the castaways might conceivably have found shelter.

The weather was clear and bright, and the view was expansive from atop the cliff where Neb and Pencroff laid out their lunch. From shore to horizon, there was not a sail to be seen, nor over the entire coastline—not a single vessel, not even wreckage. But the engineer refused to give up the search until they had explored the shoreline to the very end of Serpentine Peninsula.

They downed their meal speedily, and at eleven-thirty Cyrus Smith announced that it was time to set off again. They had a difficult trek ahead of them, for their path lay not along a clifftop or sandy beach, but through the close-huddled trees at the water's edge.

Some twelve miles separated the mouth of Falls River from Reptile End. On a beach, such a distance could be easily crossed in four hours; but it took them twice that time to reach their goal, for they were continually impeded by trees, dense brush, and troublesome lianas, and these many unavoidable detours made their journey far longer than they could have guessed.

And still they found no sign of any recent shipwreck. As Gideon Spilett observed, however, the tides could well have carried the wreckage out to sea, and the lack of debris in no way proved that a ship had not been driven onto the shores of Lincoln Island.

The reporter's reasoning was sound, and furthermore, the incident of the lead pellet proved irrefutably that a rifle had been fired on the island within the previous three months at most.

Soon it was five o'clock, and the colonists were still two miles from the end of Serpentine Peninsula. By the time they reached Reptile End, there would not be enough daylight left to see them back to their campsite beside the Mercy. They would thus have no choice but to spend the night on the promontory itself. But they had a good supply of provisions—fortunately for them, as the woods along the shore were apparently devoid of furred game. On the other hand, there were birds in profusion: jacamars, trogons, tragopans, capercaillies, lories, parrots, cockatoos, pheasants, pigeons, and hundreds of others. Not a single tree without a nest, not a nest unanimated by beating wings!

At about seven o'clock in the evening the exhausted colonists arrived at Reptile End, a sort of curious scalloped volute overhanging the water. Here the maritime forest came to a halt, and to the south the shoreline was once again formed of the familiar rocks, shoals, and beaches. A crippled ship might thus have foundered somewhere in this vicinity; but night was now falling, and they would have to wait until the following morning to pursue their explorations.

Pencroff and Harbert hurried off in search of a likely spot for their camp. The point was scattered with a few last trees from the forest, among which the boy found a dense thicket of bamboo.

"Well!" he said. "This is a wonderful find."

"It is?" answered Pencroff.

"Certainly," Harbert answered. "There's no point in telling you, Pencroff, that the bark of the bamboo plant can be cut into flexible strips and used to weave baskets or bushels; that the Chinese pound and macerate this same bark into a pulp to make paper; that the stalks can be used as canes, tubing, or water conduits, depending on their thickness; that the largest bamboo plants make an excellent building material, both light and sturdy, and impervious to insects. Nor will I bother to add that when it is cut with care, leaving the transverse walls at the joints, it makes fine, watertight vases, much favored in the Orient! No! that would mean precious little to you. But..."

"But?"

"But I might inform you, if you don't know it already, that in India these bamboo plants are eaten much as we eat asparagus."

"Thirty-foot-long asparagus!" cried the sailor. "And is it good?"

"Delicious," Harbert answered. "But they don't eat the thirty-foot-long stalks—only the tender shoots."

"Capital, my boy, capital!" Pencroff answered.

"And I will add that the pith of the young stalks can be pickled in vinegar to make a highly prized condiment."

"Better and better, Harbert."

"And finally that the joints exude a sugary liquor, from which a very pleasant drink can be made."

"Is that all?"

"That's all!"

"It can't be smoked, by any chance?"

"No, it can't be smoked, my poor Pencroff!"

Harbert and the sailor did not have to hunt long for a suitable camp-site. Lashed by the wind-driven waves, the rocks along the shore were wildly cracked and cloven, with a multitude of hollows offering shelter from the rigors of the weather. But just as they were about to enter one such cavity, a series of fearsome roars stopped them short.

"Back!" cried Pencroff. "We've nothing but lead shot in our rifles, and that'll be about as effective as table salt against any beast who roars like that!"

Seizing Harbert's arm, the sailor dived for cover among the rocks just as a magnificent creature appeared at the entrance to the cavern.

It was a jaguar, more or less equivalent in size to its Asian counterpart, which is to say more than five feet from the end of its nose to the root of its tail. Its tawny coat was dotted with several rows of ocellated black spots, and contrasted with the white fur of its belly. In this beast Harbert recognized a fierce rival of the tiger, far more redoubtable than the cougar, whose only rival is the wolf!

The jaguar came forward and looked from side to side, its fur bristling, its eyes aflame, as if this were not its first encounter with the scent of man.

At the same time, the reporter was coming around the high rocks, and Harbert was about to run toward him, assuming that he had not seen the jaguar; but Gideon Spilett gestured to him to stay where he was, and continued forward. This was not his first tiger. Advancing to within ten paces of the animal, he stood motionless, his rifle raised, his arm perfectly steady.

The jaguar tensed and sprang at the hunter, but at that moment a bullet struck it between the eyes, and it fell lifeless to earth.

Harbert and Pencroff hurried toward the jaguar, Neb and Cyrus Smith came running, and they all stood for a few moments contemplating the beast that lay before them, whose magnificent pelt would soon ornament the great room of Granite House.

"Oh! Mr. Spilett! How I admire you! How I envy you!" cried Harbert, in a perfectly understandable fit of enthusiasm.

"Come now, my boy," the reporter answered, "you could have done as much."

"Me! cool-headed like that!"

"Just imagine that a jaguar is a hare, Harbert, and you will shoot him down as calmly as you please."

"So!" Pencroff answered. "Is that all there is to it!"

"And now, my friends," said Gideon Spilett, "since this jaguar won't be needing its lair, I don't see why we shouldn't take it over for the night!"

"But there may be others!" said Pencroff.

"We'll light a fire at the entrance to the cavern," the reporter said, "and they won't dare cross the threshold."

"To the jaguar house, then!" the sailor answered, dragging the animal's cadaver behind him.

The colonists headed for the empty lair. Leaving Neb to skin the jaguar, his companions gathered a large quantity of dry wood in the forest and piled it at the cavern's entrance.

But Cyrus Smith, spotting the stand of bamboo plants, went and cut down a few stalks, and intermingled them with the firewood.

This done, they set up camp inside the grotto, whose sandy floor was covered with bones; they loaded their weapons as a protection against unexpected attack; they dined, and when it finally came time to sleep they set fire to the pile of wood at the entrance to the cavern.

All at once, a veritable fusillade rent the air! It was the bamboo stalks, exploding like fireworks in the heat of the flames! This din alone would have been enough to terrify the most fearless of wild beasts!

It should be said that this stratagem was not the engineer's invention. According to Marco Polo, the Tartars have used it for many centuries, and with great success, to drive the formidable wildlife of central Asia far from their campsites.

V

A Suggestion to Return by the Southern Coast.—Configuration of the Coastline.—In Search of the Presumed Shipwreck.—Wreckage in the Air.—Discovery of a Small Natural Harbor.—The Banks of the Mercy at Midnight.—A Boat Adrift.

Cyrus Smith and his companions slept like innocent dormice in the cavern so kindly left to them by the jaguar.

By sunrise they were all on the shore at the end of the promontory, their gaze once again fixed on the horizon, visible here over two thirds of its circumference. One last time, the engineer confirmed that no sail or ship's carcass lay offshore, and the telescope revealed not a single suspect dot in the sea.

The promontory's straight southern shoreline was equally deserted, over a distance of three miles at least; beyond that, a meander concealed the rest of the coast, so completely that Cape Claw itself lay hidden behind the high rocks.

The island's southern shore would thus have to be explored on foot. Should they see to this at once, and devote the entire day of November 2nd to the task?

This was not part of their original plan. On abandoning the canoe at the source of the Mercy, they had agreed to return to that spot after their examination of the western shore, then proceed to Granite House by way of the river. At that time, Cyrus Smith was convinced that the western shores might have offered refuge to a vessel in distress or a ship still afloat and intact; but since they now knew that no boat could have landed on that side, they would have to seek on the island's southern shores what they could not find in the west.

It was Gideon Spilett who proposed that they continue the exploration, in hopes of settling the question of the shipwreck once and for all. He asked how far Cape Claw might be from the end of the peninsula.

"About thirty miles," the engineer answered, "if we account for the bends in the shoreline."

"Thirty miles!" Gideon Spilett replied. "That will be a long day's walk. Nevertheless, I believe we should return to Granite House by way of the southern coast."

"But," Harbert observed, "from Cape Claw to Granite House it must be another ten miles at least."

"Let us say forty miles total," the reporter answered. "Nevertheless, I believe we should press on without a moment's hesitation. If nothing else, we will be able to observe all the unknown shores, and that will be the end of our explorations."

"Very true," said Pencroff. "But what about the canoe?"

"The canoe has already sat unattended for one day," Gideon Spilett answered, "so it can certainly wait another! After all, we have no reason to believe that our island is infested with thieves!"

"All the same," said the sailor, "when I remember what happened with the tortoise, I'm not so sure of that as I might be."

"The tortoise! the tortoise!" the reporter answered. "Don't you understand that it was the sea that turned it over?"

"Who knows?" murmured the engineer.

"But..." said Neb.

Neb had something to say, that was clear, but no words came when he opened his mouth.

"What do you want to say, Neb?" the engineer asked him.

"If we start out along the shoreline to Cape Claw, once we've gone around the cape we'll be cut off..."

"By the Mercy! He's right," Harbert answered, "and we'll have neither bridge nor boat to help us across!"

"Oh well, Mr. Cyrus," Pencroff replied, "a few floating tree trunks will take care of that!"

"All the same," said Gideon Spilett, "a bridge would be a useful thing to have if we're planning to spend much time in the Far West!"

"A bridge!" cried Pencroff. "Well, doesn't Mr. Cyrus earn his living as an engineer? So he can build us a bridge, whenever we need one! As for getting you across to the other bank of the Mercy this evening, you can leave that to me! Don't worry, not so much as a drop of water will touch the cuffs of your trousers! We still have a day's worth of provisions, and that's all we need; besides, we might have better hunting today than we did yesterday. Let's be off!"

The reporter's suggestion, energetically supported by the sailor, met with general approval. They were all eager to settle the question of the shipwreck, and a return by way of Cape Claw would make their exploration complete. But there was not an hour to be lost, for a forty-mile day was a long one, and they could not hope to reach Granite House before nightfall.

At six o'clock in the morning, the little band set off. The rifles were loaded with bullets as a defense against unpleasant encounters of both the two-legged and four-legged variety, and Top was given orders to run on ahead and flush out any animals that might be lurking in the forest.

They set out from the tail end of the promontory, then, and followed the slow curve of the shoreline for a distance of five miles, looking around them as they walked; but still they found no trace of a landing ancient or recent, nor any wreckage, nor the remains of any campsite, nor the ashes of an extinguished fire, nor a single footprint!

Soon the colonists arrived at the point where the shoreline curved northeast to form Washington Bay. The view extended over the island's entire southern coast. Twenty-five miles away, dimly emerging from the morning fog, lay Cape Claw. A mirage effect made it seem to hover between heaven and earth, and to rise far higher than it actually did. From where the colonists now stood to the innermost point of the immense bay, the shoreline first took the form of a broad beach, very regular and very flat, edged with a line of trees; beyond that, it became far more irregular, with sharp spits jutting into the sea, and this eventually gave way to a jumbled pile of black rocks that continued as far as Cape Claw.

Such was the explorers' first view of this region, and they paused a moment to let their gaze wander over the landscape.

"Any ship that foundered here would certainly be destroyed," said Pencroff. "Sandbars offshore, and shoals beyond that! Not a pleasant spot!"

"But surely something would be left of the ship, at least," the reporter observed.

"A few pieces of wood on the shoals, perhaps, but nothing on the sandbars," the sailor answered.

"Why is that?"

"Because sandbars are even more treacherous than rocks; they swallow everything. A ship of several hundred tons can run onto a sandbar, and vanish in a matter of days!"

"So, Pencroff," the engineer asked, "if a ship had foundered on these sandbars, there might very well remain not the slightest trace of the accident?"

"No, Mr. Smith, given time enough, or a storm. Even so, I'd be a bit surprised if no debris from the masts or spars had washed up onto the beach, beyond the wave line."

"In that case, let us continue our search," Cyrus Smith answered.

At one hour past noon, after a twenty-mile walk, the colonists came to the innermost point of Washington Bay.

They stopped for lunch.

Here the shoreline became curiously irregular and ragged, with a long line of shoals now appearing beyond the sandbars as the tide receded. The gently undulating sea broke over the rocks, leaving a long trail of foam. From here to Cape Claw, the beach was narrow and confined, tightly squeezed between shoals and forest.

Their trek would soon become more arduous still, for the shore was littered with a multitude of fallen rocks. Looking down the beach, they could see the wall of granite rising gradually higher, and all they could glimpse of its crest were the green treetops, motionless in the still air.

After a half-hour's rest the colonists resumed their journey, leaving no point unobserved between the shoals and the beach. Pencroff and Neb waded out into the shoals whenever some object caught their eye, but each time, they found that they had been deceived by some odd configuration of the rocks, and there was no wreckage to be seen. On the other hand, they were delighted to discover an abundance of edible shellfish along the beach; but they could not take advantage of this windfall until a link had been established between the two banks of the Mercy, and until they had devised a more convenient means of transport.

Thus, no sign of the supposed shipwreck could be found along the shore. Any sizable object lying in the water—the hull of a ship, for instance—would have been exposed by the receding tide; any debris would have washed ashore, like the crate they had found less than twenty miles from where they now stood. And yet there was nothing.

At around three o'clock, Cyrus Smith and his companions arrived at a narrow, well-protected cove. No stream flowed into the ocean here. They had come across a veritable natural harbor, invisible from offshore, accessible from the sea only by way of a narrow channel through the shoals.

Within the cove, some violent convulsion of the earth had rent the wall of rock, and through that rift lay a gentle slope leading up to the plateau, which might have been less than ten miles from Cape Claw, and consequently four miles, as the crow flies, from Longview Plateau.

Gideon Spilett suggested a brief halt. His proposal was gladly accepted, for the walk had sharpened their hunger, and although it was not yet dinnertime, no one could refuse a fortifying piece of venison to sustain them until their supper at Granite House.

A few minutes later the colonists were sitting beneath a majestic stand of maritime pines, devouring the provisions that Neb had taken from his sack.

From where they sat, some fifty to sixty feet above sea level, they enjoyed an extensive view over the last rocks of the cape and beyond to Union Bay, lying hazily in the distance. But neither the islet nor Longview Plateau was visible—nor would they ever be from this spot, for the northern horizon was concealed behind the hills and the tall trees' dense foliage.

Nor, it need hardly be added, was there any sign of a ship in the surrounding waters. They had before them a great expanse of sea, and the engineer took up his spyglass and painstakingly examined every point along the curving line where the sky met the water. He found nothing.

Now he turned his spyglass to the shoreline, examining the area yet to be explored from beach to shoals, and still the instrument's lens revealed no wreckage.

"My friends," said Gideon Spilett, "we've got to face facts. At least we know our ownership of Lincoln Island will never be disputed, and that's some consolation!"

"But what about the lead pellet?" said Harbert. "I don't think we imagined that!"

"By all the devils, no!" cried Pencroff, thinking of his missing molar.

"What are we to think, then?" asked the reporter.

"This," the engineer answered. "Sometime within the last three months at most, voluntarily or otherwise, a ship landed..."

"What! You believe a ship could have washed ashore and then vanished without a trace, Cyrus?" cried the reporter.

"No, my dear Spilett. Understand me well: it is certain that some human being has set foot on this island, and it seems equally certain that he is no longer here."

"Then, if I understand you rightly, Mr. Cyrus," said Harbert, "the ship has sailed away?..."

"Obviously."

"And we've forever lost a chance to go home?" said Neb.

"I'm afraid so."

"Well! Since we've missed our chance, let's be on our way," said Pencroff, already homesick for Granite House.

But no sooner had he stood up than Top began to bark violently, and soon the dog came running from the woods with a shred of mud-stained fabric between his teeth.

Neb pulled the rag from the dog's mouth. It was a piece of thick canvas.

Top continued to bark, running back and forth before his master, as if there were something in the forest he urgently wanted him to see.

"This might explain my lead pellet!" cried Pencroff.

"A castaway!" answered Harbert.

"Wounded, perhaps!" said Neb.

"Or dead!" the reporter added.

And with Top leading the way they raced into the tall pines, weapons at the ready in case of an unexpected encounter.

They pressed ever farther into the woods, but to their great disappointment they still found no trace of a footprint. The vines and undergrowth were undisturbed, and they were forced to cut their way through with their hatchets as they had done in the dense forest the day before. It thus seemed quite unlikely that some human creature had passed this way before them, and yet Top ran back and forth, to and fro, not like a dog hunting randomly but like a being endowed with a will of its own, and pursuing a particular notion.

After seven to eight minutes' walk, Top stopped and waited for them. They had come to a sort of clearing, ringed with tall trees; they looked

It was a piece of thick canvas.

around them and saw nothing, neither in the undergrowth nor among the thick trunks.

"What is it, Top?" said Cyrus Smith.

Top barked still louder, leaping upward from the foot of a giant pine tree.

Suddenly, Pencroff cried out:

"Oh! that's good! Oh! that's perfect!"

"What are you talking about?" asked Gideon Spilett.

"We were looking for wreckage on the sea and on land!"

"Yes?"

"When in fact we should have been looking in the air!"

And the sailor pointed to a sort of huge, whitish rag hanging from high atop a pine tree. It was a piece of this rag, fallen to earth, that Top had brought them.

"But this isn't wreckage!" cried Gideon Spilett.

"Beg pardon!" Pencroff answered.

"What? it's? . . ."

"It's what's left of our airship, our balloon! This is where she foundered, up at the top of that tree!"

Pencroff was not mistaken, and he let out a magnificent hurrah, adding:

"Look at all that fine canvas! That'll give us clothes for years to come! Just the thing for our shirts and handkerchiefs! Tell me, Mr. Spilett, what do you think of an island where shirts grow on trees?"

This was a happy circumstance indeed: after its final bound through the air, the aerostat had fallen to earth on the island, and now the colonists had had the great good fortune to come across its remains. They could repair the envelope of the balloon in hopes of making another aerial escape, or perhaps remove the layer of varnish that coated it and put those several hundred ells of first-quality cotton canvas to a more immediate and practical use. As we might well suppose, Pencroff's joy was heartily shared by all.

But first they would have to disengage the envelope from the tree over which it was draped, and then store it away for safekeeping. This would be no small task. Neb, Harbert, and the sailor scaled the tree and set to work; only by the most prodigious acrobatic feats did they succeed in freeing the immense deflated aerostat from the branches.

After some two hours, the balloon lay before them on the ground: not only the envelope, complete with valve, springs, and copper fittings, but also the net—a great tangle of ropes and cords—the retaining ring, and the anchor. The envelope was in fine condition, apart from the fateful tear, only its lower appendix had been damaged by the trees.

A vast fortune had fallen from the skies.

"But in the end, Mr. Cyrus," the sailor said, "if we do ever set out to leave the island, surely it won't be in a balloon, will it? As we well know, you can't choose your direction when you're navigating through the air. So if you want my opinion, we'd do better to build a good sturdy ship of, say, twenty tons. I can cut the foresail and jib from this canvas, and the rest we can use for clothes!"

"We shall see, Pencroff," answered Cyrus Smith, "we shall see."

"In the meantime, we've got to find somewhere safe to keep it," said Neb.

For it was true that they could not hope to transport this heavy, cumbersome load of canvas, ropes, and cords back to Granite House until they had constructed a vehicle capable of carrying it all. In the meantime, they could not afford to leave their treasure exposed to the vagaries of the weather. Working together, the colonists succeeded in dragging the huge bundle to the shore, where they located a suitable cavity in the rock, sheltered from wind, rain, and ocean waves.

"We needed a linen chest, and we've found a linen chest," said Pencroff; "but it doesn't have a lock on it, so we'd best be sure to conceal the entrance. Not that I'm worried about two-legged thieves; I'm thinking more of the four-legged variety!"

By six o'clock in the evening everything was stowed away, and after giving the little cove the very suitable name of "Port Balloon," they resumed their journey to Cape Claw. Along the way, Pencroff and the engineer discussed the various projects they would soon have to undertake. They would need a bridge over the Mercy for easy travel to the south of the island; then, once the bridge was in place, they would take the cart and pick up the balloon, since they could not hope to transport it in the boat; then they would build a decked launch, which Pencroff would rig as a cutter, and they would attempt to circumnavigate the island; and then, etc.

Meanwhile night began to come on, and the sky was already dark when the colonists reached Flotsam Point, where they had discovered the precious crate. But here, as everywhere else, they found no sign that any kind of shipwreck had occurred, and no reason to challenge the conclusion that Cyrus Smith had asserted some time before.

A distance of four miles separated Flotsam Point from Granite House, and the colonists completed that final stage of their journey as quickly as they could. Nevertheless, it was past midnight when the colonists finally reached the first bend in the Mercy.

Here the river measured some eighty feet wide, and they knew they would have no easy time crossing it. But Pencroff had taken it upon himself to surmount that difficulty, and his companions authorized him to carry on as he saw fit.

It cannot be denied that the colonists were thoroughly exhausted. The day had been long, and the incident of the balloon had not been easy on their arms and legs. They were understandably impatient to find themselves back inside Granite House, to sup and sleep, and they would have been home in fifteen minutes if only the bridge were already in place.

The night was very dark. Mindful of his promise, Pencroff set about making a sort of raft to ferry them across the Mercy. Taking up their hatchets, he and Neb found two suitable trees near the riverbank and began to chop away at their trunks.

Cyrus Smith and Gideon Spilett sat on the bank, ready to lend assistance if necessary. Harbert came and went, never wandering too far away.

The boy had walked a short distance upstream, but suddenly he came running back to the others, and, pointing behind him:

"What is that drifting there?" he cried.

Pencroff looked up from his work and saw a moving object, only vaguely visible through the gloom.

"A boat!" he said.

They approached and, to their great surprise, found a small craft drifting along on the current.

"Ahoy there!" cried the sailor, out of professional habit, never thinking that it might have been wiser to keep his silence.

No answer. The craft drifted farther downstream, and it was only some ten paces away when the sailor cried out:

"It's our canoe! It must have broken its mooring and floated on the current! It couldn't have picked a better time, that you can't deny!"

"Our canoe?..." the engineer murmured.

Pencroff was not mistaken; it was indeed their boat. The mooring must have torn, freeing it to drift to the mouth of the Mercy of its own accord!

Their task now was to catch it as it passed by, before the river's current carried it into the bay; this Neb and Pencroff now did, skillfully wielding a long rod.

The boat was pulled to the bank. The engineer climbed in and picked up the mooring line, running his fingers over the rope in search of a frayed spot no doubt caused by friction against the rocks.

"This," the reporter said to him in a low voice, "this is what we might call a very..."

"Curious happenstance!" Cyrus Smith rejoined.

Curious or no, it was surely fortunate! One by one, they all embarked. They never doubted that the line had been worn too thin to hold the boat; but they were astounded that the canoe had come along just when it did, just when they were there to seize it as it passed, for fifteen minutes later it would have been lost to the open sea.

Had they been living in the age of genies, this incident might well have convinced them that some supernatural being haunted the island, using all his magical powers to serve the castaways!

A few oar strokes brought the colonists back to the mouth of the Mercy. The boat was towed onto the beach and left near the Chimneys, and they all headed for the ladder, eager to enter their home at last.

But just then Top gave an angry bark, and Neb, attempting to set his foot on the lowest rung, let out a cry...

The ladder was gone.

VI

*Pencroff Hails.—A Night in the Chimneys.—Harbert's Arrow.—
Cyrus Smith's Plan.—An Unexpected Solution.—What
Happened at Granite House.—How a New Domestic Entered the
Colonists' Service.*

Cyrus Smith stopped short, without a word. His companions searched in the dark for the ladder, both along the rock wall, in case the wind had blown it aside, and on the surface of the ground, in case it had come detached... But the ladder had simply and completely vanished. Perhaps some sudden gust of wind had lifted it up and deposited it on the first landing, halfway up the wall, but the darkness was too profound for them to say.

"If this is supposed to be a joke, I don't find it particularly amusing!" cried Pencroff. "Coming home to find someone's taken the staircase to your bedroom—that's no way to make weary folk laugh!"

All the while, an endless stream of exclamations poured from Neb's mouth!

"But there's no wind!" Harbert observed.

"I'm beginning to believe that some very singular things are happening on Lincoln Island!" said Pencroff.

"Singular?" Gideon Spilett answered. "Not at all, Pencroff, nothing could be more natural. Someone came along while we were absent, took possession of our home, and pulled up the ladder!"

"Someone!" cried the sailor. "Who?"

"Why, the hunter who fired the lead pellet," answered the reporter. "What is that pellet but the explanation of this whole misadventure?"

"Well, if someone's up there," answered Pencroff with an oath, his patience growing thin, "I'll hail him, and he'll have to answer me."

And in a thundering voice, the sailor let out a prolonged "Ahoy!" that echoed forcefully against the rock.

The colonists listened closely, and from high above them they thought they could hear a sort of cackling of uncertain origin. But no voice responded to Pencroff's voice, and he resumed his vigorous shouting in vain.

This was enough to confound the most indifferent soul, and the colonists were in no way indifferent. Unexpected events could have serious consequences in their situation, and in all their seven months on the island no event had been quite as unexpected as this.

In any case, oblivious to their own exhaustion, lost in perplexity, they stood at the foot of Granite House, not knowing what to think, not knowing what to do, posing endless unanswerable questions, considering a thousand hypotheses, each more unlikely than the next. Deeply distressed to find himself barred from his own kitchen, Neb lamented that they had run through their supply of provisions, with no way of restocking for the moment.

"My friends," said Cyrus Smith, "we have only one possible course of action: to wait for daylight, then consider our next move. But if wait we must, let us at least wait in the Chimneys. There we will have shelter, and there we can sleep, even if we cannot eat."

"This is pure brazen effrontery! Who could have done this to us?" Pencroff asked again, unable to reconcile himself to this vexing turn of events.

Whoever this "brazen" party may have been, the colonists had no choice but to return to the Chimneys and wait for daylight, as the engineer had recommended. Nevertheless, Top was commanded to keep watch under the windows of Granite House, and when Top was given an order, Top neither shirked nor answered back. The noble dog stayed behind, at the foot of the granite wall, while his master and his companions took refuge among the boulders.

Despite their great weariness, it cannot be said that the colonists slept soundly on the Chimneys' sandy floor. Their minds struggled to grasp the meaning of this new incident, whether caused by a simple accident, easily explained in the light of day, or by the actions of a human being; and as if these troublesome questions were not enough, the sand was some-

Top was commanded to keep watch under the windows.

thing less than comfortable. In any case, for one reason or another, they were for the moment forbidden access to their home; beyond that nothing could be known.

But Granite House was more than their home; it was their storehouse. All the colony's equipment was there: weapons, instruments, tools, ammunition, foodstuffs, etc. If Granite House were pillaged, they would have to begin everything anew, to build other weapons, other tools. A most unsettling prospect! Little wonder, then, that at every moment one colonist or another, goaded on by his anxieties, stepped outside to be sure that Top was keeping a vigilant eye on the windows of their home. Cyrus Smith alone waited for morning with his customary patience. Nevertheless, his dogged sense of reason was exasperated to find itself faced with such a thoroughly inexplicable event, and he raged at the thought that around him, or perhaps above him, lurked an influence he could not define. Gideon Spilett shared his feelings in every way, and now and then the two of them spoke in low tones of all the curious happenings that had defied their perspicacity and experienced wisdom. There was undeniably a mystery on this island; how would they ever unravel it? Harbert was equally confounded, and his mind teemed with questions for Cyrus Smith. As for Neb, he finally told himself that none of this concerned him, that this was his master's affair, and were it not for his reluctance to irritate his companions, the worthy Negro could have slept no less soundly on the Chimneys' sandy floor than if he were back on his bunk in Granite House!

And then there was Pencroff: a sense of righteous rage welled up inside him, far beyond what any of the others were feeling.

"This is a joke," he said. "Someone is playing a joke on us! Well, I don't like jokes, not one little bit, and it'll go hard for that joker when I get my hands on him!"

When the first gleams of dawn appeared in the east, the colonists emerged onto the shore and stood at the water's edge, weapons at the ready. Soon the first gleams of the rising sun hit the facade of Granite House, and by five o'clock the closed shutters over the windows could be seen through the curtain of foliage.

On that side everything appeared to be in order, but a shout burst from the colonists' breasts when they saw the door standing wide open. They knew full well that they had locked it before their departure.

It was no longer in doubt: someone had broken into Granite House.

The upper ladder remained in place, stretched from the landing to the door; but the lower ladder had been withdrawn, and hoisted up to the threshold. The intruders had clearly taken all possible measures to guard against surprise attack.

But for the moment they could not say who these intruders might be, nor how numerous, for none had yet shown himself.

Pencroff hailed again.

No answer.

"Those blackguards!" the sailor cried. "Sound asleep, just as if they owned the place! Ahoy! pirates, bandits, brigands, sons of John Bull!"

For Pencroff, a born-and-bred American, there could be no greater insult than this.

Now day broke over the ocean, and sunlight poured over the facade of Granite House. And still all was peaceful and silent, both inside and out.

The colonists began to wonder if Granite House truly was occupied. But the position of the ladder proved unambiguously that it was; furthermore, with the ladder raised, the occupants, whoever they were, could not possibly have fled! Their doubts were resolved, then; but how were they to resolve the situation?

Harbert now had the idea of tying a rope to an arrow and shooting it through the lowest rungs of the ladder, which could be seen hanging just below the threshold. With one tug on the rope they could unfurl the ladder to its full length, and access to Granite House would be reestablished.

They could think of no other solution, and with a steady aim Harbert's plan might well meet with success. Happily, they had taken the precaution of storing a number of bows and arrows in the Chimneys, along with several fathoms of light hibiscus-fiber cord. Pencroff uncoiled the cord and tied one end to a well-feathered arrow. With this, Harbert armed his bow and took careful aim at the ladder's hanging end.

Cyrus Smith, Gideon Spilett, Pencroff, and Neb had taken a step back to watch for any reaction at the windows of Granite House. The reporter raised his rifle and trained his sights on the door.

The bowstring was released. The arrow whistled away, pulling the rope behind it, and passed between the last two rungs.

Harbert's plan had succeeded.

Immediately he grasped the end of the rope; but just as he was giving it a good tug to bring the ladder down, an arm shot through the open doorway, seized the ladder, and pulled it back inside Granite House.

"Triple blackguard!" the sailor cried. "If it's a bullet you want, you won't have long to wait!"

"Who is it?" asked Neb.

"What? You can't tell?..."

"No."

"Why, it's a monkey, a macaque, a capuchin, a guenon, an orangutan, a baboon, a gorilla, a marmoset! Our home has been invaded by monkeys! They must have climbed the ladder while we were away, and in they went!"

And just then, as if to confirm the sailor's explanation, three or four quadrumanes appeared at the windows, pushing open the shutters and greeting the rightful owners with a thousand contortions and grimaces.

"I knew it was only a joke!" cried Pencroff. "But here's a joker who'll pay for all the rest!"

The sailor quickly took aim at one of the apes and fired. The others scattered at once, but Pencroff's victim fell onto the beach, mortally wounded.

It was a tall ape, unmistakably of the primate order—of that there was no doubt. Whether chimpanzee, orangutan, gorilla, or gibbon, it could clearly be classified among the anthropomorphs, so named for their resemblance to the members of the human race. In any case, Harbert declared it to be an orangutan, and as we know, the boy was well versed in zoology.

"What a magnificent animal!" cried Neb.

"If you like!" Pencroff answered. "But I still don't see how we're going to get back inside!"

"Harbert is a fine marksman," the reporter said, "and he has his bow! He only has to try again..."

"Come now! these monkeys are no fools!" Pencroff cried. "They're not about to show themselves at the windows again, and we have no way of killing them! Oh, when I think of the damage they must have done to our quarters, our storeroom..."

"Patience," answered Cyrus Smith. "They won't be able to hold us off for long!"

"I'll believe that when I see every last one of them lying dead on the ground," the sailor shot back. "To begin with, Mr. Cyrus, do you have any idea how many dozens of these jokers might be hiding up there?"

This was a difficult question to answer. As for a second attempt to pull down the ladder, it seemed an unlikely proposition at best. The lower end had been drawn inside, and their cord abruptly snapped when they tugged at it again, leaving the ladder just where it was.

This was a most bewildering situation. Pencroff fumed. Their plight was not without its comical side, but he at least did not find it at all amusing. In the end, of course, the colonists would find a way into their home, and they would certainly rid themselves of the intruders, but when and how? That they could not say.

Two hours went by. The apes were careful not to show themselves again, but clearly they had not left Granite House, for three or four times a paw or muzzle fleetingly appeared at a window, immediately greeted with rifle fire.

"We must conceal ourselves somewhere," the engineer said. "The apes might think we've gone away, and show themselves again. Spilett and Harbert will lie in ambush behind the rocks, and fire on anything that comes into sight."

The engineer's orders were carried out forthwith. The reporter and the boy, the colony's surest shooters, positioned themselves within firing range but out of the apes' line of sight. Meanwhile, Neb, Pencroff, and Cyrus Smith climbed to the plateau to hunt for game in the forest, for the breakfast hour had come, and their provisions were entirely exhausted.

The hunters returned a half-hour later with a modest number of rock doves, which they roasted as best they could. Not a single ape had shown itself in the meantime.

Gideon Spilett and Harbert joined the others for breakfast, leaving Top to keep watch from beneath the windows. Once they had eaten, they returned to their post.

Another two hours went by with no change in the situation. No further sign of the quadrumanes' presence had been detected, and the colonists began to wonder if they had finally decamped; but it seemed more likely that the death of one of their number and the sound of the rifle shots had sent them fleeing in terror to one of Granite House's interior rooms, or even to the storeroom. And when the colonists thought of the many treasures locked away in that storeroom, all the engineer's entreaties could not prevent their patience from degenerating into a violent irritation—and not without good reason, if the truth be known.

"This is simply too absurd," the reporter finally said, "and there's no reason to believe it's ever going to end!"

"But we have to get those rascals out of there!" cried Pencroff. "If we could only fight them hand to hand, I know we could prevail! The five of us could easily take on twenty or thirty of them! Oh! is there really no way to get at them?"

"Yes, one," replied the engineer, an idea flashing suddenly through his mind.

"Just one?" said Pencroff. "Well, if there are no others, that must be the right one! What is it?"

"We might try to enter Granite House through the old spillway," the engineer answered.

"By all the devils and as many more!" cried the sailor. "Why didn't I think of that!"

This was indeed their only means of entry, and their only hope of evicting the apes. To be sure, the entrance was sealed off by a wall of cemented stones, which would have to be sacrificed, but this they could easily rebuild. Fortunately, Cyrus Smith had not yet acted on his plan to conceal the opening beneath the waters of the lake, for that would have greatly slowed their progress.

It was already past noon when the colonists left the Chimneys with a load of picks and pickaxes. Passing beneath the windows of Granite House, they ordered Top to remain at his post, and turned onto the bank of the Mercy to begin the climb to Longview Plateau.

But before they had gone fifty paces they heard the dog barking furiously, as if urgently calling them back.

The stopped in their tracks.

"Hurry!" said Pencroff.

They turned around and ran downstream again, as fast as their legs could carry them.

Reaching the mouth of the river, they found that the situation had changed.

The apes had suddenly taken fright for some unknown reason, and were desperately trying to flee. Two or three of them could be seen jumping from one window to the next with the agility of veteran circus performers. They made no attempt to return the ladder to its usual position and climb down to safety; perhaps in their terror they had forgotten the existence of this easy escape route. Soon five or six apes were in full view, leaving the colonists ample opportunity to take aim and fire. Some, crying shrilly, fell backward into Granite House, either wounded or dead.

Others were thrown to their doom from inside. A few moments later, the colonists could assume that not a single living quadrumane remained in their dwelling.

"Hurrah!" cried Pencroff. "Hurrah! hurrah!"

"It's too early for hurrahs!" said Gideon Spilett.

"Why? We've killed them all," the sailor answered.

"That's true, but we still have no way into our home."

"Let's go to the spillway!" Pencroff replied.

"Yes, of course," said the engineer. "Still, I would have preferred…"

Just then, as if in response to Cyrus Smith's observation, the ladder slipped over the threshold and unrolled to its full length.

"Oh! By gad! That was lucky!" cried the sailor, looking at Cyrus Smith.

"Too lucky!" the engineer answered, hurrying toward the ladder.

"Be careful, Mr. Cyrus!" Pencroff shouted. "If any of those apes are still up there…"

"We shall see," the engineer answered, climbing as quickly as he could.

His companions followed, and a minute later they had reached the threshold.

They looked everywhere. No one in the rooms, no one in the storeroom—which happily the apes had not entered.

"Well, I'll be… what about the ladder?" cried the sailor. "Whoever sent it back down to us was a real gentleman—but where is he?"

Just then a cry rang out, and a large ape that had taken refuge in the hallway rushed into the room, with Neb in hot pursuit.

"Oh! you bandit!" Pencroff shouted.

And he was about to stave in the animal's skull with his hatchet when Cyrus Smith laid his hand on his arm and said:

"Spare him, Pencroff."

"You want me to pardon this blackamoor?"

"Yes! He was the one who threw down the ladder!"

And the engineer said this in a tone so singular that his companions could not decide whether he was joking or not.

Nevertheless, they threw themselves on the ape, which, despite a valiant defense, was soon tackled and hogtied.

"Whew!" said Pencroff. "And what shall we do with him now?"

"We'll make him our servant!" Harbert answered.

The boy was not speaking entirely in jest, for he knew how useful to man that intelligent race of quadrumanes can be.

The ape was soon tackled and hogtied.

The colonists examined the ape with great attention. His facial angle was not perceptibly inferior to that of an Australian or Hottentot, which confirmed his place in the ranks of the anthropomorphs. He was an orangutan, and as such possessed neither the ferocity of the baboon, nor the heedlessness of the macaque, nor the slovenliness of the marmoset, nor the impatience of the Barbary ape, nor the fierce instincts of the cynocephalus. This race exhibits many traits that suggest an almost human intelligence. Put to work in houses, they can serve at table, clean the rooms, care for the laundry, wax shoes, skillfully use a knife, fork, and spoon, even drink wine...much like any other bipedal, featherless domestic. It is known that Buffon owned just such an ape, a faithful and zealous servant who remained in his employ for many years.

The ape that now lay hogtied in the great room of Granite House was a large beast, six feet tall, with an admirably proportioned body, a broad breast, a head of average size, a facial angle of sixty-five degrees, a rounded skull, a protruding nose, and a soft, lustrous pelt—the very model of an anthropomorph, in short. His eyes, slightly smaller than human eyes, shone with an intelligent vivacity; his white teeth gleamed beneath his mustache, and he wore a short curly beard of hazelnut color.

"Lovely fellow!" said Pencroff. "If only we knew his language, we could talk to him!"

"Is this true, master?" said Neb. "Are we really going to take him on as a servant?"

"Yes, Neb," the engineer responded with a smile. "But there's no need to be jealous!"

"And I hope he'll make a first-rate domestic," Harbert added. "He seems to be young, and we should have no difficulty educating him without resorting to brute force or pulling out his canines, as is often done in such cases! He can't help but grow attached to masters who treat him with kindness."

"And that's just what we'll do," answered Pencroff, who had forgotten all the rancor he felt for the "jokers."

Then, approaching the orangutan:

"Well, my lad," he asked him, "how are you feeling?"

The orangutan's only response was a faint growl, not entirely ill-humored.

"Do we want to join the colony, then?" the sailor asked. "Are we going to enter into the service of Mr. Cyrus Smith?"

Another growl of assent from the ape.

"And we won't ask for any salary but room and board?"

A third affirmative growl.

"His conversation is a little dull," Gideon Spilett observed.

"Nothing wrong with that!" Pencroff answered. "The best domestics are the ones who talk the least. And he doesn't quibble over the wages!— You understand, my lad? You'll get no wages at first; but later, if we're happy with you, we'll double your salary!"

Thus it was that the colony acquired a new member, who would be of service to them on more than one occasion. As for his name, the sailor asked that they call him Jupiter, and Joop for short, in memory of another ape he had known.

And so Master Joop became a part of the daily life of Granite House.

VII

Plans for the Future.—A Bridge over the Mercy.—Isolating Longview Plateau.—The Drawbridge.—A Wheat Harvest.—The Stream.—Two Footbridges.—The Poultry Yard.—The Dovecote.—The Two Dauws.—Hitching up the Cart.—An Excursion to Port Balloon.

The colonists of Lincoln Island had recaptured their home, and had not been forced to enter by the spillway, which would have involved a substantial demolition project. They were on their way to begin this task when, by an astonishing stroke of luck, the band of apes was overcome by some sudden and inexplicable terror, which sent them fleeing from Granite House. Did the animals suspect that they would soon come under attack from a different direction? This seemed the only half-conceivable interpretation of their abrupt retreat.

The colonists spent the last few hours of this day transporting the apes' cadavers into the woods for burial; then they turned to the task of undoing the disorder left by the intruders—disorder and not damage, for at least nothing was broken, even if every piece of furniture had been overturned. Neb relit his ovens and dipped into their reserves to prepare a substantial meal, heartily enjoyed by all.

Joop was not forgotten; he was offered a large helping of pine nuts and rhizomes, which he devoured with great appetite. Pencroff had untied his arms, but thought it best to leave his legs hobbled until the animal's acceptance of his fate was no longer in question.

Before they went to bed, Cyrus Smith and his companions lingered around the table for some time, discussing the most pressing of the many tasks that lay ahead.

The most urgent were a bridge over the Mercy, which would make the southern half of the island accessible from Granite House, and a sheepfold to hold the mouflons and any other woolly animals they might capture.

Both of these projects, we should note, were motivated by the need for new clothing, which was then their most serious concern. The bridge would ease the transportation of the deflated balloon, which would give them cloth, and the sheepfold would offer a continual supply of wool with which to make warm winter clothes.

Cyrus Smith's intention was to situate the sheepfold just by the source of Red Creek, an area of fine pastureland where the ruminants would find fresh and abundant nourishment. The path from Longview Plateau to the source was partially cleared already, and with a good cart the animals could easily be transported back and forth—and all the more easily if the colonists had the good fortune to capture a beast of burden.

The sheepfold could thus conveniently be placed at some distance from Granite House, but the same was not true of the poultry yard, as Neb reminded his companions, for the birds would have to be within easy reach of the chef. They could do no better than to house them on the lakeshore, not far from the entrance to the spillway. Aquatic birds could be raised here along with the others, and the brace of tinamous they had caught during their last excursion would serve as subjects for their first attempts at domestication.

On the next day—November 3rd—they turned to the first and most important project, the construction of the bridge. Every arm was pressed into service. Saws, axes, chisels, and hammers were hoisted onto the colonists' shoulders, and, thus transformed into builders, they climbed down to the beach.

There, Pencroff made a remark:

"What if, while we're away, Master Joop gets a notion to pull in the ladder he so kindly sent down to us yesterday?"

"We'll have to tie down the lower end," Cyrus Smith answered.

This they now did with two stakes sunk deep into the sand, and then the colonists set out along the left bank of the Mercy toward the first bend in the river.

They stopped to judge the area's suitability for their new bridge, and found it an ideal spot.

For from here southward to Port Balloon, which they had discovered the day before, the distance was only three and a half miles, and they could easily clear a road wide enough for a cart from the bridge to the port, greatly easing travel between Granite House and the southern reaches of the island.

Cyrus Smith then presented an idea he had been contemplating for some time, both simple to realize and highly useful to their cause: to cut off access to Longview Plateau, protecting it from the depredations of quadrupeds and quadrumanes alike. Granite House, the Chimneys, the poultry yard, and the future crops would thus be safe from any form of animal intrusion.

The engineer's proposal could not have been more simply carried out. Here is how he intended to proceed.

On three sides, the plateau was already defended by water, either artificial or natural in origin:

—on the northwest side, from the spillway to the rift blasted into the rock, by the waters of Lake Grant;

—on the north, by the new waterway that ran from that rift to the sea, coursing over the plateau and down onto the beach, and which could be made impassible for animals if its bed were slightly deepened and broadened;

—over the entire eastern edge, from the mouth of the new creek to the mouth of the Mercy, by the sea itself;

—and on the south side, from the mouth to the bend where the bridge was to be built, by the flowing waters of the Mercy.

Only the western edge was left unprotected, from the bend to the southern corner of the lake, a distance of less than one mile. But a wide, deep trench could easily be dug and filled with a diverted stream of lake-water, which would then cascade over the plateau and flow into the Mercy. The lake's water level would drop slightly, to be sure, but by Cyrus Smith's calculations the flow of Red Creek would sufficiently compensate for this change.

"In this way," the engineer added, "Longview Plateau will become a veritable island, surrounded by water on all sides, linked to the rest of our domain only by our new bridge over the Mercy, the two small bridges we have already laid on either side of the falls, and finally two more small bridges I propose to build: one over the new trench, the other on the right bank of the Mercy. If each of these bridges can be raised at will, Longview Plateau will be perfectly protected from any surprise attack."

Cyrus Smith had drawn a map of the plateau to show his companions the full extent of his project. It was approved by unanimous consent, and Pencroff, brandishing his woodsman's ax, cried out:

"First, the main bridge!"

This was indeed the most urgent task. Trees were chosen, felled, stripped, and sawed into girders, beams, and planks. On the right bank of the Mercy the bridge would be fixed, but on the other end it could be raised by means of counterweights, like the bridges one sometimes sees over the locks of a canal.

This would of course be a considerable undertaking, and no matter how efficiently planned and carried out, it would require some time, for the Mercy measured eighty feet across. They would have to sink piles into the riverbed to support the structure and the heavy loads it would be called upon to bear; and for this they would need a piledriver.

Fortunately, they had a fine collection of woodworking tools, as well as iron strips to reinforce the beams; and in addition to this they had the ingenious mind of a practiced engineer, surrounded by conscientious and devoted companions, who had grown quite adept at physical labor over the past seven months. And it must be said that Gideon Spilett was not the clumsiest of the lot, for his skill could rival that of the sailor himself, who "would never have expected so much of a mere journalist!"

Three weeks of intensive labor were devoted to the construction of the bridge over the Mercy. They ate their lunch at the worksite, taking full advantage of the magnificent weather, and returning to Granite House only for their evening meal.

In the meantime, Joop was quickly adapting to his new life, as well as to his new masters, whom he continually watched with a deeply curious eye. Nevertheless, cautious Pencroff did not yet offer him complete freedom of movement, rightly choosing to wait until their work had closed off the perimeter of the plateau. Top and Joop got along famously, and spent many hours in play, although everything Joop did was done with great seriousness.

The bridge was finished on November 20th. The counterweights allowed one end to be raised and lowered with ease; a distance of twenty feet separated the pivot from the support on the other side, leaving a gap far too wide to be crossed by any animal.

The next task was to bring back the envelope of the aerostat and store it securely away; but for this they would have to drive a cart to Port Bal-

This would be a considerable undertaking.

loon, and consequently, to clear a broad path through the dense Forests of the Far West. This would all take some time. Neb and Pencroff surveyed the proposed route, and since they found the "supply of canvas" safe and undamaged in the grotto where they had left it, the decision was made to complete the isolation of Longview Plateau before moving on to that new task.

"This way," Pencroff observed, "we'll have a perfect site for a poultry yard, well protected from marauding foxes and any other predators that might be lurking."

"And then," added Neb, "we can clear the plateau, transplant the sprouts we find in the forest..."

"And lay out our second wheatfield!" cried the sailor in a triumphal tone.

For the first wheatfield, sown with that one single grain, had proved remarkably fruitful under Pencroff's ministrations. It had indeed produced the ten ears of wheat promised by the engineer, and since each ear bore eighty grains, the colony now found itself with a capital of eight hundred grains—after six months!—and the prospect of a double harvest every year.

These eight hundred grains, less fifty or so that were stored away as a precaution, would thus be sown in a second field, just as lovingly as the solitary grain with which they began.

The field was tilled and ringed with a sturdy palisade whose great height and sharp points would hold off any quadruped. As for the birds, Pencroff's whimsical imagination had devised a panoply of gaudy pinwheels and frightening mannequins to keep them away. The seven hundred fifty grains were then laid in small, regular furrows, and the rest was left up to nature.

On November 21st, Cyrus Smith began to draw up his plans for the trench that would close off the western edge of the plateau from the southern corner of Lake Grant to the bend in the Mercy. He examined the terrain, and found two to three feet of topsoil atop a granite bedrock. Therefore, he mixed up a second batch of nitroglycerine, which soon produced its customary effect. In less than two weeks, a trench twelve feet wide and six feet deep had been dug from the hard terrain of the plateau. A second breach was made in the granite lakeshore by the same method. The water poured out to form a new tributary of the Mercy, and this small stream was given the name "Glycerine Creek." As the engineer had predicted, the lake's water level fell, but almost imperceptibly. Finally, to complete the barrier around the plateau, the streambed on the beach was broadened, and a double palisade was erected to shore up the sandy banks.

These works were finally completed in the first half of December. Longview Plateau—a sort of irregular pentagon with a perimeter of approximately four miles, and girdled with water—was now safe from all forms of aggression.

The month of December was intensely hot from beginning to end. Nevertheless, the colonists were loath to suspend their work, and they now proceeded to the urgent task of setting up their poultry yard.

Once the plateau had been closed off definitively, Master Joop was naturally given his freedom. He never left his masters' side, and showed no desire to escape. He was a gentle animal, but very energetic, and surprisingly dextrous. Oh! None of them could have hoped to compete with him at scaling the ladder to Granite House. Already a number of chores had been entrusted to him: he pulled the sledge when it was loaded with wood, and carried away the rocks as they were removed from the bed of Glycerine Creek.

"He's not a mason yet, but he's already a monkey!" Harbert liked to joke, remembering that masons often refer to their apprentices as "monkeys." And if ever a nickname was justified, it was this one!

The poultry yard would occupy an area of two hundred square yards on the lake's southeastern shore. They put up a palisade and built shelters for the various animals to be housed there. Soon a number of small huts, built of branches and divided into compartments, stood ready and waiting for their lodgers.

First came the pair of tinamous, who were not slow to produce numerous offspring. A half-dozen ducks, well acclimated to the lakeside, kept them company. Some of these were of the Chinese variety, with fan-shaped wings and a plumage whose brilliant sheen makes them every bit the equal of the golden pheasant. A few days later, Harbert succeeded in catching a pair of gallinaceans with rounded tails formed of long plumes, two wonderful "curassows," which were soon domesticated. As for the pelicans, kingfishers, and moorhens, they came to the lakeside yard of their own accord. There were a few squabbles at first, to be sure, but soon they all learned to get along, coalescing into a single cooing, squawking, clucking menagerie that boded well for the colony's future nourishment.

As a finishing touch, Cyrus Smith built a dovecote in one corner of the yard. Here they housed a dozen of the pigeons that haunted the high rocks of the plateau, who quickly fell into the habit of returning to their new home every evening, and displayed a greater propensity for domestication than their relatives the ringdoves, who, moreover, only reproduce in the wild.

And now at last the time had come to think of making cloth from their aerostat. Only the most desperate of castaways would dream of reinflating it and sailing away over a virtually limitless ocean, and Cyrus Smith, ever practical in his intelligence, would not even consider such a proposition.

For this they would have to bring the balloon's sheath back to Granite House; thus, they made modifications to their heavy cart to make it lighter and more easily maneuvered. The vehicle now stood at the ready, but they had yet to find an engine! Were there no indigenous ruminants on this island that might take the place of a horse, ass, ox, or cow? That was the question.

"No doubt about it," said Pencroff, "a draft animal would be a very useful thing while we're waiting for Mr. Cyrus to build us a steam-powered cart, or even a locomotive—for I've no doubt that one day we'll have a railway from Granite House to Port Balloon, with a spur to the top of Mount Franklin!"

And the worthy sailor spoke these words in all good faith! Oh! What the imagination can do, when fueled by confidence!

But, exaggerations aside, a simple quadruped would have been quite sufficient for Pencroff's needs, and since Providence had a weak spot for him, he would not have long to wait.

One day, December 23rd, the colonists were busy in the Chimneys when the sound of Neb shouting and Top barking, each louder than the other, brought them running to their companions' side, sure that some terrible incident had occurred.

What did they see? Two beautiful animals, of considerable size, which had imprudently ventured over a lowered bridge and onto the plateau. They looked like two horses, or at least two asses, male and female: delicate in form, with a light tan pelt, white legs and tails, and black stripes over their heads, necks, and trunks. They came forward calmly with no sign of fear, their bright eyes fixed on these men, whom they could not yet recognize as potential masters.

"Dauws!" cried Harbert. "Quadrupeds, halfway between zebras and quaggas!"

"Why not asses?" asked Neb.

"Because their ears aren't as long, and they're far more graceful!"

"Asses or horses," Pencroff replied, "they're 'engines,' as Mr. Smith would say, and that makes them worth capturing!"

Taking care not to frighten the two beasts, the sailor slithered through the grass to the small bridge over Glycerine Creek and raised it. The dauws were trapped.

Now, would they capture them by force, and domesticate them with the rod? No. It was decided that the dauws would be allowed to spend a few days wandering freely over the plateau, where grass was plentiful. A stable was quickly erected near the poultry yard, offering shelter and a comfortable litter for the night.

And so the beautiful beasts were left free to roam as they pleased, and the colonists carefully kept their distance so as not to frighten them. Several times the dauws manifested a desire to leave the plateau, too confined for their tastes, for they were accustomed to wide-open spaces and deep forests. At such moments they could be seen walking alongside the water at the perimeter of the plateau: finding themselves before this insurmountable barrier, they brayed raucously and ran galloping through the grass. Then, regaining their composure, they stood for hours at a time looking toward the great woods, now barred to them forever!

Meanwhile the colonists fashioned harnesses and plant-fiber traces, and a few days after the dauws had been captured, not only was the cart ready to be hitched up, but a direct route, or rather a small road, had been cleared through the Far West from the bend of the Mercy to Port Balloon. They were thus ready to attempt the voyage in the cart, and toward the end of December they tried to harness the dauws for the first time.

Pencroff had already cajoled the animals into eating from his hand, and they did not object as the colonists approached them; but once they were harnessed they began to buck, and the colonists struggled valiantly to hold them back. Nevertheless, they quickly came to accept this new constraint, for the dauw, less rebellious than the zebra, is often used as a draft animal in the mountainous regions of southern Africa, and has even been acclimated to the cooler zones of Europe.

And so the entire colony—with the exception of Pencroff, who walked ahead of the animals—climbed into the cart and set off toward Port Balloon. It goes without saying that their hastily cleared route was full of jolts and bumps; but the vehicle arrived at its destination without incident, and they were able to load the areostat's sheath and hardware onto their conveyance that very day.

At eight o'clock in the evening the cart crossed the bridge over the Mercy a second time, rolled along the left bank of the river, and came to a stop on the beach. The dauws were unharnessed and returned to their stable; and before he went to sleep, Pencroff let out a sigh of satisfaction that echoed loudly through the halls of Granite House.

VIII

New Linen.—Seal-Leather Shoes.—Fabrication of Pyroxylin.—
Sowing.—Fishing.—The Tortoise Eggs.—Master Joop's
Progress.—The Sheepfold.—Hunting for Mouflons.—New Plant
and Animal Discoveries.—Memories of a Distant Homeland.

The colonists spent the first week of January tailoring the new linen they so desperately needed. The needles from the crate were manipulated with vigor, if not delicacy; and we need not doubt that whatever was sewn was sewn sturdily.

There was no lack of thread, thanks to Cyrus Smith's idea of reusing the stitching from the balloon. The long strips of canvas were unstitched with admirable patience by Gideon Spilett and Harbert, for Pencroff found the task exceedingly irritating, and soon abandoned it. Nevertheless, when it came time to sew he had no equal, for it is well known that sailors have a remarkable aptitude for the seamstress's art.

Next the canvas was stripped of its varnish with soda and potash obtained from incinerated plants; this left them with a cloth both supple and elastic, which quickly acquired an impeccable whiteness when exposed to the decolorizing action of the sun.

Several dozen shirts and stockings were thus fashioned—the latter not knitted, of course, but made of stitched canvas. Imagine the colonists' joy at finally changing into crisp white linens—a very rough sort of linen, to be sure, but they were not the kind to complain about such trifles—and to lie between real sheets, which transformed the bunks of Granite House into very respectable beds.

The colonists finally changed into crisp white linens.

Along with their linens, they found a way to make new shoes out of seal leather, a welcome replacement for the shoes and boots they had brought from America. Their new shoes were both wide and long, and let it at least be said that they never pinched the walkers' feet!

The year 1868 opened with a long period of extreme heat, but the colonists hunted without respite. The forests were full of agoutis, peccaries, capybaras, kangaroos, all sorts of game both furred and feathered, and Gideon Spilett and Harbert were too handy with their rifles to waste a single shot.

As always, Cyrus Smith cautioned them to use their ammunition sparingly. He set about finding a substitute for the powder and lead they had found in the crate, as he was anxious to maintain a reserve of ammunition for future needs. Someday, after all, he and his companions might attempt to leave their new home, and how could he know where their fortunes might take them? They would have to be prepared for any eventuality; hence the necessity of fabricating some renewable substance that would allow them to leave their supply of ammunition untouched.

Cyrus Smith had found no trace of lead on the island, but this could be replaced with granulated iron, easily produced and reasonably effective. The fragments of iron were not as heavy as lead shot; he thus had to make them larger, meaning that every shot contained a smaller number of fragments. Nevertheless, the skill of the hunters would surely compensate for this deficiency. As for powder, Cyrus Smith could easily have made his own, since he had saltpeter, sulfur, and coal at hand; but this is a very delicate process, and without specialized tools it is difficult to produce a powder of good quality.

For this reason, Cyrus Smith chose instead to make pyroxylin, also known as guncotton—a substance in which cotton is not indispensable, for any other form of cellulose will do just as well. And cellulose is nothing other than the elementary tissue of all vegetal matter, existing in a more or less pure state not only in cotton, but also in the textile fibers of hemp and linen, in paper, rags, the pith of elder bushes, etc. As it happened, elder bushes grew in great numbers around the mouth of Red Creek; indeed, the colonists had already used the berries of these shrubs, which belong to the family Caprifolaceae, to make a substitute for coffee.

The cellulose could thus be collected from the pith of the elder plants; the only other substance they would need to make pyroxylin was fuming nitric acid. As we know, Cyrus Smith had sulfuric acid already, and this could be used to produce nitric acid. He merely had to allow the sulfuric acid to react with saltpeter, of which nature offered him a plentiful supply.

Thus, he resolved to arm their weapons with pyroxylin. He understood that this substance was not without its weaknesses: a highly uneven efficacity; an excessive inflammability, since it ignites at 170 degrees rather than 240 degrees; and finally an overly rapid detonation, which can damage the weapon. On the other hand, the advantages of pyroxylin were these: it could not be harmed by humidity; it did not clog the rifle barrels with deposits; and its propulsive force was four times that of ordinary powder.

To make pyroxylin, cellulose is soaked in fuming nitric acid for a quarter of an hour, then throughly rinsed and allowed to dry. As we see, nothing could be simpler.

Now, what Cyrus Smith had was only ordinary nitric acid, and not fuming or monohydrate nitric acid, which is an acid that emits a whitish vapor on contact with humid air; but by replacing the fuming nitric acid with three units of ordinary nitric acid mixed with five units of concentrated sulfuric acid, the engineer believed he would obtain the same result, and so he did. Each of the island's hunters was soon offered a supply of the engineer's compound, and when used with some caution it proved wonderfully effective.

At about this same time, the colonists cleared away a three-acre* area on Longview Plateau, leaving the rest as rangeland for the dauws. Several excursions were made into Jacamar Woods and the Far West, from which they brought back a veritable bounty of wild plants: spinach, cress, horse-radish, and turnips. With careful cultivation, these could be made to produce a plentiful supply of fresh greens—a welcome supplement to the nitrogenous diet to which the colonists of Lincoln Island had heretofore been limited. Considerable quantities of wood and coal were brought back as well; and in addition to all this, each excursion served to improve their pathways over the island, as the trail became more beaten down with every passage of the cart's wheels.

The warren continued to supply the kitchens of Granite House with a daily contingent of rabbits. It lay not far from the source of Glycerine Creek, which prevented its denizens from entering onto the protected plateau and ravaging the new crops. The new oyster bed was flourishing,

* One acre is equivalent to 0.4046 hectares.

nestled among the rocks on the beach; the colonists took care to restock it regularly, and in return they had an inexhaustible supply of delicious mollusks. Fish now became a regular part of their diet as well, for Pencroff had installed a number of ledger lines in the lake and in the flowing waters of the Mercy. The iron hooks offered a daily catch of trout, as well as another sort of fish, with small yellow spots scattered over its silver flanks, which proved extremely flavorful. Master Neb, who had taken on the culinary responsibilities, could thus vary the menu for every meal, much to his companions' delight. All they lacked now was bread, and, as we have said before, this was a privation that they found difficult to bear.

It was during this same era that they first attempted to hunt sea turtles, frequent visitors to the beaches of Cape Mandible, whose sands were peppered with small mounds. Each of these contained a number of hard, white, spherical eggs, full of an albumen that differs from that of birds' eggs only in that it does not coagulate. An impressive number of these eggs had been left on the beach to hatch in the warm sunlight, for a single turtle can lay as many as two hundred fifty each year.

"A veritable field of eggs," Gideon Spilett observed, "just waiting to be gathered."

But they did not content themselves with the product alone; they hunted the producers as well, and so returned to Granite House with a dozen of these chelonians, greatly esteemed by epicureans. Neb's turtle soup, spiced with aromatic herbs and supplemented with a few cruciferous plants, earned its creator an endless stream of enthusiastic praise, and rightly so.

By another happy circumstance, the colonists were able to make a significant addition to their store of winter provisions. Schools of salmon had found their way into the Mercy, following the river several miles upstream. The females had come looking for suitable places to spawn, causing a great to-do in the fresh waters as they awaited the arrival of the males. A thousand such fish, each measuring up to two and a half feet in length, thus passed through the mouth of the river, and the colonists had only to erect a number of dams to detain them. Several hundred salmon were caught in this way, then salted and stored away for the coming winter, when the freezing of the river would make fishing an impossibility.

Meanwhile, the very intelligent Joop had been elevated to the position of manservant. He was decked out in a morning coat, white canvas knee pants, and an apron whose pockets brought him great joy, for he loved to thrust his hands inside them, and jealously guarded their contents. Neb had taken great pains to train the nimble orangutan in his daily tasks, and the Negro and the ape genuinely seemed to understand each other when they spoke. Joop felt a great sympathy for Neb, which Neb fully reciprocated. Whenever the colonists did not require him to carry wood or climb into a treetop, Joop could nearly always be found in the kitchen, attempting to imitate Neb's every move. The master instructed his pupil with great patience and zeal, and the pupil applied these teachings with what truly seemed to be remarkable intelligence.

Imagine, then, the delight of the dinner guests when, quite unexpectedly, Joop first appeared with a napkin over his arm to serve them at table. Skillful, attentive, he acquitted himself of his duties impeccably—changing the plates, bringing in the dishes, pouring drinks—and all of this with a gravity that amused the colonists no end, and moved Pencroff to new heights of enthusiasm.

"Joop, more soup!"

"Joop, a bit of agouti!"

"Joop, a plate!"

"Joop! Good Joop! Fine Joop!"

Such were the words on everyone's lips; ever unruffled, Joop answered every call, looked after every need, and nodded his intelligent head when Pencroff repeated a pleasantry from the early days, saying:

"Really, Joop, we're going to have to double your wages!"

It need hardly be said that the orangutan had taken readily to his new life in Granite House. He often accompanied his masters into the forest, never manifesting any desire to flee. Pencroff had fashioned a cane for him, and what a sight he was, walking along in the most amusing manner possible, carrying it over one shoulder like a rifle! If they needed some fruit to be plucked from the top of a tree, how quickly he scaled it! If the cartwheel became stuck in its rut, how vigorously Joop set it right with one shove from his shoulder!

"What a strapping fellow he is!" Pencroff often cried. "If he were as wicked as he is good, there'd be no stopping him!"

Toward the end of January, the colonists began a very ambitious project in the island's central region. They had resolved to build a sheepfold for their ruminants, and more particularly for the mouflons, which would provide wool for their winter clothes. The sheepfold would be built not far from the source of Red Creek, for the presence of these beasts in the immediate vicinity of Granite House might well have proved bother-some.

Every morning a group of colonists set out for the source of the creek—sometimes all of them, more often only Cyrus Smith, Harbert, and Pencroff. Now that they had the dauws to help them, this was an easy five-mile jaunt beneath the arching greenery, along the newly laid out route that they named Sheepfold Road.

The site of the future sheepfold lay hard against the mountain's south-ern flank. It was a broad grassy meadow strewn with scattered clumps of trees, and closed off on one side by the sloping foothill. A small rill rushed down the slopes and flowed diagonally across the meadow before pouring into Red Creek. The grass was lush, and fresh breezes swept through the sparse trees. They had only to surround the meadow with a semicircular palisade, abutting the mountainside at both ends, of suffi-cient height to keep out even the most agile animals. The enclosure could easily hold a hundred-some horned animals—mouflons or wild goats—and all the young that they would later bear.

The perimeter of the sheepfold was thus laid out by the engineer, and the next step was to find sufficient wood for the construction of the pal-isade. A good number of trees had had to be sacrificed for the creation of the road, and these were brought to the sheepfold; from them the colonists derived some hundred uprights, which were thrust deep into the ground.

A rather wide entryway was cut into the front of the palisade, kept closed by a double-sided door made of thick planks, which they would later reinforce with iron bars on the outside.

The construction of the sheepfold took no less than three weeks, for, in addition to the palisade, Cyrus Smith had erected huge barns made of planks as shelter for the ruminants. These structures had to be as sturdy as possible, for mouflons are very strong animals, and Cyrus Smith feared that they might react to their new confinement with some violence. The uprights of the palisade had been sharpened at the upper end and hard-ened by fire; they were now bolted together with crosspieces, and braces were installed every few feet to ensure the structure's solidity.

With the sheepfold finished, it was now time to organize a great roundup at the foot of Mount Franklin, through the pasturelands favored by the ruminants. This was done on February 7th, a beautiful summer day, and all the colonists participated. Gideon Spilett and Harbert mounted the two dauws, now thoroughly domesticated, and their assistance proved invaluable.

Their task was simple: to drive the mouflons and goats into a single herd by surrounding them and slowly tightening the circle. Cyrus Smith, Pencroff, Neb, and Joop were posted at various points in the woods; meanwhile, Gideon Spilett and Harbert, with Top running beside them, galloped around the sheepfold in a great circle with a radius of some half-mile.

The mouflons were numerous in this part of the island. They were beautiful animals, roughly the size of bucks, with stout horns thicker than a ram's. Their grayish fleece was overlaid by a coat of long hairs, and on the whole they looked rather like argalis.

How exhausting this long roundup turned out to be! How many comings and goings, how many races and counterraces, how many shouts! More than two thirds of the hundred mouflons they attempted to drive into the sheepfold escaped; but in the end, thirty-some such ruminants, along with about ten wild goats, were gradually pushed along toward the pen, whose open door seemed to offer them an escape route. Soon they were within the enclosure; the door was closed, and they were imprisoned.

On the whole, this was a very satisfactory result, and the colonists had no reason to complain. Most of the mouflons were females, some of them not far from giving birth. The colonists did not doubt that their flock would thrive in its new home, and that not only wool but also leather would be in plentiful supply in the not too distant future.

That evening, the hunters returned exhausted to Granite House. Nevertheless, they revisited the sheepfold the next day to be sure that all was well. The prisoners had attempted to topple the palisade, but without success, and soon they would learn to stay peacefully within its confines.

No events of any great importance occurred over the month of February. The colonists methodically pursued their daily work, and, even as they improved the roads to the sheepfold and to Port Balloon, they now started work on a third, running from the sheepfold toward the western shore. Only one part of Lincoln Island had yet to be explored: the great forests of Serpentine Peninsula, the domain of the felines of which Gideon Spilett hoped to purge their domain.

The colonists lavished their attentions on the wild plants they had brought to Longview Plateau from the forest, hoping to acclimate them to their new surroundings before the cold weather set in again. Harbert rarely came back from an excursion without some useful new flora. One day it was specimens of the Chicoraceae tribe, whose seeds produce an excellent oil when pressed; another, it was a common sorrel, whose antiscorbutic properties were not to be disregarded; then a few of those precious tubers grown since time immemorial in the American south, potatoes, whose species today number more than two hundred. The kitchen garden, well maintained, well irrigated, well defended against birds, was divided into small squares, with lettuce, kidney potatoes, sorrel, turnips, horseradish, and other cruciferous vegetables. The soil of the plateau was prodigiously fertile, and they had every reason to hope that the harvests would be abundant.

Nor were the colonists deprived of variety in their beverages. So long as no one demanded wine, even the most difficult tastes were satisfied. They already had the Oswego tea furnished by the *Monarda didyma* and the fermented liqueur extracted from the roots of the dragon tree; but now Cyrus Smith provided real beer, concocted from the young sprouts of the *Abies nigra* plant, which, when boiled and fermented, produce a pleasant and particularly healthful drink known to Anglo-Americans as "spring beer," which is to say spruce beer.

By summer's end, their population of fowl was augmented with a fine pair of bustards of the houbara species, characterized by a sort of ruff of feathers; a dozen spoonbills, with membranous extensions protruding from either side of their upper jaws; and some magnificent roosters with black crests, black wattles, and black skin, like the black roosters of Mozambique, which paraded haughtily along the lakeshore.

The colony was flourishing, then, thanks to the tireless labor of these brave and intelligent men. Providence had done them many favors, to be sure; but, faithful to the great precept, they helped themselves first, and only then did Heaven come to their aid.

When the hot summer sun had set, when all their many labors were done, when the sea breezes began to blow, they liked to spend the evening sitting on the edge of Longview Plateau under a sort of veranda covered by climbing plants, which Neb had constructed with his own hands. There they chatted, they taught each other, they made plans, and the sailor's hearty good humor brought continual merriment to the little band, among whom the most untroubled harmony had never failed to reign.

Often they spoke of their country, of their great, beloved America. What events had transpired in the War between the States? It must have been long since over! Richmond had surely fallen, no doubt into the hands of General Grant! The takeover of the Confederate capital must have been the final act of that cursed battle! Now the North had triumphed, and the cause of justice with it. Oh, how welcome the sight of a newspaper would have been to the exiles of Lincoln Island! It had now been eleven months since they had lost contact with the rest of mankind, and soon, on March 24th, they would mark the anniversary of their landing on these unknown shores! They had begun as mere castaways, fighting the elements for their wretched lives, and unsure of their prospects for success! And now, thanks to their leader's knowledge, thanks to their own intelligence, they were true colonists, equipped with weapons, tools, and instruments; and they had taken the island's various plants, animals, and minerals—elements from each of nature's three kingdoms—and turned them to their own advantage!

Yes! they often spoke of these things, and dreamed of still greater plans for the future!

Cyrus Smith generally kept his peace, listening more often than he spoke. Sometimes he smiled on hearing some observation made by Harbert, or some quip from Pencroff; but, no matter what the hour, no matter where he was, his thoughts remained fixed on one single preoccupation: the inexplicable events that they had witnessed, the strange enigma whose secret eluded him yet!

IX

Bad Weather.—The Hydraulic Elevator.—Creation of Glass for Windows and Goblets.—The Bread Tree.—Frequent Visits to the Sheepfold.—Growth of the Flock.—A Question from the Reporter.—Precise Coordinates of Lincoln Island.—Pencroff's Suggestion.

The weather changed during the first week of March. There was a full moon at the beginning of the month, and the heat remained intense. It was as though the atmosphere were impregnated with electricity, and they did not doubt that a long period of stormy weather was at hand.

And, indeed, the thunder began to roar with great violence on the second. The wind blew from the east, and a shower of hail pelted the facade of Granite House, crackling like a volley of grapeshot. The shutters over the doors and windows were closed and carefully latched, for otherwise the interior of their dwelling would surely have been flooded.

Seeing the hailstones fall, some of them as large as pigeon eggs, Pencroff suddenly realized to his horror that his wheat was in serious danger.

And he ran at once to the field, where the wheat plants were already beginning to hold up their little green heads, and laid out a thick canvas tarpaulin to protect his precious crops. The hailstorm's wrath fell on him rather than on the wheat, but he never once complained.

The bad weather lasted eight days, and the thunder never stopped rolling through the distant reaches of the heavens. Even between storms they could hear a quiet rumbling from somewhere beyond the horizon; then it all began again, with renewed fury. The sky was streaked with lightning bolts, and several trees on the island were struck, among them a huge pine standing near the lake just at the edge of the forest. The beach,

Pencroff ran at once to the field.

too, was struck several times by the electric current, melting the sand and vitrifying it in an instant. The sight of these fulgurites inspired an idea in the engineer's mind: to make thick, sturdy panes of glass that could be installed in the window frames as a protection against wind, rain, and hail.

With no pressing tasks awaiting them outside, the colonists took advantage of the rain to make further improvements inside Granite House, which grew more comfortable and livable every day. The engineer set up a lathe, with which he was able to turn tools for cooking or grooming—and particularly buttons, which the colonists sorely missed. They did not want for shelves or cupboards, and a rack was installed to hold their weapons, which they looked after with loving attention. They sawed, they planed, they rasped, they turned, and through it all the creaking of the tools or the whirring of the lathe were continually answered by the grumbling thunder.

Master Joop was never left out. He had a room of his own near the main storeroom, a sort of cabinet furnished with a simple wooden bed frame. The colonists were careful to keep it filled with good, clean litter, and Joop could not have been more content.

"Never a word of recrimination from our fine friend Joop," Pencroff often said, "never a disrespectful remark! What a servant he is, Neb, what a servant!"

"My pupil," Neb answered, "and soon my equal."

"Your better," the sailor replied with a laugh, "for, after all, you talk, Neb, and he never does!"

Joop had mastered his responsibilities with remarkable ease. He beat the linens, he turned the spit, he swept out the rooms, he served at table, he stacked the wood, and—to Pencroff's great delight—he never failed to tuck the worthy sailor into bed before he himself retired.

All of the colonists, bipeds or bimanes, quadrumanes or quadrupeds, enjoyed the most robust good health. With plenty of pure, fresh air, a salubrious environment, a temperate climate, and no lack of occupations both intellectual and physical, the colonists could well believe that illness would never strike them.

In short, the colony was thriving. Harbert had grown two inches in the past year. His face was becoming more mature and more virile, and by all indications he would soon be a man as distinguished in physique as in character. He took advantage of every lull in his manual labors to further his education. He read the handful of books they had found in the crate, and, in addition to the practical knowledge daily afforded by his current situation, he enjoyed the company of masters who took pleasure in instructing him: the engineer tutored him in the sciences, the reporter in the arts of language.

The engineer strove to transmit everything he knew to the boy, to instruct him both by example and by word of mouth, and Harbert profited greatly from his teacher's lessons.

"If I should die," thought Cyrus Smith, "he is the one who will take my place!"

By March 9th the storms were ending, but the sky was veiled with dense clouds over this entire last month of summer. After the violent electrical disturbances of the preceding weeks, the atmosphere was slow to recover its purity, and rain and fog were a nearly constant threat. Only three or four fine days offered the colonists the opportunity for excursions.

At about this same time, the female dauw gave birth to a foal of the same sex as the mother, which thrived wonderfully in its new life. The flock of mouflons had grown as well, and already several lambs could be heard bleating from within the barns, to the great joy of Neb and Harbert, who each had his own favorite among the newborns.

The colonists now attempted to domesticate the peccaries, and succeeded admirably. A shed was built near the poultry yard, and soon it housed a number of piglets, lovingly civilized—which is to say fattened up—by Neb. Master Joop was charged with the task of bringing them their daily rations, table scraps, peelings, etc., and acquitted himself of his responsibilities with wonderful assiduity. To be sure, he could not always resist the temptation to pull his little boarders' tails, but this was out of a spirit of fun, not cruelty, for he found those curling little appendages endlessly amusing, and his instincts were those of a child.

One day during that month of March, Pencroff reminded Cyrus Smith of a promise that he had not yet had time to make good.

"You once made mention of a machine that could take the place of the long ladders at Granite House, Mr. Cyrus," he said to him. "Are you still planning to build that someday?"

"You mean a sort of elevator!" Cyrus Smith answered.

"We can call it an elevator, if you like," the sailor replied. "The name's of no importance, as long as it will lift us effortlessly into our house."

"Nothing could be simpler, Pencroff, but is it really so important?"

"It certainly is, Mr. Cyrus. Now that we've seen to the necessities, we can afford to think of our own comfort a bit. It might seem a luxury for ourselves, if you like; but for our things, we can't do without it! It's not easy climbing a ladder with your hands full and a heavy load on your back!"

"Well, Pencroff, we'll try to make your dream come true," answered Cyrus Smith.

"But we have no engine."

"We'll make one."

"A steam engine?"

"No, a water engine."

For the engineer knew that he had a powerful natural force at his disposal, ready to use and relatively easy to harness.

He had only to increase the flow of liquid through the small channel that brought their water into Granite House. To this end, he enlarged the opening among the rocks and grasses near the upper extremity of the spillway. The trickle of water flowing into the cave at the far end of the corridor was now a powerful cascade, whose excess continued to pour down the shaft and so out to sea. The engineer installed a bladed cylinder at the bottom of the cascade, and this was connected to a wheel outside Granite House; a stout cable was coiled around this wheel, and attached to a small wooden cabin. A long rope ran down to the beach, allowing them to engage or disengage the hydraulic engine at will, and in this way the cabin could be made to rise straight to the front door of Granite House.

The elevator made its first run on March 17th, to the great satisfaction of all. Thanks to this simple device, the colonists could now hoist aloft all manner of heavy loads: wood, coal, provisions, and even themselves. To no one's regret, the elevator had rendered the ladder obsolete. Top was particularly delighted with this innovation, for no matter how he tried he would never climb the rungs with the easy grace of Master Joop, and many times he was forced to ride on Neb's back, or even the orangutan's, for the climb to Granite House.

Now Cyrus Smith's mind turned to the problem of glass. As a first step, the former pottery kiln would have to be adapted for a new use. This was no easy project, and the engineer failed more than once, but in the end he succeeded in constructing a functioning glassworks shop, ably seconded by his born assistants, Gideon Spilett and Harbert, who devoted several days to this new undertaking.

In order to make glass, one needs nothing more than sand, chalk, and soda (sodium carbonate or sulfate). There was no lack of sand on the beach; chalk could be derived from lime, and soda from marine plants; the pyrites would give them sulfuric acid, and the earth itself offered the coal necessary to heat the oven to the proper temperature. Cyrus Smith had everything he needed to proceed.

Among the instruments required for this procedure was one that proved quite difficult to construct: the glassblower's "pipe," an iron tube some five to six feet long, on which the molten glass is collected and blown. After some hesitation, Pencroff finally thought of taking a long, narrow strip of iron and rolling it like a rifle barrel. His plan succeeded admirably, and soon the pipe was ready for use.

On March 28th, the kiln was heated to a high temperature. Into the heat-resistant clay crucibles were deposited one hundred parts sand, thirty-five parts chalk, forty parts sodium sulfate, and two or three parts powdered coal. Once the heat of the kiln had reduced this substance to a liquid, or more precisely a paste, Cyrus Smith "collected" a certain quantity on the end of the pipe. He held it close to an upright metal sheet and turned it around and around, shaping it roughly in preparation for the blowing, then passed the pipe to Harbert, telling him to blow into the other end.

"As if I were making soap bubbles?" the boy asked.

"Precisely," the engineer answered.

Harbert puffed his cheeks and blew into the pipe, careful to keep it turning all the while, and at once the force of his breath caused the vitreous mass to swell. Another dab of molten material was now added on, and they soon had a bubble measuring one foot in diameter. Cyrus Smith took the pipe from Harbert and began to swing it back and forth like a pendulum. The elastic bubble gradually grew longer and thinner, and soon it had taken on a cylindro-conical form.

They were left, then, with a glass cylinder rounded on either end by two hemispherical caps. These were easily cut away from the cylinder with a sharp blade previously plunged into cold water; next the knife was used a second time to split the cylinder lengthwise down one side. The glass was now briefly returned to the kiln to restore its malleability, then laid out on a sheet of metal and flattened with a wooden roller.

Thus they made their first windowpane, and they would only have to repeat this operation fifty times to make fifty more. Soon, then, the window frames of Granite House were fitted with diaphanous sheets of glass, not perfectly clear perhaps, but sufficiently transparent for their needs.

Now they attempted to make various sorts of vessels, glasses, and bottles, which proved mere child's play after their windows. Anything that came off the end of the pipe was judged quite acceptable. Pencroff asked to be allowed to "blow" a few of his own, and this gave him endless pleasure; he blew so hard that his products took on the most remarkable forms, which he found thoroughly wonderful.

One of the excursions they made during this month brought the discovery of a new sort of tree, whose products offered yet another contribution to the colony's alimentary resources.

Cyrus Smith and Harbert had wandered into the Forests of the Far West in search of game. As always, the boy asked the engineer a thousand questions, and he answered them all quite willingly. But hunting is like any other occupation in this world: when one does not pursue it with the necessary zeal, one stands an excellent chance of failing. And since Cyrus Smith was no hunter, and since Harbert could not stop discussing matters of chemistry or physics, many kangaroos, capybaras, and agoutis had passed within range of the boy's rifle but escaped unharmed. It was now quite late in the day, and it was beginning to appear that their excursion would prove fruitless, when suddenly Harbert stopped short and let out a cry of joy:

"Oh! Mr. Cyrus, do you see that tree?"

And he pointed at something that seemed more plant than tree, for it consisted only of a single stalk sheathed in a squamous bark, bearing leaves striated with small parallel veins.

"What could it be? It looks like a small palm tree more than anything else," said Cyrus Smith.

"It's a *Cycas revoluta*, whose portrait I've seen in our dictionary of natural history!"

"It bears no fruit?"

"No, Mr. Cyrus," Harbert answered, "but its trunk contains a sort of flour, already milled by nature and ready for use."

"So this is the bread tree?"

"Yes! the bread tree."

"Well, my child," the engineer answered, "this is a very precious discovery, and it will tide us over nicely while we're waiting for our wheat harvest. Let's get to work, and I hope to Heaven you're not mistaken!"

Harbert was not mistaken. He broke open a cycad stalk, and within its glandulous tissue he found a good quantity of floury pith, with woody fibers running through it from top to bottom and concentric rings of the same material at regular intervals. The starch was intermingled with a mucilaginous sap of disagreeable flavor, but this could easily be pressed out. This cellular substance formed a veritable flour of the finest quality, an extremely nourishing flour whose export was once forbidden under Japanese law.

Cyrus Smith and Harbert carefully studied the area of the Far West where these cycads grew, taking note of certain landmarks that would help them find it again, and returned to Granite House to announce their discovery.

The next day the colonists set off to harvest their flour, and Pencroff, ever more enamored of his island, said to the engineer:

"Mr. Cyrus, do you believe in castaways' islands?"

"What do you mean by that, Pencroff?"

"Well, I mean islands specially designed for shipwrecks, where a poor wretch can always make good!"

"I suppose such places might exist," the engineer answered with a smile.

"It's a certainty, sir," Pencroff answered, "and it's just as certain that Lincoln Island is one of them!"

They returned to Granite House with an great bundle of cycad stalks. The engineer built a press for the extraction of the mucilaginous sap, and so he obtained a notable quantity of flour, soon transformed into cakes and puddings by Neb's able hands. They did not yet have a true wheat bread, but they were not far from it.

In the sheepfold, the dauw, the goats, and the ewes were now producing a daily supply of milk for the colonists' needs. Thus, the cart, or rather the light cariole that had taken its place, made frequent trips to the sheepfold. Whenever it fell to Pencroff to make this journey, he always brought Joop along and had him drive; and Joop, cracking his whip, performed this task with his usual intelligence.

Everything was prospering, then, both at the sheepfold and in Granite House, and the colonists had no complaints save the distance separating them from their homeland. Indeed, they had grown so accustomed to their new life on this island, so perfectly at home, that they could not think of leaving its hospitable shores without a twinge of regret!

Nevertheless, so strong is the love of country in the hearts of men that if some ship had unexpectedly appeared on the horizon, the colonists would not have hesitated to signal it, attract it to them, and sail away!...But in the meantime, their existence was a happy one, and it was more with fear than desire that they told themselves it would one day come to an end.

But can any man be so bold as to believe that he has mastered his own destiny, and freed himself from the whims of fate?

Lincoln Island had now been their home for a full year, and their new life here was a frequent topic of conversation. One day, in just such a discussion, an observation was made that would later have momentous consequences.

It was April 1, Easter Sunday. Cyrus Smith and his companions had marked the date with rest and prayer. It had been a beautiful day, much like a fine October day in the boreal hemisphere.

After dinner, as evening was coming on, they gathered under the veranda at the edge of Longview Plateau to watch the darkness descend over the horizon. Neb had served several cups of the elder-seed infusion that was their substitute for coffee. They spoke of the island and its isolation in the Pacific, and Gideon Spilett was led to say:

"My dear Cyrus, now that we've found the sextant in the crate, have you taken another reading of our island's location?"

"No," the engineer answered.

"Do you not think it would be wise to do so? It's a far more accurate instrument than the one you used before."

"Why trouble ourselves?" said Pencroff. "The island is where it is!"

"To be sure," Gideon Spilett replied, "but with such crude tools our observations might not have been entirely accurate, and since we can now easily verify them..."

"You're right, my dear Spilett," the engineer answered. "I should have confirmed my readings long ago, although I'm quite sure that I couldn't have erred by more than five degrees longitude or latitude."

"Well! who knows?" the reporter answered. "Who knows if we aren't much closer to some inhabited land than we thought?"

"We'll know tomorrow," Cyrus Smith replied, "and we would know already if our other occupations had offered me the leisure."

"Come now!" said Pencroff. "Mr. Cyrus is too good an observer to have

They spoke of the island and its isolation.

made a mistake, and unless the island has moved in the meantime, I've no doubt it's just where he put it!"

"We shall see."

And so, the next day, the engineer used the sextant to verify the coordinates he had already obtained, and these were the results of his operation:

The first observation had situated Lincoln Island at:

west longitude: from 150 degrees to 155 degrees;

south latitude: from 30 degrees to 35 degrees.

From the second observation he obtained these precise figures:

west longitude: 150 degrees 30 minutes;

south latitude: 34 degrees 57 minutes.

Thus, even with his rough, handmade tools, Cyrus Smith had performed his observations with such skill that the margin of error did not exceed five degrees.

"Now," said Gideon Spilett, "since we possess an atlas as well as the sextant, let us see, my dear Cyrus, just where in the Pacific Lincoln Island lies."

Harbert went to fetch the atlas, which, as we know, had been published in France, and whose nomenclature was consequently in French.

The map of the Pacific was spread out, and the engineer took up his compass to determine their precise location.

Suddenly the compass went still, and he said:

"But there's already an island in this part of the Pacific!"

"An island?" cried Pencroff.

"Ours, no doubt?" answered Gideon Spilett.

"No," Cyrus Smith replied. "This island is situated at one hundred fifty-three degrees longitude and thirty-seven degrees eleven minutes latitude, which is to say two and a half degrees west and two degrees south of Lincoln Island."

"And what is this island called?" Harbert asked.

"Tabor Island."

"Is it a large island?"

"No, only an islet in the middle of the Pacific. It might well never have been visited before!"

"Well, we'll visit it," said Pencroff.

"Us?"

"Yes, Mr. Cyrus. We will build a decked boat, and I'll volunteer to steer her. —How far are we from this Tabor Island?"

"About one hundred fifty miles northeast," Cyrus Smith answered.

"A hundred fifty miles! What's that to us?" Pencroff answered. "With a good wind, we can cover that in forty-eight hours!"

"But what good would it do?" the reporter asked.

"We don't know. We just have to see!"

And with that it was decided that they would build a boat, and attempt the voyage the following October, when the good weather returned.

X

*Building the Boat.—A Second Wheat Harvest.—A Kola Hunt.—
A New Plant, More Pleasant Than Useful.—A Whale in
Sight.—The Harpoon from the Vineyard.—Butchering the
Whale.—Uses for Whalebone.—The End of May.—Pencroff's
Dream Come True.*

Once Pencroff had made up his mind to do something he would not rest, nor allow anyone else to rest, until it had been carried out. He wanted to visit Tabor Island, and since a craft of some size would be required for such a voyage, it was now necessary to construct it.

Here is the plan devised by the engineer, in accordance with the sailor.

The boat's keel would measure thirty-five feet and its beams nine feet—which would make it a good sailer, if its bilge and waterlines were designed with care—and would draw no more than six feet of water, just enough to keep it from drifting. It would be decked over its entire length, with two hatchways for access to two separate cabins; it would be rigged as a sloop, with a spanker, staysail, pole, jib—a very maneuverable set of sails, easily struck in case of squalls, ideal for sailing close-hauled. Finally, its hull would be constructed with freeboards, which is to say that the planking would be abutted rather than superimposed, and as for its frame, it would be installed after the planking had been laid out over temporary timbers, using heat to bow the wood.

What wood should be used for the construction of this boat? Elm or pine, both of which grew abundantly on the island? They decided on pine, a rather "splitty" wood, as carpenters say, but easily worked, and no less water-resistant than elm.

Having worked out these details, the colonists now agreed that Cyrus

Smith and Pencroff would work on the boat alone, since the fine weather would not return for another six months. In the meantime, Gideon Spilett and Harbert would continue hunting, and Neb and his assistant, Master Joop, would see to the domestic chores.

Pencroff and Cyrus Smith set about finding suitable trees, and these they felled, stripped, and sawed into planks, like seasoned pit sawyers. Eight days later a shipyard had been established in the recess between the Chimneys and the granite wall, and a thirty-five-foot-long keel lay on the sand, fitted with a sternpost behind and a stem before.

Cyrus Smith did not approach this new project blindly. He was well acquainted with the shipbuilder's trade, as he was with nearly every field of human endeavor, and he had drawn up the design and dimensions of his boat with great care. Pencroff's assistance was of course invaluable, since he had worked for several years in a Brooklyn shipyard, and so knew the procedures by heart. Acting not by instinct, then, but in accordance with the most rigorous and exacting specifications, they attached the temporary timbers to the keel and prepared to begin their work in earnest.

As we might well expect, Pencroff burned to see his new enterprise come to fruition, and he was loath to interrupt his work for a single moment.

Only one responsibility could tear him away from his shipyard, and only for one single day. This was the second wheat harvest, which was carried out on April 15th. It proved no less successful than the first, and provided precisely the proportion of grains Cyrus Smith had predicted.

"Five bushels, Mr. Cyrus!" said Pencroff, when he had meticulously measured out his wealth.

"Five bushels," the engineer replied, "and, at one hundred thirty thousand grains per bushel, that makes six hundred fifty thousand grains."

"Well then, we'll sow it all this time," said the sailor, "keeping a small supply in reserve, of course!"

"Yes, Pencroff, and if the same proportions hold for the next harvest, we'll have four thousand bushels."

"And we'll have bread to eat?"

"We will have bread to eat."

"But we'll have to build a mill?"

"We'll build a mill."

The third wheat field was thus of much greater size than the first two.

The soil was carefully prepared, the precious seeds were sown, and Pencroff returned to his work.

Meanwhile, Gideon Spilett and Harbert undertook a series of hunting expeditions into the unexplored areas of the Far West, loading their rifles not with shot but with bullets, for they never knew what sorts of beasts they might meet up with. The trees were magnificent, the forest dense; it was as if the vegetation were locked in a continual battle for space. This made the exploration of these woods an arduous pursuit, and the reporter never entered the area without his pocket compass, for the sun could scarcely penetrate the interlaced branches, and it would be no easy thing to find their way out again if they became lost. Naturally, game was not as plentiful here as elsewhere, for the forest was as impenetrable to animals as to men. Nevertheless, three large herbivores were killed in the latter half of April. These were kolas, like the beast previously sighted north of the lake, and they offered an easy target as they lumbered into the branches for refuge. Their hides were brought back to Granite House and tanned with sulfuric acid.

Another discovery resulted from these excursions, this time thanks to Gideon Spilett. A very precious discovery it was, but not in the same sense as the others.

It was April 30th. The two hunters had wandered into the southwestern reaches of the Far West, and as the reporter was walking some fifty paces ahead of Harbert he came upon a sort of clearing. The trees were more widely scattered here, and a few rays of sunlight filtered through the verdure.

Gideon Spilett was surprised to find a curious odor emanating from a bed of plants with straight, cylindrical stems, whose many ramifications produced clusters of flowers and very small seeds. The reporter pulled up one or two such stalks and returned to the boy, saying:

"What do you suppose this might be, Harbert?"

"Where did you find that plant, Mr. Spilett?"

"Over there, in a clearing. There are a great many of them."

"Well, Mr. Spilett," said Harbert, "you've just made a discovery that will earn you Pencroff's undying gratitude!"

"So this is tobacco?"

"Yes—not of the finest quality, perhaps, but tobacco nonetheless!"

"Oh! good old Pencroff! Won't he be happy! But we won't let him smoke it all, by God! He'll have to leave us our share!"

"Oh! I have an idea, Mr. Spilett," Harbert answered. "Let's not mention this to Pencroff. Let's take the time to prepare the leaves, and one fine day we'll offer him a pipe all loaded and ready to smoke!"

"Right you are, Harbert, and that day our worthy companion will have nothing more to desire in all the world!"

The reporter and the boy gathered a good supply of the precious plant and returned to Granite House, warily "smuggling" it inside, just as if Pencroff were the strictest of all customs agents.

Cyrus Smith and Neb were let in on the secret. Over the next two months, the slender leaves were carefully dried, chopped, and torrified on hot stones; and all the while the sailor suspected nothing. Ever occupied with the construction of his boat, Pencroff returned to Granite House only at bedtime, leaving them all the time they needed for their covert preparations.

Once more, however, whether he liked it or not, Pencroff had to tear himself away from his beloved boat; for on the first of May all the colonists were called to a great fishing expedition.

For several days they had observed an enormous animal swimming in the seas around Lincoln Island, some two or three miles offshore. It was a whale of the most monumental proportions, very likely a member of the austral species known as the "right whale."

"What a fine thing it would be to get our hands on that whale!" the sailor cried. "Oh! if only we had a good boat and a working harpoon, how I would love to cry out: 'After her boys, whatever it takes she'll be worth it!' "

"My friend Pencroff," said Gideon Spilett, "I would certainly like to see you wielding a harpoon. That must be a very curious sight!"

"Very curious indeed, and not without its dangers," said the engineer; "but since we have no way of attacking the beast, there's no point troubling ourselves about it."

"I'm surprised," the reporter said, "to see a whale at so high a latitude."

"Why, Mr. Spilett?" Harbert answered. "The English and American fishermen call this part of the Pacific the 'whale field,' and for a very good reason: nowhere in the southern hemisphere can whales be found in greater numbers than between New Zealand and South America."

"That's exactly right, my boy," Pencroff answered. "I'm only surprised we haven't seen more of them. But after all, we've no way to get close to it, so what does it matter!"

And Pencroff returned to his work, not without a sigh of regret, for in every sailor lives a fisherman, and if the pleasure of fishing is directly proportional to the size of the animal, we can only imagine what a whaler feels in the presence of a whale!

Now, if it were only a question of pleasure, that would be one thing! But the colonists could not help thinking of the precious new resources that a whale would offer, of all they could do with the oil, blubber, and bone!

But now they found that the whale seemed reluctant to leave the island's waters. Between hunting expeditions, Harbert and Gideon Spilett stood at the windows of Granite House or on Longview Plateau, endlessly eyeing the whale through their telescope. Neb displayed a similar preoccupation, observing the whale's every move even as he watched over his ovens. The cetacean had entered Union Bay, and spent its days speeding back and forth from Cape Mandible to Cape Claw. Thrusting its prodigiously powerful tail fin into the water, it hurtled forward at a speed that sometimes reached twelve miles per hour. Sometimes it approached the islet, allowing the colonists a more extensive view of its gigantic bulk. It was indeed a southern right whale, completely black, and with a head more concave than those of the north.

They could see it spouting from its spiracles, filling the air above its head with steam ... or water, for—however odd it may seem—naturalists and whalemen are not yet in agreement on this point. Is it warm air or water that the whale spouts? It is generally believed to be the former, which suddenly condenses on contact with the cold air and falls like rain into the sea.

The presence of this sea mammal was a continual preoccupation, particularly irritating to Pencroff, who many times found himself distracted from his work. He longed for that whale as a child does for some forbidden object. He dreamed of it at night, calling out in his sleep, and there is no doubt that if he had had the means to go after it, if the sloop had been ready to take to sea, he would not have hesitated for a moment.

But what the colonists could not do for themselves was finally done for them by chance. On May 3rd, from his post at the kitchen window, Neb excitedly shouted that the whale had washed onto the shore.

Harbert and Gideon Spilett were about to leave for a hunting trip, but now they dropped their rifles at once. Pencroff threw down his hatchet, Cyrus Smith and Neb joined their companions, and they all hastened to the spot where the whale had washed ashore.

The beaching had occurred at Flotsam Point, three miles from Gran-

"What a monster!" cried Neb.

ite House, at high tide. This suggested that the cetacean would have great difficulty finding its way into the water again; nevertheless, should it attempt to do so, they would have to hurry to cut off its retreat. They came running with picks and pikes, crossed the bridge over the Mercy, ran down the right bank, turned onto the beach, and in less than twenty minutes the colonists were approaching the enormous animal, as a great population of seabirds wheeled overhead.

"What a monster!" cried Neb.

And the expression was well chosen, for it was a southern right whale, eighty feet long, a giant of the species, whose weight was clearly no less than 150,000 pounds!

Meanwhile, the monster made no attempt to return to the deep water, but merely lay motionless on the sand.

When the tide had dropped sufficiently, the colonists came to the animal's side, and soon discovered the explanation for its immobility.

It was dead. A harpoon emerged from its left flank.

"There must be whaling ships hereabouts!" Gideon Spilett immediately said.

"Why do you say that?" asked the sailor.

"Because the harpoon is still in it..."

"Why, Mr. Spilett, that proves nothing," Pencroff replied. "Whales have been known to travel thousands of miles with harpoons in their sides, and I wouldn't be at all surprised to learn that this one was hit in the North Atlantic and came to die in the South Pacific!"

"Nevertheless..." said Gideon Spilett, unsatisfied by Pencroff's claim.

"It's perfectly possible," Cyrus Smith answered; "but let's have a look at that harpoon. I believe it's customary for whalers to engrave their names on these weapons?"

And indeed, Pencroff, pulling the harpoon from the animal's flank, read this inscription:

Maria-Stella
Vineyard.

"A ship from the Vineyard! A ship from my country!" he cried. "The *Maria-Stella!* A fine whaling ship, by gad! I know her well! Oh, my friends, a ship from the Vineyard, a whaling ship from the Vineyard!"*

---

* A port in the state of New York.

And the sailor brandished the harpoon, repeating the beloved name with great emotion, a name from his native land!

But since there would be no point in waiting for the *Maria-Stella* to come along and claim the animal she had harpooned, they resolved to dismember the whale before decomposition set in. The birds of prey had been eyeing this bounty for the past several days, eager to take possession. The colonists were forced to scatter them with rifle shots.

It was a female, whose teats would provide a great quantity of a milk that, according to the naturalist Dieffenbach, could easily be mistaken for cow's milk; indeed, the two are indistinguishable in taste, color, and density.

Pencroff had once served aboard a whaling ship, and he was able to direct the dismembering process with great efficiency—a rather disagreeable operation, lasting three days, but before which no colonist recoiled, not even Gideon Spilett, who, to hear the sailor tell it, would someday become "a very fine castaway."

The blubber was cut into parallel slices some two and a half feet thick, then divided into slabs of a thousand pounds each. This was melted down in great earthenware urns that had been brought to the site for this purpose, since they did not want to befoul the air of Longview Plateau. The whale lost about a third of its weight in the process. But there was still a great deal of flesh to deal with: the tongue alone produced six thousand pounds of oil, and the lower lip four thousand. In addition to the fat, which offered them an endless supply of stearin and glycerine, there was the whalebone, for which some use would no doubt be found, although umbrellas and corsets were in no great demand at Granite House. The upper part of the cetacean's mouth was lined on both sides with eight hundred very elastic blades of a fibrous consistency, tapering at the ends like two enormous combs. The teeth of these combs serve to capture thousands of tiny organisms, along with fish and mollusks, which make up the whale's diet.

Once this operation was over—much to the colonists' relief—the animal's remains were left to the birds. Soon nothing would be left of the beast, and so the colonists resumed their daily tasks at Granite House.

Nevertheless, before returning to the shipyard, Cyrus Smith had the idea of using the whalebone to construct a device that greatly excited his companions' curiosity. He took a dozen of the blades, cut them into six equal pieces, and sharpened them at both ends.

"Tell me, Mr. Cyrus," asked Harbert, "what will we do with these once you've finished?"

"We'll kill wolves, foxes, even jaguars," the engineer replied.

"Now?"

"No, this winter, when we have ice."

"I don't understand..." answered Harbert.

"You will, my boy," the engineer replied. "I did not invent these devices; they are frequently used by the Aleutian hunters of Russian America. Once the cold weather sets in, my friends, I will curve these blades double, then sprinkle them with water until they are sheathed in a coating of ice. This coating will hold them as they are, and I will scatter them over the snow, beneath a thick layer of blubber. Now, what will happen when a hungry animal swallows the bait? The heat of its stomach will melt the ice, and the whalebone will spring open, plunging its sharpened points into the animal's belly."

"Most ingenious!" said Pencroff.

"And it will spare us powder and bullets," answered Cyrus Smith.

"It's better than the pit traps!" added Neb.

"So now we wait for winter!"

"We wait for winter."

In the meantime, their ship was slowly taking form, and by the end of the month the planking was half done. Already its graceful lines showed that it would handle a sea voyage without difficulty.

Pencroff's ardor for his work could not be equaled, and only a man as robust as he could have endured the physical strain; but his companions were secretly preparing a capital reward for his labors, and, on May 31st, he would experience one of the greatest joys of his life.

That day, as dinner was ending, just as he was about to leave the table, Pencroff felt a hand on his shoulder.

It was the hand of Gideon Spilett, who said to him:

"Just one moment, Master Pencroff. Where do you think you're going? You'll miss dessert!"

"Thank you kindly, Mr. Spilett," the sailor answered, "but I have to get back to work."

"Well, what about a cup of coffee, my friend?"

"No, thank you."

"A pipe, then?"

Pencroff suddenly leaped up, and his fine ruddy face grew pale when he saw the reporter holding out a well-packed pipe, and Harbert a burning ember.

The sailor attempted to speak, but no words came to his lips. Nevertheless, he seized the pipe, brought it to his mouth, touched the ember to the tobacco, and quickly took six puffs in a row.

A perfumed, bluish cloud enveloped him, from within which a delirious voice could be heard to repeat:

"Tobacco! Real tobacco!"

"Yes, Pencroff," answered Cyrus Smith, "and very fine tobacco too!"

"Oh! Merciful Providence! Sacred Author of all things!" cried the sailor. "Now we've nothing more to wish for!"

And Pencroff smoked, smoked, smoked!

"Who made this wonderful discovery?" he finally inquired. "No doubt it was you, Harbert?"

"No, Pencroff, it was Mr. Spilett."

"Mr. Spilett!" cried the sailor, clasping the reporter to his breast. Spilett had never known so vigorous an embrace.

"Oof! Pencroff," said Gideon Spilett, catching his breath after this brief strangulation. "You owe your thanks to Harbert as well, for having identified the plant, and to Cyrus, who prepared it, and to Neb, who struggled so mightily to keep the secret!"

"I promise you all, I'll make this up to you someday!" the sailor answered. "Now I'm yours forever, in this life and the next!"

XI

Winter.—Fulling the Wool.—The Mill.—Pencroff's Obsession.—The Whalebone.—An Experiment with an Albatross.—The Fuel of the Future.—Top and Joop.—Storms.—Damage to the Poultry Yard.—An Excursion to the Marsh.—Cyrus Smith Alone.—Exploration of the Shaft.

Now June had come, and with it the beginning of winter, for that month is the equivalent of December in the boreal zones, and the colonists found themselves in urgent need of warm, sturdy clothes.

The mouflons had been shorn of their wool, and that precious textile material had now only to be transformed into cloth.

Of course, Cyrus Smith had no mechanical means for carding the wool, nor combing it, nor smoothing it, nor drawing it out, nor spinning it; he had neither a "Crompton's mule" nor a "self-acting" mule spindle to spin the wool, nor a loom to weave it. He would have to find a simpler procedure, requiring neither spinning nor weaving. It then occurred to him that he could use a property inherent to wool filaments: when tightly pressed together, they naturally interlock, and the inextricable tangle that results is nothing other than the fabric known as felt. Felt could thus be produced by fulling the wool—a very simple operation, which robs the cloth of some of its softness but notably increases its ability to preserve warmth. And, by a happy circumstance, the mouflons' wool was formed of very short fibers, ideal in every way for felting.

The engineer enlisted his companions, including Pencroff—forced to abandon his boat once again!—and began the preliminary operations. The first step would be to rid the wool of the oily, fatty substance that impregnates it, which is known as suint. This degreasing process was accomplished by soaking the wool for twenty-four hours in basins filled with water at a temperature of seventy degrees centigrade. Next they washed it thoroughly in soda baths and wrung it dry. Now it was ready to be fulled, after which the colonists would have a good, sturdy cloth, rather coarse no doubt, and worthless in an industrial center of Europe or America, but which would be highly prized on the "Lincoln Island market."

The invention of this material must surely date back to the most distant reaches of human history; indeed, the earliest woolen fabrics were created by the very process Cyrus Smith had in mind.

Now he would need a machine to full the wool. Drawing on his training as an engineer, he realized that the kinetic energy of the cascade of water falling onto the beach—an energy heretofore untapped—could be used to power a fulling mill.

The design of the machine could not have been simpler. A framework of stout beams supported a wooden camshaft, by which a series of heavy upright pestles were alternately raised and allowed to drop into the trough that held the raw wool. Such was the engineer's device, and such, no doubt, were the fulling mills of centuries past, before some inventor thought of replacing the pestles with compression cylinders, producing the felt not by beating but by lamination.

The procedure was carried out under Cyrus Smith's watchful eye, and the results were everything he had hoped. They began by soaking the wool in a soapy solution to soften the fibers and make them more compressible, greatly facilitating their slippage and interweaving, while at the same time damping the impact of the falling pestles; next the machine was set in motion, and soon the wool was transformed into a thick sheet of felt. The rough, ridged wool fibers were now tightly interlocked, clinging together to form a cloth no less suitable for clothing than for blankets. To be sure, it was not merino, nor muslin, nor Scottish cashmere, nor stuff, nor reps, nor Chinese satin, nor orleans, nor alpaca, nor broadcloth, nor flannel! It was "Lincoln felt," and yet another industry had come to Lincoln Island.

Thus, the colonists now had thick blankets and fine, warm clothes, and the oncoming winter of 1866–67 was no longer cause for trepidation.

The cold of winter first made its appearance around June 20th, and to his great regret Pencroff was forced to suspend work on his boat, consoling himself with the knowledge that it could not fail to be completed by the following spring.

The sailor had become obsessed with the idea of an exploratory excursion to Tabor Island. On this Cyrus Smith and Pencroff disagreed, for the engineer was sure they would find nothing of use to them on that deserted, semiarid rock, and he refused to consider making such a journey for curiosity's sake alone. A one-hundred-fifty-mile voyage on a relatively small boat through unknown waters was simply too dangerous to attempt. Suppose the craft were stranded on the open sea, unable to reach Tabor Island nor return to Lincoln Island—what would become of it, lost in the middle of the Pacific Ocean, a place long known for maritime disasters?

Pencroff's idea was a recurrent theme in his conversations with Cyrus Smith, who found the sailor curiously obstinate on this point, perhaps more so than he realized himself.

"Really, now, my friend," the engineer said to him one day, "does it not strike you as odd that after all the praise you've lavished on Lincoln Island, after all your expressions of regret at the very idea of leaving it, suddenly you're the first to want to go away?"

"To go away for a few days, nothing more," Pencroff answered. "Just a few days, Mr. Cyrus! Only as long as it takes to go and come back, just to see what the islet looks like!"

"But it can't be as good as Lincoln Island!"

"I know that already!"

"Then why do you want to risk your life to go there?"

"To know what's happening on Tabor Island!"

"But nothing is happening there! Nothing can happen there!"

"Who knows?"

"Suppose you find yourself caught in a storm?"

"Not likely in springtime," Pencroff answered. "But, Mr. Cyrus, I know we have to plan for any eventuality, so if you please I'll take no one with me but Harbert."

"Pencroff," the engineer answered, putting his hand on the sailor's shoulder, "if something were to happen to you and that child, whom chance has made our son, do you believe we would ever be able to console ourselves?"

"Mr. Cyrus," Pencroff answered with unshakable confidence, "we'd never do such a thing to you. But we can talk about this later, when it comes time to make the voyage. I have a feeling that once you've seen our beautiful boat with all her rigging out, and all her fittings, once you've seen the way she takes to the sea, once we've taken her out for a trip around the island—for that's just what we will do—I have a feeling you won't hesitate to let me go! I don't mind saying, Mr. Cyrus, your boat is going to be a masterpiece!"

"You might at least say 'our boat,' Pencroff!" the engineer answered, momentarily disarmed.

So the conversation ended for the moment, with the sailor and the engineer equally unpersuaded.

The first snows fell toward the end of June. The sheepfold had been amply stocked with food, and no longer required daily visits; nevertheless, it was decided that they would not let a week go by without checking on the animals.

The pit traps were baited again, and Cyrus Smith put his Aleutian contrivances to the test. Imprisoned in a sheath of ice and covered with a thick layer of whale fat, the curved whalebones were set out at the edges of the forest, on a route regularly followed by animals on their way to the lake.

To the engineer's great satisfaction, the devices were a complete success. A dozen foxes, a few wild boars, and even a jaguar took the bait, and soon lay dead, their stomachs perforated by the sharp whalebones.

And we must not neglect to mention another experiment carried out at this same time, for this was the colonists' first attempt to communicate with their fellow men.

Gideon Spilett had sometimes thought of sealing a message away in a bottle and casting it into the sea in hopes that the current would carry it to some inhabited shore; sometimes, too, he thought of tying such a message to the leg of a pigeon. But could he seriously believe that a pigeon or a bottle might somehow cross the twelve hundred miles of ocean that lay between him and the nearest land? No, that would be madness.

But on June 30th they succeeded in capturing an albatross, slightly wounded in the foot by a shot from Harbert's rifle. It was a magnificent creature, belonging to a family of long-flight birds whose enormous wings, measuring up to ten feet across, allow them easy passage over the Pacific.

The wound soon healed, and Harbert was hoping to keep the bird and domesticate it; but Gideon Spilett asserted that the arrival of this courier offered them an unparalleled opportunity to make their presence known to their fellow men, somewhere across the Pacific. Harbert had no choice but to agree, for if the albatross had indeed come from an inhabited land, it could not fail to return there once it was free.

Perhaps it tickled the chronicler in Gideon Spilett to be sending off a fascinating account of their adventures on Lincoln Island, however uncertain its final destination may be! What a triumph for the *New York Herald*'s star reporter, and for the issue containing his account, if ever it reached the desk of his editor, the honorable John Benett!

Gideon Spilett thus wrote up a succinct message and sealed it inside a sack of heavy gummed canvas with a request that it be forwarded at once to the offices of the *New York Herald*. This small sack was attached not to the albatross's leg but to its neck, for these birds are in the habit of sitting on the water's surface for their rest; then the swift courier of the air was given its freedom, and it was not without a certain emotion that they watched the bird disappear into the fog toward the west.

"Where is he headed?" asked Pencroff.

"Toward New Zealand," Harbert answered.

"Bon voyage!" the sailor cried, although he had no great hopes for the success of this enterprise.

With the return of winter, the colonists resumed their work inside Granite House: mending their clothing, cutting sails for their boat from the inexhaustible sheath of the aerostat, sewing...

July was a month of bitter cold, but they spared neither wood nor coal. Cyrus Smith had built a second fireplace in the great room, and here they gathered for the long winter evenings. They chatted as they worked, they read when their hands were idle, and slowly the time went by to the profit of all.

What a pleasure to sit in that room after a restorative dinner, in the glow of the candlelight and the warmth of the hearth, with elder coffee steaming in their cups and plumes of aromatic smoke streaming from their pipes, and hear the howling of the wind outside! They might well have felt completely content, if such were possible for ones so far from their fellow men, and so utterly cut off from the outside world! Inevitably their conversations turned to their homeland, the friends they had left behind, the greatness of the American republic, the ineluctable spread of its influence throughout the world; and Cyrus Smith, as one deeply involved in the Union's affairs, never failed to arouse his companions' interest with his stories, insights, and predictions.

One day, Gideon Spilett remarked to him:

A small sack was attached to the albatross's neck.

"My dear Cyrus, with all your predictions of endless progress for our world's vast commerces and industries, do you not see that one day, sooner or later, it must come to an end?"

"An end! Why?"

"For lack of coal, of course, which we might well call the most precious of all minerals!"

"Yes, the most precious, indeed," the engineer answered. "Nature herself has proclaimed it so, by creating the diamond, which is nothing other than pure crystallized carbon."

"You're not trying to tell us, Mr. Cyrus," the sailor shot back, "that one day we'll burn diamonds instead of coal in our boilers?"

"No, my friend," Cyrus Smith replied.

"To return to my question," Gideon Spilett resumed, "surely you can't deny that one day the earth's supply of coal will be exhausted?"

"Oh, the world still has plenty of coal. Every year a hundred thousand workers excavate a hundred million metric quintals of coal from deposits all over the earth, and they're nowhere near exhausting them!"

"With the growing rate of coal consumption," Gideon Spilett answered, "we might well predict that those hundred thousand workers will soon be two hundred thousand, and that the rate of extraction will be doubled."

"No doubt; but when the deposits in Europe have been depleted—and soon we shall have machines to mine that coal more efficiently that we had ever dreamed possible—even then, the coalfields of America and Australia will still furnish an ample supply for many years to come, more than enough to meet our industries' needs."

"How many years?" asked the reporter.

"At least two hundred fifty or three hundred years."

"That's all very well for us," Pencroff replied, "but very worrisome for our great-great cousins!"

"People will find something to replace it," said Harbert.

"Let us hope so," answered Gideon Spilett, "for without coal, no more machines, and without machines, no more railways, no more steamships, no more factories, no more of anything that the progress of modern life requires!"

"But what could take its place?" asked Pencroff. "Do you have any idea, Mr. Cyrus?"

"More or less, my friend."

"And what will people burn in place of coal?"

"Water," answered Cyrus Smith.

"Water," cried Pencroff, "water to run the steamships and locomotives, water to heat water?"

"Yes, but water broken down into its component elements," answered Cyrus Smith, "and broken down, no doubt, by electricity, which will by then have become a powerful force, easily harnessed; for, by some inexplicable law, it seems that the great discoveries always arise together, as if the one were meant to complement the other. Yes, my friends, I believe that water will one day be used as fuel, that the hydrogen and oxygen of which it is constituted will be used, simultaneously or in isolation, to furnish an inexhaustible source of heat and light, more powerful than coal can ever be. One day, the holds of steamships and the tenders of locomotives will be filled with those two compressed gases, powering their engines with an incalculable calorific force. We've no need to worry. As long as this earth is inhabited it will fulfill its inhabitants' every need, and man will never lack for light or heat, no more than for the various productions of the vegetal, animal, and mineral kingdoms. I believe, then, that once the coal deposits have been exhausted, we will warm our homes and ourselves with water. Water is the coal of the future."

"That I'd like to see," said the sailor.

"You got up too early, Pencroff," Neb answered, and this was his only contribution to the discussion.

Nevertheless, it was not Neb's words that put an end to this conversation, but Top, barking with that strange intonation that had more than once troubled the engineer. And as he barked, Top circled the entrance to the vertical shaft, at the far end of the central corridor.

"What could be making Top bark like that?" asked Pencroff.

"And making Joop growl so?" added Harbert.

For the orangutan had now come to the dog's side, unequivocally signaling his agitation, and—curiously—both animals seemed more frightened than angry.

"Clearly," said Gideon Spilett, "this shaft communicates directly with the ocean, and every now and then some sea creature finds its way inside to breathe."

"That's obvious," Pencroff answered. "There's no other explanation for it...Come on now, Top, be quiet!" he added, turning toward the dog, "and as for you, Joop, go to your room!"

The dog and the ape fell silent. Joop went off to bed, but Top stayed in the great room and spent the rest of the evening growling quietly.

There was no further discussion of this incident, which nevertheless brought a furrow to the engineer's brow.

July ended with alternating periods of rain and cold. The temperatures were somewhat warmer than the previous winter's, and the thermometer did not fall below 8 degrees Fahrenheit (13.33 degrees centigrade below zero). Nevertheless, it was a winter full of storms and high winds. Once again, the sea violently lashed at the shoreline; once again, the installations at the Chimneys were threatened. Monstrous waves crashed against the exterior wall of Granite House, like a series of tidal waves set off by some great undersea disturbance.

Sometimes the colonists stood at their windows to watch the enormous masses of water crashing against the shore, admiring in spite of themselves the magnificent spectacle of the ocean's impotent fury. The waves rebounded from the rocks in a shower of dazzling spume. The entire beach disappeared beneath the raging flood, and the granite wall seemed to emerge from the sea itself, whose spray sometimes shot more than a hundred feet into the air.

These tempests made any attempt at travel difficult, and even dangerous, for falling trees were a frequent occurrence. Nonetheless, the colonists never let a week go by without a visit to the sheepfold. Fortunately, the enclosure was sheltered by the southeastern foothills of Mount Franklin, and its trees, barns, and palisade were never endangered by the violence of the gales. But the poultry yard on Longview Plateau was directly exposed to the easterly winds, and suffered considerable damage over the course of the winter. Twice the dovecote lost its roof, and the fence was toppled as well. Clearly, these structures would have to be rebuilt more sturdily than before; for as we see, Lincoln Island lay in one of the wildest regions of the Pacific. The island seemed a veritable focal point for cyclones, which lashed it as a string lashes a top. But here it was the top that stayed motionless, and the whip that spun.

The fierce winds gradually abated over the first week of August, and the atmosphere regained a calm that it seemed to have lost forever. This brought about an abrupt drop in temperature; the bitter cold had returned, and the thermometric column fell to eight degrees Fahrenheit below zero (twenty-two degrees centigrade below freezing).

For several days the colonists had been planning an excursion to Shel-duck Fens, tempted by the varied aquatic birds that had taken up residence there for the winter. Wild ducks, snipes, pintails, teals, and grebes were to be found in abundance, and it was decided that they would spend the third of August in pursuit of feathered game.

Pencroff and Neb joined Gideon Spilett and Harbert for this expedition. Only Cyrus Smith stayed behind at Granite House, on the pretext of some work he had left unfinished.

And so, with Top and Joop accompanying them, the hunters set out for the marsh by way of the Port Balloon road, promising to be home by nightfall. Once they had crossed the bridge over the Mercy, the engineer raised it and returned home, his thoughts full of a project for which he wished to be alone.

The project in question was a thorough exploration of the shaft that opened up in the floor of Granite House and no doubt continued to the sea, since it had once served as a conduit for the waters of the lake.

What was the source of Top's fascination with this shaft? What was the nature of the anxiety that drew him to it, and why did he bark so strangely as he endlessly circled around it? Why did Joop join in, as if gripped by the same sort of terror? Did the shaft branch off as it fell vertically toward the sea? Did these ramifications run beneath the surface of the ground, to other regions of the island? Cyrus Smith desperately wanted to know the answers to these questions—and to be the only one to know. For this reason, he had resolved to explore the shaft while his companions were away, and now the opportunity had finally presented itself.

He could easily descend to the bottom of the shaft with the long rope ladder, which had fallen into disuse since the construction of the elevator. This the engineer did. He dragged the ladder to the hole, whose diameter measured about six feet; he solidly anchored its upper end, then let it drop. Next he lit a lantern, took up a revolver, thrust a cutlass through his belt, and began to descend the rungs.

The wall was solid and smooth; nevertheless, a few outcroppings could be seen here and there, and perhaps a sufficiently agile creature could use these natural footholds to reach the top of the shaft.

The engineer took note of this; but, carefully shining his lantern over the outcroppings, he found no mark, no fracture to suggest they had been used to scale the wall, neither recently nor in the past.

He found nothing suspicious.

Cyrus Smith continued his descent, illuminating every inch of the wall.

He found nothing suspicious.

The surface of the water lay just below the final rungs, calm and untroubled. Neither here nor at any point in his descent had he seen a lateral corridor running through the mass of granite. Cyrus Smith knocked the shaft wall with the handle of his cutlass, and judged it to be perfectly solid. Clearly, no living creature could pass through this dense block of granite. In order to reach the bottom of the shaft and climb up to its opening, it would have to come through the submerged tunnel that ran through the bedrock to the open sea, and only an aquatic creature would be capable of this. Where the tunnel's other endpoint emerged from the shoreline, and at what depth below the waves, that he could not hope to discover.

His exploration had come to an end, and so Cyrus Smith climbed to the top again, pulled in the ladder, and covered the opening; then, lost in thought, he wandered back into the great room, saying to himself:

"I saw nothing, and yet something is there!"

XII

The Rigging of the Boat.—An Attack of Culpeos.—Joop Wounded.—Joop's Convalescence.—Joop Healed.—The Boat Is Finished.—Pencroff's Triumph.—The Bonadventure.*— Maiden Voyage South of the Island.—A Surprising Message.*

The hunters returned triumphant that evening with as much game as four men can carry, their legs literally buckling under the weight of their catch. Top had a string of pintails around his neck, and Joop was belted with snipes.

"Look here, master," cried Neb, "here's something to help us pass the time! Pâtés, hams, many fine meals in store! But someone will have to help me. I'm counting on you, Pencroff."

"No, Neb," the sailor answered. "I've got to rig the boat. You'll have to make do without me."

"What about you, Mr. Harbert?"

"Well, I've got to go to the sheepfold tomorrow," the boy answered.

"So, Mr. Spilett, you're the one who's going to help me!"

"Anything to oblige you, Neb," the reporter answered. "But I must warn you, if you reveal your recipes to me, I shall most certainly publish them."

"As you like, Mr. Spilett," Neb answered, "as you like!"

And so it was that the next day Gideon Spilett entered Neb's culinary laboratory as his humble assistant. Not long before, the engineer had revealed to Spilett the results of the previous day's explorations, and the reporter found himself in complete agreement with Cyrus Smith: despite the lack of evidence, there was clearly some mystery about the shaft that would have to be uncovered!

The cold persisted for another week, and the colonists never set foot outside Granite House except to repair the damage at the poultry yard. Their house was suffused with delectable aromas emanating from the kitchen, where Neb and the reporter were still hard at work. Nevertheless, only a portion of their catch was put up as preserves, for in this cold weather the game would be very slow to spoil. Thus they enjoyed many meals of fresh wild duck and other fowl, which were deemed superior to any other aquatic birds in the known world.

Pencroff now enlisted Harbert to help him sew the sails for their boat. Harbert proved a dab hand with a sailmaker's needle, and by week's end the two diligent workers had finished the sails. The rigging from the balloon offered all the hemp rope they needed. The cables and ropes from the net were made of a fine cord, which the sailor put to good use. The sails were edged with strong boltropes, leaving a plentiful supply left over for the halyards, shrouds, sheets, etc. Cyrus Smith used his lathe to make the pulleys, under Pencroff's guidance, and soon the rigging was ready, well before the boat itself was finished. Pencroff even sewed a red, white, and blue flag, deriving the colors from certain dye-producing plants that grew abundantly on the island. American yachts fly a flag with thirty-seven shining stars, representing the thirty-seven states of the Union; to his flag, however, the sailor added a thirty-eighth, the star of "the state of Lincoln," for he considered his island a part of the great republic.

"It's already a state in spirit," he liked to say, "if not yet by law!"

In the meantime, the flag was displayed in the central window of Granite House, and the colonists saluted it with three hurrahs.

The cold season was now nearing its end, and the colonists were beginning to believe that this second winter would pass by without serious incident; but then, during the night of August 11th, an invasion of Longview Plateau threatened to devastate their crops and poultry yard.

The colonists were sleeping soundly after a very full day, when, at around four o'clock in the morning, they were suddenly awakened by the sound of Top's bark.

They found the dog not circling the shaft, but at the entrance to Granite House, throwing himself against the door as if he wanted to break it down. Joop shrieked savagely all the while.

"Why, Top!" cried Neb, who was the first one awake.

But the dog only barked with greater fury.

"What is it?" asked Cyrus Smith.

They hastily threw on their clothes, ran to the windows, and opened the shutters.

A thick blanket of snow covered the ground, faintly white in the darkness. The colonists saw nothing, but a series of strange barks resounded through the still night air. The beach had clearly been invaded by animals, but what sort of animals, and how many, the colonists could not say.

"What is it?" cried Pencroff.

"Wolves, or jaguars, or monkeys!" answered Neb.

"Damnation! There's nothing stopping them from climbing up to the plateau!"

"What will happen to our poultry yard," cried Harbert, "and our fields?..."

"How did they get here?" asked Pencroff.

"Probably by the bridge on the beach," the engineer answered. "One of us must have forgotten to raise it."

"You're right," said Spilett, "I remember leaving it down..."

"Well, thank you very much, Mr. Spilett!" cried the sailor.

"What's done is done," answered Cyrus Smith. "We must counter this attack—nothing else matters for now!"

Such was the quick exchange of questions and answers between Cyrus Smith and his companions. It was clear that the bridge had been crossed, that the beach had been invaded by animals, and that the latter, whatever they were, could easily reach the plateau by the left bank of the Mercy. The colonists did not have a moment to lose: they would have to confront the beasts at once, and, if need be, fight them off.

"But what sort of animals are they?" someone asked again, as the barks grew still fiercer and louder.

This sound sent a shiver down Harbert's spine, for he had heard it before, during his first visit to the source of Red Creek.

"They're culpeos—they're foxes!" he said.

"Forward!" cried the sailor.

And taking up their hatchets, rifles, and revolvers, they raced into the elevator and descended to the beach.

A large pack of hungry culpeos is a fearsome and redoubtable foe. Nevertheless, the colonists threw themselves unhesitatingly into their midst, and a volley of gunshots soon repelled the first wave of assailants, piercing the dark night with brief, blinding flashes of light.

It was vitally important that the marauders be kept away from

Longview Plateau, for if they discovered the defenseless wheat fields and poultry yard, the result would be catastrophic. The wheat field, particularly, might never recover from the damage they would wreak. And since Longview Plateau could only be reached by the left bank of the Mercy, the colonists would have to position themselves on the narrow stretch of land between the river and the granite wall, and fight off the foxes at all costs.

This same thought flashed through every colonist's mind, and, on an order from Cyrus Smith, they hurried to the designated spot, with the band of foxes bounding through the darkness behind them.

Cyrus Smith, Gideon Spilett, Harbert, Pencroff, and Neb positioned themselves to form an impenetrable barrier. Top ran on ahead, his formidable jaws wide open, with Joop on his heels brandishing a knotty branch like a bludgeon.

The darkness was profound. They had only briefly glimpsed their assailants by the light of the gunshots. No doubt several culpeos had been hit by their fire. Nevertheless, there might easily have been a hundred such beasts, and their eyes shone like hot embers.

"We can't let them get through!" cried Pencroff.

"They will not get through!" the engineer replied.

But if they did not get through, it would not be for lack of trying. The foxes at the back of the pack pushed the first ones forward, and there ensued an interminable melee of revolver shots and ax blows. The ground must already have been littered with fox cadavers, but the horde surged forward undiminished, as if an endless column of reinforcements were pouring over the little bridge on the beach.

Soon the colonists were reduced to fighting the foxes hand to hand, so to speak. They could not hope to emerge from this battle unscathed, but fortunately their wounds were slight. A culpeo pounced on Neb's back, just as an Australian quoll might do, of which Harbert delivered him with a shot from his revolver. Top fought furiously, leaping at the foxes' throats and crushing them between his jaws. Joop would not allow himself to be held back, and rained savage blows on all sides. His sharp eyes must have been able to penetrate the darkness, for he was ever in the thick of the combat, and sometimes let out a shrill whistle, as he often did to express great joy. Indeed, at one point he threw himself into the fray with such abandon that the flash of a gun muzzle revealed him surrounded by five or six enormous culpeos, fighting them off with remarkable coolness.

Eventually the battle turned to the colonists' advantage, but only after two hours of stubborn resistance! Finally the assailants retreated, no doubt urged on by the first glimmers of dawn. They hurtled off to the north, once again crossing the bridge, which Neb hurried to raise behind them.

Once the light of the sun had illuminated the battleground, the colonists counted some fifty corpses strewn over the beach.

"What about Joop?" cried Pencroff. "Where's Joop?"

Joop had disappeared. His friend Neb shouted his name, and for the first time Joop did not answer his call.

They began a search for Joop, trembling at the thought that they might find him among the dead. They separated the piled corpses, dragging them through the bloodstained snow, and found Joop lying beneath a veritable mound of culpeos, whose shattered jaws and broken backs bore witness to the terrible force of the intrepid ape's bludgeon. Poor Joop was still clutching the stump of his broken stick; seeing him disarmed, the horde must have set upon him with renewed fury, for his breast was scarred by deep, slashing wounds.

"He's alive!" cried Neb, kneeling over him.

"And we'll save him," the sailor answered, "we'll care for him just as if he were one of us!"

Joop seemed to understand these words. He rested his head on Pencroff's shoulder as if in thanks. The sailor himself was wounded, as were they all, but not seriously, for their firearms had kept most of the assailants at bay. Only the orangutan was gravely hurt.

Neb and Pencroff carried Joop to the elevator, and scarcely did a single quiet moan escape his lips. They gently brought him into Granite House. There they laid him on a mattress from one of the bunks, and cleaned his wounds with great care. The vital organs appeared undamaged, but Joop was greatly weakened by the loss of blood, and he was now running a high fever.

They laid him down, then, and after bandaging his wounds they put him on a strict diet, "like for a natural-born person," said Neb, and they gave him several cups of a restorative tisane, drawn from the vegetal pharmacy of Granite House.

Joop now fell into a restless slumber; but little by little his breathing became more regular, and they let him rest, taking every precaution to

Top came to visit his friend.

avoid disturbing him. From time to time, walking "on tiptoe," we might say, Top came to visit his friend, and seemed satisfied with the care he was being given. One of Joop's hands hung over the side of his bed, and Top licked it with an air of deep contrition.

That morning the colonists set about cleaning up the beach, dragging the bodies to the Forests of the Far West and burying them deep within the earth.

This attack could have had serious consequences indeed. The colonists took it as a lesson, and vowed never again to sleep before one of them had verified that the bridges were raised, and that invasion of their lands was impossible.

Joop's condition alarmed them greatly for a few days, but soon his body found the strength to combat the infection. His strong constitution triumphed in the end; the fever gradually diminished, and Gideon Spilett drew on his practical medical expertise to pronounce him out of danger.

Joop began to eat again on August 16th. Neb made some fine little sweetmeats for him, and the patient greedily bolted them down, for if he had a small weakness it was a slight tendency to gluttony, a failing that Neb had never attempted to correct.

"What can I do?" he often said to Gideon Spilett, who sometimes reproached him for spoiling the orangutan. "Food is poor Joop's only pleasure, and I'm only too happy to repay him for all he's done!"

On August 21st, ten days after taking to his bed, Master Joop arose at last. His wounds had healed, and he would not be slow to recover his customary vigor and agility. Like all convalescents, he was gripped by a ravenous hunger, and the reporter let him eat all he pleased, trusting in the animal's instinct—all too often absent in sentient beings—to protect him against excess. Neb was delighted to see his pupil's appetite return.

"Eat," he said to him, "eat, my friend Joop, take anything you like! You shed your blood for us, and it's the least I can do to help you get it back!"

Finally, on August 25th, Neb was heard calling to his companions.

"Mr. Cyrus, Mr. Gideon, Mr. Harbert, Pencroff, come quick!"

The colonists were sitting in the great room; hearing Neb's call, they leaped to their feet and raced to join him.

"What is it?" asked the reporter.

"Look!" answered Neb, with a great, resounding laugh.

And what did they see? Master Joop, squatting like a Turk in the doorway of Granite House, calmly and gravely smoking a pipe!

"My pipe!" cried Pencroff. "He's taken my pipe! Oh, my fine friend Joop, it's yours! Smoke, my friend, smoke!"

And Joop ceremoniously exhaled a thick cloud of tobacco, which seemed to give him a pleasure without equal.

Cyrus Smith showed no great astonishment at this incident, citing numerous other examples of domesticated apes habituated to the use of tobacco.

But from that day onward, Master Joop had a pipe of his own—the sailor's ex-pipe—which he hung on the wall of his room next to his tobacco. He filled it himself, lighting it with a glowing ember, and seemed to be the happiest of all quadrumanes. As we might well believe, this shared enthusiasm only strengthened the close bonds of friendship uniting the worthy ape and the good sailor.

"Sometimes you'd think he was a man like you or me," Pencroff said to Neb from time to time. "Would you be surprised to find him talking to us one day?"

"Oh my, no!" Neb answered. "I'm only surprised he doesn't talk now, because that's the only thing he can't do!"

"Still, I'd find it very amusing," the sailor went on, "if one fine day he asked me 'What do you say we trade pipes, Pencroff!' "

"Yes," answered Neb. "Too bad he was born dumb!"

September marked the long-awaited end of winter, and now the colonists earnestly took up their work again.

Considerable progress was made on their boat. With the planking done, the next step was to install the interior ribs, which hold the hull together and solidify its structure. Steam was used to help them bend the beams, and with these in place another crucial stage in the process was complete.

Given their plentiful supply of wood, Pencroff suggested that the interior of the hull be lined with a watertight inner planking, to make their boat as sturdy as she could possibly be.

Never knowing what the future might bring, Cyrus Smith heartily approved of the sailor's idea to make the safest boat they knew how to make.

The inner planking and the deck were completed around September 15th. Now the seams would have to be caulked, and so they made oakum from dried eelgrass. Using mallets, they pounded the oakum into the joints of the hull, the inner planking, and the deck, then painted the seams with hot tar, generously offered to them by the pines in the forest.

The final steps in the construction were extremely simple. First the boat was ballasted with heavy pieces of granite—some twelve thousand pounds' worth, set into a bed of lime. A lower deck was laid over that ballast, and the boat's interior was divided into two cabins, whose sidewalls were lined with benches that also served as storage chests. The foot of the mast would shore up the interior wall between the two cabins, which could be entered by two hatchways cut into the deck and fitted with protective covers.

Pencroff had no difficulty finding a suitable tree for the mast. He chose a young pine, very straight, without knots; he had only to square off its base and round off its head. The iron fittings for the mast, rudder, and hull had been forged at the Chimneys; their appearance was somewhat crude, but they were wonderfully strong and sturdy. The rest was finished by the first week of October—yards, topmast, boom, spars, oars, etc.— and plans were made for a trial run in the immediate vicinity of the island, to gauge their new boat's seaworthiness and determine whether they could entrust her with their lives.

Their daily labors were never neglected while all this was going on. The sheepfold was expanded, for the herd of mouflons and goats now included a number of young that had to be fed and housed. Nor had the colonists failed to visit the oyster bed, the warren, the coal and iron deposits, and certain previously unexplored regions of the Far West forests, home to yet more game with which to stock their kitchens.

Two new native plants were discovered, of no immediate use perhaps, but nevertheless a welcome contribution to Granite House's fine and varied store of vegetables. They were both a variety of ficoid; one had fleshy edible leaves, like those found on the cape, and the seeds of the other could be used to produce a sort of flour.

The boat was finally launched on October 10th. Pencroff beamed in delight. Their undertaking was a complete success. The craft, now fully rigged, was pushed to the water's edge on rollers, then lifted by the rising tide; soon, to the applause of the colonists, it was afloat. Pencroff applauded louder than the rest, abandoning every pretense of modesty for the moment. And his vanity was soon to be flattered yet again, for now that he had constructed the boat, he would be called upon to command it. By common consent, he was awarded the rank of captain.

At Captain Pencroff's insistence, they now had to find a name for their craft. Several suggestions were made, and after a long discussion the vote

The boat was finally launched on October 10th.

went unanimously to the *Bonadventure,* which was the good sailor's Christian name.

As the *Bonadventure* bobbed on the water in the rising tide, they could see that its waterline was perfectly even, and that it would sail untroubled no matter what the trim.

And that judgment would be put to the test this very day with an excursion through the island's waters. The weather was fine, the wind fresh, and the sea calm, especially off the southern coast, for the wind had been blowing from the northwest for the past hour.

"Come aboard! come aboard!" cried Captain Pencroff.

But their excursion would have to wait until after breakfast, and further provisions would have to be brought on board in case they decided to prolong the journey until nightfall.

Cyrus Smith was every bit as impatient as Pencroff. He was the author of the boat's design, although he had modified his plans many times at the sailor's suggestion; nevertheless, his faith in their craft was not as entire as Pencroff's. The sailor had not spoken of the trip to Tabor Island for some time now, and Cyrus Smith had begun to hope that he had given up on the idea. For it pained him deeply to think of two or three of his companions sailing off on that boat—such a small boat, in the end, weighing no more than fifteen tons.

By ten-thirty everyone was on board, even Joop, even Top. Neb and Harbert pulled the anchor from the sands at the mouth of the Mercy, the spanker was raised, the flag of Lincoln fluttered gaily atop the mast, and the *Bonadventure* put out to sea, with Pencroff at the helm.

They had to run before the wind in order to leave Union Bay, and they judged the speed of the vessel quite satisfactory in such conditions.

Rounding Flotsam Point and Cape Claw, Pencroff followed along the southern coastline, sailing close-hauled. He tacked this way and that a few times, observing that the *Bonadventure* could easily keep a course within about five points of the wind, with no tendency to drift. She came about like a dream, for she was yare, as sailors say, and gained ground even as she tacked.

The passengers of the *Bonadventure* were genuinely enchanted. What a fine craft this was! And how invaluable such a boat might prove! And on a day as fine as this, with these ideal winds, the excursion could not fail to delight.

Pencroff turned away from the island until they were some three or four miles from shore, with Port Balloon abeam. From here they could see the island in its entirety, as they never had before: the whole varied panorama of the coastline, from Cape Claw to Reptile End, and beyond that the forests, where the conifers contrasted with the budding foliage of the surrounding trees, and finally, looking down on it all, Mount Franklin, still crowned with white by the last lingering snows.

"How beautiful!" cried Harbert.

"Yes, our island is beautiful and good," answered Pencroff. "I love her like I loved my poor mother! Our island took us in when we were bereft, when we had nothing; and has she ever failed the five children who fell from the sky that day?"

"Never!" answered Neb. "Never, captain!"

And the two fine fellows let out three great hurrahs in honor of their island!

In the meantime, Gideon Spilett sat with his back against the mast and sketched the panorama that lay before him.

Cyrus Smith stared in silence.

"Well, Mr. Cyrus," asked Pencroff, "what do you think of our boat?"

"She seems to handle well," the engineer replied.

"Yes indeed! And now do you believe she's ready for a real voyage?"

"What sort of voyage, Pencroff?"

"To Tabor Island, for instance?"

"My friend," answered Cyrus Smith, "I would gladly entrust my life to the *Bonadventure* in case of emergency, even for a longer journey than you now propose; but as you well know, there's no pressing need for a trip to Tabor Island, and I would be greatly distressed to see you attempt it."

"It's always nice to know who your neighbors are," Pencroff answered, still clinging to his idea. "Tabor Island is our neighbor—our only neighbor! Common courtesy requires us to go and pay a call, at least!"

"Well, what do you think of that!" said Gideon Spilett. "Suddenly our friend Pencroff is a stickler for the social niceties!"

"I'm not a stickler for anything at all," the sailor shot back, slightly put out at the engineer's opposition but reluctant to cause him any pain.

"Remember, Pencroff," Cyrus Smith answered, "there's no way you can go to Tabor Island alone."

"I'll only need one companion."

"I see," the engineer answered. "So that makes two of the five colonists we might well lose forever?"

"Six colonists!" Pencroff answered. "You're forgetting Joop."

"Seven!" added Neb. "Top's as good as any of us!"

"There's no danger, Mr. Cyrus," Pencroff resumed.

"That's possible, Pencroff; but I'm telling you again that you would be needlessly risking your life!"

The obstinate sailor did not answer; there he let the matter drop, fully intending to return to it later. Little did he know that his argument was about to be bolstered by an incident that would make a humanitarian mission of what was otherwise no more than a whim, and a rather questionable one at that.

For after standing offshore for a time, the *Bonadventure* returned toward the coast, heading for Port Balloon. Their plan was to survey the layout of the channels through the shoals and sandbars, and perhaps to mark them out, for this little cove was to be the boat's home port.

They were only a half-mile from shore, tacking to remain ahead of the wind. Their speed had slowed somewhat, for the breeze was partially blocked by the highlands, and scarcely filled the *Bonadventure*'s sails. The sea was as smooth as glass, only occasionally rippled by an unpredictable little breeze dancing by.

Harbert was standing in the bow, pointing out the route through the channels, when suddenly he cried out:

"Luff, Pencroff, luff!"

"What is it?" the sailor answered, standing up. "A rock?"

"No...wait," said Harbert. "...I can't quite see...luff again...that's good...bear away a little..."

And with this Harbert lay down at the edge of the deck, suddenly thrust his arm into the water, and leaped to his feet again, saying:

"A bottle!"

He had plucked a sealed bottle from the water, several cable-lengths from shore.

Cyrus Smith took it from his hands. Silently he pulled the cork, drew out a damp piece of paper, and read the following words:

"Shipwrecked...a castaway on Tabor Island: 153° W. long.—37° 11′ S. lat."

XIII

*The Departure Now Decided.—Hypotheses.—Preparations.—
The Three Passengers.—First Night.—Second Night.—Tabor
Island.—A Search of the Beach.—A Search of the Forest.—No
One.—Animals.—Plants.—A House.—Deserted.*

"A castaway!" cried Pencroff. "All alone, a hundred miles away on Tabor Island! Oh! Mr. Cyrus, you can't refuse me now!"

"No, Pencroff," answered Cyrus Smith. "You must sail to Tabor Island as soon as you possibly can."

"Tomorrow?"

"Tomorrow."

The engineer still held the paper he had found in the bottle. For several moments he stared at it in silence; then:

"From this message, my friends," he said, "simply from the manner in which it is written, we may draw the following conclusions. First, the castaway of Tabor Island has some experience as a seafarer, since he has given us the island's latitude and longitude down to the minute, precisely as they appear in our atlas. Second, he is an American or an Englishman, since the message is written in the English language."

"That seems perfectly logical," answered Gideon Spilett. "Furthermore, the existence of this castaway might well explain the sudden appearance of the crate. If there is a castaway, there was clearly a shipwreck. And whoever that castaway may be, he may thank his lucky stars that Pencroff thought of building a boat, and that this was the day we chose for her maiden voyage. One day later, the bottle might have shattered against the shoals."

"Indeed," said Harbert. "What a stroke of luck that the bottle happened to be floating just in the *Bonadventure's* path!"

"And you don't find that odd?" Cyrus Smith asked Pencroff.

"I find it fortunate, nothing more," the sailor answered. "Surely you don't see anything out of the ordinary in all this, Mr. Cyrus? The bottle had to go somewhere, and this is as good a place as any!"

"Perhaps you're right, Pencroff," the engineer replied. "All the same..."

"But," Harbert observed, "there's no proof that the bottle has been floating in the ocean for any length of time."

"None," Gideon Spilett answered. "In fact, by the look of it, this note seems to have been written quite recently. What do you think, Cyrus?"

"It's difficult to say with any certainty. In any case, we shall soon find out!" Cyrus Smith replied.

Pencroff had not remained idle during this conversation. He had turned the boat about, and now the *Bonadventure* found herself on a broad reach, speeding toward Cape Claw with all sails unfurled. Thoughts of the castaway occupied every colonist's mind. Would they be able to rescue him in time? A great event in the colonists' lives! They were castaways themselves, but they knew that not every castaway could be as fortunate as they, and they were duty-bound to assist those in distress in any way they could.

Soon they rounded Cape Claw, and by four o'clock the *Bonadventure* was moored at the mouth of the Mercy.

That evening they settled the details of the next day's expedition. Pencroff and Harbert were both practiced in the art of sailing, and so it was resolved that they would make this voyage alone. If they left the following day, October 11th, they would arrive after daylight on the thirteenth, for with the current wind conditions it could take no more than forty-eight hours to make the one-hundred-fifty-mile crossing. One day on the island, three or four for the return trip: they would be expected back at Lincoln Island on the seventeenth. The weather was fine, the barometer rising steadily, and the winds seemed unlikely to shift. Fortune was smiling on the worthy colonists as they prepared for this mission of mercy.

It had been agreed that Cyrus Smith, Neb, and Gideon Spilett would remain at Granite House, but now this decision was contested. Ever the conscientious reporter for the *New York Herald,* Gideon Spilett declared that he would sooner swim to Tabor Island than let such an opportunity pass by; at his insistence, then, it was decided that he would board the *Bonadventure* along with his two companions.

The evening was spent loading the boat with bedding, utensils, weapons, ammunition, a compass, and some eight days' provisions. Soon their work was done, and once more the elevator lifted the colonists to the front door of Granite House.

At five o'clock the next morning they said their farewells, not without a certain emotion on all sides. Then Pencroff filled his sails and set off in the direction of Cape Claw, which he would round before turning due southwest for the island.

The *Bonadventure* was already a quarter-mile from shore when her passengers saw two men standing atop Granite House, waving goodbye. It was Cyrus Smith and Neb.

"Our friends!" cried Gideon Spilett. "The first time we've been apart in fifteen months!..."

Pencroff, the reporter, and Harbert made one last sign of farewell, and Granite House soon disappeared behind the high rocks of the cape.

For the first few hours of the journey, the *Bonadventure* remained within view of Lincoln Island's southern coast, now reduced to a mere blanket of greenery with Mount Franklin rising from its middle. Seen from this distance, the island could not appear particularly attractive to passing ships.

At around one o'clock they lay some ten miles off Reptile End. From there to the flanks of Mount Franklin, the western coastline was now virtually invisible; three hours later, all trace of Lincoln Island had vanished behind the horizon.

The *Bonadventure* sailed like a dream. Its prow lifted easily over the waves, and the sailors made rapid progress. Pencroff had rigged the topsail, and with the wind at their backs they sped due southwest, frequently checking their heading with the compass.

From time to time Harbert relieved Pencroff at the helm, and the boy proved a first-rate steersman. Not a single yaw would have escaped Pencroff's critical eye, but under Harbert's steady hand the boat sailed straight and true.

Gideon Spilett chatted sometimes with one, sometimes with the other, readily lending a hand when required. Captain Pencroff could not have been more pleased with his crew, and promised "tankards of wine all around" as a reward for their excellent service!

It was Cyrus Smith and Neb.

The moon would not be at first quarter until the sixteenth; only a slender crescent appeared in the last gleams of the setting sun, and soon faded from sight. The night was dark, but the sky was full of stars, and the next day promised to be fine.

Pencroff now took the precaution of striking the topsail, lest a sudden freshening of the wind catch them with sails at the masthead—perhaps an unnecessarily prudent measure to take on a night as calm as this, but Pencroff preferred to avoid undue risk, and his companions could not blame him.

The reporter slept for part of the night. Pencroff and Harbert took turns at the helm every two hours. The sailor trusted Harbert as entirely as he trusted himself, and the boy's cool clear-headedness never let him down. Pencroff called out the bearing, just as a commander does to his helmsman, and Harbert never strayed from it by so much as an inch.

The night passed peacefully, and the day of October 12th went by in the same way. They carefully maintained their southwesterly course all day, and, barring some unexpected current, the way was clear to Tabor Island, dead ahead.

The seas were utterly deserted. Now and then an albatross or a frigate bird passed within range of their rifles, and each time Gideon Spilett could not help but wonder if it might be the one carrying his chronicle for the *New York Herald.* In any case, birds seemed to be the only living things that frequented the waters between Tabor Island and Lincoln Island.

"And to think," Harbert observed, "at this time of the year the whaling ships should all be heading for the South Pacific! I've never seen an ocean as empty as this!"

"It's not as deserted as all that!" answered Pencroff.

"How do you mean?" asked the reporter.

"Well, we're here, aren't we? Do you take our boat for a wreck, and our persons for porpoises?"

And Pencroff laughed at his own quip.

That evening they calculated that the *Bonadventure* had traveled a distance of one hundred twenty miles since casting off from Lincoln Island thirty-six hours before, which indicated a speed of three and one third miles per hour. The winds were slight, and seemed to be calming. Nevertheless, if their estimations were accurate and their heading true, they could rightly hope to cast their eyes on Tabor Island at dawn the next day.

For this reason, none of them slept the night of October 12th, trembling with anticipation as they waited for sunrise. So many uncertainties hung over their present endeavor! Were they near Tabor Island? Was the island still inhabited by the castaway they had come to rescue? And who was this man? Might his presence introduce an instability into the colony's daily life, hitherto so harmonious? Indeed, would he consent to exchange his current prison for another? Sleep was impossible as they awaited the answers to these many questions, and the first glimmers of dawn found them feverishly scanning the horizon.

"Land ho!" cried Pencroff at about six o'clock in the morning.

And if Pencroff's unerring eye had spotted land, then land was unquestionably there.

Imagine the joy that now gripped the crew of the *Bonadventure*! A few hours to go, and they would be standing on the islet's shore!

The low coastline of Tabor Island lay some fifteen miles ahead, scarcely visible over the crests of the waves. The sailors corrected their bearing, for the *Bonadventure*'s current course would take it slightly south of the island. As the sun rose in the east a number of scattered hilltops appeared, silhouetted against the clear blue sky.

"It's only an islet, much smaller than Lincoln Island," Harbert observed. "It must have been formed by an upthrust of the seabed."

By eleven o'clock in the morning the *Bonadventure* was only two miles offshore, and Pencroff searched for a safe passage to land, sailing with all possible prudence through these unknown waters.

They could now see the whole of the islet, crowned with the greenery of gum trees and other tall trees, much like those on Lincoln Island. To their surprise, however, no plume of smoke rose heavenward to show that the island was inhabited, no signal appeared at any point along the shore!

And yet the message they had found left no doubt: there was a castaway here, who should have been on the lookout for approaching ships!

Meanwhile, the *Bonadventure* followed a rather sinuous channel through the shoals, with Pencroff very attentively observing every curve and bend. He had given Harbert the helm while he stood in the bow, eyes glued to the water, the halyard in his hand, ready to strike the sail at any moment. Gideon Spilett held the spyglass to his eye, scanning the entire shoreline but finding nothing.

Finally, at about noon, the stem of the *Bonadventure* ran onto a sandy beach. The anchor was dropped, and the little craft's crew came ashore.

There could be no doubt that this was indeed Tabor Island, for the most recent maps showed no other land in this area of the Pacific, from New Zealand to the American coastline.

Their boat was made fast so that the tide would not carry it out to sea; then Pencroff and his two companions armed themselves and climbed up the beach toward a sort of mound, two hundred fifty to three hundred feet tall, a half-mile from shore.

"From the top of that hill," said Gideon Spilett, "we'll have a good view over the island, which will greatly speed our search."

"In other words," said Harbert, "we'll do just what Mr. Cyrus first did on Lincoln Island, when he climbed Mount Franklin."

"Precisely," the reporter answered. "I can think of no better way to proceed!"

And as they talked the explorers wended their way through a meadow that led to the very foot of the mound. Flocks of rock doves and sea swallows, similar to those of Lincoln Island, fled as they approached. To their left lay an area of dense forest, and the rustling of the undergrowth and trembling of the tall grasses betrayed the presence of large numbers of reclusive animals; but nothing so far suggested that the islet was inhabited.

Soon they had reached the foot of the mound, and a few moments later they stood at its summit, sweeping the horizon with their gaze.

They were indeed on an islet, no more than six miles across. Its form was that of an elongated oval, altered only here and there by a jutting cape or promontory, only rarely indented by a cove or inlet. An empty sea surrounded it, stretching off to the very edges of the heavens. No other patch of land, not a single sail in sight!

The islet was heavily wooded from one end to the other, but its appearance was far less diverse than that of Lincoln Island. It was not arid and wild in one area and rich and fertile in another; it was simply a uniform mass of greenery overlooked by two or three low hills. A stream ran diagonally across the oval, flowing over a broad plain and emptying into the sea by way of a narrow mouth on the western shore.

"None too large," said Harbert.

"Yes," answered Pencroff, "it would have been a bit small for us!"

"And furthermore," the reporter replied, "it doesn't seem to be inhabited."

"Indeed," Harbert answered, "I see no sign of any human presence."

"Let's go back down and have a look," said Pencroff.

The sailor and his two companions returned to the shore, where they had left the *Bonadventure*. They decided to walk the perimeter of the islet before venturing into the interior, so that not a single point would escape their investigations.

An occasional pile of boulders blocked their way as they walked along the beach, but they had no difficulty finding a way around them. The explorers followed the shoreline southward, and with every step they scattered great flocks of birds before them, and sent whole herds of seals scurrying into the sea.

"This is not the first time these animals have seen men," the reporter observed. "They fear us, so they must have seen our like before."

An hour later the three men came to the narrow cape at the southern end of the islet; now they turned northward along the western shore, still formed of sand and boulders, with a line of dense forest in the background.

After four hours, they had walked the entire perimeter of the island. Nowhere did they find any trace of human habitation, nowhere the print of any human foot.

They found this curious, to say the least, and were led to conclude that Tabor Island was never or was no longer inhabited. The message they had found might after all have been written months or years before, and if so, the castaway might have been repatriated, or might have since died.

Pencroff, Gideon Spilett, and Harbert had a quick dinner on board the *Bonadventure*. The conversation never strayed from the mystery of the castaway's existence; they were eager to resume their search, and to continue until darkness fell.

They set out again at five o'clock in the evening, this time heading into the woods.

Once again, their approach set off a small stampede of wild animals, primarily—one could even say uniquely—goats and pigs, visibly of European origin. No doubt some whaling ship had brought them here, and they had quickly multiplied. Harbert vowed to capture two or three pairs of these beasts and bring them back to Lincoln Island.

Men had thus visited this islet at some point. They grew ever more convinced of this as they made their way into the forest, for now they found trails, trees that had been felled with an ax, and other signs of human activity; but the rotting trunks had toppled many years before, the gashes left by the ax were now velveted with moss, and the grass grew long and thick over the trails, soon to obliterate them entirely.

"Nevertheless," Gideon Spilett observed, "this proves not only that men have come ashore on this island, but also that they lived here for some time. Who were these men? How many were there? How many remain?"

"The message we found speaks of only one castaway," said Harbert.

"Well, if he's still on the island," answered Pencroff, "we can't possibly fail to find him!"

Thus they pursued their explorations. The sailor and his companions followed a path that cut diagonally across the islet, and soon found themselves beside the stream that flowed toward the sea.

The European animals, like the trails and ax marks, proved that man had come to this island before; and now this hypothesis was bolstered by evidence from the vegetal kingdom, for here and there the explorers found clearings where crops had been planted some time in the past.

Imagine Harbert's joy at finding potatoes, chicory, sorrel, carrots, cabbages, turnips—welcome additions to the gardens of Lincoln Island, and he had only to collect the seeds!

"Very nice indeed!" cried Pencroff. "A great pleasure for Neb, and for us as well. If we don't find the castaway, at least our voyage won't have been for naught. God will have rewarded us for our pains!"

"To be sure," answered Gideon Spilett; "but from the condition of these vegetable plots, it seems very likely that the islet has not been inhabited for a great while."

"That's true," answered Harbert. "They would surely be better tended than this if someone were still here!"

"Yes!" said Pencroff. "The castaway is gone!... That's the only explanation..."

"So we must assume that the message in the bottle was written long ago?"

"Clearly."

"And that the bottle reached Lincoln Island only after several years in the waters of the sea?"

"Why not?" Pencroff answered. "But night's coming on," he added, "and I think we'd best break off the search."

"Let's go back to the boat, and tomorrow we'll start afresh," said the reporter.

This was indeed the wisest course of action, and they were about to turn around when Harbert, pointing at a vague form between the trees, cried:

"A house!"

The three explorers hurried toward it. In the fading light, they saw that the house was built of planks covered with thick, tar-soaked canvas.

The door was ajar. Pencroff pushed it open, and quickly stepped inside...

The house was empty!

XIV

Inventory.—Night.—Letters.—The Search Continues.—Plants and Animals.—Harbert in Danger.—On Board.—Casting Off.—Bad Weather.—A Glimmer of Instinct.—Lost at Sea.—A Fire Opportunely Lit.

Pencroff, Harbert, and Gideon Spilett stood silent in the darkness.

Pencroff loudly called out.

No answer came.

The sailor then struck his flint and lit a twig. Its brief light revealed a small room, apparently abandoned. At one end stood a crude fireplace, with an armload of wood piled atop a bed of cold ashes. Pencroff threw his burning twig into the fireplace, and the wood caught fire at once, crackling as it cast a bright glow over the room.

Now the sailor and his two companions saw an unmade bed whose damp, yellowed covers bore witness to a long period of disuse; to one side of the fireplace, two rusty kettles and an overturned pot; a cabinet containing a few moldering articles of sailor's clothing; on the table, a tin plate and a Bible slowly rotting in the humid air; in one corner, a few tools, shovel, pickax, pick, and two hunting rifles, one of them broken; on a plank that served as a shelf, a keg of powder, still full, a keg of lead shot, and several boxes of caps—all of this covered with what appeared to be several years' accumulation of dust.

"There's no one here," said the reporter.

"No one!" Pencroff replied.

"This room was abandoned a long time ago," Harbert observed.

"Yes, a very long time ago!" the reporter answered.

"Mr. Spilett," said Pencroff, "I think we might do better to spend the night in this house instead of going back to the boat."

"You're right, Pencroff," Gideon Spilett answered, "and if the owner comes back, well! perhaps he won't be so unhappy to find someone's taken his place!"

"He won't come back!" said the sailor, shaking his head.

"You think he's left the island?" the reporter asked.

"If he'd left the island, he would have taken his weapons and tools with him," Pencroff replied. "You know how a castaway values the last remnants of his wrecked ship. No! No!" the sailor repeated adamantly. "No! He never left the island! Even if he'd managed to build some sort of boat, he wouldn't have left all this behind. His survival would depend on it! No, he's here on the island!"

"Alive? ..." asked Harbert.

"Alive or dead. But if he's dead, I don't imagine he buried himself," Pencroff answered. "His remains are still here, if nothing else!"

And so they agreed to spend the night in the abandoned house. They found a supply of firewood in one corner, which would provide ample heat for the night. Shutting the door, Pencroff, Harbert, and Gideon Spilett sat down on a bench, speaking little but thinking a great deal. In their present state of mind nothing seemed impossible, nothing unimaginable, and they listened with rapt attention to the sounds outside. Despite the dwelling's abandoned air, they would not have been overly surprised to see the door thrown open to reveal a man standing before them on the threshold. How their hands yearned to press the hands of that man, that castaway, that unknown friend so eagerly awaited by friends!

But no sound was heard, the door did not open, and slowly the hours went by.

How long this night seemed to the sailor and his two companions! Harbert alone slept for two hours, for at his age sleep is indispensable. How great was their impatience to resume the search they had begun the day before, to comb the most secret recesses of the islet! Pencroff's deductions could not be refuted; since the house had been abandoned, and the tools, utensils, and weapons left behind, the occupant must surely have perished. The only thing to do was search for his remains and at least give his body a Christian burial.

The new day dawned, and Pencroff and his companions made a closer inspection of the house.

The site could not have been better chosen: at the foot of a small hill, in the shelter of five or six magnificent gum trees. An ax had been used to create a clearing before the front door, from which the sea could be glimpsed. A small lawn ran down to the shore, edged by a wooden fence now fallen into pieces. The mouth of the stream lay just to the left.

The house was built from planks that had clearly been pulled from the hull or deck of a ship. From this it could be deduced that a crippled vessel had run onto the island's shore, that at least one of its crew members had survived, and that this man had salvaged the necessary tools and used the ship's wreckage to build this dwelling.

This hypothesis was confirmed when Gideon Spilett, walking around the outside of the house, found a plank—no doubt from the prow of the ruined ship—bearing these letters, now half worn away:

BR.TAN..A

"*Britannia!*" cried Pencroff, when the reporter had called him to his side. "A common enough name for a ship, and I couldn't tell you if this one was English or American!"

"It hardly matters, Pencroff!"

"It hardly matters, you're right," the sailor answered. "We'll rescue the survivor no matter where he's from, assuming he's still alive! But before we start exploring again, let's go back to the *Bonadventure!*"

A sudden shiver of anxiety had run down Pencroff's spine as he thought of his boat sitting unattended on the beach. Suppose the island was inhabited after all, and suppose whoever lived here had taken...But no, this seemed really too unlikely, and he quickly shrugged the idea off.

Nevertheless, the sailor very much wanted to return to the boat for breakfast. She lay little more than a mile away, down an easy path through the woods. They began to walk, all the while carefully searching the undergrowth and the surrounding forests, and finding nothing but goats and pigs.

Twenty minutes after they had left the house, Pencroff and his companions were within sight of the islet's eastern shore, and of the *Bonadventure*, its anchor still sunk deep into the sand.

Pencroff could not hold back a sigh of relief. After all, this boat was his child, and surely a father can be forgiven the occasional bout of irrational anxiety.

They boarded their boat again and ate a copious breakfast, for they expected to dine quite late. The meal was soon over, and they returned to their exploration with renewed vigor.

They no longer doubted that the island's sole inhabitant had perished long before; the object of their search was now not so much a man as a body! Still they found nothing, however, and after a fruitless half-day hunt through the island's forests, they were forced to conclude that no trace would ever be found of the castaway's corpse, no doubt long since picked clean by wild animals.

"We'll cast off at first light tomorrow," said Pencroff to his two companions that afternoon, as they lay resting in the shade of a stand of pine trees.

"I believe we can take the castaway's tools with a clear conscience?" Harbert added.

"I believe so," answered Gideon Spilett, "and they'll be of great use to us at Granite House. As I remember, there was a good supply of lead and powder in the house."

"Right you are," answered Pencroff, "and we mustn't forget to capture two or three pairs of pigs. That's one thing Lincoln Island sorely lacks!..."

"Nor to collect some seeds," added Harbert. "With what we've found here, we'll soon have vegetables from the Old World as well as the New!"

"In that case," said the reporter, "perhaps we should extend our stay by a day, so that we can gather everything we might require."

"No, Mr. Spilett," Pencroff replied. "I'll ask you to be ready to leave at first light tomorrow. The breeze seems to be shifting to the west, and that's just the thing to speed us on our way. We had a fair wind to bring us here, and tomorrow we'll have a fair wind to take us home."

"Then let's waste no time!" said Harbert, standing up.

"Let's waste no time," Pencroff answered. "You, Harbert, you can gather the seeds, since you know them better than we do. In the meantime, Mr. Spilett and I will go on a pig hunt, and I wager we'll capture our share, even without Top to help us!"

And so they went their separate ways, Harbert toward the vegetable plots, the sailor and the reporter into the forest.

As they advanced, the hunters sent pigs fleeing in all directions, leaping nimbly through the undergrowth, seemingly terrified of men. A half-hour was spent in vain pursuit; they had just cornered a pair of them in a dense thicket when shouts suddenly erupted several hundred paces to the north. These cries were mingled with a horrible snarling sound, clearly not of human origin.

The sailor was readying his rope to hog-tie their catch, but now he and the reporter leaped to their feet, and the pigs, seizing the moment, immediately made good their escape.

"That's Harbert's voice!" said the reporter.

"Run!" cried Pencroff.

And the sailor and Gideon Spilett sped off toward the source of the shouting, as fast as their legs could carry them.

They arrived not a moment too soon. Rounding the final bend in the path, they discovered the boy laid out flat on the ground. Some sort of wild creature, an enormous ape no doubt, was crouched over him, about to strike a terrible blow.

It was but a moment's work for Pencroff and Gideon Spilett to throw themselves on this monster, cast it to the ground, pull Harbert from its grasp, and immobilize it. The sailor was a man of Herculean strength, the reporter very robust as well, and in spite of the monster's struggles it was soon bound so tightly that it could not make a single move.

"You're not hurt, Harbert?" asked Gideon Spilett.

"No! no!"

"Oh, if that ape had injured you!..." cried Pencroff.

"But he's not an ape!" answered Harbert.

Hearing these words, Pencroff and Gideon Spilett turned their gaze toward the strange creature at their feet.

It was true: this was no ape! It was a human creature—it was a man! But what a man! A wild man, in the full horrible sense of that word, all the more terrifying in that he seemed to have sunk to the very depths of brutishness!

Bristling hair, an unkempt beard down to his waist, naked but for a rag over his loins, wild eyes, enormous hands, extraordinarily long nails, skin as dark as mahogany, feet so calloused that they seemed to be made of horn: such was the wretched creature whom they nevertheless had to call a man! But well might they have wondered if a soul survived within that body, or if the wretch was animated only by the basest instincts of the beast!

"Are you quite sure that this is a man, or once was?" Pencroff asked the reporter.

"Alas, of that there's no doubt," he answered.

"So this is the castaway?" said Harbert.

"Yes," answered Gideon Spilett, "but the poor fellow has lost every last vestige of humanity!"

The reporter spoke the truth. If this castaway had ever been a civilized being, isolation had clearly made him a savage, and even, perhaps, a veritable wild man. A hoarse growl emerged from between his teeth, which were as sharp as any carnivore's, suited to raw meat and nothing more. He must have lost his memory long before, and with it the knowledge required to use his tools, his weapons—even the knowledge required to make fire! He was remarkably quick and agile, but clearly his moral qualities had atrophied as his physical prowess grew!

Gideon Spilett attempted to speak to him. He seemed not to understand, not even to hear ... And yet, looking deep into his eyes, the reporter thought he saw a small remaining glimmer of reason.

The prisoner neither struggled nor attempted to break his bonds. Had the sight of men—his former fellows—robbed him of his savagery? Had some fleeting memory in the recesses of his mind recalled to him his own humanity? Would he attempt to flee if given his freedom? There was no way to know, and the colonists made no attempt to find out. Gideon Spilett carefully examined the wretch, then looked at his companions and said:

"Whatever he may be, whatever he has been, whatever he might become, it is our duty to bring him back to Lincoln Island!"

"Yes! yes!" answered Harbert. "And perhaps, with care, we can begin to reawaken his intelligence!"

"The soul does not die," said the reporter, "and it would be a great satisfaction to wrest this creature of God from the grip of bestiality!"

Pencroff shook his head with a skeptical air.

"We must try, nevertheless," the reporter answered. "Humanity demands it."

Such was indeed their duty as civilized Christian beings. On that point they could not disagree, and they knew that Cyrus Smith would approve this course of action.

"Shall we leave him tied up?" the sailor asked.

"Perhaps he would walk if we untied his feet?" said Harbert.

"Let's give it a try," Pencroff replied.

The ropes hobbling the prisoner's feet were undone, but his arms remained firmly tied. He stood up of his own accord, making no attempt to flee. His cold eyes gazed questioningly at the three men walking beside him, but nothing in his demeanor suggested any awareness that he was or ever had been their equal. A continuous hiss emerged from between his lips, and his air was wild, but he made no resistance as they walked on.

At the reporter's suggestion, the wretch was led back to his house. Perhaps the sight of familiar surroundings might make some impression on him! Perhaps one single spark would suffice to reanimate his clouded mind, to give new light to his extinguished soul!

The house was not far away. Soon they were standing inside it; but the prisoner remained oblivious, as if his every memory had been erased!

What explanation could there be for this descent into animality, if not a long period of isolation on the island? No doubt he had arrived here with his reason intact, but had been gradually reduced to this state under the effects of his solitude!

It then occurred to the reporter that the sight of fire might rouse him from his stupor, and in an instant the hearth was lit by a beautiful blaze—an irresistible attraction even for a mere animal.

At first, the sight of the flames seemed to attract the poor devil's attention; but soon he drew back, and his gaze grew dim once more.

Clearly, there was nothing to be done, at least for the moment, but bring him on board the *Bonadventure*. This they now did, and there he remained under Pencroff's watchful eye.

Harbert and Gideon Spilett set off to finish their work, and a few hours later they returned to the shore with the castaway's tools and weapons, a collection of vegetable seeds, a few pieces of game, and two pairs of pigs. These were promptly stowed away, and the *Bonadventure* sat ready to weigh anchor with the next morning's tide.

The prisoner sat in the forward room, calm, silent, deaf, and mute.

Pencroff offered him some food, but he pushed away the cooked meat, for which he had evidently lost his taste. Now the sailor offered him a duck that Harbert had killed, and he threw himself upon it with bestial gluttony and devoured it at once.

"Do you really believe he'll ever recover?" said Pencroff, shaking his head.

"Perhaps," the reporter answered. "Our attentions might well have some effect in the end. Isolation has made him what he is, and henceforth he is no longer alone!"

"The poor man has probably been in this state for quite some time!" said Harbert.

"Perhaps," answered Gideon Spilett.

"What do you suppose his age might be?" asked the boy.

"It's difficult to say, with that beard hiding his face," answered the reporter. "Nevertheless, he is not a young man. I would guess that he must be at least fifty years old."

"Have you noticed, Mr. Spilett, how deep his eyes are sunk into their sockets?" asked the boy.

"Yes, Harbert, but I would add that there is a humanity in those eyes that belies his general appearance."

"Well, we shall see," Pencroff replied. "I'm curious to know what Mr. Smith will think of our savage. We went off to find a human being, and we come home with a monster! Ah well! we're doing what we can!"

The night went by. They had no way of knowing if the prisoner was sleeping; in any case, even though he was untied, he never stirred. Wild animals often fall into a state of mute dejection in the first few days of their captivity, only to regain their ferocity a few days later, and the same might well prove true of the wretch they had brought aboard their *Bonadventure*.

By dawn of the next day—October 15th—Pencroff's meteorological predictions had come to pass. The wind was now in the northwest, favoring the *Bonadventure*'s return trip; but it was freshening as well, and this would make their navigation more difficult.

The anchor was raised at five o'clock in the morning. Pencroff reefed in his great sail and set the bearing at east-northeast, directly toward Lincoln Island.

The first day of the crossing passed without incident. The prisoner sat silent in the forward cabin. He had once been a sailor, and the agitations of the sea seemed to have a salutary effect on his mood. Was some memory of his former trade coming back to him? In any case, he kept his peace, more dazed than downcast.

The next day—October 16th—the wind freshened considerably, backing still further northward, slowing the *Bonadventure*'s progress and kicking up a heavy swell. Pencroff soon found himself forced to sail close-hauled, and although he said nothing of it to his companions, he watched the waves crashing over the deck with growing alarm. He knew that their return would take longer than the outbound journey if the wind did not shift again.

Indeed, as morning broke on October 17th, the *Bonadventure* had been sailing for forty-eight hours with no sign that they were nearing the island, and no means of estimating the distance they had traveled, for their speed and direction were far too irregular.

Another twenty-four hours went by, and still no land in sight. The seas were heavy, and their boat was sailing straight into the wind. They reefed, they changed tack again and again, they struggled to manipulate the sails as the wild waves tossed the little boat this way and that. Indeed, one such wave, even larger and more powerful than the others, washed straight over the *Bonadventure* during this gale of October 18th, and if they had not taken the precaution of lashing themselves to the deck they would surely have been swept off.

Desperately bailing the flooded deck in the wake of this near-calamity, Pencroff and his companions were astonished to see their prisoner burst through the hatchway, as if impelled to action by his seafarer's instincts. With a powerful blow of the spar, he smashed the bulwarks to speed the draining of the water; then, once the deck was dry again, he disappeared back into his room without a word.

Pencroff, Gideon Spilett, and Harbert could only look on in silent stupefaction.

But their situation remained no less perilous than before, for the sailor had every reason to believe that the storm had driven them far off course. And if they were indeed lost in this great wide sea, they could not hope to find their bearings again!

The night of the eighteenth was dark and cold. Nevertheless, at around eleven o'clock the wind calmed, the swell lessened, and the *Bonadventure* began to pick up speed. In spite of it all, she had held her own on the storm-tossed sea.

Sleep was out of the question, even for a single hour. Pencroff, Gideon Spilett, and Harbert kept a vigilant watch, for Lincoln Island might not be far off now, and perhaps they would see it at daybreak; perhaps, too, the *Bonadventure* had lost her way, pushed far to leeward by the winds and storm currents, in which case there was no telling where they might be, nor any way to determine the direction of Lincoln Island.

A deep apprehension filled Pencroff's soul—apprehension and not

"A fire! A fire!" Pencroff cried.

despair, for he was blessed with a hardy and intrepid soul. He merely sat at the helm, staring stubbornly through the thick gloom that enveloped his boat.

Suddenly, at about two o'clock in the morning, he stood up:

"A fire! A fire!" he cried.

And indeed, a brilliant light had come into view some twenty miles to the northeast. This was Lincoln Island, and thanks to that signal, obviously lit by Cyrus Smith, the way home was now clear.

Their present bearing would take them well to the island's north; thus, Pencroff corrected his course, steering directly toward the fire, which shone over the horizon like a star of the first magnitude.

XV

*The Return.—A Discussion.—Cyrus Smith and the Stranger.—
Port Balloon.—The Third Harvest.—A Windmill.—The First
Flour and the First Bread.—The Engineer's Devotion.—A
Moving Experiment.—Flowing Tears!*

And so, at seven o'clock on the morning of October 20th, after a journey of four days, the *Bonadventure* gently came ashore at the mouth of the Mercy.

Greatly alarmed by the bad weather and the prolonged absence of their companions, Cyrus Smith and Neb had climbed onto Longview Plateau at dawn to find that the long-awaited boat was now in sight at last!

"God be praised! There they are!" Cyrus Smith cried.

Overcome with joy, Neb immediately broke into a dance, spinning in circles, clapping his hands, shouting: "Oh! Master!"—a pantomime more touching than the most eloquent speech!

Counting the passengers on the deck of the *Bonadventure*, the engineer concluded that Pencroff had not found the castaway of Tabor Island, or perhaps that he had chosen to remain where he was, refusing to exchange one prison for another.

For Pencroff, Gideon Spilett, and Harbert were alone on the deck of the *Bonadventure*.

The engineer and Neb were waiting on the beach when the boat pulled to shore, and even before her passengers had leaped onto the sand, Cyrus Smith cried out:

"You've caused us a great deal of worry, my friends! Did you meet with some sort of misfortune?"

"No," answered Gideon Spilett, "on the contrary, everything went wonderfully. We'll tell you all about it."

"All the same," the engineer replied, "I see there are still only three of you. You found no one on the island?"

"Beg pardon, Mr. Cyrus," the sailor answered, "there are four of us!"

"You found the castaway?"

"Yes."

"And you've brought him back?"

"Yes."

"Alive?"

"Yes."

"Where is he? Who is he?"

"He is," answered the reporter, "or rather he was, a man! And that's all we know for now, Cyrus!"

With this the events of the journey were hastily related to the engineer. They told him of their search, of the long-abandoned house, and finally of their encounter with a castaway who seemed no longer a member of the human race.

"And I sometimes wonder," added Pencroff, "if we've done the right thing by bringing him here."

"You most certainly did do the right thing, Pencroff!" the engineer answered warmly.

"But the wretch has lost his reason!"

"For the moment, perhaps," Cyrus Smith replied; "but just a few short months ago, this poor devil was a man like you or me. Could not a similar fate await the last survivor of our own colony, after years of isolation on this island? Unhappy is the man who finds himself alone, my friends, and this poor creature's condition is nothing other than proof of the devastating effects of solitude!"

"But, Mr. Cyrus," asked Harbert, "what makes you believe that he's been in this state for no more than a few months?"

"Because the message we found was written quite recently," the engineer answered, "and only the castaway could have written it."

"Unless, that is," Gideon Spilett observed, "it was written by a companion of his who has since died."

"That is impossible, my dear Spilett."

"Why?" the reporter asked.

"If there were two castaways, the note would have said so," Cyrus Smith replied, "and it mentions only one."

Harbert now briefly recounted the events of their return voyage, placing particular emphasis on the curious, fleeting resurrection that had taken place in the prisoner's mind at the height of the tempest, when for one brief moment he had become a sailor again.

"That's fine, Harbert," the engineer replied. "This is a very significant development indeed. Clearly the wretch is not beyond rehabilitation. Despair alone made him what he is; but here he will rediscover what it means to live among his fellow men. He still has a soul within him, and it's up to us to help him recover it!"

Now, as Neb looked on in astonishment and the engineer in deep compassion, the castaway of Tabor Island was brought from his cabin in the bow of the *Bonadventure*. Finding himself on land again, his first impulse was to flee.

But Cyrus Smith approached him and put a hand on his shoulder with quiet authority, looking into his eyes with infinite tenderness. The engineer's commanding presence produced an immediate effect: the wretch now stood quiet and still, his eyes downcast, his head inclined, and he made no further resistance.

"Poor outcast!" the engineer murmured.

Cyrus Smith examined him with great attention. Judged solely by his outward appearance, the creature had lost every last trace of his former humanity; and yet, like the reporter, Cyrus Smith glimpsed an elusive gleam of intelligence in his eyes.

It was decided that the outcast, or rather the stranger—for it was thus that his new companions would speak of him henceforth—would be given a room at Granite House, from which, moreover, escape was impossible. He made no objection as they led him to his new quarters. Perhaps, with proper care and attention, he might one day become a fine companion for the colonists of Lincoln Island.

Quickly Neb prepared a nourishing breakfast—for the reporter, Harbert, and Pencroff were dying of hunger—and as they ate they gave Cyrus Smith a detailed account of the voyage. He agreed with his friends that the stranger must be English or American, both because of his ship's name—*Britannia*—and because, through that unkempt beard, beneath the bushy mass of hair, the engineer thought he had descried the characteristic traits of the Anglo-Saxon.

"Incidentally," said Gideon Spilett to Harbert, "you never told us how you met the savage. All we know is that he would have throttled you if we hadn't been so lucky as to reach you in time!"

"On my word," answered Harbert, "I don't know that I could tell you what happened. I believe I was gathering plants when something fell from a high tree. It sounded like a small avalanche. I scarcely had time to turn around...He must have been crouching on a branch in the tree, and in less time than it takes to say it, he was upon me. If it weren't for Mr. Spilett and Pencroff..."

"My dear child!" said Cyrus Smith, "you were in grave danger, but were it not for this incident the poor creature might have forever eluded your search, and we would not now have a new companion."

"You believe that we can make him a man again, then?" asked the reporter.

"Yes," the engineer replied.

With breakfast finished, Cyrus Smith and his companions left Granite House and returned to the beach. They proceeded to the unloading of the *Bonadventure;* the engineer carefully examined the tools and weapons, but found nothing that might serve to establish the stranger's identity.

The captured pigs were hailed as a most welcome addition to Lincoln Island's supply of livestock, and the animals were led off to the stables in hopes of a rapid domestication.

The fulminating caps and the kegs of lead and powder were greeted with equal enthusiasm. Plans were made for a small powder magazine, perhaps outside Granite House, perhaps even in the upper cavern, where the possibility of an explosion posed no threat to their safety. Nevertheless, they would continue to load their weapons with pyroxylin, for the engineer's invention had proved most effective, and there was no reason to replace it with ordinary powder.

When the ship had been completely unloaded:

"Mr. Cyrus," said Pencroff, "I'd be much obliged if we could find a more secure harbor for the *Bonadventure.*"

"You don't believe she's safe at the mouth of the Mercy?"

"No, Mr. Cyrus," the sailor answered. "Half the time she's grounded on the beach, and that doesn't do her any good. She's a very fine boat. I wish you could have seen how she handled that squall on our way home!"

"Could we not keep her afloat in the river itself?"

"No doubt we could, Mr. Cyrus, but there's no shelter at the mouth of the river, and I fear she might be damaged by the waves when the east wind blows."

"Well then, where would you like to keep her, Pencroff?"

"At Port Balloon," the sailor answered. "The little cove is nicely protected by the rocks, and I believe it's just the port she needs."

"You don't think it a bit far away?"

"Oh, it's no more than three miles from Granite House, and we have a fine, straight road to take us there!"

"Very well, Pencroff, do as you think best, although I'd rather keep the *Bonadventure* where we can watch over her. Nevertheless, we shall build a little harbor for her at Port Balloon, when we have time."

"Wonderful!" cried Pencroff. "A port with a lighthouse, a breakwater, and a dry dock! Oh, with you, Mr. Cyrus, everything seems so easy!"

"Yes, my good Pencroff," the engineer replied, "but only with you to help me. We owe three fourths of our accomplishments to your tireless hands!"

Harbert and the sailor thus reboarded the *Bonadventure*, raised anchor, hoisted the sails, and sped toward Cape Claw with the offshore winds. Two hours later, she was resting in the quiet waters of Port Balloon.

Did the stranger give any indication of a change in his savage nature over his first few days at Granite House? Had some brighter gleam begun to shine in the depths of that darkened mind? Was his soul returning to his body? It was, to be sure; and Cyrus Smith and the reporter were increasingly convinced that the poor man's reason had never been fully extinguished.

Accustomed as he was to the open air, and to the unbounded freedom of his life on Tabor Island, he spent the first few days in a state of muted fury, and his companions rightly feared that he might at any moment throw himself out of a window and onto the beach. But gradually a sort of calm settled over him, and soon they were able to offer him his freedom of movement.

There was room for hope, then, and a great deal of it. Already the stranger was forgetting his carnivorous ways. The food they set before him was of a far less bestial nature than his sustenance on Tabor Island, but he did not refuse it. Not even cooked meat repulsed him now, as it had his first night on board the *Bonadventure*.

Cyrus Smith had taken advantage of the stranger's profound slumber to cut off his unkempt beard and tangled hair, and once rid of this unruly mane his air seemed far less savage. He had also removed the shred of tattered fabric from the wretch's loins and dressed him in more civilized apparel. The stranger's appearance became far more human as a result; even his gaze seemed gentler now. Surely, in times past, illuminated by the light of human intelligence, there must have been a kind of beauty in this man's face.

Cyrus Smith had resolved to spend several hours each day in the stranger's company. He sat down beside him to work, busying himself with various tasks that might attract his attention and occupy his mind. For one single spark of light might have sufficed to reilluminate that soul; one single memory flashing through his brain might reanimate his reason. Indeed, they had already seen the proof of this during that stormy night on board the *Bonadventure*!

The engineer spoke constantly as he worked, hoping to penetrate that benumbed intelligence by way of the organs of both sight and sound. Sometimes one of his companions joined in, sometimes another, sometimes all of them together. Their conversations generally revolved around questions of sailing, calculated to touch a seafarer's soul. At times the stranger seemed to follow the conversation in a vague sort of way, and the colonists soon concluded that he could understand their words, at least in part. Sometimes an expression of the most profound distress came over his face, and the colonists interpreted this change in his physiognomy as proof of a deep, intimate suffering. But he never spoke, although they sometimes thought a word was about to escape his lips.

How subdued, how melancholy the poor creature seemed! But was this subdued air merely an illusion? Was his melancholy caused solely by his confinement? For the moment they could not say. He was kept within limited, familiar surroundings; he was continuously cared for by the colonists, to whose company he would soon become accustomed; his every need was satisfied; he was fed a healthier diet, given more suitable clothes, and all of this could not fail to bring about a modification in his physical health and appearance. But had he truly taken to this new life, or—to use a word that seems particularly appropriate here—had he simply been tamed, as an animal by its master? That was the real question, and Cyrus Smith yearned to find its answer, despite his reluctance to push his patient too far and too fast! For to him, the stranger was ill, and nothing more! But what were his chances for recovery?

Thus, with what attention the engineer observed him! How he waited for a glimpse of his soul, if one can say such a thing! How eager he was to grasp that soul when at last it made its appearance!

The colonists followed the various phases of this cure with great emotion. Alongside Cyrus Smith, they struggled to restore the patient back to health, and all of them, except perhaps the skeptical Pencroff, soon found themselves sharing his hope and his faith.

The stranger was deeply calm, as we have said, and he clearly felt a sort of affection for the engineer, whose influence had a visible effect on him. For this reason, Cyrus Smith resolved to test him by transporting him to some other setting: facing the ocean, perhaps, to which his gaze had become so thoroughly accustomed, or into the forest, which could not fail to recall his former home!

"But," said Gideon Spilett, "how can we be sure he won't try to escape once we give him his freedom?"

"Only by experiment can we be sure," the engineer answered.

"Come now!" said Pencroff. "The moment our fine friend here smells the fresh air and sees the wide open spaces in front of him, he'll be off like a jackrabbit!"

"I don't think so," answered Cyrus Smith.

"Let's give it a try," said Gideon Spilett.

"Let's give it a try," answered the engineer.

It was now October 30th, and the castaway of Tabor Island had been imprisoned in Granite House for nine days. The weather was warm, and a brilliant sun cast its rays over the island.

Cyrus Smith and Pencroff went to the stranger's room and found him lying near the window, looking at the sky.

"Come, my friend," the engineer said to him.

The stranger immediately stood up. He never took his eyes from Cyrus Smith, and he followed him obediently out of the room. The sailor brought up the rear, with no great hopes for the experiment's success.

Cyrus Smith and Pencroff escorted him into the elevator while Neb, Harbert, and Gideon Spilett awaited them below on the beach. The basket descended, and a few moments later they stood together at the foot of Granite House.

The colonists took a few steps away from the stranger to give him a sense of freedom.

Uncertainly he approached the water, and his gaze shone with great

A heavy sigh escaped his breast.

animation, but he made no attempt to escape. He watched as the little waves washed gently onto the sand, their force broken by the islet.

"This is only the ocean," Gideon Spilett observed. "Perhaps he knows there's no use trying to escape here!"

"Yes," answered Cyrus Smith, "we shall have to take him to the plateau, and to the edge of the forest. There the experiment will be more conclusive."

"And in any case, the bridges are all raised," Neb observed, "so he won't be able to escape."

"Oh! yes," said Pencroff, "he's just the sort of fellow to let a little stream like Glycerine Creek stand in his way! I'll wager he could cross it with a single bound!"

"We shall see," was Cyrus Smith's only reply, his gaze still fixed upon his patient.

The stranger was then led to the mouth of the Mercy, and together the little band turned onto the left bank. Soon they were standing on Longview Plateau.

No sooner had he come to the first fine trees of the forests, shimmering slightly in the breeze, than the stranger took a series of deep breaths, as if intoxicated by their penetrating perfume, and a heavy sigh escaped his breast!

The colonists stood a few paces behind him, ready to hold him back if he made any move to escape!

And indeed, the poor creature was on the verge of diving into the creek, the only obstacle between him and the forest. He tensed his legs, he began his spring... But suddenly he caught himself and sank to the ground, with a single tear flowing from each eye!

"Ah," cried Cyrus Smith, "you can weep! Now you are a man again!"

XVI

A Mystery to Be Resolved.—The Stranger's First Words.—
Twelve Years on the Islet!—An Uncontainable Confession!—The
Disappearance.—Cyrus Smith's Confidence.—Construction of a
Mill.—The First Bread.—An Act of Devotion.—Honest Hands!

Yes! the wretch had wept! Some memory had surfaced in his mind, and, to use Cyrus Smith's expression, his tears had made him a man again.

The colonists let him linger on the plateau for some time, and took a few more steps back to convince him he was truly free; but he never thought of seizing the opportunity to escape, and soon Cyrus Smith decided to bring him back to Granite House.

Two days after these events, the stranger began to show a desire to involve himself in the colony's daily life. It was clear that he heard and understood their words. He never answered, but they soon learned that behind his silence lay nothing more than a curious refusal to speak, for one evening Pencroff, listening at his door, heard these words escape his lips:

"No! here! me! never!"

The sailor reported this to his companions.

"Something is haunting this man, something we may never know!" said Cyrus Smith.

The stranger had begun to work in the vegetable gardens, using the colony's tools. He often paused in his labors, standing motionless as if lost in his own inner world. The engineer sensed his desire to be left alone, and urged his companions never to disturb him at such moments. If by chance one of the colonists approached him, he inevitably backed away, his breast racked by sobs, as if his body could not hold back the powerful emotions stuffed away inside!

Was it some sort of remorse that tormented him so? This seemed not unlikely, and one day Gideon Spilett was led to make this observation:

"If he doesn't speak, I believe it must be because what he has to say is too serious!"

They would have to be patient and wait.

A few days later, on November 3rd, the stranger was working on the plateau when suddenly, as before, he stood motionless and let his spade fall to the ground. Cyrus Smith was watching him from nearby, and once again he saw tears flowing from his eyes. Drawn to his side by the irresistible force of compassion, he lightly touched the stranger's arm.

"My friend?" he said.

But when Cyrus Smith tried to take his hand, the stranger only recoiled, his gaze averted.

"My friend," said Cyrus Smith more firmly, "I command you to look at me!"

The stranger looked at the engineer. Just as a skilled mesmerist can instantaneously place his subject under his influence, the stranger seemed now entirely in the engineer's power. At first he tried to flee, but suddenly a change came over him, utterly transforming his physiognomy. His eyes flashed. Words struggled to escape his lips. He could not hold back any longer!... Finally, he crossed his arms; then, in a quiet voice:

"Who are you?" he asked Cyrus Smith.

"Castaways, like yourself," the engineer answered, deeply moved. "We have brought you here to rejoin your fellow men."

"My fellow men!... I am fellow to no man!"

"You are among friends..."

"Friends!... me! friends!" the stranger cried, burying his face in his hands... "No... never... leave me alone! leave me alone!"

He fled to the edge of the plateau overlooking the sea and stood motionless for a great while.

Cyrus Smith returned to his companions and told them what had happened.

"Yes! there is a mystery in this man's life," said Gideon Spilett. "It would seem that remorse alone can lead him back into the fold of humanity."

"I don't know what manner of man we've brought to our island," said the sailor. "He has secrets..."

"Which we shall respect," quickly answered Cyrus Smith. "If he has indeed committed some offense, he has done his penance in the cruelest way, and in our eyes he is absolved."

For two hours the stranger remained alone on the beach, apparently lost in memories of a dark and tortured past. The colonists were careful not to let him escape their sight, but never attempted to trouble his solitude.

Nevertheless, after two hours, he seemed to have made some sort of resolution, and he came to find Cyrus Smith. His eyes were red from a long flow of tears, but now he no longer wept. His demeanor had changed, suddenly suffused with deep humility. He seemed fearful, ashamed, abject, and he never raised his eyes from the ground.

"Sir," he said to Cyrus Smith, "are you and your companions Englishmen?"

"No," the engineer answered, "we are Americans."

"Ah!" the stranger replied, and he murmured these words:

"It's better that way!"

"And you, my friend?" the engineer asked.

"English," he quickly answered.

And as if it had cost him dearly to speak these few words, he walked away again, pacing in restless agitation from the waterfall to the mouth of the Mercy.

At one point he passed by Harbert and stopped to ask, in a strangled voice:

"What month is it?"

"December," answered Harbert.

"What year?"

"1866."

"Twelve years! twelve years!" he cried. And once more he quickly strode away.

Harbert told the colonists of the stranger's questions, and of the answers given.

"Poor devil!" Gideon Spilett observed. "His long isolation has robbed him of his sense of time—of the passing months, even the years!"

"Yes," added Harbert, "and he had been on the islet for twelve years when we found him!"

"Twelve years!" answered Cyrus Smith. "Oh! twelve years of isolation, and perhaps a cursed existence before that—how could this fail to compromise a man's reason?"

"I'm beginning to think," said Pencroff, "that it wasn't a shipwreck that brought this man to Tabor Island. I believe he was abandoned there as punishment for some misdeed."

"You must be right, Pencroff," the reporter answered, "and if that's the case, whoever left him on the island might well return for him one day!"

"And they won't find him," said Harbert.

"But then," answered Pencroff, "we'll have to go back there, and…"

"My friends," said Cyrus Smith, "we cannot consider such questions until we know the history of our unhappy friend. I believe that he has suffered, that he has expiated his crimes in the harshest possible conditions—whatever those crimes may be—and that he now feels an overwhelming need to open himself to us. But we must not push him! I've no doubt he'll tell us his story one day, and when he does we will consider how best to proceed. Perhaps he dreams of repatriation, perhaps he knows it will come one day—although I doubt it. In any case, only he can say."

"But why do you doubt it, Cyrus?" asked the reporter.

"Because if he knew he would be delivered at some specific time, he would never have thrown the bottle into the sea, but simply waited for the hour of his liberation. No, I find it much more likely that he was banished to that islet for life, never again to set eyes on his fellow men, and condemned to die alone!"

"But," the sailor observed, "there's one thing I can't understand."

"And what is that?"

"If this man was abandoned on Tabor Island twelve years ago, then he must have been in this degenerate state for several years at least?"

"Very likely," answered Cyrus Smith.

"Which means that the note was written several years ago!"

"No doubt…and yet it looked so recent!…"

"Furthermore, how can we believe that the bottle took several years to come from Tabor Island to Lincoln Island?"

"That's not entirely out of the question," the reporter answered. "Could it not have been floating in the vicinity of the island for some time?"

"No," answered Pencroff, "it would never have survived. It could not even have washed ashore and then been pulled out to sea again at high tide. The southern shoreline is nothing but rocks, and it would surely have shattered!"

"Indeed," answered Cyrus Smith, pensively.

"And furthermore," added the sailor, "if the message were written several years ago, if it had spent several years floating in a bottle on the sea, it would have been damaged by the water. And yet it wasn't damaged in any way when we found it. It was in perfect condition."

The sailor's observations could not be disputed. Something incomprehensible lay behind these events, for the note the colonists found in that bottle did indeed seem to have been written quite recently. Furthermore, it indicated the precise latitude and longitude of Tabor Island, which implied that its author had an extensive knowledge of cartography, more extensive than one would expect to find in a simple sailor.

"Once again, we find ourselves confronted with an unanswerable question," said the engineer. "Nevertheless, we must not compel our new companion to speak. When he is ready, my friends, we will be there to hear him!"

For the next few days the stranger did not speak a single word, and never once left the enclosure on the plateau. He endlessly worked the fields, never resting for an instant, but always well away from the others. He did not return to Granite House at mealtimes, although he was often invited to do so; he ate his dinner of raw vegetables in solitude. When night fell, he did not return to his bed, but slept in the open air beneath a stand of trees, or, when the weather was bad, in some cavity among the rocks. Thus, he continued to live the life he had led in the forests of Tabor Island, and since every attempt to change him had proven fruitless, the colonists simply waited with all the patience they could muster. But soon the imperious, half-involuntary urgings of his troubled conscience would wrest from him a terrible confession.

At around eight o'clock on the evening of November 10th, as darkness was slowly settling over the island, the colonists were sitting together under the veranda when the stranger unexpectedly appeared. An odd light shone in his eyes, and his demeanor was once again that of the wild, tormented creature they had found on Tabor Island.

Cyrus Smith and his companions were astonished to find the stranger in the grips of a terrible emotion, his teeth chattering feverishly. What was the matter with him? Had the sight of his fellow men grown unbearable to him? Had he had enough of an existence in civilized surroundings? Could a nostalgia for his brutish state have swept over him? Such were they led to believe when he began to speak in a stream of incoherent sentences:

"Why am I here?...What right did you have to take me from my island?...How can we ever be companions?...Do you know who I am...what I've done...why I was there...alone? And how do you know I wasn't abandoned there...left there to die?...What do you know of my past?...how do you know I'm not a thief, a murderer...a filthy wretch...a cursed thing...fit to live like a wild beast and nothing more...far from the rest of humanity...tell me...how do you know?"

The colonists listened, never interrupting the stranger as—in spite of himself, it seemed—these half-spoken confessions escaped his lips. Cyrus Smith came forward to reassure him, but he quickly leaped back.

"No! no!" he cried. "Just one word...Am I free?"

"You are free," the engineer replied.

"Farewell, then!" he cried, and off he ran, like a madman.

Neb, Pencroff, and Harbert ran after him toward the edge of the woods...but they returned alone.

"We must let him do as he wishes!" said Cyrus Smith.

"He'll never come back..." cried Pencroff.

"He will come back," answered the engineer.

Many days went by; but Cyrus Smith, as if blessed with some sort of foreknowledge, never wavered in his belief that the wretch would sooner or later return.

"He is a hard man," he sometimes said, "and this is his final revolt against an overpowering remorse. Isolation will only bring him greater suffering now."

In the meantime the colonists resumed their various labors, both on Longview Plateau and at the sheepfold, where Cyrus Smith intended to build a complete farm. The seeds Harbert had gathered on Tabor Island were carefully sown. The plateau was now one vast vegetable garden, carefully planned, scrupulously maintained, and never did the colonists lack for honest work, for there was always more to be done. With the new crops came the need for new fields, and soon their little plots of tilled earth had become a vast spread of cultivated land, replacing the pastures that once covered the plateau. But forage could be found in plentiful supply elsewhere on the island, and the dauws would not want for fodder.

Besides, the girdle of protective creeks made Longview Plateau an ideal location for their vegetable plots, and since there was no need to protect the grazing lands from quadrumanes and quadrupeds, the colonists could easily find another area to devote to that purpose.

On November 15th they completed their third harvest of wheat. How the wheat fields had spread since the first grain was sown, eighteen months before! The second harvest of six hundred thousand grains had now produced four thousand bushels, which is to say more than 500 million grains! Never again would they be forced to do without wheat; henceforth, an annual sowing of some ten bushels would ensure them a plentiful yearly harvest, and food for men and beasts alike.

Soon the harvest was over, and so, in the first half of November, they considered how best to transform their wheat into bread.

For while they had grain, they did not yet have flour; for that they would need a mill. Cyrus Smith could have used the Mercy's second waterfall to drive its mechanism, just as he had used the first to move the pestles of the fulling mill; but after some discussion, they decided on a simple windmill atop Longview Plateau. A windmill was no more difficult to build than a water mill, and they knew their mill would never want for wind on this plateau, exposed as it was to the continual breezes of the open sea.

"Not to mention," said Pencroff, "that a windmill's far prettier than a water mill. What a handsome landmark it will make!"

And so they set to work. The first step was to find stout wood for the mill's housing and mechanism. Several large slabs of sandstone were discovered north of the lake, which they could easily fashion into millstones. As for the windmill's sails, the inexhaustible balloon would supply all the canvas they needed.

They resolved to build their mill near the lakeshore, slightly to the right of the poultry yard; and with this decided, Cyrus Smith began to draw up the plans. The housing would rest on a pivot held in place by massive beams, so that the entire mill could be turned as necessary to face the prevailing winds.

This work was swiftly carried out. Neb and Pencroff had become skillful builders, and had only to follow the dimensions supplied by the engineer. Thus, a sort of cylindrical guardhouse, a real pepper pot topped with a pointed roof, soon stood at the chosen location. The four frames that supported the sails were joined to the driveshaft at a slight angle, and fixed with iron clasps. The mill's various internal components posed no great difficulty: a box to house the upper and lower millstones; a hopper, which is to say a sort of large square basket, wide at the top and narrow at the bottom, to direct the grains as they fell onto the millstones; the oscillating trough, which regulates the flow of grain, and whose endless click-clack sound has earned it the nickname "chatterer"; and finally the sieve, which filters the bran from the flour. Their tools were fine and the work undemanding, for in the end a windmill is a very simple device. It was simply a question of time.

Every colonist gladly contributed his skill, and so the work proceeded smoothly and quickly. On December 1st their windmill was complete.

As always, Pencroff was delighted with his handiwork, and found the machine perfect in every way.

"Now all we need is a good strong wind," he said, "and we'll mill our first harvest pretty as you please!"

"A good wind, yes indeed," the engineer answered, "but not too strong, Pencroff."

"Oh! our mill will only turn the faster!"

"There's no need for it to turn quickly," answered Cyrus Smith. "Experiments have shown that a windmill performs with greatest efficiency when the number of revolutions the sails make in one minute is six times the number of feet traveled in one second by the wind. With a medium breeze of twenty-four feet per second, the windmill's sails will turn sixteen times per minute, and no more than that is required."

"And here we are!" cried Harbert. "There's a fine breeze blowing from the northwest—the very thing we need!"

There was no reason to delay the inauguration of the new windmill, and the colonists were impatient for their first taste of Lincoln Island bread. Thus, two or three bushels of wheat were ground that very morning, and at lunch the next day a magnificent round loaf—rather dense, perhaps, despite having been leavened with beer yeast—was to be seen on the dining table at Granite House. This was soon devoured with great enthusiasm, and, as we might easily understand, with the deepest of pleasure!

The stranger had not yet reappeared. Several times Gideon Spilett and Harbert had wandered through the surrounding forests, but he was nowhere to be seen, and not a trace of him could be found. This pro-

Pencroff was delighted with his handiwork.

longed disappearance caused them no small alarm. To be sure, the former savage of Tabor Island could easily survive in the game-filled woodlands of the Far West, but was it not greatly to be feared that he had returned to his old ways, and that his independence had revived his savage instincts? Nevertheless, Cyrus Smith clung to his predictions, and insisted that the fugitive would one day return.

"Yes, he will come back!" he repeated with a confidence that his companions could not share. "When that poor creature was on Tabor Island, he knew he was alone! Here, he knows that his fellow men are awaiting him! Already he has begun to tell us of his former life; one day the penitent will return to tell us the rest, and that day he will be ours!"

Events were soon to prove Cyrus Smith right.

On December 3rd, Harbert left Longview Plateau for a fishing trip to the southern shore of the lake. He was unarmed; until then they had felt no real need for such precautions, since dangerous animals had never been spotted in this part of the island.

Pencroff and Neb were working in the poultry yard, while Cyrus Smith and the reporter were at the Chimneys making soda to replenish their supply of soap.

Suddenly they heard a shout:

"Help! Help me!"

Cyrus Smith and the reporter were too far away to hear the cries. Pencroff and Neb threw down their tools and ran breathlessly toward the lake.

No one had suspected that the stranger might be nearby; but now he preceded Neb and Pencroff in their race to the lake. He dashed through Glycerine Creek, which separated the plateau from the forest, and leaped onto the opposite bank.

Harbert had found himself face to face with a fearsome jaguar, much like the one that had been killed at Reptile End. Caught unawares, the boy was standing with his back to a tree, while the animal tensed its powerful legs, about to pounce... But now, armed with nothing more than a knife, the stranger bounded toward the redoubtable beast, which turned to face this new adversary.

The combat was brief. The stranger's strength and agility were nothing short of prodigious. He seized the jaguar by the throat with a hand like a powerful vise, and, oblivious to the claws digging into his flesh, he plunged his knife into the animal's heart.

The jaguar fell. The stranger pushed him away with one foot, and he was about to flee as the colonists arrived on the scene of the battle; but Harbert, grasping him, cried out:

"No! no! you can't go now!"

Cyrus Smith went to the stranger, whose brow furrowed as he saw him approach. Blood was flowing over his shoulder from beneath his torn jacket, but he paid it no mind.

"My friend," said Cyrus Smith, "we owe you a debt of gratitude. You risked your life to save our child!"

"My life!" the stranger murmured. "What's it worth? Less than nothing!"

"You're wounded!"

"It doesn't matter."

"Will you give me your hand?"

Harbert tried to grasp the hand that had saved his life, but the stranger only crossed his arms. His breast swelled, his gaze grew veiled, and he seemed about to flee once again; but, struggling to contain himself, he spoke, his voice harsh and brusque:

"Who are you? And what do you wish to be for me?"

Never before had he inquired into the colonists' history. Perhaps, if they told him their story, he might tell them his?

In a few words, Cyrus Smith recounted the events since their departure from Richmond, how they had survived their ordeal, and what resources now lay at their disposal.

The stranger listened with rapt attention.

Then the engineer told him who they were, Gideon Spilett, Harbert, Pencroff, Neb, himself, and he added that they had known no greater joy since coming to Lincoln Island than the moment of Pencroff's return from the islet, when they realized that they had gained a new comrade.

Hearing these words, the stranger reddened, his head fell onto his breast, and a great wave of emotion shook him from head to foot:

"And now that you know us," added Cyrus Smith, "will you give us your hand?"

"No," the stranger answered in a quiet voice, "no! You are all decent and honorable people! Whereas I!..."

XVII

Still at a Distance.—A Request from the Stranger.—A Farmhouse at the Sheepfold.—Twelve Years Before!—The First Mate of the Britannia.—Abandoned on Tabor Island.—Cyrus Smith's Hand.—The Mysterious Note.

These last words had justified the colonists' suspicions. The stranger was haunted by some dark deed, expiated in the minds of others perhaps, but still unpardoned by his own conscience. Nevertheless, the criminal had now proven the depths of his remorse. He had repented, and had he offered his new friends his hand, as they asked, they would have clasped it warmly; but he did not think his hand worthy of being pressed by decent people! Nevertheless, he did not flee into the forest again after the incident of the jaguar, but remained forever in the vicinity of Granite House.

What secret lay in the stranger's past? Would he ever reveal it? Only time would tell. In any case, it was agreed that they would ask him no questions, and that they would live with him as if they suspected nothing.

For a few days, then, their life together continued as it always had. Cyrus Smith and Gideon Spilett pursued their various projects, working now as chemists, now as physicists. The reporter left the engineer's side only to go hunting with Harbert, for it would not have been prudent to let the boy wander through the forest on his own, and they had to be careful not to let down their guard. As for Neb and Pencroff, they never lacked for work, one day at the stables or poultry yard, another at the sheepfold, not to mention their various tasks inside Granite House.

The stranger still worked at some distance from the others, and he had returned to his old ways, never dining with them, never joining them beneath the veranda, sleeping among the trees on the plateau. The company of his rescuers genuinely seemed an unbearable torment for him!

"But in that case," Pencroff often observed, "why did he ask for help? Why did he throw that bottle into the sea?"

"He will tell us one day," Cyrus Smith invariably replied.

"When?"

"Perhaps sooner than you think, Pencroff."

And indeed, the day of his confession was near.

On December 10th, one week after his return to the vicinity of Granite House, the stranger came to Cyrus Smith and said in a quiet, humble voice:

"Sir, I have a request."

"Speak," the engineer replied; "but first, let me ask you something."

The stranger's face reddened on hearing these words, and he seemed to be on the point of walking off again. Cyrus Smith understood full well what was happening in the stranger's guilt-riddled soul. No doubt he feared that the engineer was about to inquire into his past!

Cyrus Smith held him back by the hand:

"Friend," he said to him, "we are not only your companions; we are your comrades. I wanted to tell you that; and now I'm listening."

The stranger passed a hand over his eyes. A sort of tremor racked him from head to foot, and he stood for a few moments, unable to speak a single word.

"Sir," he finally said, "I've come to ask you a great favor."

"What is it?"

"Four or five miles from here, at the foot of the mountain, there is a pen where you keep your domesticated animals. Those animals need to be looked after. Would you allow me to live there with them?"

Cyrus Smith stared at the wretch for a few instants with the deepest sympathy. Then:

"My friend," he said, "there's nothing at the sheepfold but barns and sheds, scarcely fit for the animals..."

"They will do for me, sir."

"My friend," Cyrus Smith replied, "we will never deny you what you wish. You would like to live at the sheepfold. So be it. And of course you will always be welcome at Granite House. But if you're to live at the sheepfold, allow us to take the necessary steps to give you a proper home."

"There's no need. I'll be fine there."

"My friend," answered Cyrus Smith, deliberately repeating this cordial epithet, "let us judge how best to proceed in this matter!"

"Thank you, sir," the stranger answered, withdrawing.

The engineer immediately informed his companions of the stranger's proposition. A decision was made to build him a wooden house, furnished as fully and comfortably as they could.

The colonists set out for the sheepfold that very day with all the necessary tools, and before the week was out the house was ready to receive its lodger. It had been erected some twenty feet from the barns, where the stranger could easily watch over the flock of mouflons, of which there were then more than eighty. Some simple furniture was fashioned—a bunk, a table, a bench, a cupboard, a chest—and the house was amply stocked with weapons, ammunition, and tools.

The stranger had never come to see his new home; he left the colonists to their work while he busied himself on the plateau, no doubt eager to finish what he had begun. And indeed, thanks to his labors, all the fields had been tilled and lay ready for sowing, as soon as the time was right.

By December 20th the construction and furnishing of the house at the sheepfold was complete. The engineer announced to the stranger that his home was ready to receive him, and he replied that he would sleep there that very night.

As always, the colonists retired to the great room after their dinner. It was then eight o'clock—the hour at which their companion was to be on his way. Their intention was to spare him the difficulty and perhaps the pain of taking his leave of them, and so they had left him alone on the plateau and made their way back to Granite House.

They had been conversing in the great room for a few moments when a light rap was heard at the door. Almost immediately the stranger entered and said, without preamble:

"Gentlemen, before I leave you, it is only right that you know my story. Here it is."

Cyrus Smith and his companions were deeply moved to hear these simple words.

The engineer stood up.

"We ask nothing of you, my friend," he said. "You have every right not to speak..."

"It is my duty to speak."

"Sit down, then."

"I'll stand."

"We're ready to hear you," answered Cyrus Smith.

The stranger stood in one corner of the room, half hidden in the shadows. He had removed his hat and crossed his arms over his breast, and in a muted voice, speaking as one who forces himself to speak, he set out the following account, which his audience never once interrupted:

"On December 20th, 1854, a steam-powered pleasure craft, the *Duncan,* belonging to the Scottish laird Lord Glenarvan, cast anchor at Cape Bernoulli, which lies at the thirty-seventh parallel on the western coast of Australia. Aboard that yacht were Lord Glenarvan, his wife, a major in the British army, a French geographer, a girl, and a boy. The last two were the children of Captain Grant, whose ship, the *Britannia,* had gone down with all hands one year before. The *Duncan* was commanded by Captain John Mangles, with a crew of fifteen men.

"Now, here is why the yacht had come to this Australian shore.

"Six months earlier, a bottle had been spotted in the Irish Sea and picked up by the *Duncan.* It contained a message written in French, German, and English, which said, in short, that three men had survived the wreck of the *Britannia*—Captain Grant and two crew members—who were now stranded on an island in the Pacific. The note gave the island's latitude, but the paper had been damaged by seawater, and the longitude could not be made out.

"The latitude was thirty-seven degrees eleven minutes south. Therefore, if a rescue party simply followed the thirty-seventh parallel over land and sea, they were sure to arrive at the island where Captain Grant and his two companions could be found.

"The British Admiralty was reluctant to undertake such a search; thus, Lord Glenarvan himself resolved to set out to find the captain. Mary and Robert Grant had been informed of his intentions. The lord's family and the captain's children asked to be allowed to participate, and so the yacht the *Duncan,* which was fully equipped for such an endeavor, sailed from Glasgow across the Atlantic, past the Straits of Magellan, and onward through the Pacific to Patagonia, where, according to a preliminary interpretation of the document, they might suppose Captain Grant had been taken prisoner by natives.

"The *Duncan* left its passengers on the western coast of Patagonia, and set off again to pick them up on the eastern coast, at Cape Corrientes.

"Lord Glenarvan made his way across Patagonia along the thirty-seventh parallel; finding no trace of the captain, he reembarked on November 13th to continue his search across the ocean.

"The *Duncan*'s route passed by Tristan da Cunha and the Amsterdam Islands, but here, too, the search was fruitless. Finally, as I have said, they arrived in Australia, at Cape Bernoulli, on December 20th, 1854.

"Lord Glenarvan's intention was to cross Australia as he had crossed Patagonia, and so he began his trek. Some miles from shore stood a farm belonging to an Irishman, where the travelers were offered hospitality for the night. Lord Glenarvan told the Irishman of his business in this area, and asked him if he had heard any news of an English three-master, the *Britannia*, which might have gone down off the west coast of Australia sometime within the previous two years.

"The Irishman had heard nothing of the shipwreck; but, to his guests' great surprise, one of the Irishman's servants interjected:

" 'Milord, praise and thanks be to God. If Captain Grant is still alive, he is living on Australian soil.'

" 'Who are you?' asked Lord Glenarvan.

" 'A Scotsman like yourself, milord,' the man answered. 'I am one of Captain Grant's companions, a survivor of the wreck of the *Britannia*.'

"This man was named Ayrton. As his papers proved, he had indeed been the first mate on board the *Britannia*. But he had been separated from his captain as the ship broke up over the reefs, and until this moment he was sure that the captain had perished with the rest of the crew, and that he, Ayrton, was the calamity's sole survivor.

" 'Except,' he added, 'the *Britannia* was lost not on the west coast of Australia, but on the east. If Captain Grant is still alive, as your note suggests, he has surely been captured by the Australian aborigines, and you must seek him on the other coast.'

"The man spoke with an artless voice and a steady gaze. They could not doubt the veracity of his words. The Irishman, in whose employ he had been for over a year, vouched for him without hesitation. Lord Glenarvan judged the man to be trustworthy, and in light of his revelations he resolved to follow the thirty-seventh parallel across Australia. Ayrton would lead the small band—Lord Glenarvan, his wife, the two children, the major, the Frenchman, Captain Mangles, and a few deckhands—in their overland journey, while the *Duncan*, commanded by the second

Ayrton.

mate, Tom Austin, would sail for Melbourne and await Lord Glenarvan's instructions.

"They set out on December 23rd, 1854.

"The time has come to say that Ayrton had deceived them. He had indeed been the *Britannia*'s first mate; but, after a series of altercations with his captain, he had tried to incite the crew to mutiny, and to take over the ship. On April 8th, 1852, Captain Grant had put him off on the west coast of Australia, then continued on his way, leaving Ayrton behind—which was only right.

"Thus, the wretch knew nothing whatsoever of the wreck of the *Britannia*. Lord Glenarvan's account was the first he had heard of it! Since his arrival in Australia, he had taken the name Ben Joyce and became the leader of a gang of escaped convicts; and the reason for his brazen claim that the shipwreck had occurred on the east coast, and for his suggestion that Lord Glenarvan strike out in that direction, was that he intended to abandon the rescue party, take over the *Duncan,* and set out into the Pacific as a pirate."

Here the stranger's voice faltered, and he was forced to interrupt his narration for a moment; but he soon resumed his tale in the following terms:

"The expedition set off through the Australian interior. With Ayrton or Ben Joyce—however you might wish to call him—as its leader, the fate of the rescuers was sealed. He had informed his cohorts of his treacherous plans, and they kept a close eye on the little troop, sometimes preceding them, sometimes following behind, but never far away.

"Meanwhile, the *Duncan* had put in at Melbourne to await further orders. Ayrton would now have to persuade Lord Glenarvan to order the crew to leave Melbourne and proceed to the east coast of Australia, where the yacht would be the more easily taken over. He led the expedition toward those shores, through vast and inhospitable forests, and soon he had convinced the lord to order his boat out of Melbourne. He dictated a letter, to be delivered by Ayrton himself to the *Duncan*'s second mate, asking that the yacht proceed immediately to Twofold Bay on the continent's eastern coastline, which is to say several days' journey from the rescue party's present location. It was there that Ayrton had arranged to meet his accomplices.

"But Ayrton was unmasked just as the lord was placing the letter into his hands, and he had no choice but to flee. Nevertheless, he refused to abandon his plans. With the letter, the *Duncan* would be his, and he was prepared to do whatever it took to recover it. In this Ayrton soon succeeded, and two days later he arrived in Melbourne.

"The criminal's odious scheme had triumphed, for the moment. He would now lead the *Duncan* to Twofold Bay, where the convicts would easily capture it; once the crew had been slaughtered, Ben Joyce would become the master of the seas...But God was to stop him just as his wicked designs were about to become a reality.

"Arriving in Melbourne, Ayrton delivered the letter to the second mate, Tom Austin, who read it and immediately set sail; but imagine Ayrton's fury and dismay when, the day after their departure, he discovered that the ship was sailing not for the east coast of Australia, but for the east coast of New Zealand. He questioned the second mate, and Austin showed him the letter!... Thanks to a miraculous error by the French geographer who took down the message, the *Duncan's* orders were indeed to set sail for the east coast of New Zealand.

"All Ayrton's careful plans had come to naught! He tried to incite a revolt. They locked him up. And so he was taken to the east coast of New Zealand, never knowing what might become of his accomplices, nor of Lord Glenarvan.

"The *Duncan* cruised along the coastline until March 3rd. That day, Ayrton heard a series of detonations. The *Duncan's* carronades were being fired, and soon Lord Glenarvan and all his entourage came aboard.

"This is what had happened.

"After much exhaustion and many dangers, Lord Glenarvan had finally reached the east coast of Australia and Twofold Bay. No *Duncan*! He telegraphed Melbourne. The answer came back: '*Duncan* departed eighteenth this month destination unknown.'

"Lord Glenarvan had only one thought in his mind: that his noble yacht had fallen into the hands of Ben Joyce, and become a pirate ship!

"In spite of this, Lord Glenarvan refused to give up his search. He was an intrepid man, with a great and generous heart. He booked passage on a merchant ship bound for the west coast of New Zealand and set out across the island, still following the thirty-seventh parallel. Again he found no sign of Captain Grant, but on reaching the other shore, to his great surprise, and by the will of Heaven, he found the *Duncan*, under the command of the second mate. For five weeks the yacht had remained in these waters, faithfully awaiting his arrival!

"It was March 3rd, 1855. Lord Glenarvan boarded the *Duncan,* only to find that Ayrton was on board as well. He was brought before the lord, who tried to drag from the bandit everything he might know concerning Captain Grant. Ayrton refused to speak. Lord Glenarvan informed him that he would be handed over to the British authorities at the first port of call. Ayrton remained silent.

"The *Duncan* resumed its journey along the thirty-seventh parallel. As they traveled, Lady Glenarvan attempted to break down the bandit's resistance. Finally her influence won out, and Ayrton offered to tell everything he knew in exchange for Lord Glenarvan's assurance that he would not be turned over to the British authorities, but left on an island in the Pacific. Lord Glenarvan was prepared to make any sacrifice in order to learn Captain Grant's whereabouts, and readily consented.

"Ayrton then told his story, revealing that he knew absolutely nothing of the events that had transpired after Captain Grant put him off on the Australian shoreline.

"Despite Ayrton's trickery, Lord Glenarvan kept his word. The *Duncan* continued its journey, and soon they came to Tabor Island. This was where Ayrton would be left off, and, by a genuine miracle, it was here—on the thirty-seventh parallel, just as the note had said—that they found Captain Grant and his two men. The convict was left to take their place on this deserted islet, and as Ayrton left the yacht, Lord Glenarvan spoke these parting words:

" 'Here, Ayrton, you will be far from any other land, without means of communication with your fellows. You will see that escape is impossible. You will be alone, in the gaze of God who sees deep into human hearts; but you will not be lost, as Captain Grant was, and unlike his your fate will not be unknown to others. However unworthy you are of remaining in the memory of men, men will remember you. I know where you are, Ayrton, and I know where to find you. I will never forget!'

"And so the *Duncan* set sail and vanished over the horizon.

"The date was March 18th, 1855.*

"Ayrton was alone, but he was left a good supply of weapons, ammunition, tools, and seeds. The good Captain Grant had built a house, now to

---

* The events that have just been succinctly recounted are taken from a work that some of our readers have no doubt read, entitled *The Children of Captain Grant.* Such readers may notice certain discrepancies in the dates, both here and further on; but it will eventually be clear why the true dates could not have been provided previously. *(Publisher's note.)*

become his own. The time would pass, and in his isolation he would expiate his terrible crimes!

"Gentlemen, he repented. He looked on his criminal past with horror, and his unhappiness was profound. He told himself that if ever men came to look for him here, he would have to prove himself worthy of returning to their midst! How the poor wretch suffered! How he worked, hoping to rebuild himself through constant labor! How he prayed, hoping to remake himself through prayer!

"Such was his life for two years, three years; but Ayrton, defeated by his isolation, forever staring out to sea in hopes of sighting an approaching ship, wondering if the time of his atonement might be nearing its end, Ayrton suffered as no man ever suffered before! Oh! how hard a thing is solitude for a soul racked by remorse!

"But no doubt Heaven did not consider him sufficiently chastised, for he soon found himself gradually descending into savagery! He could feel himself becoming a mere brute! He cannot say if this occurred after two or four years of abandonment, but in the end he became the wretch you found!

"I needn't tell you, gentlemen, that Ayrton, Ben Joyce, and I are one and the same!"

Cyrus Smith and his companions rose to their feet as Ayrton fell silent. How this account had stirred their souls! Such pain, such misery, such despair there were in Ayrton's tale, unvarnished and undisguised!

"Ayrton," Cyrus Smith then said, "your crimes have been great, but now Heaven has judged them duly expiated! And as proof of your redemption, Providence has brought you once more among your fellows. Ayrton, you are forgiven! And now, will you be our companion?"

Ayrton had taken a step back.

"Here is my hand!" said the engineer.

Ayrton leaped toward Cyrus Smith's outstretched hand, and heavy tears flowed from his eyes.

"Will you live with us?" asked Cyrus Smith.

"Mr. Smith, let me be for a little longer," answered Ayrton, "let me live alone in the house at the sheepfold!"

"As you wish, Ayrton," answered Cyrus Smith.

Ayrton was about to withdraw, but now the engineer posed one final question:

"One last word, my friend. Since you had resolved to live out the time

"Here is my hand," said the engineer.

of your punishment in isolation, why did you write the note that finally brought us to your rescue?"

"Note?" answered Ayrton, as if he did not understand the engineer's words.

"Yes, that note we found sealed inside a bottle, which gave us the precise location of Tabor Island!"

Ayrton passed his hand over his forehead. Then, after some thought:

"I never threw a bottle into the sea!" he answered.

"Never?" asked Pencroff.

"Never!"

And, bowing slightly, Ayrton walked to the door and disappeared into the night.

XVIII

"The poor man!" said Harbert, returning to the great room. He had run to the door as Ayrton went out, only to see him slip down the elevator rope and flee into the darkness.

"He will be back," said Cyrus Smith.

"By gad, Mr. Cyrus," Pencroff cried, "what does this mean? What! it wasn't Ayrton that threw the bottle into the sea? But who was it, then?"

And if ever there were a question that needed asking, this was it!

"It was him," Neb replied, "but the wretch was already half-mad."

"Yes!" said Harbert. "He was no longer aware of his actions."

"This seems the only possible explanation, my friends," Cyrus Smith quickly replied, "and now I understand how Ayrton was able to give us the location of Tabor Island with such precision. It was engraved in his mind by the very events that had led to his abandonment."

"Nevertheless," Pencroff observed, "if he was still in his right mind when he wrote that message, and if he threw the bottle into the ocean seven or eight years ago, how could the paper not have been damaged by the seawater?"

"This proves," Cyrus Smith replied, "that Ayrton's intelligence deserted him much more recently than he believes."

"That must be how it happened," Pencroff answered. "There's no other explanation."

"Indeed," answered the engineer, seemingly reluctant to prolong the conversation.

"But was Ayrton telling the truth?" the sailor asked.

"Yes," the reporter replied. "His story is true in every respect. I well remember the newspaper accounts of Lord Glenarvan's travels, and of the castaways' rescue."

"Ayrton was telling the truth," added Cyrus Smith. "Do not doubt it, Pencroff, for this story cost him dearly. A man who accuses himself as he did tonight is a man who speaks the truth!"

The next day, December 21st, the colonists descended to the beach and climbed up to the plateau. Ayrton was nowhere to be seen. He had clearly proceeded to his new house on leaving the colonists, and for the moment they thought it best not to disturb him with their presence. No doubt time would accomplish what all their encouragements could not.

Harbert, Pencroff, and Neb returned to their habitual occupations; meanwhile, a common project called Cyrus Smith and the reporter to the workshop at the Chimneys.

"Do you know, my dear Cyrus," said Gideon Spilett, "I'm not at all satisfied by your explanation of the message in the bottle! How are we to believe that the wretch could have written the note and thrown it into the sea with no memory of having done so?"

"Then he must not have been the one who wrote it, my dear Spilett."

"So you still believe..."

"I believe nothing, I know nothing!" Cyrus Smith answered, interrupting the reporter. "I simply see this as yet another in a long series of incidents I cannot explain!"

"Truly, Cyrus," said Gideon Spilett, "we've seen things here that defy belief! Your rescue, the crate washing up on the shore, Top's adventures, and now this bottle... Will we ever have the key to these enigmas?"

"Yes!" the engineer answered briskly. "Yes! Even if I have to search this island down to its very entrails!"

"Perhaps chance will give us the solution we seek!"

"Chance! Spilett! I don't believe in chance, no more than I believe in earthly mysteries. There is a cause for every inexplicable event that has happened here, and one day I shall discover that cause. But in the meantime, let us watch and let us work."

January came, and with it the year 1867, and the colonists duly turned to the labors of summer. Early in the month, Harbert and Gideon Spilett traveled to the sheepfold and found that Ayrton had indeed settled into his new lodgings. He spent his time looking after the multitudinous flock that had been entrusted to him, thus sparing his companions the fatigue of coming to check on their animals every two or three days. Nevertheless, the colonists often called on Ayrton, reluctant to leave him in isolation for too long.

Furthermore, it was of no little value—given certain suspicions shared by the engineer and Gideon Spilett—to have a watchful eye surveying this region of the island, and to know that Ayrton would not neglect to alert the inhabitants of Granite House in the event of unusual happenings.

But such incidents could well occur with great suddenness, and the engineer might have to be informed at once. Aside from the very real possibility of events related to the mystery of Lincoln Island, any number of circumstances might arise requiring the colonists' immediate intervention: the spying of a ship off the western shoreline, a shipwreck in the waters to the west, the arrival of pirates, etc.

For this reason, Cyrus Smith resolved to establish a means of instantaneous communication between the sheepfold and Granite House.

On January 10th, he presented his project to his companions.

"Good Lord! how are you going manage that, Mr. Cyrus?" asked Pencroff. "You wouldn't be thinking of putting in a telegraph line?"

"Precisely," answered the engineer.

"Electrical?" cried Harbert.

"Electrical," replied Cyrus Smith. "We have everything we need to make a battery; the most difficult part will be drawing out the iron wire, but with a sturdy drawplate I believe we might well succeed."

"Well, if we can do this," the sailor answered, "I've no doubt I'll be touring the island by railway someday!"

And so they set to work, beginning with the most difficult task, which is to say the making of the wires, for if they failed in this there would be no point in constructing the battery and the rest.

As we know, the soil of Lincoln Island offered an iron of excellent quality, easily worked and so easily drawn out. Cyrus Smith's first step was to fabricate a drawplate, which is a steel plate drilled with conical holes of various calibers; the iron would be successively pulled through the various holes, gradually reducing it to the desired thinness. The plate was forged and tempered "full hard," as metallurgists say, then solidly fixed to a frame sunk deep into the ground a few feet from the waterfall, whose mechanical force the engineer intended to exploit once again.

This procedure was to be performed at the site of the fulling mill. The mill was not currently in use, but the powerful waterfall still turned the drive shaft, and that power would now be harnessed for this new purpose. One end of the wire would be attached to the shaft, and as it turned the wire would inexorably be pulled through the drawplate and wound around the shaft.

This was a complicated operation, requiring great care and close attention. The iron was pounded into long, thin rods, filed down at both ends, and fed into the largest perforation of the drawplate, stretching to a length of twenty-five or thirty feet as it wound around the drive shaft; then it was unwound and run through each of the other holes in turn, and slowly the strand grew thinner and thinner! By this process the engineer obtained wires some forty to fifty feet long, which could then be linked together to form a single strand connecting the sheepfold to Granite House, a distance of five miles.

This entire procedure took no more than a few days. Indeed, once the machine had been set in motion Cyrus Smith left his companions to their new occupation as wire drawers and turned to the fabrication of his battery.

In specific terms, his present purpose required a constant-current battery. As we know, the elements of modern batteries generally include retort carbon, zinc, and copper. The engineer had no copper at his disposal; no matter how he searched, he had never found the slightest trace of that metal on the island, and he would have to make do without. He could have produced retort carbon, which is to say the hard graphite left in the retorts of gas factories after the coal has been dehydrogenated, but for this he would need to construct a special apparatus, which seemed too onerous an undertaking. As for the zinc, we might recall that the crate found at Flotsam Point was lined with a sheet of that very metal, for which there could be no better use than this.

After much reflection, Cyrus Smith finally settled on a very simple battery of the sort devised by Becquerel in 1820, which requires neither carbon nor copper, but only zinc. The battery would be powered by the reaction of nitric acid and potash, of which he already had a plentiful supply.

Here, then, is how this battery was made.

A certain number of glass flasks were fashioned, and filled with nitric acid; the engineer then stopped each flask with a cork transpierced by a glass tube. The lower end of this tube was sealed with a wad of clay held in place by a strip of cloth, and then submerged into the acid. Into the upper end he poured a solution of potash derived from the incineration of various plants; the acid and the potash would now react through the permeable clay.

Cyrus Smith then submerged a small strip of zinc in the nitric acid, and another in the potash solution. An electrical current now flowed between the two strips—one in the flask, the other in the tube. He joined the two strips with a piece of metallic wire, making the strip in the glass tube the battery's positive pole, and the other the negative pole. Each flask thus produced its own current, and when these were united they would produce all the energy needed to power the electrical telegraph.

Such was Cyrus Smith's simple and ingenious apparatus. With this he could establish instantaneous and permanent communication between Granite House and the sheepfold.

The installation of the poles began on February 6th. Each was fitted with a glass insulator to support the wire, and one by one they were erected alongside Sheepfold Road. A few days later the wire had been hung, ready to transmit an electrical current that would race from one end to the other at a speed of one hundred thousand kilometers per second, then return to its point of departure through the earth.

Two batteries had been made, one for Granite House, the other for the sheepfold, for if the sheepfold was to communicate with Granite House, no doubt Granite House should be able to communicate with the sheepfold as well.

Two receivers and two keys were now devised, one for either end of the telegraph line—a task of no great difficulty, for the elements are very simple. The line ended at an electromagnet, which is to say a piece of soft iron wrapped with a wire. When a message was sent, the current flowed from the positive pole, traveled the length of the wire, passed into the electromagnet, temporarily magnetizing it, and returned to the negative pole through the ground. When the circuit was broken, the electromagnet was immediately demagnetized. Now a plate of soft iron was placed before the electromagnet; when the current was flowing the plate would be attracted to the magnet, and when the current was interrupted it would fall away from it. On each plate Cyrus Smith painted the letters of the alphabet in a circle, at whose center he affixed a small revolving pointer, like a clock hand. In this way, each station could easily correspond with the other.

The installation was completed on February 12th. That very day, Cyrus Smith sent the current coursing through the wire to ask if all was well at the sheepfold; a few moments later, he received Ayrton's affirmative response.

Pencroff could scarcely contain his joy. Every morning and every evening, without fail, he sent a telegram to the sheepfold, which never went unanswered.

This invention had two great advantages: first, it allowed them to verify Ayrton's presence at the sheepfold, and second, it left him far less isolated than before. All the same, Cyrus Smith never let a week go by without paying a visit to his new companion, and from time to time Ayrton came to Granite House as well, where he always found a hearty welcome.

And so the summer passed, with the usual round of daily chores. The colony's resources grew from day to day; their grains and vegetables flourished, and the sprouts brought back from Tabor Island thrived wonderfully in their new surroundings. Longview Plateau was a fine and reassuring sight to behold. The fourth wheat harvest was prodigious, and as we might well imagine, no one attempted to count the 400 billion grains that, in theory, the harvest had brought in. Pencroff briefly thought of doing so, but Cyrus Smith informed him that even at a rate of three hundred grains per minute, which is to say nine thousand an hour, he would need some 5,500 years to see his task through, and the good sailor thought it best to abandon this plan.

The weather was superb, the daytime temperatures quite warm; but in the evening the sea winds blew and moderated the heat of the atmosphere, offering pleasantly cool nights for the residents of Granite House. There were a few storms, relatively short-lived but extraordinarily violent, illuminating the heavens with a blaze of lightning and sending endless peals of thunder through the air.

The little colony's prosperity was great. The poultry yard teemed with feathered beasts, and the colonists, forced to reduce their numbers, lived on the excess fowl for some time. The pigs had farrowed, and Neb and Pencroff devoted many long hours to the care of the piglets. The dauws, which had now borne two beautiful calves, were often mounted by

Gideon Spilett and Harbert for their hunting expeditions, and under the reporter's expert tutelage Harbert had become an excellent horseman. The dauws were also called upon to draw the cart whenever Granite House required a fresh supply of wood or coal, or of some other mineral needed for the engineer's projects.

The colonists pursued their explorations as well, primarily into the depths of the Far West. The summer heat never hampered these excursions, for the forest was so dense that the solar rays could scarcely penetrate the interlaced boughs. The right bank of the Mercy was surveyed in its entirety, from the riverbank to the road that ran from the sheepfold to the mouth of Falls River.

In all their wanderings, the colonists were careful never to set out unarmed; for this region was home to a certain kind of wild boar, very savage, very fierce, and very tenacious in battle.

That summer also saw a merciless campaign to eradicate the jaguars. Gideon Spilett felt a particular loathing for these beasts, and his pupil, Harbert, seconded him enthusiastically. The jaguars' ferocity proved no match for their expertly handled weapons. Harbert's bravery was unmatched, and the reporter's coolheadedness remarkable. Already some twenty magnificent pelts hung on the walls of their great room, and if the killing continued at this rate the island would soon be rid of its jaguars forever—which was precisely the two hunters' intention.

Sometimes the engineer participated in these explorations of the island's unknown forests. He observed the area with the closest possible attention, in search of something very different from wild animals, but nothing he saw struck him as odd or untoward. Top and Joop walked close beside him, and never once did their demeanor suggest unusual goings-on in the vicinity. Nevertheless, the dog still sometimes returned, agitated and barking, to the opening of the shaft that the engineer had so fruitlessly explored.

Gideon Spilett now thought of using the photographic kit they had found in the crate, and together with Harbert he produced a fine series of views of all the island's most picturesque localities.

The kit was admirably complete. In addition to a powerful lens, it contained every substance necessary for photographic reproduction: collodion to prepare the glass plate, silver nitrate to sensitize it, sodium hyposulfate to fix the image thus obtained, ammonium chloride to prepare the paper on which the image would be printed, sodium acetate and gold chloride to impregnate the print. There was even a generous supply of paper, already primed with chloride, needing only to be soaked for a few minutes in dilute silver nitrate before it was placed in the printing frame beneath the negative.

The reporter and his assistant soon became skillful photographers, and they obtained some rather remarkable images of the landscape: the whole of the island from Longview Plateau, with Mount Franklin on the horizon; the mouth of the Mercy, picturesquely framed by the towering rocks; the clearing and the sheepfold at the base of the mountain; the wild outline of Cape Claw seen from Flotsam Point, etc.

Nor did the photographers neglect to capture the likenesses of each and every inhabitant of the island.

"That'll give us some company," said Pencroff.

The sailor was enchanted to see his visage, faithfully reproduced, ornamenting the walls of Granite House. He often paused as he passed by, staring at his image as if he were standing before the most elegant shopwindow on Broadway.

But the most successful likeness was incontestably that of Master Joop. He had posed with indescribable gravity, and his portrait could not have been more lifelike!

"You expect him to break into one of his grimaces at any moment!" Pencroff cried.

Master Joop would have been a very demanding ape indeed if he had found this portrait not to his liking; but in fact it was entirely to his liking, and he often contemplated his picture with a sentimental gaze, in which a slight trace of smugness could be detected.

The summer heat ended with the month of March, which is the September of the austral latitudes. The air remained warm, but now the rains began to fall, and March proved not as fine a month as they had hoped. Perhaps this presaged a harsh and early winter.

Indeed, one morning—the twenty-first—they thought the season's first snow had fallen. For that morning, Harbert arose and looked out the windows of Granite House, suddenly crying:

"Look! The islet is covered with snow!"

"Snow, at this time of year?" the reporter answered, joining the boy at the window.

Master Joop posed with indescribable gravity . . .

Soon their companions came to see; to be sure, they found that not only the islet but also the entire beach below Granite House was covered with a uniform blanket of white.

"It's snow all right!" said Pencroff.

"Or something very like it!" Neb replied.

"But the thermometer says it's fifty-eight degrees outside (14° centig. above zero)!" Gideon Spilett observed.

Cyrus Smith gazed silently at the expanse of white, unable to explain such a phenomenon at this time of year and at this temperature.

"By all the devils!" cried Pencroff. "Our crops are going to freeze!"

And the sailor made ready to descend to the beach, preceded by the agile Joop, who leaped over the threshold and swiftly slid to the ground.

But no sooner had the orangutan set foot on the beach than the vast layer of snow rose into the air and scattered, in a flurry so dense that the light of the sun was obscured for several minutes.

"Birds!" cried Harbert.

And so they were: great swarms of seabirds with brilliant white plumage. Hundreds of thousands of them had landed on the islet and the beach, and now they disappeared into the distance. The colonists were left utterly dumbfounded; it was as if they had witnessed a wondrous change of scenery at the theater, miraculously transforming winter into summer. Unfortunately the change had come quite suddenly, leaving no time for the boy or the reporter to shoot down one of the avians, whose species they did not recognize.

A few days later came March 26th. It was now two years since the castaways from the skies had been thrown onto Lincoln Island!

XIX

*Memories of Home.—Outlook for the Future.—Plans for an
Exploration of the Shoreline.—Departure on April 16th.—
Serpentine Peninsula, Seen from Offshore.—The Basaltic
Boulders of the Western Coast.—Bad Weather.—Oncoming
Night.—Another Incident.*

Two years already! Two years without communication with their fellow
men! Two years cut off from the civilized world, stranded on an island as
lonely as the remotest asteroid of the solar realm!

What was happening in their mother country? Their minds were full
of memories of home, of a nation they had left in the grip of a terrible
civil war, a nation still bleeding, perhaps, from the wounds dealt by the
Southerners' rebellion! Such thoughts lay heavy on their minds, and
many an evening was spent discussing their fears for their homeland.
Through it all, however, they never once doubted that the Northern
cause would prevail, to the greater honor of the American union.

In two years, not a single ship had passed within sight of the island—
or at least no sail had been spotted. Clearly, Lincoln Island lay far from
any shipping route; clearly, too, it was entirely unknown to the outside
world, as the atlas confirmed. Even a small island without a port is sometimes visited by ships in search of fresh water, but never once in two years
had such a visit been paid to Lincoln Island: as far as the eye could see, all
was emptiness and desolation, and if the colonists truly hoped to return
to their homeland, they could only rely on themselves.

One single hope for deliverance was left to them now, and one evening
in early April they sat in the great room discussing this possibility.

As so many times before, their conversation had turned to the subject of America, and their despair of ever seeing their native land again.

"It would seem that we have only one course of action open to us," said Gideon Spilett, "only one hope for leaving Lincoln Island, and that is to build a ship capable of withstanding a voyage of several hundred miles. If we can build a boat, we can certainly build a ship, it seems to me!"

"And if we can go to Tabor Island, we can certainly go to the Pomotous!" added Harbert.

"I don't dispute it," said Pencroff, whose voice carried a particular weight in all discussions of seafaring matters, "I don't dispute it, although close by and far away aren't quite the same thing! If we found ourselves in heavy seas on the way home from Tabor Island, at least we knew that land wasn't far off, in one direction or the other; but twelve hundred miles is quite a little trip, and the nearest land is at least that far away!"

"A risky venture, indeed. But would you not attempt it, Pencroff, should the occasion arise?" the reporter asked.

"I'll attempt anything you like, Mr. Spilett. You must know me well enough to realize I'm not afraid of a little risk!"

"And let's not forget that we have one more sailor among us," Neb observed.

"Who would that be?" asked Pencroff.

"Ayrton."

"That's true," answered Harbert.

"If he's willing to leave with us!" Pencroff observed.

"Come now!" said the reporter. "Do you think he would have refused to leave Tabor Island if Lord Glenarvan's yacht had returned to take him home?"

"You're forgetting, my friends," said Cyrus Smith, "that Ayrton's reason had deserted him in his final years on the island. But that is not the question. We must determine whether the return of the Scottish ship can be counted among our possible hopes for rescue. Lord Glenarvan promised Ayrton that he would come back for him one day, when he believed the criminal had atoned for his crimes. I firmly believe that he will return to Tabor Island."

"Yes," said the reporter, "and soon, I daresay. It's been twelve years now since Ayrton was abandoned!"

"Well, yes," Pencroff replied, "I quite agree with you that the lord will return, and soon. But return where? To Tabor Island, not Lincoln Island."

"And he can hardly be expected to visit an island that's not recorded on any map," said Harbert.

"This, my friends," the engineer resumed, "is why we must at all costs return to Tabor Island and leave some indication of our presence here, and Ayrton's as well."

"Of course," the reporter answered. "We have only to leave a message in Ayrton's cabin. Lord Glenarvan or his crew cannot possibly fail to find it."

"Come to mention it," the sailor observed, "it's very irksome that we didn't think of that on our first trip to Tabor Island."

"How could we have?" Harbert answered. "We knew nothing of Ayrton's past at the time. We had no idea that someone would return for him one day, and by the time we learned his story it was too late in the season to return to Tabor Island."

"Yes," answered Cyrus Smith, "too late. And now we shall have to wait for spring to attempt the journey again."

"But what if the Scottish yacht comes back between now and then?" said Pencroff.

"That seems unlikely," the engineer replied. "I don't believe Lord Glenarvan would set out for such remote seas in winter. Either he has already come and gone in the five months since Ayrton joined us, or else he has not yet returned, leaving us time to sail to Tabor Island in October, as soon as the weather turns fine."

"There's no denying," said Neb, "it would be a sad thing for us if the *Duncan* had come just a few months ago!"

"I dearly hope she hasn't," Cyrus Smith answered, "and I trust that Heaven would not deprive us of our one real chance for rescue!"

"In any case," the reporter observed, "I believe a return to Tabor Island will at least give us a clearer idea of our situation; for if the Scotsmen have already returned we will surely find some trace of their passage."

"Most certainly," answered the engineer. "This may be our best chance to return home, my friends, and we must wait patiently to discover whether it is a real chance. If we find that it is not, then we shall consider another course of action."

"In any case," said Pencroff, "I'd like it understood that if we ever do find a way off Lincoln Island, it won't be because we're displeased with our life here!"

"No, Pencroff," the engineer replied, "it will be because we are far from everything that a man must cherish above all else: his family, his friends, his homeland!"

With this they set aside their plans to build a ship and make for the archipelagoes to the north or New Zealand to the west, and resumed their preparations for a third winter at Granite House.

Nevertheless, they resolved to make a trip around the island in their boat before the bad weather set in. Much of the shoreline remained unexplored; they had only the vaguest sense of the northern and western coastlines from the mouth of Falls River to the two Capes Mandible, and little knowledge of the narrow bay that lay between those capes, as between the jaws of a shark.

It was Pencroff who had suggested this excursion, wholeheartedly supported by Cyrus Smith, no less eager than he to expand his acquaintance with their domain.

This was a season of variable weather, but the barometer's oscillations were slow and gentle, and no doubt conditions would be acceptable for such a trip. The barometric pressure fell precipitously in the first week of April, in advance of a strong westerly gale of five or six days' duration; but the storm presaged a return to high pressure, and soon the barometer's needle stood stationary again, at twenty-nine and nine-tenths inches (759.45 millimeters), and the time was right to begin their exploration.

The departure was set for April 16th, and the *Bonadventure,* now anchored in Port Balloon, was stocked for a voyage of several days.

Cyrus Smith informed Ayrton of their plans, and invited him to participate; but Ayrton preferred to remain on land, and it was resolved that he would stay at Granite House for the duration of his companions' absence, in the company of Master Joop, who expressed no objections to this proposal.

The colonists boarded their boat on the morning of April 16th, with Top at their side. A fresh breeze blew from the southwest quadrant, and the *Bonadventure* was forced to tack as it left Port Balloon in the direction of Reptile End. Between the port and the southern promontory lay twenty of the ninety miles that made up the island's perimeter, and these twenty miles would have to be sailed close-hauled, for the wind was dead ahead.

It took them the entire day to reach the promontory. For the first two hours of their voyage the ebb tide sped the boat along, but soon the current reversed and they found themselves faced with six hours of incoming tide, which they found very difficult to stem. Thus, night had already fallen when the craft passed by the promontory.

Pencroff suggested that they continue through the night, taking two reefs in the sail to slow their progress to a crawl. But Cyrus Smith preferred to drop anchor where they were, a few cable lengths from land, for a closer examination of the shore by daylight. The task at hand, after all, was a thorough exploration of the island's shores, and so it was agreed that they would never sail by night, but—weather permitting—drop anchor just offshore when evening came.

And so the night passed by, with the boat lying off the promontory. The wind had died down, and a fog descended, enveloping them in unbroken silence. The sailor excepted, the *Bonadventure*'s passengers slept not quite so well as in their bunks at Granite House, but nevertheless they slept.

Pencroff got under way at dawn the next day—April 17th—and, on a broad reach, tacking to port, he was able to keep close to the western coastline.

The colonists knew this magnificent wooded coastline well, having walked it from end to end in a previous excursion; even now, though, they could not help but wonder at the sight of it. They kept as close to shore as possible, moderating their speed to observe every detail, all the while taking care to avoid the tree trunks floating here and there in the water. Several times they dropped anchor, and Gideon Spilett captured the image of this marvelous shoreline on his photographic plates.

The *Bonadventure* came to the mouth of Falls River at around noon. The forest continued onto the right bank, growing ever sparser, and three miles farther on the trees stood in isolated stands on a ridge of the mountain's westernmost foothill, which sank down to the water's edge.

What a contrast between this coastline's southern and northern halves! Wooded and green on one side, harsh and savage here—much like what are sometimes referred to as "iron coasts"! Its tormented look seemed to indicate a sudden crystallization of molten basalt deep in the geological past. What a fearsome pile of stones, and how horrified the colonists would have been if chance had dropped them here in the beginning! The profoundly sinister aspect of this landscape had eluded them from the summit of Mount Franklin, for details could not be made out from such an elevation; seen from offshore, however, the coastline displayed a strangeness whose equivalent might not be found in any corner of the globe.

The *Bonadventure* sailed along this curious shoreline for a distance of a half-mile. It was composed of stone blocks of varying dimensions, from twenty to three hundred feet tall, and of varying forms: some cylindrical, like towers, some prismatic, like church steeples, some pyramidal, like obelisks, some conical, like smokestacks. These wildly capricious forms infused the place with a sublime horror unmatched by any ice field in any arctic sea! Here, bridges running through the air from one boulder to the next; there, vaults like the vaults of a nave, receding darkly into the distance; here, broad hollows in the stone, with arches on a monumental scale; there, a veritable chaos of points, pyramidions, and spires such as no Gothic cathedral ever possessed. Nature's every fancy—stranger and more varied even than men's—lay before the colonists' eyes, strewn over the shoreline for a distance of eight or nine miles.

Cyrus Smith and his companions looked on with a sense of wonder not far from awe. They stared in silence, but all at once Top began to bark, and a thousand echoes rebounded from the wall of basalt. The engineer noticed a strange tone to Top's barks—not unlike the sounds he produced as he prowled around the shaft in Granite House.

"Bring us closer in," he said.

And the *Bonadventure* drew as near to the rocky shore as Pencroff dared. Might there be some grotto worth exploring here? Cyrus Smith saw nothing; not a cavern, not a single cavity that could have served as a dwelling, for the base of the rocks plunged straight into the sea. Soon Top fell silent, and the boat was once again steered to a distance of several cables from shore.

The shoreline became flat and sandy again in the island's northwestern quadrant. A few sparse trees stood in a marshy plain that the colonists had glimpsed once before. In stark contrast to the region they had just visited, this shore teemed with life in the form of myriads of aquatic birds.

That evening, the *Bonadventure* dropped anchor in a small inlet on the north side of the island. The water was deep, and so they spent the night quite near the shore. This second night went by peacefully, for the breeze had, so to speak, faded along with the last gleams of daylight, and it returned only with the first glimmers of dawn.

A landing could easily be made from so close to shore. Thus, the colony's master hunters, Harbert and Gideon Spilett, went for a two-hour

They returned with several strings of ducks and snipes.

stroll in the early morning, and returned with several strings of ducks and snipes. Top had outdone himself; thanks to his zeal and skill, not a single piece of game had been lost.

At eight o'clock the *Bonadventure* set sail again and speeded toward Cape Mandible North, for it now enjoyed a rear wind, and the breeze was freshening.

"I wouldn't be at all surprised," said Pencroff, "if a westerly gale was on its way. The horizon was very red yesterday at sunset, and this morning there are 'mare's tails,' which bode nothing good."

What Pencroff called mare's tails were elongated cirrus clouds, stretched through the heavens at an altitude of never less than five thousand feet. They resemble light pieces of cotton in appearance, and their presence ordinarily presages some meteorological disturbance in the near future.

"Well," said Cyrus Smith, "let us put up as much sail as we can, and find shelter in Shark Gulf. I believe the *Bonadventure* will be safe there."

"Perfectly," answered Pencroff. "Besides, there's nothing much to see on the northern coast—nothing but sand dunes."

"I wouldn't be unhappy," added the engineer, "if we spent tonight and all day tomorrow in that bay. I believe it deserves a very careful exploration."

"I don't think we'll have a choice one way or the other," answered Pencroff. "There's a very threatening look to the western skies. Look how dark it's become!"

"In any case, we have a fair wind to take us to Cape Mandible," the reporter observed.

"A very fair wind," the sailor answered, "but we'll have to tack if we want to enter the gulf, and I'd much rather sail in head-on, since I've never been there before!"

"The water will likely be full of shoals," added Harbert, "judging by what we saw on the southern coast of Shark Gulf."

"Pencroff," Cyrus Smith then said, "do the best you can. You have our complete confidence."

"Don't you worry, Mr. Cyrus," the sailor answered, "I won't do anything foolhardy! I'd sooner have a knife in my vitals than a submerged rock in the vitals of my *Bonadventure*!"

And by "vitals" Pencroff meant his boat's hull, more precious to him than his own flesh!

"What time is it?" asked Pencroff.

"Ten o'clock," answered Gideon Spilett.

"And what's the distance from here to the cape, Mr. Cyrus?"

"About fifteen miles," the engineer answered.

"That will take us two and a half hours," the sailor said. "We'll be off the cape between noon and one o'clock. Unfortunately, the tide will be going out, and there'll be a strong ebb current in the gulf. It's not going to be easy making our way in, with the wind and the sea both against us."

"Furthermore, there's a full moon today," Harbert observed, "and these April tides are very strong."

"Well, Pencroff," asked Cyrus Smith, "could you not drop anchor just off the end of the cape?"

"Drop anchor near land, with bad weather coming!" cried the sailor. "You don't really mean that, Mr. Cyrus? You might as well run yourself straight into the shoreline!"

"What will you do, then?"

"I'll try to keep offshore until the tide comes in again, about seven o'clock this evening, and if there's still daylight I'll try to put us into the gulf; if not, we'll stay out tacking back and forth all night, and we'll come into the gulf at sunrise tomorrow."

"I've told you before, Pencroff, you have our complete confidence," Cyrus Smith answered.

"Oh!" said Pencroff. "If only there were a lighthouse here, things would go so much easier for navigators!"

"Yes!" answered Harbert, "and this time we won't have a kindly engineer to light a fire and guide us into port!"

"Yes, incidentally, my dear Cyrus," said Gideon Spilett, "we've never thanked you for that; but frankly, without that fire, we would never have been able to reach…"

"Fire?" asked Cyrus Smith, astonished at the reporter's words.

"We mean, Mr. Cyrus," Pencroff answered, "that we were very confused for the last few hours of our journey back from Tabor Island, and we would have gone well leeward of our own island if you hadn't been so kind as to light a fire on the plateau that night of October nineteenth."

"Yes, yes!… What a very fortuitous idea that was!" the engineer replied.

"And this time," the sailor added, "unless it occurs to Ayrton, there will be no one to do us that little favor!"

"No! no one!" answered Cyrus Smith.

And a few moments later, finding himself alone with the reporter in the bow of the craft, the engineer leaned toward him and said:

"If there is one thing certain in this world, Spilett, it is that I never lit a fire the night of October nineteenth, neither on the plateau nor anywhere else on the island!"

XX

A Night at Sea.—Shark Gulf.—Secrets.—Preparations for Winter.—An Early Onset.—Bitter Cold.—Working Inside.— After Six Months.—A Photographic Image.—An Unexpected Incident.

Things went just as Pencroff had predicted, for his experience never steered him wrong. The wind freshened, and soon the fresh breeze became a fresh gale, which is to say that it acquired a speed of forty to forty-five miles per hour,* requiring a boat on the open sea to ride at low reef, with its topgallant sail struck. At six o'clock, the *Bonadventure* lay with the gulf abeam; but as the ebb current was flowing against them, they could not hope to enter. They had no choice but to stay offshore; no matter how he might try, Pencroff could not even have sailed to the mouth of the Mercy. Thus, he ran his staysail up the mainmast to serve as a storm jib; then he waited, with the bow of the boat pointed toward land.

The wind was quite strong, but fortunately the seas were not overly heavy in the shelter of the shoreline. A small boat is always vulnerable to sudden swells or waves, but here they had nothing to fear. To be sure, the *Bonadventure* was well ballasted, and would no doubt not have capsized under such an assault; nevertheless, a great mass of water falling onto the deck could pose a real danger if the hatches were not watertight. Pencroff, ever the able sailor, took precautions against any eventuality. His confidence in his boat was complete and unshakable; nevertheless, it was not without apprehension that he waited out the night.

* Approximately 106 kilometers per hour.

Cyrus Smith and Gideon Spilett had had no occasion to speak together for the moment, and yet the engineer's words made it clear that once again a mysterious influence had exerted itself over Lincoln Island, and this merited further discussion. Gideon Spilett could not take his mind off the inexplicable appearance of that bonfire on the island's coastline. He had seen that fire with his own eyes! His companions, Harbert and Pencroff, had seen it along with him! Through the darkness, the fire had showed them the way to the island. They had never doubted that it was lit by the engineer's hand, and now Cyrus Smith stated categorically that he had done no such thing!

Gideon Spilett resolved to bring the incident up again as soon as the *Bonadventure* had returned to port, in hopes of encouraging Cyrus Smith to present these strange facts to the others. Perhaps, by common agreement, they would decide to carry out an exhaustive search of every corner of Lincoln Island.

But in any case, there were no fires now burning on the gulf's unexplored shoreline, and the little boat stood offshore all through the night.

When the first gleams of dawn appeared on the eastern horizon, the wind had calmed slightly and shifted by two quarters, easing Pencroff's passage through the narrow entrance to the gulf. The *Bonadventure* now bore off Cape Mandible North, and by seven o'clock she had carefully entered the channel. Onward they ventured between the curious walls of hardened lava.

"Now, this would make a capital roadstead!" said Pencroff. "It's big enough for an entire fleet!"

"What I find most remarkable," Cyrus Smith observed, "is that these capes must have been created by two separate lava flows, then built up by successive eruptions, protecting the gulf on every side. Even in the strongest winds, the waters must be as calm as a lake."

"No doubt," the sailor replied. "The only way in for the wind is through the bottleneck between the two capes, and even there the northern cape covers the southern, so we're not likely to see many gales in here! Our *Bonadventure* could lie in this gulf from January to December, and never so much as tug at her anchors!"

"It seems a bit large for her!" the reporter observed.

"Why! Mr. Spilett," the sailor answered, "I don't deny that it's a bit roomy for the *Bonadventure,* but if ever the Union fleet needs a safe harbor in the Pacific, I don't think they could do better than this!"

"We're in the jaws of the shark," Neb then observed, alluding to the gulf's strange form.

"Right between them, dear Neb!" Harbert answered. "You're not afraid they're going to close down on us, are you?"

"No, Mr. Harbert," Neb answered, "but all the same I don't much care for this gulf! It's got a wicked physiognomy!"

"Well now!" cried Pencroff. "So Neb has taken to impugning my gulf, just as I was thinking of offering it to America in homage!"

"But tell me, are the waters very deep?" asked the engineer. "After all, what's sufficient for the keel of the *Bonadventure* may not be enough for our armored battleships."

"We can easily find out!" Pencroff answered.

And the sailor took up his sounding line—a long rope with an iron weight tied to one end—and sent it plunging into the depths. A moment later the fifty-fathom line had unfurled to its full length, and still the iron weight had not hit bottom.

"So you see," said Pencroff, "our armored ships can come here whenever they like! There's no risk of running aground!"

"Indeed," said Cyrus Smith, "the gulf is a veritable abyss. But, considering our island's plutonian origins, deep depressions in the seabed are only to be expected."

"The walls seem to sink straight down into the water," Harbert observed. "At the base of the cliffs, a sounding line five or six times longer than Pencroff's might still not hit bottom."

"That's all very well," the reporter then said, "but I must inform Pencroff that his roadstead is missing one thing!"

"What would that be, Mr. Spilett?"

"Some sort of passage through the rock for access to the island's interior. I don't see a single spot where someone could set foot!"

Indeed, the towering walls of solidified lava rose perfectly straight and sheer, and no matter how carefully the colonists scrutinized the perimeter of the gulf, they could find no suitable landing site—only an unbroken and insurmountable curtain of rock, reminiscent of a Norwegian fjord, but without the lush greenery. Sailing almost within arm's reach of the walls, the passengers of the *Bonadventure* found not so much as an outcropping on which to clamber out of their boat.

Pencroff consoled himself that they might one day disembowel that wall with explosives; but since there was clearly nothing worthy of their attention in this gulf, he steered his vessel back toward the entrance and emerged around two o'clock in the afternoon.

"Whew!" said Neb, sighing with relief.

The good Negro seemed to feel a genuine unease within those enormous jaws!

A distance of eight miles separated Cape Mandible from the mouth of the Mercy. Pencroff set the heading for Granite House, and with sails unfurled the *Bonadventure* followed the coastline from one mile offshore. Soon the great volcanic rocks gave way to the expanse of wild dunes where the engineer had so mysteriously reappeared, now frequented by hundreds of seabirds.

At about four o'clock, Pencroff guided his boat into the channel between the islet and the shore, and at five o'clock the *Bonadventure*'s anchor sank into the sand at the mouth of the Mercy.

The colonists had been away for three days. They found Ayrton awaiting them on the beach, and Master Joop came running to meet them, growling with hearty satisfaction.

They had now explored the whole of the island's shoreline, and nothing suspicious had been uncovered. If some mysterious being were indeed living on their island, it could only be within the cover of the impenetrable woods of Serpentine Peninsula, where the colonists' investigations had not yet led them.

Gideon Spilett now spoke with the engineer, and they agreed to call to their companions' attention all the many troubling events that had so far occurred on the island, the most recent of which was among the most inexplicable.

Thus, still dwelling on the mystery of the fire lit by an unknown hand, Cyrus Smith could not prevent himself from repeating to the reporter, for the twentieth time:

"You're quite sure your eyes did not deceive you? It couldn't have been a partial eruption of the volcano, or some kind of meteorological oddity?"

"No, Cyrus," the reporter answered, "it was most certainly a fire lit by a human hand. You can ask Pencroff and Harbert. They saw what I saw, and they will confirm what I've told you."

And so it was that a few days later, on the evening of April 25th, as the colonists sat together on Longview Plateau, Cyrus Smith spoke the following words:

"My friends, I believe I must bring to your attention certain events that have occurred on the island, of which I would gladly hear your opinion. These are events of a highly curious nature—I might almost say supernatural..."

"Supernatural!" cried the sailor, letting out a great puff of tobacco smoke. "You don't believe our island is supernatural?"

"No, Pencroff, but it is surely mysterious," the engineer answered, "unless you can explain what Spilett and I have thus far been unable to comprehend."

"Speak, Mr. Cyrus," the sailor replied.

"Well, do you understand," the engineer then said, "how, after falling into the sea, I was found a quarter-mile inland, with no memory of such a trek in my mind?"

"Unless, in your unconsciousness..." said Pencroff.

"That cannot be," the engineer answered. "But let us go on. Do you understand how Top could have discovered your refuge, five miles from the grotto where I lay?"

"The dog's instinct..." answered Harbert.

"That's quite an instinct!" the reporter observed. "Through all that night's fierce wind and rain, Top arrived at the Chimneys with his fur perfectly dry, and not so much as a single splash of mud!"

"Let us go on," the engineer continued. "Do you understand how our dog was so mysteriously thrown from the lake after his battle with the dugong?"

"No! Not really, I must admit," Pencroff answered. "Nor do I understand why the wound in the dugong's side looked so much like something made by a sharp blade."

"Let us go on," Cyrus Smith now said. "Do you understand, my friends, how the lead pellet came to be in the body of the baby peccary; how that crate so opportunely washed onto our shores with no trace of a shipwreck; how the bottle containing the message appeared just as we were first testing out our *Bonadventure;* how the canoe happened to break its moorings and drift down the Mercy to meet us just when we needed it; how, after the invasion of the apes, the ladder was so conveniently sent down from the heights of Granite House; and how, finally, a note that Ayrton claims never to have written came into our hands?"

And so Cyrus Smith enumerated all the strange events that had occurred on their island, omitting none. Harbert, Pencroff, and Neb merely looked at one another, unable to reply, for the succession of incidents now laid out before them had plunged them into the most profound astonishment.

"My word," Pencroff finally said, "you're right, Mr. Cyrus. These are difficult things to explain!"

"Well, my friends," the engineer replied, "one last event must now be added to the list, no less incomprehensible than the rest!"

"What is it, Mr. Cyrus?" Harbert asked breathlessly.

"When you returned from Tabor Island, Pencroff," the engineer continued, "you say that a fire appeared to you from Lincoln Island?"

"Indeed," said the sailor.

"And you're quite certain you saw it?"

"As sure as I see you now."

"You too, Harbert?"

"Oh! Mr. Cyrus," cried Harbert, "that fire shone like a star of the first magnitude!"

"Could it not have been a star?" the engineer asked insistently.

"No," answered Pencroff. "The sky was covered with thick clouds, and in any case a star wouldn't have appeared so low on the horizon. But Mr. Spilett saw it along with us, and he can confirm what we say!"

"I would add," said the reporter, "that the fire was extremely brilliant, and it cast a sort of electrical field around it."

"Yes! Yes! Precisely…" answered Harbert, "and it was clearly on the plateau above Granite House."

"Well, my friends," Cyrus Smith replied, "during that night of October nineteenth, neither Neb nor myself lit any such fire."

"You didn't?…" cried Pencroff, too astonished to finish his sentence.

"We never set foot outside Granite House," answered Cyrus Smith, "and if you saw a fire burning on the plateau, it was lit by some hand other than ours!"

Pencroff, Harbert, and Neb were stunned. It was no illusion; a fire had most certainly dazzled their eyes that night of October 19th!

Yes! they had to agree, there was a mystery here! An inexplicable influence—obviously favorable to the colonists, but highly irritating to their curiosity—had made itself felt on numerous occasions, and always just when it was needed most. Did some strange being lurk in the deepest recesses of Lincoln Island? This was a question to which they must imperatively find the answer, no matter what the cost!

Cyrus Smith went on to remind his companions of Top and Joop's curious obsession with the shaft that led from Granite House to the sea, and told them of his fruitless exploration of the shaft some time before. The conversation concluded with a unanimous vow to make an exhaustive search of the island when the fair weather returned.

A sort of cloud hung over Pencroff from that day forward. He had come to see the island as his personal property, but now it seemed no longer fully his. Like it or not, he was forced to share it with another, with one who truly seemed his master. He and Neb often spoke of these mysteries. Inclined by their nature to a certain belief in the fantastic, they were all but convinced that some superhuman force controlled Lincoln Island.

The weather deteriorated in the month of May, as in the boreal November. All signs pointed to a harsh and early winter, and certain tasks would have to be performed if they hoped to survive over the coming months.

On the whole, however, the colonists were well prepared for the onset of winter, no matter how harsh it might prove. Their cabinets were full of felt clothing, and their prolific flock of mouflons offered an abundant reserve of wool for the future.

Ayrton had of course been provided with a full wardrobe of warm winter clothes. Cyrus Smith invited him to spend the season at Granite House—a place far more comfortable than the sheepfold in cold weather—and Ayrton promised to do so, once he had finished a few final projects. He came and joined his companions around the middle of April, sharing in their daily existence, never failing to make himself useful; yet his quiet sadness still remained, and he could never truly enjoy the simple pleasures of the colonists' life!

They remained confined to Granite House for the greater part of their third winter on Lincoln Island. Great storms and terrible gales seemed to shake the granite cliff down to its very foundation. Immense waves threatened to inundate vast stretches of the island's surface, and any ship moored offshore would most surely have been destroyed. Twice the bridges over the rain-swollen Mercy were menaced by the river's roaring waters; meanwhile, the storm-driven waves crashed over the small bridges on the beach, requiring immediate reinforcement of their structure if they were not to be swept away by the raging sea.

The gales whirled around their island like gigantic waterspouts, their winds driving a mixture of rain and snow. As we might well expect, they wrought severe damage on Longview Plateau, particularly to the mill and the poultry yard. Urgent repairs were more than once required to protect the lives of their domesticated fowl.

As winter neared its peak, several pairs of jaguars and bands of quadrumanes appeared at the edge of the plateau, apparently driven from their homes by the storm. Urged on by hunger, the most agile and daring among them might well have attempted to cross the stream; indeed, when the surface was frozen, there was nothing to stop them. The colonists were thus forced to keep a continuous watch over their crops and animals, firing rifle shots to keep the unwelcome visitors at bay. Between these outdoor duties and the thousand projects always awaiting them within Granite House, it should be clear that the colonists never lacked for occupations.

Even in the depths of winter there was hunting to be done in Shelduck Fens, where myriads of ducks, snipes, teals, pintails, and lapwings had taken shelter for the season. Ably assisted by Top and Joop, Gideon Spilett and Harbert never wasted a shot. The fens offered a never-ending supply of fresh game, only two or three miles from Granite House, easily reached by way of the Port Balloon road or the rocks at Flotsam Point.

Thus passed four rigorous months of winter, June, July, August, and September. Granite House had suffered no real harm from the violent weather; nor had the sheepfold, far less exposed than the plateau, sheltered as it was by the mass of Mount Franklin and protected from strong winds by the forests and the high rocks of the shoreline. Whatever minor damage the storms had caused was promptly repaired by Ayrton's skillful and energetic hands during a brief return to the sheepfold in the latter half of October.

The winter passed with no new inexplicable events, no strange happenings of any sort, even with Pencroff and Neb forever on the lookout for the most insignificant occurrence of a mysterious nature. Never once had Top and Joop come prowling around the shaft; never once had they shown the slightest sign of anxiety or anger. The string of supernatural events seemed to have been interrupted, but remained a frequent topic of evening conversation at Granite House, and the colonists never thought of abandoning their plans for an exhaustive search of the island when spring returned. Soon, however, an event of the greatest significance—and of the gravest potential consequences—would distract Cyrus Smith and his companions from their projects.

Cyrus Smith examined the spot.

The month of October had come. Spring was approaching by leaps and bounds. Nature came back to life in the warmth of the brilliant sun, and the green shoots of the nettle trees, banksias, and deodars appeared among the deeper hues of the conifers.

As we recall, Gideon Spilett and Harbert had on several occasions taken photographic views of Lincoln Island.

At about three o'clock on the afternoon of October 17th, Harbert, delighted by the pure blue sky and dazzling sun, thought of capturing an image of Union Bay from Granite House, which offered a sweeping view from Cape Mandible to Cape Claw.

The horizon was sharply drawn, and the sea, gently rippling in the breeze, seemed as still as the waters of a lake, studded here and there with luminous glints.

He placed the lens at a window in the great room, overlooking the beach and the bay. Exposing his photographic plate, he retired to a dark closet to fix the image with the necessary chemicals.

Emerging into the light of day again, he looked closely at the glass plate and discovered a tiny dot on the horizon. He tried to wash it away, but found that he could not.

"There must be a flaw in the glass," he thought.

And then his curiosity impelled him to examine the dot with a strong lens unscrewed from one of the telescopes.

But no sooner had he bent over it than he let out a shout, nearly dropping the plate.

He ran at once to find Cyrus Smith and handed him the plate and lens, pointing out the small black spot.

Cyrus Smith examined it; then, seizing his spyglass, he hurried to the window.

The spyglass slowly moved over the horizon, finally stopping on a suspicious dark point. Cyrus Smith lowered the telescope and said simply: "A ship!"

For it was true: a ship lay within sight of Lincoln Island!

PART THREE
THE SECRET OF THE ISLAND

I

*Salvation or Doom?—Ayrton Summoned.—An Important
Discussion.—Not the Duncan.—A Suspicious Craft.—
Precautions to Be Taken.—The Ship Approaches.—A Cannon
Shot.—The Brig Moors Within Sight of the Island.—
Darkness Falls.*

In all their two and a half years on Lincoln Island, the castaways from the balloon had had no communication with the outside world. The reporter had once tried to contact his fellow men with a message tied to the neck of a seabird, but little faith could be placed in such an uncertain enterprise. Ayrton was the only outsider to have set foot on their island, in the circumstances we remember. And now, this very day—October 17th—other men had suddenly appeared on the eternally deserted sea!

There was no doubt about it! It was a ship! But would it pass by or drop anchor? The colonists would have their answer in a matter of hours.

Cyrus Smith and Harbert immediately called Gideon Spilett, Pencroff, and Neb to the great room of Granite House and told them what had happened. Pencroff seized the spyglass and quickly ran his eye over the horizon; then, discovering the object that had made the imperceptible dot on the photographic plate:

"By all the devils! It's a ship, to be sure!" he said, in a voice that did not betoken great pleasure.

"Is it coming this way?" asked Gideon Spilett.

"I can't tell you for the moment," Pencroff answered. "I can only see her masts above the horizon, and not a bit of her hull!"

"What should we do?" said the boy.

"Wait," answered Cyrus Smith.

And for some time the colonists stood in silence, their minds full of a thousand thoughts, a thousand emotions, a thousand fears, a thousand hopes aroused by this incident—the most momentous by far since their arrival on Lincoln Island.

To be sure, they did not find themselves stranded on a sterile islet, struggling to win a meager existence from implacable nature, devoured by an insistent yearning to return to inhabited lands. Pencroff and Neb would have felt a particular sorrow on leaving the island, for they found their life here a rich and happy one. They had come to love their new existence, in a new domain civilized, so to speak, by their intelligence! Nevertheless, a ship meant news from the inhabited world, and perhaps a bit of their homeland coming to greet them! It carried beings like themselves, and we need not wonder that their hearts quivered uncontrollably at the sight of it!

From time to time Pencroff took up the spyglass and stood at the window, carefully examining the ship, which lay twenty miles to the east. For the moment the colonists had no way to attract its attention. A flag would not have been seen; a gunshot would not have been heard; a fire would not have been visible.

Nevertheless, the towering form of Mount Franklin could not have escaped the gaze of the ship's watchmen. But why should the ship land here? Had it not been driven purely by chance to this area of the Pacific, where maps indicate no land save the tiny Tabor Island, which lay well off the routes normally traveled by the sea liners of the Polynesian archipelagoes, New Zealand, and the American coast?

This question was on every mind, and Harbert suddenly provided an answer.

"Could it not be the *Duncan*?" he cried.

It will be remembered that the *Duncan* was the yacht of Lord Glenarvan, who had abandoned Ayrton on the islet and would return to pick him up one day. And the islet was close enough to Lincoln Island that a ship traveling toward the one might well pass within sight of the other. Only one hundred fifty miles separated them in longitude, and seventy-five in latitude.

"We must alert Ayrton," said Gideon Spilett, "and send for him at once. He alone can say if this is the *Duncan* or not."

This sentiment was shared by all. Hurrying to the telegraphic apparatus linking the sheepfold to Granite House, the reporter now sent this telegram:

"Come at once."

A few moments later, the iron plate clanked against the electromagnet.

"On my way," Ayrton answered.

"If this is the *Duncan*," said Harbert, "Ayrton will have no trouble recognizing it, since he sailed aboard it for some time."

"And if he does," added Pencroff, "it's going to give him quite a shock!"

"Yes," answered Cyrus Smith, "but Ayrton has proved himself worthy of reboarding the *Duncan*, and may God grant that this is indeed Lord Glenarvan's yacht, for any other ship may be cause for great concern! There are many brigands in these seas, and my fears of a visit from Malay pirates are as strong as ever."

"We'll fight them off!" cried Harbert.

"No doubt, my boy," the engineer answered with a smile, "but I would prefer not to be forced to do so."

"A simple observation," said Gideon Spilett. "Lincoln Island is unknown to seamen, since even the most recent maps make no mention of its existence. Do you not believe, Cyrus, that this in itself is enough to attract any ship that catches sight of this new land?"

"Certainly," answered Pencroff.

"I agree," the engineer added. "The captain would be duty-bound to record, and thus to come and survey, any unknown land or island such as ours."

"Well," said Pencroff, "suppose the ship comes into our waters and moors a few cables from shore. What shall we do?"

Pencroff's abrupt question met with no immediate response. But after a moment's thought, Cyrus Smith answered in his usual steady tone:

"What we will do, my friends, what we must do, is this: we will make contact with the ship, we will take passage aboard it, and we will leave our island, after claiming it in the name of the Union. Then we will return with all who might wish to follow us and make of it a real colony, a Pacific outpost for our great American republic!"

"Hurrah!" cried Pencroff. "And what a fine gift for our beloved country! The island's as good as colonized already! Every feature of its landscape has a name; there's a natural harbor, fresh water, roads, a telegraph line, a shipyard, industries—all that's left is to give Lincoln Island a place on the map!"

"But what if someone captures the island in our absence?" Gideon Spilett observed.

"By all the devils!" cried the sailor. "I'll stay behind all alone to watch over it, and by Pencroff's honor, I won't let it be snatched away from me like a watch from some ninny's pocket!"

An hour passed, and still they could not say with certainty whether the ship was or was not heading toward Lincoln Island. To be sure, it was nearer now, but what was its bearing? That Pencroff could not determine. Nevertheless, since the wind was in the northeast, it was reasonable to assume that the ship was sailing on a starboard tack. Such a breeze would inevitably propel it toward the island's shores, and in these calm seas the sailors would have no reason to fear the approach toward land, even without a chart to show them the soundings of the island's waters.

Ayrton arrived at Granite House about four o'clock, an hour after he had been sent for. He entered the great room, saying:

"Present as requested, gentlemen."

Cyrus Smith extended his hand toward him, as was his custom; then, leading him to the window:

"Ayrton," he said, "we have asked you here for a very serious reason. There is a ship within sight of the island."

Ayrton paled slightly, and for a moment his gaze went blank. Then he leaned out the window and ran his eye over the horizon, but he saw nothing.

"Take the spyglass," said Gideon Spilett, "and look closely, Ayrton, for this ship might possibly be the *Duncan*, returning to pick you up."

"The *Duncan*!" Ayrton murmured. "Already!"

This last word seemed to burst from Ayrton's lips unbidden, and he buried his face in his hands.

Did he not find twelve years' isolation on a desert island punishment enough? Could the repentant wrongdoer not yet consider himself amply pardoned, either in his own eyes or in others'?

"No," he said, "no! It cannot be the *Duncan*."

"Look, Ayrton," the engineer replied. "It is vitally important that we know in advance what to expect."

Ayrton took the spyglass and aimed it in the direction he was shown. For several minutes he observed the horizon, motionless and silent. Then:

"It is indeed a ship," he said, "but I don't believe it's the *Duncan*."

"On what basis do you say that?" asked Gideon Spilett.

"The *Duncan* is a steam yacht, and I see no trace of smoke, neither above the ship nor around it."

"Perhaps she's simply traveling under sail?" Pencroff observed. "She has a fair wind for the course she seems to be taking, and at this distance from land a good captain always spares the coal when he can."

"You may be right, Mr. Pencroff," Ayrton replied, "it could be that the ship has extinguished its fires. Let's wait until it stands into the shore, and soon we'll know what to expect."

With this Ayrton went and sat down in a corner, and there he remained in deep silence. The colonists continued their discussion of the unfamiliar ship, but Ayrton took no part.

No one could think of returning to his customary chores at a time such as this. Gideon Spilett and Pencroff seemed singularly ill at ease, pacing back and forth, unable to stand still. Harbert felt more curious than anything else. Only Neb maintained his habitual composure. Was his homeland not wherever his master happened to be? As for the engineer, he remained absorbed in his thoughts; deep down, he dreaded the arrival of this ship far more than he desired it.

Meanwhile, the ship had drawn slightly nearer the island. With the aid of the spyglass, the colonists discovered that it was a sea liner, and not a Malay prau, the favored vessel of Pacific pirates. From this they concluded that the engineer's fears were groundless, and that its presence in Lincoln Island's waters did not constitute a threat. After a careful examination of the ship, Pencroff announced that it seemed to be rigged as a brig, and that it was traveling on a starboard tack at an oblique angle to the shoreline, under courses, topsails, and topgallants. This was confirmed by Ayrton.

But if it continued on that southwesterly heading, it would soon disappear behind Cape Claw, and the colonists would have to make for the highlands over Washington Bay, near Port Balloon, if they wanted to watch its progress. Unfortunately, it was already five o'clock in the afternoon, and dusk would soon make any observation difficult at best.

"What will we do when night comes?" asked Gideon Spilett. "Shall we light a fire to alert them to our presence?"

This was a weighty question; but despite the engineer's forebodings, it was soon resolved in the affirmative. The ship might disappear in the night and sail away forever; and once it had vanished, would another ever come to the waters of Lincoln Island? Who among them could predict what the future might hold?

"Yes," said the reporter, "whatever the ship may be, we must make it clear that the island is inhabited. If we refuse this opportunity we might regret it for the rest of our lives!"

And so it was decided that Neb and Pencroff would set off for Port Balloon and light a great fire, whose brilliance could not fail to attract the attention of the brig's crew.

But the ship changed course just as Neb and the sailor were about to leave Granite House. Now it was headed straight toward the island, making for Union Bay. The brig was a swift runner, and approached at a considerable speed.

Neb and Pencroff thus abandoned their plans, and the spyglass was placed in Ayrton's hands so that he might determine to a certainty whether this was the *Duncan* or not. The Scottish yacht, too, was rigged as a brig. The question, then, was whether a chimney stood between the two masts of the ship now before them, no more than ten miles away.

The water was still brightly lit by the rays of the setting sun. The ship's configuration could thus easily be verified, and a moment later Ayrton lowered the spyglass, saying:

"It's not the *Duncan*! It can't be!..."

Once more Pencroff framed the ship within the visual field of the spyglass. It was a brig of three or four hundred tons, wonderfully slender, boldly masted, admirably built for speed, a swift and agile courser of the seas. But what was its nationality? That he could not say.

"There's a flag flying at the gaffer," the sailor told them, "but I can't quite make out the colors."

"We'll know within half an hour," the reporter answered. "In any case, the captain is clearly intending to land, and we will soon make his acquaintance, if not today then at least tomorrow."

"All the same!" said Pencroff. "It would be best to know who we're dealing with before then. I'd dearly love to see our visitors' colors before we welcome them into our domain!"

And the sailor kept his eye glued to the spyglass as he spoke.

The light was beginning to fade, and the winds slowed as well. Hanging limp, the brig's flag became tangled in the halyards, making it all the more difficult to make out.

"The black flag!" said Ayrton.

"It's not an American flag," Pencroff went on, "nor British, or the red would show. It's not brightly colored like the French or German flag, or the white flag of Russia, or the yellow flag of Spain... It seems to be all one color... Let me see... in these seas... what would we be most likely to find?... The Chilean flag? No, that's a tricolor... Brazilian?... That's green... Japanese?... That one's black and yellow... whereas this one..."

Just then a gust of wind drew out the unknown flag to its full length. Pencroff had lowered the spyglass. Ayrton now took it from him and raised it to his eye; then, in a quiet voice:

"The black flag!" he said.

For a dark bunting fluttered from the brig's gaffer, and at once the ship appeared to them in a very different light!

Had the engineer's fears been realized? Was this indeed a pirate ship? Did it scour the South Pacific in competition with the Malay praus? Why had it come to the shores of Lincoln Island? Had the pirates realized they had stumbled onto undiscovered land, where they could store their stolen goods in safety? Would they use the island as a winter harbor for their ship? Was the colonists' honest domain destined to become a sordid refuge for brigands and bandits—a capital of Pacific piracy?

Such were the questions that flashed through the colonists' minds. The meaning of the ship's flag, at least, was not in doubt. It could only be a pirate flag! The very flag the *Duncan* would have flown, if the convicts had succeeded in their criminal designs!

The colonists lost no time in vain discussions.

"My friends," said Cyrus Smith, "perhaps the ship merely intends to observe the island's coastline; perhaps the crew will not come ashore. This is possible. Nonetheless, we must do everything we can to conceal our presence! The mill on Longview Plateau is too visible from the sea. Ayrton and Neb, I want you to go and take down the sails. And we must find leafy branches to cover the windows of Granite House. All fires are to be extinguished at once. Let nothing betray the presence of men on these shores!"

"What about our boat?" said Harbert.

"Oh," answered Pencroff, "she's snug in Port Balloon, and I defy these blackguards to find her!"

The engineer's orders were immediately carried out. Neb and Ayrton climbed to the plateau and methodically concealed every sign of human habitation. In the meantime, their companions hurried to Jacamar Woods and returned with a great pile of branches and vines. These would be hung over the windows of Granite House, producing, from a distance, an effect of natural growth. At the same time, they gathered together all their weapons and ammunition for immediate use, should some unprovoked act of aggression necessitate it.

When all these precautions had been taken:

"My friends," said Cyrus Smith—and the depth of his emotion could clearly be heard in his voice—"if these wretches attempt to capture Lincoln Island, we will defend her, will we not?"

"Yes, Cyrus," the reporter answered, "and we are prepared to die in her defense, if need be!"

The engineer held out his hand, and his companions pressed it effusively.

Only Ayrton hung back, still silent in his corner. Perhaps the former convict did not yet consider himself worthy of joining in with the rest!

Cyrus Smith realized what was taking place in Ayrton's soul, and, coming toward him:

"What about you, Ayrton," he asked him, "what will you do?"

"My duty," Ayrton answered.

Then he walked to the window and stood peering through the foliage.

It was now seven-thirty. The sun had disappeared behind them some twenty minutes before, and the eastern horizon slowly dimmed. Meanwhile, the brig continued its advance toward Union Bay. It was now no more than eight miles distant, with Longview Plateau directly abeam, for after it had veered aside at Cape Claw, the current of the rising tide had quickly pushed it northward. Even at this distance it could be considered to have entered the vast bay, for a straight line drawn from Cape Claw to Cape Mandible would have lain to its west, off the ship's starboard side.

Would the brig push farther into the bay? That was the first question. Once in the bay, would it moor? That was the second. Might the pirates simply observe the shoreline and return to the open sea without making landfall? They would know within the hour. They had no choice but to wait.

A wave of anxiety had run through Cyrus Smith when he saw the black flag flying from the sinister ship. Was this not a direct threat to all that he and his companions had accomplished? Had the pirates—for such the brig's sailors surely were—set foot on this island before, since they had raised their colors as they approached? Could the strange events that had so baffled the colonists be explained by a previous landing of the pirate ship? Might there be some accomplice even now lying in wait on the island, ready to make contact with his cohorts?

Cyrus Smith pondered these questions in silence, knowing that he did not have the answers; in any case, he strongly sensed that the arrival of the brig would pose a serious threat to the little colony's very existence.

Nevertheless, he and his companions had vowed to fight to the last. Were the pirates more numerous and better armed than they? A crucial question! But how to approach them and find out?

Night had fallen. The new moon had disappeared in the wake of the solar rays. A deep darkness enveloped the island and the sea. No light filtered through the mass of thick clouds on the horizon. The winds had died away as the sun set. Not a single leaf trembled on the trees, not the slightest lapping wave murmured on the beach. Nothing could be seen of the ship, for its lights were covered, and while they knew it still lay in the island's waters, they could not determine its position.

"Who knows?" said Pencroff. "Perhaps the blasted ship will sail away in the night, and when dawn comes she'll be long gone?"

As if in response to the sailor's observation, a bright light flashed off-shore, and the sound of cannon fire echoed through the darkness.

The ship was still there, and it was armed with cannons.

Six seconds had passed between the flash and the sound of the detonation.

Thus, the brig lay some one and one-quarter miles from shore.

And now they heard the rattle of chains running through the hawse-holes.

The ship had dropped anchor in the waters before Granite House!

II

Discussions.—Forebodings.—A Proposal from Ayrton.—Ayrton's Suggestion Accepted.—Ayrton and Pencroff on Grant Islet.— Convicts from Norfolk.—Their Plans.—Ayrton's Daring.—His Return.—Six Against Fifty.

The pirates' intentions were no longer in doubt. They had dropped anchor only a short distance from the island, and the next day they would lower their launches and come ashore!

Cyrus Smith and his companions were ready to act; but however firm their resolve, they knew that caution was their greatest ally. Their presence here might yet go undetected if the pirates confined their explorations to the shores, and did not venture inland. For it could well be that they had only come to replenish their supply of fresh water at the Mercy, and it was not inconceivable that the bridge some mile and a half from the mouth would escape their notice, along with the modifications made to the Chimneys.

But why the flag flying from the brig's gaffer? Why the cannon shot? Purely for show, no doubt, unless this was their way of signifying that the island was theirs! Cyrus Smith now knew the ship to be formidably armed. And with what could the colony respond to their cannons? Nothing more than a handful of rifles.

"Nevertheless," Cyrus Smith observed, "our current position is unassailable. Our enemies will never find the entrance to the spillway under the shrubs and grasses, so they have no means of entering Granite House!"

"But our vegetables, our poultry yard, our sheepfold—everything, in short, everything!" cried Pencroff, stamping his foot. "Within a matter of hours they could pillage everything, destroy everything we've worked so hard to build!"

"Everything, Pencroff," answered Cyrus Smith, "and we have no way to stop them."

"How many are they? That's the question," the reporter said. "If there are only a dozen or so, perhaps we can hold them off; but forty, fifty, more perhaps!…"

"Mr. Smith," Ayrton then said, advancing toward the engineer, "would you allow me to try something?"

"To try what, my friend?"

"I'd like to go to the boat, and try to determine the size of her crew."

"But Ayrton…" the engineer answered hesitantly, "you would be risking your life…"

"And why shouldn't I, sir?"

"That's more than your duty."

"I have more than my duty to do," Ayrton answered.

"You'd take the canoe out to the ship?" asked Gideon Spilett.

"No, sir, I'd swim. A canoe can't travel underwater as a man can."

"You do know that the brig is a mile and a quarter from shore?" said Harbert.

"I'm a good swimmer, Mr. Harbert."

"You're risking your life, I say," the engineer repeated.

"No matter," Ayrton answered. "Mr. Cyrus, I'm begging you, as a favor. This might help to redeem me in my own eyes!"

"All right, Ayrton," the engineer answered, sensing that a refusal would have greatly pained the former convict, now become an honest man again.

"I'll go with you," said Pencroff.

"You don't trust me!" Ayrton brusquely replied.

Then, more humbly:

"Alas!"

"No! no!" Cyrus Smith quickly replied. "It's not that Pencroff doesn't trust you! You've misunderstood his meaning."

"That's right," the sailor answered. "I propose to accompany Ayrton only as far as the islet. It's possible, although not altogether probable, that one of those rogues has already left the ship. If so, we'd do well to have two men there to stop him sounding the alarm. I'll wait for Ayrton on the islet, and he'll go the brig alone, since that's what he's offered to do!"

This they all agreed to, and Ayrton prepared to set off. It was a daring plan, but under cover of darkness it could easily succeed. On reaching the ship, clinging to the bobstays or shrouds, he might well be able to determine the number of brigands on board, and perhaps discover their intentions.

Ayrton and Pencroff descended to the beach, with their companions close behind. Ayrton undressed and rubbed himself with fat as insulation against the ocean's frigid temperatures, for he might find himself forced to spend several hours in the water.

Meanwhile, Pencroff and Neb went to fetch the canoe, moored to the bank of the Mercy a few hundred paces away. They soon returned, and Ayrton was ready to set off.

A blanket was thrown over his shoulders, and the colonists stepped forward one by one to press his hand.

Ayrton climbed into the canoe alongside Pencroff.

It was ten-thirty at night when they disappeared into the darkness. Their companions headed toward the Chimneys to await their return.

The canoe quickly crossed the channel, and soon Pencroff and Ayrton stood on the islet's shore. They had landed as discreetly as they could, knowing there might be pirates lurking in the vicinity; but a careful inspection showed the islet to be deserted. Thus, they hurried to the opposite side, startling the birds that nested in the cavities among the rocks; then, without a moment's hesitation, Ayrton threw himself into the sea and swam soundlessly toward the ship, whose location was shown by lights that had been lit a few minutes before.

As for Pencroff, he took cover in a small hollow and awaited his companion's return.

Ayrton swam with great vigor, gliding through the water without a single splash. His head scarcely emerged above the surface, and he kept his eyes fixed on the somber form of the brig, whose lights were reflected in the sea. All his attention was on the task before him. Never once did he think of the risk to himself—not only on board the ship, but also in these very waters, often frequented by sharks. The current carried him forward, and soon he was far from shore.

A half-hour later, so far unseen and unheard, Ayrton dove under the surface for the last few fathoms of his journey. He drew alongside the ship

Carefully bracing himself, Ayrton listened.

and grasped the bowsprit's bobstays with one hand. After a pause to catch his breath, he hoisted himself up on the chains and worked his way to the end of the cutwater, where he found several pairs of sailor's trousers that had been left to dry. He pulled on a pair; then, carefully bracing himself, he listened.

The passengers of the brig were not asleep. On the contrary, they talked, they sang, they laughed. And these were the exchanges, freely sprinkled with oaths, that struck Ayrton most particularly:

"A fine acquisition, this brig!"

"She's a good runner, our *Speedy* is! She more than lives up to her name!"

"Let every ship in Norfolk come after her! Just let them try and catch us!"

"Hurrah for her commander!"

"Hurrah for Bob Harvey!"

We can only imagine the effect that these words had on Ayrton, for as it happened this Bob Harvey was no stranger to him. He was an old companion from his Australian days, a daring seaman who had returned to his criminal ways. Somewhere near Norfolk Island he had seized this brig, bound for the Sandwich Islands with a load of ammunition, utensils, and tools. His cohorts had come to join him, and now these convicts-turned-pirates scoured the Pacific, destroying ships and slaughtering their crews, more bloodthirsty than the Malays themselves!

The convicts were loudly recounting their exploits, drinking immoderately all the while, and from their words Ayrton gleaned the following information:

The *Speedy*'s crew was composed solely of English prisoners, newly escaped from Norfolk.

A brief description of Norfolk might now be necessary.

At 29 degrees 2 minutes south latitude and 165 degrees 42 minutes east longitude, off the east coast of Australia, there lies a small island six leagues in circumference, overlooked by Mount Pitt, which stands eleven hundred feet above sea level. This is Norfolk Island, which has become the site of a prison colony housing some five hundred of the most hardened convicts of the British judicial system. An unyielding system of discipline governs their existence, and the prisoners live under the constant threat of terrible punishments. They are guarded by one hundred fifty soldiers, and the camp is administered by one hundred fifty employees, answering to a governor. It would be difficult to imagine a more detestable gathering of scoundrels. Sometimes—although this is rare—a small band of prisoners succeeds in eluding the guards' unsparing surveillance and mounts a surprise attack on a ship moored in the island's waters; once the ship falls into their hands, they make their escape and set out to wander the Polynesian archipelagoes in search of plunder.

This is precisely what Bob Harvey and his companions had done, and this is what Ayrton had once sought to do. The *Speedy* had been captured as it stood at anchor near Norfolk Island; the crew was massacred, and for the past year, this ship, now a pirate vessel, had plied the Pacific seas under the command of Bob Harvey, once an honest long-haul sea captain, now a marauding pirate well known to Ayrton!

Most of the convicts had gathered on the poop deck, in the stern, but a few of them lay on the decks in raucous conversation.

Their discussion continued amid shouts and libations, and Ayrton learned that chance alone had brought the *Speedy* to Lincoln Island. Bob Harvey had not seen this land before; rather, as Cyrus Smith had supposed, he had simply stumbled onto this unknown island, unmarked on any map, and resolved to explore it, and perhaps make of it the brig's home port.

As for the black flag at the *Speedy*'s gaffer and the firing of the cannon—in imitation of the shots fired by warships as they raise their flag—this was nothing more than sheer pirate bravado. It was not a signal, and for the moment no communication existed between Lincoln Island and the escapees from Norfolk.

The colony was thus in great danger. With its convenient supply of fresh water, its small harbor, a wealth of resources uncovered by the colonists' labors, the hidden recesses of Granite House—with all these advantages, the island could not fail to please the convicts. It would make an ideal lair, secret and unknown, offering an easy existence out of reach of the law, perhaps for many years to come. No respect would be owed the lives of the colonists; Bob Harvey and his accomplices would slaughter them forthwith. The colonists could not hope to flee and take shelter elsewhere on the island, since the convicts were planning to make of it their home. Even when the *Speedy* set off for an expedition, several men would likely stay behind to maintain their new settlement. The colonists thus had no choice. They must attack the pirates with all possible force, and they must exterminate them down to the very last man, for such wretches deserve no mercy, and any means of countering their wicked designs is a good one.

Such were Ayrton's thoughts, and he knew that Cyrus Smith would agree.

But could they truly hope to resist this invasion? Was victory within their reach? This would depend on the brig's complement of arms and the number of men aboard.

This Ayrton resolved to determine at any cost, and since, an hour after his arrival, the vociferations had begun to calm somewhat—for a good number of the convicts had fallen into a deep, drunken slumber—Ayrton did not hesitate to venture onto the deck of the *Speedy,* now left in complete darkness by the extinguishing of the lanterns.

He worked his way up the cutwater again, and came to the brig's forecastle by way of the bowsprit. Stepping over the prostrate convicts, he made a quick tour of the ship and found that the *Speedy* was armed with four cannons, capable of firing balls of eight to ten pounds. By touch, he discovered that these were breechloaders, of modern design and fabrication, easily used and terrible in their effects.

Some ten men could be seen sleeping on the deck, but presumably there were others within. Indeed, by the sound of their voices, Ayrton had reckoned their number at about fifty—a formidable opponent for the six colonists of Lincoln Island! But at least, thanks to Ayrton's devotion, Cyrus Smith would not be caught unawares; he would know the strength of his adversaries, and he would take steps accordingly.

The time had come for Ayrton to rejoin his companions and report his findings. He prepared to return to the bow and slip back into the water.

But, as Ayrton had said, he wished to do more than his duty, and into his mind there now came a heroic thought. It would mean sacrificing his own life, but at least he would save the island and its colonists. He knew that Cyrus Smith could not hope to fight off fifty heavily armed brigands. Perhaps they would force their way into Granite House, or perhaps they would besiege it and slowly starve the colonists to death; either way, they would surely prevail in the end. He thought of those who had made him a man again, and an honest man; they were his saviors, and he owed them everything. He imagined them dead, mercilessly slaughtered, all their work destroyed, their island become a pirate lair! He blamed himself for these disasters, since his former companion Bob Harvey was nothing other than what he himself had once hoped to become, and a shudder of horror ran through his entire being. Suddenly he was overcome with an irresistible desire to blow up the brig, and all its passengers with it. He too would perish in the explosion, but he would have done his duty.

Ayrton did not hesitate. He could easily find the powder magazine, which always lies in the stern. A ship of this sort would carry a considerable supply of powder, and a single spark would be enough to demolish it instantaneously.

Silently he slipped between decks and found his way through another crowd of dozing bodies, immobilized more by drunkenness than by sleep. A single lantern glowed at the foot of the mainmast, to which was slung a rack holding all manner of weapons.

Ayrton took a revolver from the rack and verified that it was loaded and primed. This was all he would need to bring about the destruction of the brig. He slunk toward the stern, knowing he would find the powder magazine just below the poop deck.

He made his way into the profound darkness of the between-decks. He found it difficult to crawl without brushing against the outstretched convicts, some of whom were only half asleep; hence a number of oaths and blows aimed in his direction. More than once Ayrton was forced to stop and wait, keeping as still as he could. But at last he arrived at the wall of the rear compartment, and here he discovered the door to the powder magazine itself.

He soon saw that he would have to force his way in; he thus set to work, attempting to break the padlock—not an easy task to accomplish in silence. But thanks to the extraordinary strength of his hands the padlock soon cracked, and the door was opened...

Just then, Ayrton felt a hand on his shoulder.

"What are you doing there?" asked a tall, shadowy figure in a cold voice, bringing his lantern near Ayrton's face.

Ayrton threw himself backward. The sudden brilliance of the lantern had revealed his former accomplice, Bob Harvey. Nevertheless, he felt sure that Harvey had not recognized him, having no doubt long since concluded that Ayrton was dead.

"What are you doing there?" said Bob Harvey again, holding Ayrton back by his belt.

Ayrton made no response. Roughly he pushed the pirate away, trying to throw himself into the magazine. One single gunshot into the barrels of powder, and it would all be over!

"Rally 'round, lads!" Bob Harvey cried.

Awakened by his voice, two or three pirates leaped to their feet and threw themselves on Ayrton, attempting to bring him down. Ayrton struggled vigorously and escaped their grasp. Two shots rang out from his revolver, and two convicts fell; but he could not dodge the knife that soon sank into the flesh of his shoulder.

Ayrton realized that his plan was doomed to failure. Bob Harvey had closed the door to the magazine, and the decks came alive as the pirates awoke. Ayrton knew he would have to save himself at all costs, for Cyrus Smith would need every hand to combat the pirate invasion. Flight was his only recourse!

But was flight still possible? Very likely not. Nevertheless, Ayrton would spare no effort to rejoin his companions.

Four bullets remained in his revolver, and two shots now echoed through the night. One was aimed at Bob Harvey, but appeared to have missed its target; at best, the head convict might have been slightly wounded. In any case, seeing that his adversaries had momentarily stepped back a pace or two, Ayrton raced toward the hatchway ladder in hopes of reaching the upper decks. He struck the lantern with the butt of his revolver, plunging the ship into darkness and greatly facilitating his flight.

Awakened by the commotion, two or three pirates were coming down the ladder at that very moment. A fifth shot from Ayrton's revolver sent one of them plummeting toward the bottom, and the others ran off, baffled and terrified at this turn of events. With two leaps, Ayrton reached the deck of the brig; three seconds later, firing his revolver one last time in the face of a pirate who had seized him by the neck, he vaulted the railing and dived into the sea.

Ayrton had not swum six fathoms before a hail of bullets began to rain down all around him.

Imagine his companions' emotions on hearing these gun blasts from aboard the brig—Pencroff concealed amid the islet's rocks, Cyrus Smith, the reporter, Harbert, and Neb huddled in the Chimneys! At once they raced out onto the beach and raised their rifles, ready to repel the attackers.

For there was no doubt in their minds! Ayrton had been caught unawares and slaughtered by the pirates, and now, perhaps, these devils would use the cover of darkness to descend on the island!

He vaulted the railing and dived into the sea . . .

A half-hour went by in mortal trepidation. In the meantime, the gun-shots had stopped, and neither Ayrton nor Pencroff had reappeared. Had the islet been invaded? Should they attempt to come to their two companions' rescue? But how could they? The tide was high, and the channel impossible to ford. The canoe was on the islet! Imagine the dread that now fell over Cyrus Smith and his companions!

Finally, at about half past midnight, a boat landed on the beach, bearing two passengers: Ayrton, slightly wounded in the shoulder, and Pencroff, safe and sound. Their friends greeted them with open arms.

They ran at once to take shelter in the Chimneys. There Ayrton told them everything that had happened, including his failed plan to blow up the brig.

All hands were extended toward Ayrton, who made no attempt to conceal the gravity of their present situation. They could no longer hope to go undetected. The pirates knew that Lincoln Island was inhabited. They would come ashore in great numbers, and well armed. They would respect nothing. If the colonists fell into their hands, they could expect no mercy!

"Well then, we shall die as we must!" the reporter said.

"But for the moment, let us stay in our shelter and keep watch," the engineer replied.

"Do we have any chance of finding a way out of this, Mr. Cyrus?" the sailor asked.

"Yes, Pencroff."

"Hm! Six against fifty!"

"Yes … six! … not including …"

"Who?" asked Pencroff.

Cyrus did not answer, but he gestured toward the heavens.

III

The Fog Lifts.—The Engineer's Measures.—Three Outposts.—
Ayrton and Pencroff.—The First Boat.—Two Other Vessels.—On
the Islet.—Six Convicts Ashore.—The Brig Lifts Anchor.—
Projectiles from the Speedy.—*Situation Desperate.—An*
Unexpected Outcome.

The night passed uneventfully. The colonists remained on the alert, maintaining their position at the Chimneys; the pirates did not seem to have attempted a landing. After the last shots fired at Ayrton, not a single detonation, not a single sound had betrayed the brig's presence just off the island's shore. The colonists might almost have thought that the pirates had lifted anchor and sailed away, perhaps thinking themselves outnumbered.

But no such thing had happened, and when day began to dawn, the colonists descried an amorphous shape through the morning fog. It was the *Speedy.*

"My friends," the engineer said, "we must take certain measures before the fog lifts. For the moment, we are hidden from the pirates' eyes, and we can act without arousing their attention. Above all else, we must convince them that the island is densely populated, and that the inhabitants are ready and able to defend themselves. I suggest, then, that we divide into three groups, with one posted here in the Chimneys and the second at the mouth of the Mercy; the third, I believe, should proceed to the islet in order to prevent or at least delay any attempt at landing. We have two carbines and four rifles. Each of us will thus be armed, and our reserves of powder and bullets are such that we needn't spare our fire. We have nothing to fear from the pirates' rifles, nor even their cannons. What can they do against these rocks? And since we will not be firing from the windows of Granite House, the pirates will never think to send missiles in that direction, which could do irreparable damage to our abode. We must avoid hand-to-hand combat at all costs, for we are greatly outnumbered. In short, we must vigorously oppose any attempt at landing, but at the same time we must not show ourselves to the pirates. This is no time to be economical with your ammunition. Let us shoot freely, but let us aim true. Each of us has eight to ten enemies to kill, and kill them we must!"

Cyrus Smith had clearly and lucidly laid out the situation, all the while speaking in the calmest of voices, as if this were merely some new construction project, and not a plan of battle. His companions agreed to these measures without a word. All that remained was to take up their positions before the fog had fully dissipated.

Neb and Pencroff immediately ascended to Granite House and returned with a good supply of ammunition. Gideon Spilett and Ayrton, both fine marksmen, were armed with the two precision carbines, whose range was no less than one mile. The four remaining rifles were divided among Cyrus Smith, Neb, Pencroff, and Harbert.

The outposts were to be manned as follows.

Cyrus Smith and Harbert would lie in wait at the Chimneys, controlling a wide area of the beach beneath Granite House.

Gideon Spilett and Neb were to make for the mouth of the Mercy, whose bridge had been raised, like the others; there they would crouch among the rocks, ready to prevent any crossing of the river or landing on the opposite bank.

As for Ayrton and Pencroff, they would push the canoe into the water and set out for the islet, where they would occupy two separate positions. In this way, the colonists' fire would come from four different points, suggesting that the island was at the same time well peopled and severely defended.

Should it prove impossible to prevent a landing—and, more seriously, should they find themselves about to be outflanked by a launch from the brig—Pencroff and Ayrton were to return to the shores of the island with the canoe, and head toward the spot most threatened by the pirates' attack.

The colonists clasped hands one last time before setting out. Pencroff struggled to maintain his composure, choking back his emotion as he embraced Harbert, his child!... and then they separated.

Cyrus Smith and Harbert disappeared into the Chimneys, Neb and the reporter toward the Mercy; five minutes later, Ayrton and Pencroff had safely crossed the channel and found cover among the rocks on the islet's eastern shore.

They knew they had not been spotted, for they themselves could scarcely make out the brig through the fog.

It was six-thirty in the morning.

Now the fog gradually began to break apart in the upper atmosphere, and the brig's mastheads emerged from the mist. For a few moments more, great wreaths of fog swirled over the water's surface; then a breeze came up and quickly dissipated the veil.

The *Speedy* was now fully revealed, moored by two anchors, its stem facing north, its port side facing the island. It lay no more than a mile and a quarter from shore, just as Cyrus Smith had estimated.

The sinister black flag still fluttered at its gaffer.

Through his spyglass, the engineer saw that the ship's four cannons were now trained on the island, ready to be fired at any moment.

For now, however, the *Speedy* sat in silence. Some thirty pirates could be seen coming and going over the decks. A few stood on the poop deck; two others had climbed to the crossbars of the topgallant, keeping a close watch on the island through their spyglasses.

Bob Harvey and his crew must have been hard put to account for the night's events. A half-naked man had forced the lock of the powder magazine; they had fought him off, and he had fired six revolver shots in return, killing one of their men and wounding two others. Had he been hit by their fire as he fled? Had he succeeded in swimming to shore? Where did he come from? Why had he come aboard? Was he truly attempting to blow up the brig, as Bob Harvey believed? This incident must have raised many questions in their minds. But what they could no longer doubt was that the island before them was indeed inhabited; perhaps an entire colony lay in wait, preparing to defend themselves. And yet there was not a soul to be seen, neither on the beach nor atop the plateau. The shoreline appeared utterly deserted. Nowhere could they detect any sign of human presence. Had the inhabitants fled toward the interior?

Such must have been the questions running through the pirate captain's mind; as any prudent leader would do, he was now no doubt studying the locality before sending in his men.

An hour and a half went by, with no sign of an impending attack or landing. Bob Harvey was clearly pondering his next move. Even with the finest telescope, he could not have seen a single colonist concealed among the rocks. Nor would his eye have been caught by the tangle of green branches and lianas hanging over the bare rock at the windows of Granite House. How could he have suspected that a dwelling had been carved from the granite cliffs so high above the ground? Scanning the entire perimeter of Union Bay, from Cape Claw to the two Capes Mandible, he must have found no evidence that the island was or might be inhabited.

At eight o'clock, however, the colonists observed a burst of activity on board the *Speedy*. The hoists were manned and a launch was lowered into the water, then boarded by seven men armed with rifles. One sat at the tiller, four others took up the oars; the last two crouched in the bow, eyes trained on the island, ready to open fire. This was clearly to be a reconnaissance mission rather than a landing, for in the latter case they would surely have come in greater numbers.

From their vantage point on the crossbars of the topgallant mast, the pirates had obviously seen that the coastline was sheltered by an islet, with a half-mile channel running between the two shores. Nevertheless, by the heading of their launch, Cyrus Smith soon realized that they would not proceed directly into the channel, but first land on the islet— a wise precaution.

From their separate hiding places among the rocks, Pencroff and Ayrton observed the launch's approach, and waited for it to come within range of their rifles.

Slowly and cautiously the boat moved forward, with long, widely spaced strokes of the oars. One of the convicts in the bow held a sounding line, searching for the deep channel dug out by the Mercy's current. From this they deduced that Bob Harvey was intending to steer the brig as near the shore as he could. Scattered through the rigging, some thirty pirates kept their eyes glued to the launch's movements, noting certain sea marks that would guide them to a safe mooring.

The launch came to a stop two cables from the islet. The tillerman stood up and searched for a likely spot to come ashore.

A moment later, two gunshots rang out. Wisps of smoke drifted over the islet's rocks. The tillerman and the sounding man fell backward into the boat, struck at the same moment by Ayrton's and Pencroff's bullets.

Almost at once a more violent detonation rent the air. A great burst of smoke erupted from the flank of the brig, and a cannonball smashed into the rocks where Ayrton and Pencroff had taken shelter. The shards of rock went flying in all directions, but the two marksmen had not been hit.

Terrible imprecations could be heard coming from the boat, which immediately resumed its advance. The tillerman was replaced by one of his comrades, and the oars pulled the launch swiftly through the water.

Nevertheless, rather than returning to the ship, as one might have expected, the boat continued along the islet's shore, skirting the southern point. The pirates rowed furiously, desperate to move out of firing range.

They advanced to within five cables of the curved beach that ended at Flotsam Point, which they skirted by a semicircular route; now, still protected by the brig's cannons, they steered toward the mouth of the Mercy.

Their intention was obviously to enter the channel from this side and outflank the colonists on the islet, exposing them to gunfire from both the launch and the brig—a hopeless situation for the marksmen, no matter how numerous they might be.

The launch pursued this course for a quarter of an hour. Absolute silence, perfect calm in the air and on the water.

Pencroff and Ayrton understood full well the danger of being outflanked; nevertheless, they stayed at their posts, either because they did not want to leave their cover and expose themselves to the *Speedy*'s cannons or because they were counting on assistance from Neb and Gideon Spilett, who were watching from the mouth of the river, and from Cyrus Smith and Harbert, holed up in the rocks of the Chimneys.

Twenty minutes after the first shots had been fired, the boat lay abeam the Mercy, less than two cable-lengths away. The tide was beginning to rise. Accentuated by the narrowness of the channel, the current was drawing the convicts' launch toward the river. Only by rowing for all they were worth could they maintain their position in the middle of the channel. Soon they passed by the mouth of the Mercy, well within rifle range; two bullets came to greet them, and two more of their number were thrown to the planks of their little boat. Neb and Spilett had not missed their shots.

Immediately the brig sent a second cannonball hurtling toward the plumes of smoke from the two rifles, and again the result was only minor damage to the rocks.

The boat now held no more than three sound men. Caught in the current, it drifted through the channel with the speed of an arrow, floating past Cyrus Smith and Harbert, who nevertheless held their fire, judging the target to be out of range. Then, coming around the northern point of the islet under the force of its two remaining oars, it headed back toward the brig.

For the moment, the colonists had no reason to despair. The battle had begun badly for their adversaries. Four of their men lay seriously injured, and perhaps dead; the colonists, on the other hand, had not wasted a single bullet, and had emerged from the skirmish unscathed. If the pirates' attack continued as it had begun, if they made further attempts to land with their launch, they could be picked off one by one.

The brilliant reasoning behind the engineer's battle plan should now be clear. The pirates might well believe themselves faced with a numerous and well-armed opponent, perhaps impossible to overcome.

A half-hour went by before the boat, struggling against the offshore current, pulled alongside the *Speedy*. Terrible shouts rang out as the wounded men were hoisted aboard, and a further three or four cannon shots were fired, once again to no avail.

But now a dozen new convicts threw themselves into the launch, drunk with rage and perhaps still with the previous evening's libations. A second boat was lowered at the same time, manned by another eight pirates. The first rowed directly toward the islet to flush out the colonists, while the maneuvers of the second showed that they were planning to force their way into the Mercy.

Pencroff and Ayrton saw that their situation would soon become untenable, and that the time had come to rejoin their companions.

Nevertheless, they waited a moment longer until the first boat was within range; two more bullets, skillfully aimed, wrought new havoc among the launch's crew. Then Pencroff and Ayrton abandoned their position amid a hail of gunfire from the launch, and ran across the islet with all possible speed. They threw themselves into the canoe, crossed the channel just as the second boat was reaching the southern point, and ran for cover in the Chimneys.

No sooner had they rejoined Cyrus Smith and Harbert than the first launch made its landing on the islet. A moment later, its surface was teeming with pirates.

Almost simultaneously, yet more gunfire was heard from the Mercy, which the second boat had rapidly approached. Two of the eight men aboard were mortally wounded by Gideon Spilett and Neb, and the vessel itself, dragged onto the shoals by the irresistible current, broke up at the river's mouth. Nonetheless, the six survivors waded onto the right bank, holding their weapons above their heads to protect them from the water. Then, finding themselves exposed so near the outpost, they fled in a panic toward Flotsam Point, and at once they were out of firing range.

This, then, was the situation at that moment: on the islet, twelve convicts, some of them no doubt wounded, but still in possession of an undamaged launch; on the island, six men ashore, but cut off from Granite House by the river, whose bridges had all been raised.

"It's going well!" Pencroff had said as he raced into the Chimneys. "It's going well, Mr. Cyrus! What do you think?"

"I believe," the engineer responded, "that the battle is about to take a new form. The convicts have realized that the present circumstances place them at a great disadvantage. They will not be so stupid as to maintain the same plan of attack!"

"All the same, they can't cross the channel," the sailor said. "Ayrton's and Mr. Spilett's carbines will see to that. Remember, they have a range of over a mile!"

"No doubt," answered Harbert, "but what can two carbines do against the brig's cannons?"

"Oh! the brig isn't in the channel yet!" Pencroff answered.

"And what if it enters the channel?" said Cyrus Smith.

"That's impossible. The risk of running aground is too great!"

"It is possible," Ayrton answered. "The convicts might enter the channel at high tide, even if it meant running aground when the tide goes out; and then, once they start firing their cannons, we'll have no hope of holding our positions."

"By all the thousand devils of Hell!" cried Pencroff. "You're right! The blackguards are about to raise anchor!"

"Should we take refuge in Granite House?" asked Harbert.

"Not yet!" answered Cyrus Smith.

"But what about Neb and Mr. Spilett?..." said Pencroff.

"They'll come and join us when the time is right. Stand ready with your carbine, Ayrton. Now it's all up to you and Spilett."

This was all too true! Still riding at anchor, the *Speedy* was coming about, betraying an intention to approach the islet. The tide would rise for another hour and a half, and since the incoming current was already broken, the brig would have an easy time maneuvering. But as for entering the channel, Pencroff, unlike Ayrton, never thought the pirates would dare.

In the meantime, the convicts occupying the islet had made their way toward the shore, and now only the channel separated them from land. Their rifles could not harm the colonists in the Chimneys or at the mouth of the Mercy, and they did not realize the great danger of their own position, for they could not know that the colonists were armed with long-range carbines. Thus, they paced up and down the edge of the islet, unknowingly exposing themselves to fire from shore.

Their illusion was short-lived, for Ayrton's and Gideon Spilett's carbines soon gave two of the convicts a disagreeable surprise. Thrown backward by the force of the bullets, they lay lifeless in the sand.

The other ten fled at once in disarray. Without so much as a moment's thought for their dead or wounded companions, they beat a hasty retreat to the other side of the islet, threw themselves into the launch, and set off to rejoin the brig.

"Eight down!" Pencroff had cried. "You'd think Ayrton and Mr. Spilett had planned out every shot!"

"Gentlemen," Ayrton answered, reloading his carbine, "things are about to take a very serious turn. The brig is under way!"

"The anchor's apeak!..." cried Pencroff.

"Yes, and now it's atrip."

For the crew had begun to hoist anchor, and the pawl could be heard rattling against the windlass. The *Speedy* steered toward her anchor to put some slack in the chain; then, once it had been pulled from the bottom, the ship began to drift toward land. The wind was blowing from the sea; the standing jib and the topsail were raised, and slowly the *Speedy* advanced toward shore.

From their outposts at the Mercy and the Chimneys, the colonists silently watched the progress with understandable dread. To be exposed to cannon fire at such close range, with no effective means of response, would put them in the most terrible peril. How could they hope to prevent the pirates from coming ashore?

Cyrus Smith fully realized the gravity of the situation, and tried to find some way to fight back. Soon he would have to make a decision. But what? Should they take cover in Granite House, where they had provisions enough for a siege of several weeks, perhaps even months? Yes, but what then? This would not stop the pirates from taking over the island; they would pillage it at their leisure, and in time they would inevitably triumph over the prisoners of Granite House.

Nevertheless, one last hope remained: that Bob Harvey would not risk steering his ship into the channel, but would drop anchor off the islet. This would put them a half-mile from shore, and at such a distance the cannons might do no great harm.

"Never," repeated Pencroff, "never will a practiced sailor like Bob Harvey enter the channel! He knows the brig would be at risk if the sea turned even the tiniest bit choppy! And what would become of him without his ship?"

Now the brig had approached the islet, and they could see it was bearing toward the southern end. The breeze was light, the tidal current weakening, and Bob Harvey could easily maneuver as he wished.

The launches that had earlier attempted to land had shown him where the water was deepest, and he boldly followed the same course. His plan was all too obvious. He wanted to bring his ship broadside onto the Chimneys, and from there respond to the colonists' bullets with missiles and cannonballs, so avenging the deaths of his crew members.

Soon the *Speedy* reached the point of the islet, and quickly skirted it; the spanker billowed, and the brig, hugging the wind, found itself abeam the Mercy.

"The bandits! they're coming in!" cried Pencroff.

Just then, Neb and Gideon Spilett raced into the Chimneys to rejoin their companions.

Neb and the reporter had rightly decided to abandon their position on the Mercy, from which they could no longer attack the ship. The battle was about to take a decisive new turn, and it was best that the colonists be together. Gideon Spilett and Neb had slipped behind the rocks to make their way toward the Chimneys, unharmed by the volleys of gunfire that pursued them.

"Spilett! Neb!" the engineer had cried. "You aren't wounded, are you?"

"No!" the reporter answered. "Only a few contusions from the ricochets! But that blasted brig is entering the channel!"

"Yes!" answered Pencroff. "And within ten minutes she will have dropped anchor before Granite House!"

"Do you have a plan, Cyrus?" the reporter answered.

"We must take cover inside Granite House while we still can, and while the convicts cannot see us."

"That's my opinion as well," answered Gideon Spilett; "but once we're locked away inside..."

"Then we will consider our options," the engineer answered.

"Let's be off, then, and fast!" said the reporter.

"You wouldn't prefer Ayrton and myself to stay behind, Mr. Cyrus?" asked the sailor.

"What good would it do, Pencroff?" Cyrus Smith answered. "No. We must stay together!"

There was not a moment to be lost. The colonists left the Chimneys. A small bend in the curtain of granite concealed them from the brig; but two or three detonations and a crash of cannonballs against the rocks told them that the *Speedy* was now only a small distance away.

A moment later, they had hurtled into the elevator, hoisted themselves to their door—where Top and Joop had been awaiting them since the day before—and charged into the great room.

Their retreat came none too soon, for through the branches the colonists saw the *Speedy* racing through the channel, engulfed in smoke. The cannon roared unendingly, and the balls blindly smashed into the unoccupied outposts at the Chimneys and the mouth of the Mercy. Each blast sent a spray of pulverized stone in all directions, accompanied by loud hurrahs.

They had not lost hope that Cyrus Smith's idea to conceal the windows would protect Granite House from assault; but just then a cannonball suddenly shot into the corridor, after grazing the edge of their largest window.

"Damnation! Have we been discovered?" cried Pencroff.

Perhaps Bob Harvey had not spotted them; he might simply have thought it a good idea to attack the suspicious greenery in the upper regions of the great rock wall. But soon a second cannonball broke through the curtain of foliage, revealing a gaping hole in the granite, and with this the cannon fire suddenly doubled in intensity.

The colonists' situation was desperate. Their retreat had been discovered. They were powerless against the cannonballs, and they watched helplessly as the granite shattered around them, the shards ripping through the air like grapeshot. They had no choice: they would have to take refuge in the upper cavern, abandoning their home to unthinkable

A crash of cannonballs against the rocks . . .

devastation. But just then a muted sound was heard, followed by a chorus of horrifying screams!

Cyrus Smith and his friends ran to the window...

A great column of water had lifted the helpless brig high above the surface of the sea. All at once the ship broke in two, and in less than ten seconds it had sunk, with all its felonious crew!

IV

*The Colonists on the Beach.—Ayrton and Pencroff Attempt a
Salvage Operation.—Mealtime Conversation.—Pencroff's
Reasoning.—Careful Examination of the Brig's Hull.—The
Powder Magazine Intact.—New Wealth.—The Last Debris.—A
Fragment from a Broken Cylinder.*

"They've exploded!" cried Harbert.

"Yes! just as if Ayrton had fired into the gunpowder!" answered Pencroff, leaping into the elevator along with Neb and the boy.

"But what happened?" asked Gideon Spilett, dumbfounded by this unexpected turn of events.

"Ah! This time, we're going to find out!..." the engineer answered forcefully.

"Find what out?..."

"Later! later! Come along, Spilett. The important thing is that the pirates have been exterminated!"

And Cyrus Smith, hurrying the reporter and Ayrton along with him, joined the others on the beach.

The brig had vanished, hull, masts, and rigging. The surge of water had lifted it up and toppled it to one side, and it had sunk at once in that position, no doubt as a result of an enormous gash in the hull. Nevertheless, since the water was no more than twenty feet deep in that part of the channel, they knew the hull would be revealed at low tide.

Scattered bits of flotsam covered the water: spare masts and yards, crates, kegs, even chicken cages holding live birds. The contents of the hold must have fallen through the broken hull and risen to the surface. But nowhere could the colonists discover debris from the ship itself—no planks from the deck or hull—and the cause of the *Speedy's* abrupt disappearance remained as elusive as before.

Nevertheless, the two masts soon floated to the surface of the water, snapped off several feet above the partner once the stays and guys had given way. The sails were intact, some unfurled and others taken in. The colonists resolved not to allow the outgoing tide to carry off this treasure, and Ayrton and Pencroff ran to the canoe, intending to haul the varied flotsam onto the shores of either the islet or the island.

But just as they were about to embark, they were stopped short by a remark from Gideon Spilett.

"What about the six convicts who landed on the right bank of the Mercy?" he said.

Indeed, the colonists could ill afford to forget that six men had come ashore after their launch broke up on the shoals.

They looked toward Flotsam Point. No fugitives were in sight. They must have fled inland when they saw the brig suddenly swallowed by the waters of the channel.

"We'll deal with them later," said Cyrus Smith. "They are armed, and no doubt dangerous, but after all, six against six gives us even odds. We must attend to the most urgent tasks first."

Ayrton and Pencroff climbed into the canoe and paddled vigorously toward the wreckage.

The sea was quite smooth and the tide very high, for the moon had been new two days before. It would be an hour at least before the hull of the brig emerged from the water.

Ayrton and Pencroff would thus have time to begin the salvage. They tied long ropes to the masts and spars, then returned to the beach beneath Granite House. The colonists took up the other ends of the ropes, and, pulling together, they succeeded in hauling the flotsam ashore. With this done, the canoe set about picking up everything still afloat—chicken cages, kegs, crates—and these were immediately transported to the Chimneys.

A few cadavers surfaced as well. Among others, Ayrton recognized Bob Harvey's body, and he showed it to his companion, saying in a voice choked with emotion:

"What I once was, Pencroff!"

"But what you no longer are, my good Ayrton!" the sailor answered.

It seemed curious that such a small number of bodies had floated to

"What I once was, Pencroff!"

the surface—only five or six, no more, now drifting out to sea on the current of the ebbing tide. So sudden was the destruction of the brig, and so swift its sinking, that they never had a chance to escape; as the *Speedy* was thrown to one side, most of the pirates must have been trapped beneath the bulwarks, and so went down with their ship. And now the outgoing tide would carry the wretches' remains into the open sea, sparing the colonists the disagreeable chore of burying them in some corner of the island.

Cyrus Smith and his companions spent two hours pulling the spars ashore, removing the undamaged sails, and drying them in the sun. Absorbed in their work, they spoke little; but how full of thoughts were their minds! To possess this brig, or rather its contents, was to come into a considerable fortune. A ship is like a small world unto itself, and the colony's material wealth would burgeon with the treasures of the *Speedy*'s hull—as with the crate found at Flotsam Point, but on a much larger scale.

"And for that matter," Pencroff thought, "why shouldn't we try to refloat the brig? Perhaps there's a hole in her flank, but a hole can be repaired, and a three- or four-ton sea liner is a real ship next to our little *Bonadventure*! You can go a long way with a ship like that! Wherever you please! I'll have to convince Mr. Cyrus and Ayrton to look into this! It's more than worth the trouble!"

If the brig was indeed still seaworthy, the colonists' chances of seeing their homeland again were greatly improved. But this all-important question could not be resolved until the tide had reached its lowest ebb, for only then could they inspect the brig's hull from one end to the other.

When all the flotsam had been pulled onto the shore, Cyrus Smith and his companions allowed themselves a brief pause for breakfast. It would scarcely be an exaggeration to say that they were dying of hunger. Fortunately, the kitchen was not far off, and Neb was an efficient and expeditious chef. They ate in the shadow of the Chimneys, all the while, as we might well imagine, discussing the astonishing event that had so miraculously saved their colony.

"Miraculous is the only word for it," said Pencroff. "No question about it, those rascals couldn't have blown up at a better time! Granite House was becoming a singularly uncomfortable place to be!"

"And do you have any idea, Pencroff," the reporter asked, "how this could have happened, and what could have set off the explosion?"

"Why, Mr. Spilett, nothing could be simpler," Pencroff replied. "A pirate ship isn't kept up the way a warship is! Convicts don't make good sailors! The brig's powder magazines were obviously open, since they were firing their cannons without letup. One careless or clumsy pirate is all it would take to blow the whole thing sky high!"

"Mr. Cyrus," said Harbert, "I can't understand why the explosion wasn't more forceful. It didn't seem that strong a detonation, and all things considered we've found surprisingly little debris, and scarcely a handful of planks from the hull. The ship seems more to have sunk than exploded."

"And you find that odd, my child?" the engineer asked.

"Yes, Mr. Cyrus."

"I do too, Harbert," the engineer answered, "very odd indeed; but perhaps we'll have our explanation once we've examined the hull."

"Come now, Mr. Cyrus," said Pencroff, "you're not trying to say that the *Speedy* just sank like a ship run against a shoal?"

"Why not?" Neb observed. "Aren't there submerged rocks in the channel?"

"Really, Neb!" Pencroff answered. "You must not have been watching! Just before she sank, I saw this quite clearly, the brig was lifted up on an enormous wave. Then she capsized to port as she fell again. If she'd simply struck a shoal she would have sunk smoothly and peacefully, like any decent ship, straight to the bottom."

"Well, that's just it! This isn't a decent ship!" Neb replied.

"At any rate, we shall see, Pencroff," the engineer answered.

"We shall see," added the sailor, "but I'll bet my head there are no submerged rocks in the channel. See here, Cyrus, once and for all, do you believe this was yet another of your fantastical happenings?"

Cyrus Smith did not reply.

"In any event," said Gideon Spilett, "collision or explosion, you must agree, Pencroff, it came just when it was needed most!"

"Yes!...yes!..." the sailor answered, "...but that's not the question. I'm asking Mr. Smith if he thinks there's something supernatural behind all this."

"I have not yet arrived at an opinion, Pencroff," the engineer said. "There's nothing more I can tell you."

Pencroff was not satisfied with the engineer's response. He insisted that it was "an explosion," and he refused to back down. He dismissed out of hand the possibility of undiscovered shoals in the channel, for he had often crossed it at low tide, and he knew there was nothing but fine sand at the bottom. Besides, the brig had sunk at high tide; even if there were rocks in the channel that could not be seen when the tide was out, the water would then have been more than deep enough to let the *Speedy* pass over them unharmed. Thus, the ship could not have struck a submerged object. Thus, the ship had not simply sunk. Thus, she had exploded.

And it must be said that there was a certain logic to the sailor's reasoning.

At about one-thirty, the colonists embarked in the canoe and paddled toward the site of the sunken ship. Regrettably, the two launches could not be saved; one of them, as we know, had broken up beyond repair at the mouth of the Mercy, and the other had gone down with the brig and never returned to the surface, no doubt crushed beneath the wreckage.

The hull was now beginning to emerge above the water. The brig was not lying on its side after all; the ballast had been jarred loose by its sudden fall, and the ship now lay on the seafloor with its broken masts beneath it and the keel nearly topmost. It had thus been truly overturned by the terrible, inexplicable undersea event that had sent that mountain of water shooting into the heavens.

The colonists paddled around the hull, and as the tide receded they discovered, if not the cause of the catastrophe, at least the effect it had produced.

Beginning at the bow, seven or eight feet before the root of the stem post, the flanks of the brig had been violently ripped open over a length of at least twenty feet, on either side of the keel. Clearly, they could not dream of repairing these two huge gashes. The copper sheath and the planking had disappeared, no doubt vaporized in the blast; but, more than this, the very ribbing of the hull, the iron bolts, and the treenails had vanished without a trace. The shattered strakes hung loose from the bow right up to the rear runs. The false keel had been ripped from the hull with unimaginable force, and the keel itself had split from one end to the other, torn from the keelson in several places.

"By all the devils!" cried Pencroff. "Here's a ship that won't be easy to refloat!"

"Impossible, in fact," said Ayrton.

"In any case," Gideon Spilett observed to the sailor, "the explosion, if there was an explosion, certainly had a very curious effect! It demolished only the lower parts of the hull, and left the deck and deadwork perfectly intact! Collision with a shoal could have caused this kind of damage, but not, I daresay, the explosion of a powder magazine!"

"There are no shoals in the channel!" the sailor shot back. "I'll agree to anything you say, except that this ship hit a rock!"

"Perhaps we can find a way inside the brig," said the engineer. "We might find evidence of the cause of its destruction."

This seemed the best manner in which to proceed, not least because it would allow them to inventory the ship's contents, and to make preparations for their salvage.

They found their way into the brig with no great difficulty. With the receding tide, they could easily walk over the underside of the deck, now become the topside with the inversion of the hull. Here and there the deck had been shattered by the heavy blocks of pig iron that served as the ship's ballast. A continuous rushing sound could be heard as the water drained out through the fissures in the hull.

Cyrus Smith and his companions advanced, hatchets in hand. The deck was strewn with a great profusion of crates. Their submersion had been of brief duration, and the contents might thus well be salvageable.

And so they turned to the task of hauling the cargo to safety. The tide would not be in for several hours, and the colonists put those hours to the most profitable use. Ayrton and Pencroff had erected a hoist before the opening in the hull to speed the extraction of the kegs and crates. These were placed in the canoe and carried directly to the beach. They took everything they found, indiscriminately, planning to sort through it all at some later time.

To their great delight, they found that the brig was transporting a cargo as varied as the commercial freighters of the Polynesian archipelago: utensils, factory-made products, tools, a world of useful items. They would find a bit of everything here, they realized, and everything was precisely what the colony of Lincoln Island needed.

As we know, the hull had been seriously damaged by the force of the mysterious catastrophe; but now Cyrus Smith observed in stunned silence that the interior was equally damaged, especially toward the bow. The interior walls and stanchions were shattered, as if some formidable missile had burst inside the brig. The colonists advanced from bow to stern, clearing away the crates and hoisting them into the canoe as they went. The boxes were not heavy, and they had been thrown helter-skelter about the hold by the force of the ship's upheaval.

The colonists advanced toward the rear, and soon reached the area that had once lain beneath the poop deck. It was here, according to Ayrton, that they would find the powder magazine. Cyrus Smith was convinced it had not exploded, and that they might be able to salvage several kegs, whose powder would no doubt have remained dry inside the metal sheet with which such kegs are invariably lined.

And so it was. Amid a great quantity of cannonballs, they found some twenty copper-lined powder kegs, which they carefully extracted from the ship. Pencroff could not dispute what his eyes so clearly showed him: the destruction of the *Speedy* could not be attributed to an explosion. The portion of the hull surrounding the powder magazine had in fact suffered less damage than any other part of the ship.

"Very well!" answered the obstinate sailor. "But still I say there are no rocks in the channel!"

"What happened, then?" asked Harbert.

"I have no idea," answered Pencroff, "Mr. Cyrus has no idea, and no one has nor ever will have the faintest idea!"

Several hours had elapsed since they began this exploration, and the tide was visibly rising. They had no choice but to suspend their work. In any case, they felt sure that the brig would not be swept out to sea, for even now it was sinking into the sand, as solidly fixed in place as if it were riding at two anchors.

Thus, they could easily wait for the next ebb tide before resuming their labors. But the ship itself was indisputably beyond repair; indeed, they would have to finish their salvage operations as quickly as they could, for the brig's carcass would soon be swallowed by the channel's shifting sands.

It was now five o'clock in the afternoon, the end of a long and exhausting day. They ate with great appetite, and once dinner was over, despite their great weariness, they could not resist the temptation to delve into the crates that had made up the *Speedy*'s cargo.

Most of them held tailored clothes—warmly received by the colonists, as we might well imagine. There was enough here to clothe an entire colony, linens for all possible uses, shoes for every foot.

"We're rich, too rich!" cried Pencroff. "What are we going to do with all this?"

And the sailor let out a joyous hurrah with each new discovery: kegs of tafia, casks of tobacco, firearms and swords, bales of cotton, agricultural instruments, tools for carpenters, cabinetmakers, and blacksmiths, seeds of every species, all undamaged by their short sojourn in the water. Oh! how desperately they needed all this two years before! But even now, despite all the colonists' inventiveness, despite their great collection of hand-forged tools, their newfound wealth would surely not go unused.

There remained an abundance of storage space in Granite House; but there was no time that day to stow their treasure away. Nevertheless, they could not allow themselves to forget that six survivors from the *Speedy* had landed on the island, very probably scoundrels of the first order, and that they must think of protecting themselves. The bridges had been raised, but the convicts were unlikely to be deterred by a river or stream, and in their desperation these rogues might easily prove implacable and fearsome foes.

The colonists resolved to discuss that problem in the near future; for the moment, they would have to keep watch over the crates and packages piled up before the Chimneys, and so, by turns, they guarded their bounty through the night.

This night passed quietly, with no attempted aggression from the convicts. Master Joop and Top had been left to stand guard at the foot of Granite House, and would have sounded the alarm the moment they appeared.

The three days that followed, October 19th, 20th, and 21st, were spent salvaging anything that might prove valuable or useful in any way, both from the crates and from the ship's rigging. When the tide was low, they continued to unload the hold. When the tide was high, they stored away the objects they had found. A large sheet of copper was pulled from the hull, which sank further into the sands with each passing day. The heaviest objects would vanish first, but Ayrton and Pencroff refused to allow this to happen: several times they dived into the channel, bringing up the brig's chains and anchors, the blocks of pig iron that formed its ballast, and even four cannons, which were buoyed with empty kegs and successfully hauled ashore.

As we can see, the colony's arsenal had profited from the salvage operation no less than its kitchens and storerooms. Ever enthusiastic in his plans for the future, Pencroff conceived an artillery installation that would defend the channel and the mouth of the river. With four cannons, he promised to prevent any fleet, "no matter how mighty," from entering the waters of Lincoln Island!

The brig was now reduced to nothing more than a useless carcass, and soon the bad weather came to finish off the ship's destruction. Cyrus Smith had planned to blow the carcass up and collect the debris that landed on the shore, but a great wind from the northeast and heavy seas allowed him to spare his gunpowder.

For, during the night of the twenty-third, the hull of the brig was completely demolished, and a part of the wreckage washed up onto shore.

Of the ship's papers, no matter how meticulously he searched through the lockers on the poop deck, Cyrus Smith found no trace. The pirates had clearly destroyed all evidence of the *Speedy*'s owner and captain, and since the name of its home port was not inscribed on the rear escutcheon, there was no way to guess at its nationality. Nevertheless, by the configuration of its prow, Ayrton and Pencroff thought the brig to be of English construction.

Eight days after the catastrophe—or rather after the happy but inexplicable event to which the colony owed its salvation—there was nothing left to be seen of the ship, even at low tide. Its debris had been scattered over the seas, and nearly all its contents now lay in the storerooms of Granite House.

The mystery behind its strange destruction might never have been solved, had Neb, strolling along the beach on November 30th, not found a piece of a thick iron cylinder, bearing all the telltale traces of an explosion. The cylinder was twisted and torn at the edges, as if ripped apart by a sudden, violent force.

Neb brought this piece of metal back to his master, then at work with his companions in the Chimneys.

Cyrus Smith carefully examined the cylinder; then, turning to Pencroff:

"You still believe, my friend," he asked him, "that the *Speedy* was not destroyed by collision with a submerged rock?"

"Yes, Mr. Cyrus," answered the sailor. "You know as well as I do that there are no shoals in the channel."

"But what if it had struck this piece of iron?" the engineer said, showing him the broken cylinder.

"What, that little bit of pipe?" cried Pencroff, in a tone of the utmost incredulity.

"This?" Pencroff retorted.

"My friends," replied Cyrus Smith, "do you remember that the brig was hoisted up by a veritable mountain of seawater before it sank?"

"Yes, Mr. Cyrus!" answered Harbert.

"Well, would you like to know the cause of that curious eruption? Here it is," said the engineer, showing them the broken tube.

"This?" Pencroff retorted.

"Yes! This cylinder is all that remains of a mine!"

"A mine!" cried the engineer's companions.

"But who could have put a mine in the channel?" asked Pencroff, still reluctant to give in.

"All I can tell you is that it wasn't me!" answered Cyrus Smith. "But it was there all the same, and with your own eyes you witnessed its incredible power!"

V

The Engineer's Claims.—Pencroff's Grandiose Hypotheses.—An Aerial Battery.—The Four Projectiles.—Concerning the Surviving Convicts.—Ayrton Hesitates.—Cyrus Smith's Noble Sentiments.—Pencroff Regretfully Concedes.

Thus, everything could be explained by the explosion of the undersea mine. Cyrus Smith had had occasion to witness the terrible effects of these devices during the War between the States, and he could not have been mistaken. It was the powerful force of this cylinder, filled with an explosive material—nitroglycerine, ammonium picrate, or some other substance of the same nature—that had so violently churned up the waters of the channel. The brig had been blasted from below, sinking it at once; this was the cause of the immense damage done to the hull, destroying any hope of refloating the ship. This mine could have demolished an armored frigate as if it were no more than a simple fishing boat; the *Speedy* never stood a chance!

Yes! everything was explained, everything . . . except the presence of a mine in the waters of the channel!

"My friends," Cyrus Smith resumed, "we can no longer doubt the presence of some mysterious being on these shores, perhaps a castaway like ourselves, stranded here as we are. We have seen many inexplicable events in the past two years, and it is time that Ayrton knew of all that has happened. Who is this benevolent stranger who has so generously intervened in so many varied circumstances? I cannot imagine. What moves him to act as he does, to conceal his existence despite the many favors he has done us? I cannot say. But his favors are no less real for all that, and by their nature they depict a man of the most enormous power. Ayrton's debt to him is as great as our own, for if it was the stranger who saved me from the waves after my fall from the balloon, it was clearly him as well who wrote the message, directed the bottle into the channel, and alerted us to our companion's situation. I might add that the crate, so conveniently filled with everything we needed, must have been tugged to Flotsam Point and left there by the same stranger; that the fire on the plateau that guided you back to shore was lit by him; that the lead pellet found in the peccary was fired by him; that the mine that destroyed the brig was placed in the channel by him; in a word, that every one of these inexplicable and unaccountable happenings is the work of that mysterious being. Therefore, whatever he may be, whether castaway or exile, we must gratefully realize that we are beholden to him. We have contracted a debt, and I only hope that we may repay it one day."

"I couldn't agree more, my dear Cyrus," answered Gideon Spilett. "Yes, our island is home to some reclusive being, a being of seemingly unlimited power, whose influence has proven singularly beneficial to our colony. I might easily consider the stranger's abilities to be of a supernatural nature, if I found such a notion acceptable in the domain of practical existence. Is it he who haunts the shaft in Granite House? Does he observe us in secret? For he seems to be aware of our every undertaking. Was it he who placed the bottle in our path when we first put out to sea? Was it he who threw Top from the lake and dispatched the dugong? Was it he, as all the evidence suggests, who saved you from the waves, Cyrus, in circumstances far beyond the capacities of any ordinary man? If so, he possesses the secret of a great power, which has made him master of the elements."

This was a judicious observation, and none could disagree.

"Indeed," answered Cyrus Smith. "We can no longer doubt that some human being has intervened in our favor; but at the same time, I am forced to agree that his powers far outstrip those of the common run of men. This is another mystery; but if we discover this man, we will discover the key to that mystery as well. The question, then, is this: should we respect our benefactor's incognito, or should we take whatever steps are necessary to find him? What do you say to this?"

"I say," answered Pencroff, "that whoever he is he's a good man, and he has my wholehearted and everlasting esteem!"

"To be sure," Cyrus Smith replied, "but that's not an answer to my question, Pencroff."

"Master," Neb then said, "it seems to me that we can look all we like for the gentleman in question, but we won't find him until he wants us to."

"That's not bad thinking, Neb," Pencroff answered.

"I agree with Neb," added Gideon Spilett, "but that's no reason not to try. Whether we find this mysterious being or not, we will at least have attempted to fulfill our obligation."

"And you, my boy, give me your opinion," the engineer said, turning to Harbert.

"Oh!" cried Harbert, his eyes shining. "First he rescued you, and then he rescued us, and I'd very much like to thank him!"

"You don't ask for much, do you, my boy?" Pencroff replied. "And nor do I, nor any of us here! I'm not overly curious, but I'd give one of my two eyes to look that individual in the face! I can picture him now: handsome, tall, strong, with a fine beard, hair like rays of sunlight, lying on a bed of clouds with a great globe in his hand!"

"Why, Pencroff," answered Gideon Spilett, "you've just drawn the portrait of God Himself!"

"Perhaps, Mr. Spilett," the sailor replied, "but that's how I see him!"

"What about you, Ayrton?" the engineer asked.

"Mr. Smith," Ayrton replied, "I cannot give you my opinion. Whatever you do will be the right thing. If you want to include me in the search, I will be ready to follow you."

"I thank you, Ayrton," Cyrus Smith responded, "but I would prefer a more direct answer. You are our companion; more than once you have proven your devotion, and, no less than the rest of us, you must be consulted when there is an important decision to be made. Speak."

"Mr. Smith," answered Ayrton, "I believe we should do everything we can to find our unknown benefactor. Perhaps he is lonely? Perhaps he is suffering? Perhaps it is time he rejoined the company of men? I, too, owe him a debt of gratitude, as you say. It was he, it cannot have been another, who came to Tabor Island and discovered the wretch you found, and it was he who told you of an unhappy man in desperate need of succor!... Thanks to him, I became a man again, and that I will never forget!"

"Then it's decided," said Cyrus Smith. "We shall begin the search as soon as possible. Not a single area of the island will be left unexplored. We will delve into its most secret nooks, and may our unknown friend forgive us our curiosity and remember our good intentions!"

The colonists spent the next few days haymaking and harvesting, finishing all their most essential chores before they set out to explore the island. The sprouts found on Tabor Island had now matured, and the vegetables they produced had to be harvested and stocked in the vast larders of Granite House. Despite the colony's increasing wealth, the storerooms offered ample space for this new abundance. Within those walls lay all the fruits of the colony's labors, methodically arranged, perfectly safe, protected from animals and men alike, sheltered from the weather by the thick granite that enclosed them. Several of the natural recesses in the upper corridor were made broader or deeper with picks and explosives. Granite House had become a veritable warehouse, generously stocked with provisions, ammunition, spare tools, and utensils—in a word, everything the colony could need.

The cannons removed from the brig had been expertly fashioned from cast steel, and at Pencroff's insistence they were hoisted to the threshold of Granite House with a crane and winding tackle. Small gunports were cut between the windows, and soon the cannons' gleaming muzzles could be seen emerging from the granite wall. From this height, the guns could command the whole of Union Bay. Pencroff had devised a miniature Gibraltar, and no ship lying broadside off the islet would escape the fire of his aerial battery.

"Mr. Cyrus," Pencroff said one day—it was November 8th—"now that our artillery is in place, I believe we should test its range."

"Do you really think that's worthwhile?" the engineer answered.

"It's more than worthwhile, it's necessary! Otherwise, we'll never know how far we can fire those lovely cannonballs!"

"All right, then, Pencroff, we shall put them to the test," the engineer replied. "Nevertheless, for the purposes of this experiment, I would prefer not to break into our supply of gunpowder. I propose that we arm the cannons with pyroxylin, for which we will never lack."

"Are you sure they can withstand the force of a pyroxylin detonation?" asked the reporter, who longed to test their new artillery every bit as ardently as Pencroff.

"I believe so. Besides," the engineer added, "we will take every precaution."

The engineer had judged the cannons to be of first-rate design and construction, and he had considerable experience in this domain. Breech-loading, cast from strong, forged steel, they could clearly withstand a considerable blast; consequently, their range would surely prove enormous. For the flatter the trajectory of a cannonball, the more powerful its physical effect; and a flat trajectory requires that the projectile shoot from the muzzle at a very great speed.

"Now," said Cyrus Smith to his companions, "the initial speed is directly proportional to the quantity of powder used. The great thing, in the construction of such a weapon, is to use as highly resistant a metal as possible, and steel is incontestably the strongest of them all. Thus, I believe I can say with some certainty that our cannons will safely withstand the expansion of the pyroxylin gases, and will give excellent results."

"We can say that with much greater certainty once we've tried them out!" Pencroff replied.

Needless to say, the four cannons were in perfect firing condition. The sailor himself had taken on the task of cleaning them after they were pulled from the floor of the channel, and he performed this task with admirable conscientiousness. How many hours he spent rubbing, oiling, polishing, cleaning the gas check mechanism, the bolt, the set screw! And now they shone as brightly as the artillery of any frigate in the United States Navy.

Thus, with all the colony present, Master Joop and Top included, the four cannons were successively tested that day. They had been loaded with pyroxylin, carefully measured to compensate for that substance's greater explosive force—four times that of ordinary powder, as we have said—and then armed with their projectiles, which were of a cylindro-conical form.

Pencroff held the rope, ready to ignite the quick-match.

On Cyrus Smith's command, the shot was fired. Aimed toward the sea, the cannonball passed over the islet and disappeared offshore, at a distance that they could not precisely gauge.

The second cannon was turned toward the outermost rocks of Flotsam Point; this time the projectile struck a pointed stone nearly three miles from Granite House, shattering it to pieces.

Harbert had aimed and fired this second cannon, and he felt a certain pride at his first attempt as a gunner. Only Pencroff could have been prouder! Such a fine shot, and solely to his dear child's credit!

The third projectile was launched toward the dunes along the northern shore of Union Bay. It smashed into the sand at a distance of four miles at least, then ricocheted and vanished beneath the waves in a great cloud of spray.

Cyrus Smith armed the fourth cannon with a more generous amount of ordnance, for he wished to determine the upper limits of its range. The colonists took a step back, lest the cannon be ripped apart by the blast, and the quick-match was lit with a long rope.

The detonation was quite violent, but the steel withstood the blast. Running to the window, the colonists saw the projectile clip the rocks at Cape Mandible, some five miles from Granite House, and disappear into Shark Gulf.

"Well now, Mr. Cyrus," cried Pencroff, whose hurrahs could easily rival the explosions of the cannons, "what do you think of our battery? Let every pirate in the Pacific come calling at Granite House! Not a one of them will land without our permission!"

"If you want my opinion, Pencroff," the engineer replied, "that's an experiment I'd rather not undertake."

"Speaking of which," the sailor resumed, "what about those six rogues on the prowl somewhere on our island? What are we going to do about them? Should we let them roam freely through our forests, our fields, and our grazing lands? Those pirates are no better than jaguars, and I say we should treat them as such! What do you think, Ayrton?" added Pencroff, turning to his companion.

At first Ayrton made no reply, and Cyrus Smith regretted the thoughtlessness of Pencroff's question. He was thus greatly moved to hear Ayrton answer, in a humble voice:

"I was once one of those jaguars, Mr. Pencroff, and I have no right to speak . . ."

And off he walked with a heavy step.

Pencroff realized his error.

"What a damn fool I am!" he cried. "Poor Ayrton! He has just as much right to speak as anyone here! . . ."

"Yes," said Gideon Spilett, "but his reserve is greatly to his credit. We must never forget his feelings about his unfortunate past."

"Right you are, Mr. Spilett," the sailor answered. "You won't catch me making that mistake again! I'd sooner swallow my own tongue than aggrieve our friend Ayrton! But let's return to the question. It seems to me those bandits deserve no mercy. We should rid the island of their presence as soon as we can."

"Is that truly your opinion, Pencroff?" the engineer asked.

"Indeed it is."

"You wouldn't prefer to wait for some new sign of hostile intentions before we set after them in merciless pursuit?"

"What they've already done isn't enough?" asked Pencroff, confounded by the engineer's reticence.

"They might mend their ways!" said Cyrus Smith. "And perhaps repent..."

"Repent! Them!" cried the sailor with a dismissive shrug.

"Pencroff, think of Ayrton!" said Harbert, taking the sailor's hand. "He became a decent man again!"

Pencroff looked at his companions, one after the other. He would never have thought his suggestion might meet with the slightest dissent. His was a rough and ready soul, and he could envisage no compromise with the scoundrels who had landed on their island—Bob Harvey's accomplices, willing members of the *Speedy*'s murderous crew! He saw them as nothing more than wild animals, to be destroyed without hesitation and without remorse.

"So!" he said. "Everyone is against me! You want to show forgiveness to blackguards like that! Fine. May we never live to regret it!"

"What do we risk," said Harbert, "if we take care not to let down our guard?"

"Hm!" said the reporter, who had as yet expressed no particular opinion. "These are six well-armed men. If each were assigned to ambush one of us, they'd soon be the masters of the island!"

"Why haven't they done so already?" answered Harbert. "Because they have no reason to do so, surely. Besides, there are six of us as well."

"All right! all right!" answered Pencroff, whom no amount of reasoning could convince. "We'll just leave these fine fellows to their little occupations, and not give them a moment's thought from now on!"

"Come now, Pencroff," said Neb, "you know you're not that heartless! If one of those poor men were standing here before you, not three paces away, you'd never..."

"I would shoot him down like a mad dog, Neb," Pencroff answered coldly.

"Pencroff," the engineer then said, "you have often shown great deference for my opinions. May I ask you to rely on my judgment once again?"

"I will do as you see fit, Mr. Smith," the sailor replied, in no way convinced.

"Well then, let us wait, and let us attack only if we are attacked."

The question of the remaining pirates was thus resolved, although Pencroff believed no good could come from this decision. They would not attack the pirates, but they would stay on the alert. After all, the island was large and fertile. If some sense of decency remained deep within their souls, the wretches might well mend their ways. Indeed, was it not in their best interests to begin their lives anew, given their present circumstances? In any case, if only for reasons of humanity, the colonists had no choice but to wait. Perhaps they would not feel as carefree as they once did, nor as able to come and go as they pleased. Until then their only concern had been wild animals, and now six convicts were at large on their island, perhaps desperate and highly dangerous. This was a serious thing, to be sure, and for folk less doughty than the colonists, it would have shattered all sense of security.

No matter! For the moment, the colonists had good reason to oppose Pencroff's plans. Would the future prove them right? That remained to be seen.

VI

Plans for the Expedition.—Ayrton at the Sheepfold.—A Visit to Port Balloon.—Pencroff's Remarks Aboard the Bonadventure.*— A Message Sent to the Sheepfold.—No Response from Ayrton.— Departure the Following Day.—Why the Message Had Not Gone Through.—A Gunshot.*

The colonists remained greatly preoccupied with their plans for a full exploration of the island, an exploration that had now taken on two purposes: first, to discover the mysterious being whose existence was no longer in doubt, and, second, to determine what had become of the pirates, what repair they had chosen, what sort of life they were living, and what threat they might pose.

Cyrus Smith wanted to set out at once, but first the cart would have to be loaded with the various camping effects and utensils they might require for a journey of several days. Furthermore, one of the dauws had injured its leg, and would need an extended period of rest before it could be called upon to pull the cart. Thus, the colonists had no choice but to delay their departure for another week or so, until November 20th. At Lincoln Island's latitude, the month of November resembles the boreal May, and the weather was fine indeed. The sun was approaching the Tropic of Capricorn, giving them the longest days of the year—an auspicious moment for their expedition, for which they had the highest of hopes. Even if the excursion did not accomplish its principal goal, it might well offer them a host of new discoveries, most particularly new wealth from nature's bounty; for, at Cyrus Smith's suggestion, the search would be focused on the dense Forests of the Far West, and would be pursued straight to the end of Serpentine Peninsula.

By common agreement, the colonists would use the nine days preceding their departure to attend to a few unfinished tasks on Longview Plateau.

Meanwhile, Ayrton would return to the sheepfold, where the flocks required his attention. He would devote two days to his various chores, and amply stock the stables with food before returning to Granite House.

As he was leaving, Cyrus Smith asked if he would like one of the others to accompany him, reminding him that the island was not as safe as it once was.

Ayrton saw no need for this; he could easily tend to the flocks on his own, and he feared no harm from the pirates. He promised to send a telegram to Granite House at once in case of untoward incident.

Ayrton left at dawn on November 9th, with a single dauw hitched to the cart. Two hours later, a telegram announced that all was in order at the sheepfold.

Cyrus Smith spent these two days working on a project to guard Granite House against future surprise attacks. His intention was to seal off the upper entrance to the spillway, now barricaded with cemented rocks and half-hidden by grasses and shrubs. His plan was simplicity itself: he had only to raise the water level in Lake Grant by two or three feet, and the orifice would be completely submerged.

Raising the water level meant building dams at the two outlets they had blasted from the lake's granite shore, which now fed Glycerine Creek and the waterfall. He called his companions to work, and soon two small stone-and-mortar dams, eight feet wide and three feet high, slowed the outward flow of the lakewater.

The water level gradually rose, and soon no one could have guessed that the entrance to a vast underground gallery might lie at one end of the lake.

It goes without saying that their supply of fresh water remained undiminished, for they had been careful not to disturb the small deviation that fed Granite House's reservoir and powered their elevator. They now had a safe and comfortable retreat, impervious to attack and impossible to enter unbidden once the elevator had been raised to the top.

With this project finished, Pencroff, Gideon Spilett, and Harbert found time for an excursion to Port Balloon. The sailor was anxious to see whether the convicts had visited the cove where the *Bonadventure* was moored.

The colonists were called to work.

"Let us remember that those gentlemen happened to come ashore on the southern coast," he observed, "and if they continued along the shoreline they might well have found our little port, in which case I wouldn't give four bits for our *Bonadventure*'s chances."

Pencroff's apprehensions seemed not unfounded, and a visit to Port Balloon was deemed an excellent idea.

The sailor and his companions set out after lunch on November 10th. They did not neglect to bring their weapons. Pencroff ostentatiously slipped two bullets into the barrels of his rifle, shaking his head in a manner that boded ill for any being who tried to come too close, "whether man or beast," as he said. Gideon Spilett and Harbert loaded their weapons as well, and the trio set out at about three o'clock.

Neb accompanied them to the bend in the Mercy and raised the bridge after seeing them across. It was agreed that they would announce their return with a rifle shot, whereupon Neb would come and allow them across the river again.

The little band followed the port road toward the southern coastline. The journey was no longer than three and a half miles, but Gideon Spilett and his companions took two hours to complete it. They searched the environs of the road with great care, both in the dense forests and in the marshes of Shelduck Fens. They found no trace of the fugitives. Not knowing the number of colonists, nor the size and nature of their defenses, the six convicts must have made directly for the island's least accessible regions.

Arriving at Port Balloon, Pencroff looked with delight on the *Bonadventure*, still peacefully moored in the narrow cove. Indeed, Port Balloon was so well hidden amid the towering rocks as to remain invisible from both sea and land, unless the viewer was above or inside it.

"So," said Pencroff, "the scoundrels haven't yet found their way here. Snakes have a natural liking for tall grass, so the Far West will be the place to look if we want to find them."

"And it's a good thing, too," added Harbert, "because if they'd found the *Bonadventure* they would have taken it and fled, and we could never hope to return to Tabor Island."

"Indeed," the reporter answered. "And it is vitally important that we leave a message there with Lincoln Island's location and Ayrton's new address, in case the Scottish yacht should return."

"Well, the *Bonadventure* is still here, Mr. Spilett!" the sailor replied. "She and her crew are ready to leave at a moment's notice!"

"I believe this should be our first task once we have finished the exploration of the island, Pencroff. After all, should we finally meet up with the stranger, he might have a great deal to tell us about both Lincoln and Tabor Islands. He was clearly the author of the message in the bottle; perhaps he knows when we might expect the yacht to return!"

"By all the devils!" cried Pencroff. "Who can that character be? He knows us, and we don't know him! If he's just a castaway, why is he hiding? We're all fine people, I do believe, and no one spurns the company of fine people! Did he come here of his own free will? Can he leave the island if he pleases? Is he still here? Is he gone? . . ."

Pursuing their conversation, Pencroff, Harbert, and Gideon Spilett boarded the *Bonadventure* and walked the length of the deck. Suddenly, glancing at the bitt around which the anchor cable was wrapped, Pencroff cried out:

"Why! Well, I'll be . . . What is the meaning of this?"

"What is it, Pencroff?" the reporter asked.

"It's just that I never tied this knot!"

And Pencroff showed them the rope that secured the anchor cable to the bitt.

"You didn't tie it?" asked Gideon Spilett.

"No! On my oath. This is a reef knot, and my knot is two half hitches."*

"You must have made a mistake, Pencroff."

"I did not make a mistake!" the sailor stated. "Tying knots is in your hands. It comes naturally, and your hands never make a mistake!"

"Then the convicts must have come aboard?" Harbert asked.

"I have no idea," Pencroff answered. "All I know is that someone has raised the *Bonadventure*'s anchor, then moored her again! And look! here's further proof. They've paid out the anchor line, and the chafing gear† is no longer at the rim of the hawsehole. I'm telling you, someone has used our boat!"

"But if it was the convicts, they would have either pillaged the boat or used it to flee . . ."

---

* A knot commonly used by sailors, prized for its great resistance to slippage.

† The chafing gear is a piece of old canvas wrapped around the anchor line to prevent abrasion as the cable rubs against the hawsehole.

"To flee!...where?...to Tabor Island?" Pencroff retorted. "Do you seriously believe they would have tried to put out to sea on a boat as small as this?"

"And furthermore, they would have had to know that the islet existed," the reporter added.

"In any event," said the sailor, "as sure as my name is Bonadventure Pencroff from the Vineyard, someone has sailed our *Bonadventure* without us!"

Gideon Spilett and Harbert could not contest the sailor's allegation. It seemed obvious that the boat had been sailed—for a distance great or small—since Pencroff had last returned her to Port Balloon. There was no question in the sailor's mind that the anchor had been raised and then sent to the bottom again. And why would that be, if not because the boat had been used for some sort of expedition?

"But wouldn't we have seen the *Bonadventure* pass by offshore?" the reporter observed, attempting to find every possible objection to this hypothesis.

"Oh! Mr. Spilett," the sailor answered, "if they set off in the night with a fresh breeze behind them they'd be out of sight within two hours!"

"Very well," Gideon Spilett continued, "but for what purpose would the convicts have taken the *Bonadventure*, and why would they have brought her back to port when they were finished? That I cannot understand."

"Well, Mr. Spilett," the sailor answered, "let's just call this one more inexplicable event, and not give it another moment's thought! What matters most is that the *Bonadventure* remain in our possession, and so she does, for the moment. Unfortunately, if the convicts take her out a second time, we might not find her again!"

"Then, Pencroff," said Harbert, "perhaps it would be wise to moor the *Bonadventure* within sight of Granite House?"

"Yes and no," Pencroff replied, "or rather no. The mouth of the Mercy is no place for a boat, and the sea is too rough."

"What if we hauled her onto shore, or even up to the base of the Chimneys?"

"Perhaps...yes..." answered Pencroff. "But we're about to leave Granite House for a long expedition, and while we're away I believe the *Bonadventure* will be safer here than there. This is where we shall leave her, until we're done purging the island of those scoundrels."

"I agree," said the reporter. "At least she won't be as exposed as at the mouth of the Mercy in case of bad weather."

"But what if the convicts board her again?" said Harbert.

"Well, my boy," Pencroff replied, "if they didn't find her here, they wouldn't be slow to come looking for her at Granite House, and with us gone, nothing would stand in their way! No, I agree with Mr. Spilett: we must leave her at Port Balloon. But perhaps it would be best to bring her back to Granite House when our search is over, and leave her there until the villains have been vanquished."

"Agreed. Off we go!" said the reporter.

Returning to Granite House, Pencroff, Harbert, and Gideon Spilett informed the engineer of their discovery. Cyrus Smith agreed to their plans for the boat, both present and future, even promising Pencroff that he would study the waters between the islet and the coastline to see if a system of dikes could be built to create an artificial harbor. In this way, the *Bonadventure* would always be close at hand, within the colonists' view, and if need be under lock and key.

That evening a telegram was sent to Ayrton, asking that he bring back a pair of goats that Neb intended to acclimate to the pastures of the plateau. Oddly, Ayrton did not respond at once, as he usually did. The engineer found this rather surprising, but of course Ayrton could simply have been out; perhaps he was even on his way back to Granite House, for two days had now passed since his departure, and he had agreed to return the evening of the tenth or the morning of the eleventh at the latest.

The colonists waited for Ayrton on the plateau above Granite House. Neb and Harbert kept watch over the roads, ready to allow their companion across the creek as soon as he came into view.

But soon it was ten o'clock at night, and Ayrton had still not appeared. They decided to send another message, requesting an immediate response.

The receiver at Granite House remained silent.

The colonists were now deeply concerned. What could have happened? Had Ayrton left the sheepfold? If not, was something preventing him from responding? Should they attempt a trip to the sheepfold on a night as dark as this?

They held counsel. Some wanted to go, others to stay.

"But," said Harbert, "perhaps something's happened to the telegraph to put it out of service?"

"That could be," said the reporter.

"I believe we should wait until tomorrow," Cyrus Smith answered. "It may well be that Ayrton failed to receive our message, or even that we failed to receive his."

And so they waited, not without some perfectly understandable trepidation.

Very early on the morning of November 11th, Cyrus Smith sent the electric current running once more through the wire, and still there came no reply.

He tried again; the result was the same.

"To the sheepfold!" he said.

"And don't forget the rifles!" added Pencroff.

Hastily they resolved not to leave Granite House unattended. Neb would see his companions as far as Glycerine Creek; then, raising the bridge behind them, he would conceal himself among the trees to await their return, or Ayrton's.

Should the pirates appear and attempt to force their way onto the plateau, he would do his best to hold them back with rifle fire. If this should fail, he would take refuge in Granite House, raising the elevator to the top to guarantee his absolute safety.

Cyrus Smith, Gideon Spilett, Harbert, and Pencroff would make directly for the sheepfold, and search the surrounding woods if they failed to find Ayrton there.

The engineer and his three companions crossed Glycerine Creek at six o'clock in the morning, and Neb took up position on the stream's left bank, behind a small escarpment crowned by towering dragon trees.

Reaching the edge of Longview Plateau, the colonists turned onto Sheepfold Road. Two carbines and two rifles had been loaded with bullets, and the colonists carried their weapons over their forearms, ready to fire at the first sign of hostility.

The road was edged with dense thickets in which a number of outlaws could easily have found cover. Armed as the colonists knew them to be, they could pose a truly formidable threat.

The colonists walked quickly and silently. Top ran on ahead, sometimes speeding straight down the road, sometimes making a detour into the woods, but always mute, apparently sensing nothing suspect in the environs. And they knew they could count on their faithful dog to bark at the first sign of danger, and never to let down his guard.

The telegraph line linking the sheepfold and Granite House lay just alongside the road. Some two miles into their walk, Cyrus Smith and his companions had still found no break in the connection. The poles were in good condition, the insulators intact, the wire evenly stretched from one pole to the next. Nevertheless, the engineer here observed the first signs of a slackening in the wire, and finally, on arriving at pole 74, Harbert stopped and shouted back to the others:

"There's a break in the wire!"

His companions hurried forward to join the boy.

They found the toppled pole lying across the road. Their hypothesis of a malfunction in the telegraph was thus confirmed; clearly no message from Granite House could have been received at the sheepfold, nor from the sheepfold at Granite House.

"It wasn't the wind that uprooted this pole," Pencroff observed.

"No," answered Gideon Spilett. "The soil beneath it has been dug out. It was brought down by a human hand."

"And the line has been deliberately pulled apart as well," added Harbert, holding up the broken ends of the iron wire, which had been violently snapped in two.

"Does the break appear to be recent?" asked Cyrus Smith.

"Yes," Harbert replied, "it can't have been long ago."

"To the sheepfold! to the sheepfold!" cried the sailor.

The colonists were then halfway between Granite House and the sheepfold, with another two and a half miles to go. They set off at a run.

They now had reason to believe that some serious incident had occurred at the sheepfold. To be sure, Ayrton could have sent a telegram that never arrived; this was not the cause of his companions' concern. Considerably more troubling was the fact that Ayrton had not reappeared at Granite House after promising to return the previous evening. Worse yet, they felt sure that the telegraph line had been broken for some specific purpose, and who other than the convicts could have a reason to interrupt communications between the sheepfold and Granite House?

On and on the colonists ran, profoundly shaken by their discovery. They had become sincerely attached to their new companion. Would they find him massacred by those who had once looked to him as their leader?

Soon the road was joined by the little stream deviated from Red Creek to irrigate the sheepfold's grazing lands. They relaxed their gait on reach-

A gunshot echoed off the palisade, and a cry of pain came in response.

ing this point, for they did not want to enter into combat in their present breathless condition. Their rifles were cocked, ready to be fired at any moment. Each man kept watch over a separate area of the forest. Every now and them Top let out a quiet growl that did not bode well.

Finally the palisade appeared through the trees, apparently undamaged. The gate remained closed, as usual. A profound silence hung over the sheepfold; neither the mouflons' bleats nor Ayrton's voice could be heard.

"Let's go in!" said Cyrus Smith.

The engineer strode forward. His companions covered him from twenty paces behind, watching intently for any sign of suspicious movement.

Cyrus Smith raised the interior latch of the gate. He was about to push it open when Top suddenly let out a furious bark. A gunshot echoed off the palisade, and a cry of pain came in response.

Struck by the bullet, Harbert lay outstretched on the ground!

VII

The Reporter and Pencroff in the Sheepfold.—Harbert Carried Inside.—The Sailor's Despair.—The Reporter and the Engineer Consult.—The Treatment.—Hope Returning.—How to Inform Neb?—A True and Faithful Messenger.—Neb's Response.

Hearing Harbert's shout, Pencroff dropped his weapon and ran to his side.

"They've killed him!" he cried. "My child! They've killed him!"

Cyrus Smith and Gideon Spilett came forward at once. The reporter tried to make out the poor child's heartbeat.

"He's alive," he said. "But we've got to take him…"

"To Granite House? Impossible!" the engineer answered.

"Into the sheepfold, then!" cried Pencroff.

"Just one moment," said Cyrus Smith.

He ran off to the left, skirting the perimeter of the enclosure. A moment later he found himself face to face with a convict, who hastily aimed his weapon and sent a bullet through the engineer's hat. But before he could fire a second shot he fell dead, struck in the heart by Cyrus Smith's dagger—a weapon even more trustworthy than his rifle.

In the meantime, Gideon Spilett and the sailor climbed up the corners of the palisade, threw their legs over the top, and jumped into the enclosure. They knocked away the stays blocking the gate from inside and ran into the house, which they found to be empty. Soon Harbert was lying on Ayrton's bed.

A few moments later, Cyrus Smith stood at his side.

Truly terrible was the sailor's grief as he looked on Harbert's inanimate body. He sobbed, he wept, he tried to smash his head against the walls. Neither the engineer nor the reporter could console him. Their own emotion was far too great. They could not speak.

Nevertheless, they did everything in their power to wrest from death's grip the poor child who lay agonizing before them. Gideon Spilett had seen many emergencies in the course of his life, from which he had acquired some knowledge of basic medical practice. He knew a bit of everything, and many a time he had been called upon to treat bullet or saber wounds. Thus, with the aid of Cyrus Smith, he considered the measures that Harbert's treatment would require.

To begin with, he was struck by the general stupor into which the child had been plunged. This could have had two causes: either a hemorrhage or the terrible concussion of a bullet striking a bone.

Harbert was extremely pale, and only at long intervals could Gideon Spilett feel the faint beating of his pulse. It seemed to be on the point of stopping altogether. The child had lost all sensibility and awareness as well. These were very serious symptoms.

Harbert's breast was laid bare, and washed with cold water once the flow of blood had been stanched with handkerchiefs.

Now the contusion, or rather the wound, was revealed. An oval-shaped hole could be seen between the third and fourth ribs of his breast. It was here that the bullet had struck him.

Now Cyrus Smith and Gideon Spilett turned the poor child over, and so faint was his moan of pain that they might well have believed it his last.

Blood flowed over Harbert's back from a second contused wound. The bullet had run straight through his body.

"God be praised!" said the reporter. "The bullet didn't remain inside, and we won't have to extract it."

"But what about his heart?..." asked Cyrus Smith.

"The heart has not been hit, or Harbert would be dead!"

"Dead!" cried Pencroff, letting out a great roar.

The sailor had heard only a part of the reporter's reply.

"No, Pencroff," Cyrus Smith answered, "no! He is not dead. His heart is beating! He even moaned just now. But, for the very sake of your child, be calm. We need to keep our wits about us now. Don't make us lose them, my friend."

Pencroff fell silent, but the great tears pouring down his face betrayed the violent emotions inside him.

Meanwhile Gideon Spilett attempted to summon his memories, so that he might proceed in the most methodical way. He surmised that the bullet had entered Harbert's chest, and exited through his back. But what ravages had the bullet caused as it passed through? What vital organs had been hit? For the moment, even a professional surgeon would have been hard put to answer such questions, and the reporter all the more.

Nevertheless, one thing he knew: it was vital to protect the damaged organs from any constriction caused by swelling, and to fight the local inflammation and fever that would ineluctably result from the wound—a wound that might well prove fatal! And what could he use as a topical antiphlogistic? How was he to go about reducing the inflammation?

In any case, the most crucial task was to bandage the two wounds without delay. Washing them in warm water and pressing the edges together would inevitably result in a new outpouring of blood, and this Gideon Spilett rightly chose to avoid. The hemorrhaging was quite abundant as it was, and Harbert had been all too seriously weakened by the blood he had already lost.

The reporter thus resolved to wash the two wounds with cold water.

Harbert was placed on his left side and held in that position.

"We must not let him move," said Gideon Spilett. "In this position the wounds in his back and chest will suppurate properly. He must stay just as he is, without the slightest disturbance."

"What! We can't transport him to Granite House?" asked Pencroff.

"No, Pencroff," said the reporter.

"Damnation!" cried the sailor, raising his fist toward Heaven.

"Pencroff!" said Cyrus Smith.

Gideon Spilett had resumed his examination of the wounded child. The reporter was deeply troubled by Harbert's frightful pallor.

"Cyrus," he said, "I'm not a doctor...I'm so terribly unsure of myself...I need you to help me, I need your advice, your experience!..."

"Stay calm, my friend," answered the engineer, grasping the reporter's hand. "Keep your wits about you, and think...Think of this alone: we must save Harbert!"

These words restored Gideon Spilett's self-possession, stolen away from him in a moment of weakness by the realization of his awesome responsibility. He sat near the bed. Cyrus Smith remained standing. Pencroff had ripped off his shirt, and sat mechanically tearing it into strips for the purpose of dressing the wounds.

Gideon Spilett then told Cyrus Smith of the treatment he thought it best to attempt. The hemorrhage would have to be stopped at all costs; but they must not close the two wounds, nor allow them to heal immediately, for certain internal organs had surely been punctured, and the suppuration from those internal wounds must not be allowed to accumulate inside the chest.

Cyrus Smith fully endorsed the reporter's plan, and they resolved to dress the two wounds without attempting to close them by coaptation. Happily, it appeared that they would not have to be incised.

And now, did the colonists possess any effective agent to combat the ensuing inflammation?

Yes! they did, offered in abundance by nature herself. They had cold water, which is the most powerful remedy for inflammation known to man, the most effective therapeutic agent in such cases, widely used by doctors the world over. In addition to its other virtues, cold water does not disturb the wound, but protects it without bandaging; and this is of no small importance, for experiments have shown that contact with air is detrimental for the first few days.

Such was Gideon Spilett and Cyrus Smith's reasoning, founded on simple common sense, and the finest surgeon would have chosen no other treatment. Canvas compresses were applied to poor Harbert's wounds, and continually moistened with cold water.

The sailor's first act was to light a fire in the hearth. The house at the sheepfold had been stocked with all of life's essentials. Maple sugar and medicinal plants—the very ones the boy had gathered on the shores of Lake Grant—were used to brew refreshing infusions; but Harbert lay utterly insensible even as these were administered to him, and his fever remained alarmingly high. The day went by, and then the night, and still the child did not regain consciousness. Harbert's life was hanging by a single thread, and that thread could break at any moment.

The next day, November 12th, hope returned to Cyrus Smith and his companions. Harbert had emerged from his prolonged stupor. He opened his eyes and recognized Cyrus Smith. He had no idea what had happened. They recounted the previous day's events, and Gideon Spilett entreated him to remain perfectly calm, assuring him that his life was not in danger and that his wounds would begin to heal in a few days. Harbert felt little pain, and the continuous application of cold water prevented any inflammation of his wounds. The suppuration was proceeding regularly, the fever showed no signs of increasing, and they began to hope that no catastrophe would result from this terrible wound. Pencroff's heartache gradually eased. He was like a Sister of Mercy, or a mother at her child's sickbed.

Harbert lost consciousness again, but his sleep seemed sounder now.

"Tell me again that your hopes are high, Mr. Spilett!" said Pencroff. "Tell me again that you'll save Harbert!"

"Yes, we shall save him!" the reporter answered. "The wound is serious, and the bullet might have passed through the lung, but the perforation of that organ is rarely fatal."

"Oh! may God hear your words!" said Pencroff.

All through these twenty-four hours, as we might well suppose, the colonists' only thought was for Harbert's recovery. They never once considered the danger that might face them if the convicts returned, nor the precautions to be taken to guard against future attacks.

But that day, as Pencroff watched over the patient, Cyrus Smith and the reporter discussed their present situation.

First of all, they walked the sheepfold from one end to the other, finding no trace of Ayrton. Had the poor devil been carried off by his onetime accomplices? Had he been ambushed at the sheepfold? Had he struggled, only to be overcome in the end? This last conjecture seemed all too likely. As he scaled the palisade, Gideon Spilett had clearly seen one of the convicts fleeing into the southern foothills of Mount Franklin, with Top in pursuit. He was unmistakably one of the six whose boat had broken up on the shoals, as was the man Cyrus Smith had killed, whose body they found outside the enclosure.

The sheepfold had suffered no damage in the attack. The gates were still closed, and the animals had not fled into the forest. No sign of combat or pillage could be found, and the house and palisade were just as they last saw them. Only Ayrton's store of ammunition had disappeared.

"They must have caught the poor fellow unawares," said Cyrus Smith, "and since he was not one to go down without a fight, he must have perished at their hands."

"Yes! I'm afraid that seems most likely!" the reporter answered. "Then, finding ample supplies of everything they needed, the convicts must have settled in at the sheepfold, and taken flight only when they found us approaching. And it seems equally clear that Ayrton, whether dead or alive, was no longer here by then."

"We shall have to search the forest and rid the island of these wretches," said the engineer. "We should have listened to Pencroff when he urged us to hunt them down like wild beasts. That would have spared us a great deal of grief!"

"Yes," said the reporter, "but now we have earned the right to show no mercy!"

"In any case," said the engineer, "we have no choice but to wait here until Harbert can be safely transported to Granite House."

"What about Neb?" asked the reporter.

"Neb is perfectly safe."

"Suppose he becomes alarmed by our long absence, and tries to come join us?"

"He must not!" Cyrus Smith briskly answered. "He would be murdered on the way!"

"Nevertheless, I wouldn't be at all surprised if he tried!"

"Oh! if only the telegraph were working, we could warn him! But there's nothing to be done about that. And we certainly can't leave Pencroff and Harbert alone here!... Very well. I will go to Granite House myself."

"No, no! Cyrus," the reporter answered, "you mustn't lay yourself open to attack! Your courage is no match for their weapons. The wretches are obviously watching the sheepfold from somewhere in the woods, and if you left we'd soon have not one but two misfortunes to lament."

"But what about Neb?" the engineer repeated. "It's been twenty-four hours since he last heard from us! He's sure to come looking for us!"

"And he'll be far less wary than we would be ourselves," Gideon Spilett added, "so he might well be shot down!..."

"Have we no way of warning him?"

As he pondered this question, the engineer's gaze landed on Top, who was pacing back and forth as if to say, "Am I not here?"

"Top!" cried Cyrus Smith.

The animal bounded forward in response to his master's call.

"Yes, Top will go!" the reporter said, reading the engineer's thoughts. "Top can get through where we cannot! He'll bring Neb the news from the sheepfold, and then he'll return with news from Granite House!"

"Quickly!" answered Cyrus Smith. "Quickly!"

Hurriedly tearing a page from his notebook, Gideon Spilett wrote these lines:

"Neb, Top! Neb!" the engineer repeated.

"Harbert wounded. We are at the sheepfold. Be on your guard. Do not leave Granite House. Any sign of the convicts? Answer by Top."

This laconic message contained everything Neb needed to know, and at the same time asked him everything his companions wished to learn. The paper was folded and prominently attached to Top's collar.

"Top! my dear dog," said the engineer, petting the animal's head. "Neb, Top! Neb! Go! go!"

Top leaped up on hearing these words. He immediately understood what they wanted from him. He knew the way home from the sheepfold. The trip would take him less than half an hour, and while the dangers of such a journey would have been great for Cyrus Smith or the reporter, Top would very likely go unnoticed as he ran through the grass or under the canopy of trees.

The engineer went to the gate and pushed back one of the swinging doors.

"Neb, Top! Neb!" the engineer repeated once again, pointing in the direction of Granite House.

Top bounded off and disappeared almost at once.

"He'll make it!" said the reporter.

"Yes, and he will return, faithful animal that he is!"

"What time is it?" asked Gideon Spilett.

"Ten o'clock."

"He should be back in an hour. We will watch for his return."

The gate was closed again, and the engineer and the reporter returned to the house. Harbert remained in a state of profound unconsciousness. Pencroff carefully kept the compresses damp. Seeing that there was nothing more to be done for the moment, Gideon Spilett set about preparing some nourishment, all the while keeping a watchful eye on the foothill at the far end of the enclosure, from which an attack might be launched at any moment.

Not without anxiety, the colonists awaited Top's return. A little before eleven o'clock, Cyrus Smith and the reporter took up their carbines and posted themselves behind the gate, ready to open it at the dog's first bark. They knew that Neb would send Top back immediately if he reached Granite House unharmed.

After some ten minutes' wait a gunshot rang out, followed by a great flurry of barks.

The engineer opened the gate. Seeing a wisp of smoke in the woods a hundred paces away, he immediately fired in that direction.

Just then Top came bounding into the sheepfold, and the gate was quickly closed behind him.

"Top, Top!" cried the engineer, embracing the dog's fine large head.

A note had been tied to his neck, and Cyrus Smith read these words, written in Neb's rough handwriting:

"No pirates around Granite House. I will not move. Poor Mr. Harbert!"

VIII

*The Convicts in the Area of the Sheepfold.—A Prolonged Stay.—
Harbert's Treatment Continues.—Pencroff's Jubilation.—A Look
Back.—What the Future Holds.—Cyrus Smith's Ideas on This
Subject.*

The convicts were still in the area, then, still keeping a close watch on the sheepfold, still determined to kill the colonists one by one! Sooner or later the pirates would be hunted down like the savage beasts they were; but for the moment they had the upper hand—seeing but unseen, ready to attack at any instant but safe from ambush—and the only measures the colonists could take were defensive ones.

Thus, Cyrus Smith prepared for a long stay at the sheepfold, whose reserves could fortunately sustain them for some time to come. Ayrton's house had been furnished with everything they needed; if the pirates had not yet carried off its precious resources, it was only because of the colonists' sudden and timely arrival. Gideon Spilett attempted to piece together the events following the convicts' landing: they must have followed the southern shore around Serpentine Peninsula, avoiding the dense Forests of the Far West, and soon arrived at the mouth of Falls River. From there they must have followed the right bank into the foothills of Mount Franklin, where they might naturally be expected to seek shelter. They would not have been slow to discover the sheepfold, then unoccupied, and they must have settled in at once, biding their time before carrying out their abominable plans. Caught unawares by Ayrton's arrival, they nevertheless succeeded in overpowering the poor fellow, and . . . the rest was all too easy to guess!

Now the convicts were lurking in the woods—their numbers reduced by one, to be sure, but nevertheless armed and hostile. Any colonist who attempted to enter the forest would lay himself open to vicious attack, a defenseless target for the pirates' rifles.

"We must wait! There's nothing else we can do!" said Cyrus Smith. "As soon as Harbert has recovered, we will assemble a hunting party, and we will vanquish the convicts. That will be the object of our great expedition, along with…"

"The search for our mysterious protector," added Gideon Spilett, finishing the engineer's sentence. "Oh! we can't deny it, my dear Cyrus: this time his protection seems to have failed us, just when it was needed most!"

"Who knows?" answered the engineer.

"What do you mean?" asked the reporter.

"That our troubles are not yet over, my dear Spilett, and that he might well exert his powerful influence yet. But that's of no concern to us now. Harbert's life takes precedence over all."

This was indeed their most painful preoccupation. Several days went by with no aggravation of the poor child's condition, and at this they rejoiced, for to hold off infection for a single day was a victory in itself. The cold compresses, scrupulously maintained, had prevented any inflammation of his wounds. Indeed, the reporter found this water—slightly sulfurous, owing to the proximity of the volcano—even more beneficial to the healing process than ordinary water. The suppuration had slowed, the fever was abating, and thanks to the attentions lavished upon him Harbert was coming back to life. He had been placed on a strict liquid diet, and consequently was and would remain extremely weak; but the herbal infusions were not spared, and what he needed most for the moment was untroubled rest.

Cyrus Smith, Gideon Spilett, and Pencroff had become quite adept at dressing the boy's wounds. Every bit of cloth in the house had been sacrificed for this purpose. Compresses and linen bandages were expertly applied, bound neither too tightly nor too loosely, speeding the healing process without provoking an inflammatory reaction. The reporter tended to this task with loving attention, knowing its crucial place in the overall treatment, and repeating to his companions what most doctors readily accept: that a successful bandaging is a far rarer thing than a successful operation.

By November 22nd, ten days after his injury, Harbert's condition had noticeably improved. He had begun to eat again; the color was returning to his cheeks, and his kindly eyes smiled at his nurses. He spoke a few words now and then, although Pencroff did his best to prevent this with an incessant stream of utterly outlandish tales. Harbert once asked after Ayrton, believing him to be at the sheepfold and surprised not to find him at his side. Anxious not to cause the child any grief, Pencroff merely answered that Ayrton had gone to join Neb and aid in the defense of Granite House.

"Well now!" he said. "What about those pirates! No need to show those gentlemen any consideration now! And to think Mr. Smith wanted to spare their tender feelings! I'll give them tender feelings, from the muzzle of a high-caliber rifle!"

"And they haven't been seen since that night?" asked Harbert.

"No, my child," the sailor answered, "but don't worry, we'll find them. So they like to shoot from behind, do they? Well, once you're healed we'll see how those cowards fight face to face!"

"I'm still so weak, my poor Pencroff!"

"Oh! don't you worry, your strength will come back! What's a bullet through the chest? Child's play! I've been through worse than that, and it's done me no harm!"

Thus, things were proceeding as well as could be expected, and so long as no complications developed, Harbert's recovery could be considered a certainty. But imagine the colonists' plight if his wounds had been more serious than they were—if the bullet had remained inside his body, for instance, or if they had been forced to amputate an arm or a leg!

"The mere thought of such things sends a shiver down my spine!" said Gideon Spilett more than once.

"And yet, if it had been necessary," Cyrus Smith answered one day, "you would not have hesitated to do so?"

"No, Cyrus!" said Gideon Spilett. "But God be praised for having spared us that!"

As they had so many times before, the colonists had relied on the unfailing logic of simple common sense, and once again their wide knowledge of the world had served them well! But might there come a time when all their learning would come to naught? They were alone on this island. And it is only in society that humanity can flourish, for men need nothing so much as the aid and company of other men. Cyrus Smith knew this full well, and he sometimes wondered if they might one day meet with some circumstance that they could not overcome!

Indeed, he began to sense that the good fortune they had so long enjoyed had now come to an end, and that dark days lay ahead. It had been more than two and a half years since their escape from Richmond, and until now everything had gone their way. The island had offered up an abundance of minerals, vegetables, and animals; nature had never failed to meet their needs, and their own learning had allowed them to make good use of her gifts. The colony's material well-being was virtually complete, and on top of this there was the inexplicable influence that had so often come to their aid!...But this could not be expected to last forever!

In short, Cyrus Smith was convinced that their luck was about to turn.

For the pirate ship had appeared in the island's waters, and while the convicts had been, so to speak, miraculously destroyed, six had nonetheless escaped the catastrophe and come ashore. The five who survived had eluded their every search. The wretches had undoubtedly murdered Ayrton, and the first shot they had fired with their rifles had left Harbert near death. Were these only the first of many adversities to come? So Cyrus Smith wondered, and so he often repeated to the reporter! They could not help but conclude that the string of troubling but timely interventions had come to an end, and that no further assistance would come from that quarter. Whoever he was, the mysterious being had proved himself real; but had he now left the island? Had he himself perished?

These were questions without answers. Nonetheless, no matter how often they spoke of such things, let no one believe that Cyrus Smith and his companions had given in to despair! Far from it. They faced their situation head on, they analyzed their chances, they prepared for any eventuality, they stood up straight and tall before the future, and should adversity strike one day, they would be ready to resist it.

IX

No News from Neb.—A Suggestion from Pencroff and the Reporter, Rejected.—Gideon Spilett's Outings.—A Shred of Cloth.—A Message.—Hurried Departure.—Arrival at Longview Plateau.

The young patient's convalescence was proceeding regularly. All they needed now was an opportunity to transport him to Granite House. However well furnished and supplied was the house at the sheepfold, it did not offer the comfort of their fine granite home. Nor was the house at the sheepfold as safe as the other; despite all their watchfulness, its inhabitants lived under the constant threat of attack. At Granite House, on the other hand, protected by an impregnable and inaccessible mass of stone, they would have nothing to fear. Thus, they eagerly awaited the moment when Harbert would be well enough to make the trip, and they resolved to depart at the earliest opportunity, despite the many dangers of a trek through Jacamar Woods.

No news had come from Neb, but they did not worry for his safety. Entrenched in the depths of Granite House, the courageous Negro would not be caught off guard. Top had not been sent back to him, for there could be no point in exposing the faithful dog to the convicts' fire, and risking the life of the colonists' most useful aide.

Thus, they waited, deeply impatient to be back inside Granite House. The engineer was unhappy to see his forces divided, for this only strengthened the pirates' hand. With Ayrton gone, it was now four against five. It goes without saying that Harbert could not be asked to fight at their side—much to the chagrin of the doughty child, who well understood the disadvantage of which he was the cause!

The question of an offensive against the convicts was carefully considered on November 29th by Cyrus Smith, Gideon Spilett, and Pencroff. Harbert lay sleeping, unable to hear.

"My friends," said the reporter, after a discussion of the impossibility of communicating with Neb, "I believe, as you do, that to attempt the trip home by Sheepfold Road would be to put ourselves in an unacceptably vulnerable position. Does this mean that our only reasonable course of action is to go after the wretches with all possible force?"

"That's just what I was thinking," answered Pencroff. "I don't believe any of us are men to quail at the thought of a bullet. Speaking only for myself, if Mr. Cyrus agrees, I'm quite prepared to storm the forest! What the devil! One man's as good as another!"

"But is he as good as five?" asked the engineer.

"I'll gladly second Pencroff," the reporter answered. "With the two of us well armed, and Top by our side..."

"My dear Spilett, and you too, Pencroff," Cyrus Smith replied, "let us try to think this through objectively. If we knew the convicts to be hiding in some specific location, I would gladly agree to a direct assault; we might well succeed in driving them out. But as you well know, they could be anywhere around us. Do you not fear that they would have the first shot?"

"Oh! Mr. Cyrus," cried Pencroff, "a bullet doesn't always go where it's sent!"

"The one that hit Harbert didn't go astray, Pencroff," the engineer answered. "And I would ask you to consider this: with both of you away, I would have to defend the sheepfold single-handed. Do you believe the convicts would fail to notice your departure? Do you not believe they would wait for you to vanish into the forest, then take advantage of your absence to attack the sheepfold, knowing there is no one to defend it but one man and a wounded child?"

"You're right, Mr. Cyrus," answered Pencroff, his breast swelling with quiet rage, "you're right. They'll do whatever they must to recapture the sheepfold, and all its supplies and provisions! And you'll never be able to hold them off all alone. Oh! if only we were at Granite House!"

"If we were at Granite House," the engineer replied, "everything would be different! I would not hesitate for a moment to leave Harbert in the care of one of our companions while the other three set out to search the forests. But we are at the sheepfold, and here we must remain until we can all leave together!"

Cyrus Smith's reasoning was unassailable, and his companions knew it.

"If only Ayrton were still with us!" said Gideon Spilett. "Poor devil! His return to society was all too short-lived!"

"Assuming he's dead, that is…" added Pencroff in an odd tone of voice.

"You still believe those scoundrels might have spared his life, Pencroff?" asked Gideon Spilett.

"Yes! if they had a reason to do so!"

"What! you're not suggesting that Ayrton might have fallen in with his accomplices again! That he might have forgotten everything he owes us!…"

"Who knows?" answered the sailor, who had put forward this troublesome supposition only with great reluctance.

"Pencroff," said Cyrus Smith, taking the sailor's arm, "this is a wicked thought, and I would be very sorry to hear you go on speaking this way! I guarantee Ayrton's fidelity!"

"And I too," the reporter quickly added.

"Yes…yes!…Mr. Cyrus…I'm wrong," answered Pencroff. "You're right, it was a wicked thought, and an unjustified one! But what can you expect? I'm not quite in my right mind. This long imprisonment has been very hard for me. I've never known such a trial!"

"Be patient, Pencroff," the engineer answered. "How soon do you believe Harbert can be transported to Granite House, my dear Spilett?"

"That's difficult to say, Cyrus," the reporter answered. "We mustn't be hasty, for the consequences could be severe. Nonetheless, his convalescence is progressing regularly, and if in a week's time he has regained his strength, well then, we shall see!"

A week! That would delay their return until the first days of December.

Spring had come two months before. The weather was fine, and the heat grew from day to day. The forests were in full leaf, and harvest time was not far off. They would have much to do in the fields on their return to Longview Plateau, with only a brief pause for their expedition into the island's interior.

Gideon Spilett was armed with his carbine against unexpected attack.

We might easily imagine how painful this sequestration must have been for the colonists. They fully understood the need to stay on, but all the while they yearned to be away.

Once or twice, with Top at his side, the reporter emerged and walked the perimeter of the palisade, armed with his carbine against unexpected attack.

But he met with no misfortune, and found no sign of suspicious activity. The dog would have warned him of any imminent danger; from Top's silence he concluded that for the moment at least there was nothing to fear, and that the convicts were off in some other part of the island.

But on November 27th, in the course of a second outing that brought him some quarter-mile into the woods south of the mountain, Gideon Spilett was surprised to find that Top had picked up a scent. The dog's indifference vanished at once; now he began to run to and fro, sniffing through the grass and undergrowth as if his sense of smell had alerted him to the presence of something suspicious in the area.

Gideon Spilett followed close behind, urging the dog on with his voice, warily observing the environs, his rifle raised, careful never to leave the cover of the sheltering trees. It was probably not a human scent that Top had picked up, for if it were he would have announced it with half-contained barks and a sort of muted fury. And since no growl escaped his lips, the danger must not have been immediate, nor nearby.

For five minutes Top followed the trail, with the reporter watchfully following. Suddenly the dog bounded toward a dense bush and returned with a small piece of cloth.

Tattered and stained, it had clearly been torn from an article of clothing. Gideon Spilett immediately brought it back to the sheepfold.

A close examination revealed it to be a shred of Ayrton's jacket, for it was a patch of felt of the kind produced exclusively by the workshops of Lincoln Island.

"As you see, Pencroff," Cyrus Smith observed, "poor Ayrton clearly put up some resistance. He struggled as they dragged him off! Do you still doubt his integrity?"

"No, Mr. Cyrus," the sailor answered. "Perhaps I mistrusted him for a moment, but I've long since reconsidered! In any case, I believe Top's discovery tells us something."

"What is that?" asked the reporter.

"That Ayrton was not killed at the sheepfold! If he was struggling against his captors, he had to be alive when they carried him off. And he might still be alive today!"

"Perhaps so," answered the engineer, who remained pensive.

Thus, Ayrton's companions now had some hope to cling to. Their first conclusion could only have been that Ayrton was felled by a bullet in the course of a surprise attack, just as Harbert had fallen on their arrival at the sheepfold. But if the convicts had not killed him straight off, if they had merely captured him and taken him to some other part of the island, was it not conceivable that he might yet remain their prisoner? Perhaps one of them had recognized Ayrton as a former companion from Australia—as Ben Joyce, the leader of the escapees! And who could say that they had not conceived the impossible hope of bringing Ayrton back into their fold? How useful he might be to them if they could convince him to betray his companions!

This incident was thus interpreted as a favorable sign, and it no longer seemed impossible that they might be reunited with Ayrton one day. Meanwhile, if he was indeed the convicts' prisoner, he would no doubt do everything he could to escape their grasp, and this might very well work to the colonists' advantage!

"At any rate," Gideon Spilett observed, "if ever Ayrton escapes, he'll go directly to Granite House, since he knows nothing of the attempt on Harbert's life, and so has no reason to believe we are imprisoned at the sheepfold."

"Oh! I wish he were there right now, at Granite House!" cried Pencroff. "And us as well! Even if those rogues are powerless to attack our fortress, they could still lay waste to the plateau, our fields, our poultry yard!"

Pencroff had become a real farmer, with a heartfelt devotion to his crops. But none could have been more impatient than Harbert to return to Granite House, for he knew how desperately his companions were needed there. And he was the only thing holding them back! Thus, one single idea occupied his mind: to leave the sheepfold, to leave it in spite of everything! He believed he could withstand the trip to Granite House. He assured his companions that his strength would return all the faster in his own room, with the fresh ocean breezes and a fine view of the sea!

Several times he begged Gideon Spilett to agree to this, but the reporter rightly feared that Harbert's half-healed wounds might reopen along the way, and he could not be convinced.

But what happened next compelled Cyrus Smith and his friends to grant Harbert's wish despite themselves. God alone could predict the pain and remorse this decision would bring them!

It was seven o'clock, on the morning of November 29th. The three colonists were talking in Harbert's room when they heard Top barking energetically.

Cyrus Smith, Pencroff, and Gideon Spilett picked up their rifles, loaded as always, and emerged cautiously from the house.

They found Top at the base of the palisade, leaping into the air and barking loudly—not in anger but in joy.

"Someone's coming!"

"Yes!"

"Not an enemy!"

"Neb, perhaps?"

"Or Ayrton?"

No sooner had these words been spoken than a figure hurtled over the palisade and landed on the ground before them.

It was Joop, Master Joop in person, warmly welcomed by Top like the dearest of friends!

"Joop!" cried Pencroff.

"Neb must have sent him!" said the reporter.

"In that case," the engineer replied, "he must have a message for us."

Pencroff hurried toward the orangutan. If Neb had important news to relate, he could not have chosen a faster or more trustworthy messenger, nor one more likely to get through where the colonists—where even Top himself—could not.

As Cyrus Smith suspected, a small sack hung from Joop's neck; and in that sack they found a message written in Neb's hand.

Imagine their despair on reading these words:

> Friday, 6 A.M.
> Plateau invaded by convicts!
> Neb.

They stared at one another in silence, and slowly walked back to the house. What were they to do now? If the convicts were on Longview Plateau, then disaster, devastation, and ruin would inevitably follow!

One glance at Cyrus Smith and his companions was enough to tell Harbert that some new calamity had taken place; and when he caught sight of Joop, he deduced that Granite House had come under attack.

"Mr. Cyrus," he said, "I want to leave. I can withstand the trip! I want to leave!"

Gideon Spilett came to Harbert's side. Then, after a careful examination: "Very well. I believe he's ready!" he said.

Should Harbert be transported in a stretcher, or in the cart Ayrton had brought to the sheepfold? This question was quickly considered. The stretcher would offer the wounded child a more comfortable ride; nevertheless, it required two bearers, which meant two fewer rifles with which to defend themselves in case of assault.

The cart, on the other hand, would leave every arm free and unburdened. Could they not place Harbert's bedding in the cart, and, if it was steered with great care, could he not be protected against sudden jolts? This seemed entirely possible.

The cart was brought to the house. Pencroff hitched up the dauw. Cyrus Smith and the reporter laid Harbert's mattress and bedding between the two rails.

The weather was fine. Bright rays of sunlight streamed through the trees.

"Are the weapons ready?" asked Cyrus Smith.

They were. Pencroff and the engineer were armed with double-barreled rifles, Gideon Spilett with his carbine. Everything was ready for departure.

"Are you all right, Harbert?" the engineer asked.

"Oh! Mr. Cyrus," the boy answered, "don't worry, I won't die on the way!"

All too clearly, it had cost the poor child every last ounce of his energy to speak these words. Only by a supreme effort of will had he summoned up the last of his failing strength.

Grief flooded the engineer's heart. He was still reluctant to leave, but to stay at the sheepfold was to condemn Harbert to a despair that might well prove fatal.

"Let's be off!" said Cyrus Smith.

The gate was opened. Joop and Top ran ahead in silence, as the situation dictated. The cart started forward, the gate was closed, and Pencroff kept the dauw at a gentle walk.

To be sure, they would have preferred not to return by the road, but it would have been nearly impossible to guide the cart over through forest's rugged terrain. The road was exposed and well known to the convicts, but they had no other choice.

Cyrus Smith and Gideon Spilett walked beside the cart, ready to respond to any attack, but in all likelihood the convicts were still on Longview Plateau. Neb's message had clearly been written and sent the moment the convicts appeared. It was dated six o'clock that morning, and the swift orangutan had covered the familiar five-mile path to the sheep-fold in only three quarters of an hour. Thus, the road was very likely safe for the moment, and not until they neared Granite House would their rifles be required.

But the colonists did not let down their guard. No cries of warning were sounded by Top and Joop, the latter armed with his club, as they raced down the road or through the surrounding woods.

Slowly the cart moved on. They had left the sheepfold at seven-thirty. An hour later, four of the five miles had been covered without incident.

The road was deserted, as was the whole of Jacamar Woods from the Mercy to the lake. No suspicious activity had been spotted. The forest seemed as uninhabited as the day of the colonists' landing.

They were now nearing the plateau. One more mile, and they would see the bridge over Glycerine Creek. Cyrus Smith felt sure that the bridge would be down. The convicts might well have crossed that bridge to invade the plateau; if not, if they had forded one of the other water-ways to gain access to the area, they would very likely have lowered the bridge in preparation for a hasty retreat.

Finally they glimpsed the ocean through a gap in the trees. The cart continued its advance, still surrounded by its defenders.

Just then, Pencroff stopped the dauw, and in a thundering voice he cried:

"Oh! those wretches!"

And with one hand he pointed toward a thick column of smoke rising from the mill, the stables, and the various constructions of the poultry yard.

A human form could be seen amid the swirling smoke.

It was Neb.

His companions let out a shout. Hearing this cry, he came running to meet them . . .

The convicts had fled the plateau about a half-hour before, leaving only devastation behind them!

"How's Mr. Harbert?" cried Neb.

Gideon Spilett returned to the cart.

Harbert had lost consciousness!

X

Harbert Carried into Granite House.—Neb's Story.—Cyrus Smith Visits the Plateau.—Ruin and Devastation.—The Colonists Powerless Against an Illness.—Willow Bark.—A Deadly Fever.—Top Barks Again!

No further mention was made of the convicts, the dangers facing Granite House, or the ruins on the plateau. Harbert's condition took precedence over everything. Had the journey caused some sort of dangerous interior lesion? The reporter could not say, but he and his companions despaired.

The cart was brought to the bend in the river. Branches were laid out to form a stretcher, atop which were placed the mattresses and Harbert's lifeless body. Ten minutes later, Cyrus Smith, Gideon Spilett, and Pencroff stood at the foot of the granite wall while Neb took the cart back to Longview Plateau.

The elevator was set in motion, and moments later Harbert was lying on his bunk in Granite House.

He soon returned to consciousness under his companions' care. He smiled briefly at finding himself in his own room again, but his weakness was such that it was all he could do to murmur a few words.

Gideon Spilett examined his wounds, fearing they might have opened again, incompletely healed as they were...but no. Whence, then, Harbert's prostration? Why had his condition so suddenly deteriorated?

The boy fell into a sort of feverish slumber, and the reporter and Pencroff remained at his bedside.

In the meantime, Cyrus Smith told Neb of the events at the sheepfold, and Neb recounted the arrival of the pirates on the plateau.

The elevator was set in motion.

The convicts had emerged from the forest the previous night, on the opposite bank of Glycerine Creek. Standing guard at the poultry yard, Neb immediately fired as one of them waded into the water; but in the deep darkness of the night he could not see whether he had hit the wretch or not. In any case, this did not drive the marauders away, and Neb scarcely had time to return to Granite House, where at least he would be safe.

But what to do then? How to prevent the devastation of the plateau at the convicts' hands? How might Neb attempt to contact his master? And for that matter, what was the situation of his companions at the sheepfold?

Cyrus Smith and the others had left Granite House on November 11th, and it was now the twenty-ninth. For nineteen days, then, Neb's only communication with them had been the disastrous news brought by Top: Ayrton missing, Harbert grievously wounded, the engineer, the reporter, and the sailor virtually imprisoned at the sheepfold!

What to do? poor Neb wondered. He himself was in no danger, for the convicts were powerless against the natural defenses of Granite House. But the buildings, the fields, all the fruits of their labor at the mercy of a gang of pirates! Should he not let Cyrus Smith decide what must be done, or at least warn him of the dangers that faced him?

It was then that Neb thought of entrusting a message to Joop. Time and again, the orangutan had proven his extreme intelligence. Joop understood the word *sheepfold*, having heard it spoken many times, and we might even recall that he had driven the cart there on several occasions, with Pencroff at his side. Day had not yet dawned. The agile orangutan could easily make his way through the woods unnoticed; indeed, even if they did catch sight of him, the convicts would surely take him for a natural inhabitant of the region.

Neb did not delay. He wrote the message, tied it to Joop's neck, and led the ape to the door of Granite House, throwing a long rope down to the beach; then he repeated these words several times:

"Joop! Joop! sheepfold! sheepfold!"

The animal understood at once. He grasped the rope, quickly slipped down to the beach, and vanished into the night, without in any way arousing the convicts' suspicions.

"You did well, Neb," Cyrus Smith answered, "but if you hadn't warned us you might have done even better!"

And as he spoke these words he thought of Harbert, and of the severe setback the journey had apparently dealt to his recovery.

Neb finished his account. The convicts never came to the beach. Not knowing the island's population, they no doubt assumed Granite House to be defended by a large contingent of colonists. They must have remembered the relentless rifle fire directed against the brig from several points on the shoreline, and hesitated to expose themselves to further attack. But all of Longview Plateau lay open to them, protected by the cliff face from any defensive positions on the beach. There they indulged their destructive instincts, sacking, burning, doing evil for evil's sake, and they withdrew only a half-hour before the colonists' arrival, no doubt supposing them to be still imprisoned at the sheepfold.

Neb rushed from his retreat the moment he saw them leave. He climbed to the plateau, braving the bullets fired back by the departing pirates. He tried to extinguish the fires consuming their buildings, and he kept up this fruitless struggle until the cart appeared at the edge of the woods.

Such were the morning's events. No more could the colonists dismiss the threat posed by the pirates' presence. So many blessings had been bestowed on the colony in the past, but now the future promised only misfortunes, perhaps still greater than these!

Gideon Spilett remained at Granite House with Harbert and Pencroff while Cyrus Smith set out with Neb to gauge the extent of the disaster.

It was fortunate indeed that the convicts had not dared come to the foot of Granite House. The workshops at the Chimneys would not have escaped their depredations. Nonetheless, how much more difficult to repair would be the ruination of Longview Plateau!

Cyrus Smith and Neb walked toward the Mercy and turned onto the left bank. No trace of the convicts' passage could be found, neither there nor in the dense forest on the opposite bank.

Two hypotheses now occurred to the engineer: either the convicts knew of the colonists' return to Granite House, having glimpsed them on Sheepfold Road, or they had fled along the Mercy into Jacamar Woods after sacking the plateau, and thus had no idea of the colonists' where-abouts.

In the first case, they must have headed back toward the sheepfold, where they would find a wealth of valuable resources awaiting them, undefended.

In the second, they would have returned to their campsite to await the opportunity for further destruction.

This could surely be prevented; but Harbert's recovery would take precedence over any attempt to rid the island of their presence. Every hand would be needed to launch this assault, and for the moment no one could leave Granite House.

The engineer and Neb arrived on the plateau. As far as the eye could see, all was devastation. The fields had been trampled. The wheat was nearly ready for harvest, but now it lay crushed on the ground. The other crops had suffered in equal measure. The vegetable garden was a total loss. Fortunately, this could be repaired with Granite House's ample reserve of seeds.

As for the mill, the outbuildings, and the dauws' stable, these had been completely consumed by the flames. A few terrified animals still wandered over the plateau. The birds had taken refuge from the fire on the waters of the lake; now they were slowly returning to their customary spots along the shore. Everything would have to be rebuilt.

Cyrus Smith's face paled, expressing his ill-contained rage; but he did not speak a single word. He cast one last look over his ravaged fields. Then, with the smoke still rising from the ruins, he returned to Granite House.

The following days were the saddest the colonists had yet spent on the island! Harbert's weakness grew before their eyes. It seemed that his profound physiological shock had opened the way for a very serious illness, and Gideon Spilett foresaw a worsening of his condition that he would be powerless to combat!

For Harbert had fallen into an unbroken torpor, and signs of delirium were beginning to appear. Refreshing infusions were the only remedies at the colonists' disposal. His temperature was not yet very high, but the series of regular attacks that soon began to shake his frail body showed that the fever was attempting to take hold.

So Gideon Spilett realized on December 6th. The child's fingers, nose, and ears became extremely pale, and soon he was overtaken by shivers, horripilations, and trembling. His pulse was weak and irregular, his skin dry, his thirst intense. This was followed by a period of warmth; his face grew more animated, his skin redder, his pulse quicker. Then he began to sweat abundantly, and the fever seemed to diminish. The attack had lasted some five hours.

Gideon Spilett had not left Harbert's side. It was all too obvious that the child was now in the grip of an intermittent fever, which would have to be broken at all costs before it became more serious.

"And in order to break the fever," said Gideon Spilett to Cyrus Smith, "we need a febrifuge."

"A febrifuge!..." the engineer replied. "But we have neither cinchona nor quinine sulfate!"

"No," said Gideon Spilett, "but there are willows growing on the lakeshore, and willow bark makes a reasonable substitute for quinine."

"Let's not waste a moment, then!" answered Cyrus Smith.

Indeed, willow bark is sometimes used as a replacement for cinchona, along with horse chestnut, holly leaf, snakeroot, etc. This was clearly their only hope. Nonetheless, willow bark is far less effective than cinchona, and lacking the means to extract its salicin—the alkaloid that is its active ingredient—they would have to use it in its natural form.

Cyrus Smith himself went to cut a few pieces of bark from the willows that grew by the lake. He brought these back to Granite House and reduced them to a powder, which was administered to Harbert at once.

The night went by without serious incident. Harbert was slightly delirious, but the fever did not recur in the night, nor the following day.

Hope returned to Pencroff's breast. Gideon Spilett said nothing. It could be that the fever would no longer recur at daily intervals—that it was a tertian fever, in a word, and would return the next day. Thus, they awaited the dawn with the deepest anxiety.

They had noticed that even in his apyrexic periods he seemed completely broken, his mind clouded and prone to confusion. And another symptom had begun to appear, to the reporter's great alarm: Harbert's liver was becoming congested, and soon an intensification in his delirium showed that his brain had been affected as well.

Gideon Spilett was dismayed at this new complication. He took the engineer aside.

"It's a pernicious fever!" he told him.

"A pernicious fever!" cried Cyrus Smith. "You must be mistaken, Spilett. A pernicious fever never arises spontaneously. It can only be contracted from a germ!"

"I am not mistaken," the reporter answered. "Harbert must have been exposed to the germ in the island's swamps. He has suffered one attack already. If there is now a second attack, and if we do not find a way to prevent a third...he is finished!..."

"But what about the willow bark?..."

"It will not be enough," the reporter answered. "A third attack of pernicious fever is always fatal unless it is broken with quinine."

Fortunately, Pencroff had heard none of this conversation. He would have lost his reason.

We might well imagine the depth of the engineer's and the reporter's anxiety that December 7th, and throughout the following night.

The second attack finally came around noon. It was a terrible crisis. Harbert knew he was done for! He stretched out his arms toward Cyrus Smith, Spilett, Pencroff! He did not want to die!... It was a heart-wrenching scene. Pencroff had to be pulled away.

The attack lasted five hours. It was clear that Harbert would not survive a third.

It was a horrific night. In his delirium, Harbert said things that broke his companions' hearts! He raved, he struggled against the convicts, he called for Ayrton! He pleaded with their mysterious protector, now vanished, whose image obsessed him... Then he fell once more into a deep, devastating prostration... More than once, Gideon Spilett believed that the poor boy was dead!

By the next day, December 8th, all Harbert's strength had drained from his broken body. His frail hands clutched at the sheets. Further doses of crushed bark were administered, but the reporter had lost all faith in the drug's efficacity.

"If we haven't found a more potent febrifuge by tomorrow morning," said the reporter, "Harbert will be dead!"

Night came on, no doubt the last night on earth for this brave child, this unfailingly good-hearted child, a child wise beyond his years, a child loved by his companions as if he were their own! There was only one known remedy for that terrible pernicious fever, only one specific that could defeat it, and it was not to be found on Lincoln Island!

Harbert's delirium redoubled in intensity during the night of December 8th. His liver was horribly congested, his brain inflamed; he stared blankly at his companions, no longer able to recognize them.

Would he survive until the next day, when the third attack would inevitably carry him off? Even this had begun to seem unlikely. His forces were utterly depleted, and between crises he lay very nearly inanimate.

At around three o'clock in the morning Harbert let out a terrifying scream. He writhed as if racked by one final convulsion. Neb had been left to watch over him, and now he ran in terror to summon his companions!

Just then, Top barked in a curious way...

Together they hurried to Harbert's bedside. The dying child was trying to throw himself from his bed, and they held him down as Gideon Spilett took his wrist. The pulse was gradually quickening.

It was five o'clock in the morning. The rays of the rising sun were streaming into Granite House. A beautiful day was dawning, and that day would be poor Harbert's last!...

A ray of sunlight landed on the bedside table.

Suddenly Pencroff let out a shout, pointing to an object sitting on that table...

It was a small oblong box, whose lid bore these words:

Quinine sulfate.

XI

Gideon Spilett picked up the box and opened it to reveal some two hundred grains of white powder. He collected a few particles on his fingertip and brought it to his lips. Its extreme bitterness removed all doubt. This was indeed the precious alkaloid component of cinchona, the finest remedy for periodic fevers known to man.

The powder would have to be administered to Harbert without delay. The question of its sudden appearance on the table could be discussed later.

"Coffee," Gideon Spilett requested.

Neb hurried off and returned at once with a cup of the warm infusion. Gideon Spilett added some eighteen grains* of quinine, and, not without difficulty, they succeeded in pouring the mixture down Harbert's throat.

It was not too late, for the third attack of the pernicious fever had not yet begun!

And let it now be said that it never would!

A new sense of hope arose in the colonists' breasts. The mysterious influence had exerted itself once again, at the last possible moment, when all hope for salvation seemed lost!...

A few hours later, Harbert was resting peacefully in his bed, and the

---

* Ten grams.

colonists took advantage of this respite to discuss the incident. The stranger had intervened more overtly than ever before. But how had he entered Granite House in the night? This they found absolutely inexplicable. Truly, the workings of the "genie of the island" were no less mysterious than the genie himself.

Harbert was given a fresh dose of quinine sulfate every three hours for the rest of the day.

By the following morning he was showing visible signs of improvement. To be sure, he was not yet cured, and serious relapses are always a danger with intermittent fevers; but his companions spared no effort in their attempt to nurse him back to health. And of course the specific was close at hand, and he who had brought it surely not far off! In the end, then, the colonists' hopes for a complete recovery were high indeed.

Those hopes were not disappointed. Ten days later, on December 20th, Harbert's convalescence began in earnest. He was still weak, and limited to a strict diet, but the attacks had ceased. And how willingly the docile child accepted his prescriptions! He was so eager to be cured!

Pencroff was like a man pulled from the bottom of a profound abyss. He sometimes succumbed to fits of joy that bordered on delirium. When the threat of a third attack had passed, he gave the reporter an embrace powerful enough to knock the wind out of him. From that day on, he always referred to him as Doctor Spilett.

But they had yet to find the real doctor.

"We'll find him yet," the sailor often said.

And that man, whoever he was, had in store a still more formidable embrace from the good Pencroff!

December came to an end, and with it the year 1867—a year in which the colonists of Lincoln Island had been cruelly tested indeed. The year 1868 began with marvelous weather, delightful sunshine, tropical temperatures pleasantly freshened by the sea breeze. Harbert was slowly returning to life. His bed had been placed near a window, and there, caressed by the wholesome saline emanations of the sea air, he found his way back to full health. He had begun to eat again, and God knows what fine dishes, both savory and light, Neb prepared for him!

"It's enough to make you wish you'd been at death's door yourself!" said Pencroff.

The convicts had not been sighted again in the environs of Granite House. Nor had the colonists had any word of Ayrton, and while the engineer and the boy still harbored some hope of seeing him again, their companions were all but convinced he had perished. Nevertheless, they were eager to put their uncertainties to rest. As soon as Harbert was fit again, they would set out on their exploration, whose outcome might well determine their future. But the departure might have to be delayed by as much as a month, for the colony would need all its strength if it hoped to win out over the convicts.

Meanwhile, Harbert's condition continued to improve. The congestion of his liver had disappeared, and his wounds could now be considered well and truly healed.

Much work was done on Longview Plateau over the month of January; but the object of these labors was simply to save what could be saved of their devastated wheat and vegetable crops. Seeds and sprouts were collected in hopes of a second harvest in the next half-season. As for rebuilding the outbuildings, the mill, the stables, for that Cyrus Smith preferred to wait. The convicts might well return to the plateau while he and his companions were engaged in their search, and they must not be given an opportunity for further arson and vandalism. Only after they had purged the island of these villains would they turn to the task of rebuilding.

In the latter half of January, the young convalescent began to arise from his bed, first for one hour a day, then two, then three. His strength was visibly returning, thanks to the great vigor of his constitution. He was then eighteen years old. He had grown tall over the past few years, and promised to become a man of fine and noble bearing. From then on, while he still required some care—and Doctor Spilett proved a very strict physician—his convalescence proceeded continuously.

By the end of the month, Harbert was taking long walks on the plateau and the beach. He sometimes bathed in the sea with Pencroff and Neb, and this did him a world of good. Cyrus Smith believed they could now set a date for their departure. It was fixed for February 15th. Darkness fell late at that time of year, and this would be of no small help to their ambitious explorations.

And so they began to prepare for the journey. This proved a considerable task, for the colonists had vowed not to return until they had attained their two goals: first, to destroy the convicts and rescue Ayrton, if he was still alive; second, to discover the mysterious benefactor who had so masterfully guided the colony's destiny.

The colonists now had a thorough knowledge of the island's eastern

The young convalescent began to arise from his bed.

shore, from Cape Claw to the two Capes Mandible, as well as the vast Shelduck Fens; the environs of Lake Grant; Jacamar Woods between Sheepfold Road and the Mercy; the course of the Mercy and of Red Creek; and finally the foothills of Mount Franklin, where they had built their sheepfold.

They had also explored—albeit only partially—the long shoreline of Washington Bay from Cape Claw to Reptile End, the line of forests and marshes on the west coast, and the endless dunes that led to the half-open jaws of Shark Gulf.

But as yet they had no reckoning whatever of the broad wooded expanses of Serpentine Peninsula, the entire right bank of the Mercy, the left bank of Falls River, and the intricate network of foothills and valleys to the west, north, and east of Mount Franklin—an area no doubt rich in secluded hiding places. Several thousand acres of the island's surface had escaped their investigations, then, and it was here that they must concentrate their efforts.

The expedition would thus traverse the Far West, allowing an exploration of all the unknown expanses on the right bank of the Mercy.

They briefly considered heading first for the sheepfold, to which the convicts might well have been expected to return, perhaps in search of shelter, perhaps with pillage in mind. But either the devastation of the sheepfold was now a fait accompli, and it was too late to prevent it, or else the convicts had made of it their permanent entrenchment, in which case the colonists could wait, and attack at their leisure.

With this question resolved, they settled on the former route, which would take them to Reptile End by way of the forests. They would cut their way through with hatchets; this excursion would thus also serve to lay out the beginnings of a new road linking Granite House to the far end of the peninsula, a distance of sixteen to seventeen miles.

The cart was in perfect condition. The dauws were well rested, and could be relied on for a journey of considerable distance. Foodstuffs, camping equipment, the portable kitchen, and various utensils were loaded onto the cart along with weapons and ammunition, chosen with care from Granite House's now abundant arsenal. But they must not forget that the convicts might well be lurking within the woods themselves. In such dense forests a rifle could be fired at any moment, and a bullet could quickly find its victim; hence they resolved to stay close together at all times, and not to split up for any reason whatever.

They further resolved to leave no one behind at Granite House. Top and Joop would participate along with the rest. Their inaccessible dwelling could easily protect itself.

The fourteenth of February, the eve of their departure, fell on a Sunday. They made this a day of rest, sanctified with prayers addressed to their Creator. Harbert's recovery was now complete, but he was still rather weak; thus, a special place would be reserved for him in the cart.

The next day, at first light, Cyrus Smith took the necessary measures to protect Granite House from invasion. The ladders they once scaled to reach their front door were brought to the Chimneys and buried deep beneath the sand to await the colonists' return, for the wheel of the elevator was to be dismantled, and all trace of their apparatus concealed. Pencroff stayed behind to see to this task after the others had left Granite House. He then descended to the beach by way of a rope whose end was held fast below; once this rope was pulled down, there was no way to climb to the landing from the beach.

It was a magnificent day.

"Warm day coming!" the reporter said merrily.

"Pshaw! Doctor Spilett," Pencroff replied, "the trees will give us plenty of shade. We won't even know the sun is out!"

"Let's be off!" said the engineer.

The cart was waiting on the shore, by the Chimneys. The reporter insisted that Harbert stay seated, for the first few hours at least, and the boy had no choice but to accede to his doctor's prescription.

Neb walked beside the dauws. Cyrus Smith, the reporter, and the sailor took the lead. Top frolicked joyously. Harbert offered Joop a seat beside him, and Joop accepted with unassuming grace. The moment had come, and the little band set off.

The cart turned at the mouth of the river, then followed the left bank for a mile, crossing the bridge to enter the Port Balloon road. But from here they struck out obliquely to the right, and so began to make their way beneath the huge, overarching trees that made up the Forests of the Far West.

For the first two miles, the widely scattered trees did not impede the cart's progress; from time to time they were forced to cut through lianas and tangles of brush, but no serious obstacle slowed their advance.

The dense network of branches cast a cool shade over the forest floor. Deodars, Douglas pines, gum trees, banksias, dragon trees, and other familiar species surrounded them on all sides. Among the trees they glimpsed a host of birds, of all the varieties native to the island: capercaillies, jacamars, pheasants, lories, and the whole chattering family of cockatoos, budgerigars, and parrots. Agoutis, kangaroos, and capybaras dashed through the grass. The colonists could not help but think of their first excursions, soon after their arrival on the island.

"Nevertheless," Cyrus Smith observed, "we should note that these animals, both quadrupeds and avians, seem more easily frightened than they once did. The convicts must have recently passed through these woods. No doubt we will discover their trail."

And indeed, they found a great many signs of human presence, more or less recent; here, broken branches, perhaps intended to mark the way; there, ashes from an extinguished campfire and footprints preserved in the mud. But nothing suggesting a fixed campsite.

The engineer had urged his companions to refrain from hunting, for the convicts might well be lurking in the forest, and a gunshot would alert them to the colonists' presence. Furthermore, the pursuit of game would necessarily take the hunters some distance from the cart, and it was strictly forbidden to walk alone.

Travel became more difficult in the latter half of the day, after a trek of some six miles from Granite House. Here the forest grew considerably denser, and the explorers were sometimes forced to fell trees in order to pass through. Before proceeding, Cyrus Smith sent Top and Joop to reconnoiter, and they conscientiously carried out their task. Once the dog and orangutan returned, they knew there was nothing to fear from convicts or wild beasts—animals all, equally bloodthirsty in their instincts.

The colonists stopped for the night some nine miles from Granite House, beside a small tributary of the Mercy whose existence had hitherto escaped their notice—another element of the vast hydrographic system that gave this soil its astonishing fertility.

They supped copiously, for their appetite was keen after the rigors of the day; next, steps were taken to ensure an untroubled night. If their only enemies had been wild animals, jaguars or the like, Cyrus Smith could easily have defended their campsite by surrounding it with small fires; but the convicts were more likely to be drawn to fire than repelled by it, and given the circumstances it would be wiser to cloak themselves in the deepest darkness.

The campsite would be vigilantly guarded. Two colonists would keep watch together, to be relieved by their comrades every two hours. Despite his entreaties, Harbert was excused from this task; thus, Pencroff and Gideon Spilett first stood watch at the edge of the campsite, then the engineer and Neb, and so on by turns.

The darkness, however, lasted no more than a few hours, for it was caused more by the thickness of the leafy canopy than by the disappearance of the sun. Occasionally the silence was broken by the husky roar of a jaguar or the mocking laughter of apes, which Master Joop seemed to find particularly irritating.

The night went by without incident, and the next day, February 16th, they resumed their march through the forest, a march more slow than arduous.

That day they were able to travel only six miles, for they were continually forced to hack their way through the forest with their hatchets. Veritable "settlers," the colonists spared the tallest and finest trees—whose felling would furthermore have required enormous exertion—and sacrificed only the smaller ones; but consequently the path's direction was far from rectilinear, and their route was made all the longer by the many detours they were forced to make.

In the course of that day, Harbert discovered several species of plants not yet sighted on the island, such as arborescent ferns, whose drooping fronds seemed to pour out like water from a basin, and carob trees, whose elongated pods were greedily nibbled at by the dauws, for they produced a sugary pulp of wonderful flavor. The colonists also found stands of magnificent kauris, whose cylindrical trunks, crowned with a cone of foliage, can rise to a height of two hundred feet. These are the kings of the New Zealand forests, as justly celebrated as the cedars of Lebanon.

They found no species of fauna they had not already encountered. Nevertheless, at one point they glimpsed a pair of enormous birds, of a type commonly found in Australia: a variety of cassowary known as the emu, five feet tall and covered with brown plumage. Top set off in pursuit as fast as his four legs could carry him, but with their prodigious gait the cassowaries effortlessly outran him.

They also found further traces of the convicts' presence in the forest. The remains of a fire were discovered, apparently extinguished not long before, and surrounded by footprints that they examined with particular care. Measuring them one after the other, in both length and width, they determined that these footprints had been left by five different men.

The night went by without incident.

Thus, the five convicts had clearly camped here; but—and this was the object of an exhaustive search!—they could not find a sixth footprint, which would have been left by Ayrton's foot.

"Ayrton was not with them!" said Harbert.

"No," answered Pencroff, "and, if he wasn't with them, it must be because the wretches have already murdered him! But never fear, we will track them down like tigers, and kill them in their lair!"

"No," the reporter answered. "They're more likely to be roving the island than hiding in some secret repair. It's in their best interests to keep moving until they can make themselves the masters of the island."

"The masters of the island!" cried the sailor. "The masters of the island!..." he repeated, and his voice was choked as if an iron fist had seized him by the throat. Then, regaining his composure:

"Mr. Cyrus," he said, "do you know what bullet I've put in my rifle?"

"No, Pencroff!"

"It's the bullet that went through Harbert's chest, and I promise you this one will go straight to the heart!"

But such reprisals, however justified, would never bring Ayrton back; and their inspection of the footprints had, alas! shown all too clearly that they would never see their friend again!

That evening they set up camp fourteen miles from Granite House, and Cyrus Smith estimated the remaining distance to Reptile End at no more than five miles.

And so it was. They reached the end of the peninsula the following morning. They had now crossed through the forest from one end to the other, but nowhere had they found any clue to the convicts' whereabouts, nor to the location of the mysterious stranger's secret lair.

XII

Exploration of Serpentine Peninsula.—A Campsite at the Mouth of Falls River.—Six Hundred Paces from the Sheepfold.— Reconnaissance by Gideon Spilett and Pencroff.—Their Return.—Forward!—An Open Door.—An Illuminated Window.—By the Light of the Moon!

The next day, February 18th, was spent exploring the coastal woods from Reptile End to Falls River. The colonists made a thorough search of the forest between the two shorelines of Serpentine Peninsula, whose breadth varied from three to four miles. The great size and dense foliage of the trees attested to the prodigious fertility of the soil, richer here than anywhere else on the island. It was as if a piece of the virgin forests of South America or Central Africa had somehow been transported to the island's shores. Damp and cool at the upper levels, the soil must have been heated from below by the volcanic fires, offering this magnificent flora a warmth not otherwise to be found in such temperate climes. The predominant species were kauris and eucalyptus, and they grew to the most colossal dimensions.

Still, the colonists had not come here to admire the wondrous plant life. They already knew full well that in this domain Lincoln Island could be ranked alongside the Canaries, formerly known as the Islands of Fortune. But now, alas! their island was no longer entirely theirs; others had usurped their place. Even now its soil was trodden by scoundrels, and it was the colonists' duty to hunt them down, and destroy them to the very last man.

No trace could be found of the convicts' presence on the western shore, no matter how the colonists searched. No footprints, no broken branches, no cold ashes, no abandoned campsites.

"This doesn't surprise me," said Cyrus Smith to his companions. "The convicts came ashore near Flotsam Point, and they immediately fled through Shelduck Fens and into the Forests of the Far West. Thus, their path was more or less the one we followed after leaving Granite House. That explains the traces we found in the woods. But once they reached the coastline the convicts must have realized they would find no suitable shelter here, and so they turned north, and soon they came upon the sheepfold..."

"To which they've no doubt returned..." said Pencroff.

"I don't think so," the engineer answered, "for that's just where they would expect us to begin our search. The sheepfold is a storehouse for them, not a dwelling."

"I share Cyrus's opinion," the reporter said. "If the convicts were seeking a hiding place, I believe they would naturally head for the foothills of Mount Franklin."

"In that case, Mr. Cyrus, it's time we paid a visit to the sheepfold!" cried Pencroff. "We have to put an end to this, and so far we've been wasting our time!"

"No, my friend," the engineer answered. "You forget that we have an interest in searching for signs of life in the Forests of the Far West as well. Our exploration has two goals, Pencroff. On the one hand, we must punish a crime; but on the other, we have a debt of gratitude to repay!"

"Well said, Mr. Cyrus," the sailor replied. "All the same, I don't believe we'll find that gentleman unless he wants it that way!"

And in this Pencroff expressed an opinion shared by all. No doubt the stranger's lair would prove every bit as elusive as the man himself!

That evening the cart drew to a halt at the mouth of Falls River. Their campsite was set up as usual, and they took the customary precautions for the coming night. The sea breezes and the invigorating atmosphere of the forests did wonders for Harbert's health; he had once more become the robust, active boy that he was before his illness. His place was no longer in the cart, but at the head of the caravan.

The next day, February 19th, the colonists turned away from the shoreline, away from the picturesque chaos of basalt beyond the mouth of the river, and followed the left bank toward the interior of the island. The path had been partially cleared in their previous excursion from the sheepfold to the western shore. The colonists now found themselves six miles from Mount Franklin.

The engineer's plan was as follows: to carefully observe the entire river valley, and make their way discreetly toward the sheepfold; if the sheepfold was occupied, to retake it by force; if not, to make of it their base for the upcoming search of Mount Franklin's environs.

This proposal was unanimously approved by the colonists. How great was their impatience to regain possession of their domain!

And so they advanced through the narrow valley between the two largest foothills of Mount Franklin. The trees were dense along on the riverbanks, but became sparser on the volcano's upper slopes. This was a rugged, hilly area, well suited to ambushes, and they observed their surroundings with a wary eye. Top and Joop led the way; leaping left and right into the thick undergrowth, they proved closely matched in intelligence and agility. But nothing suggested that this riverbank had recently been visited by men, and nothing hinted at the presence nor even the proximity of the convicts.

At around five o'clock in the evening, the cart stopped some six hundred feet from the palisade, which lay hidden behind a semicircular curtain of tall trees.

Their goal was to watch for signs of human occupation at the sheepfold. Should the convicts be lying in wait, any attempt to storm the enclosure outright in broad daylight would likely result in terrible misfortune, such as had already befallen Harbert. Prudence dictated that they wait for nightfall.

Nevertheless, Gideon Spilett wanted to investigate the area around the sheepfold at once, and Pencroff, his patience wearing thin, offered to accompany him.

"No, my friends," the engineer replied. "You must wait until darkness falls. The risk of being seen is too great."

"But Mr. Cyrus..." answered the sailor, reluctant to obey.

"Pencroff, please," said the engineer.

"Very well!" the sailor replied; and then, to vent his wrath, he apostrophized the pirates with a stream of the harshest terms in the sailor's vocabulary.

And so the colonists remained with the cart, their eyes trained on the forest around them.

Three hours went by. The wind had died down, and beneath the tall trees all was unbroken silence. They would clearly have heard the snapping of the thinnest branch, the most stealthy footstep over the dry leaves, the most cautious slithering of a body through the grass. But everything was perfectly quiet. Lying on the ground, his head resting on his outstretched front legs, Top showed not the slightest sign of agitation.

By eight o'clock, darkness had begun to settle over the land, and the conditions seemed suitable for their reconnaissance mission. Gideon Spilett now proposed to set off, with Pencroff by his side. Cyrus Smith consented. Top and Joop would stay with the engineer, Harbert, and Neb, for any inopportune bark or cry might alert the convicts and greatly jeopardize their safety.

"Take no unnecessary risks," Cyrus Smith exhorted the sailor and the reporter. "Your task is not to reconquer the sheepfold, but only to determine whether it is occupied."

"Agreed," answered Pencroff.

And off they went.

The dense foliage cast deep shadows on the forest floor, reducing the visibility to some thirty to forty feet in any direction. Pencroff and the reporter advanced with all possible caution, halting in their tracks whenever any remotely suspicious sound reached their ears.

They kept a certain distance between them, so as not to offer an easy target for gunfire. And, truth to tell, they expected a shot to ring out at any moment.

Five minutes after leaving the cart, Gideon Spilett and Pencroff arrived at the edge of the wood. The palisade stood at the far end of the clearing.

Here they stopped. The treeless meadow was still bathed in the last vague gleams of daylight. The gate was thirty feet away. These thirty feet from the edge of the woods to the enclosure constituted what is known in the science of ballistics as the danger zone. Within that area, the colonists would be easy targets, effortlessly felled by a bullet from atop the palisade. And this was precisely the area that Gideon Spilett and the sailor would now have to cross.

They were by no means fainthearted men; nevertheless, they knew that one single careless act on their part could well have fatal consequences, first for themselves, and then for their companions. For if they were to perish, what hope could be left for Cyrus Smith, Neb, and Harbert?

Greatly excited to find himself so near the sheepfold, where he assumed the convicts had taken refuge, Pencroff was about to start forward, but the reporter firmly held him back.

"In a few moments it will be completely dark," Gideon Spilett murmured into his ear. "That will be the time to act."

Convulsively gripping the stock of his rifle, Pencroff restrained himself and settled in to wait, grumbling all the while.

Soon the last glimmers of dusk faded entirely. The gloom that seemed to emanate from the dense forest now spread over the clearing. The towering mass of Mount Franklin blocked off the western horizon, and night seemed to fall all at once, as it often does at this low latitude. The time had come.

From the moment of their arrival at the edge of the woods, Pencroff and the reporter had never once taken their eyes off the sheepfold. Everything appeared to be completely deserted. The crest of the palisade was dimly visible in the darkness, its outline perfectly straight and unbroken. Nevertheless, if the convicts were indeed at the sheepfold, this is where they would post a guard to sound the alarm in case of unexpected incident.

Gideon Spilett pressed his companion's hand, and together they crawled forward, ready to fire at any moment.

They arrived at the gate; not a single ray of light could be seen piercing the darkness.

Pencroff tried to push open the gate, but, as he and the reporter expected, it proved to be locked. Nevertheless, the sailor found that the exterior bars had not been lowered.

From this they concluded that the convicts were inside, having in all likelihood secured the gate to prevent its being forced open from without.

Gideon Spilett and Pencroff stopped to listen.

No sound from within the enclosure, nor from the stables, where the goats and mouflons were no doubt fast asleep.

Hearing nothing, the reporter and the sailor wondered whether they should climb the palisade and slip inside, despite Cyrus Smith's explicit instructions.

Such an operation might well meet with success, but it might just as well fail. And if the convicts suspected nothing, if they were as yet unaware of the colonists' plans to attack, and, finally, if they now had a chance to catch them off guard, should they compromise that chance by risking an unplanned invasion?

The reporter thought not. The reasonable course of action would be to wait until the colonists were all together before attempting to enter the sheepfold. In any case, they could now be certain that it was possible to reach the palisade undetected, and that the enclosure was apparently unguarded. Having resolved that question, they could only return to the cart and consider their next move.

The same idea must have occurred to Pencroff, for he made no objection as the reporter retreated into the woods, but simply followed behind.

A few minutes later, the engineer was informed of the situation.

"Well," he said, after a few moments' thought, "I believe we can now assume that the convicts are not watching the sheepfold."

"We'll find that out once we're over the palisade," said Pencroff.

"To the sheepfold, my friends!" said Cyrus Smith.

"Shall we leave the cart in the woods?" asked Neb.

"No," answered the engineer, "this is our munitions and supply wagon, and if need be, we can use it as cover."

"Forward, then!" said Gideon Spilett.

The cart emerged from the woods and rolled soundlessly toward the palisade. The darkness was impenetrable, the silence as complete as when Pencroff and the reporter had first set off. The thick grass muffled the sound of their steps.

The colonists walked on, ready to fire at any moment. Pencroff had ordered Joop to bring up the rear. Neb kept Top on the leash to prevent him from bounding forward unexpectedly.

Soon they were within sight of the clearing, still perfectly deserted. The little troop wasted no time, but continued directly toward the sheepfold. Soon they were across the danger zone. Not a single shot had been fired. The cart drew alongside the palisade and came to a halt. Neb stayed with the dauws to keep them quiet. The engineer, the reporter, Harbert, and Pencroff then stole toward the gate, intending to determine whether it was barricaded from inside . . .

One of the two doors was open!

"What did you tell me?" asked the engineer, turning to the sailor and Gideon Spilett.

They looked on, dumbstruck.

"I swear on my eternal soul," said Pencroff, "this door was closed not a moment ago!"

Now the colonists hesitated. Were the convicts inside after all when Pencroff and the reporter first came to the sheepfold? That could not be in doubt; the gate was then closed, and only by one of them could it have been opened! Were they all still inside, or had one of their number recently emerged?

The same questions flashed through every colonist's mind. But how were they to find the answers?

Harbert had ventured a few paces into the enclosure. Now he suddenly leaped back and seized Cyrus Smith's hand.

"What is it?" asked the engineer.

"A light!"

"In the house?"

"Yes!"

They drew nearer the gate, and to be sure they saw a dim light trembling in the nearest window.

Cyrus Smith made his decision at once.

"This is a unique opportunity," he told his companions. "The convicts are gathered inside the house, off guard, unsuspecting! They are ours! Forward!"

Raising their rifles, the colonists slipped quietly into the enclosure. Top and Joop stayed outside to guard the cart, tied to the axle as a precautionary measure.

The colonists now broke into two groups. Cyrus Smith, Pencroff, and Gideon Spilett walked along the palisade to one side, Harbert and Neb to the other, all of them closely watching for signs of movement; but the sheepfold remained entirely dark and deserted.

A few moments later they were together again, standing before the closed door of the house.

With a gesture, Cyrus Smith signaled his companions not to move. He approached the window, only faintly illuminated by the light within.

His looked into the room that occupied the entire ground floor.

A lantern sat glowing on the table; nearby he saw the bed once used by Ayrton.

On the bed lay the body of a man.

Suddenly Cyrus Smith stepped back, and in a muffled voice:

"Ayrton!" he said.

At once, the door was not so much opened as bashed in, and the colonists rushed into the room.

Ayrton seemed to be asleep. His face bore witness to a long and cruel suffering. Large, painful abrasions could be seen on his wrists and ankles.

Cyrus Smith bent over him.

"Ayrton!" cried the engineer, seizing the arm of the companion with whom they had been so unexpectedly reunited.

Hearing the engineer's voice, Ayrton opened his eyes and looked straight at Cyrus Smith, then at the others:

"You!" he cried. "You?"

"Ayrton! Ayrton!" repeated Cyrus Smith.

"Where am I?"

"In the house at the sheepfold!"

"Alone?"

"Yes!"

"But they'll be back!" cried Ayrton. "Defend yourselves! defend yourselves!"

And Ayrton fell back, all his forces depleted.

"Spilett," said the engineer, "we could be attacked at any instant. Bring the cart into the sheepfold and bar the gate. And then I want everyone inside the house."

Pencroff, Neb, and the reporter hurried to carry out the engineer's orders. There was no time to lose. The cart might already have fallen into the convicts' hands!

A short while later, the reporter and his two companions were at the gate. Top could be heard growling quietly on the other side.

Leaving Ayrton's bedside for a moment, the engineer hurried out of the house, ready to fire. Harbert stood beside him. They kept their eyes on the foothill overlooking the sheepfold. If the convicts had found cover somewhere in those hills, they could easily cut down the colonists one by one.

Just then the moon appeared in the east, rising over the black curtain of the forest, and its pale light streamed into the enclosure, illuminating the entire enclosure: the stands of trees, the little stream, the broad expanse of grass. Looking back toward the mountain, they could see the house and the far end of the palisade, white amid the darkness. In the opposite direction, toward the gate, everything was bathed in shadows.

Soon a dark form appeared. The cart now entered the circle of light,

"But they'll be back!" cried Ayrton.

and Cyrus Smith heard his companions closing the gate and barring it from inside.

Just then, however, Top suddenly broke free of his leash, barking furiously and bounding off to the right of the house toward the far end of the sheepfold.

"Look out, my friends! Take aim!..." cried Cyrus Smith.

Rifles raised, the colonists stood ready to fire. Top continued to bark, and Joop hurtled after him, whistling shrilly.

The colonists set out on his heels, and soon they came to the bank of the little stream, in the shadows of the tall trees.

And there, in the moonlight, what did they see?

Five bodies lying on the grass!

It was the convicts who had landed on Lincoln Island four months before!

XIII

Ayrton's Story.—His Former Accomplices' Designs.—Settling in at the Sheepfold.—The Defender of Lincoln Island.—The Bonadventure.*—Exploration of Mount Franklin.—The Upper Valleys.—Subterranean Rumbles.—Pencroff's Reply.—At the Bottom of the Crater.—The Return.*

What had happened? Who had struck down the convicts? Was it Ayrton? No, for only a moment before he still feared their return!

But Ayrton now lay in a deep slumber, from which he could not be awakened. An intense torpor had come over him after the few words he had spoken, and he sank back onto the bed unconscious.

With a thousand unsettled thoughts running through their minds, still shaken by the shock of their discovery, the colonists spent the night in Ayrton's house, never once returning to the spot where the convicts' bodies lay. Ayrton could doubtless tell them nothing of the manner of their death; indeed, he seemed not even to know where he was. But at least he could recount the events leading up to that terrible execution.

Ayrton awoke from his torpor the following day, and his companions warmly expressed their joy at seeing him again, more or less unharmed, after a separation of one hundred four days.

Ayrton then briefly told them what had happened, or at least what he knew of it.

The day after his arrival at the sheepfold, November 10th of the preceding year, the convicts had scaled the fence at nightfall and launched a surprise attack. He was bound and gagged, then taken to a dark cavern at the foot of Mount Franklin, which the convicts had made their refuge.

It was resolved that he must die; but the next day, just as he was about to be executed, one of the convicts recognized him and addressed him by the name he bore in Australia. The wretches would gladly have slaughtered Ayrton! But they respected Ben Joyce!

From that moment on, Ayrton became an enduring obsession for his former accomplices. They burned to bring him back into their midst, for with his assistance they could storm the impregnable fortress of Granite House, wrest it from the colonists' grasp, lay waste to the colony, and make of themselves the masters of the island!

Ayrton resisted. Repentant and absolved, he would sooner have died than betray his companions.

Ayrton lived in that cavern for four months, bound, gagged, closely watched at every moment.

The convicts had discovered the sheepfold soon after landing on the island, and its store of provisions sustained them for many months, although they never attempted to make of it their lair. On November 11, suddenly surprised by the colonists' arrival, two of the bandits fired on Harbert. One of them returned to the cavern boasting of having killed a colonist, but he returned alone. As we know, his companion had fallen victim to Cyrus Smith's dagger.

Imagine Ayrton's fear and despair on hearing of Harbert's death! There were now only four colonists left, at the mercy—so to speak—of the convicts!

After this incident and throughout the colonists' sequestration at the sheepfold, the pirates remained in hiding at the cavern. Indeed, after the pillage of Longview Plateau, they thought it might prove most unwise to leave it.

Ayrton's torment grew more unbearable with each passing day. His hands and feet still bore the bloody marks of the ropes that bound him day and night. He had no hope of escaping his fate, and expected to die at any moment.

And so it continued until the third week of February. Concerned for their own safety, the convicts rarely left their repair; nevertheless, they sometimes went hunting in the island's interior or in the area of the southern shore. No news of his friends had reached Ayrton's ears; he was sure he would never see them again!

Finally, his forces drained by his ill treatment, Ayrton fell into a deep prostration, losing both his sight and hearing. Thus, from that moment on—which is to say two days before—he could not tell them what had transpired.

"But, Mr. Smith," he added, "after so many months imprisoned in the cavern, why do I now find myself in the sheepfold?"

"Why is it that the convicts are all lying dead in the pasture?" the engineer replied.

"Dead!" cried Ayrton, suddenly sitting up despite his weakness.

His companions helped him arise from his bed, and together they made their way to the little stream.

Bright sunlight shone down over the meadows.

There on the bank lay the five convicts' corpses! Death must have come upon them with lightning speed, for their attitudes were those of their last moment of life!

Ayrton was thunderstruck. Cyrus Smith and his companions looked at him wordlessly.

On the engineer's signal, Neb and Pencroff examined the bodies, already cold and stiff.

They found no visible wounds.

However, after a careful examination, Pencroff discovered that—whether on the forehead, breast, back, or shoulder—they were each marked with a small red dot, a sort of scarcely visible contusion whose origin he could not determine.

"This is where they were hit!" said Cyrus Smith.

"But with what sort of weapon?" cried the reporter.

"A weapon entirely unknown to us, possessed of the most awesome force!"

"And who did this to them?..." asked Pencroff.

"The defender of the island," answered Cyrus Smith, "he who brought you here, Ayrton, he whose power we have just witnessed once again, he who does everything for us that we cannot do ourselves, and then flees from view."

"We've got to look for him!" cried Pencroff.

"Yes, we shall look for him," answered Cyrus Smith, "but we'll never find a man capable of miracles like this unless he calls us to him!"

The engineer was both moved and irritated by this invisible protective force, for next to this their own actions paled into insignificance, and this relative inferiority could not fail to test a soul as proud as his. A benevolence that refused any expression of thanks suggested a sort of disdain for its beneficiary, and to a certain extent this sullied the wonder of the blessing in Cyrus Smith's eyes.

"Let us look for him," he resumed, "and may God grant that we might one day prove our gratitude to our sovereign protector! What would I not give to repay our debts, to do him some signal favor in our turn, even if it cost us our lives!"

From that day on, this search was the colonists' sole preoccupation. An irresistible compulsion drove them to discover the enigma's solution, a solution that could not be other than the name of a man endowed with a genuinely inexplicable and virtually superhuman power.

But for the moment the colonists returned to the house at the sheepfold, for Ayrton required prompt treatment if he was to recover his mental and physical strength.

Neb and Pencroff carried the bodies of the convicts into the forest and buried them deep in the ground at some distance from the sheepfold.

Ayrton was told of the events that had taken place during his imprisonment. He learned of Harbert's misfortunes, and of the many tribulations that had beset the colonists. He learned that they had lost all hope of seeing him again, and had justly feared that he had been mercilessly slaughtered.

"And now," said Cyrus Smith, finishing his account, "we still have one vital task before us. Half of our work is done; nevertheless, if the convicts no longer pose a threat, and if we are once more the masters of the island, it must be said that this was not our doing."

"Well," answered Gideon Spilett, "we must search the entire labyrinth of foothills beneath Mount Franklin! We will not leave a single hollow unexplored, not a single hole! Oh! my friends, reporters love a mystery, and I believe we've stumbled onto the most mysterious of them all!"

"And we will not return to Granite House," answered Harbert, "until we have discovered our benefactor's repair."

"Yes!" said the engineer. "We will do everything it is humanly possible to do...but, I repeat, we will not find him unless he wishes it so!"

"Shall we stay at the sheepfold?" asked Pencroff.

"Yes, let us stay here," answered Cyrus Smith. "We're at the very heart of the area we plan to investigate, and the sheepfold's supply of provisions will sustain us. And we can easily return to Granite House whenever the need might arise."

"Very well," the sailor answered. "One observation, however."

"And what is that?"

"Summer is moving on, and we have an important trip to make."

"A trip?" asked Gideon Spilett.

"Yes! to Tabor Island," Pencroff answered. "The Scottish yacht could return at any time, and we must inform the crew of Ayrton's new whereabouts, and of our island's coordinates. Who knows, perhaps it's too late already?"

"But Pencroff," asked Ayrton, "how are you intending to make the trip?"

"On the *Bonadventure!*"

"The *Bonadventure!*" cryed Ayrton... "The *Bonadventure* is no more."

"No more! My *Bonadventure!*" howled Pencroff, leaping up.

"Yes!" Ayrton answered. "The convicts found her moored in the harbor not eight days ago; they sailed out to sea, and..."

"And?" said Pencroff, his heart aflutter.

"And without Bob Harvey to guide them they ran her into the rocks, and now there's nothing left of her!"

"Oh! those brutes! those bandits! those vile wretches!" cried Pencroff.

"Pencroff," said Harbert, taking the sailor's hand, "we'll build a new *Bonadventure*, bigger and better. We already have the fittings and rigging from the brig!"

"But do you realize," Pencroff answered, "that it takes at least five months to build a ship of thirty or forty tons?"

"We'll take all the time we need," the reporter answered, "and we shall have to abandon our plans for a trip to Tabor Island this year."

"Nothing to be done, Pencroff, we have to face it," said the engineer. "Let us hope the delay will not harm our chances."

"Oh! my *Bonadventure*! My poor *Bonadventure!*" cried Pencroff, genuinely heartbroken at the loss of his pride and joy!

The destruction of the *Bonadventure* was a cruel blow indeed, and the colonists resolved to repair the loss as soon as they were able. With this decided, they once more turned their full attention to the exploration of the island's hidden recesses.

The search began that very day, February 19th, and continued through the next week. The complex folds of the foothills at the mountain's base formed an unpredictable labyrinth of valleys and ravines. It was clearly here, deep in these narrow gorges, and perhaps somewhere on Mount

Franklin itself, that they must concentrate their efforts. Nowhere else on the island could a recluse have so easily found a secluded and secret repair. Cyrus Smith planned out their route with the most exacting care; otherwise, they might easily overlook more than one likely spot among the intricate network of hills.

The colonists began with the deep valley on the south side of the volcano, which brought the snowmelt from the mountainside to Falls River. Here Ayrton showed them the cavern where the convicts had taken refuge, the place of his imprisonment before his removal to the sheepfold. The cavern was precisely as Ayrton had last seen it; the convicts' stolen supply of ammunition and foodstuffs was found hidden away within.

The grotto lay at the head of a valley shaded by luxuriant trees, principally conifers, and this entire valley was now explored with the greatest possible attention. Then, making their way around the southwestern foothill at its far end, the colonists found themselves in a narrower gorge, which ran directly down to the chaos of basalt on the shoreline.

Here the trees were sparser. The grass was replaced by stone. Wild goats and mouflons gamboled over the rocks. Here began the island's arid regions, and from this spot they could see that, of the entire network of valleys at the foot of Mount Franklin, only three, between the Falls River valley on the west and the Red Creek valley on the east, were richly wooded and grassy like the environs of the sheepfold. These two streams originated in the mountain's melting snow; farther on, fed by various tributaries, they became rivers, and this was the source of the fertility of the island's southern half. As for the Mercy, it was more directly fed by fast flowing springs, no doubt buried deep in the density of Jacamar Woods; the same sort of spring, percolating through the soil in a thousand little rivulets, must have irrigated Serpentine Peninsula.

Any one of these three valleys might have served as the recluse's repair, for with the presence of flowing water they offered all the requirements of life. But each of them had already been explored with great thoroughness, and nowhere within them had the colonists found any sign of human presence.

Was it thus deep within the arid gorges, amid the chaos of rocks, in the harsh ravines to the north, among the streams of hardened lava, that they would find the strange lair and its occupant?

On its northern side, the base of Mount Franklin divided into two valleys, wide and relatively shallow, apparently devoid of greenery, strewn with erratic boulders and slashed by long moraines. The surface was paved by long lava flows, studded here and there by great mineral excrescences sprinkled with shards of obsidian and labradorite. The exploration of this area proved a long and difficult process. A thousand cavities could be found among the rocks, cramped and uncomfortable no doubt, but nonetheless well hidden and resistant to uninvited entry. The colonists inspected a number of dark tunnels burrowing deep into the mountainside, and clearly dating back to the island's plutonian era, for the walls were still black from the passage of burning lava. By the light of pine-branch torches, they carefully made their way down the dark galleries, searching the tiniest recesses, probing the slightest cranny. But everywhere they found silence and darkness. No human seemed to have set foot in these ancient corridors; no arm had ever pushed aside the stones that obstructed the path. They remained exactly as the volcano had created them in the island's earliest days, when the continuous flow of molten material caused land to appear in what was once an expanse of open sea.

Nevertheless, while the substructures were clearly deserted, while their darkness was complete, Cyrus Smith could not help but notice that the silence was not absolute.

They had followed one such cavity several hundred feet into the mountainside. Arriving at the end of the tunnel, Cyrus Smith was surprised to hear a muted rumbling, its intensity magnified by the resonant walls of rock.

At his side, Gideon Spilett heard the same distant murmurs, which indicated that the subterranean fires were beginning to return to life. Listening closely, they agreed that some chemical reaction seemed to be taking place in the entrails of the island.

"Does this mean that the volcano is not entirely extinct?" the reporter said.

"It could be that some process has been set in motion deep within the earth since we first explored the crater," said Cyrus Smith. "Any volcano can come back to life, even one long considered extinct."

"But if Mount Franklin were to erupt," asked Gideon Spilett, "would that not place Lincoln Island in some considerable danger?"

"I believe not," answered the engineer. "The crater already exists. A crater serves as a safety valve; the vapors and lava will simply escape by their usual outlet, as they have so often done in the past."

The colonists inspected a number of dark tunnels . . .

"Unless the lava takes a new route, and flows toward the fertile regions!"

"Why, my dear Spilett," Cyrus Smith answered, "why would the lava not follow the route that is already laid out for it?"

"Well! volcanoes are unpredictable things!" the reporter answered.

"Do not forget," the engineer resumed, "the slopes of Mount Franklin are inclined toward these valleys; it is here that ejected matter will flow. Their direction could be altered only by an earthquake powerful enough to change the mountain's center of gravity."

"But earthquakes can never be ruled out when volcanic activity is present," said Gideon Spilett.

"To be sure," the engineer answered, "especially when, after their long slumber, the reawakening subterranean forces cause an obstruction in the entrails of the globe. Therefore, my dear Spilett, an eruption would be a serious matter, and all things considered I would prefer that the volcano showed no sign of awakening! But there's nothing we can do about it, is there? In any case, no matter what happens, I do not believe our domain on Longview Plateau will be in any real danger. There is a notable dip in the terrain between the plateau and the mountain, and if the lava were to travel toward the lake, its flow would be diverted into the dunes and the region of Shark Gulf."

"And we have seen no smoke at the top of the mountain to suggest that eruption is imminent," said Gideon Spilett.

"No," Cyrus Smith answered. "Only yesterday I was looking closely at the mountaintop, and I saw not a single puff of steam from the crater. Nevertheless, an accumulation of rocks, ashes, and hardened lava could have slowly built up in the lower extremities of the chimney, and so obstructed the valve I spoke of just now. But with the first subterranean upheaval these obstacles will be dislodged, and you can be certain, my dear Spilett, that neither the island, which is the boiler, nor the volcano, which is the chimney, will explode from the pressure of the gases. Nevertheless, I repeat, I would greatly prefer that the volcano not erupt."

"And yet there's no doubt about it," the reporter continued. "What we are now hearing are indeed muted rumblings from the very entrails of the volcano!"

"Yes," the engineer answered, still listening intently, "there's no mistaking that... There is a reaction taking place here, and for the moment we can judge neither its significance nor its ultimate effects."

Emerging from the gallery, Cyrus Smith and Gideon Spilett rejoined their companions and informed them of these developments.

"So!" cried Pencroff. "The volcano is planning to throw a tantrum! Just let it try! It'll soon find out who the master is!…"

"Who is that?" asked Neb.

"Our genie, Neb, our genie! He'll put a gag in that crater the moment the volcano tries to open it!"

As we can see, the sailor's faith in the island's private deity was absolute. Unlimited indeed appeared the hidden force that had so inexplicably exerted itself time after time; and now it had proven itself once again, by eluding the colonists' most painstaking searches. In spite of all their efforts, in spite of all the zeal—and, more than zeal, the tenacity—that they brought to their explorations, the strange repair could not be found.

From February 19th to the 25th the circle of their investigations slowly expanded, finally embracing the entire northern region of Lincoln Island. Once again, even the slightest niche was methodically and thoroughly scrutinized. The colonists found themselves knocking on every rock wall, like policemen searching a suspect house. The engineer made a painstaking survey of the mountain, then led his investigators through every fold in its foundation, up to the truncated cone atop the rocks on the first plateau, and onward to the upper ridge of the enormous hat within which lay the open crater.

And they did not stop here: they searched the abyss itself, still lifeless, from whose depths the rumbling could distinctly be heard. Nevertheless, finding no smoke, no steam, no heat emanating from the rock walls, they concluded that no eruption was imminent. But in any case, neither here nor anywhere else on Mount Franklin did they find a trace of the one they sought.

They carefully combed the broad expanse of dunes. With great difficulty and at the price of great exertion, they inspected the sheer lava walls of Shark Gulf from base to peak. No one! Nothing!

Such was the reward for all their fruitless efforts, for all their ill-paid obstinacy: no one and nothing. There was a certain tinge of anger in the colonists' deep disappointment.

The time had come to return to their home, for the search could not go on forever. They might well be forgiven for concluding that the mysterious being did not live on the surface of the island, and now their

And they did not stop here: they searched the abyss . . .

overexcited imaginations gave birth to the wildest conjectures. Pencroff and Neb, especially, could not confine their ideas to the domain of the merely strange, but soon wandered into the realm of the supernatural.

On February 25th, the colonists returned to Granite House. One end of the rope was attached to an arrow fired to the level of the threshold, and soon they were inside.

One month later, on the twenty-fifth day of March, they marked the third anniversary of their arrival on Lincoln Island!

XIV

*Three Years Have Passed.—The Question of the New Ship.—
The Decision.—The Colony's Prosperity.—The Shipyard.—The
Cold of the Austral Hemisphere.—Pencroff Resigns Himself.—
Washing the Linen.—Mount Franklin.*

Three years had passed since the prisoners' flight from Richmond. How often, in the course of those three years, did they speak of their homeland, forever present in their minds!

They did not doubt that the Civil War had now come to an end, and they could not conceive that the just cause of the North might have been defeated. But by what terrible incidents had this fearsome war been marked? How much bloodshed had it cost? What friends had perished in the battle? They often spoke of such things, and wondered when they might once more look upon their native land. To return, if only for a few days, to reestablish the social bond with the outside world, to create a link between their homeland and their island, and then to spend the greater part of their existence—perhaps the finest part—in the colony they had founded, now become a satellite of the mainland: was this truly an impossible dream?

But only in two ways could that dream be made a reality: the unexpected appearance of a ship in the waters of Lincoln Island or the construction of a ship by the colonists themselves—one mighty enough to withstand the rigors of an ocean voyage, and powerful enough to bring them to some inhabited land.

"Unless," said Pencroff, "our genie himself offers us the means to return home!"

And indeed, the others could have told Pencroff and Neb that a three-hundred-ton ship awaited them in Shark Gulf or at Port Balloon, and they would not have batted an eye. Nothing could surprise them where the island's genie was concerned.

Cyrus Smith did not share their confidence; he urged them to return to reality, and to turn their minds to the urgent task of building a ship themselves. There was no time to lose, for a message would have to be left on Tabor Island at the earliest opportunity.

At least six months would be required to build a replacement for the vanished *Bonadventure*; and, with winter coming on, the voyage would have to be delayed until the following spring.

"This gives us all the time we need," said the engineer to Pencroff. "We can be ready to sail when the fair weather returns. And, my friend, since we have no choice but to build a new vessel, I believe we should consider a far more ambitious construction than the last. We cannot count on the Scottish yacht's return to Tabor Island. It could well have come already, sometime in the past few months, and sailed off again after a fruitless search for Ayrton. Do you not agree that it would be best to build a real ship, large enough to take us to the Polynesian archipelagoes or New Zealand? What do you think?"

"I think, Mr. Cyrus," the sailor responded, "I think you might just as easily build a large ship as a small one. We have wood, and we have tools. It's only a question of time."

"And how many months would we need to build a ship of two hundred fifty to three hundred tons?" asked Cyrus Smith.

"Seven or eight months at least," Pencroff answered. "But we mustn't forget that winter is coming, and wood isn't easy to work with in the cold. Let's count on a few weeks of idleness, and, if our boat is ready by November next, we can consider ourselves very lucky."

"And that," answered Cyrus Smith, "will be the perfect time for a voyage of some distance, either to Tabor Island or to a more faraway land."

"Indeed, Mr. Cyrus," the sailor replied. "Well then! Draw up your plans. The workmen are ready, and with Ayrton beside us the work should go all the easier."

The colonists were consulted. They approved the engineer's plan, and indeed this was the best thing they could have done. It is true that the construction of a two- to three-hundred-ton ship was an enormous undertaking; nevertheless, the colonists were blessed with a self-confidence more than justified by a long history of success.

And so Cyrus Smith turned to the task of drawing up the plans and determining the ship's dimensions. His companions spent this time felling and transporting the trees they would use for the knees, timbers, and planking, venturing into the Forests of the Far West for the finest oaks and elms. An entrance into the forest had already been made in their last excursion; this was used as a beginning for a fully practicable road through the woods, which they soon called the Far West Road, and which allowed them to transport the trees to the Chimneys, where the shipyard had been established. The path of their new road was rather sinuous, as it was for the most part the availability of wood that had determined its course; nevertheless, it greatly eased their access to a large area of Serpentine Peninsula.

The trees had to be felled and stripped as soon as possible, for they could not be used while they were still green, and would require time to harden. The woodsmen labored incessantly throughout the month of April. Save for a few rather violent equinoctial gales, the weather in no way impeded their work. Master Joop proved an invaluable assistant, whether clambering up a tree to attach the felling ropes or lending his robust shoulders to the transport of the stripped trunks.

This wood was stacked under a large lean-to that had been built with planks just alongside the Chimneys, and there it sat, waiting for the moment when it would be used.

April was a month of delightful weather, much like a fine October in the boreal zones. They had devoted no less time to their agricultural endeavors than to the ship, and soon all trace of devastation had been erased from Longview Plateau. The mill was rebuilt, and the poultry yard was graced with a number of new hen coops. Indeed, these were rebuilt on a considerably larger scale, for the population of fowl was growing at a remarkable rate. Five dauws were now housed in the stables, four of them vigorous and well trained, easily hitched or mounted; the fifth had just been born. The colony had come into possession of a plow, and the dauws were used to till the fields, like the finest oxen of Yorkshire or Kentucky. Every colonist lent his hand to these tasks, and no arm was idle. Consequently, how robust was the colonists' health, and with what fine spirits they animated their evenings in Granite House, imagining a thousand plans for the future!

It need hardly be said that Ayrton now participated fully in their common existence, and the possibility that he might return to live at the sheepfold was never considered. All the same, he remained vaguely melancholy and rather quiet, and joined in his companions' labors more readily than in their pleasures. But he was a tireless worker, energetic, dextrous, ingenious, and intelligent. He was esteemed and loved by all, and he could not fail to see it.

Nevertheless, the sheepfold was not abandoned. Every two days, one of the colonists hitched up the wagon or mounted a dauw and went off to tend to the mouflons and goats, returning with buckets of fresh milk for Neb's kitchens. These excursions offered ample opportunity for hunting as well, and so Harbert and Gideon Spilett—with Top in the lead—could be seen on Sheepfold Road far more often than the others. Thanks to their excellent weapons, the colony never wanted for fresh game, both big and small: capybaras, agoutis, kangaroos, boars, and wild pigs in the former case; ducks, black grouse, capercaillies, jacamars, and snipes in the latter. What with the warren, the oyster beds, the occasional capture of a tortoise, the seasonal return of the salmon to the waters of the Mercy, the vegetables from Longview Plateau, the natural fruits of the forest, with all of this it was a time of plenty upon plenty, and their master chef, Neb, had his hands full merely trying to find room for it all.

The telegraph line from the sheepfold to Granite House had of course been repaired, and it was put to use whenever one or another colonist had gone to check on the animals and found it necessary to spend the night. But the island was safe now, and they had no cause to fear further aggression—not from human hands, at least.

Nevertheless, the future might well bring a recurrence of the recent unhappy events. The possibility of another invasion by pirates, or even escaped convicts, was not to be dismissed. Bob Harvey's companions and accomplices still captive at Norfolk could well have been let in on his plans, and might try to emulate him. For this reason, the colonists kept up their constant observation of the island's shores, and every day the spyglass scanned the broad horizon at the outermost limit of Union and Washington Bays. The seas to their west were scrutinized with equal care on each visit to the sheepfold, for the nearby foothill offered a view over a broad sweep of the western horizon.

Never once did they find anything out of the ordinary; nonetheless, they knew they would have to remain vigilant.

Thus, one evening, the engineer informed his friends of a plan he had conceived to fortify the sheepfold. He thought it a good idea to raise the palisade and adjoin to it a sort of bunker, from within which they could repel an invasion if necessary. Granite House's unusual location made it a nearly impregnable stronghold; inevitably, then, the sheepfold—with its house, its store of supplies, its flocks—would become the target of any pirates who might land on the island. Should the colonists find it necessary to take shelter there, they must be prepared to resist any aggression. They would do well, then, to give themselves every possible advantage.

Such a project would require some thought, and in any case they could not hope to begin work until the following spring.

By the middle of May, the keel of their new vessel lay on the sand in the shipyard, and soon the stem and the sternpost had been mortised to either end at an angle of nearly ninety degrees. This keel was made of the finest oak; it measured one hundred ten feet in length, allowing a midship beam twenty-five feet wide. This was as much as the shipbuilders could accomplish before the storms and cold set in. Over the following week they installed the first timbers in the stern, but then they were forced to suspend their work.

The weather turned foul in the last days of the month. The wind blew from the east, sometimes with the force of a hurricane. The engineer feared for the sheds at the shipyard—which, let us note, he could not have built anywhere else in the area of Granite House—for the islet only partially protected the shoreline from the fury of the open sea, and when the storms were severe, the waves hammered the very base of the granite wall.

Happily, however, his fears were not borne out. The wind shifted somewhat to the southeast, and in such conditions the shoreline beneath Granite House was thoroughly sheltered by the natural redan of Flotsam Point.

Pencroff and Ayrton, the most zealous of the shipbuilders, continued to work as long as they possibly could. The wind whipped their hair, the rain soaked through to their bones, but such trifles meant precious little to men such as these, and a hammer can be wielded in good and bad weather alike. But the rain soon gave way to a period of bitter cold, making the wood fibers as hard as iron and extremely difficult to work with; thus, around June 10th, they had to abandon their project for the rest of the season.

More than once, Cyrus Smith and his companions had remarked on the harshness of the Lincoln Island winter. It was a cold much like that of the New England states, which lie at a comparable distance from the Equator. Now, in the boreal hemisphere—or at least in the occupied regions of New Britain and the northern United States—the low temperatures are explained by the unrelieved flatness of the lands around the pole, whose sweeping plains offer no obstacle to the hyperborean winds; but some different explanation would have to be found for Lincoln Island.

"Indeed, it has been observed," Cyrus Smith told his companions one day, "that winter is notably harsher in the Mediterranean lands than on islands and seacoasts at similar latitudes. I have often heard it claimed that winters are more rigorous in Lombardy, for instance, than in Scotland, and this is explained by the fact that in winter the sea releases the warmth it has collected over the summer, much to the benefit of any islands within it."

"But, Mr. Cyrus," asked Harbert, "why should Lincoln Island be an exception?"

"That is a difficult question," the engineer answered. "Nevertheless, I would suggest that it is because the island lies in this austral hemisphere, which, as you know, my child, is colder than the boreal."

"Yes," said Harbert. "Floating ice can be found at lower latitudes in the South Pacific than in the North."

"That's true," answered Pencroff. "Back in my whaling days, I saw icebergs even off Cape Horn."

"Perhaps, then, we could explain the bitter cold on Lincoln Island by the presence of icebergs or ice floes relatively near our shores," said Gideon Spilett.

"Very likely, my dear Spilett," answered Cyrus Smith. "Clearly, the proximity of the ice floes has a profound effect on our temperatures. But I would also have you notice that a purely physical cause makes the austral hemisphere colder than the boreal. Since the sun is nearer that hemisphere in summer, it is necessarily farther away in winter. This explains why the high temperatures on our island should be as extreme as the lows, for while it is true that our winters are very cold, we must not forget that our summers are conversely very hot."

"But, if you please, Mr. Smith," asked Pencroff with furrowed brow, "why should fortune so disfavor our hemisphere, as you say? It doesn't seem fair!"

"My friend Pencroff," the engineer replied with a laugh, "fair or no, we must simply bear our lot. But here is the source of this oddity. In its rotation around the sun the earth describes not a circle but an ellipse, as the laws of rational mechanics tell us it must. The earth occupies one focus of the ellipse; consequently, one stage of its journey brings it to apogee, which is to say the greatest distance from the sun, and another to perigee, which is to say the shortest distance. As it happens, the moment of apogee occurs during the winter of the austral lands, and so those regions are subjected to a cold more intense than the others. I'm afraid there's nothing to be done about that, Pencroff. No matter how wise they be, men will never change even a single element of the cosmographical order created by God Himself."

"All the same," added Pencroff, unable to resign himself to this fact, "there's such a lot of wisdom in this world! What a great, thick book could be made from everything we know, Mr. Cyrus!"

"And a still thicker book from what we do not!" answered Cyrus Smith.

In any case, for one reason or another, winter returned with its usual violence in the month of June, and more often than not the colonists could be found inside Granite House, sheltering against the cold.

Oh! how they chafed against their captivity! And none of them so impatiently, perhaps, as Gideon Spilett.

"My friend," he said to Neb one day, "I would gladly give you a notarized document signing over any inheritance that might someday come my way, if you would only be so kind as to go somewhere, anywhere, and get me a subscription to a newspaper! I really cannot think of a more serious obstacle to my happiness than the impossibility of arising each day to learn what happened in distant lands the day before!"

Neb began to laugh.

"My goodness," he answered, "all I need to keep me busy are my daily chores!"

And it was true that, both inside and out, there was plenty of work to be done.

After three years of continuous hard work the colony of Lincoln Island found itself more prosperous than ever before. The destruction of the brig had greatly increased their wealth. The rigging would be invaluable for the ship under construction; but even leaving that aside, their storerooms were full to bursting with weapons, ammunition, clothing, instruments, and all manner of utensils and tools. No more were they forced to make thick felt for their clothes. The cold was a source of constant torment in their first winter on the island, but now they snapped their fingers at its rigors. Nor did they lack for linen, and they took great pains to care for it. From sodium chloride, which is nothing other than sea salt, Cyrus Smith had easily extracted soda and chlorine. It was a simple task to transform the soda into hydrated sodium carbonate, or washing soda; the chlorine, meanwhile, was used to make lime chloride, among other things. And these two substances have many domestic uses, most particularly the cleaning of linens. Furthermore, their supply of clothing was such that they did their laundry only four times a year, just as many families did in the old days. And, it should be added, Pencroff and Gideon Spilett—the latter still waiting for the mailman to bring him his newspaper—proved to be very distinguished launderers.

Thus passed the months of winter: June, July, and August. It was a time of bitter cold, and the average reading observed on the thermometer was never more than 8 degrees Fahrenheit (13.33 degrees centigrade below zero), lower than the year before. A fine fire thus incessantly burned in the hearth of Granite House, staining the granite wall with long black streaks of soot! They never spared the firewood, which grew in great abundance only a few steps away. Furthermore, they had felled more trees than they needed for their ship, and this allowed them to economize on coal, which was considerably more difficult to transport.

Men and animals alike, all were in fine health. Master Joop, it must be said, had one small shortcoming: he was rather sensitive to cold, and his companions had to make him a fine quilted dressing gown. Nonetheless, what a good servant he was: nimble, zealous, tireless, never indiscreet, never too talkative. He could have served as a model for all his bipedal peers, in the Old World as well as the New!

"Well," Pencroff liked to say, "when you have four hands to work with, there's no excuse for not doing a proper job!"

And the fact is that the intelligent quadrumane did it well!

Seven months had passed since their search through the environs of Mount Franklin, and now September brought the return of fair weather. No sign of the genie had since been seen. Never was his influence felt. To be sure, there had been no need for his intervention, for this was a time marked by no untoward incidents, and never once did the colonists find themselves in danger.

Had the mysterious being once used the shaft as a spyhole into Granite House? Was Top's agitation a sign that his instincts had sensed the stranger's presence? Perhaps; but as Cyrus Smith now observed, Top had remained remarkably calm throughout this entire period. No more did his bark resound through the chambers of Granite House; no more did he and the orangutan fall into fits of furious agitation. The two friends—for friends they were—no longer prowled around the entrance to the shaft, nor growled or groaned in that curious and troubling way that had first aroused the engineer's concern. Would nothing more ever come of this mystery? Would they never have the solution to the enigma of the stranger's existence? Could they be certain that no future turn of events might bring the mysterious personage back to the fore? Who could say what the future might hold?

Winter had finally come to an end, but with the first fine days of the returning spring there occurred an event whose potential consequences were grave indeed.

On September 7th, gazing at the summit of Mount Franklin, Cyrus Smith saw a vaporous plume writhing over the crater, as jets of steam shot high into the air.

XV

The Volcano Reawakens.—Fair Weather.—The Work Resumes.— The Evening of October 15th.—A Telegram.—A Question.—A Response.—Departure for the Sheepfold.—The Note.—The New Wire.—The Basalt Coast.—High Tide.—Low Tide.—The Cavern.—A Dazzling Light.

Alerted by the engineer, the colonists paused in their labors and silently contemplated the summit of Mount Franklin.

The volcano had thus reawakened, and the gases had broken through the pile of mineral rubble at the bottom of the crater. But did this mean that a violent eruption was at hand? That they could not say.

Nevertheless, even if the volcano should erupt, the consequences for Lincoln Island as a whole were unlikely to be serious. An outpouring of magma is not always a catastrophe. The island had undergone such tribulations many times before, as the streaks of hardened lava on the mountain's northern slopes clearly showed. Furthermore, thanks to the deep gash in the crater's upper rim, any material thrown from the volcano would be directed away from the fertile areas of the island.

Nevertheless, things past are not always signs of things to come. Old volcanic craters can close up, and new ones open. Such a phenomenon has been seen in both the Old World and the New—at Mount Etna, Popocatepetl, Orizaba—and on the eve of an eruption anything is possible. It would require only an earthquake, a common accompaniment to volcanic activity, to modify the form of the mountain's interior and open new paths for the incandescent lava.

This Cyrus Smith explained to his companions, and, avoiding any

The colonists contemplated the summit of Mount Franklin.

exaggeration, he laid out their situation: what they could hope for, and what they must fear.

In any case, there was nothing they could do. Barring an earthquake forceful enough to rattle the island's foundation, Granite House seemed in no immediate danger. But the same could not be said of the sheepfold if a new crater were to open in the southern flanks of Mount Franklin.

From that day onward, a plume of steam and hot gases continually hovered over the mountaintop. Indeed, the density and altitude of the vapors seemed to be increasing, even if no flame had yet appeared in their midst. The fires were thus still confined to the lower part of the central chimney.

With the return of fair weather came a resumption of the shipbuilding. They hastened the construction as best they could. Using the force of the water falling onto the beach, Cyrus Smith built a hydraulic saw, which cut the trunks into planks and beams more quickly than they ever could have done by hand. The mechanism could not have been simpler; indeed, this technique is in common use in the rustic lumber mills of Norway. It was simply a matter of imparting a horizontal movement to the piece of wood, and a vertical movement to the saw; with a wheel, two cylinders, and a number of pulleys, the engineer easily made his plan a reality.

Toward the end of September, the skeleton of the ship could be seen standing in the shipyard. The timbers were almost all in place, and with each pair of ribs held fast by a temporary truss, the form of the vessel was already clear to see. It would be rigged as a schooner, slender at the bow, very graceful in its rear runs, perfectly suited to a long sea journey should the need arise. Nonetheless, the hull, the interior planking, and the deck had yet to be installed, and this would take some considerable time. It was fortunate indeed that the brig's fittings had been salvaged after the under-sea explosion, and that Pencroff and Ayrton had pulled the pegs and copper nails from the ship's mutilated knees and planking. This greatly eased the blacksmiths' task, but the builders still had much to do.

Work on the ship was suspended for a week, as the colonists' hands were required on Longview Plateau. There was harvesting to be done, and haymaking, and the bounty had to be carefully stored away. Once this was behind them, they devoted every available moment to the completion of the schooner.

Great was the workers' exhaustion at the end of their day. Their meal-times were modified in an effort to save time: they dined at noon and supped only when all light had faded from the sky. They then returned to Granite House and retired at once.

Sometimes, however, caught up in conversation, they liked to linger in the great room before going to their beds. The colonists often spoke of the future, and of the great changes to come as they contemplated a journey to inhabited lands. Nevertheless, through it all, one idea was ever present: the hope of an eventual return to Lincoln Island. After so many trials, and so many triumphs, they could not think of abandoning their colony. And how much greater it could become, once regular communication with America was established!

Pencroff and Neb, especially, hoped to live out their lives there.

"Harbert," the sailor sometimes said, "you'll never leave Lincoln Island?"

"Never, Pencroff, particularly if you're intending to stay on yourself!"

"I am indeed, my boy," Pencroff answered. "I'll be waiting for you! You can bring back your wife and children, and I'll make jolly rascals of your youngsters!"

"Agreed, Pencroff," Harbert replied, laughing and blushing at the same time.

"And you, Mr. Cyrus," Pencroff went on with great excitement, "you will be the governor of the island! Just think! How many inhabitants can it feed? Ten thousand at least!"

And on they went, giving free rein to Pencroff's exuberant fancies, and with one thing leading to another the reporter was eventually to found a newspaper, the *New Lincoln Herald*!

Such are the hearts of men. The imperious need to produce some lasting work—something that will live on when we are gone—is the sign of mankind's superiority over every other creature that lives on this earth. This is the very foundation of our dominance, justified every day the world over.

But then, how can we be sure that Top and Joop did not harbor their own little dreams for the future?

Ayrton sat in silence, fondly imagining the moment when he would see Lord Glenarvan again, and show himself, fully rehabilitated, to the outside world.

On the evening of October 15th a conversation of this nature persisted deeper into the night than usual. It was nine o'clock. A number of long, ill-concealed yawns suggested that sleep could be postponed no more;

but just as Pencroff was wandering off to bed, a metallic clank was heard from the telegraph machine.

Cyrus Smith, Gideon Spilett, Harbert, Ayrton, Pencroff, Neb—every last colonist was here in the great room, and none at the sheepfold.

Cyrus Smith stood up. Sure that their ears had deceived them, his companions looked on in silence.

"What does this mean?" cried Neb. "Is that the devil calling us?"

No one answered.

"It's a stormy night," Harbert observed. "Perhaps the electricity in the atmosphere could have..."

But Harbert did not finish his sentence. All eyes were turned to the engineer, but he only shook his head.

"I believe we should do nothing for the moment," said Gideon Spilett. "If someone is trying to contact us, they will surely try again."

"But who do you think it could be?" cried Neb.

"Well," Pencroff answered, "the man who..."

The sailor's sentence was cut short by a second metallic ringing.

Cyrus Smith walked to the apparatus. Activating the flow of electrical current through the wire, he sent this question to the sheepfold:

"What do you want?"

A few moments later, the needle moved over the alphabetical dial to spell out this response:

"Come to the sheepfold at once."

"Finally!" cried Cyrus Smith.

Yes! Finally! The mystery was about to be solved! The colonists' fatigue instantly evaporated. They had been summoned to the sheepfold! How could they think of sleep? An instant later, they had gathered on the beach, never speaking a single word. Only Top and Joop stayed behind in Granite House. For the moment, their presence was not required.

It was a pitch-dark night, for the moon was new, and had set at the same time as the sun. Furthermore, as Harbert remarked, a great mass of low, heavy storm clouds veiled the sky, blocking out the glimmering stars. Flashes of heat lightning sometimes lit the horizon, reflections of a distant storm.

Within a few hours, the worst of it would be over the island itself. A vague sense of menace hung over the atmosphere.

But the colonists knew Sheepfold Road like the backs of their hands, and the darkness proved no obstacle. They turned onto the left bank of the Mercy, climbed to the plateau, crossed the Glycerine Creek bridge, and entered the forest.

Their pace was brisk, their souls stirred by a powerful emotion. There could be no doubt: the long search was at an end. They were about to discover the solution to the enigma—the name of the mysterious being who had so profoundly affected the course of their lives, so benevolent in his influence, so powerful in his actions! Indeed, was this stranger not an integral part of their colony? Was it not plain to see that he knew every detail of their day-to-day existence, that he heard every word spoken at Granite House? How could it be otherwise, since he had never failed them when they needed him most?

They raced through the forest, lost in meditation. The darkness was complete beneath the canopy of trees; even the edges of the road were swallowed by the shadows. Not a sound could be heard in the forest. Subdued by the heavy atmosphere, the animals were silent and still. No breeze shook the leaves. The only sound to be heard in the night was the colonists' footfalls over the hard ground.

Only once in the first fifteen minutes of their walk was this silence broken, by an observation from Pencroff:

"We should have brought a lantern."

And the engineer's reply:

"We'll find one at the sheepfold."

Cyrus Smith and his companions had set out at twelve minutes past nine. By 9:47, they had traveled three of the five miles from the mouth of the Mercy to the sheepfold.

The sky was ablaze with vast, bright sheets of lightning. Every few moments, the dark forms of the foliage were starkly silhouetted against a blinding flash of light. The storm would soon be upon them. The lightning was slowly growing brighter and more frequent. Low rumblings rolled through the distant reaches of the heavens. The air was still and almost stiflingly heavy.

The colonists continued ever onward, as if moved by some irresistible force.

At ten-fifteen, a bright flash of lightning revealed the outline of the palisade; a deafening peal of thunder greeted them as they entered the enclosure.

An instant later they had crossed the sheepfold, and Cyrus Smith now stood at the door of the small house.

No doubt the stranger was within at this very moment, for only from here could the telegram have been sent. Nevertheless, no light shone at the windows.

The engineer knocked.

No response.

Cyrus Smith opened the door and the colonists entered the house, feeling their way through the dark.

Neb struck a light, and the glow of the lamp flooded into every corner of the room...

No one was there. The room was just as they had last seen it.

"Could it all have been some sort of illusion?" murmured Cyrus Smith.

No! that could not be! The telegram had said quite clearly: "Come to the sheepfold at once."

They approached the telegraph, sitting on its table. Everything was in its place, the battery, its case, the transmitter and receiver.

"Who was the last one here?" asked the engineer.

"I was, Mr. Smith," answered Ayrton.

"And that was?..."

"Four days ago."

"Oh! a note!" cried Harbert, pointing to a piece of paper lying on the table.

On it they read these words, written in English:

"Follow the new wire."

"Come!" cried Cyrus Smith, realizing that the message had been sent not from the sheepfold but from the stranger's abode. A new wire must have been connected to the old one, establishing a direct link to Granite House.

Neb took up the lamp and they left the house at once.

The storm was now nearing the island, in all its terrible fury. Flashes of lightning were succeeded by thunderclaps, at ever shorter intervals. Soon the disturbance would be over Mount Franklin, and then over the entire island. The continual flashes of lightning revealed the summit of the volcano, still plumed with gaseous vapors.

They searched the enclosure from the house to the palisade, but found no telegraphic connection. Cyrus Smith raced through the gate toward the first of the poles, and there, in a flash of lighting, he saw a wire hanging down from the insulator.

"There it is!" he said.

The wire trailed off along the ground. Much like an undersea cable, it was sheathed in a protective layer of insulation. It seemed to lead westward through the woods and the mountain's southern foothills.

"Follow it!" said Cyrus Smith.

And the colonists raced along the wire, lit now by their lantern, now by the flash of a lightning bolt.

The thunder rolled incessantly, and they could not hope to make their voices heard over its deafening roar. But this was no time for conversation; this was a time to go forward.

Cyrus Smith and his friends climbed the foothill that stood between the sheepfold and Falls River, which they then crossed at its narrowest point. Now hung over the low branches of the trees, now running along the ground, the wire showed them the way.

The engineer assumed that the wire would lead only as far as the head of the valley, where the unknown repair must lie.

But this was not the case. They climbed the southwestern foothill, then descended to the arid plateau at the end of the curious wall of basalt. From time to time they had to kneel down and feel for the wire, altering their course accordingly. Nevertheless, it was now quite clear that the wire ran directly toward the sea. It was no doubt there, in some cavity of the igneous rocks, that they would find the stranger they had so long sought in vain.

The sky was ablaze with lightning, one flash coming hard upon the last. Now and then a bolt struck the summit of the volcano, shooting into the crater amid dense clouds of steam. At times it almost seemed the mountain was spewing flames.

At ten minutes before eleven o'clock, the colonists arrived at the high ridge overlooking the ocean to the west. A strong wind had come up. The surf roared five hundred feet below.

Cyrus Smith calculated their distance from the sheepfold at a mile and a half.

Here the wire threaded its way among the rocks, down the steep slope of a narrow, capricious ravine.

The colonists began to make their way down the ravine. It was a perilous descent, for the hillside was formed of precariously balanced rocks; a single footstep might provoke an avalanche and send the colonists plummeting into the sea. But they cared little for the dangers they faced. They were not their own masters, for an irresistible attraction drew them toward that mysterious point, just as a magnet attracts iron.

Thus, nearly unconscious of their own actions, they descended the ravine, virtually impassable even in broad daylight. Loose stones rolled past them from above, shooting like celestial fireballs through the lantern's beam of light. Cyrus Smith walked at the head of the group, Ayrton brought up the rear, and on they went, their eyes ever on the uneven ground before them, step by step, sometimes slipping on the smooth rocks, then standing up at once and continuing onward.

Finally, on reaching a jumble of stones overlooking the water, the wire took a sudden turn. The colonists were now at the bottom of the slope, amid a chaos of basalt boulders, no doubt lashed by the waves when the tide was high.

The wire led them onto a narrow, horizontal ledge that ran parallel to the sea. Soon the ledge took on a very slight downward inclination, and not a hundred steps farther on they found themselves at the level of the water.

The engineer picked up the wire and saw that it vanished into the sea.

Drawing alongside him, his companions looked on in utter incomprehension.

A cry of disappointment sprang from their breasts—almost a cry of rage! Would they have to dive into the water in search of some undersea cavern? In their current state of physical and emotional frenzy, they would not have hesitated for a moment.

A remark from the engineer held them back.

Cyrus Smith led his companions into a hollow in the rocks, and there:

"Let us wait," he said. "The tide is high. At low tide, the way will be clear."

"But what makes you think?..." asked Pencroff.

"He would not have summoned us if we had no way to find him!"

The tone of conviction in Cyrus Smith's voice silenced all objections, and his logic could not be denied. There must have been some opening in the base of the wall, submerged for the moment but negotiable at low tide.

With a wait of several hours before them, they huddled beneath a sort of portico sunk deep into the rocks. Rain began to fall, and soon, as the lightning ripped through the clouds, a veritable torrent poured down from the heavens. The crashing thunder echoed off the rocks in grandiose reverberations.

A riot of emotions now stirred the colonists' souls, and a thousand strange and supernatural fancies raced through their minds. They tried to picture the great, superhuman apparition awaiting them below; for in their minds the mysterious genie of their island could have been nothing less.

At midnight, Cyrus Smith took up the lantern and went off to observe the shoreline. The tide had been receding for two hours.

The engineer was not mistaken. The upper vault of a vast cavern was now revealed above the water's surface, and he saw that the wire now made a ninety-degree turn and entered the gaping hole.

Cyrus Smith returned to his companions and told them simply:

"In one hour, the opening will be passable."

"So it exists?" asked Pencroff.

"Did you ever doubt it?" Cyrus Smith replied.

"But the cavern will still be at least partially filled with water," Harbert observed.

"If the cavern's water drains out completely at low tide," answered Cyrus Smith, "we will enter it on foot; if not, some means of transportation will surely have been left for us."

Another hour went by. In the rain, they made their way to the water's edge. The tide had fallen fifteen feet in the previous three hours. The top of the vault was now at least eight feet above the water, like the arch of a bridge. Topped with white foam, the waves passed underneath and on into the cavern.

Leaning over, the engineer now saw a dark object afloat in the water. He reached out and pulled it closer.

It was a rowboat, made of riveted sheet metal, and moored by a rope to an outcropping in the rock. Two oars lay on the bottom, beneath the benches.

"We have only to embark," said Cyrus Smith.

And so they did. Neb and Ayrton manned the oars, Pencroff the rudder. Cyrus Smith sat in the bow, resting the lantern on the stem to illuminate their route.

The boat passed under the low vault that was the cavern's entrance. Once inside, the ceiling suddenly soared far above their heads; but the

The colonists climbed into the rowboat.

darkness was too profound and the lantern's light too faint to allow them to gauge the cavern's width, height, and depth. An awesome silence reigned within the vast grotto of basalt. No sound could be heard from outside; not even the crashing thunder could penetrate its thick walls.

More than one such vast cavern has been found in the recesses of our globe—natural crypts, formed deep in the geological past. Some have been invaded by the waters of the sea; others hold entire lakes within their flanks. Such is Fingal's Cave on the Isle of Staffa in the Hebrides; such are the grottoes of Morgat on the Bay of Douarnenez in Brittany, the grottoes of Bonifacio in Corsica, or of the Lyse Fjord in Norway; such is the immense Mammoth Cave in Kentucky, five hundred feet high and more than twenty miles long! Here and there, all over the earth, nature has created such crypts, and preserved them for the admiration of men.

Could the cavern in which the colonists now found themselves extend to the very center of the island? For fifteen minutes the boat moved on. Every now and then the engineer's ringing voice ordered a change of course; then, all at once:

"More to the right!" he cried.

The craft pulled toward the cavern's right-hand wall. The engineer wanted to be sure that the wire was still running along the face of the rock.

And indeed, there was the wire, slung from one outcropping to the next.

"Forward!" said Cyrus Smith.

Once more the two oars sank into the black water, pulling the vessel ever onward.

This continued for a further fifteen minutes. The boat now lay some half-mile from the entrance to the cavern; but suddenly, Cyrus Smith's voice was heard again.

"Stop!" he said.

The boat stopped. A bright light had now appeared, illuminating the enormous crypt so deep within the island's living rock.

Now they could make a closer inspection of the cavern, whose existence they had never so much as suspected.

A hundred feet above, they saw a rounded ceiling supported by shafts of basalt, all seemingly cast from the same mold, from atop which grew irregular imposts and ribs of the most fantastic shapes. A thousand such pillars filled the caverns, erected by nature in the earliest days of the earth's formation. The shafts were constructed of basalt sections, some forty to fifty feet high, stacked one atop the other; their bases were sunk into the water, calm despite the agitation outside. The dazzling light played off the innumerable prismatic edges, dappling them with fiery gleams, seeming almost to penetrate the walls, just as if they were translucent, and making of every protrusion a sparkling cabochon.

These brilliant gleams of light were reflected atop the water's surface, and the boat truly seemed to hover between two endless scintillations.

There was no mistaking the nature of the luminous rays refracted over every rib and angle of the crypt. Their directness and perfect whiteness clearly showed them to be of electrical origin. This was the sun of the caverns, and its light poured into every hollow and recess.

On Cyrus Smith's signal, the oars sank once more into the water, setting off a veritable shower of glittering carbuncles. Now the boat made directly for the light, and soon it was only a half-cable from the source.

Here the water measured some three hundred fifty feet wide, and beyond the dazzling light they saw only an enormous wall of solid basalt. The cavern had thus grown considerably broader, and within it the ocean waters formed something like a small lake. But, bathed in the electrical emanations, everything—the vaulted ceiling, the lateral walls, the wall that formed the apse, so many prisms, so many cylinders, so many cones—everything seemed to glow from within! Faceted like the finest diamonds, the stones could truly have been said to exude pure light!

A fusiform object floated in the middle of the lake, silent and motionless. Light poured from two openings in its flanks, as if from the mouths of two white-hot kilns. Similar in form to the body of an enormous cetacean, this vessel measured some two hundred fifty feet long, and its upper flanks rose to a height of ten or twelve feet above the water's surface.

Slowly the boat approached. Cyrus Smith stood upright in the bow. He stared straight ahead, gripped by a violent agitation. Then, suddenly, grasping the reporter's arm:

"It's him! There's no one else it can be!" he cried. "Him!…"

Then he sank back onto his bench, murmuring a name that only Gideon Spilett could hear.

This name must not have been unknown to the reporter, for it produced a prodigious effect on him, and he answered in a muted voice:

"Him! an outlaw!"

"Himself!" said Cyrus Smith.

On the engineer's order, the boat approached the curious apparatus, drawing alongside its left flank. A great beam of light poured through a thick porthole.

Cyrus Smith and his companions climbed onto the platform and raced through an open companionway.

At the bottom of the ladder they found an interior gangway, lit by electricity. At the far end stood a door. Cyrus Smith strode forward and pushed it open.

The colonists first passed through a richly decorated anteroom, which led to a library, flooded with light from a luminous ceiling.

Across the room stood another door, soon thrown open by the engineer.

The colonists now found themselves in a vast salon—indeed, a sort of museum, crammed with great works of art, marvels of human industry, and all the treasures of the mineral realm. They might well have thought themselves magically transported to a world of dreams.

A man lay stretched out on a luxurious divan, apparently unaware of their presence.

Now Cyrus Smith spoke, and, to the great surprise of his companions, these were his words:

"You sent for us, Captain Nemo? We have come."

"You sent for us, Captain Nemo?..."

XVI

*Captain Nemo.—His First Words.—The Story of a Hero of
Independence.—A Hatred of the Invaders.—His Companions.—
Life Underwater.—Alone.—The Last Refuge of the* Nautilus *at
Lincoln Island.—The Mysterious Genie of the Island.*

Hearing these words, the man arose from his divan, and all at once his
face was bathed in light: a magnificent face, with a high forehead, a proud
gaze, a white beard, and a thick, swept-back mane of hair.

He supported himself with one hand on the back of the divan. His
gaze was calm. A lingering disease had visibly wasted his body, but his
voice was strong as he said in English, in a tone of surprise:

"I have no name, sir."

"I know you!" answered Cyrus Smith.

Captain Nemo fixed the engineer with a fiery gaze, as if to silence him
at once.

Then, falling back onto the pillows of the couch:

"After all, what does it matter?" he murmured. "I am a dying man!"

Cyrus Smith drew nearer Captain Nemo, and Gideon Spilett took his
hand, which he found to be burning hot. Ayrton, Pencroff, Harbert, and
Neb kept a respectful distance in one corner of the magnificent salon,
whose atmosphere was saturated with electrical effluences.

Meanwhile, Captain Nemo had quickly withdrawn his hand, and gestured to the engineer and the reporter to sit down.

The colonists gazed on him with genuine emotion. So this was the one
they called the "genie of the island," the all-powerful being whose intervention had so often rescued them from peril, the protector to whom they

owed their undying gratitude! Pencroff and Neb had fully expected to find a god; but the one before them was nothing more than a man, and a man not far from death!

But how came it that Cyrus Smith knew of Captain Nemo? And why, on hearing him speak that name—a name he seemed to think known to none—why had he so abruptly risen to his feet?

The captain returned to his place on the divan. Leaning on one arm, he looked at the engineer, who sat nearby.

"You know the name that once was mine?" he asked.

"I know it," answered Cyrus Smith, "just as I know the name of this remarkable undersea vessel."

"The *Nautilus*?" said the captain, half-smiling.

"The *Nautilus*."

"But do you know... do you know who I am?"

"I do."

"But for thirty years I have had no contact with the outside world! Thirty years in the depths of the sea, the one place on earth that offers me my independence! Who could have betrayed my secret?"

"A man not bound to you in any way, Captain Nemo, and consequently one who cannot be accused of betrayal."

"That Frenchman who happened onto my ship sixteen years ago?"

"Himself."

"Then he and his two companions did not die as the *Nautilus* plunged into the Maelstrom?"

"They did not die, and an account of your history has since been published, under the title *Twenty Thousand Leagues Under the Sea*."

"A few months of my history, sir, nothing more!" the captain briskly replied.

"That is true," Cyrus Smith answered, "but those few months of your strange life have established your fame..."

"As a great criminal, no doubt?" Captain Nemo replied, a haughty smile playing over his lips. "Yes, a rebel, an outcast, perhaps an exile banished from the world of men!"

The engineer did not answer.

"Well, sir?"

"It is not my place to judge Captain Nemo," answered Cyrus Smith, "or rather to judge the life he once led. Whatever motivations might lie behind that strange existence are as unknown to me as to my fellows, and

I cannot judge effects without knowing their causes; but what I do know is that a benevolent hand has unfailingly protected us since our arrival on Lincoln Island, and that each one of us owes his life to a good, generous, powerful being, and that that powerful, good, and generous being is you, Captain Nemo!"

"It is," the captain answered simply.

The engineer and the reporter had risen to their feet. Their companions drew near, ready to express with words and gestures all the gratitude that filled their hearts...

Captain Nemo signaled them to stop, and in a voice more emotional than he might well have wished:

"Wait until you've heard me out," he said.*

His story was brief, and yet it took all his remaining strength to tell it through to the end. His weakness was clearly extreme, and he strove mightily to surmount it. Several times Cyrus Smith begged him to rest for a few moments, but as one who has lost all hope for the morrow, he only shook his head; and when the reporter offered his medical expertise:

"There is no use," he answered, "my hours are numbered."

Captain Nemo was born in India as Prince Dakkar, son of a rajah of the then-independent territory of Bundelkund, and nephew of the great Indian hero Tippu Sahib. His father sent him to be educated in Europe at the age of ten, secretly hoping that this would prepare him to do battle with those he considered the oppressors of his land.

Remarkably gifted, great in both heart and mind, Prince Dakkar devoted the years between his tenth and thirtieth birthdays to the study of letters, the sciences, the arts, striving ever higher and further in his thirst for new knowledge.

Prince Dakkar traveled widely on the Continent. His great wealth and high birth were much prized in society, but the seductions of this world held no appeal for him. Young and handsome, he was nonetheless serious, sober, ever hungry for learning, and, deep within his heart, consumed by an implacable resentment.

For Prince Dakkar felt a hatred. He hated the one country where he had never consented to set foot, the one nation whose advances he con-

---

* The story of Captain Nemo has indeed been published under the title *Twenty Thousand Leagues Under the Sea*. Here we must reiterate a remark made in the narration of Ayrton's adventures, concerning certain chronological discrepancies. Readers in search of further information are requested to refer to that previous note.

tinually spurned: he hated England, and the admiration he bore her in more than one regard only strengthened that hatred all the more.

Within the Indian's breast was concentrated all the loathing of a vanquished people for their conquerers. The invader could find no forgiveness among the invaded. As the son of a sovereign only nominally bound to the United Kingdom, the young prince—with the blood of Tippu Sahib coursing through his veins, an upbringing that inculcated undying dreams of revenge and redress, and a heartfelt love for his poetic land now enchained by the British oppressors—had made a vow never to set foot on the cursed soil of the nation to which India owed her subjection.

Prince Dakkar became an artist with a fine and sensitive eye, a scientist to whom no field of human inquiry was unknown, a statesman forged in all the royal courts of Europe. To those who did not know him well, he must have seemed some mere cosmopolite, eager for learning but disdainful of action—one of those proud Platonic souls who spend their opulent lives traveling the world from one end to the other, and call no nation home.

But in fact nothing could have been further from the truth. This artist, this scientist, this statesman had remained Indian in his heart, Indian in his longing for revenge, Indian in his dreams of reclaiming his native land, driving out the invaders, and inaugurating a new era of independence.

Thus, Prince Dakkar returned to Bundelkund in the year 1849. He married a woman of noble birth, whose heart bled as his did for the torments of her homeland. He fathered two children, whom he cherished above all else. Nevertheless, domestic contentment could not drive thoughts of India's enslavement from his mind. He waited for his moment. Finally it came.

The British yoke had grown increasingly heavy for the Hindu population. Prince Dakkar became the voice of the downtrodden, and instilled into their minds all his own hatred for the foreigners. His travels took him not only through the independent regions of the Indian peninsula, but also into provinces under British control. He reminded his audiences of the great feats of Tippu Sahib, and of his heroic death at Seringapatam in the defense of his homeland.

The great rebellion of the Sepoys erupted in 1857. Prince Dakkar was the soul of this revolt, for it was he who had organized the entire uprising. He had given freely of his wealth and talents to support the Sepoys' cause. Nor did he recoil from combat; indeed, he fought in the first ranks, risking his life like the humblest of his fellow rebels and seekers after freedom, and he was wounded ten times in twenty skirmishes. Soon the last insurgents for the cause of independence were felled by English bullets, but he survived unharmed, ready to continue the fight.

Such a challenge had never been mounted against the British forces in India. If, as the Sepoys had hoped, the outside world would now champion their cause, then perhaps the influence and dominance of the United Kingdom would be a thing of the past in Asia.

The name of Prince Dakkar was now an illustrious one. The hero who bore it did not conceal himself, but struggled openly against the oppressors. A price was put on his head. No traitor came forward to deliver his corpse into the hands of the British; nevertheless, before he fully understood the peril they faced on his account, his wife and children paid the ultimate price in his stead.

Once again, right had been conquered by might. But the tide of civilization can never be reversed, and necessity knows no law. The Sepoys were vanquished, and the land of the ancient rajahs fell once more under British domination, more strictly subjugated than ever before.

Prince Dakkar alone had been spared. He returned to the mountains of Bundelkund, alone forevermore. Overcome by an enormous disgust for everything that bore the name of Man, consumed by hatred and horror of the civilized world, he yearned to quit the society of humankind. Gathering together what small fortune he had left, he summoned twenty of his most faithful companions, and one day he disappeared with them forever.

Where had Prince Dakkar gone to seek the independence refused him by the civilized world? To the very depths of the sea, where none could follow.

The valiant soldier now made way for the scientist. A deserted island in the Pacific served as a shipyard for the construction of an undersea vessel of his own design. One day we will understand how he harnessed the immeasurable mechanical force of electricity for his ship's needs, on what inexhaustible source he drew to power her engines and fill her with light and warmth. The sea, with its infinite riches, its myriads of fish, its endless supply of kelp and sargasso, its enormous mammals—all the vast reserves offered by nature, but also everything lost to the sea by men themselves—proved more than enough to sustain the prince and his crew.

He had longed to rid himself of human society, and now his desires were fulfilled. He christened his machine the *Nautilus,* took for himself the name Captain Nemo, and vanished beneath the waves.

The captain traveled every ocean from one pole to the other in the many succeeding years. A pariah throughout the inhabited universe, he found unheard-of treasures in these unknown realms. The millions lost to the waters of Vigo Bay by the Spanish galleons in 1702 offered him incalculable riches, which, always in complete anonymity, he used to further the cause of peoples fighting for the independence of their homeland.*

And then, on the night of November 6th, 1866, after many years' isolation from his fellows, fate brought three men on board his ship: a French professor, his servant, and a Canadian fisherman, cast into the sea by a collision of the *Nautilus* and the American frigate *Abraham Lincoln,* then in pursuit of Nemo's vessel.

From the professor, Captain Nemo learned that the *Nautilus*—sometimes mistaken for a giant mammal of the cetacean order, sometimes for an undersea pirate ship—had become the object of a great search throughout all the oceans of the earth.

Chance alone had brought these three men into his mysterious life, and he could easily have returned them to the ocean whence they had come. But no; he chose to hold them captive on his ship, and for the next seven months they witnessed all the wonders of a twenty-thousand-league voyage beneath the sea.

On June 22nd, 1867, these three men, who knew nothing of Captain Nemo's past, succeeded in seizing the *Nautilus*'s launch, and so made their escape. But at that moment the *Nautilus* was caught up in the whirling Maelstrom off the Norwegian coast, and the captain could only assume that the terrible eddy had dragged the three fugitives to their watery doom. He could not have known that the Frenchman and his two companions were miraculously thrown onto the shoreline and rescued by fishermen from the Lofoten Islands, nor that the professor, on his return to France, had offered up to a curious public the narration of those strange and eventful seven months.

Nemo pursued this existence for some considerable time, endlessly plying all the oceans of the earth. One by one, his companions died and

* It was in such conditions that Captain Nemo supported the uprising of the Candiots.

went to their rest in the coral cemeteries at the bottom of the Pacific. Every year the *Nautilus* grew emptier, until finally Captain Nemo found himself alone on his ship, the last of the small band who had sought independence in the depths of the sea.

Captain Nemo was then sixty years old. On the death of his last companion, he steered the *Nautilus* to one of the undersea harbors he had sometimes used as ports of call.

The harbor lay deep in the bowels of Lincoln Island, and the *Nautilus* was never to leave this shelter again.

For six years the *Nautilus* remained in this port, as the captain waited for death to reunite him with his companions; but then, by chance, he witnessed the fall of the balloon carrying the prisoners of the Secessionists. Protected by his diving suit, he was walking on the sea floor a few cable lengths from the island's shore when the engineer was thrown into the sea. The captain's benevolent instincts were aroused...and he rescued Cyrus Smith.

At first he tried to flee the five castaways; but soon he discovered that his ship was imprisoned in its harbor. The volcanic forces had brought about an uplifting of the basalt, and the *Nautilus* could no longer pass over the threshold to the crypt. A lighter vessel could have navigated the shallow waters at the cavern's entrance, but the *Nautilus*'s weight and bulk were such that he was forced to abandon all hope of escape to the open sea.

And so Captain Nemo remained. Taking care not to be seen, he observed the men whom fate had thrown unarmed onto this desert island. Little by little, finding them to be upright, energetic, and bound by brotherly affection, he began to take an interest in their efforts. As if in spite of himself, he soon learned every secret of their existence. Wearing his diving suit, he could easily walk to the bottom of the shaft that opened in the floor of Granite House, then climb up the outcroppings to the top. There he listened as the colonists recalled their past and contemplated their present and future; there he learned of the terrible war between the two Americas, and of the struggle for the abolition of slavery. Truly, no men could have been more likely to reconcile Captain Nemo to the rest of humanity, and none could have represented human society more worthily!

It was Captain Nemo who rescued Cyrus Smith. It was Captain Nemo who guided the dog to the Chimneys, who threw Top from the waters of the lake, who sent the providential crate toward Flotsam Point, who returned the launch to the mouth of the Mercy, who threw down the rope from Granite House during the invasion of apes, who wrote the message alerting the colonists to Ayrton's presence on Tabor Island, who laid the mine that destroyed the pirate brig, who saved Harbert from certain death with the gift of a box of quinine sulfate, and who, finally, felled the convicts with electrical bullets, a secret weapon he had devised for his undersea hunting expeditions. Each of these seemingly supernatural incidents was thus explained, and each of these actions bore eloquent witness to the captain's extraordinary goodness and power.

Nevertheless, the great misanthrope still hungered to do good, and he had much important advice to offer his protégés. He now ran a wire from his own telegraph apparatus to the sheepfold; then, feeling the beat of a heart restored to life in the shadow of death, he sent for the colonists, as we have seen… And perhaps he would never have done so if he had known that Cyrus Smith was aware of his story, and would greet him as Captain Nemo.

Here the captain ended his tale. Now it was Cyrus Smith's turn to speak; one by one, he recalled each of the captain's humanitarian acts, and in the name of his companions and himself he thanked the benefactor to whom they owed so much.

But Captain Nemo had not summoned them here to bask in their gratitude. One final thought preoccupied his mind, and before he would take the engineer's outstretched hand, he said to him:

"Now, sir, now that you know the story of my life, you may judge of my actions!"

These words clearly alluded to a serious incident witnessed by the three foreigners aboard his ship—an incident that the French professor would inevitably have recounted in his work, and for which the captain must have been fiercely condemned.

For, several days before the flight of the professor and his two companions, Captain Nemo had found himself pursued by a frigate in the North Atlantic. The *Nautilus* had deliberately rammed this ship, sinking it at once.

Cyrus Smith understood the allusion, and kept his silence.

"It was an English frigate, sir," cried Captain Nemo, becoming Prince

Dakkar again for a moment, "an English frigate, you understand! I was under attack, cornered in a tight, shallow bay!... I had to escape, and... I escaped!"

Then, more calmly:

"I was within the law and within my rights," he added. "Throughout all my travels, I did whatever good was possible, and whatever evil was necessary. Justice does not always mean forgiveness!"

These words met only with silence, and again Captain Nemo spoke:

"What do you think of me, gentlemen?"

Cyrus Smith stretched out his hand and answered gravely:

"Captain, your mistake was to believe you could bring back the past. You struggled against progress, which is a good and necessary thing. This is an error that some admire and others condemn, but God alone can judge of its virtue, and human reason can only pardon it. A man who errs through what he believes to be good intentions may well be denounced, but he will always be esteemed. Some may find much to praise in your error, and your name has nothing to fear from the judgment of history. History loves heroic follies, even as it condemns their consequences."

Captain Nemo's breast heaved, and he raised his hand heavenward.

"Was I right, was I wrong?" he murmured.

Cyrus Smith answered:

"All great actions redound to God, for it is from Him that they come! Captain Nemo, you are surrounded by good men whose lives you have saved, and they will grieve for you forever!"

Harbert approached the captain. He knelt down, took his hand, and kissed it.

A tear fell from the eye of the dying man.

"My child," he said, "bless you!..."

XVII

*Captain Nemo's Final Hours.—A Dying Man's Wish.—A
Keepsake for His New Friends.—Captain Nemo's Coffin.—Advice
for the Colonists.—The Supreme Moment.—At the Bottom of
the Sea.*

Day had now dawned, but no ray of sunlight could enter the profound
crypt, for the tide had come in, and the entrance was entirely submerged.
Nevertheless, great beams of artificial light still poured from the flanks of
the *Nautilus*, and the cavern still gleamed with the fire of a thousand diamonds.

Captain Nemo had sunk back onto the divan, overcome with fatigue.
They could not think of transporting him to Granite House, for his stated
intention was to await his impending death in the company of the many
priceless wonders housed within the *Nautilus*'s walls.

There followed a long period of prostration, and as their patient lay
virtually unconscious, Cyrus Smith and Gideon Spilett carefully
observed his condition. It was clear that Captain Nemo would soon be
gone. The strength was fast ebbing from the body before them, once so
robust, now a mere frail envelope for a soul soon to be set free. Only his
heart and head were yet animated by some lingering sign of life.

The engineer and the reporter discussed his case in quiet tones. Was
there nothing to be done? Could they, if not save him, at least prolong his
life for a few days? He himself had said there was no cure, and he awaited
his death in perfect tranquillity, serene and unafraid.

"There is nothing we can do," said Gideon Spilett.

"But what is he dying of?" Pencroff asked.

"He is simply fading away," answered the reporter.

"All the same," the sailor replied, "if we were to bring him into the open air, perhaps he would come back to life?"

"No, Pencroff," the engineer answered, "there is no point in trying! Besides, Captain Nemo would never leave his ship. For thirty years the *Nautilus* has been his only home, and it is on the *Nautilus* that he wishes to die."

No doubt Captain Nemo had heard Cyrus Smith's words, for he raised himself up a little, and in a voice grown weaker, but still intelligible:

"You're right, sir," he said. "I must and I wish to die here. Therefore, I have a request to make of you."

Cyrus Smith and his companions had approached the divan again, arranging the cushions so that the dying man might sit up more comfortably.

They watched as his gaze wandered over the marvels of his salon, lit by the electrical rays filtering through the arabesques of the luminous ceiling; one after another, he contemplated his paintings, masterpieces of Italian, Flemish, French, and Spanish art set off by the splendid tapestries that lined the walls; then he turned his eyes toward the sculptural miniatures of marble or bronze that stood here and there on pedestals; then the magnificent organ against the back wall, then the great central aquarium, teeming with all the wonders of the sea: aquatic plants, zoophytes, strings of pearls of inestimable value. Finally his gaze landed on this device, inscribed into the pediment of his museum, the device of the *Nautilus* herself:

Mobilis in mobili.

One last time, it seemed, he wanted to caress with his eye the many masterworks of art and nature that had accompanied him in his endless travels through the oceanic abyss!

Cyrus Smith respected Captain Nemo's desire for silence. He waited for the dying man to speak again.

For several minutes Captain Nemo lay mute, no doubt reliving the life that had once been his. Then he turned toward the colonists and said:

"Do you believe yourselves to be in my debt, gentlemen?"

"Captain, we would gladly give our lives to prolong yours!"

"Very well," Captain Nemo resumed, "very well!... Promise that you will faithfully execute my last wishes, and I will consider myself repaid for all that I have done for you."

"We promise," answered Cyrus Smith.

And with this promise he committed himself and his companions.

"Gentlemen," the captain resumed, "tomorrow I shall be dead."

Harbert began to protest, but he silenced him with a gesture.

"Tomorrow I shall be dead, and I want no other tomb than the *Nautilus.* This will be my grave! My friends rest at the bottom of the sea, and that is where I wish to rest as well."

Profound silence greeted Captain Nemo's words.

"Listen well, gentlemen," he continued. "The *Nautilus* is trapped in this grotto, with no hope of escape. But if my ship cannot leave her prison, she can at least sink into the abyss beneath it, to preserve my mortal remains."

The colonists listened reverently to the words of the dying man.

"Tomorrow, Mr. Smith, after my death," the captain went on, "you and your companions will leave the *Nautilus,* for the riches she holds must disappear along with me. You will have one single keepsake of Prince Dakkar, whose story you have just learned. That jewel box...there... contains a fortune in diamonds—reminders of my life as a husband and father, and of a time when I almost believed in happiness—as well as a collection of pearls gathered deep in the sea by my friends and myself. Someday this treasure will allow you to do much good. Money can never be a danger, Mr. Smith, in hands such as yours and your companions'. I will be watching your endeavors from above, and I have no fear of what I may see!"

After a few moments' rest, required by his extreme weakness, Captain Nemo went on in these terms:

"Tomorrow you will take the jewel box and leave this room, closing the door behind you; then you will climb to the upper platform and close the hatch, screwing down the bolts to seal it shut."

"As you wish, Captain," answered Cyrus Smith.

"Good. You will then reembark in the boat that brought you here. But before you leave the *Nautilus,* go astern and open the two large taps you will find at the waterline. The reservoirs will soon be flooded, and the *Nautilus* will slowly sink to its final resting place at the bottom of the abyss."

"That jewel box ... there ... contains a fortune ..."

And in response to a gesture from Cyrus Smith, the captain added:
"Do not fear! You will only be burying a dead man!"

None would have dared question Captain Nemo's request. These were his final wishes, and it was their duty to comply.

"Do I have your word, gentlemen?" added Captain Nemo.

"You do, Captain," answered the engineer.

Gesturing his thanks, the captain asked to be left alone for a few hours. Gideon Spilett wanted to stay at his side in case of some crisis, but the captain refused, saying:

"I shall live until tomorrow, sir!"

They left the salon, walking through the library and dining room to the bow. Here they found the machine room, which housed the electrical power source for the *Nautilus*'s engines, heaters, and lights.

The *Nautilus* was a masterpiece full of masterpieces, and the engineer gazed around him in awe.

The colonists climbed to the exterior platform, some seven or eight feet above the water. They sat down on the metal surface near a sort of large oculus. Light poured from its thick pane of lenticular glass, and inside they saw the wheels that controlled the ship's rudder. It was from this cabin that the steersman once guided the *Nautilus* through the sea, with the brilliant electrical light to show him the way.

For some time Cyrus Smith and his companions sat in silence, dumbstruck by all they had just seen and heard. A great sadness filled their hearts as they thought of the man lying below—a man who had never failed to deliver them from danger, a protector, a newfound friend soon to be lost forever, a man on the eve of his death!

However posterity might judge the course of what could be called his extrahuman existence, Prince Dakkar would forever remain engraved in the minds of men, a unique and unparalleled figure in human history.

"Now that's what I call a man!" said Pencroff. "Can you believe it! A life at the bottom of the ocean! And to think, even there he might not have found the peace he sought!"

"With the *Nautilus*," Ayrton observed, "we might have left Lincoln Island, and found our way to inhabited lands."

"By all the devils!" cried Pencroff. "You'll never find me at the helm of a ship like that! There's nothing finer than sailing the seven seas, but underneath the seven seas, no thank you!"

"I would guess," the reporter said, "that an undersea vessel such as the *Nautilus* must be very simple to use, Pencroff; I'm sure we would take to it quite readily. No fear of storms or pirates, and below the surface the water must be as calm as any lake."

"Could be!" the sailor shot back. "But I'd be happier in a good gale on a well-rigged ship. Boats are made to go over the water, not under it."

"My friends," the engineer intervened, "there is no point in pursuing this discussion, at least where the *Nautilus* is concerned. She does not belong to us, and we cannot do with her as we please. And in any case, she is useless to us now, both because the uplifting of the basalt has imprisoned her in this cavern and because Captain Nemo has asked us to sink her after his death. His wishes are explicit, and we must respect them."

After some further conversation, the colonists reentered the *Nautilus.* There they took some nourishment and returned to the salon.

Captain Nemo had emerged from his prostration; his eyes had regained their glow, and a sort of smile could be seen on his lips.

The colonists drew near.

"Gentlemen," the captain said, "you are courageous, good, and upright men. You have devoted yourself unreservedly to the task that fate has dealt you. How often I observed you in your labors! I grew to love you, and I love you still!... Your hand, Mr. Smith!"

Cyrus Smith offered him his hand, and the captain pressed it with great affection.

"How good it is!" he murmured to himself.

Then, addressing the others again:

"But enough of me! I wish to speak to you of yourselves and of the island that offered you shelter... Do you intend to leave this place?"

"And then come back, Captain!" Pencroff warmly replied.

"Come back?... Indeed, Pencroff," the captain answered with a smile, "well I know how you love this island. You have transformed it with your hard work, and now it is yours!"

"Our plan, Captain," said Cyrus Smith, "is to offer the island to the United States, and to establish a harbor in the Pacific for our navy's ships."

"You think of your country, gentlemen," the captain replied. "You work for her prosperity and for her glory. You are right to do so. The homeland!... we must always return to our homeland! It is there that we must die!... And I, I die far from everything I have ever loved!"

"Do you have some last message to be sent on?" the engineer quickly asked. "Some remembrance and farewell for the friends you left behind in the mountains of India?"

"No, Mr. Smith. I have no friends left! I am the last of my race … those who once knew me have long thought me dead … But let us return to you. Man was not meant for solitude … I die here because I believed it was possible to live alone! … You must do everything you can to leave Lincoln Island, and to look once more on the soil where you were born. I know that those wretches destroyed your boat …"

"We plan to build a ship," said Gideon Spilett, "a ship large enough to carry us to the nearest land; but if we ever succeed in leaving Lincoln Island, we will most certainly return. We will never abandon this place. Too many memories have bound us to it!"

"It was here that we came to know Captain Nemo," said Cyrus Smith.

"Only here will your memory live on undiminished!" added Harbert.

"And it is here that I will lie in eternal slumber, if …" the captain answered.

Here he hesitated, and rather than finish his sentence, he merely said:

"Mr. Smith, I would like to speak to you … to you alone!"

Respecting the wish of the dying man, the engineer's companions withdrew.

For a few minutes, Cyrus Smith remained closeted with Captain Nemo; he soon called his friends into the room again, but he did not reveal what he had heard.

Gideon Spilett observed the invalid with close attention. Only his great mental vitality sustained him now, and this last remnant of strength would soon be powerless to combat his physical weakness.

The day ended with no change in his condition. Not for a moment did the colonists leave the *Nautilus*. Night had come again, still indiscernible from within the crypt.

Captain Nemo was not in pain; he was simply fading away. Although pale with the approach of death, his noble face was serene. From time to time a word escaped his lips, nearly inaudible, but clearly related to some moment of his strange existence. The colonists watched helplessly as the life ebbed from his body. Already his extremities were growing cold.

Once or twice more he spoke to the assembled colonists, smiling with that final smile that continues even unto death.

A little after midnight, Captain Nemo made one last movement, crossing his arms as if it was thus that he wanted to die.

Slowly the Nautilus *began to sink ...*

By one o'clock, life had receded to his eyes alone. A final flame flickered in the pupils that had once burned with such an ardent fire. Then he gently expired, murmuring these words:

"God and homeland!"

Cyrus Smith bent down to close the eyes of the one who was once Prince Dakkar, now no longer even Captain Nemo.

Harbert and Pencroff wept. Ayrton wiped away a furtive tear. Neb knelt beside the reporter, who stood motionless as a statue.

Cyrus Smith raised one hand over the dead man's head.

"May God keep his soul!" he said, and, turning to his friends again, he added:

"Let us pray for the one we have lost!"

———

A few hours later, the colonists fulfilled their promise to the captain, and faithfully executed his final wish.

They left the *Nautilus,* bearing the keepsake willed to them by their benefactor, the jewel box that held a hundred fortunes.

The marvelous salon was carefully sealed, still flooded with light, and the metal door of the hatchway was screwed shut. Not a single drop of water could now enter the chambers of the *Nautilus.*

With this, the colonists climbed into the rowboat, still moored to the side of the undersea ship.

They rowed to the stern of the *Nautilus.* There, on the waterline, they found the two taps that controlled the reservoirs and allowed the ship to surface and dive at will.

The taps were opened, the reservoirs filled with water, and slowly the *Nautilus* began to sink.

The colonists watched it drift gently to the bottom, its powerful lights shining through the transparent waters as the crypt gradually dimmed. Finally those electrical effluences faded in turn, and soon the *Nautilus,* now the grave of Captain Nemo, lay at the bottom of the sea.

XVIII

The Colonists' Meditations.—The Shipbuilding Resumes.—
January 1st, 1869.—A Plume of Smoke at the Volcano's
Summit.—First Symptoms of an Eruption.—Ayrton and Cyrus
Smith at the Sheepfold.—Observations at Dakkar Crypt.—What
Captain Nemo Told the Engineer.

At daybreak, the colonists silently rowed to the entrance of the cavern, henceforth to be known as "Dakkar Crypt," in memory of Captain Nemo. The tide was low, and they slipped effortlessly through the archway as the water lapped at its basalt piers.

The boat was left at the entrance, well protected from the waves. As an added precaution, Pencroff, Neb, and Ayrton hauled it onto a small beach to one side of the crypt, where no harm could come to it.

The storm had ended as daylight returned. A few final rumbles of thunder could be heard faintly in the west. The rain had stopped, but clouds still covered the sky. October, the first month of the austral spring, had not begun in a promising way, and the wind's tendency to jump from one point of the compass to another suggested unstable weather ahead.

Cyrus Smith and his companions set out from Dakkar Crypt toward the sheepfold. Neb and Harbert carefully disconnected the wire the captain had laid, for which a use might be found at some later time.

The colonists spoke little as they walked. The events of the night of October 15th had left a profound impression in their minds. Captain Nemo was no more—the man they had once imagined as a genie, the stranger in whose protective shadow they had so long lived. He and his *Nautilus* lay deep in the abyss, leaving them with a sense of isolation more intense than ever before. In a sense, they had come to rely on his powerful influence, and now they were forced to accept that they would never feel that influence again. Not even Gideon Spilett, not even Cyrus Smith himself could banish that thought from his mind. Thus, in deep silence, they walked homeward along Sheepfold Road.

By nine o'clock in the morning, the colonists were back in Granite House.

They had agreed to devote all their energy to the construction of the ship, and Cyrus Smith threw himself into this task far more vigorously than before. They could not know what the future might hold, but with a seaworthy vessel, sturdy enough for a voyage of some duration and able to withstand the weather's rigors, their safety would be assured. If, on completing the ship, the colonists still hesitated to set out for the Polynesian archipelagoes or the shores of New Zealand, they could at least sail to Tabor Island and leave word of Ayrton. The Scottish yacht might return at any time, and this was a precaution they could ill afford to neglect.

And so they returned to their project. Cyrus Smith, Pencroff, and Ayrton worked without respite, assisted by Neb, Gideon Spilett, and Harbert when no other pressing task occupied them. The ship would have to be ready in five months, which is to say at the beginning of March, if they wanted to visit Tabor Island before the equinoctial gales made the journey impossible. Thus, not a moment was wasted. Fortunately, their careful salvage operation had preserved the rigging from the *Speedy*; they could thus concentrate all their efforts on their vessel's hull.

These important labors occupied the last weeks of 1868, to the virtual exclusion of all others. After two and a half months, the timbers had been put in place, and the first planking was fitted. Already they could see that Cyrus Smith had designed a first-rate ship, both swift and sturdy. Pencroff's passion for his work was all-consuming, and he grumbled openly whenever one of his fellow workers dropped the carpenter's hatchet to take up the hunter's rifle. To be sure, it was important that they maintain their reserves for the coming winter; nonetheless, the doughty sailor was never pleased to see his workers absent from the shipyard. On such occasions, muttering under his breath all the while, he did the work of six men, fueled purely by anger.

It was a summer of wild weather. Again and again the same ritual was repeated: after a few days of stifling heat, the accumulated electricity saturating the atmosphere was suddenly discharged in the form of fearsome and violent storms. Only rarely was the rolling of distant thunder not to be heard, a slow, quiet rumble, muted but unrelenting, such as one often finds in the equatorial regions of the globe.

January 1st, 1869, was marked by a storm of particular severity. Bolts of lighting rained down on the island, and a number of great trees were sheared off by the force of the electrical current, including one of the enormous nettle trees that shaded the poultry yard at the southern end of the lake. Could this meteorological disturbance somehow be related to the phenomena then taking place in the island's entrails? Was the aerial commotion a response to the commotion deep within the earth? Cyrus Smith came to think this quite likely, for the development of these storms was accompanied by a recrudescence of the volcanic symptoms.

It was on January 3rd that Harbert, climbing to Longview Plateau at dawn to saddle one of the dauws, noticed an enormous plume of smoke unfurling from atop the volcano.

He immediately alerted the others, and they came running to observe the summit of Mount Franklin.

"Oh," cried Pencroff, "so it's not just steam anymore! The giant isn't merely breathing now; he seems to have taken up smoking!"

The sailor's image quite accurately captured the new developments at the volcano's mouth. For three months the crater had emitted great clouds of steam—sometimes quite thick, sometimes less so—released by the boiling mineral substances within. Now the steam had given way to a gray column of dense smoke, more than three hundred feet wide at its base and spreading like an enormous mushroom some seven to eight hundred feet above the mountaintop.

"The chimney's caught fire," said Gideon Spilett.

"And we have no way of extinguishing it!" added Harbert.

"Volcanoes need to be swept out now and then," said Neb, in all apparent seriousness.

"Well, Neb," cried Pencroff, "would you like to take on the job?"

And he let out a great roar of laughter.

Cyrus Smith walked a few steps away and closely observed the dense smoke that streamed from Mount Franklin, cocking his ear as if to listen for distant rumblings. Then, returning to his companions:

"My friends, we must face the fact that our situation has undergone a great change. No longer is the magma merely boiling; it has now caught fire, and we may expect an eruption at any time!"

"Well then, Mr. Smith, we'll all watch the eruption," cried Pencroff, "and if it's a good one we'll all applaud! I don't see why this should concern us overmuch!"

"I do not disagree, Pencroff," answered Cyrus Smith. "The lava's usual route is still clear, and until now the shape of the crater has always directed the flow to the north. Nevertheless…"

"Nevertheless, nothing good can come from an eruption, and it would be a far better thing for us if this one never happened," said the reporter.

"Who knows?" the sailor answered. "There might be some sort of useful or precious materials inside that volcano, and as soon as the mountain kindly spits them out for us, we can put them to good use!"

Cyrus Smith shook his head, seeing no possible benefits from this sudden development. He could not look on the consequences of an eruption as lightly as Pencroff. For while the orientation of the crater would no doubt protect their forests and fields, other, more dangerous complications were still to be feared. Eruptions are not infrequently accompanied by earthquakes, and an island such as theirs, of such varied composition—basalt on one side, granite on the other, lava fields in the north, loose soil in the south, forming an assemblage none too solidly interlinked—might conceivably be ripped apart by a formidable seismic force. Thus, while the eruption itself posed no very serious threat, any major shift in the island's terrestrial structure might well have the gravest of consequences.

Ayrton lay down and pressed his ear to the ground; then, turning to his companions, he said: "I hear a sort of muted rumble, like a rolling cart loaded with iron bars."

Listening intently, the colonists realized that Ayrton was not mistaken. Sometimes the rumbling was mingled with subterranean roars, suddenly swelling in a sort of *rinforzando* and then gradually fading away, as if a strong gust of wind had blown through the depths of the globe. For the moment, however, they heard no detonations in the proper sense of the word. From this they deduced that the vapors and smoke were flowing freely through the chimney, and given the great size of the safety valve, there was no cause to fear sudden dislocation or explosion.

"Well then!" said Pencroff. "Could we not go back to work now? Mount Franklin may smoke, bellow, moan, vomit fire and flame; that's no excuse to be idle! Come along, Ayrton, Neb, Harbert, Mr. Cyrus, Mr. Spilett— today we need every available hand! We're going to install the ribbands, and twelve arms won't be too many. Two months from now, I want to see our new *Bonadventure*—because we will keep that name, won't we?—floating in the waters of Port Balloon! There's not an hour to be wasted!"

With their arms thus requisitioned by Pencroff, the colonists walked down to the shipyard and proceeded to the installation of the ribbands, which are stout planks that girdle the ship's hull, securely maintaining the timbers of its frame. This was a formidable undertaking, requiring all the strength the six colonists could muster.

They thus spent January 3rd hard at work, little thinking of the volcano, which in any case they could not see from the beach below Granite House. A bright sun shone in a brilliant blue sky, but once or twice its light was dimmed by a passing cloud of dense smoke, carried westward by the winds from the sea. Cyrus Smith and Gideon Spilett took note of these brief veilings of the sun, and remarked on the development in the volcanic phenomenon that they suggested; nevertheless, the work went on unabated. Clearly, from every point of view, it was in their best interests to finish the boat as quickly as possible. A cloud of uncertainty hung over their future, and the ship would more fully guarantee their safety. Indeed, might it not one day be their only refuge?

After their evening meal, Cyrus Smith, Gideon Spilett, and Harbert returned to Longview Plateau. Night had fallen, and only in darkness could they see if the vapors and smoke were now mingled with flames or incandescent materials thrown out by the volcano.

"The crater is on fire!" cried Harbert, arriving at the plateau before his less sprightly companions.

Six miles from where they stood, Mount Franklin appeared as a gigantic torch, topped with a number of writhing, sooty flames. Through the smoke, no doubt mingled with scoria and ash, the fire only dimly illuminated the night. A sort of tawny glow hung over the island, silhouetting the tangled forms of the woods. Immense wreaths of smoke obscured the heavens, here and there punctuated by shining stars.

"It's making very rapid progress!" said the engineer.

"That's no surprise," answered the reporter. "It's been quite some time since the volcano awoke. You remember, Cyrus, we first saw the steam as we were searching the foothills for Captain Nemo's retreat. And if I'm not mistaken, that was around October 15th?"

"Yes!" answered Harbert. "Two and a half months ago!"

"For ten weeks the subterranean fires have smoldered," Gideon Spilett continued. "I'm not surprised that they've finally burst through to the top!"

"Do you feel a vibration in the earth?" asked Cyrus Smith.

"I do," answered Gideon Spilett, "but that's a long way from an earthquake..."

"I'm not suggesting there's an earthquake at hand," answered Cyrus Smith. "May God protect us from that! No, these vibrations are caused by the ferment of the central fire. The earth's crust is nothing other than the wall of a boiler, and as you know, the wall of a boiler vibrates like a sounding board under the pressure of the gases within. And that is precisely what is now happening."

"Look at the wonderful spray of fire!" cried Harbert.

For at that moment the crater seemed to have released a sort of fireworks display, its brilliance undiminished by the smoke and steam. Thousands of sparks and glowing fragments flew in all directions. Some of them shot higher than the dense shroud of smoke, and as they burst through it they left behind a trail of incandescent dust. These bursts of fire were accompanied by a long string of loud blasts, like the thundering of a machine-gun installation.

After an hour, Cyrus Smith, the reporter, and the boy left Longview Plateau and returned to Granite House. The engineer seemed pensive, even preoccupied, so much so that Gideon Spilett was compelled to ask if he sensed some imminent danger, caused directly or indirectly by the eruption.

"Yes and no," answered Cyrus Smith.

"Nevertheless," the reporter went on, "the only real catastrophe that could befall us would be an earthquake, would it not? And since the hot gases and lava have an unobstructed passage to the exterior, I don't believe that's an immediate threat."

"And for that very reason," answered Cyrus Smith, "I do not fear an earthquake in the usual sense of convulsions provoked by an expansion of gases under the ground. Nevertheless, a disaster could well come about from other causes."

"What causes, my dear Cyrus?"

"I am not entirely sure...I shall have to see...I must return to the mountain...Within a few days I will know more fully what we might expect."

Gideon Spilett did not press the engineer further, and soon, despite the increasing intensity of the volcano's resounding blasts, the inhabitants of Granite House were sound asleep.

Three days went by—January 4th, 5th, and 6th. The construction of the ship continued, and, without explaining his reasons, the engineer urgently hurried his companions on. A dark cloud of sinister aspect hung over Mount Franklin, and the crater spewed flames and incandescent rocks. Some of these stones were thrown straight into the air, then fell back into the crater at once; and Pencroff, who looked on the volcanic phenomenon purely as entertainment, was led to say:

"Look! the giant is playing cup-and-ball! the giant is juggling!"

These stones were immediately swallowed by the abyss, and this suggested that the lava had not yet been pushed to the crater's rim by the mounting pressure within the central chimney; nor did any torrent of lava flow from the great rift on the crater's northeast side, partially visible from Longview Plateau.

Meanwhile, no matter how pressing their shipbuilding tasks, other concerns required the colonists' presence elsewhere on the island. The most urgent of these was a visit to the sheepfold, to replenish the supply of fodder for their mouflons and goats. It was agreed that Ayrton would make this trip the following day, January 7th. Well accustomed to the task, he had no need of assistance, and so it was with considerable surprise that the colonists heard the engineer say to him:

"Since you're going to the sheepfold tomorrow, I'll accompany you."

"What! Mr. Cyrus!" cried the sailor. "Our workdays are numbered, and with both of you gone that makes four fewer arms to work on our ship!"

"We shall return the next day, never fear," answered Cyrus Smith. "I really must go to the sheepfold...I want to assess the progress of the eruption."

"The eruption! the eruption!" came Pencroff's irritable reply. "I've had quite enough of that blasted eruption! I assure you, it's the very last thing on my mind!"

In spite of the sailor's opinions, the engineer kept to his plan. Harbert longed to accompany Cyrus Smith, but he did not wish to vex Pencroff by his absence.

At sunrise the next day, Cyrus Smith and Ayrton hitched up the two dauws and climbed into the cart, setting out for the sheepfold at a fast trot.

Great clouds drifted over the forest, swelled by the incessant smoke from the crater of Mount Franklin. The clouds lumbered heavily through the atmosphere, clearly composed of an amalgam of heterogeneous substances. It was not to the smoke alone that they owed their strange, dense opacity, for within that smoke were suspended pulverized scoria, pozzolana dust, and gray ash as fine as cornstarch. So minute is the ash thrown out by volcanoes that it can remain floating in the air for many months; thus, after the Icelandic eruption of 1783, the atmosphere was choked for more than a year with volcanic dust, virtually impenetrable to the rays of the sun.

Generally, however, this pulverized matter settles rapidly to the ground, and so it was in this case. No sooner had Cyrus Smith and Ayrton arrived at the sheepfold than a sort of blackish snow began to fall, similar to a light gunpowder, instantaneously modifying the appearance of the ground. Trees, pastures, everything disappeared beneath a layer of ash that soon grew to a thickness of several inches. Fortunately, however, the wind was from the northeast, and the greater part of the cloud was quickly dispersed over the sea.

"That's a very strange thing, Mr. Smith," said Ayrton.

"A very serious thing," the engineer replied. "From the presence of this pozzolana, these pulverized pumice stones, in a word this mineral dust, we may conclude that a great disturbance is taking place deep within the volcano."

"Is there nothing we can do?"

"Nothing but watch as the phenomenon develops. You see to your tasks at the sheepfold, Ayrton; in the meantime, I will be on the northern slopes of the mountain, for I wish to observe the state of the eruption. And then..."

"Then, Mr. Smith?"

"Then we will make an excursion to Dakkar Crypt...I want to see...At any rate, I will return to meet you in two hours."

Ayrton entered the enclosure, and as he awaited the engineer's return he tended to the mouflons and goats. He found them vaguely uneasy and agitated, no doubt troubled by the early symptoms of the eruption.

Meanwhile, Cyrus Smith climbed to the ridge in the eastern foothills and continued along Red Creek until he arrived at the sulfurous spring they had discovered in their first exploration of this area.

Much had changed! He now counted not one column of smoke rising from the earth, but thirteen; and the vapors shot from the ground as if

Much had changed!

violently expelled by some sort of piston. The crust of the earth was clearly under a terrible pressure in this part of the globe. The atmosphere was saturated with sulfurous gases, as well as hydrogen and carbonic acid, mingled with a great quantity of steam. The plain was strewn with volcanic tufa—powdery ashes solidified over time into solid blocks of stone—and, leaning down, Cyrus Smith felt that they were trembling. Nevertheless, he found no sign of a new flow of lava.

This was confirmed by the engineer's observation of the northern flank of Mount Franklin. Eddies of smoke and fire poured from the summit, a hail of scoria fell to the ground, but no lava flowed from the crater's broken rim, proving that the volcanic materials had not yet risen to the top of the chimney.

"I'd much rather they had!" said Cyrus Smith to himself. "Then, at least, I could be certain that the flow would be confined to its established route. How can we be sure that some new crater is not about to open up? Nevertheless, that is not the real danger. Captain Nemo knew it well! No! that is not where the real danger lies!"

Cyrus Smith continued as far as the vast causeway whose two arms embraced Shark Gulf. Here he made a careful examination of the ancient striations of lava, which allowed him to date the last eruption of the volcano to a time deep in the island's past.

Now he retraced his steps, his ear attuned to the subterranean rumblings, rolling like slow thunder and punctuated by sharp detonations. By nine o'clock in the morning, he was back at the sheepfold.

He found Ayrton waiting.

"The animals have all they need, Mr. Smith," said Ayrton.

"Good, Ayrton."

"They seem uneasy, Mr. Smith."

"Yes, they listen to their instincts, and instinct is never wrong."

"Whenever you'd like to..."

"Bring a lantern and flint, Ayrton," answered Cyrus Smith, "and let us be off."

Ayrton did as he was told. The dauws were unhitched and allowed to wander freely over the pastures. The gate was locked from the outside, and Cyrus Smith led Ayrton along the narrow path that led toward the western shore.

The surface beneath their feet was soft with the powdery ash dropped by the cloud. They saw no sign of quadrupeds in the woods. Even the birds had fled. Sometimes a passing breeze stirred up the layer of ash, and the two colonists lost sight of each other amid the dense, whirling dust. They were forced to cover their eyes and mouths with handkerchiefs to avoid being blinded and suffocated.

The soft soil slowed their progress. The air was heavy, as if a part of its oxygen had been burned away, and breathing itself soon proved difficult. Every hundred steps, they had to stop and catch their breath. It was thus after ten o'clock when the engineer and his companion came to the ridge overlooking the pile of basalt and porphyry boulders that formed the island's northwestern coast.

They began to make their way down the steep slope, along the same perilous route that had led them to Dakkar Crypt that stormy night. The descent proved less treacherous by the light of day, and the layer of ash now coating the smooth rocks offered a more secure purchase on their rounded surfaces.

Soon they reached the ledge set into the flank of the slope, some forty feet above the sea, and followed its gentle inclination down to the water's edge. The tide was low, but there was no beach to be seen, and dirty waves, sullied by volcanic dust, crashed against the basalt boulders that littered the shore.

Soon Cyrus Smith and Ayrton had found the entrance to Dakkar Crypt, and they stopped under an overhanging boulder at the lower end of the ledge.

"This is where we should find the rowboat," said the engineer.

"Here it is, Mr. Smith," Ayrton replied. It was floating beneath the vault at the cavern's entrance. Ayrton now drew it toward them.

"Let us embark, Ayrton."

The two colonists climbed into the boat. A slight undulation of the waves pushed it under the low arch and into the cavern, and there Ayrton lit their lantern with the flint. Taking up the oars, he set the lantern on the stem of the boat to light their way. Cyrus Smith manned the tiller and guided the boat through the darkness of the crypt.

No more did the *Nautilus* fill the cavern with a thousand diamantine points of light. Perhaps the ship's power source still functioned; perhaps the electrical radiance continued to shine in the depths of the sea; but not a single glimmer escaped the abyss that was Captain Nemo's final resting place.

The lantern cast only a meager light; nevertheless, the engineer could easily find his way along the cavern's right-hand wall. A sepulchral silence hung over the entrance to the crypt, but as they pushed farther inside, Cyrus Smith distinctly heard rumblings from the entrails of the mountain.

"The volcano," he said.

This sound was soon accompanied by a sharp odor, given off by the chemical reactions deep within the earth. The engineer and his companion were choked by the sulfurous fumes.

"It is just as Captain Nemo feared!" Cyrus Smith murmured, his face growing slightly pale. "But we must continue to the end."

"Forward!" answered Ayrton, bending over the oars again, and propelling the boat toward the apse of the crypt.

Twenty-five minutes after they had entered the cavern, the boat stopped at the back wall.

Cyrus Smith stood up on his bench and slowly shone the lantern over the surface of the rock. This was all that stood between the crypt and the volcano's central chimney. How thick was the wall? A hundred feet, or ten? There was no way to know. But judging by the volume of the subterranean rumbling, it could not have been very thick.

The engineer carefully examined the wall along a horizontal line; then he hung the lantern from the end of an oar and once again shone it over the basalt, at a higher level than before.

There, through a series of scarcely visible cracks between the interlocking prismatic blocks, he saw a continuous stream of acrid smoke—the source of the foul odor in the cavern. The wall was riddled with such fissures; some of them, more clearly visible than the others, descended to within two or three feet of the water.

Now Cyrus Smith stood still, lost in thought. Then he once again murmured these words:

"Yes! the captain was right! This is where the danger lies, and a terrible danger it is!"

Ayrton made no response. On a sign from Cyrus Smith, he took up the oars again, and a half-hour later he and the engineer reemerged from Dakkar Crypt.

XIX

*Cyrus Smith's Account of His Observations.—The Construction
of the Ship Is Hastened.—A Final Visit to the Sheepfold.—The
Battle Between Fire and Water.—What Remains on the Island's
Surface.—The Decision to Launch the Ship.—The Night of
March 8th.*

The next morning, January 8th, after a day and a night at the sheepfold,
now replenished with food for the animals, Cyrus Smith and Ayrton
returned to Granite House.

On his return, the engineer immediately summoned his companions
and informed them that Lincoln Island was faced with a terrible danger,
which no human force could ward off.

"My friends," he said, with deep emotion in his voice, "Lincoln Island
is not destined to last as long as the Earth itself. It is fated for destruction
in the very near future. The cause of its annihilation lies within the island
itself, and it cannot be stopped!"

In mute incomprehension, the colonists looked first at one another,
then at the engineer.

"Explain yourself, Cyrus!" said Gideon Spilett.

"I will," answered Cyrus Smith, "or rather, I will pass on to you the
explanation given to me by Captain Nemo in our brief private conversation."

"Captain Nemo!" the colonists cried.

"Yes. Before he died, he was determined to do us one last favor!"

"One last favor!" cried Pencroff. "One last favor! Just you wait! He may
be dead, but I know we haven't seen the last of his favors yet!"

"But what did Captain Nemo say to you?" asked the reporter.

"Let me tell you, my friends," the engineer replied. "Lincoln Island is of a different nature from the other islands of the Pacific. Because of a certain peculiarity of its formation, which Captain Nemo revealed to me, the island's very bedrock is doomed, sooner or later, to burst apart in a violent explosion."

"Burst apart! Lincoln Island! Come now!" cried Pencroff, unable to repress a dismissive shrug, in spite of all his respect for Cyrus Smith.

"Listen, Pencroff," the engineer continued. "This is what Captain Nemo discovered, and this is what I myself confirmed yesterday in my examination of Dakkar Crypt. The cavern runs far beneath the island, up to the edge of the volcano. Only the great wall at its apse separates it from the central chimney, and that wall is riddled with fissures and cracks. Even now, the sulfurous gases that have built up within the volcano are steadily streaming into the cavern."

"And?" asked Pencroff, his brow deeply furrowed.

"And, under the pressure of those gases, the fissures are growing. Slowly but surely, the wall is breaking open, and soon the waters of the cavern will pour into the chimney."

"Well, that's fine, then!" Pencroff retorted, still trying to make light of their situation. "The water will put out the volcano, and that will be that!"

"Yes, that will be that!" answered Cyrus Smith. "The day the sea pours through the wall, into the chimney, and onto the boiling magma in the bowels of the island, that day, Pencroff, Lincoln Island will be blown into a thousand pieces, just as might happen to Sicily if the Mediterranean poured into Mount Etna!"

The colonists made no response to the engineer's forceful affirmation. The danger they faced was now clear.

It must be added that Cyrus Smith had in no way exaggerated this threat. Volcanoes are generally found in the vicinity of oceans or lakes, and it has sometimes been thought that a sudden flow of such waters into the volcano's chimney might very well extinguish them forthwith. But any attempt to carry out this plan would incur a strong risk of shattering a vast area of land, for the effect would be not unlike firing a bullet into a hot boiler. Rushing into an enclosed area whose temperature might be measured in the thousands of degrees, the water would be vaporized instantly, with such force that no wall of rock could ever withstand the pressure.

There could thus be no doubt. An explosion of monumental proportions now threatened the colony's home, and the island would continue to exist only as long as the wall of Dakkar Crypt survived. It was not a matter of months, nor of weeks; it was a matter of days, perhaps hours!

Great was the colonists' grief on hearing the engineer's words! It was not the thought of their own peril that affected them so deeply, but the imminent destruction of the shores that had offered them shelter, of an island grown fertile under their patient hands, an island they had come to love, and dearly hoped to see flourish one day! So much exertion expended in vain, so much wasted labor!

Pencroff could not hold back a tear, and he made no attempt to conceal it as it rolled down his cheek.

The conversation continued some moments longer. They discussed their prospects for salvation; in the end, however, they realized that their time was fast running out, and that the shipbuilding would have to be accelerated at a prodigious rate, for that half-finished vessel was now the only hope for the colonists of Lincoln Island!

All hands would henceforth be required at the shipyard. What could be gained from harvesting their wheat or vegetables, from hunting, from adding to their supply of provisions? Already their storerooms and kitchens held enough—and indeed more than enough—to stock their ship, no matter how long the voyage might last! Only one task remained to them now: to finish the ship before disaster struck.

And so they returned to the shipyard and set to work at a frenzied pace. The planking was half finished by January 23rd. Until that day, no change had been observed at the volcano's summit. Steam and smoke continued to pour from the crater, shot through with flames and incandescent stones. But on the night of the twenty-third, the cone that once formed the volcano's hat was blown off under the effect of the rising lava. A deafening crash echoed through the air. Believing that the island had been rent asunder, the colonists rushed out of Granite House.

It was about two o'clock in the morning.

The sky was ablaze. The upper cone—a mass of stone a thousand feet high, weighing billions of pounds—had been thrown onto the island, and the earth trembled under the blow. Fortunately, the cone was inclined toward the north, and it fell onto the plain of sand and tufa that stretched from the volcano to the sea. A broad crater lay in its former place, from which poured a brilliant, fiery light, reflected and diffused throughout the heavens, bathing the island in an incandescent glow. The magma had risen up to the new crater, and now a torrent of lava spilled out in long cascades, like water overflowing a basin, and a thousand serpents of fire slithered over the mountain's rocky flanks.

"The sheepfold! the sheepfold!" cried Ayrton.

For the orientation of the new crater was indeed sending the lava directly toward the sheepfold. Red Creek, Jacamar Woods, and all the fertile regions of the island were now under threat of immediate destruction.

Ayrton's shout sent them running to the dauws' stable, where they hitched up the cart at once. A single thought occupied every colonist's mind: to race to the sheepfold and give the animals their freedom!

They arrived shortly before three o'clock in the morning. The desperate bellows that greeted them eloquently expressed the depth of the animals' terror. An incandescent torrent of liquefied minerals was pouring from the foothill onto the pasture, steadily eating away at the palisade. Ayrton threw open the gates, and the animals fled in all directions, wild with panic.

An hour later, the boiling lava had spread over the sheepfold. The little rill was instantly vaporized, and the house burst into flames, blazing like a pile of thatch. The lava consumed everything in its path, down to the last upright of the palisade. Soon there was nothing left!

The colonists had tried to fight off this invasion; they had tried, but all their efforts went for naught. Man is no match for such cataclysms, and mad indeed is he who struggles against the forces of nature!

A new day had dawned—January 24th. Before returning to Granite House, Cyrus Smith and his companions attempted to determine the course the lava would now take. The ground sloped steadily from Mount Franklin to the eastern shore, and despite the dense growth in Jacamar Woods, they feared that the torrent would soon be upon Longview Plateau.

"The lake will protect us," said Gideon Spilett.

"I hope so!" was Cyrus Smith's only reply.

The colonists had sought to continue as far as the plain where Mount Franklin's upper cone had fallen, but the lava barred their route. Streams of molten rock flowed through the valleys of Red Creek and Falls River, turning the water to steam as the lava advanced. The colonists could not hope to cross this torrent, and soon they realized that they had no choice but to retreat. The loss of its crown had profoundly altered the volcano's appearance. What had once been its summit was now merely a long, flat expanse. Two separate streams of lava poured over the southern and eastern sides. A thick cloud of smoke, ash, and steam gathered above the new crater, and great crashes of thunder punctuated the mountain's deep rumble. Igneous rocks spewed from its mouth, shooting a thousand feet into the air and bursting amid the clouds, sending a spray of shards rocketing through the sky. Bolts of lightning streaked through the heavens, as if in response to the volcano's fury.

By seven o'clock in the morning the colonists' position had become untenable, and they retreated to Jacamar Woods. White hot stones were raining down all around them; worse yet, the lava had now overflowed the bed of Red Creek, and threatened to cut off Sheepfold Road. The outermost trees of the forest had caught fire, bursting like firecrackers under the pressure of their boiling sap; here and there, a tree more desiccated than the others still stood, surrounded by a lake of molten rock.

And so the colonists returned to Sheepfold Road. They walked slowly, looking over their shoulders to observe the lava's advance. The ground's inclination was speeding the torrent eastward. The lava hardened as it cooled, only to be covered a moment later by a fresh wave of boiling magma.

The situation in the valley of Red Creek had greatly deteriorated. The forest had become a blazing inferno, and enormous wreaths of smoke rolled through the air as the flames licked at the trunks of the trees.

The colonists stopped near the lake, a half-mile from the mouth of Red Creek. A question of life or death was about to be decided.

Long practiced in the appraisal of desperate situations, Cyrus Smith turned to his companions. Knowing them to be men who did not fear the truth, no matter how disturbing it might be, he then said:

"Either the lake will stop the flow and a part of the island will be spared complete devastation, or else the lava will enter the Forests of the Far West, and not a single tree, not a single plant will survive. We will then find ourselves on a pile of denuded rocks, with nothing to hope for but death. And we shall not have long to wait, for soon the island will be no more!"

"In that case," cried Pencroff, crossing his arms and stamping his foot, "there's no point working on the ship, is there?"

"Pencroff," answered Cyrus Smith, "a man must do his duty, right to the bitter end!"

The colonists' position had become untenable ...

The river of lava had now found a path through the magnificent trees of the forest. Leaving behind it a trail of devastation, it arrived at the edge of the lake. Here the ground inclined slightly upward; if the slope were more pronounced, it might be enough to hold back the torrent.

"To work!" cried Cyrus Smith.

The engineer's companions had divined his intentions at once: the flow of lava must be canalized, so to speak, and forced to run into the lake.

The colonists ran to their workshop at the Chimneys, returning with armloads of shovels, picks, and axes. The next several hours were spent felling great trees, then piling them up to build earth-covered terraces. In the end—after what seemed like no more than a few minutes—they had erected a dike three feet high and several hundred paces long.

None too soon had they finished their work, for moments later the liquefied stone encountered the base of their embankment. The lava surged up like a swollen river about to overflow its banks, threatening to submerge the last remaining obstacle protecting the Far West... But no, the dike held back the flow. For a few chilling moments the lava seemed to hesitate; but then it began to pour into Lake Grant in a cascade twenty feet high.

Breathless, motionless, silent, the colonists looked on as the two elements battled it out.

What a spectacle was this combat between water and fire! What pen could depict the marvelous horror of the scene, and what brush could paint it? A sharp hiss filled the air as the water evaporated on contact with the boiling lava. Vast clouds of steam poured high into the heavens, as if the valves of a colossal boiler had been abruptly thrown open. Nevertheless, however great the volume of water, it could not fail to be absorbed in the end; for no stream now replenished the lake, whereas an inexhaustible source fed the flow of lava with continuous floods of fresh incandescent stone.

The first streams of lava instantly solidified on falling into the lake, and soon a pile of hardened rock arose from the waters. A new stream of lava poured onto this surface, glowing red for a few moments more, then gradually turning to stone. Little by little a sort of jetty was formed, spreading over the surface of the lake, replacing the vaporized water with stone. The air was filled with sharp cracks and a deafening hiss. Swept offshore by the wind, the huge clouds of steam condensed in the cool air, and rain began to fall over the sea. The jetty grew longer and broader as each drop of lava solidified upon the last. What had once been a tranquil expanse of water now appeared as a vast sheet of smoking rocks, as if some geological upheaval had thrust thousands of buried boulders to the surface. Imagine a body of water whipped up by a hurricane, then suddenly frozen by a blast of twenty-degree air; such was the look of the lake three hours after the coming of the lava.

This time, fire would prove stronger than water.

Nevertheless, the diversion of the lava into Lake Grant offered the colonists a reprieve of several days. For the moment, Longview Plateau, Granite House, and the shipyard were out of danger. These few days would be spent hastily finishing the ship's planking and sealing the joints as best they could. They could then launch the ship and take refuge on the sea, even if it meant attempting to rig her as she floated in the water. The final explosion could come at any moment, and no part of the island was safe. The very walls of Granite House, once so invincible, might come tumbling down around them without a moment's notice!

Over the next six days, from January 25th to the 30th, the colonists worked on the ship with the speed of twenty men, and precious few were their moments of rest. The brilliant flames that shot from the crater allowed them to work both night and day. The flow of lava had not ceased, but might have abated somewhat—a fortunate thing indeed, for Lake Grant was almost entirely full, and a fresh flow of lava over the solidified surface would inevitably have streamed onto Longview Plateau, and from there to the beach.

But while this side of the island was thus partially protected, the same could not be said of the regions to the west.

For nothing stood in the path of the second lava flow as it coursed through the valley of Falls River. The valley was wide and open, and allowed the incandescent liquid to spread throughout the Far West. Parched by the baking heat of summer, the forest blazed like a tinderbox; the flames leaped from one trunk to the next, and raced through the tree-tops high above the ground. Indeed, fed by the canopy of interlacing branches, the fire spread through the air well ahead of the flowing lava below.

Every furred and feathered beast of the forests—wildcats, jaguars, boars, capybaras, kolas—had fled in terror toward the Mercy and Shelduck Fens, just across the Port Balloon road. Urgently occupied with their labors, the colonists were little concerned by the proximity of dangerous animals. They themselves had abandoned Granite House; their pressing tasks left no time to settle into the Chimneys, and they now lived at a campsite near the mouth of the Mercy.

Cyrus Smith and Gideon Spilett climbed to Longview Plateau every day. Harbert sometimes accompanied them, but never Pencroff. He knew full well what devastation the volcano had wrought, and he could not bear to look on his island in its current lamentable state!

It was indeed a wrenching sight. The forests had been leveled; one single stand of green trees remained, at the very end of Serpentine Peninsula. Here and there stood a gnarled, blackened trunk, branchless and forlorn. Nothing had survived the relentless flow of liquid fire. What was once a luxuriant woodland was now more desolate than Shelduck Fens; what was once a riot of greenery was now a wasteland strewn with mounds of volcanic tufa. Neither Falls River nor the Mercy would ever again carry a single drop of water toward the sea, and the colonists might surely have died of thirst were it not for the last waters of Lake Grant. For the southern end of their lake had mercifully been spared; the small pond that remained held their entire supply of potable water. To the northwest lay the jagged, inhospitable ridges of the foothills, like a gigantic claw sunk the earth. How appalling was the spectacle before them! How fearsome the prospect! How bitterly the colonists wept for the island they had known—fertile, forested, a place of flowing waters and bountiful harvests, now a bleak and ravaged land of stone, a place where survival itself would have been impossible without their reserves!

"It's heartbreaking!" Gideon Spilett said one day.

"Yes, Spilett," answered the engineer. "May Heaven give us time enough to finish the ship, our last hope, our only refuge!"

"Do you not agree, Cyrus, that the volcano seems to be quieting? The lava still flows, but not as abundantly as before, if I am not mistaken!"

"No matter," answered Cyrus Smith. "Deep in the mountain, the fires are still burning. The wall could crumble at any time. We are like the passengers of a burning ship, unable to extinguish the flames, and knowing that sooner or later the fire will be at the door of the powder magazine! Come, Spilett, come, we must not lose a single hour!"

The lava continued to flow for another week, until February 7th; nevertheless, the eruption's violence never exceeded what they had witnessed in the first few days. Cyrus Smith's greatest fear was that the liquefied rock would find its way onto the beach, for if it did, they could not hope to save the shipyard. But now there arose a new cause for alarm: the colonists had begun to feel vibrations in the island's substructure that disturbed them very deeply indeed.

Soon it was February 20th. The ship could be ready in a month. Would the island hold until then? Cyrus Smith and Pencroff intended to launch the ship as soon as the hull had been made watertight. The decks, the rigging, and the interior could well wait; above all else, the colonists needed a safe refuge away from the island. Perhaps they might moor in Port Balloon, as far as possible from the center of the eruption, for at the mouth of the Mercy, caught between the islet and the wall of granite, their new *Bonadventure* could easily be crushed should the island blow apart. Thus, sparing no effort, they labored to complete the hull.

By March 3rd, they could legitimately hope to launch the ship within ten days.

Hope now returned to the colonists' hearts, so sorely tried indeed in this, their fourth year on Lincoln Island! Even Pencroff seemed to emerge somewhat from the brooding silence inspired in him by the devastation of his beloved domain. His only thoughts now were for his ship, and his only hope.

"We will finish her," he told the engineer, "we will finish her, Mr. Cyrus, and high time too! The equinox will be here before we know it. If we have to, we can put in at Tabor Island and spend the winter there! But Tabor Island after Lincoln Island! Oh! it's too much to bear! I never thought I'd see this day!"

"We must make haste!" the engineer invariably replied.

And so they worked, never wasting a single instant.

"Master," asked Neb a few days later, "do you think this would be happening if Captain Nemo were still alive?"

"Yes, Neb," answered Cyrus Smith.

"Well, I don't!" Pencroff murmured into Neb's ear.

"Nor I!" Neb gravely answered.

The first week of March brought a renewed threat from Mount Franklin. Thousands of strands of glass, made of fluid lava, fell like rain over the ground. A fresh flood of magma rose to the crater, spilling out over the flanks of the volcano, pouring over the hardened tufa and toppling the frail skeletons of the few trees that had withstood the first eruption. New streams of lava flowed along the southwest shore of Lake Grant; soon they had crossed Glycerine Creek and invaded Longview

The air was rent by an explosion.

Plateau, with devastating results. The mill, the outbuildings, the stables, everything the colonists had worked so hard to construct now vanished under the onslaught of the liquid fire. Panic-stricken, the birds fled in all directions. Signs of the most intense terror could be read in the demeanor of Top and Joop, as if their instincts had warned them of impending catastrophe. Much of the island's wildlife had perished in the earlier eruption; most of the survivors huddled in Shelduck Fens, but a few had found shelter on Longview Plateau—a last retreat now lost to them forever. The river of lava flowed over the granite wall, and cataracts of fire began to fall onto the beach. The sublime horror of that spectacle defies all description. At night, with incandescent vapors above and boiling masses below, it seemed a Niagara of molten steel!

The colonists were forced into their retrenchment of last resort. The upper seams of the ship had yet to be sealed; nevertheless, they now had no choice but to launch her into the sea!

The launch was planned for the following morning—the morning of March 9th—and Pencroff and Ayrton quickly saw to the final preparations.

But that night, amid a succession of tremendous explosions, a huge column of steam shot from the crater, rising to an altitude of more than three thousand feet. The wall of Dakkar Crypt had given way at last, and the seawater had poured into the fiery abyss, instantly turning to steam. The pressure mounted within the chimney as the vapors built up far faster than they could escape. The air was rent by an explosion that might have been heard a hundred miles away. Pieces of mountain plummeted into the Pacific, and a few moments later there was only water where Lincoln Island once lay.

XX

An Isolated Rock in the Pacific.—The Last Refuge of the Colonists of Lincoln Island.—Near Death.—An Unexpected Rescue.—Why and How This Came About.—The Last Act of Kindness.—An Island on a Continent.—Captain Nemo's Tomb.

An isolated rock, thirty feet long and fifteen wide, rising scarcely ten feet above the water: such was the one trace of land not swallowed by the Pacific waves.

This was all that remained of the great cliff of Granite House! The wall had toppled to one side and smashed into pieces; piling one atop the other, the huge boulders of the great room had formed a tiny ridge above the waters. Everything else had disappeared into the abyss: the shattered lower cone of Mount Franklin, the lava-stone jaws of Shark Gulf, Longview Plateau, Safety Island, the granite boulders of Port Balloon, the basalt of Dakkar Crypt, even Serpentine Peninsula, so distant from the center of the blast! Nothing was left of Lincoln Island but a single patch of stone, the final refuge for the six colonists and their dog, Top.

The catastrophe had left no other survivors. Birds, apes, quadrupeds, every last living creature had been crushed or drowned. Poor Joop himself had, alas! met his doom as the ground opened up beneath his feet!

But Cyrus Smith, Gideon Spilett, Harbert, Pencroff, Neb, and Ayrton had survived. Huddling beneath their tent, they had been thrown into the sea as the debris of the island began to rain down around them.

They struggled to the surface some half-cable from that wretched pile of rocks. Swimming furiously, they soon hoisted themselves out of the water.

For nine days now they had lived on this barren rock! A few provisions taken from their storerooms before the cataclysm, a bit of fresh water left by the rain among the rocks, such were their sole possessions. Their ship, their last hope, lay shattered on the ocean floor. Escape was out of the question. No fire, and nothing to make fire with. Their fate was no longer in doubt. They were doomed!

It was now March 18th. They had taken great care to spare their meager provisions, but only two days' rations remained. All their learning, all their intelligence were useless to them now. They were helpless, in the hands of God.

Cyrus Smith maintained his usual calm. Gideon Spilett, more agitated, and Pencroff, in the grips of a simmering rage, paced endlessly over the rock. Harbert never left the engineer's side, staring into his face as if to beg for a deliverance that he could not provide. Neb and Ayrton had simply resigned themselves to their fate.

"Blast! blast! blast!" Pencroff often cried. "Oh, for a dinghy, a dory, even a raft! It's only a hundred miles to Tabor Island! But we have nothing, nothing!"

"Captain Nemo was right to die!" Neb said once.

For five days more Cyrus Smith and his wretched companions struggled on, weak with hunger and fatigue, eating only enough to stave off starvation. Harbert and Neb had begun to show signs of delirium.

Could they not harbor some faint glimmer of hope deep within their hearts? They could not! From what source could salvation come? A passing ship? But their experience had taught them all too well that no ship ever plied these waters! Could they hope that the Scottish yacht might even now be steaming toward Tabor Island in search of Ayrton? The coincidence would be nothing short of miraculous, and hence highly unlikely; and in any case they had never left the required message with the coordinates of Ayrton's new home. After a fruitless search of the island, the commander would waste no time before sailing off toward lower latitudes.

No! they must abandon all hope of rescue. Here, alone on this miserable rock, they would slowly die of hunger and thirst—a terrible death indeed!

Already their last strength was failing them, and they lay inanimate and insensible, blind to the world around them. Only Ayrton, pushing himself to the very limit, could still summon the force to raise his head and cast a desperate eye over the deserted seas! . . .

Ayrton mutely reached out...

But now, on the morning of March 24th, Ayrton mutely reached out toward some distant point. He struggled to his knees, then to his feet, gesturing weakly as if to make some sort of signal...

There was a ship within sight of the island! A ship, not idly wandering the oceans, but steaming straight toward their rock! A ship they would surely have seen hours before, if only they had had the strength to watch the horizon!

"The *Duncan*!" murmured Ayrton, and he sank lifeless onto the stone.

———

Nursed back to consciousness, Cyrus Smith and his companions awoke to find themselves safely on board a steamship. They stared at their new surroundings in dazed incomprehension. How had this happened? How did they escape what had seemed an inevitable death?

A single word from Ayrton told them all they needed to know.

"The *Duncan*!" he murmured.

"The *Duncan*!" answered Cyrus Smith.

And, raising his hands to Heaven, he cried:

"Oh! all-powerful God! So it was Your will that we be saved!"

For this was indeed the *Duncan*, Lord Glenarvan's yacht, now commanded by Captain Grant's son, Robert, sent to Tabor Island to bring Ayrton home after twelve years of atonement!...

The colonists were saved, and soon they would see their homeland again!

"Captain Robert," asked Cyrus Smith, "how did you come to this place? Having failed to find Ayrton on Tabor Island, what could have moved you to continue the search one hundred miles to the northeast?"

"Mr. Smith," answered Robert Grant, "my search was for you—not only for Ayrton, but for you and your companions!"

"For us?"

"Why, yes! On Lincoln Island!"

"Lincoln Island!" cried Gideon Spilett, Harbert, Neb, and Pencroff with one voice, profoundly astonished to hear this name spoken.

"How could you know of Lincoln Island," asked Cyrus Smith, "when it does not appear on any published map?"

"I learned of it from the message you left on Tabor Island," answered Robert Grant.

"Message?" cried Gideon Spilett.

"Of course! I have it here," answered Robert Grant, showing them a paper on which were written the latitude and longitude of Lincoln Island, "now home to Ayrton and five American colonists."

"Captain Nemo!..." said Cyrus Smith, reading the note, unmistakably written in the same hand as the message they had found at the sheepfold!

"Oh," said Pencroff, "so it was him who took our *Bonadventure*! He sailed off alone to Tabor Island!..."

"In order to leave this note!" Harbert rejoined.

"So," the sailor cried, "I was right to say that we hadn't yet seen the last of Captain Nemo's good deeds!"

"My friends," said Cyrus Smith in a tone of deep emotion, "may merciful God forever keep the soul of our savior, Captain Nemo!"

The colonists doffed their hats as Cyrus Smith spoke these words, and together they murmured the captain's name.

Just then, Ayrton approached the engineer, saying simply:

"What shall I do with this box?"

It was the jewel box. Ayrton had risked his life to save it in the island's final moments, and now he faithfully delivered it into the hands of the engineer.

"Ayrton! Ayrton!" said Cyrus Smith, deeply moved.

Then, turning to Robert Grant:

"Sir," he added, "you left on that island a guilty man, but you see here before you one who has atoned for his sins, a man who has found his way back to righteousness, a man to whom I am proud to give my hand!"

Robert Grant then heard the strange story of Captain Nemo and the colonists of Lincoln Island. A careful survey was made of the island's remains, for inclusion on future maps of the Pacific; then Captain Grant called out a new heading to his steersman.

Fifteen days later, the colonists disembarked on American soil, returning to a land newly at peace, after a terrible war that had ended with the triumph of justice and liberty.

Of the immense fortune left to them by Captain Nemo, the greater part was used to acquire a vast domain in the state of Iowa. One single pearl, the finest of all, was taken from the jewel box and sent to Lady Glenarvan, in the name of the castaways repatriated by the *Duncan*.

There, to their new domain, the colonists invited all those they had hoped to bring to Lincoln Island, offering them a life of wholesome labor, which is to say a rich and happy life. They founded a great colony, named for the island now vanished beneath the Pacific waves. On their lands lay a river they called the Mercy, a mountain to which they gave the name Mount Franklin, a small lake that became Lake Grant, and a vast expanse of forest, rechristened the Forests of the Far West. It was like an island in the middle of a continent.

There, in the intelligent hands of the engineer and his companions, a prosperous new life was born. Not one of the former colonists was absent, for they had sworn to stay together forever, Neb still at his master's side, Ayrton ever ready to sacrifice himself for any cause, Pencroff more a farmer than he had ever been a sailor, Harbert completing his studies under the direction of Cyrus Smith—even Gideon Spilett, now the editor of the *New Lincoln Herald,* and a better-informed newspaper was not to be found the world over.

There, Cyrus Smith and his companions were sometimes visited by Lord and Lady Glenarvan, by Captain John Mangles and his wife, the sister of Robert Grant, by Robert Grant himself, by Major MacNabbs, by all those involved in the intertwining stories of Captain Grant and Captain Nemo.

There, finally, they lived happily, united in the present as they had been in the past; but they never forgot their island, an island to which they had come bereft and naked, an island that for four years had met their every need, an island of which there now remained only a small slab of granite lashed by the Pacific waves, the tomb of a man who was once Captain Nemo!

A Note on the Illustrations

The wood-engraved illustrations reproduced in this volume are from the original 1875 French edition of *L'Île mystérieuse*, published in Paris by Pierre-Jules Hetzel. They are the work of artist Jules-Descartes Ferat (1829-1889) and his collaborator, the engraver Charles Barbant. Ferat, who studied at Paris's l'École des beaux arts in the 1850s, gained a reputation for his portrayals of the Parisian working-class milieu, which are evident in the roughened, shadowy faces and landscapes in his illustrations for *L'Île mystérieuse* and several other titles in Verne's fantastic adventure series *Les voyages extraordinaires*, including *Une ville flottante* (A Floating City), *Les forceurs du blocus* (The Blockade Runners), *Michel Strogoff*, and *Les Indes noires* (The Black Indies), published from 1871 to 1877. In addition to his work on Verne's books, Ferat also contributed his talents to the texts of Victor Hugo, Edgar Allan Poe, Émile Zola, and Eugène Sue, among others. The lavishly produced 1875 original edition of *L'Île mystérieuse* appeared in the wake of what historians refer to as the period of the "Romantic" book. Characterized by rich typographical ornamentation and innovative designs, many of these books, popular in France and Britain in the mid-nineteenth century, were initially issued in inexpensive installments, with wood- or metal-engraved illustrations by fine artists, and later published as complete volumes. Ferat's illustrations for *L'Île mystérieuse*, considered to be his masterwork, are a remarkable contribution to a golden period in the history of bookmaking.

THE MODERN LIBRARY EDITORIAL BOARD

Maya Angelou
·
Daniel J. Boorstin
·
A. S. Byatt
·
Caleb Carr
·
Christopher Cerf
·
Ron Chernow
·
Shelby Foote
·
Stephen Jay Gould
·
Vartan Gregorian
·
Richard Howard
·
Charles Johnson
·
Jon Krakauer
·
Edmund Morris
·
Joyce Carol Oates
·
Elaine Pagels
·
John Richardson
·
Salman Rushdie
·
Arthur Schlesinger, Jr.
·
Carolyn See
·
William Styron
·
Gore Vidal

A NOTE ON THE TYPE

The principal text of this Modern Library edition
was set in a digitized version of Janson,
a typeface that dates from about 1690 and was cut by Nicholas Kis,
a Hungarian working in Amsterdam. The original matrices have
survived and are held by the Stempel foundry in Germany.
Hermann Zapf redesigned some of the weights and sizes for Stempel,
basing his revisions on the original design.